MARMADUKE HERBERT

VALANCOURT CLASSICS

MARMADUKE HERBERT;

OR,

THE FATAL ERROR.

A NOVEL, FOUNDED ON FACT.

by

The Countess of Blessington

THREE VOLUMES IN ONE

Edited with an introduction by
Ross G. Arthur

𝕶𝖆𝖓𝖘𝖆𝖘 𝕮𝖎𝖙𝖞:
VALANCOURT BOOKS
2008

Marmaduke Herbert by Marguerite, Countess of Blessington
Originally published in 3 vols. by Richard Bentley, 1847.
First Valancourt Books edition 2008

Library of Congress Cataloging-in-Publication Data

Blessington, Marguerite, Countess of, 1789-1849.
Marmaduke Herbert, or, The fatal error : a novel, founded on fact
/ by the Countess of Blessington ; three volumes in one ; edited
with an introduction by Ross G. Arthur. – 1st Valancourt Books ed.
p. cm. – (Valancourt classics)
Originally published: London : Richard Bentley, 1847.
ISBN 1-934555-33-9 (alk. paper)
I. Arthur, Ross Gilbert, 1946- II. Title.
PR4149.B5M37 2008
823'.5–dc22

2007046588

Design and typography by James D. Jenkins
Published by Valancourt Books
Kansas City, Missouri
http://www.valancourtbooks.com

INTRODUCTION

DURING her lifetime, Marguerite Gardiner, Countess of Blessington, was widely known as a versatile, successful and prolific novelist, a charming and witty hostess, and one of the most engaging women of the age. Her literary output includes broad satirical portrayals of characters from all walks of society, searing social and political commentary, searching psychological examinations of a whole range of self-absorbed men and women,—and stray epigrams, occasional articles, and memoirs. She wrote single-volume novels and three-deckers; first-person narratives, third-person narratives, short stories, lyric poems, a "long poem" and an epistolary novel. Her literary successes would have seemed, at her death in 1849, to assure a permanent place in the canon of English literature.

That her works are not better known today is in large measure a result of excessive interest in the details of her life. She began life in Ireland as the daughter of a rather disreputable man who married her off for profit; her first husband died in a drunken brawl; her second husband, the Earl of Blessington, was one of the richest men in England; she knew Byron, and wrote about him; from Blessington's death in 1829 until her own, she maintained a relationship of an uncertain nature with Alfred Count d'Orsay, one of the most prominent dandies of the age and the estranged husband of the Countess's stepdaughter; she died bankrupt.

One might hesitate to hold up England in the 1840s as an era of balance and toleration in such areas; but the near unanimity of writing about the Countess since her death does make one long for the greater variety, at least, of attitudes expressed in the newspapers, journals, and memoirs of that age. Reviews of her novels and anecdotes about her life from the 1840s and 1850s are not, of course, uniformly positive, but they do display an interest in her *work*; today, too many of her supporters treat her as an appendage to Byron, or speak of her as a victim of patriarchy; too many of her detractors revel in the scurrilous speculations which in the past would have been found only in the gutter press. Of proper literary criticism there is precious little; it is in the hope that such may be encouraged that this publication of *Marmaduke Herbert* has been undertaken.

Experienced readers of early nineteenth-century texts will not be surprised to find rather more commas (usually to mark vocal pauses) than would be allowed in modern prose, and unusual spellings—"corse" where we would expect "corpse," "sunk" and "shrunk" where "sank" and "shrank" would now be expected—or words which require different syntax—a person may whisper another rather than whisper to another, or be expelled college rather than expelled from college, and may partake *tout court* rather than partake in or partake of. Such things may be found, of course, in Scott, Dickens, and Austen, although it must be admitted that the Countess is rather less attentive than many of her contemporaries to the newly imposed rules of grammar which forbade dangling modifiers and would have replaced many of her "whos" with "whoms" and vice versa. "Correcting" her language, as occasional modern editors of other texts have done, would not only falsify history; it would also diminish the effect of the *voice*—or, since we hear Louisa as well as from Marmaduke in the extended quotation from her diary—the *voices* which the Countess constructed so vividly.

The text presented here follows the first edition, published by Richard Bentley in 1847, with two small exceptions. An overzealous editor or typesetter seems to have removed three examples of the word "like" from the speech of the vulgar Mrs. Mordaunt in chapter 23; they survive in the otherwise inferior Tauchnitz edition, which is flawed by rather more typographical errors than are usual in the works from that press.

ROSS G. ARTHUR

A CHRONOLOGY OF THE MAJOR WRITINGS OF THE COUNTESS OF BLESSINGTON

Journal of a Tour through the Netherlands to Paris in 1821 (1822)
Sketches and Fragments (1822)
The Magic Lantern (1822)
Rambles in Waltham Forest (1827)
Journal of Conversations of Lord Byron with the Countess of Blessington (1832)
Grace Cassidy, or, The Repealers (1833)
The Two Friends (1835)
Confessions of an Elderly Gentleman (1836)
Flowers of Loveliness (1836)
Gems of Beauty (1836)
The Victims of Society (1837)
Confessions of an Elderly Lady (1838)
Desultory Thoughts and Reflections (1839)
The Governess (1839)
The Idler in Italy (1839)
The Belle of a Season (1840)
The Idler in France (1841)
The Lottery of Life (1842)
Meredith (1843)
Strathern: or, Life at Home and Abroad (1845)
The Memoirs of a Femme de Chambre (1846)
Marmaduke Herbert; or, The Fatal Error (1847)
Country Quarters (1850)

Marmaduke Herbert;

OR,

THE FATAL ERROR.

MARMADUKE HERBERT.

CHAPTER I.

WELL has it been observed, that truth is often stranger than fiction. The one fatal event that has destroyed my happiness, and cast its gloomy influence over a life that without it might have been peaceful, is an exemplification of this assertion. I do not seek relief by recapitulating the cause, and results of my long years of misery, for well do I know the recurrence will add to, rather than diminish my chagrin; neither do I expect that my story can serve as a warning, for as the one event that led to my wretchedness was involuntary, neither example nor precept can be derived from its narration.—A motive urges me to lay bare the agonies that have long tortured my heart. I have a child, dearer to me than life itself, who, when I am laid in the grave, will peruse these pages, and comprehending much that, during my existence, was incomprehensible to her, will learn to feel for the misery of her father. Oh my child, my dear child! how often has my heart yearned to trust thee with the cause of those frequent fits of moodiness and abstraction which were uncontrollable, and which I feared must alienate thy affections, (his sole blessing,) from thy wretched parent.—But even this dread, bitter as it was, was preferable to the risk of poisoning thy young life with a secret which might effect a baleful influence over it, so I have borne in silence suspicion and coldness, where I had been wont to meet only confidence and love. I have seen the wife of my bosom fade and die under the baleful influence exercised over her by my moodiness, yet I dared not reveal the truth to her; and I have marked the alienation of friends, produced by a conviction that madness had seized me, a conviction founded on my wayward humour, my despondency, my inexplicable changes from forced and unnatural gaiety to the deepest gloom. Oh! the misery of having a terrible secret, like a vulture preying on the vitals, yet not daring to pluck it out. To feel the dire necessity of everlastingly wearing a mask, of trying to force the jaded spirits when they refuse to own control, and of being aware that their sudden and violent changes will inevitably confirm

suspicions that one would suffer death, to remove.—Oh! the wretchedness
of brooding over one terrible event,

> "One fatal remembrance, one sorrow that throws
> Its bleak shade alike o'er our joys and our woes,"

through days, weeks, months, and years! To have sleep become as unbearable as waking, by being haunted with hideous dreams from which I awake
to know that they are all based on one terrible truth.

But to my story.—My father, a man of ancient family, possessed of a
small estate in Wales, was early left an orphan. The guardian to whom he
was confided took care that he received good education, but lived not to
see its completion. Arrived at his majority, my father determined to travel,
and after having explored France and Italy, visited Spain, where he became
enamoured of a youthful Spanish girl, with *sangre azula** flowing through
her veins, but with little worldly wealth.—Beautiful, high-spirited, and
impetuous, she resembled in her nature one of those fine Arabian cours-
ers, so rare and so prized even in their own country. Acting ever upon the
impulse of the moment, she waited not for reason to examine, or approve
what it prompted, but so good, so noble were her feelings, that seldom did
she err, and so passionate was her love for her husband, and so entire her
devotion, that he sought not to correct a peculiarity, said to appertain to her
nation, and which decidedly in his eyes, lent her new charms. I was born in
Spain, and inhaled my infant nurture from the breast of my mother. Her
delicacy of structure, and nervous temperament, ill fitted her for fulfilling
this maternal function, and anxiously did her doting husband desire that she
should confide it to another. But she would not listen to his pleadings, and
I imbibed with her milk much of the impetuous nature of my Andalusian
parent, who, as she marked my precocious vivacity and impatience, would
smile and say I was a true Spaniard. My father, too, was rather of a quick
and fiery disposition, as most Cambrians are, and this similarity of temper,
far from producing any disagreements, seemed to endear them still more
to each other. My father died when I was little more than ten years old. His
illness was short, and from the first baffled the skill of all the neighbouring
medical men called in to his aid. Well do I remember the unceasing care,
the almost breathless anxiety with which my poor mother hung over his
couch, or flew to prepare, with her own hands, the remedies ordered by
his physicians. But the fiat had gone forth—he expired in her arms, and

---

* Blue blood, said to belong exclusively to the ancient noblesse of Spain. [Author's
note.]

for many days it was deemed that her life could not be saved. I followed as chief mourner to the grave. It seemed incomprehensible to me that the dear father, who, only a few days before, I had seen in the bloom of health and manhood, walking on the very path along which his corse was now borne, my mother leaning fondly on his supporting arm, while holding by his hand, I moved by his side, his voice still ringing in my ears, should now be shut up in the black coffin, which I could not look at without a shudder, while the sky looked as blue, the trees and earth as green as before.—And yet with this deep sense of childish grief and terror was mingled a pride in my new black garments, the crape on my hat, and the mourning cloak that swept to my feet. I fancied myself nearer to manhood, I saw that I was an object of attention and sympathy, and when my tears for a few minutes ceased to flow, I conjured up fresh ones by dwelling on all the proofs of affection my lost father had been wont to lavish on me—so early do we prolong natural sorrow by appealing to the imagination and memory to nurse it, and so learn to become actors in the pageant of grief. While tears flowed down my cheeks, I was conscious that I was enacting my part in the ceremony, with all due propriety, that those around felt it, and that my sables produced a striking effect. Nevertheless, when we entered the church, and when the coffin was let down into the dark and dreary vault, never more to be visited by the light of day, and I heard the earth fall on it, I forgot everything, but that I should never more see the pleasant face that never looked on me but with a smile of affection, never again hear that sonorous but sweet voice, and that in the dark cavern yawning before me, must my dead father remain shut out for ever from the blue sky, and green fields, from the breath of flowers, and the song of birds; and, my grief becoming desperate, I uttered a cry and rushed to throw myself on the coffin, then being let down by ropes into the vault.

I remember no more until I again found myself in the open air, which revived me, and as the gentle breeze stirred my hair, and played over my brow and burning eyelids, I turned from it, recollecting that never more could it visit that dear head shut up for ever in the black coffin in the dark vault into which I had tried to precipitate myself.

My mother's grief was at once deep and passionate. She *would* not be consoled. She could not be induced to leave the chamber, it was their nuptial one, in which my poor father died. There, giving way to the violence of her sorrow, she would pass all her hours, by turns weeping, and apostrophizing the dead. She shrank from the light of day, as if, to enjoy it when *he* could see it no more, were an infidelity to the departed. Nor would she suffer anything that had been his to be removed from the room. In vain did those around her preach resignation to the will of God. They spoke to ears that heeded them not. His death could not be viewed by her impatient mind in any other light than as a terrible, an irrecoverable blow, from the effects of which she did not desire to escape; nay, she accused her own heart of hardness and ingratitude, for not breaking when the heart of her husband had ceased to beat. She would detain me for whole days in her darkened chamber, by turns embracing me, and steeping my cheeks with her burning tears, until I involuntarily betrayed some symptom of uneasiness, inevitable to childhood under such circumstances, when she would banish me from her presence, saying, "I knew not how to grieve for such a loss as I had sustained, that if I did, she would not weep alone." Then she would summon me to her, embrace me fondly, acknowledge that she had been unreasonable in expecting that a child like me could feel grief as she did, and say, "That if she consented to live, it was for me alone." Her frantic sorrow, and passionate tenderness, alike alarmed me. I might, perhaps, have shared a gentler grief, have sympathized with a less vehement affliction, but the darkened chamber, and the half-phrenzied mourner, became, after some weeks, objects of dread to me, the more intolerable from knowing I could not escape them. But let it not be supposed that I had ceased to regret, or remember, my poor father. Never did a day, indeed I may say an hour, pass, that he was not thought of. I enjoyed no pleasure without recollecting that _he_ never more could share it. I missed him from all his accustomed haunts, and, for many months, never saw the spire of the church where he was laid, glittering in the sunbeams or tinged by the moonlight, without a tear starting to my eye; never inhaled the odour of his favourite flowers, nor heard the carol of the birds which was wont to please him, without being melted into tenderness. My melancholy was of a mild and gentle character, which, if it burst not into violent paroxysms of grief, was not likely to pass away rapidly; while that of my poor mother resembled the sorrow of Joanna of Castile for Philip the Handsome, so engrossing and so uncontrollable were its effects.

Oh! what a relief it was when I was dismissed from the dark chamber, and rushed into the sunshine, and breathed the fresh air. It seemed ungrateful to Providence, nay, almost wicked, to abandon oneself to woe, while all nature was rejoicing, and yet, as I have before stated, the view of the beautiful scenery around appealed to my feelings with a force and tenderness, that the gloomy chamber and intense sorrow of my mother could not awaken. Childhood is ever prone to seek, and to find, relief from affliction. "The sunshine of the breast" will break forth from grief, even as the sun pierces and disperses the clouds that would obscure its brightness; but this my poor mother could not comprehend, and often was I rebuked, because I felt not as she did, until I incurred the danger of becoming a hypocrite, and assuming the demonstrations of a more violent sorrow than I really experienced.

A year wrought little change in her regret. It is true she would now venture forth, but it was to visit the vault where the remains of her husband reposed, and to saunter and weep over his favourite haunts. At this time, the guardian appointed by my father happening to make a tour through Wales, paid a visit to my mother. Mr. Trevyllan was a cold-hearted, selfish, matter-of-fact man, wholly destitute of sentiment, and totally incapable of comprehending it in others. He expected to find my mother reconciled to the loss she had sustained, or at least, the bitterness of regret melted down to a gentle melancholy. He expected, too, to find at Llandover the creature comforts, to which no one attached more importance than he did; and was consequently both disappointed and vexed, when he discovered that the sorrow of his hostess rendered her alike incapable of companionship and of superintending her household affairs, as was proved, by her granting him only a brief interview, which was passed on her part in unchecked tears and lamentations, and by a repast of so frugal a character, that not even the keen appetite given by the air of the Welch mountains could enable the epicure to tolerate it. He questioned the servants whether their mistress always pursued the same course as at present; and, being informed that since her husband's death she had wholly abandoned herself to sorrow, he formed the conclusion that her intellects must be deranged by grief; how else could her utter carelessness about her repasts be accounted for, by one who considered his daily fare as one of the most important affairs imaginable. Such an inconceivable neglect would at any time have satisfied him of the necessity of a verdict of insanity; but as the widow of his friend did not throw away her money, nor permit any extravagance in her expenditure, he felt it would be difficult to establish a case of mental derangement, on the mere grounds that she made no effort to check her grief, or pamper her appetite: so he contented himself with the determination of exerting his authority to have me placed at school, with as little delay as possible, lest, as he thought, my poor mother should make me as mad as herself. He expected much opposition from her, in the adoption of this scheme, and was agreeably surprised when none was offered. Having repeatedly heard my father express his intention of sending me to a public school, and being determined religiously to fulfil every wish of his, she yielded to Mr. Trevyllan's proposal, and I accompanied him the following day, when he left. The parting with my mother greatly affected us both. The passionate love I had borne her before her grief had interposed a barrier between us, revived when I was leaving her; and my unrepressed regret seemed to awaken afresh her tenderness for me.

Now it was that, for the first time, I blamed myself for not having evinced a deeper sympathy in her overwhelming grief during the last year. It might have lightened the burthen of her sorrow; at all events, it must have soothed it to see that it was shared. If the tears that often fell from my eyes in secret, when thinking of my dear lost father, had been shed on her breast, they might have cooled its feverish sorrow, and I should not now have had to deplore that, checked by the sternness of her grief, I had not, as I ought to have done, partaken it. Pressed to her heart, its tumultuous throbbings seemed to communicate a magnetic influence to mine. I comprehended the extent of her sufferings, and would have given worlds to be permitted to stay with her another year, to prove that I was not cold nor forgetful, as I believe she had thought me. She, too, appeared now to understand my feelings, as our tears mingled together. She imprinted burning kisses on my brow, which was wet with her tears. She implored blessings on me—prayed that I might resemble my father—blamed herself for not having sooner comprehended me; and then, gently pushing me from her, said, "Go, while I have yet courage to let you leave me;" and, retreating into the little oratory inside her chamber, I heard her sobs, while sinking on her knees she prayed for strength to bear this new trial; and I left the home of my fathers, never more to behold my poor mother in life.

CHAPTER II.

"What's the use of crying, child?" demanded Mr. Trevyllan, when, having reached the first milestone on our journey, he found I still continued to weep. He could not have asked a question that I was more incapable of answering; and the brusquerie of the tone in which it was made, far from checking my regret, only increased it. "Come, come," said he, "you must learn to be a man, and get over this absurd habit of shedding tears. Tears are fit only for women, and they but show their weakness in indulging them."

This observation seemed to me to be nothing short of an insult offered to my poor mother, which I would gladly have resented, but my ignorance how to do so prevented the attempt, and, hurt and offended, I dried my eyes, and put my handkerchief in my pocket.

"You are a good boy," said Mr. Trevyllan, and he took my hand and shook it. "Never betray your feelings before strangers; they will only mock your distress, or envy you for any demonstrations of happiness. You will learn this as you grow older; but, in the meanwhile, it is my duty, as your guardian, to give you the benefit of my experience; whether you will profit by it, depends wholly on yourself. Be ever on your guard against the world. Conceal your errors from it, as you would from a relentless judge, whose condemnation you should tremble for; but remember it is almost as necessary to conceal, likewise, any weakness of your nature, as to hide your faults. By weakness, I mean that foolish good nature, or kindness, to which some men are prone, and which renders them through life the dupes of the artful and designing, and objects of derision to men of sense. Learn betimes to resist every hasty impulse of compliance, either with the entreaties of others, or the dictates of your own heart, and you will find cause to rejoice at this self-control hereafter. A school is a faithful miniature picture of the world. In it you may acquire the art of governing yourself, and making use of those around you. 'The boy is father to the man,' and betrays the seeds of those vices or weaknesses which are to mark his career in manhood. Study the characters of your companions; and this study will enable you to judge men in general when you go forth into the busy world, where you will find it so difficult to steer clear of suffering by them."

I listened to this counsel with a distaste that increased my dislike to the giver of it. His peering and malicious eyes, looking out from under protruding and deeply-marked brows, the hard and stern expression of his mouth, and the harsh tones of his voice, produced an unconquerable sentiment of aversion in my heart. The advice, too, so different to the opinions of my dear parents, accorded so well with the countenance of Mr. Trevyllan, and the whole manner of the man was so repulsive, that I wondered how he could have been selected by my father to fill the trust confided to him. In the course of conversation he accounted for this, by explaining to me that he had never seen my father but once since they had parted at school, and then only for a few hours.

"Your poor father was one of those warm-hearted youths who plunge headlong into friendship with the first companion chance throws in their way," observed Mr. Trevyllan. "He loved me, or fancied he did, which amounts much to the same thing, and I preferred him to any of the other lads in the school. This same proneness to rush headlong into affection without weighing the prudence of the measure, or analyzing the qualities of the object, led him to form a rash marriage, which he, however, in all his letters to me declared had secured his happiness. This was his affair, and not mine, so I never exposed to him, as some meddling fools would have done, how much wiser a choice he might have made in wedding a country-woman of his own, with a good fortune and family connexions, that might have forwarded his interests in the world. The same want of perception and credulity which induced him to believe me endowed with all his own peculiar qualities, no doubt, led him to think that his wife was a paragon of perfection."

I drew up my head offended, and was about to pronounce an eulogium on my poor mother, when he cut me short, by adding—

"I don't want to say anything against either of your parents; I only have come to the conclusion, that as his friendship for me made your father give me credit for the possession of peculiarities the most opposite to *my* character, and congenial to his own, so may his mad passion for his wife have induced an equally false appreciation of hers. One thing is quite certain, which is, that this extravagant passion of his for her renders his death an insupportable calamity to its object, to whom life is now an unbearable burthen; whereas, had her husband been a cool, calculating, reasonable man, he would not have been blind to those manifold defects from which no woman is exempt; he would have endeavoured to correct them, and, when he died, his widow would have found consolation by the reflection, that if she had lost a husband, she had likewise lost a Mentor, whose strictures, however just, were never palatable."

Such were the observations addressed by my guardian to me. It was plain he had not been used to children, or he would have selected topics more suited to my comprehension. How, at this time, I remember his words, surprises me, as much as it will doubtlessly astonish you, my dear child; but my memory was a peculiarly retentive one; and however distasteful the subject might be, I was flattered that he considered me old enough to be so confidential and communicative; I fancied myself more of a man, and, in consequence, assumed a more manly demeanour. I observed, that however Mr. Trevyllan prided himself on his habits of self-control with regard to his sentiments, he abandoned himself to the enjoyments of the table with the gusto of an epicure, and the gluttony of a *gourmand*.

In this particular, nothing could be so different from the habits of my father, who might be said to eat to live, and not to live to eat, so temperate was his appetite, and so frugal his repasts. He had taught me to partake sparingly of the simple fare set before me, and to satisfy my thirst with no other beverage than what was supplied by the cooling spring. Mr. Trevyllan remarked, and disapproved this system. A man, he said, should be able to live on the hardest fare, when compelled to it; but it was folly to adopt the habits of an anchorite, when opportunities offered for enjoying the pleasures of the table. He counselled, nay, insisted on my partaking the food always the most luxurious the inns could afford, or set before us; made me drink wine, to which I had previously been a stranger; and, by the time we arrived at his residence in Serle-street, near Lincoln's Inn, neither my mind nor my taste retained the purity they possessed when, only a few days before, I left my native mountains. I began to relish the flavour of wine, which at first displeased my palate, nor did the feverish thirst it excited, prevent my indulging in it, when pressed by Mr. Trevyllan. I could hear without disgust the worldly, if not misanthropic, sentiments and opinions he loved to utter, and I began to think him a wise, though not a generous-minded man. Such are the deleterious effects on a youthful and ductile mind from an association with the unworthy, even for a short period. Many a time in after days did I find the harsh precepts of Mr. Trevyllan recur to my mind, weakening, if not vanquishing, the noble sentiments instilled by my parents, which partook much more of the chivalrous than of the worldly wise.

Death, my father taught me was infinitely preferable to dishonour, nay, even to incurring its suspicion, and crime he looked on as an irrefragable proof of insanity, which entitled its perpetrator to an asylum in a mad-house. When excited into confidence by wine, I ventured to reveal these opinions to my guardian, he laughed them to scorn, said that my father had from childhood been a visionary filled with Utopian systems of the perfectibility of human nature, to which, had he lived in the busy world, he must inevitably have fallen a victim, and added that the sooner I got such folly out of my head the better.

"See," observed Mr. Trevyllan, the day after I entered his house, "the advantages derived by my system, over that of your father—look around, the walls of my dwelling are covered with pictures by the best masters, ancient and modern. Their fine colours, and beautiful scenery give me pleasure I confess, but I derive even greater gratification from the reflection that I owe them to my own prudence, and that worldly wisdom which I have through life made the guide of my actions. I admire good pictures, but I laugh in my sleeve when I visit the galleries of collectors, and hear the prices they pay. I bide my time until they are either ruined, or dead, and then at sales, I pick up for pounds what they paid hundreds for; and when these treasures are hung up in my rooms, I look on them with double satisfaction from the recollection of my paying so little for what the original owners paid so much. In the same way, I buy plate at melting prices, for which the previous possessors gave the most enormous sums by the ounce for workmanship. What say you, my lad, to giving four or five shillings an ounce for what cost thirty-five? Books, furniture, glass, china, in short, everything I require, I purchase at sales for less than a quarter of their value, and so the wise man profits by the folly of the foolish."

Such were the subjects on which Mr. Trevyllan loved to descant for the few days I remained in his house. I have cited his sayings for two reasons: the first is, that this trifling diverts my attention for the moment from myself, just as a truant schoolboy lingers by the wayside on his route to school, to snatch a few minutes of enjoyment from idleness, though certain that he must a little later perform his allotted task; and the second, that although I had perception enough not to adopt the selfish and narrow-minded principles of Mr. Trevyllan in all things, one of his tenets, namely, the determination to conceal errors or sins from the world, exercised in after life an influence over me that has given a colour to my fate.

I entered a public school in a short time after my arrival in London, and here I began to perceive the result of my guardian's advice. Naturally shy and reserved, I had never previously detected in myself the slightest tendency to suspicion; but now, I involuntarily found myself analysing the characters of those around me, and searching for motives for their conduct. Did a schoolfellow, with the unceremonious frankness peculiar to boyhood, make advances of goodwill towards me, a suspicion that some secret motive actuated him instantly crossed my mind, and however open and natural might be his looks and manners, I held back, fearful of giving way to the sympathy he excited in my breast. This I considered to be a proof of prudence and good sense that would, if revealed to my guardian, command his esteem; and although occasionally I might yield to the temptation of a growing friendship, I soon remembered the precepts of Mr. Trevyllan, and kept aloof from placing any confidence in those who confided every thought to me. Nevertheless, when any of my schoolfellows betrayed coldness or reserve towards me, my pride was wounded, and I felt disposed to consider such treatment as an insult. Such were the results of Mr. Trevyllan's counsel and opinions. I never enjoyed the frank companionship which among boys of the same years grows into regard, and cements the friendship that often forms one of the blessings of after age.

My mother's letters were more frequent than I had anticipated. They breathed the warmest affection, and inculcated the strongest caution of preserving the high and chivalrous sense of honour that had been the guiding principle of my father. "He," would she write, "thought an unspotted fame of such vital importance, that I have heard him say he could not survive even the suspicion of a bad action, however conscious he might be of his own freedom from it; and he blessed Providence that he had never been exposed to such a trial."

The opposite opinions of my high-minded and romantic mother, who had all the pride of the noble blood of her country, and the narrow policy and unblushing selfishness that marked those of my guardian, produced the most contending feelings in my breast. My pride, encouraged by that of my mother, gradually increased in proportion to the deterioration of the qualities that might have furnished an excuse, if they could not have redeemed it. I ought to have known that nothing is more incompatible with a high sense of honour, the only stable basis for pride, than suspicion; but, alas! the counsel and the self-complacency of the rich and worldly-minded Mr. Trevyllan had tainted and blinded me to this fact, and I continued proud, when an impartial self-examination would either have taught me humility or prompted me to merit self-esteem.

My reserve, by degrees, alienated from me the companions who were at first desirous of forming a friendship. They drew back, disappointed by the coldness with which I met their advances, and listened with complacency, if not with avidity, to the ill-natured remarks of those youths who had from the commencement manifested an ill will towards me. One, however, of my schoolfellows, remained firm in his attachment. He was precisely the best-natured, and most generous boy in the whole establishment. He shared his purse and all his possessions, with a lavish hand, with his companions; assisted them in their tasks, submitted to punishment for their faults, rather than reveal the real culprits, and in short, was one of the least selfish of human beings. Did any boy get into debt, he had recourse to Neville to extricate him. Did he neglect his lessons, Neville aided him to pass muster. Did a strong boy tyrannize over a weak, Neville protected the latter. Consequently, there was not a dissentient voice to be heard when he was acknowledged to be the best fellow in the world, and the kindest-hearted. It happened one day that Neville was present when I received a letter from my mother, enclosing me five pounds. The note dropped from the letter, and he stooped, took it up, and handed it to me.

"I am glad, Herbert, you are in cash, for I want half these five pounds," said he, as frankly and as carelessly as he would have given them away.

My first impulse was to say, "keep the whole, if you want it;" but after a moment's reflection, I checked myself, and asked, "what he wanted the money for?"

"Hang it! A lender should not question a borrower," replied he; "it looks as if he would as soon keep his money as lend it. But the truth is, Bentley is dunned for four pounds, and I have only thirty shillings to give him, so I want your two pounds ten to make up the sum."

"If you wanted it for yourself, I should readily lend it," replied I; "but for another, and that other an extravagant——"

"Hold!" interrupted he, "not another word. If we were entitled to lecture, and censure those we assist, who would ever accept aid at our hands? I
have a pleasure in helping my friends out of scrapes. It is, I think, one of the
pleasures as well as privileges of friendship. You think otherwise, so there's
an end of the matter," and he walked away, looking disappointed, leaving me utterly ashamed myself. I followed him, entreated him to take the
money, nay, would have forced him to accept it, but I could not prevail.

"No, my good fellow, it is impossible! *You* have *your* notions, and I, *mine;*
and now that I know yours, I could not touch your money."

The reflection that Mr. Trevyllan would have approved my conduct
on this occasion, failed to silence my self-reproaches, and as I really was
not a lover of money, the having saved my two pounds ten offered me no
consolation under them. What must Neville think of me? was a question
that occurred to my mind several times during that day, and I longed for
an opportunity of explaining to him my self-imposed system of prudence
and caution, in order to exonerate myself from the charge of avarice. It
became evident that from this time he avoided me, and though mortified
by his doing so, will it be believed, that instead of thinking he was justified
by my conduct, I began to imagine that Neville, the profuse, the generous Neville, had only formerly shown a friendship towards me to furnish
a claim on my purse, should his prodigality to others render such a step
necessary. Do not, my beloved child, hate your unfortunate father for thus
revealing the defects of his character, defects which he would fain attribute
to the unworthy counsel of his guardian, yet which conscience sometimes
whispers may have originated in a taint in his nature, which left him but
too open to evil impressions. Pride prevented my seeking the wished for
explanation with Neville. Why urge it when it was quite evident *he* desired
it not? No, he had formed his opinion of me, had misjudged my motives,
and kept away from me, and I certainly would not humble myself by further parley on the subject. By gradual, but not slow degrees, I became more
and more isolated in the school. I fancied that this proceeded from Neville
having disclosed the fact of my refusing to lend him the trifle he asked for.
This belief increased my suspicion of him until it ripened into dislike; and
in the indulgence of this sentiment I lost sight of the cause of my former
self-reproaches, and believed myself an injured person.

After having passed a year at school, I expected to return to my mother,
to spend the vacation with her, but when I wrote to my guardian to propose it, he stated, that he had decided I should not return to Wales until
my education was completed. He urged that my mother had now got
accustomed to my absence, and that a visit to her would but renew her

regret at parting from me again. This reasoning by no means satisfied me, but from his decision Mr. Trevyllan allowed no appeal. He arranged that I should pass the vacation with him, and thus, unhappily, an opportunity was afforded him of inculcating still more profoundly in my mind, those suspicions of mankind, and that dread of its censure, which, henceforth, became rooted in my heart. Mr. Trevyllan insinuated himself into my confidence, he plied me with wine until I laid bare to him every thought, even to the self-reproaches I had made myself on the subject of Neville; and he laughed to scorn my weakness, as he termed it, while he applauded my prudence in refusing his request.

"This Neville," said he, "is evidently a fool, or a hunter after popularity. He lavishes his money on his companions, thus encouraging their extravagance in order that he may lay them under obligations, and when he no longer has sufficient to satisfy their demands, he has recourse to you, and finding you too wise to comply with his exactions, he resents it, forsooth, and avoids you."

Thus, he imprinted still more deeply on my ductile mind, those feelings which so greatly deteriorated his character and sullied mine.

We generally travelled during my vacations, and the long *tête-à-têtes*, shut up in a carriage, furnished my guardian with ample time to descant on the cunning, deception, and artifices of mankind as well as on the necessity of guarding against them. "It is the custom;" would he say, "to censure selfishness as something to be despised, but never was there a greater mistake. Selfishness is the armour furnished us by Providence as a defence against that weakness denominated sympathy, which lays us open to feel for, and assist, persons in misfortune, to the injury of our personal comfort, and often to the detriment of our fortunes."

How many stories had he to tell illustrative of this theory! The generous, the kind, the noble-minded were, according to his system, the certain dupes of the designing; and the poor and unfortunate, merited reproof for the errors that led to their destitution, rather than pity or assistance, he being convinced that poverty must invariably originate in want of prudence—a crime of deep dye in his eyes. Oh! the sin of clouding over the gay sunshine of childhood by the worldly wisdom that experience should alone bring, tempered as it ever is, by the peculiar character of him who acquires it! But to receive it second-hand, coloured by the prejudices of a selfish mind glorying in its own crude, unwholesome wisdom, is indeed a misfortune! Better were it to suffer all the penalties that originate in inexperience, and a too favourable opinion of mankind, than to become prematurely soured, and suspicious, afraid to trust in our fellow-creatures for sympathy, or to show them our own.

By degrees, the desire to visit my mother faded away from my mind. Perhaps her letters unconsciously aided the wishes of Mr. Trevyllan on this point, for they were filled with a regret as poignant for the loss of her husband, as when I left her, and I dreaded the dark chamber and ceaseless lamentations to which I believed a meeting with her would inevitably expose me. I was the less compunctious for not urging my guardian to allow me to visit her, as her recent letters informed me that an old friend of her's, lately become a widow like herself, had come to see her. "We were intimate friends in happier times," wrote my mother, "at Seville, where she, then a young wife, accompanied her husband. They were as happy, and loved each other almost as much as your dear father and I did. This worthy man died, leaving her with two daughters—lovely creatures—ill provided with the goods of fortune, and she came to seek sympathy and companionship near me. Similar affliction has drawn closer the bond of friendship between us. Our tears often mingle together, and we find a consolation, mournful though it be, in dwelling on the memory of other days, and on those who formed our happiness. I have fitted up the pretty cottage you may remember at Llantrisant, for Mrs. Maitland, and few days pass in which we do not meet."

The knowledge that she was no longer alone, quieted my conscience, and afforded me pleasure. I wrote to her frequently, and so affectionately, that my letters, which she showed to Mrs. Maitland, interested that lady deeply in my favour. Her daughters, too, were told what a good son I was, and joined, as my mother wrote me, in longing to see the son of their kind friend, their second mother—for so they considered her.

CHAPTER III.

THE attention with which I listened to the worldly counsel of Mr. Trevyllan, and the docility with which I adopted it, flattered his *amour-propre*, and conciliated his friendship. Young as I was, he was delighted to have instilled into my mind the defects and prejudices of his own, and judged more and more favourably of me in proportion as he remarked my suspicion and distrust of mankind. The coldness of my companions, on which I sometimes animadverted to him, he declared to be caused by their anger at not being able to dupe me; and he asserted that, at school, as in the world, a popular person must either be a dupe or a duper; and, as I was too proud to be the last, and too sensible to be the first, I must never expect popularity.

"But Neville," said I, "is the most popular boy in the school, yet, I assure you, *he* does not want for cleverness. He invariably upholds his own opinions when he believes himself to be in the right, flatters no one, appears to be regardless of flattery; and although his superiority is undisputed, excites no envy."

"I see you are dazzled by this same Neville," replied Mr. Trevyllan; "but, remember, you judge only from appearances. Whatever may be the envy he excites,—and that he does excite it there can be no doubt, as never did superiority of any kind escape envy,—the obligations he confers on his companions preclude them from betraying any symptom of their entertaining such a sentiment, and he, poor dupe, will go on lavishing favours on them, and believing in their affection, until some fine day discovers he has been their dupe."

And yet so inclined was I to like and esteem Neville, that the good feeling he excited in my own breast rendered me well inclined to give credit to the sincerity of the regard professed, or rather evinced towards him by others, that it required all the sophistical warnings and suspicions, so continually instilled into my mind by my guardian, to prevent me from opening my whole soul to him, and endeavouring to win his friendship. It pained me to be thought ill of by Neville; and had he not plainly let me see that he wished to avoid me, I do believe that, in spite of the opinions and advice of Mr. Trevyllan, I would have laid bare to him all that was passing in my heart, and allowed the influence of his healthy mind to heal the canker that was corroding mine. But here, too, pride and mistrust, the besetting sins engendered in my nature, operated to vanquish this strong desire. What, was *I* to pursue one who evidently shunned me? Was I to expose my failings to one who had already judged, and condemned me, as was proved by his avoidance of all intercourse between us? No, this would be too humiliating even were I sure that my advances towards a renewal of our former good intelligence would be well received; but with a chance of the possibility that he might decline my offered civility, refuse my confidence, and tell his companions that he had done so, I could not stoop to such a step, though my heart yearned for his friendship. I stood alone in the school. I had no friend to share my pleasures, or my pains. The boy, whom Neville had broken off intimacy with, no one else wished to seek; and this coldness on the part of my schoolfellows, acting on my pride, operated still more strongly than the advice of Mr. Trevyllan, to increase the hauteur and indifference towards them which I had assumed.

Years rolled on, but my position in the school remained unchanged; for though many of my contemporaries left it for college, or to enter professions, some remained behind; and the new comers who replaced those who departed had imbibed their prejudices against me. Often did I propose to Mr. Trevyllan that I should be placed in another school, where, having no prejudices to contend with, I might make friends; but *he* laughed these proposals to scorn, declared it would be weak and unmanly to be conquered by those who only avoided, because they could not make me their dupe. He said I must support my position with fortitude, and show no deference to the opinions of persons who felt no good-will towards me, and for whom I consequently could experience none.

"You ought to remember," added he, "that persons who wish to learn to fence must begin with foils. Consider your schoolfellows as foils. Do not let them touch you; and by this means you will be prepared for the more serious combats to which in society every man is exposed, when the foils being thrown away, he must defend himself with real weapons. Leave school, and your enemies will say 'we drove him away;' and when you meet them in the world, they will be ready to attempt the same game with you that succeeded at school. But maintain your place, let them see you attach no importance to their opinions, and though in future years they may not feel inclined to cultivate your intimacy, they will at least be deterred from molesting you."

Who that has not experienced it, can judge the misery of a youthful heart yearning for affection, but checked by pride from avowing it, and deploring the errors that preclude its growth; errors, too, not natural to the soil, but the forced fruit of an evil cultivator, against whose unhealthy influence the heart has never ceased to rebel? "Put not confidence in man," was the often repeated caution of Mr. Trevyllan. "Never let even your friend—your wife, when you are old enough to have one—acquire the knowledge of any circumstance, the betrayal of which could injure or give you pain. If you commit a fault, conceal it within the most secret recess of your heart, for be assured that man's happiness can never be secure who trusts another."

Such were the reiterated maxims of the person to whom my noble-minded father confided his only son; such the man entrusted with my destiny; and who, fearful that the romantic turn of my poor mother, and the chivalrous feelings that governed her, might counteract his counsels, kept me away from her; and thus not only destroyed the happiness of my youth, but laid up for my maturity the seeds of those failings which have given a colour to my after life. During the long and tedious years passed at school, I never had an opportunity of enjoying the humanising influence of female society. No woman, save his servants, and they were as unfeminine as aught in woman shape could be, ever passed the threshold of Mr. Trevyllan. He invariably spoke of the sex in terms of unmitigated contempt, as weak, capricious, giddy creatures, fit only to be made the toys of our lighter hours, but wholly incapable of becoming rational companions or friends. Often did the image of my absent mother, in her devoted and all-engrossing love to my father while he lived, and her passionate and enduring grief for his loss, rise up to destroy his calumnies of her sex; but I dreaded to name her, lest he should, in his cynicism, utter some taunt that I could not have borne to hear applied to her. This total seclusion from all female society rendered the sex much more attractive in my eyes. Every pretty face I saw, when passing through the streets, appeared almost angelic in my sight, and I endowed its possessor with every amiable and engaging quality, and formed in my mind a little romance, of which she was the imaginary heroine. My dreams were haunted by these ambulating beauties, a chance encounter with whom in the streets made my heart beat quicker, and sent the blood to my cheeks; but such was my timidity, that had I met one of them alone, and far from the ken of mortal, I should have wanted courage to address her, nay more, would probably have fled from her had she addressed me.

And now I entered college, filled with hope that I might find none of my schoolfellows there, and consequently that a chance remained of forming a favourable impression on my new acquaintances. But this hope was of brief duration. No less than seven of my former companions, if indeed those with whom I held no companionship could thus be termed, had entered Christ Church before me; and not one of the seven possessing the generosity of mind or goodness of heart which characterised Neville, my unpopularity at school, and its causes were soon revealed, probably exaggerated, and I found no one desirous to extend to me the hand of amity, or to question the sentence of exclusion from intimacy, which here, as at school, kept me apart from my contemporaries. How often have I wished that some tangible slight, some premeditated offence, gave me the right to demand reparation from some one of these young men, who, while avoiding all intimacy, were so studiously on their guard not to furnish me with an excuse for questioning their motives, that I could not demand satisfaction. My sensitiveness and susceptibility to take offence now became irritated into morbidness, and was only kept within bounds by the dread of any demonstration of it exposing me to ridicule—a dread which tortured me. My progress in my studies was more rapid as well as more solid from the seclusion in which I lived. I had none of the interruptions springing from sociability which so frequently draw others from their tasks: hence my success, which was also probably aided by a strong desire to excel those who evinced indifference towards me. The reputation attained by my assiduity, and its results, did not tend to diminish the coldness, of my fellow collegians. I was sneered at as a pedant, a bookworm, a fellow devoid of spirit who set myself up as a model to be cited when the professors wished to reproach the idle and dissipated. Conscious of the dislike of those around me, and anxious to seize on some mark of it that would justify my demanding satisfaction for the affront, I furnished, by the constraint and hauteur of my manner, fresh cause for their dislike and avoidance. Among the young men were some, however, who after a time made advances towards acquaintanceship with me. But they were not the companions I would have chosen, being precisely in positions so humiliating that an intimacy with them must have for ever sunk me in my own esteem. They had incurred the dislike and contempt of those under whose avoidance I smarted, and believing that this circumstance would be a passport to my favour, they made their approaches by severely animadverting on them.

I felt the blow aimed at my pride, and repulsed their advances with a *fierté*, that rendered them, from that hour, my most implacable enemies. They had been suspected, if not openly accused, of profiting by the inexperience of certain of their companions at play; and, though aware of the suspicion, took no steps to justify themselves, or, if wronged, to call to account those who entertained such suspicions. That such men should presume to seek acquaintance with me, was one of the severest blows ever inflicted on my pride, and while recoiling from it, it increased my sense of injury towards those, who, by their avoidance, had subjected me to it.

My vacations, as when at school, were passed at Mr. Trevyllan's. Sometimes I accompanied him to the continent, but there, as in London, he lived apart from society, and I, consequently, had no opportunity afforded me of entering it. We spent the mornings in sight-seeing, the evenings in theatres, and returned to England as ignorant of the manners and customs of the persons in whose country we had been sojourning, as if we had never entered it. Among the prejudices of Mr. Trevyllan was a strong dislike to foreigners. "If England contains many bad men, be assured the continent possesses no good ones," would he say. "Foreigners cover over their defects with a thick coating of politeness, that helps to conceal them, rendering them thereby more dangerous, because hidden; whereas, an Englishman is less adroit. You soon find him out; therefore, if I always put forth my feelers before I admit a countryman to acquaintanceship, I take especial care to shun foreigners, as I would plague and pestilence."

Strange to say, these illiberal prejudices failed to make any unfavourable impression on my mind, easily as it had hitherto yielded to the opinions

of my guardian. He acknowledged, that he had no personal experience
to lead him to the conclusions he had formed with regard to the general
turpitude of foreigners; and this acknowledgment, induced me, not only
to disbelieve his assertions with regard to them, but also, to question their
justice with regard to our own countrymen. An oppressive weight seemed
removed from my breast, the moment I began to think better of mankind,
and I looked on him who had so long poisoned my mind against my fellow
men as a slanderer; a sorcerer, who had robbed my youth of happiness, by
covering all that was fair and bright with a dark pall, which had chilled and
separated me from sympathy. His wise saws, his constant cautions, became
odious to me; and not unfrequently did I incur his anger, by defending mankind against his unceasing attacks on it. He declared that after all the pains
he had taken to bestow on me the fruit of his own experience, he began to
fear I should nevertheless become as credulous a victim to the wicked and
designing, as if he had never armed me against them; and added, that my
obstinacy in pursuing my own erroneous opinions, unbased as they were
by the experience, which a long contact with society can alone bestow, was
a new proof of the unworthiness of human nature. In escaping from the
misanthropy that had so long enthralled me, I was rushing into an opposite
error. The world assumed as fair an aspect to my view, after the mental
blindness that had obscured my vision, as the blue sky and bright verdure,
does to one, who, long suffering from cataract, is at length restored to sight.
I felt disposed to think all men good, all women fair and pure. The conven-
tional sentiments of virtue, uttered on the stage, not only found an echo in
my breast, but I was disposed to believe that the actor who spoke them felt
them as profoundly as I did; and the actresses were perfect heroines in my
eyes. Their beauty dazzled, their address in enacting their rôles, charmed
me. Mr. Trevyllan surmised this, though I did not express it. He divined it
as accurately, as persons who have an antipathy to cats become conscious
that one of those animals is in a room, however carefully concealed it may
be.

   "I dare be sworn," said he, "that you think that girl, who has just left
the stage, little less than a divinity. Come, you shall see her!" and taking my
arm, he led me out of the box where we sat, spoke to one of the box-keep-
ers, into whose hand he slipped a piece of silver, was guided by him to a
private door, through which, after some few minutes parleying on the part
of the said box-keeper, we were permitted to enter; and on a piece of gold
being given to another man behind the scenes, we were conducted to the
dressing-room of the actress, I had only a few minutes previously thought
so transcendantly lovely. A silver coin to the *femme de chambre*, gained us

admission to the sanctuary of her mistress, who, panting and exhausted, reclined in an easy chair, and presented a most appalling, and fearful contrast, to her I expected to see. The light of a flaring lamp, the odour of which infected the chamber with a most offensive smell, revealed to me a woman, past the meridian of life, whose face was covered with white and red paint, so coarsely laid on, as to leave no doubt of the unskilful artifice, whose lips were smeared with red, and whose eyebrows with black. The gaudy tinsel of her dress, the false stones stuck in her hair, and the care-worn and haggard countenance, struck me with such disgust and dismay, that I involuntarily turned away with a loathing I cannot describe.

"Tell the Signora," said Mr. Trevyllan, "that we ask her pardon for the interruption, occasioned by mistaking her, when on the stage, for an acquaintance," and we hurried from the room.

"That poor painted woman," resumed he, "differs not more from the attractive person she appeared to be when we beheld her at a distance, enacting her part, than do men and women when they are approached closely, and their artifices and deceptions are exposed. Had I not conducted you near that woman, you would have left the theatre with the impression that she was young and beautiful. Let this serve as a lesson to you, not to be imposed on by appearances, and I shall not grudge the money I bestowed, to gain you admission to the dressing-room of Signora Malatesta."

Mr. Trevyllan was as delighted at having exposed to me the sad reality of the poor actress's face and person, as he always was when he laid bare the errors and vices of human kind, and I thanked him as little for this last act of friendship, as I had done for former ones of a similar nature. Few are ever pleased by the destruction of an illusion, and fewer still are grateful to the destroyer.

CHAPTER IV.

I RETURNED to college after my last tour on the continent, almost as ignorant of mankind as when I left it. I had no friend to welcome me back, to question me about what I had seen in foreign lands, or to draw my attention from self, by interesting me about others. The same cold civilities, limited to the common courtesies of life, which, while they never approach cordiality, leave no opening for questioning why it is withheld, met me at every side, except on that of the masters', who distinguished me by an attention as marked as the avoidance of my fellow-collegians. A few days after my return to Christ Church, walking alone one fine evening, as was

my wont, by the banks of the Isis, I picked up a reticule, and seeing two
ladies in advance of me, I concluded that it must appertain to one of them.
I hurried on until I overtook them, and presenting the reticule, found that
my conjecture had been right; it belonged to the elder of the ladies, who
thanked me so warmly for its restoration, that instead of pursuing my walk
alone, I entered into conversation with the ladies, and continued with them.
The younger was about sixteen, and so extremely beautiful and graceful,
that it was impossible for any man to behold, without admiring her. She
mingled little in the conversation carried on by her companion and myself,
but the few words she uttered were marked by good sense.

"You are not quite unknown to me, Mr. Herbert," observed the elder
lady. "My friend Mr. Everett has often spoken to me of your attention to
your studies, and the success with which it has been crowned; but are you
not too much engrossed by them, and might you not sometimes find lei-
sure to enter society?"

I blushed, stammered, and made some only half-intelligible reply, and
this led the lady into a few civil speeches on the pleasure my society would
afford the circumscribed, but not unintellectual circle of which she formed
a member, and to which every student of good acquirements and irreproachable conduct was welcome. I thought, but perhaps it might only be
fancy, that the fair young creature who walked by the side of the elder lady,
looked at me, as if she too would have been glad if the reasoning of her
friend induced me to enter that social circle ready to open for my reception, but a deep blush and down-cast lids prevented my ascertaining, from
a further inspection of that fair face, how far my conjecture was correct.

"This is my niece, Miss Melville, Mr. Herbert, who only arrived last
evening, at Oxford, from London, where she has been finishing her education, if such a task can indeed ever be finished; for do we not find, every day
that passes over our heads, bring us some fresh knowledge, notwithstanding that the more we acquire, the less we find we possess."

The deep blush had faded from the cheek of Miss Melville, leaving it
so delicately fair (not pale) that I thought she looked even more lovely than
when it was suffused with rose colour. I was assenting to the justice of
the elder lady's observation, when suddenly two of my fellow-collegians
approached us, and saluted my new acquaintance. They were, by her, presented to her niece, to whom they immediately addressed some very animated compliments, expressed their long impatience to have the happiness
of being made known to her, and their satisfaction at her becoming an
inhabitant of Oxford. The young lady appeared to be more embarrassed
than pleased by their attentions, which her aunt, observing, came to her

aid, and told the gentlemen that Miss Melville, not being accustomed to compliments, would, she was sure, readily dispense with them, and prefer a more rational conversation. The truth was, that both the young men being passionate admirers of female beauty, were evidently captivated by hers, and each, fearful of being rivalled by his friend, endeavoured to surpass him in the dangerous art of flattery, in the hope of propitiating her favour. She received their compliments with as much coldness and reserve as was consistent with politeness, while I, an anxious observer of what was passing, felt as much pleased with her maidenly and dignified behaviour, as I was displeased by their forwardness and presumption. A formal bow was the only recognition of acquaintance that passed between these gentlemen and myself, and they, confining all their attention to Miss Melville, left her aunt to maintain a conversation with me. Mrs. Scuddamore, for such I discovered was the name of this lady, was a widow, and resided with brother, a well-known and much-respected Professor at Christ Church. Her husband had been a colonel in the army, and a very distinguished officer, with whom she had not only constantly lived with his regiment, but with whom she had actually made more than one campaign. A well-informed and sensible woman—she had many excellent qualities, which had endeared her to the brother officers of her husband—the elder ones considering her in the light of a sister, while the younger looked on her as a mother, whose good advice and kind offices were ever at their service. This familiarity of many years with camps and barracks had considerably detracted from the reserved manners peculiar to well-bred Englishwomen, without, however, abating one particle of the high principle and strict morality for which they are remarkable. A woman who has "roughed it," as the military phrase is, in a barrack, in some out of the way country quarter, making the best of a position requiring no ordinary share of good humour to sustain, and who has not only shared the dangers of her husband and his brother officers in perilous campaigns, but assisted to dress the wounds and nursed the wounded among them, can hardly he expected to retain the decorous reserve and feminine gentleness which form so great a charm in her sex. It was only strangers who found fault with the absence of these womanly qualities, for those who had opportunities of knowing Mrs. Scuddamore well, thought their loss amply compensated for by the cordial kindness of her nature, and the frank and unceremonious friendliness of her manners. It was these peculiarities that led her at once to enter freely into conversation with me, and to encourage my joining her without any previous introduction, on an occasion when most, if not all other women would have merely bowed or curtsied their thanks for the restoration of the reticule;

but I was so ignorant of the usages of society, that this *manque des convénances* did not strike me as it would have done others, and relieved by her frankness from the shyness and constraint under which I always laboured, I felt more disposed to be grateful for her good nature than inclined to question the unceremonious proof of it extended to me. I continued to walk by Mrs. Scuddamore's side, listening to her animated and interesting conversation, while the two gentlemen, whose presence afforded me anything but pleasure, remained by the side of Miss Melville, who never for a moment quitted the arm of her aunt.

Mrs. Scuddamore made several ineffectual attempts to make the conversation general, but my fellow-collegians avoided entering into it, confining themselves to a complimentary strain of remarks addressed exclusively to Miss Melville, and I took especial care to show as decided a desire to refrain from any interchange of words with them, as they did towards me. I could see that Mrs. Scuddamore observed this mutual avoidance with surprise. She became silent and *distraite*, proposed returning home, and I was more than half-tempted to make my bow and retire, but a dread lest such a step might be construed to my disadvantage checked me, and I continued by the side of Mrs. Scuddamore until she reached her abode, at the door of which, although invited to enter, I took my leave. I was glad to find that my fellow-collegians also declined entering the house, as it would retard the explanation Mrs. Scuddamore could not fail to demand relative to the marked coldness existing between them and me. They could only explain it by some statements disadvantageous to me. The simple fact, which they would be sure to assert, that I had no friends in college, that, in short, I was avoided, would in itself be ample cause to justify Mrs. Scuddamore for declining any further acquaintance with me. All these thoughts presented themselves vividly to my mind as I left the door, and pursued my way to Christ Church, the two gentlemen crossing to the opposite side of the street, though pursuing the same direction. The beautiful face and thoughtful eyes of Miss Melville haunted me, and mingled with the painful emotions excited by reflecting on the evil impression which the conduct of the young men was calculated to make on the minds of those who witnessed it. I almost regretted that I had formed any acquaintance with the ladies, greatly as I admired one of them, so certain did I feel that some disagreeable termination would inevitably attend it, owing to the dislike entertained towards me in college; and I deliberated with myself whether it would not be more dignified and consistent with the respect due to myself to avoid all further intercourse with Mrs. Scuddamore, and her fair niece, than to wait the chance of their taking a similar step towards me. And then came the thought that my refraining from taking advantage of the invitation of Mrs. Scuddamore, pressed too with a warmth and friendliness that had evidently displeased the young men present when it was given, would amount to a tacit acknowledgment that I was unworthy of her kindness, and this thought added to my chagrin. After much deliberation I determined to pay her a visit the following day, and let her reception decide my future intercourse with these ladies. I would judge whether or not they had imbibed any prejudice against me from the coolness of my fellow collegians, and if I found them as well disposed as before, I would certainly cultivate an acquaintance which possessed so much attraction for me. I dreamt of Miss Melville that night, and perpetrated a sonnet addressed to her next morning. These two unusual occurrences to one so inexperienced in the tender passion as myself, convinced me that I was indeed in love, and such a conviction goes far to accomplish that which may be, in truth, but a mere passing fancy. Ignorant of the world as I was, I knew not that the seclusion in which I had dwelt, the absence of all female society, and, above all, never having lived in habits of confidential intimacy with any of my own sex, had prepared my heart to receive an impression from the first pretty face that chance might throw in my way, but that it required time, and a knowledge of the individual, to ripen admiration into affection.

No; I believe that Love full grown, and ready armed with all his darts, was to jump into my heart with as great facility as Minerva had sprung into life from the brain of Jove, and I yielded to what I fancied was my destiny, and cherished a foolish passion for a girl I had seen but once, and with whom I had never exchanged three words. Strange infatuation of youth, fruit of inexperience!

I was, however, far from viewing my sudden passion for Miss Melville in its true light. Nay, had any one attempted to explain it to me as the natural result of my previous mode of existence, I would have resented the suggestion with anger, as an insult. I persuaded myself that she, and she only, could have awakened the dormant passion in my heart, which at sight of her burst into an unextinguishable flame. I endowed her with every charm, every accomplishment, with the reckless profusion with which only youthful lovers can enrich the object of their first attachment, and having created this idol, I, like Pygmalion, became in love with my own work. A new world opened to me, and Miss Melville was the enchantress, at the touch of whose magic wand the doors of this Paradise flew asunder to give me entrance. All nature seemed changed. The skies were brighter, the earth greener, the trees more beautiful, the flowers more fragrant. And all this had been effected by one with the tones of whose voice my ear was yet unfamiliar, with whose character, disposition, and modes of thinking I was a stranger! Oh! ye young beauties, who, when ye regard your images in a mirror, count on the triumphs the lovely faces reflected in it can achieve, how little do ye doubt that the charms on which ye gaze with delighted vanity, potent though they may be, are far less so, than those with which the ardent imagination of a lover can endow ye. Never did nature create aught so transcendently fair as that ideal "which youthful poets fancy when they love," and every youthful lover becomes a poet. As I dwelt on the image of Miss Melville, so rapidly did its loveliness increase in my mind's eye that I became dazzled, intoxicated. She appeared a miracle of beauty, and after I had indulged several hours' reverie on her charms, I felt surprised that I had been able to contemplate them so coldly when she was present. I could now comprehend the admiration excited by the first glance at her in my fellow collegians, and almost excuse the compliments they had addressed to her, and which, on the previous day, had appeared so fulsome and impertinent, when I listened to them.

"How flat, stale, and unprofitable,"

appeared the long hours of that day, until released from college, I was at liberty to go forth in search of the object which occupied all my thoughts. Never had I before taken any pains about my appearance beyond what propriety required, but now I could not satisfy myself, so anxious was I to appear to advantage in her eyes, and for the nonce, I was in danger of becoming a fop. I looked in my mirror frequently before I went forth, and never felt so dissatisfied with my own appearance, so plain and forbidding did it look after the bright image that filled my thoughts. How could one so fair, so matchless, condescend to glance with a favourable eye on aught so rude as me? was the next thought, and such a sense of my own personal demerits flashed on my mind, that I almost dreaded to meet her, whom a few minutes before I longed to behold. If humility be one of the proofs of love, then indeed might I well believe in the depth and sincerity of my passion, for never did the plainest of my sex feel a stronger consciousness of his own want of attraction than did I.

CHAPTER V.

I CALLED at Mrs. Scuddamore's, and was admitted. My reception was more than polite, it was cordial. That lady had a frankness of demeanour as well as of manner that soon set every one at his ease. Miss Melville was seated at her tambour frame when I entered, and a soft blush mantled her face as she raised it to return my salute. If I had thought her beautiful the previous evening, how much more lovely did she now appear in my eyes, her finely shaped head no longer, as then, concealed by a bonnet, and her exquisitely modelled bust, uncovered by a shawl, its delicate proportions revealed by the close fitting white morning robe in which she was attired. Her snowy throat, round as a pillar of marble, supported her head with a peculiar grace and dignity. I could hardly withdraw my eyes from her; and she, as if conscious that they were fixed on her face, seldom raised hers, but pursued her work, her small, rounded, white hand and taper fingers appearing to singular advantage while employed in passing and repassing the gay-coloured silken threads.

"I was afraid you would not come," said Mrs. Scuddamore, "for you are, I have taken it into my head, a little *sauvage*—come, confess, am I not right? You must get over this; for nothing mars a man's success in life so much as shyness."

The colour rose to my face as well as to Miss Melville's at this well meant but *brusque* remark of her aunt's, and I felt my admiration of her increased by this sympathy between us.

"You are going to tell me it is constitutional—that you can't help it," resumed the lady; "but that is all nonsense. I have known young ensigns join their regiments, to whom one could not say 'Good morrow,' without their blushing like a boarding-school girl; just as Georgina did two minutes ago—I suppose for the sake of keeping you company—yet before they had been a month at mess, they would have been the first to have laughed at the *mauvaise honte* of a new comer, so completely had they conquered their shyness."

Miss Melville's face was now a deep rose-colour, and she bent lower than before over her embroidery frame to conceal it, while I muttered something almost as incomprehensible to myself as to Mrs. Scuddamore, about the seclusion of a college life tending to encourage shyness.

"But your fellow-collegians—and I know several—are not shy," said the lady. "On the contrary, I think they seem rather in the other extreme. For example, the two young men who joined us last evening, and who nearly overpowered Georgina, whom they had never previously seen, with compliments."

I felt my embarrassment increase every moment during this scene. I knew not what to say, and Mrs. Scuddamore was not a woman to let a subject drop once she had commenced it. I endeavoured to divert her attention to other topics talked of—the environs, the walks, the rides, and that unfailing subject to an Englishman—the weather.

"Come, come," replied Mrs. Scuddamore, "I see you want to shirk the subject, and I won't let you. I was so long a sort of mother to a set of young men like yourself, in my dear husband's regiment, that I can't help thinking myself still privileged, as then, to give advice, or call to account. Why were you so distant and reserved with your fellow-collegians last evening?"

"We know little of each other, and therefore are on very distant terms," was my stupid answer.

"And whose fault is it?" demanded my persecutor. "Do they avoid your acquaintance, or is it you who will not encourage theirs?"

"I believe the avoidance is mutual."

"But there must be some cause, some motive for this; and as a man of spirit, the person conscious of being avoided ought to come to an explanation with him or them who showed him such a slight. I am the widow of an old soldier, as brave a man as ever commanded a battalion; and he, I am sure, would have thought very ill of a young officer who allowed another to avoid him without demanding satisfaction. It won't do to say 'he avoids me, and I avoid him.' No; a man must permit no one to have the air of declining his acquaintance, however he may be disposed to undervalue the person offering such a slight. The laws of honour—and I admit no other in such affairs—are very strict in such matters. I have known a hundred quarrels, and as many duels, for similar causes; and I advise you, if you wish to maintain the respect due to every gentleman, never to allow a man to assume the air of avoiding your acquaintance."

"Dear aunt!" interrupted Miss Melville, casting an appealing glance at the soldier-like Mrs. Scuddamore.

"Dear aunt, what?" reiterated the aunt. But the bashful girl became silent, and the lady resumed: "Ah! I see, that foolish Georgy is afraid I may get you into a duel. And what if I do? Better one now than several perhaps hereafter, when some of those young men who believe they shun you, while you believe you avoid them, may hereafter meet you in society, and their air of avoidance may lead to disagreeable results. Honour before everything, is my maxim. It was that of Colonel Scuddamore, than whom a better judge on such points never existed. I remember once, when a young officer joined his regiment, some of the juniors took a dislike to his dress, the cut of his hair, his accent, or some other equally efficient cause of objection, and arranged among themselves to send him to Coventry, as it is called, but which means, shunning intercourse with a man. The young fellow, a brave lad too, took fire at this marked coldness; and not knowing on which, of some six or eight young men, he was to fix a quarrel, wrote a challenge to each. The Colonel discovered it, called a meeting of the officers in question, and insisted on knowing the cause of the challenge. They confessed it had originated in their avoidance of the young ensign. He demanded the cause. No reason could be assigned, except that the new comer's air and manner had not pleased them. 'I consider myself as good a judge on this point, gentlemen,' said he, 'as you. I see nothing to find fault with in the air and manner of Mr.——; and much as I disapprove duelling in my regiment, I am forced to admit that Mr.—— could do nothing less than what he has done, after the slight offered to him. I will allow no man to be sent to Coventry in my regiment; for, should he merit such a proceeding, I will take care he does not remain in it. I will speak to this young officer, and bring him to reason; and I insist that every one of you who have shown him a slight, will apologise. Men of honour should ever be as ready to express regret when in the wrong, as to maintain their opinions when in the right. I will dine at the mess to-day, where I expect to see perfect harmony restored; and this young man, who has proved his sense of honour, and courage, treated with the cordiality to which, as a brave brother soldier, he is entitled.' This was the way in which Colonel Scuddamore settled such matters, and this is the way in which I would advise every man to act when a slight is offered him."

Mrs. Scuddamore had hardly concluded this last sentence, when Percival and Mordaunt, my two fellow-collegians, were announced, and entered the room. They looked surprised and displeased when they perceived me, and their bow of recognition was so slight as to exempt me from the necessity of returning it. Both approached Miss Melville, and, drawing a chair on each side of her, seemed disposed to forget the presence of Mrs. Scuddamore and myself. I felt that lady's eyes were on me, and this increased my perturbation. I was inclined to leave the room; indeed, I arose for that purpose, but a moment's reflection induced me to resume my seat, fully determined to take an early opportunity of seeking an explanation with the gentlemen present. It was no want of courage that had hitherto withheld me from such a measure, and often and often had I contemplated it, but pride—ungovernable pride—strange as the assertion may seem, had prevented my putting it into execution. What, was I to give them the triumph of thus acknowledging that *they* had offended me, when I had invariably maintained the air of having avoided *them*? But *now* that I had been told by another, and that other a woman too, what was the right conduct to pursue, I determined no longer to submit to what in my secret soul I felt to be a premeditated train of slights.

"I was just repeating to Mr. Herbert," said Mrs. Scuddamore, "an incident that occurred in the regiment of my husband relative to a young officer, who, for no earthly reason, some of his brother officers were disposed to send to Coventry, and for which the young officer called them out."

"They probably had some cause for wishing to send him to Coventry?" observed Percival.

"None—positively, none; except the absurd and puerile one of not approving his dress, his voice, the cut of his hair, or some other foolish motive for dislike."

"You know the verses, Madam," said Mordaunt:—

> "'I do not like thee, Dr. Fell;
> The reason why, I cannot tell;
> But this I know, I feel full well—
> I do not like thee, Dr. Fell.'

Be assured that there is much meaning in these often quoted lines. One cannot always explain, even to one's self, the precise motive for dislike, nor conquer a repugnance."

"For my part," remarked Percival, "I see no reason why one should. The world is large enough for every man to find persons who do not inspire him with dislike, without compelling the necessity of his associating with those who do."

"Ah, well! had you been in my husband's regiment, he would have insisted on your behaving with politeness to your brother officers, however you might have disliked them, unless they had indeed behaved ill to you. Colonel Scuddamore never allowed symptoms of dislike to be displayed towards each other by his officers."

"Perhaps the officers of his regiment were not over fastidious in their tastes, and consequently were not given to entertain dislikes?" said Mordaunt, assuming a supercilious air.

"They were as gentlemanly a corps of officers as any in the army," replied Mrs. Scuddamore, turning red in the face; "and his example and knowledge of discipline were too well calculated to render them so, to admit a doubt of the fact."

"Heaven forbid that I should call the merit of the colonel or his regiment in question! It would be unpardonable in me who have so often been enlightened on the subject!" observed Mordaunt, with a sarcastic smile.

"It would be unpardonable in any one who ever heard of Colonel Scuddamore," retorted his widow, warmly; "for his bravery and gentlemanlike conduct were acknowledged, not only by those who knew him, but by all who ever heard his name mentioned."

"Your suffrage on these points, Madam, is quite sufficient to satisfy Mordaunt and myself. Ladies, and particularly those who have gone
through a campaign, and lived in barracks, must be excellent judges, not
only of discipline and gentlemanly manners, but also of refinement." And
Percival assumed a mock gravity while uttering this remark, that indicated
his intention of quizzing Mrs. Scuddamore.

"I don't think that you, Sir, can be much of a judge on the subject we
are conversing on," replied Mrs. Scuddamore; "for a knowledge of gentlemanly conduct, or refinement, would prevent your attempting to banter a
woman."

"*I* attempt to banter *you?*" interrupted Percival. "By Jove, I would as
soon attempt it with the most experienced field-officer in the army!"

"And I," said Mordaunt, "who look on you, Madam, as the best authority on all military subjects, only regret that you do not give to the world at
large the fruits of your experience. Don't you, Percival?"

"I feel that I was wrong, gentlemen, to waste my time in attempting to
make you sensible on points in which, it is now clear to me, you are very
defective in knowledge; and, to prevent my making a similar mistake again,
I must request that in future you will not honour me with your visits."

"A request, which, had it been made two days before,"—(and here
Mordaunt looked in a peculiar manner at Miss Melville,)—"I should have
acceded to with much more readiness than at present, although it must
have deprived me of the advantage of hearing the admirable exordium on
military discipline, with which I have this day been favoured." And here he
bowed to Mrs. Scuddamore with mock humility.

This impertinence towards a woman, and one, too, whose age entitled
her to respect, I could no longer resist from noticing. I was not sorry either,
for, being furnished with a plausible excuse for resenting my own private
wrongs, while apparently only defending those of a woman. I therefore
stood up, and addressing Mr. Percival said, that, "As Mrs. Scuddamore
desired a discontinuance of the future visits of himself and his friend,
it would be, I conceived, more agreeable to her to have the present one
abridged."

"I do not see what right you have to become the interpreter of the
lady's thoughts or wishes," observed Percival, insolently.

"And I," said Mordaunt, "must request you not to meddle in anything
that has the slightest reference to me."

"Oh, no, Mr. Herbert!" exclaimed Miss Melville, standing up in evident
trepidation, and approaching me.

"Georgina, my dear, be seated; leave these gentlemen to settle their little differences," said Mrs. Scuddamore; "Mr. Herbert has acted precisely as Colonel Scuddamore would have done in a similar case."

"Then I am to understand that you are the champion of this lady?" And Percival bowed to Mrs. Scuddamore,—"that you, in short, wish to dictate to me with regard to the length of my visit?"

"Yes," answered I; "I will see no lady treated with rudeness in my presence without marking my disapproval of such conduct."

"You shall hear from me, Sir."

"And from me too," added Mordaunt, and both left the room, bowing to the ladies.

"Oh! dear aunt, how dreadful," exclaimed Miss Melville, her beautiful face pale with terror. "Surely you will not allow Mr. Herbert to expose his life about such a trifle."

"As the widow of a brave and distinguished soldier, I cannot advise Mr. Herbert, were he even my own son, to pass over the ungentlemanly conduct of these men."

"No representations, Madam, could induce me to deny these gentlemen the satisfaction they consider they have a right to demand," replied I, flattered by the interest and alarm the lovely girl before me evinced in my favour. I felt that to excite this interest, I would readily risk my life; and the thought of being able at length to prove that a want of courage was not the cause of my having hitherto allowed the marked coldness of my fellow collegians to pass unquestioned, filled me with satisfaction. The reflection that I might kill, or be killed, natural to a thinking being, at such a moment, never entered my mind. The weight of a mountain seemed removed from my breast by an opportunity having been afforded me of vindicating my wounded feelings—so long oppressed by a sense of being slighted, if not insulted. To fight, too, in the cause of Mrs. Scuddamore, was like a homage offered to her beautiful niece, and this notion added to my alacrity to meet Percival and Mordaunt.

"I am really gratified, my dear Mr. Herbert, to observe your cheerfulness under present circumstances," said Mrs. Scuddamore. "My brave husband would have approved it, and would have gladly lent his presence as your friend."

The word friend jarred on my ear, by reminding me that I had no one to whom I could appeal as mine, and as this recollection flashed on my mind, I became embarrassed.

"I hope," resumed Mrs. Scuddamore, "that you have some person worthy of confiding in on this occasion. A man brave without being overbearing or domineering, firm without being obstinate, polite without the least obsequiousness—such is the man into whose hands you ought to entrust the arrangement of this affair."

Shame prevented me from avowing that I had no friend. Might it not be received as a tacit acknowledgment that I had not merited one? I said something about not knowing any one possessed of the various qualifications which the lady had named as necessary in the person who was to act as a friend in a duel.

"I do know one," replied Mrs. Scuddamore, "who will, I am sure, at my request, take the whole management of this business into his hands. The person in question is an old brother officer of my husband, placed on half-pay, and living within a mile of Oxford. I will instantly write to him, and he will, I am quite sure, see you, and communicate with the friends chosen by Messrs. Percival and Mordaunt. You shall have the pistols of my dear husband, which I consider among the most valued of my possessions. I did not think they would ever again be used; but in defence of his widow, and to chastise an impertinence offered to her, I do not believe I am doing wrong in lending them."

It was a curious contrast to witness the perfect coolness with which Mrs. Scuddamore talked this matter over, speaking of pistols with as much indifference as other ladies speak of fans, while her niece, pale and agitated, shuddered whenever the name of these murderous instruments was pronounced, and evinced an involuntary horror that might have led even a less vain man than me to imagine that she took a more than ordinary interest in his safety. I took my leave, not however without receiving particular and repeated injunctions from Mrs. Scuddamore, to avoid being placed with my back to the horizon, when on the ground, and not to wear a light coloured waistcoat. On entering college, I found a challenge from Percival, and another from Mordaunt, desiring me to name a friend who could arrange with the gentlemen they had selected, where and when the meeting was to take place. I felt certain that both my antagonists had anticipated, with some degree of satisfaction, the difficulty in which I should be placed to find a friend, while they, living in habits of intimacy with their fellow-collegians, might choose from a number the individual who was to witness their killing, or being killed. I sat down and wrote a letter to my mother, to be sent her in case I fell. With no less than two duels on my hands, the chances of this catastrophe were against me, and as this fact occurred to me, I became conscious of an emotion as new as it was strange. It was not fear. No, not a shade of that entered in my feelings, but the thought that I might never more see my poor mother, never behold another day, sobered me, and opened a spring of tenderness towards my parent that brought a moisture to my eyes, and would have flooded hers, had they perceived the expressions it prompted.

CHAPTER VI.

How many thoughts crowd into the mind when a human being is men-aced with the possibility of a sudden summons to another world!—This rush of thoughts becomes greatly increased, when he who experiences it is in the full vigour of youth and health, when the prospects of life are but opening to him, and Hope, the Syren, points to future happiness, and whispers honeyed words. To feel the heart throbbing high, the young blood flowing swiftly through the veins, promising lengthened years, yet to know that in a few hours all may be over—that this animated frame may be but as a clod of common earth to be quickly consigned to its native clay, to be shut in for ever from the light of day, the breath of summer, to become food for the worm, is indeed an appalling thought to all, but how much more especially to one who had never before contemplated death, but as an event so distant, that no definite notion had been formed of it, no dread entertained. Neglected duties, time misspent, and oh! most terrible of all thoughts, the Almighty forgotten until one may be summoned to *His* dread presence, rise up in fearful array, filling the heart with terror of "that bourne whence no traveller returns," and of which the profound mystery, may, in a few fast fleeting hours be solved! And yet but a short time before, I had felt satisfaction in the anticipation of these duels. Not from a desire of vengeance on my adversaries, not from a vain-glorious spirit, but sim-ply and solely, from a desire of vindicating myself from the slights I had experienced, without sacrificing my pride by avowing my sense of them. How may a few hours, nay more, a few minutes change the feelings! The revolution in my mind had been effected by writing to my mother. I could not take a farewell of her that might be eternal, without sentiments of natural affection being awakened, which once aroused, give rise to serious reflections and sadness. The written words of adieu, as they marked my paper, dimmed my eyes with tears; and as I brushed them hastily away, I was glad that my door being locked, no intruder could enter to be a spy on my deep emotion, and probably to misjudge its cause, attributing that to want of courage, which in truth originated in filial affection. My letter concluded, I placed it in my desk, and had only done so, when a knock at my door announced a visitor. When admitted, a tall thin elderly man, with scanty locks, whitened by time, stood before me—he wore a black stock,

a blue coat, and military boots. "Your name, I believe, Sir, is Herbert," said
he. I bowed assent, and requested him to be seated.

"I have called on you by desire of Mrs. Scuddamore to offer my services
as a friend in a duel which I understand is to be the consequence of some
words which passed between you and two of your fellow-collegians. As
an old soldier I have had some little experience in such affairs, and will
gladly make it available to you, Mrs. Scuddamore having expressed to me
the interest she feels for you."

I bowed my thanks, and said something about my gratitude to that
lady.

"Yes, Sir, she deserves respect and esteem, not only as the widow of
one of the bravest and most honourable of men, but a lady who joins to
all the virtue and goodness of her sex, all the heroic courage and high
sense of honour that appertains to the most distinguished of ours. 'I tell
you, Captain Brady,' said she to me, 'that had you not been within reach
to go out with this young man, I do believe I would have assumed male
attire, put on for the nonce the military undress of your gallant colonel, my
ever-to-be-lamented husband, and gone to the ground with him.'

"And she would have done it, Sir, for such is her sense of honour, that
she could not bear to have you left unprovided with a friend on such an
occasion."

All this was spoken with the utmost gravity, and with a strong Hibernian
accent, and it was plain that Captain Brady, though he saw little to wonder
at, saw much to admire in the military ardour of the widow of his colonel.
I wrote a few lines to Messrs. Percival and Mordaunt, to name Captain
Brady as the friend who would be ready to meet theirs, to arrange time and
place for our rencontre; and having despatched my notes, we awaited the
result. During the time that intervened, my new acquaintance informed
me that his health having suffered from several wounds received in action,
he had been compelled to retire on half-pay, and had selected the vicinity
of Oxford solely for the purpose of being near Mrs. Scuddamore, in order
to be at all times ready to receive her commands.

"There was not an officer in her husband's regiment, Sir," continued
he, "who would not have been glad to consider himself as much under
her command, as they had been proud to serve under that of their gallant
colonel, for she was as much adored in the regiment, as he was beloved and
respected. She was the mother of the young officers, Sir, their monitress
and adviser; and the sister and friend of the old. The very private soldiers
worshipped her, while the dread of incurring her bad opinion, preserved
their wives from the levity and bad conduct which too often marks the sol-

diers' wives. She established schools for the girls, over which she presided; while the colonel personally superintended those for the men and boys, and she engaged every officer's wife to follow her good example; forming a little circle of female society in the regiment, remarkable for decorum, agreeability, and good nature. Such, Sir, was Mrs. Scuddamore. No wonder, then, that all who had opportunities of knowing her, should esteem and reverence her, and be ready, like me, to fulfil her commands."

The friends of Messrs. Percival and Mordaunt, having now come to arrange preliminaries with Captain Brady, he saw them in another room. They at first, as I afterwards learned, sought to banter the old soldier, and proposed conditions to which he would not accede, but they soon discovered that he was not a man to be imposed on; and when the arrangements for my double duel were completed, he astonished the gentlemen who acted for Percival and Mordaunt, by informing them that when my affairs were settled, he must demand satisfaction from both those individuals, for the want of respect evinced towards the widow of his late chief by them. It was in vain that the seconds declared that their friends, having had no disagreement with Captain Brady, they would not be called on to fight with him; he persisted in stating, that a want of respect towards the wife of his colonel, was the greatest offence that could be offered to him, and that he must receive the *amende honorable* for it.

I went to the ground, accompanied by Captain Brady, and an old brother in arms of his, a Captain Collyer, who lived with him. The distance was measured, I was placed opposite my adversary, Mr. Percival; Mr. Mordaunt being at a little distance, ready to take his place when I had done with his friend. We were to fire at a signal given by our seconds. My shot took away a corner of the skirt of Mr. Percival's coat, while his went through the crown of my hat, within an inch of my head. My adversary, being the challenger, was asked if he were satisfied, and having answered in the affirmative, an answer, I believe, occasioned by the certainty that he was afterwards to stand a shot from Captain Brady, we bowed to each other, and Mr. Mordaunt took the place of Percival. The same ceremony was gone through. We fired,—I was untouched, but my adversary fell on the earth. For a few moments I was horror-struck. I believed he was dead, or dying, and I rushed up to the spot where he was lying, his second and Percival supporting him. He was pale as death, but when his coat and waistcoat were opened, it was found that my ball had merely grazed the skin of his right side, over the ribs, and passed out through his garments behind, inflicting only a skin wound, which, however, dyed his clothes with blood. His fall was, I suppose, occasioned by the shock. One thing, however, was certain, which was, that he believed himself mortally wounded, nor could the assertions to the contrary made by his friends lessen his alarm.

"I know something of these matters, young gentleman," said Captain Brady, "and I can assure you your wound is only a scratch, of which, in a couple of days, you will bear scarcely a mark. I had hoped, that if you are now satisfied with regard to Mr. Herbert, you would, on the spot, afford me the satisfaction I demand, and so have the business over at once. If, however, you prefer it, I shall be at your service to-morrow, or next day."

The disconsolate countenance of Mr. Mordaunt was almost ludicrous. He shook his head, and pronounced with a tragic air,

"They jest at scars who never felt a wound."

"That cannot apply to me, Sir," replied Captain Brady, angrily, "for I have no less than fourteen wounds on my body, received in the service of my country, and three balls, which never could be extracted. But to conclude, are you satisfied with Mr. Herbert, or do you wish another shot?"

"I am quite satisfied, Sir, perfectly so; and as I have given you no offence, I really think it unreasonable that I should be expected to fight again."

"If you will apologize, that is, write a proper letter to ask pardon of the lady whom you offended by your *persiflage*, I will not insist on your fighting."

"I have no objection," was the reply, the speaker making wry faces and sundry contortions, indicative of the uneasiness he was suffering from his wound. "I will dictate the apology, Sir," resumed Captain Brady, "and my second as well as yours, will add their signatures to it."

"Hang it, Mordaunt! don't let the Captain carry it all his own way. Stand another shot, man. Your wound is only skin deep."

"Why should I stand another shot, Percival, when I am satisfied?"

"You ought to consult your second. You placed your honour in his hands, and should abide by his decision."

The second was a good-tempered, good-natured young man, and, moreover, he saw that Mordaunt had enough of fighting, so he gave it as his opinion "that Mr. Mordaunt, having been wounded, need not be expected to fight again, and that an apology to a lady, was perfectly consistent with the laws of honour;" a decision that evidently afforded perfect satisfaction to Mr. Mordaunt.

"You, I presume, Sir," said Captain Brady, addressing Mr. Percival, "will have no objection to our settling our quarrel at once."

"Not the least, Sir; the sooner the better."

The ground was again measured, the signal given, the adversaries fired. Captain Brady was not touched, but Mr. Percival had two of the fingers of his right hand shot off, when the seconds interfered, and would not allow another shot to be exchanged, as Percival proposed, after having wrapped his hand in his handkerchief with perfect *sang froid*. It was agreed on the spot, that to prevent the consequences which a knowledge of the duels would inevitably entail on collegians, the whole affair was to be kept a secret, and the bursting of a gun was to be alleged as the cause of the loss of Percival's fingers.

"But *my* wound; how is that to be explained?" inquired Mordaunt.

"It can only be discovered by your washer-woman," replied Captain Brady, "who can be told it was the scratch of a pin:" a remark which occasioned considerable hilarity in all save him at whom it was levelled. The apology was written by Captain Brady, signed by Mordaunt, and attested by his second and Captain Collyer.

"And now, young gentleman," said the worthy Irishman to me, "accept the offered friendship of an old soldier. You have conducted yourself all through this affair as an honourable and brave man, who is worthy of esteem."

And so saying, he took his departure, leaving me more self-satisfied than I had been for years, in the consciousness of having vindicated my honour.

Nor was I unmindful of the effect likely to be produced on the mind of Miss Melville by this duel. Women are prone to think favourably of him who is ready to resent any slight offered to them, and if she betrayed so much interest for my safety before the duel, might I not anticipate a kind reception when I again presented myself to her, certain as I felt that Captain Brady would not omit anything in the narration of the circumstance that could tend to raise me in the estimation of both ladies. Yes, I would certainly call on them that evening, to receive the meed of their approval.

CHAPTER VII.

FILLED with pleasurable anticipations of my coming interview with Mrs. Scuddamore and her beautiful niece, I entered my room, and found a letter in an unknown hand, which had arrived while I had been absent. It contained intelligence of the sudden death of Mr. Trevyllan, which had occurred the preceding morning, and required my presence in town for the opening of the will.

How strange and unfathomable is the heart of man! My first thought on reading the letter was regret at being compelled to leave Oxford without seeing Miss Melville; without beholding her bright eyes sparkle, and her fair cheek suffused with blushes of pleasure at our meeting, while the duel, which had, I felt certain, caused her the utmost alarm and anxiety, was still so recent, and fresh in her memory. I had looked forward to a meeting at the present time with such a conviction, that with so artless a nature as hers, it would draw forth some unconscious and involuntary demonstrations of the secret preference which I hoped I had awakened in her heart, that I could not abandon the self-promised pleasure without great disappointment and regret: and yet, unfeeling as this may appear, I was, nevertheless, shocked, if not grieved, at the news just received. There is something in the sudden death of one with whom we have been for years living in habits of intimacy, that produces a strong impression on the mind,—and I felt this; for, although the deceased was not a person to awaken affection, or to experience sympathy, nevertheless, he had been invariably kind to me; and, in the gratitude which his good nature created, I was disposed to forget the different traits in his character which had so often displeased, ay, and worse, which had produced so bad an effect on my own mind, and, by so doing, had entailed annoyances on me, the result of which might influence my destiny through life.

I notified the necessity of my departure to the proper authority, and set out immediately for London. I was received with such marked obsequiousness by the two upper servants of the late Mr. Trevyllan, that it instantly struck me that they supposed I was left heir to his property. Their alacrity to wait on me, their desire to anticipate my wants and wishes was evident, and their affected regret for their late master was so ill played, that no one could be imposed on by it. It is true, they assumed a lugubrious countenance and tone of voice when they spoke of their poor master, but no semblance of a tear moistened their eyes, no remembered acts of generosity or goodness on his part loosened their tongues to praise him, now that he was no more, and his mortal remains were left unattended, unregarded, in the solitary chamber of death, while they devoted all their thoughts and care to propitiate him whom they believed would succeed to his property.

"Two more rapacious harpies I have never encountered than the two upper servants of my poor friend," said Mr. Vise, one of the executors, to me, the day of my arrival. "I do believe they concealed his death several hours from me, in order to gain time to rob him before I could place the seals on his effects. I have been compelled several times to reprove their neglect of his remains. Ah! Mr. Herbert, if the life of an old bachelor be a cheerless and dreary one, the death-bed is an awful scene. Left to the tender mercies of hirelings, careless of his comfort now when they know he can never more reprehend or punish their neglect: no tender partner of his life to smoothe his pillow, and watch his every glance: no affectionate son, no fond and duteous daughter, to hover round the dying bed, to wipe the moisture from his brow, to lift the cup to his lip: no faltering voice, tremulous from affection, to read the word of God, or to pray: no tender hand to close his eyes: but, in the place of those dear relatives, paid menials, who served but for hire, and who wait but for death, for which they are impatient, in order to plunder; who mock the dead, who can no longer deter them from indulging in their rapaciousness and cupidity, and who long to enjoy unmolested the fruits of their dishonesty. These servants declare, that, finding their late master had not rang his bell in the morning, as usual, they had gone to his chamber, where they found him dead. Now, the usual hour of my poor friend's ringing his bell was eight in the morning, and supposing that they did not enter his room until ten o'clock, two hours after the usual hour of his awaking, how came it that they called in no physician until half-past twelve o'clock, two hours after?

"Dr. Morrington informed me that he was entering his carriage precisely at half-past twelve, when Turner, the butler of Mr. Trevyllan, came to summon him to his master, whom he stated he had just discovered, to all appearance, lifeless in his bed. This looks very suspicious, does it not? and engenders various vague and painful surmises in my mind. Who knows, but that if our poor friend had been attended to in time, he might have been saved! It is most painful to think what might have occurred in his last hours, left solely in the hands of these persons. Poor Trevyllan, too, was very imprudent. He often boasted to me of his sagacity in securing the services of his domestics for much less wages than are generally given, by holding out to them the prospect of being well provided for at his death; and I have seen him laugh in the anticipation of their disappointment when the contents of his will should be made known, and that they found he had cheated their hopes. I find that several boxes were removed from the house at six o'clock the morning of his death, that is, four hours before, as they state, they were aware of that event. I have sent to the coroner, in order that an inquest may be held, and a strict investigation be gone into, for I cannot divest my mind of very painful suspicions."

The inquest was held, and in the investigation it came out, that the housemaid heard her master's bell ring at about twelve o'clock at night, he having gone to bed at eleven. She was exact about the hour she heard the bell ring, for she had only just got into bed, having remained up later than usual to do some needlework for herself, and she heard the house-clock strike twelve, four or five minutes before. Knowing that her master's night-bell rang into the butler's room, she concluded he would hear, and attend to it, but mentioned the circumstance next morning to the housekeeper, who said she must be mistaken, for that in her room, which was very near Mr. Trevyllan's, she heard no bell.

The housekeeper appeared angry when she persisted in saying, she had positively heard the bell. The kitchen-maid told the housemaid that when she came down stairs at six o'clock in the morning she found a hackney-coach at the hall-door, nearly filled with chests and boxes, into which a man, whose face she did not see, he was so wrapped up, got, and the coach was hurriedly driven off when she appeared at the door.

The kitchen-maid, alarmed, looked around the house to see if anything was wrong, or missing, met the housekeeper on the stairs, to whom she communicated the circumstance, as also her intention of calling the butler; but was told by the housekeeper to do no such thing, and to mind her own business. The housekeeper never came down stairs before eight o'clock, but that particular day she was down at six. The butler did not make his appearance until nine o'clock, nor was the death of Mr. Trevyllan made known in the house until twelve. Several times previously to that hour, she, when in the front area, had seen the butler going backwards and forwards through the hall door with a large cloak on, beneath which he seemed to have some bulky packages. The housemaid stated, that Mr. Trevyllan's breakfast was always served at nine o'clock, but on that morning no preparation for breakfast had been made; and on her remark this fact to the housekeeper, at about half-past nine, that person had said, "True, I suppose Mr. Turner has forgotten it;" and she went herself to the butler's pantry, and placed the breakfast things ready on the tray—a thing which she, the housemaid, had never before seen her do.

The *autopsie* having taken place, it was declared that Mr. Trevyllan had died of apoplexy; and the verdict of the jury was, that suspicious circumstances having occurred, implicating the housekeeper and butler with having concealed their master's death for several hours after they must have been cognizant of that fact, and having sent packages secretly out of the house, it was advisable they should be taken into custody, and retained until a strict examination of the property, to be compared with the inventories, should prove whether or not any portion of it was deficient. It was found that the inventories given up by Turner and the housekeeper by no means corresponded with those produced by Mr. Vise, the executor, although it was stated on the back of each of these last, that the butler and housekeeper had duplicates of them. It appeared that the persons were not aware of the existence of these duplicates until their production, and had destroyed the original ones, causing false inventories to be drawn up, which omitted the various articles of value, to a very large amount, which they had from time to time abstracted, with the intention of possessing themselves of, but which they had kept ready packed in the house, lest at any time the articles should be missed, but which they had sent away when they believed themselves safe from discovery, by the death of their master; little dreaming that he had guarded against their cupidity.

They were taken into custody; a reward was offered by Mr. Vise in the public papers to the hackney coachman who had conveyed away the boxes from Mr. Trevyllan's door on the morning in question. The promised reward brought the coachman to claim it, and led to the discovery of all the stolen property worth several hundred pounds, which was restored to Mr. Vise. The two culprits were lodged in prison, to await their trial; and now the will was opened. A bequest of five thousand pounds to Mr. Vise; one of double that sum, as well as his plate, linen, china, glass, and books, to me; and the rest of his fortune, a very large one, to public charities, comprised the contents. His house, also, was bequeathed to me.

Thus died a man whose whole life had been passed in a total and reckless disregard of his fellow-men, of whom he judged so uncharitably as to believe that all who were kind and generous, were destitute of common sense, and the selfish and unfeeling alone were wise.

"How poor Trevyllan would have enjoyed his two unworthy servants having been caught in the meshes of the net which their own cupidity had wrought," said Mr. Vise; "this would have been deemed by him an illustration of his favourite theory, that most persons, and more especially servants, miss no opportunity of defrauding whenever they think they can do so with impunity."

The last solemn duties offered to the dead being over, I was on the point of returning to Oxford, leaving Mr. Vise to arrange the affairs connected with the bequest to me from Mr. Trevyllan, when a letter from Mrs. Scuddamore informed me, that owing to the weakness and imprudence of my late adversary, Mr. Mordaunt, the two duels had been made known, and the utmost commotion in the college had been the consequence. That foolish young man, persisting in believing his wound to be a dangerous one, had, *malgré* the advice, nay the entreaties of his friend Percival and the seconds, sent for a surgeon, and revealed to him not only the wound, but the cause. The surgeon happened to be addicted to gossiping. He told it to some half-dozen friends, who repeated it to as many more; and the result was, that after a few days the heads of the college became acquainted with the affair, instituted strict inquiries into it—got at the whole truth—and, desirous to prevent for the future similar events, had decided on the expulsion of the duellists from college.

"You had better remain in London for the present," wrote Mrs. Scuddamore; "for, as it is known your absence has been caused by the death of your guardian, it will not tell against you. If the affair takes a more favourable turn, and that only rustication should be the punishment, you can come back to receive the sentence. The old fograms of a college take a very different view of such matters from what military men—and I almost consider myself one—do. You have behaved like a young man of spirit, and even should you be expelled college, your character will be in no way injured by it; so do not let your spirits be affected. Captain Brady, than whom a more honourable man nor a braver soldier does not exist, highly approves your conduct; and the approval of such a man may well console you for the censure of a few old pedagogues, ignorant of the ways of the world, and of the necessity of a young man maintaining a high reputation for moral and physical courage."

Not a word was said of her niece. She was not even included in a simple "we," which often implies so much. Mrs. Scuddamore had either intentionally omitted naming her niece, or had wholly forgotten her in the earnestness of her belief, that *her* opinion, and that of Captain Brady were all that interested me.

Mr. Vise advised me to place the ten thousand pounds bequeathed me by Mr. Trevyllan, in the funds; to dispose of the house, and invest the produce in the same security; and to sell the extra plate, reserving as much as I might hereafter require for my own use, as also the pictures and library; the sale of all which would add considerably to my fortune.

This worthy man, with whom I had been acquainted ever since my first arrival from Wales, had always treated me with the greatest kindness; and on this occasion had manifested so warm an interest in my welfare, and taken so active a part in arranging my pecuniary concerns, that I could not doubt the sincerity of the friendship he professed. I made him acquainted with all that had occurred at Oxford; and he urged me so strenuously to return there, alleging that my protracted absence could not fail to prejudice my case, that I decided on adopting his advice; and after a fortnight's *séjour* in London, I returned to college. That fortnight's absence had been turned to account against me.

My first visit was to Mrs. Scuddamore, who received me with a cold civility that ill accorded with her former kindness, and with the cordiality of the letter I had received from her in London. I had heard the sound of retreating footsteps, and had caught a glimpse of white drapery, ere a door of the drawing-room, that opened on back stairs, had closed, and I instantly concluded that Miss Melville had hastily withdrawn on my being announced. This struck me as an unfavourable omen, and a presentiment of evil glanced through my mind, which was not a little increased by the gravity of Mrs. Scuddamore's demeanour, and the formality of her manner. I ventured to inquire after the health of her niece, and was answered that she was perfectly well.

"May I not hope for the pleasure of seeing Miss Melville?" asked I, in considerable trepidation.

"To be candid with you, Mr. Herbert," replied the lady, "circumstances have occurred since your departure, which render it advisable that your visits here should be discontinued. My brother has accepted proposals for our niece, of so advantageous a nature, that any thing which might interfere with the fulfilment of her engagement must be avoided. Your being on bad terms with the gentleman who is to be her husband, would naturally render your presence here disagreeable to him, and embarrassing to her; so you must excuse me for requesting that this may be your last visit here."

"May I inquire, Madam, whether anything injurious to my character, has led to your adopting this line of conduct? If so, pray furnish me with an opportunity of justifying myself; for, it would be indeed very painful to me to lose your good opinion."

"My knowledge of you, Mr. Herbert, is so slight, that I had hardly formed an opinion, except in the affair of the duel, when I certainly think you behaved perfectly well, and so I shall always say, whenever the subject is referred to in my presence; and now I will not detain you any longer, as I expect a person on business."

And Mrs. Scuddamore literally bowed me out of the room. My pride, my delicacy, and above all my deep admiration of Miss Melville, made me revolt at this unexpected and unhandsome treatment. Wounded to the quick, I heartily wished that I could avenge my mortification on some one; but to whom could I turn? I determined to pay a visit to Captain Brady, and see if he, too, were changed, or, at least, whether I could not discover through him, what had led to the alteration in Mrs. Scuddamore. He received me in a friendly manner, informed me that the person to whom Miss Melville was to be married in a short time, was no other than Mr. Mordaunt, who, being his own master and possessed of a good fortune, had proposed for her hand, and her uncle had immediately accepted the proposal. "The young lady has no fortune," said he; "her aunt and uncle have nothing to leave her, and, as she had no objection to the gentleman, the match has been arranged."

"But is it quite certain that she has no objection?" demanded I, remembering the agitation and anxiety she had betrayed on the occasion of the misunderstanding between Percival, Mordaunt, and myself; and which, to confess the truth, I had attributed wholly to her interest for me.

"Yes, young gentleman; when referred to, she positively declared that she felt a preference for Mr. Mordaunt from her first interview with him, and that it was this preference which led to her alarm and anxiety on the occasion of the quarrel. I must acknowledge," added the old soldier, "that I did not expect that a fine young girl, and, moreover, the niece of Mrs. Scuddamore, would have accepted the hand of a man, who certainly in my opinion is very deficient in courage; but women are strange creatures, Mr. Herbert, and, although Mrs. Scuddamore is aware of the want of courage of Mr. Mordaunt, she overlooks it, for the sake of securing a provision for her orphan niece: which conduct on her part, has, I confess, much surprised and disappointed me."

Shocked and disgusted at the mercenary motives of the aunt, and the duplicity of the niece, (for of duplicity I could not acquit her, although, perhaps, had I accused myself of vanity, instead of her of duplicity, I should be nearer the truth,) I named them no more, but requested Captain Brady to inform me, whether anything injurious to my honour had been said during my absence.

"Why, to be frank with you," replied he, "it has been whispered about, that you had been unpopular ever since you entered college; that at school you were likewise disliked and avoided, yet that you never evinced any symptom of surprise, or betrayed any desire to resent this general avoidance. It has been said, that it was not to resent any impertinence offered to Mrs. Scuddamore, but to avenge the long and repeated slights pointed at yourself, that you fought two duels; and this rumour has totally changed the favourable light in which the affair was previously viewed by impartial people. I can, however, give you no clue whatever, to fix this report on any particular person; and were you to charge any one with it, and so get into another duel, so far from serving yourself, you would inevitably injure your cause, and acquire the reputation of a revengeful and bad-hearted man. Be therefore advised by me, and let the matter drop, unless any offence be offered you."

CHAPTER VIII.

No sooner was my return to Oxford notified, than I was informed that the duels in which I had been engaged, and which I had by my insulting conduct towards Messrs. Percival and Mordaunt provoked and forced them into, had been made the subject of a grave investigation; the result of which was, that it was decided, that I was to be severely reprimanded, and rusticated for a year.

It had not been taken into consideration that I was the challenged, and not the challenger; consequently, while my adversaries got off with a reprimand, my punishment was much more severe, and a sense of its injustice greatly irritated me, although I experienced but little regret at leaving college, and determined on returning to it no more. The independence secured to me by Mr. Trevyllan would have led to this decision, even had I not been rusticated, for I felt no inclination towards any of the learned professions, for which a long residence in college is necessary, and rather looked to the pleasures of a tranquil home in Wales, among my native hills, and with my favourite books, than to a continuance in the busy scenes of life, for which I had no predilection. I proceeded to arrange my affairs at Oxford, and before I left it, paid one more visit to Captain Brady. He received me kindly, was evidently somewhat shocked at the cavalier treatment I had met with at the hands of his friend Mrs. Scuddamore, although he attempted to mitigate it, by pleading in excuse for it the dependent state of her fair niece, for whom she was anxious to secure a good marriage. Again I questioned him as to whether Miss Melville's own feelings were interested in the alliance now on the eve of being formed; and he assured me, that he knew for a certainty, that the young lady had acknowledged to her aunt, that her happiness depended on it. Mrs. Scuddamore had, like me, imagined, that the anxiety betrayed by her niece, on the occasion of the scene between Messrs. Percival and Mordaunt, and myself, had originated in a partiality on her part to me; and had questioned her closely on this subject, when she avowed that all her anxiety had been for Mr. Mordaunt, and that her appealing looks to me were meant to dissuade me from injuring him. Even when informed of the pusillanimity he had evinced on the ground, ("and I thought," continued the brave Hibernian, "it was my duty to state the fact,") so far from degrading him in her opinion, it seemed positively to endear him to her more, and, when he had solicited her hand, she confessed that his prudence, as she chose to term what I call by another name, would be the best guarantee for her future happiness, as it would deter him from duels. "I confess," resumed Captain Brady, "that the young lady has considerably lowered herself in my estimation. The niece too of a lady with such elevated, and I may say, soldier-like opinions on the point of honour! Indeed, I believe I may venture to say, that Mrs. Scuddamore's own notions are wholly at variance with those of her niece on the subject; but money, my dear Sir, and the prospect of a good settlement for that young person, have silenced her scruples. Her brother too, is an advocate for the match; persons of *his* profession entertaining a widely different notion on honour and courage, to those of mine."

Being now convinced that my vanity had misled me, with regard to the imagined partiality of Miss Melville for my unworthy self, my sense of disappointment became considerably abated; so true it is that self-love is generally, if not always, the basis on which male attachments are founded. I could no longer respect a woman who could love a man wanting in courage; and even her beauty, which had so captivated me, faded away from my mind from the moment I had acquired the conviction that her preference was awarded to another.

I returned to London after three days' *séjour* in Oxford, fully determined to see Alma Mater no more, and with a heart as ready to be warmed by a new flame as if the recent one had never been kindled.

The morning after my arrival in town, I received a letter informing me that my mother had been taken suddenly and dangerously ill, and urging me to hasten to her with all possible speed. I set out for Wales within half an hour after the receipt of this letter, my filial tenderness excited into a more vigorous action by the dread of losing one to whom my heart turned with greater affection from its recent disappointment. At one moment I pictured her to myself insensible—perhaps dead—and all her past fondness arose up to awaken bitter self-reproach for having consented to so long a separation from her. More firmness on my part, must have won Mr. Trevyllan's consent to my visiting her in the vacations; yet I had not sought to overcome his objections, but had let year after year pass away without seeing my only parent; and now—I might arrive too late for that happiness, might never again hear that low sweet voice, never behold those dark and loving eyes fixed fondly on mine, never receive the maternal blessing for which my heart pined. But the mind of man, and more especially while he is still young, is ever prone to turn from painful thoughts. I endeavoured to cast mine from me, and Hope whispered that I might still find my mother alive—perhaps out of danger. I pictured to myself her joy at seeing me, her words of welcome, the gentle pressure of her delicate arms, and the words of love, interrupted by kisses, dropping from her lips like dew on a parched flower. I stopped not on the road, even for food, but hurried on, every thought a prayer for the prolongation of a life grown within the last few hours dearer to me than mine own. How had I lived apart from her so long? how denied myself the happiness of being near her? were questions continually suggesting themselves to my mind, and never unaccompanied by self-reproach. The journey seemed interminable, so great was my impatience to reach home; and as the carriage flew past the hills, trees, and mountains, with a velocity that almost made me giddy, I urged the astonished postillion to redouble his speed, promising him gold for a compliance with my wishes. I longed for evening to mark how far I had progressed, yet when twilight with its soft grey mantle had veiled the surrounding scenery, rendering every object indistinct, I wished the moon to rise, that I might behold the distant country, and judge how far I had proceeded. The sighing of the wind among the trees filled me with a sadness never before experienced. It sounded like the voices of departed spirits, and seemed to my prophetic soul as a warning that she who I was hastening to was already among them,—that I should arrive too late to receive her blessing. The moon at length arose in unclouded splendour casting her silvery radiance over the grand and wild country through which I was hurrying. How cold, how stern, seemed the glance of this bright luminary, when I gazed with aching eyes on her disk, as if to read on its shining face a confirmation of my hopes or fears! I thought that perhaps at that moment its rays might be falling on the couch of my mother. Oh! why was it not given me to know whether her eyes could still view them, whether I had yet that truest and most tender friend that God bestows on man—a mother? A thousand superstitious thoughts passed through my mind, weakened as it was by anxiety and want of sustenance. When a dark cloud passed over the moon, I shuddered lest it should be an omen of the shroud that covers the dead; and when it floated away, leaving the glorious orb of night more refulgent than before, my spirits brightened with hope, until another cloud veiled it, and awakened new dread. I believe the postillions took me for a maniac, and in truth I more resembled one than a sane person, by my reiterated demands for increased speed, when, as they frequently assured me, they were driving at a pace that threatened danger to their horses and vehicle, if not to their lives. When day dawned, and an increased cold, which ever is felt when morning chases night away, announced the fact, a chill like that of the grave stole over me. Cloud after cloud faded away, leaving a sober grey more cheerless far than the moonlight had been. Another day had come, but oh! was *she* who filled all my thoughts still in life to behold it? Was *she*, like me, impatiently counting the hours, and trembling lest she should go hence before I could arrive?

How strange and unfathomable is the heart of man! Even while a prey to the deepest anxiety, tremblingly alive to fears that it was agony little less than a confirmation of their worst whispers to endure, memory brought before me a thousand proofs of maternal tenderness, the recollection of which had long slumbered in my heart, but which now awoke with a vividness that added torture to my self-accusations for having forgotten them. Who had I met in that cold and glittering world, which I had been so desirous to enter, that I consented to leave my mother's side, to love me as she had done, nay to love me at all? Had I not found all hearts closed against me? and could I count on the affection of a human being save herself? The faults, which had deterred others from liking me, had not weakened her attachment. No; the heart of a mother, like the Divinity that created it, can alone pardon the errors of her children, and look with pitying tenderness on their sins.

My burning temples throbbed with pain—my very heart ached from the force of remorse, as these bitter thoughts passed through my mind; and many, and firm were the resolves I made, that if the Almighty deigned to listen to my prayers, and to accord me a prolongation of the life of my sole parent, I would leave her no more. I would watch over her as tenderly as ever mother did over an only child; I would share her regret for my father; would listen with interest to her stories of that happy past connected with him; in short, I would live henceforth for her, and for her only, to atone for the neglect for which my conscience had within the last two days so severely accused me. Alas! we know not the depth of our affection for those dear to us, until we are in danger of losing them, or until they are gone from us for ever!

I had reached a village within about ten miles of my home, proceeding still with undiminished velocity, when the post-chaise broke down, and I received some severe contusions when thrown from it. My impatience at this delay almost maddened me; and when it was found that the carriage could not be repaired sufficiently to enable me to proceed in it for several hours, I determined to continue my route on horseback. To this project the obstinate postillion would not yield assent. His poor horses, he said, and swore, were already half dead, from the speed I had insisted on his using; and he would not allow me to ride one of them, were I even to pay him the value of both.

No horse could be had in the miserable little hamlet close to which this untoward accident occurred, and, half distracted, I determined to proceed on foot to my home, after having paid the sulky post-boy his extravagant demand for the horses and repairs of the chaise. I could procure no guide to accompany me, so was compelled to set out alone, leaving my luggage in the village ale-house.

Never shall I forget that night! An unusual stillness prevailed—unbroken, save by the occasional bark of some cottager's dog, or the cry of some bird of night. Scarcely a breeze moved the leaves of the high trees, whose long shadows fell like giants across the road, in some parts of it so close as to exclude the light. I hurried on through this solitude, my own footsteps sounding so loud as to startle me, and the beating of my heart making itself audible. Sometimes a low sighing, or moaning of the heavy branches of the trees, moved by an occasional gust of wind rushing down through some deep ravine from the mountains, struck my ear with so sad a sound, that my superstitious forebodings connected it with a supernatural warning of the danger of my mother, and I would hurry on more rapidly than before, until breathless, and exhausted, I was compelled to rest for a few minutes. These fitful gusts of the night wind, followed again by a long stillness, had something so inexpressibly solemn and imposing in them, that they made me shudder; and when some mountain torrent rushed down the precipitous path it had formed for itself, leaping wildly from crag to crag, and dashing its white foam around, I felt as if it were some mysterious agent instinct with power, from which I wished to escape, and again I hurried on until out of hearing of its deafening noise. Then, blaming my own unmanly weakness, I would turn back for a moment to behold the cataract rushing madly along, now hidden for a moment by the dark and funeral mountain pines, and the next instant, breaking into light, its white masses like huge avalanches of snow falling from some Alpine height into the valley beneath, with the sound of a mighty flood; and angry with myself for even the momentary delay, I would resume my rapid pace, while the fresh mountain air failed to cool my fevered brow, or burning lip.

At length the spire of the village church, near my home, became visible, its little vane shining brightly in the moonlight. Often, in the days of my childhood, had it guided my path home from the rambles I delighted in; and now, weary and fainting, I hailed it with an emotion that brought tears into my eyes. I trembled violently as I approached the house. I longed, yet I dreaded to pass its threshold—to know my fate. All my future happiness seemed to hang on the answer that awaited the question my tremulous lips refused to utter—"Have I still a mother?" A deathlike silence reigned around. The garden gate was unlatched, and I stealthily entered it, and passing through parterres of flowers that looked snowy white beneath the moon-beams, and whose fragrance filled the air, I approached the door, lifted the latch, hurried through the hall and into my mother's chamber. There, reclined on her bed, the curtains drawn aside, and four large waxen candles throwing their flickering light on her pallid face, I beheld the dead.—One cry escaped my agonized breast, and I fell to the ground as if bereft of life.

CHAPTER IX.

WHEN I recovered consciousness, I found myself laid on a bed to which I had been removed while insensible, the old and faithful attendant of my mother watching over me. The sight of her melted my heart, so associated was she with the days of my childhood, and with that dear mother no longer a denizen of earth. I wept long and uninterrupted, for the good Mrs. Burnet sought not to check my tears. Indeed her own fell fast, for fondly devoted to her deceased mistress, her grief at losing her was profound. She related to me every particular of the sudden and fatal illness that had snatched my mother from life. A brain fever, originating in a neglected cold, in four days, had left me an orphan.

"Oh! Sir," said Mrs. Burnet, "how often did my dear departed mistress demand you in her delirium—how frequently press her pillow in her arms, and bless it, believing she held you. Never was there so doting a mother, yet, how unselfish was her love! 'I would give worlds to have my son with me, my good Burnet,' has she often said, 'but my grief, which has now become a part of myself, would depress his spirits, and destroy that elasticity of mind, and that cheerfulness which appertains to the season of youth, and that I could not bear to witness. When he comes, and oh! how I long for that hour, I must put a constraint on my feelings, and conceal my grief for the dead, for the sake of the living.'"

And this was the mother I had so blamably acquiesced in remaining absent from, while she, longing to behold me, had sacrificed her own wishes in her desire that my cheerfulness should not receive even a temporary check. Oh! what in this cold and busy world, can be compared to a mother's heart, unless it be that fabled bird that is said to open its breast to feed its young from the spring that supports its own life, which it readily yields for the preservation of its offspring!

Mrs. Burnet forced me to take some sustenance, making my admission to the chamber of death the condition of my yielding to her wishes on this point, and on sleeping a few hours before I visited it. She administered a narcotic, and, under its soothing influence, I dropt into slumber, from which I awoke not until the next morning. How painful is the first awakening from sleep after a heavy affliction! How bewildering—how confused the sensations! Yet, even while bewildered, the sense of sorrow pervades the heart, and one dreads to turn to memory for a full explanation of its cause. But soon, alas! the terrible truth reveals itself, and as the veil that shades the senses is withdrawn, agony succeeds it. A burst of grief quickly followed my awaking, and brought Mrs. Burnet to my pillow. How the room, and every object it contained, recalled past and happier times to my mind, awaking countless tender memories.

"Ah! Sir," said the worthy woman, following my eyes, as they glanced around, "it does seem hard to see inanimate things all in their places unchanged, and fresh as when left years before, and—but no! we must not talk of this now. You have painful duties to perform, and I must not unman you."

I arose, and when dressed, went to my mother's room—that room which I had been wont to dread in former times, and the entrance to which I used to consider as a penance. How my heart smote me, as the recollection crossed my mind. A cambric handkerchief veiled the face of my mother, and for a few minutes I had not courage to remove it. When at length, and with a trembling hand I drew it aside, I was seized with an awe that checked my strong desire to embrace that pallid, but still beautiful face, so like, yet so different from what I had anticipated. It looked many years younger than when I had last seen her. Death seemed to have restored youth to those marble lineaments, to that lofty brow, and those finely modelled cheeks. For the first time I became aware of how wonderfully beautiful she must have been, and my regret increased for her loss. There was something inexpressibly tender in that delicate face, which, joined to the calm and holy character which pervaded it, flooded my eyes with tears. The hands were crossed on the breast as in prayer, and their exquisite form and proportion might have led one to suppose they were of Parian marble, fresh from the chisel of some great sculptor, had not a pale lilac tint around the tips of the fingers and nails, betrayed their mortality. And there lay the only being, beside my father, who had ever loved me. There, cold, and in her marble slumber, lay the fond mother, who but a few fleeting hours before had, even in the delirium of fever, demanded me with all the longing impatience of a doting heart. *She* who would have welcomed my coming with her latest accents, was now unconscious of my presence—of my grief. My sighs and sobs moved not the dull ear of death; my burning tears fell unheeded by her, whose hand would in life have wiped them fondly away; and I stood alone in a world, whose coldness and selfishness I had already learned by sad experience to estimate. A portrait of my father was placed on the wall that fronted the foot of my mother's bed. It had occupied that place ever since his death, that she might behold it on the first moment of awaking, and the last before she resigned herself to sleep. The eyes of the picture seemed to contemplate the pale face, the original had loved so well, with

a grave, if not sorrowful expression—that face which, until the last few
hours, had ever been turned towards it with such tender sadness. Alas! the
painted canvass was not more insensible than the recumbent image before
me. Both seemed but as a mockery to my bursting heart, which yearned to
clasp in life, if but even for a moment, that beloved mother, and to tell her
all that was passing in an agonized breast. Her bible and prayer-book were
on a table by her bedside; several silken strings marked pages in the former,
and proved how habitually it had been resorted to. Her *Prie Dieu* stood near,
and on it was inscribed in Spanish, a motto, which I remembered she had
placed soon after the death of my father. "A day nearer to thee," was the
translation, and referred to each day, bringing her nearer to the dead. How
warm, how loving had that heart been, that had so lately ceased to beat for
ever! How fondly and faithfully had it cherished, and remained true to the
memory of him who had been its sole love—its idol; and *now*, it was but
as the clod of the valley. It could never more throb with sorrow—never
beat with joy, to behold the child of *him* she was gone to join in another
world. The violence of my grief became subdued, as I contemplated that
pale face. Its heavenly expression seemed to chide my selfish sorrow, while
it offered a pledge that she, who could never know happiness on earth, was
now blest in heaven.

The next day I opened the escritoire of my mother, and in it I found
a letter addressed to me, as if anticipating that we should not meet again.
Her maternal feelings were poured out with a lavish fondness in this last
letter. She entreated me, that if it was decreed she should be taken from
me, not to mourn for her, for that while on earth a sorrow she could not
conquer must always poison her existence. She blamed herself for not having fought against it, while yet she had youth and health to aid her in the
effort, and for not having devoted the whole of those years given up to a
selfish grief to the fulfilment of her duties as a mother. But even in this
letter, and while accusing herself, her passionate love for my father broke
forth, for she added to this acknowledgment of error, that she believed no
woman who had been loved by a being so noble, so virtuous, so good, so
superior to all other men, could ever have been consoled for his loss. She
told me that she had for some years paid a pension to her old and esteemed
friend, Mrs. Maitland, whose husband had left that amiable lady and her
daughters so ill provided for, that, without the assistance she had afforded,
they would be unable to enjoy the comforts of life, and she entreated me
to continue to pay them that sum as if it were a bequest from her, in order
that Mrs. Maitland's delicacy should not be wounded. She added, that one
of the wishes nearest to her heart was that I might love, and marry one of

the daughters of her friend. She would not urge me to act in this matter contrary to my own inclinations, but if it pleased Providence that either of these amiable girls should win my heart, our marriage would have her maternal benediction bestowed in anticipation of the event. There was a solemnity in this last passage which made a deep impression on me. I determined to continue the pension she had allowed, nay more, to settle it beyond my own power of revocation, on the mother, without ever letting her know it had not been arranged by my mother, who had, in fact, no power to alienate any part of my property.

I questioned Mrs. Burnet about the family, and her answers convinced me that they merited all my mother had done for them.

"The young ladies are beautiful, Sir," said that worthy woman, "and as good as they are handsome. They have but one defect, if indeed the peculiarity to which I refer may be so called, and that may easily be accounted for by their having been brought up in such total solitude in this wild and lonely neighbourhood. They are as shy as uncaged birds, and, like them, fly off at the approach of a stranger. My blessed mistress, who loved them as if they had been her own children, often endeavoured to reason them out of this extreme shyness; but I suppose it is constitutional, for she never succeeded in conquering it."

"Mrs. Maitland," continued Mrs. Burnet, "never left your dear mother's bedside from the moment she learned her illness until all was over. She said she would come and see you, Sir, soon as her presence might not be deemed intrusive, for she, too, is a very shy lady. Indeed her daughters, my dear mistress used to say, inherited this peculiarity from her."

The last mournful duties were now to be paid to the dead. How many painful and heart-rending details do they involve! The placing the dead in the coffin, the closing of the lid that shuts for ever from our sight the object which, while we can still gaze on it, does not seem to have wholly left us, and the dark pall covering the coffin, each, and all, of these details bring their own separate agonies, the pangs of which can only be known by those who have experienced them.

Mrs. Maitland and her daughters came to take their last farewell of their departed friend before her remains were concealed for ever. I had not courage to see them, so wholly were my nerves unstrung, so retired to my own chamber while they remained; and when, two days after, I followed my beloved mother to the grave as chief mourner, so wholly engrossed was I by the intense grief to which my heart was a prey, that I did not recognise in the veiled and weeping persons who attended the solemn ceremony a single face I knew.

Who can paint the agony of seeing the coffin of one fondly loved lowered into the vault—of hearing the earth thrown on the coffin lid—of seeing the large flag replaced over the aperture, and of returning to the now
desolate home so lately occupied by the dear departed! In all this agony,
there was something soothing in the knowledge of how general was the
sympathy in my grief, for my dear mother was beloved and lamented by
the whole neighbourhood. She had received every care, every attention,
from the friends she most esteemed, all the devout and touching rites of
the Church had prepared her for the last change, and had been offered over
her grave,—there was much to be thankful for in this; and so eagerly does
the human heart, while yet youth is left, turn for consolation in its first
heavy sorrow to any source whence it can be found, that mine dwelt with
a pleasure, melancholy though it was, on these points. The clergyman
walked with me from the church to my home. He pressed me cordially to
take up my abode in his house for the present, and I had some difficulty in
declining his reiterated offers, or rather requests, to be allowed to spend the
rest of the day with me. Would to heaven that I had not declined them! for
how would this simple circumstance have changed my destiny—from what
years of agony would it not have saved me!

But we are the victims of circumstances, over which we frequently have
no control. Our happiness, or misery, depends on some trifling chance,
against which no prudence, no forethought, can guard us, and the result
of which colours our fate for the remainder of our lives. Had any one told
me that a greater misfortune, a severer trial, than that which I had gone
through on the morning of that day, awaited me before its close, I would
have slighted the notice, and disbelieved the warning. No; I fancied that
fate had done its worst by me, in snatching away my only parent ere her
age could have prepared me for such a blow; and while, with the foolish
security peculiar to youth, I counted on retaining the blessing of her existence through many a year to come. It was thus I reasoned. Fool, idiot,
that I was! little dreaming of the terrible event impending over my devoted
head, and of that of one of Nature's fairest works! Oh! why does no presentiment warn us, when Fate menaces us with one of its most appalling
strokes? Why did not some good, some pitying angel, whisper me to accept
the kind offer of the pastor to remain with me that day? Alas! we are but
tools in the hands of Providence, working out unconsciously its immutable
decrees!

When I entered my desolate home, I stole to my mother's chamber. Its
deserted air, its silence, and solitude, were congenial to my feelings; and
having locked the door, to prevent the intrusion of the worthy Mrs. Burnet,

I flung myself on the bed so lately pressed by her I had but two hours before seen laid in the dark and dreary vault by the side of my father, and yielding to grief, I wept with uncontrollable emotion, until tired nature sought relief in a sleep more resembling the stupor of disease than the refreshing slumber of health.—I awoke not until the sun was going down, and a mild and beautiful evening had replaced the glorious day. My head ached, my pulse throbbed with fever, and a burning heat parched my throat. I felt as if I could not breathe within doors, as an unfortunate bird might feel in an exhausted receiver, and dreading the officious kindness of Mrs. Burnet, while suffering under my present state of mental, and physical irritation, I determined to go forth into the open air.

I forgot, that since the previous day, I had tasted no food whatever, and during the four preceding ones, so little, as scarcely served to sustain life. This unusual abstinence had greatly excited the nervous system. I felt giddy, my eyes emitted sparks as if of fire, and when I closed their burning lids to shut out light, they felt as if they enclosed warm blood, so hot and crimson seemed all within them.

A small bottle of *Eau des Carmes* stood on a shelf in the room—a few drops of it, in water, had been occasionally used as a restorative for my poor mother when she was attacked by spasms. I seized it, and there being no water in the chamber, I hastily raised the bottle to my lips, and my parched throat had swallowed a considerable portion of its contents before I was aware of the strength of the liquid.

I opened the window, stepped from it into a portion of the garden inclosed from the rest, by a high hedge of laurestinas, and open only to the glass-door and windows of my mother's room, and a small gate that led into a grove close by. This portion of the garden had been divided from the rest to secure the privacy its owner loved. Here would she sit for hours, reading, or would sometimes ramble into the shady grove, always keeping in her own possession the key of the gate.

By going out through this little gate, I should avoid meeting Mrs. Burnet, or any of the servants; indeed, no part of the house commanded a view of it.—How vividly does every circumstance of that evening dwell in my mind! I remember the perfume that stole on my olfactory nerves as I stepped into the garden filled with flowers—I remember the deep stillness of the air, the crimson and golden glories of the curtain, beneath which the sun was hiding his last beams, and the feverish excitement of my feelings. My hand trembles so violently that it can scarcely hold the pen, for I am now, my dearest child, coming to the narrative of the dread event that has blighted all my prospects, and steeped my life in inextricable wretchedness.

CHAPTER X.

I PASSED the gate, entered the grove, and walked through a shaded lane leading to a wild and romantic spot, well remembered since my boyish days. This spot was situated on the brow of a steep and precipitous rock, at the bottom of which a rapid stream rushed wildly on amidst fragments of rocks and little islands covered with verdure, that bent into its glittering breast. On the left lay a wood that formed a beautiful back-ground, leaving only a space of ground sufficiently wide for two persons to walk, between it and the rocky precipice to the right.

Often had I gone in search of birds' nests in this wood in my childhood, and descended among the clefts of the rock to the verge of the stream. In some of these clefts, inaccessible to other visitants, from the danger of the steep and slippery descent, I had been wont to enter in the sultry days of summer, pleased to find so cool a retreat, and proud of having accomplished a feat of no little danger, as also in having discovered hiding-places unknown to all beside.

As I advanced along this path I noticed a small rustic alcove erected during my absence, and remembered that my dear mother had written to me to say she had had it raised as a resting-place for her friend, Mrs. Maitland and her daughters, in their daily visits to her, the spot being half-way between the two abodes. This led my mind to a new train of thought. I recollected the desire expressed by my departed parent that I should wed one of the daughters of her friend. I remembered that Mrs. Burnet had praised the great beauty of both, and with the heart yearning for some one to love, which had haunted me for years, my pulse beat quicker, as I pictured to myself, that in one of these young beauties I might find the long-desired object to satisfy all its cravings.

I approached the rustic alcove, and as I reached its entrance, I saw that it was occupied.—I stood speechless from emotion, unable to offer an excuse for my involuntary intrusion, but the person to whom it should have been addressed, spoke not, moved not—seemed wholly unconscious of my presence. A girl, young, and oh! how exquisitely beautiful, was before me. She reclined on a wooden bench, her arm resting on a table, and supporting her fair cheek, over which her rich brown tresses fell in luxuriant profusion. I approached nearer on tiptoe, and so softly that I could not hear my own steps; and now I discovered that the lovely being was asleep. How calm, how sweet was the expression of her face! The rosy lips were slightly parted,

revealing teeth like orient pearls; the long dark silken eyelashes shaded her
cheeks, just arriving where the delicate rose-colour tinged them; and her
full and rounded bust by its gentle but regular undulations, denoted that
she slumbered. Never had I beheld aught so lovely. Transfixed, and almost
breathless, I continued to gaze on her. I was tempted to doubt the reality
of her presence, and to accuse my senses of having deceived me.—I rubbed
my eyes like one awaking from a dream, but still there she reclined in all the
helplessness of repose, with all the innocence and beauty we attribute to a
slumbering seraph.

It flashed through my brain that the fair sleeper must be one of the
daughters of my mother's friend—perhaps the one designed by her to be
my wife, and oh! what a tumult of rapture thrilled my heart at the thought,
that the wondrous charms before me might one day become mine. I forgot
my grief, deep and sincere as it had been. How could it exist while I gazed
on the exquisite beauty, so softly slumbering near me, whose sweet breath
passing through her half-opened lips, came to me as the odour from some
balmy and fragrant flower.

Intoxicated with delight, I could no longer resist the uncontrollable
impulse to press my lips on that snowy forehead—but I would press them so
lightly, as not to awaken the sleeper, and heaven is my witness, that excited
as I was, no thought that could have wounded her purity presented itself to
my mind. No, I would retire, after having kissed that beautiful brow, and,
concealed behind the rustic alcove, watch over her safety, and prevent her
repose being intruded on. I approached close to her, trembling with emotion,—her sweet breath fanned my cheek, and tempted me almost beyond
my power of resistance to press the crimson portal whence it passed; but
there was something so pure, so innocent, in the beauteous face, that I
dare not profane her lips,—these could I only hope to touch with mine
when they should have pronounced her consent to become my wife. So,
gently bending down, I lightly imprinted a kiss on her fair forehead. No
sooner had I done so than she started up, opened her eyes wildly, uttered
a cry, and rushed from the alcove. I called to her, told my name, implored
her not to fly from me, and entreated her pardon; but all was in vain, she
heeded me not, but quickening her speed, ran madly along. The whole
consequences of the effect certain to be produced on her mind, and on that
of her mother, when, terrified and exhausted, she should reach her home,
flashed on my mind. I should be viewed by both with indignation and disgust, as a hardened libertine, who, on the very evening of the day that had
seen my dear mother consigned to the grave,—when sorrow alone should
fill my heart, had stolen upon the privacy of the daughter of her friend, and

dared to seek to take advantage of her slumber. Yes, I should be driven with abhorrence from their door; I should lose for ever this lovely being, for no explanation could justify me, or make them believe the innocence of my intentions.

These reflections passed through my brain with the velocity with which the past life is said to flash through the mind of the drowning wretch, and, maddened by the dread of losing her, I flew, rather than ran, in the direction she had taken. I gained rapidly on her steps, and she, I suppose still more terrified at hearing mine, increased her speed, keeping near the edge of the precipice. I could almost have seized her garment, so close had I got, when her foot slipt, and oh! horror of horrors, she rolled over the declivity, and in a moment was lost to my sight.

Oh God! never will the terror, the despair of that moment, be effaced from my memory! Even now, as I trace these lines, my hand trembles, my brain grows giddy at the recollection. With the rapidity of lightning, and careless of life, I rushed down one of the wild paths never, perhaps, trodden save by the feet of goats, and my own, but remembered since my childhood. I jumped from crag to crag, where one false step would have cast me into the yawning abyss beneath, until I reached the narrow band of sand which separated the base of the rock from the river. There she lay, part of her person immersed in the water. I raised her in my arms, and found she had not ceased to breathe. Oh Almighty God! how fervent was the thanksgiving I offered up that moment to thy throne, that she still lived. I placed her on the sand-bank, bathed her temples with water from the stream, and knelt down beside her to feel if her heart still beat. A few feeble pulsations proved that life was not extinct, and hope once more broke on my mind even in spite of reason. I prayed, I wept, I raved aloud—my eyes fixed on that angelic face—but in a few minutes a slight shudder passed over it, the lips opened, gasped, and breathing a deep sigh, her soul passed away.

Never, never, can the agony of that moment be effaced from my mind. To think that ten minutes, ten short minutes before, and she was alive, in health, and with the promise of many years of existence—and now, there she lay, a lifeless, mutilated corse! And I—I, was the cause of all this. I considered myself as much her murderer as if my hand had hurled her down the precipice: for had not my folly in daring to shock and terrify her, led to the frightful catastrophe that had occurred? I called down imprecations on my own head, I wept, tore my hair, flung my self by her side, and embraced her lifeless form. What was I to do? Ought I not at once to go and denounce my crime, and offer myself up to justice? Then came the deep, the inherent sense of shame. Who would believe that I had not more criminal intentions than those which God alone knew filled my heart, when I kissed her brow? How terrible, how ignominious would be the suspicions to which my self-denunciation must give rise—suspicions which I had no means of refuting, except my simple asseverations of the whole truth, asseverations which I felt assured no one would credit. No, I dared not avow the fact—I must conceal it for ever—for ever bear the dreadful secret pent up in my own breast—never more to hope for sympathy in the misery which must henceforth cloud my days. There were moments, when, turning my eyes from the still beautiful face of the departed, to the rapid river that almost laved my feet, I was tempted to lift the corse in my arms, and to plunge with it into its bosom; but an unseen hand—the hand of the Almighty, held me back, and I determined not to rush uncalled into the dread presence of my Creator.

Then the thought of consigning the corse to the river occurred to me. I reasoned that if found it would be supposed that she had accidentally fallen over the cliff into the water, and had been carried away by the current. This would be the safest of all methods not only of getting rid of the corse, but of accounting for her death; and the fearful catastrophe which had taken place had so wholly sobered me, that I was fully capable of judging it to be so. But when I gazed on the beautiful face—the exquisite form of the dead—I shrunk back with terror from the thought of exposing it to be injured by fishes, or, more horrible, to be devoured by water-rats, with which the river abounded. At length the recollection of one of the deep clefts in the rocks flashed on my mind. Yes, I would bear her there to take her everlasting rest, never more to be seen by mortal eye save mine. I lifted her in my arms, and tottering beneath the weight of my precious burthen, I bore her in the direction of the well-remembered opening. The moon had risen, so I was enabled to find the place, which was not far distant; and laying the corse close to its entrance, I first crept in on my hands and knees, and then drew it after me by the shoulders, as gently as if I moved a sleeping child, trembling lest I should injure it. Having drawn it to the innermost part of the cavern, I composed the limbs with as scrupulous a delicacy as if the departed had been my sister or my daughter. I covered it over as carefully, with the shawl tied around her slender waist, as if the night air could chill that lifeless form; and I placed small fragments of the rock that had from time to time fallen in, on the edge of the shawl, to prevent any reptiles that the cavern might contain, from touching her. Many a tear flowed down my cheeks while I performed this sad, sad duty, and reflected on how rude a bed now reclined that lovely form, which had hitherto been watched over by a mother's love.

I left the cavern, and with rapid but stealthy steps, keeping always in the shadow of trees or rocks, reached the little gate so lately passed, crossed the garden, creeping close to the continuous high screen of laurestinas, pushed open the lattice, and entered the chamber as noiselessly as a midnight robber. I carefully examined my clothes and boots by the light of the lamp which I had left burning in the chimney. I removed every fragment of clay and sand that had adhered to them, and collecting these last, consigned them to one of the most distant beds of the garden, there to mingle with the earth. I brushed my clothes until no trace of soil remained, and then believed my task accomplished; when examining my hands, I discovered that they were stained with blood! Her blood! The murderer who for the first time has dyed his hand with human gore, and discovers it when a witness may in a moment detect this proof of his crime, never experienced more horror and terror than I did, when I gazed on my ensanguined fingers. Shuddering I removed the stains, emptied the water into the garden, carefully closed the lattice, unlocked the door of the chamber, flung myself on my bed, and rang my bell. Mrs. Burnet soon answered the summons.

"O, Sir," observed she, "I was never before so rejoiced to hear the sound of a bell, for I was most fearful that you were very unwell. I have been to your door frequently, but would not open it, lest I might awake you." (She could not open it, as it was locked inside, but I was glad to find *she* did *not* know this circumstance.)

"I have been asleep," said I, "but my head aches sadly. Let me have a little weak wine and water."

"I am afraid, Sir, you are more ill than you think," observed the worthy woman, "for your voice sounds so husky, and, altogether, you look so unlike yourself; but it's not to be wondered at, after all you have gone through this day."

When Mrs. Burnet brought me the wine and water I detained her in my chamber, for I dreaded being alone, and it also occurred to me that her presence there on this eventful night might, should suspicion of the tragedy which had occurred ever be pointed towards me, be received as a proof of my innocence. I loathed myself for this base and selfish cunning, even while obeying its dictates to preserve a life that must henceforth be one of wretchedness. I talked to her of my mother, drew from her details of her mode of passing her time, but I shuddered when I found all of these details were mixed up with particulars of her friend Mrs. Maitland and her daughters.

"Never, Sir, was there a more charming family. The mother so kind, so considerate. She loved my dear mistress as a sister, nursed her and watched over her health and comfort so tenderly and unceasingly. There never was so devoted a mother. Her life is bound up in her children, and, I must say, they well deserve all her fondness. Miss Maitland is the most lovely, amiable young creature alive. So sweet tempered, so gentle, so charitable! Often has your dear blessed mother said to me, 'Ah Burnet, how happy I should be if my son were to marry Miss Maitland. I am sure he can't help loving her the moment he sees her, she is so beautiful and engaging.'"

How tumultuously my agonized heart beat as I listened to Burnet repeating my departed mother's words, and remembered that the creature she spoke of was now numbered with the dead, her cold remains concealed in the rude cavern where I had placed them!

"I'm sure," resumed Mrs. Burnet, "that I can't tell which of the two young ladies my dear mistress loved the best. She often said she did not know, *both* were so dear to her. Miss Louisa is as handsome as her sister, and as amiable also, and more, yielding-like, than Miss Maitland. My mistress used to call them her 'gazelles;' they were so shy, flying away from the sight of a stranger like those pretty animals."

And *I*, who had learned this peculiarity in both the sisters, had, like a maniac, provoked it into action,—had terrified, and caused the death of *her* my mother had destined to be my wife,—and was now compelled to assume an air of indifference, while listening to the praises of my victim! Well had my dear mother judged, that I could not resist loving Miss Maitland as soon as I had seen her! Who *could* resist loving such a creature? How I shuddered when I reflected what must be the alarm of the fond mother and sister when they found the dear absent girl returned not to her home,—an alarm to be followed by the agony of prolonged fear and suspense, when no tidings of her could be gained! How my heart bled for them!—and oh, how I execrated myself as the cause of their affliction!

While Burnet was resuming her praises of the young ladies, a loud knocking came to the hall door. I half started from my bed, and terror filled my breast. Had my guilt been discovered by some unseen spectator, who had marked my pursuit of the flying and terrified girl, and had seen the terrible catastrophe? was the first thought that flashed on my mind. Had the officers of justice come in search of me? was the second; and I trembled so violently that, had not Mrs. Burnet quickly left the room, my evident terror must have awakened her curiosity, if not her suspicions. I ran to the door of the chamber, which opened into the hall, and heard her demand "who knocked?"

"It is I, Mrs. Burnet," answered a man's voice. "Is Miss Maitland here?"

"Here?" reiterated Burnet; "What should bring her here at this hour?" And she unlocked the door, and a man entered.

"Then our last hope is gone!" exclaimed the man; and I heard him fling himself into a chair.

"Good God, what has occurred?" demanded Mrs. Burnet, now greatly excited.

"Miss Maitland left home this evening to take a walk, did not return at her usual hour, and night coming on, and my mistress getting alarmed, she sent me off in search of her. I have been in every direction, but cannot find her. John Jones's boy said he saw her walking towards the half-way seat, and there, sure enough, I found her pocket-handkerchief, which showed the poor dear young lady had been a-crying, for it was wet with her tears. Indeed, for that matter, all the three ladies have done nothing but cry since the death of Mrs. Herbert."

How my heart smote me!

"Good God, Ap Owen, this is very alarming!" said Mrs. Burnet.

"I've been to the churchyard," resumed Ap Owen; "for it struck me, that, mayhap Miss had gone there to see the spot where her kind friend was laid,—for you know, Mrs. Burnet, she doted on Mrs. Herbert,—but there was no sign of her there, so I returned home, thinking that she might have got back, but, woe's me, she had never been near her home, and so I came off here!"

"My master has been very poorly, and in bed, ever since he came from the funeral," said Mrs. Burnet; "but I'll go and tell him this heavy news; and I'm sure he'll get up at once and join in the search for Miss Maitland."

I had barely time to rush into my bed, and assume as calm an air as I could command, when Mrs. Burnet hurried into my chamber to tell me the news. "I will get up at once," said I, "and join the search."

"Ah, I knew you would!" observed she. "God grant you may discover where the dear young lady is, and restore her safely to her poor distracted mother and sister!"

I dismissed the good woman, and, while I hurried on my clothes, I could hear her telling Ap Owen "how good it was of me, so ill as I had been all the evening, to leave my sick-bed and expose myself to the night air—but it was just like me—I had all the kindness of my dear mother, and never considered self."

"Good heavens," thought I, "if she but knew the truth, how would she shun and hate me!" What a hypocrite—what a wretch have I become! How am I to meet the unhappy mother, and sister, whose grief I have caused? How bear to hear them speak of the angel whose evil destiny it was that I should cross her path! I felt my spirit quail before the honest servitor Ap Owen, when I joined him in the hall, and was glad that Mrs. Burnet had accounted for my agitation by having told him of my illness.

CHAPTER XI.

"In what direction had we best proceed," said I to Ap Owen. "Do your suspicions point to any particular spot?"

"In truth no, Sir. We have no bad people about this place. We are so far from any high road, that no strangers come here, and the neighbourhood is so honest, that I can't suspect any one: indeed, for the matter of that, my mistress and the young ladies are so beloved, that there is not a man, woman, or child in the whole parish that would harm them. What I fear is, that Miss Maitland may have missed the path in the dark, and have fallen over the rock into the water. God grant I may be wrong in this surmise; but I don't know how otherwise to account for her disappearance."

This natural suspicion on the part of Ap Owen quieted, in some measure, my selfish alarm; but then came the dread that the river would be drawn, and when no corse was discovered, suspicion must point elsewhere.

"I think, Sir, it will be well for us to go first to the cottage. She *may* have returned since I left it."

I trembled at the thought of confronting the mother and sister of my victim. How could I sustain their glances? Would not my countenance reveal to them that I was, if not guilty of her death, cognizant of the fact? Well has it been said, that "a guilty conscience needs no accuser;" and deeply did I feel the truth of the axiom, for I fancied that every eye might detect in my face the fearful secret that pressed like a mountain of lead on my breast. I dared not offer any excuse for a non-compliance with Ap Owen's proposition, lest it might lead to suspicion, so I roused my courage to its utmost extent, and accompanied him to the residence of Mrs. Maitland. As we approached the cottage, I was struck with its beautiful and romantic aspect. What a contrast did it offer to the feelings of its occupants, and to my own. Embosomed in trees, and surrounded by a garden filled with odoriferous plants and flowers, it looked the picture of peace; and except that lights flashed from the windows, one might have supposed that its inhabitants had long sunk in repose. No sooner, however, had Ap Owen opened the garden gate, than the bereaved mother and daughter rushed forth; the former exclaiming, "my child! my child!" while the latter pronounced the word "sister," in accents so full of hope, that my heart sickened at the thought of how soon that hope must be destroyed.

"Oh, God! Oh, God!" said the distracted mother, grasping the arm of Ap Owen, "do you bring me no tidings of my child! Does she live? Oh! say but that she is still alive, and I will bear all else, and will bless you."

I could not, had my life depended on the effort, have spoken to Mrs. Maitland at that moment. I felt ready to throw myself at her feet and avow the truth, so deep was the emotion her maternal agony had produced in my breast.

"I wish, Ma'am, I could give you any news," replied Ap Owen, in trembling accents. "This gentleman is Mr. Herbert, who left his sick-bed to come and help me in the search, and ill enough he is, God knows, for he has had many fits of trembling since we left his house, and see now how he shakes."

I made a desperate effort to recover self-composure, and approached Mrs. Maitland.

"Ah! I ought to have guessed who you were," said she, "for you resemble my friend; but my brain is so tortured, that I remember nothing but my child—the dearest, sweetest, but——"

Here a violent paroxysm of tears impeded her utterance, and she fell, half fainting, into the arms of her daughter. In a few minutes she revived, and though still tottering from weakness, she approached me and grasped my arm.

"We lose time!" exclaimed she. "Every moment is precious; let us set out in different directions in search of my child. Let us call her name aloud. She may have over-fatigued herself and fallen asleep in some sequestered spot. She has told me that this has occurred to her more than once in her long rambles."

O! how quick beat my heart at this truthful guess.

"Yes! it must be so," resumed the distracted mother, her death-like face lighting up with excitement at this new hope. Hitherto I had not looked at the daughter. Indeed I avoided it from two motives: the first that of dreading to increase the agitation I already felt; and the second, a fear of exposing it to her. But at this moment, a dark cloud, which had for some time obscured the moon's disk, floated away, leaving that glorious luminary revealed in all its splendour, and involuntarily my eyes turned on the young lady, whose pale face was illumined by its silvery light. So striking was her resemblance to her sister, that I started violently, and uttered a cry, before my reason could check the sudden impulse. Then recollecting myself, I pressed my hand to my side, and in answer to the inquiries from Mrs. Maitland, feigned a sudden spasm at my heart, to which I asserted I had lately been subject. Alas! there was a greater, a more lasting agony in that heart, than ever physical suffering inflicted.

"I am sorry to be compelled to allow you to stay in the night air, when you ought to be in your bed," said Mrs. Maitland; "but such is my intense anxiety about my child, that I have not courage enough to dispense with your aid in the search of her."

I hurried from the presence of the distracted mother and daughter, and with Ap Owen again renewed the unavailing pursuit.

"Somehow, Sir," said he, "the notion that the poor, dear young lady has tumbled down one of the precipices, grows stronger and stronger in my mind. It's difficult, and very dangerous too, to descend, the rocks are so slippery, and besides, though gentlemen like you may laugh at such superstitions, poor men like me can't quite get the better of 'em. It has been said for years and years, that among the steep rocks there are caverns from which unearthly sounds have been heard to proceed, and that those who attempted to explore them, soon came to a violent end. So general is the belief entertained in these parts of the truth of these stories, that I don't think there is a man in the whole neighbourhood who could be induced to descend, however great the reward offered."

What a weight seemed lifted from my heart at this intelligence! for ever since he had expressed his belief that Miss Maitland had fallen down the precipice, I had concluded that a careful search would inevitably be made, and that her remains would be discovered.

How did I regret having removed them from the spot where the corse had dropped and where, if found, the belief that she had accidentally fallen over the cliff would be universally received. Less terrible would be the grief of the bereaved mother and sister, when the fact of the death of her so dear to them was actually proved, than to have to bear for ever the agonies of suspense. I was half tempted to steal to the cavern the moment I could free myself from Ap Owen, and to remove the corse to the spot where I had found it.

"You, Sir, I suppose, don't believe in ghosts or fairies," resumed my companion, "but I assure you, that among the poor people about here, there is not a single person who doubts that there are such things. Yes, Sir, and warnings too. Why, it was only last night that a raven kept flapping his wings near the bed-room windows of the young ladies, and uttered such wild cries as awoke my mistress, who told my sister, who has lived with her ever since she came to Wales. My sister was quite frightened when she heard of it, for we all look on a raven crying near a house as a sign of the death of one of the inhabitants. She told it to me this morning, after she had dressed her mistress. 'I'm afraid,' said she, 'it will be the old lady, for she grieves so for the loss of her friend, Mrs. Herbert, that she'll make herself ill.' Who'd have thought it could be one of the young ladies? so healthy, so active, so likely to live for years and years. And now I think of it, would you believe it, Sir, that no later than last night, my sister showed me a winding-sheet on the candle, as plain a one as ever I saw in my life, with all the fine narrow plaits running down it, and turning over: yes, Sir, no later than last night; and whoever saw a winding-sheet on a candle without hearing of a death soon after?"

Such were the topics on which the superstitious Ap Owen spoke, while we explored every leafy nook, every moss-covered stone, or rustic seat, where she, for whom our vain search was making, could be supposed to stop to rest. I frequently proposed that we should separate, and continue our search in different directions; but so strongly had his mind been infected by his own superstitious tales, that Ap Owen dreading to be left alone, started at every breeze that moved the branches of the surrounding trees, and trembled at the sight of any object on which the moon-beams fell more strongly.

We abandoned not our search until day broke in the east, when, worn down by fatigue and mental anguish, I returned home, to fling myself on my bed. I fell into a slumber from exhaustion; but the fearful event of the previous evening haunted me in my sleep. Again I stood in the rustic alcove, gazing on the lovely slumberer; again I stole on tip-toe to press my lips to her forehead, and once more I beheld her start from her repose in terror, and wildly rush from the spot. In vain I tried to overtake her, and avert the doom that with an almost supernatural prescience, I foresaw awaited her, but my feet seemed to be of lead, I could not move, although I saw her with unsteady steps approach the giddy height, stumble, and then fall into the abyss beneath. I uttered so wild a cry, that Mrs. Burnet hurried into the chamber, and found me with drops of cold perspiration rolling from my brow, my frame trembling violently, and my mind wandering. These symptoms were the precursors of a brain fever. For several days my life was despaired of, and I was unconscious of all that was passing around me, but the one fixed and terrible scene was repeated in my dreams, never failing to produce the most violent emotions, until the fever, yielding to the skilful treatment of the doctor, summoned from the next town, left me, reduced to a state of such extreme weakness, that, helpless as an infant, I seemed to hover between life and death.

It was during these days of physical exhaustion that a reprieve from agony was granted to my mind. I scarcely could recall the circumstances of the event that had led to my illness. All was vague and dreamy in my memory, and I resigned myself to this half-oblivious state, which afforded a temporary relief to the mental pangs I had been previously suffering, as a worn out patient yields himself to the torpor produced by opiates administered to dull the sense of pain. Female forms glided with noiseless steps around my couch, but I experienced no curiosity to know who they were. I took the medicines or sustenance held to my lips, without examining who offered them, or uttering a word of thanks, and sank back on my pillow again in all the supineness peculiar to persons reduced by long illness to extreme weakness, careless of and ungrateful for the trouble I had given.— But this state of torpid existence was too much happiness for me long to enjoy. With returning strength came back memory, like a giant refreshed by slumber, and armed to wound. My recollections became clear and distinct, and misery was the result. Yet I did not abandon myself to the vain regret and corroding self-reproach that were preying on my mind, without many an effort to subdue them. Human beings are ever prone to pluck from their hearts the poisoned arrow of remorse that has pierced them, and seek to heal the wound by applying the salve of oblivion. How many excuses did I make for the share I had borne in the late terrible catastrophe! How much sophistry did I expend in the endeavour to prove myself guiltless!

I would mentally argue, "Was it *my* fault that the lovely creature, now no more, had rushed upon death, from a shyness, a *sauvagerie* I called it, that prevented her heeding my earnest prayers and entreaties to her to stop? Could I have done otherwise than pursue her, under the circumstances? Would she not have told her mother and sister, in terms exaggerated by her terror, that I had stolen on her slumber, and dared to profane with my lips, that face which never before had been pressed by man, save by her father? Should I not have been viewed as a reckless, heartless libertine, who, on the evening of the day that consigned my mother to the grave, could thus invade the privacy of one she loved as her own child?" There were moments when this vain sophistry could silence my bitter self-reproaches; but soon came back the truth, armed with its stings. It whispered that had I forborne to indulge the impulse of my ill-regulated mind, had I unseen, guarded her slumber, until she had awakened, and then followed her steps to prevent molestation or alarm to her from others; she, whose cold remains were now hastening to decay in a wild spot, where the solemn rites of the church, the sacred words of the minister of religion had never been heard to sanctify it, would now be alive and well, happy, and dispensing happiness; and then a paroxysm of remorse and despair would overpower me.

I had been indulging these bitter reflections one day, when Mrs. Burnet, for the first time since my convalescence, addressed me more at length than in the usual few words of inquiry about my health, which she was in the habit of making daily, "Have you not noticed, my dear master?" said she, "that you have had another nurse, beside me, during your illness?"

"Yes, now you name it, I have a vague notion of having seen some one else hovering around my bed, but I have felt so strangely of late that I hardly knew how to distinguish between dreams and what was actually passing around me."

"Ah! Sir, you have a heart full of sensibility and kindness, and you have met with those who can truly appreciate it. Many a tear has Mrs. Maitland shed by your bed-side, when she heard you in your sleep lamenting the loss of her daughter."

I started, and was filled with terror, lest I had revealed my terrible secret.

"What did I say?" demanded I; "I now have a dim recollection, that I had some fearful dreams about a young lady falling down from a high rock and my trying to save her!" said I, anxious to account for any strange disclosure I might have made in my sleep. But there was no occasion for this *ruse*. Those who had listened to my wild and broken exclamations, had attributed them to the shock produced on my nervous system, by finding my mother dead, after my long and hurried journey to catch her last sigh, followed, by the sudden and alarming disappearance of the daughter of her friend; the severe affliction in which I had beheld the mother and daughter plunged, and the fatigue I had encountered in the search, with their servant Ap Owen, which he had rather over-rated, in order to prove his own zeal. The brain fever that followed accounted to Mrs. Maitland and the worthy Mrs. Burnet for the strange words I had uttered, and had gained me credit with them for a more than usual degree of tenderness of heart and sympathy with the affliction that had befallen my mother's friend.

"But what did I say? my good Burnet," demanded I again, anxious to know how far I might have revealed my dreadful secret.

"Why Sir, you cried out, 'Oh! she has fallen over the rock. She will be killed. Oh! God! I have driven her to this. It is I who killed her!' And then, Sir, you talked so wildly, about having hidden her corse."

I was chilled by terror, while Burnet calmly repeated my wild ravings; ravings, which alas! had but too much truth in them.

"Mrs. Maitland," resumed she, "was filled with gratitude, for the deep interest, which it was plain from your words, you had taken in her misfortune. How strange, Sir, are the ravings of delirium! There were you, accusing yourself of a terrible crime, which, if committed at all, must have been while you were sleeping that evening, worn down as you were by grief, and I in the next room, ready to answer the first ring of your bell. Lord, bless us, thought I, if a poor man, or a man of bad character, who had no one to answer for where he was during that evening, and to prove he had not left his home, had uttered these self-accusations, he would have been apprehended, and probably his life put in jeopardy."

A shudder passed over my frame as I listened to these observations, and I became sensible how essential it must henceforth be for me to avoid having any one near enough to overhear me while I slept, lest I should betray myself.

"And has no intelligence of the young lady been had?" inquired I, trembling, while I asked the question.

"Alas! no, Sir, though every place has been searched, advertisements inserted in several newspapers, and rewards offered for tidings of her, or for finding the body, no accounts have been received. Is it not a surprising, a wonderful thing, Sir?"

I longed, but dared not inquire, whether the clefts among the rocks had been searched, and yet it seemed so likely that they must have been examined, owing to the supposition entertained by Ap Owen, from the first moment of her being missed, that there could be little doubt of it. How fortunate it had been, that, as I had the folly of moving it, I had concealed the corse so securely. It was madness of me to have removed it from the place where it had dropped. Found there, it would naturally have been surmised that she had accidentally fallen over the cliff, her dear remains would have received the rites of Christian burial, her poor mother and sister would have had the melancholy consolation of weeping over her grave, and the terrible suspense in which they now were, would be over.

How strange that all these obvious facts had not presented themselves to my mind on that fatal night! But I was maddened by the event, and incapable of thinking.

CHAPTER XII.

THE following day, Mrs. Burnet told me that Mrs. Maitland intended to come and see me. "I assure you, Sir, this good lady entertains for you a warm sentiment of affection," said that faithful creature. She perceived by my countenance that I was little disposed for the interview, which she attributed solely to the weak state of my health rendering me nervous, and unwilling to receive visitors.

"She will be much mortified and hurt, if you decline seeing her, Sir, after her unceasing attention during your illness, and at a period, too, when she was suffering under so heavy an affliction."

"I will see her, my good Burnet, for I am truly sensible of all her kindness."

"And the young lady, too, Sir, has, I assure you, in spite of all her own affliction for the loss of a sister she positively doted on, shown the deepest interest about you, and has told me repeatedly she never could forget the sensibility you betrayed on that fatal night. She has always accompanied her mother here in her daily visits while you were so ill."

I shuddered at what ears had listened to my ravings, and was grateful to Providence that they passed but as the promptings of delirium. When I learnt that Mrs. Maitland had come, I screwed my courage to its utmost pitch to enable me to meet her with calmness; but when, on entering, she approached the sofa on which I reclined, and kindly clasped my hand within hers, inquiring in the gentlest tone of voice about my health, I felt ready to sink to the earth. Suspense and sorrow had made terrible inroads on her health since the eventful night on which I had seen her; and the fatigue of her frequent vigils by my sick couch, had, I felt sure, added to the weakness of her frame. I attempted to say something about the late mysterious and terrible affair, but ere I could form the words, she entreated me not to refer to that subject, for "although," added she, "it occupies all my thoughts, I have not yet acquired sufficient self-control to speak of it, without its bringing on such violent paroxysms of grief, as nearly to destroy me."

"I have still a child on earth," said she, "though my first-born has been snatched from me. For the sake of my remaining daughter, I would fain live until she shall have found a protector; but God's will be done; and all I pray for is resignation to bear it as I ought."

The mortal pallor of her face, the tremulous motion of her lips, and her difficult breathing, convinced me that her health had received so severe a shock as to leave but little chance of its ever recovering.

Mrs. Maitland had been very lovely; and pale and attenuated as she now was, her face still retained much of its pristine beauty, and her figure, though fragile, was graceful and dignified. Whether it was the force of imagination or not, I could not decide; but every time I looked at her I was struck with her strong resemblance to that lost and lovely being, who, although only beheld for a few brief minutes, had left an impression on my mind never to be effaced. I felt drawn towards the bereaved mother by an irresistible impulse, and she, grateful for my attention, soon learned to repay it with an unfeigned regard. She visited me daily, often bringing her daughter to see me; and although, during the first few interviews, the sight of this beautiful creature, owing to her striking resemblance to her lost sister, moved and greatly agitated me, I had sufficient self-control to conceal my emotion, and by degrees habituated myself so much to her presence, that after some weeks it became indispensable to my happiness.

Happiness! and dared I to aspire to this boon?—was it possible, with the terrible secret pent up in my heart, and bowed down by the consciousness of having caused the death of one of the fairest and purest beings that ever lived—of having steeped her mother and sister in a grief that was preying on the life of one, and embittering that of the other, that I could hope for happiness? Yet such is man. So prone is he to forget the evil he brings on others, and to look for enjoyment, that not even the severest trials can long subdue this inherent selfishness and presumption!

Louisa Maitland was exceedingly lovely, and allowed by all who knew her to be the very image of her sister. This strong resemblance which, during the first weeks of my acquaintance, produced so trying an effect on my nerves, became at last to have a soothing one on them. When she looked at me mildly and sweetly, I used to fancy that it was a sign that the *departed* one had pardoned me for being the involuntary cause of her untimely death; and as my passion for her increased until it engrossed my whole soul, I cheated myself into the belief, that, by seeking her hand, and becoming a son to the bereaved mother, I should best atone for the misfortune I had brought on both. It was long ere I had sufficient strength to leave the house, and I was so anxious to continue to enjoy the daily visits, now become absolutely necessary to my peace, that even after I was able to move abroad, I was so fearful of a discontinuance of them, that I still assumed the semblance of weakness and langour, which kept these dear beings for several hours every day by my sofa. Days, weeks, and months glided away, my passion for the lovely Louisa hourly increasing. She seemed not insensible to the attachment she had inspired. There were moments when her glance met mine with answering tenderness, and her delicate white hand trembled when I touched it, but with the coyness peculiar to the most faultless of her sex, and which, when not assumed, forms one of their greatest charms, her eyes would immediately seek the ground, her fair cheeks would become suffused with blushes, and for hours after she would avoid meeting my glance.

Oh! those were delicious days, when I awoke with the certainty of seeing her, of hearing that dulcet voice which thrilled me, and made my very heart-strings vibrate; of catching those deep and thoughtful eyes fixed on my face, to be hastily withdrawn if mine met them, and of noting, with all an impassioned lover's rapture, various indications, unconscious on her part, of the progress I was making in her affections! Engrossed and selfish as I was, I noticed not that the health of Mrs. Maitland was daily becoming more impaired, until she at length avowed that she was no longer equal to the exertion of making her diurnal visit to me. I looked at her when she owned this sad truth, and her altered face but too plainly bore evidence to it. How did I reproach myself for having permitted her to undergo this fatigue, when I was perfectly able to have gone to her house; and the uncontrollable burst of tears which the avowal drew from her daughter, although it proved that she, too, had not been aware of the increased indisposition of her mother, and thereby gave me the heartfelt gratification of guessing that *her* thoughts, like my own, had all been directed to another point, could not mitigate my self-reproach. We glanced for a moment at each other, and in that glance all was revealed.

"Don't weep, dearest," said Mrs. Maitland, "I cannot bear your tears. I have long been wishing to make you aware of the truth, but I have not had courage."

"Oh! mother! dearest mother!" exclaimed Louisa, leaving her seat, and clasping her arms around her parent, and the tears of mother and child mingled together. "Do not say that you are in danger. Oh! do not hint that you, too——"

And here her violent emotion impeded her utterance. I arose from the sofa, and, kneeling before Mrs. Maitland, seized her attenuated hand, and implored her to listen to me with indulgence.

"I have loved Louisa since the first hours of our acquaintance," I said: "We have all three experienced such affliction, that I waited until the heavy sense of it had been softened before I dared to avow the deep, the devoted tenderness, I entertain for her. Suffer me to entreat, if I may hope for a return of affection on her part; and if I am to be so blessed, give me the right of becoming your son, and let one roof henceforth shelter us. Speak, dear, adored Louisa; will you accept my hand, and give your dear, your excellent mother, the most devoted and dutiful of sons, whose study from this hour shall be to ensure her comfort and your happiness?"

Louisa, disengaging one of her white arms from the neck of her mother, her face still hidden on the maternal breast, put her hand into mine, but was incapable of uttering a single word. The grace, the innocent confidence of her gesture, melted me to tears. I pressed the little, dimpled hand to my lips, to my heart, and implored Mrs. Maitland to say that she would not oppose my happiness.

"This is all so sudden, so unexpected," said she, "that it has taken me by surprise. But I will not be disingenuous with you. I at once grant my consent, and feel, in doing so, that I can now die whenever it pleases the Almighty to call me hence, without any anxiety about my child. Your dear departed mother often expressed to me her desire that you should wed one of my daughters, and in according my consent, I feel I am acting in consonance with her wishes. Take Louisa's hand, and with it my blessing on both your heads, my dear children."

Louisa sank on her knees by my side, while her mother, placing her trembling hands on our heads, breathed a heart-felt prayer that our union might be crowned with as much happiness as is ever allotted to creatures of earth. I embraced my future mother-in-law, and pressed my betrothed to my heart; while she, her beautiful cheeks suffused with blushes, over which her pearly tears shone like dew-drops on a rose leaf, hid her face on my shoulder. Mrs. Burnet, the faithful attendant of my mother, was called in to hear the happy tidings, and wept tears of joy as she listened.

How blissful were the days that followed! I went to Mrs. Maitland's house early, and remained there until reminded by my Louisa that it was time for her mother to retire for the night. Who can describe the delight of listening to beautiful lips murmuring admissions, rather than avowals of affection—referring to the first consciousness of love, and to the hopes and fears that ever accompany it—to the sleepless hours, and to the dreams that follow them of the beloved one—of the thousand nameless incidents and thoughts, that mark a growing tenderness hidden in the youthful heart that trembles lest its secret should be revealed. How vapid, how uninteresting does the whole world appear, in comparison with the circumscribed circle which contains all one dotes on! What power, that dignity and wealth could bestow, would one accept in exchange for the rapture of feeling oneself beloved by a creature lovely as our mother Eve ere she sinned, and pure and guileless as an infant!

The rapture that succeeded my betrothal with Louisa for some days banished the recollection of her unburied sister, save when, on proceeding in my daily visit to Mrs. Maitland, I had to pass the scene where the terrible catastrophe that had caused her death, had occurred. Then it would break on me, inflicting such pain on my heart, that the smiles and joyous welcome of my betrothed could alone chase the gloomy remembrance from my mind. There were moments, too, when, in all the *épanchements* of confiding love, Louisa would speak to me of her sister—would dwell on her perfections, on her tenderness, and weep her loss, her tears falling on my breast; where with almost infantine simplicity she would rest her head when aught excited her feelings.

"Oh! how you would have loved her," would she say; "she was so beautiful, so good, so far superior to me in every respect."

The emotion I could not conceal at such references to the dead, was believed by my Louisa to originate in my sympathy with her regret, and she loved me the more, as she often artlessly confessed, for this proof of affection.

And now the few necessary preparations for our marriage having been made, an ample provision for my future mother-in-law and wife, in case of my death, being secured, our nuptials were to be celebrated with the privacy desired by us, and suitable to the afflictions we had all undergone six months before.

Previous to this ceremony, I wished to visit the cavern, in order to conceal more securely the corse of the lovely and unfortunate girl, there hidden. I had, ever since my recovery, been haunted by the desire to do this, but had postponed the sad visit through a moral cowardice, that made me shrink from it with dismay. The passion that had taken possession of my heart, filling it with visions of delight and aspirations of happiness, was little calculated to sober down my mind to such a trial. I dreaded it. I feared that it would chase away the voluptuous feelings that had grown on me of late; that it would cloud the bright prospect of happiness that had opened to me, and that it might produce a revulsion of feeling from which I should not be able to emancipate myself. Who is it that has not, after some heavy trial, some severe affliction which has occasioned long hours of mental agony, feared to open again the wounds only beginning to close, but not yet healed? Who has not dreaded to look on a picture, a lock of hair, or the garments of the dear departed object, aware that the sight of them will renew the bitterness of grief, and occasion the wounds to bleed afresh? There are cells in the brain, the doors of which, heaven, in mercy to our weakness, permits to close, but which, if touched by memory, fly open, and "wakes the nerve where agony is born." We know, we feel, that in those cells our sorrow slumbers, and we tremble lest aught should arouse it, and interrupt the reprieve we have enjoyed. On the slightest symptom of memory awaking, we try to divert her attention to other points; we endeavour to silence her whispers—for so prone is man to selfishness, and so anxious to seek enjoyment, that he shrinks from all that can interrupt it.

I wished to be secure from the possibility of the corse being discovered at any future period, not that I apprehended any danger at present, but I fancied my mind would be easier, more at liberty to enjoy the bliss that awaited my union with the lovely Louisa, if the remains of her sister were consigned to a grave. I had provided myself with a lantern to guide my path in the moonless nights returning from Mrs. Maitland's, and I secretly conveyed a spade and pickaxe from the gardener's shed, as well as a portion of some new matting, found in the same place. Feigning a headache, I left my betrothed much earlier than was my wont, two evenings previous to the day fixed for our marriage, and stealthily entering my garden, I took the matting, spade, and pickaxe, as also a small prayer-book, which I had put in my pocket in the morning, and stole to the spot known only to myself. I had great difficulty in reaching it, encumbered as I was. My feet slipped several times in the dangerous descent, and a dread of being hurled to the bottom, like her who thus met her death, chilled me with terror every time I stumbled. Six months ago, on that terrible night when I last visited this spot, I would have hailed death as a release from the misery and remorse that had seized me. Life then showed me nothing but a protracted state of suffering. But now the blooming bride, who was to bless my arms in two days more, seemed to stand before me arrayed in all her witching charms, and to live with her, to call her mine, rendered existence a boon that I shuddered at the bare possibility of risking.

At length I reached the opening of the cavern; I entered it, laid down the lantern, which cast its faint but lurid light on the grotesque rocks around. A sickening dread stole over me at the thought of the change which six months must have effected in the corse I was about to touch, and I drew back with instinctive disgust and horror at the task I had to fulfil. Nevertheless, that task must be performed, however loathsome, however appalling the operation might be, and I moved towards the opening of the inner cavern, with the intention of drawing out the body, when the loud hooting of an owl so startled me, that I nearly fell to the earth. Ashamed of my pusillanimity, I once more approached the spot, knelt down, and, though shuddering while I did so, drew forth the corse by the feet. At that moment, a huge bat flew against the lantern, which I had placed on a projecting rock, upset it, and extinguished the light. For some time I felt unable to move, and almost incapable of thinking, my hand still clasping the icy feet. At length I recovered myself sufficiently to grope in the direction in which the lantern had fallen; and, after a considerable time spent in searching for it, I found it, and struck a light with a tinder-box, which I had fortunately put into my pocket in fear of accidents. I dared not look on the face of the dead. The shawl I had wrapped around it still enveloped it, and most thankful was I that I was saved the horror of beholding its altered state. I commenced digging a grave, large drops of perspiration dropping from my forehead, while, with the pickaxe, I endeavoured to loosen the compact earth to enable the spade to penetrate it. While I thus laboured, huge bats were continually flitting around me, and from time to time the screech owls sent forth their lugubrious cries.

I dug deep into the earth, and though ready to drop with fatigue, from the hard and unusual labour, I desisted not until I had penetrated some five feet beneath its surface. I then, averting my head while I did so, raised the body in my arms. Its extreme lightness astonished me, but the cause was revealed when the shawl accidentally falling aside, exposed one of the arms and hand of the deceased, which, owing, I suppose, to some peculiar quality in the earth or air in which the corse had rested, had become dried up like those of a mummy. Though shocked at beholding the withered, discoloured limb, it was less dreadful than to see it in an advanced state of decomposition as I expected, and emitting that fearful odour which marks the decay of mortality. Nothing of this assailed my olfactory nerves, and I was grateful to Providence for being spared it. I placed the matting as a lining in the grave, and then descending into it with my lifeless burthen, using as much tenderness towards it as if it were still susceptible of feeling, I placed it gently in its last earthly resting-place, and read the burial service over it.

The sound of my own voice as I pronounced the solemn words of that sacred and touching service, powerfully affected me; no human accent gave the responses, but the birds of night shrieked dismally while I prayed. I then covered the corse with a remaining piece of the matting, and, commenced filling up the grave with the earth I had previously dug, shrinking during the operation at the thought that the cloak and matting alone intervened between the corse, and the clay I was shoveling over it. I would have given heaps of gold had I possessed them, to have had a coffin in which to place the cold remains, but this was not possible; and although I shuddered at every spadeful of earth I threw into the grave, I nevertheless, continued my painful labour until the floor of the cavern resumed its former appearance. I then strewed dust over the spot, and arming myself with the pickaxe, spade, and lantern, bade an eternal farewell to it.

Oh! thought I, as I ascended the cliffs, could I but see her grave in some consecrated spot, where the mild air of summer could visit, or the moon-beams play over it; where those who knew her spotless life, and fair form, could bestow a passing sigh, or breathe a prayer, I should feel less wretched. But alas! it may not be; and thou, lovely and guileless being, art denied a fitting sepulchre, though thy memory will ever be cherished in the hearts of those who loved thee, and of him, who, by a terrible fatality, caused thy death!

CHAPTER XIII.

WITH stealthy steps I reached my home, replaced the pickaxe and spade in the garden house, rubbed the dust and earth off my clothes, and entered by a key with which I had provided myself, at the commencement of my visits to Mrs. Maitland, in order to save my good Burnet the necessity of getting up to let me in. On entering my bed-room, I again carefully examined and brushed my garments, and then, worn out by emotion and fatigue, I sought my pillow, and fell into a deep slumber, from which I awoke not, until the beams of a bright sun had illumined my chamber.

On first awaking, I was almost disposed to question whether all that had occurred the previous night had not been a dream; but as the whole scene passed through my memory, its reality was evident, and, strange to say, my mind felt more at ease than before.

The chances of the possibility of detection, now that the corse was hidden in the deep grave, seemed less than ever, and I felt satisfied with myself for having had courage enough to carry my resolution of consigning it to the earth into effect.

I arose from my bed with unusual alacrity, to superintend the arrangements for the reception of my bride and her mother on the ensuing day, and busied myself as only a lover can do, in seeing everything set in order. For the first time since my poor mother's death the house assumed a cheerful aspect. Several articles of modern fashion and elegance had been sent down from London to render the apartments allotted for my bride more suitable to her age and taste, and I took almost a childish pleasure in placing them. Nothing was neglected that could administer to the comfort of my future mother-in-law. It was a relief to the remorse that haunted me, to show her all the duty and affection of a son, as an atonement for the affliction I had involuntarily drawn on her. It was this sentiment which had induced me to overrule all her objections to give up her own house and to become an inmate of mine, where she could enjoy the constant society and attention of her only daughter, and be relieved from all the cares of housekeeping. Mrs. Burnet, who entertained a sincere affection for her, was greatly pleased with this arrangement, and did all in her power to contribute to its being carried satisfactorily into effect. Two chambers, opening into each other, and on the same floor with mine, were fitted up as a bed-room and sitting-room for Mrs. Maitland. Comfortable sofas and easy chairs were placed in each, for the use of the invalid, her prie-Dieu stood near her bed; Mrs. Burnet, who was well acquainted with her personal habits, having attended to all these matters. I looked around when everything had been completed, and was struck with the air of elegance and comfort which the whole house presented. I felt sure it would be a most agreeable surprise to my sweet Louisa, and that the pains I had taken to render her mother's apartments all that could be desired, would be received by her as the most delicate and acceptable proof of affection to herself. A cook had been engaged from the next town a few days before, and the savoury odours sent forth from the kitchen, bore evidence that she was busy in culinary arrangements for the wedding dinner. In short, all wore the aspect of preparation and cheerfulness, for though occasionally the good-natured face of Mrs. Burnet would be clouded by a momentary sadness at the thought of her departed mistress, who, had she lived, would have been so well pleased at my marriage, or, by the recollection of the mysterious fate of the lovely creature whom she had loved since her early childhood, she saw much to be thankful for in the coming union, and hailed it with unfeigned satisfaction. I left my house to dine and spend the evening with my future bride, rejoicing at the thought that this was to be the last time I should leave her at night. I found her with the traces of tears in her beautiful eyes, and felt chilled at the sight. Was there so little sympathy between us that, while I was rejoicing in the anticipation of the coming day, and the happiness it would bring me, she had passed the hours in weeping? Something of my annoyance was revealed in my face, although my lips expressed nothing of it, and the quick eye of affection instantly detected the feeling. Louisa placed her hand in mine, and leaning her lovely face on my shoulder, said:—

"Do not, dearest, be offended by my tears. In the preparations for leaving the home of my childhood, I have had to open drawers never looked into since the fatal evening that snatched from me a sister so dearly, fondly loved, that not even the happiness in store for me, in a union with you, can check the renewed agony awakened in my breast by the sight of these memorials of her; and I wonder how I have been able to overcome, in a few brief months, the anguish of such a blow, sufficiently to think of happiness, nay, to have felt it. Oh! my beloved, how engrossing must my attachment to you have been, when I could forget *her*, even for an hour?" and here a fresh shower of grief streamed down the cheeks of the lovely girl.

Every one of these tears seemed to inflict a wound on my heart. I pressed Louisa to my breast, and, melted into tenderness by her deep emotion, which but too powerfully excited my remorse for its cause, I mingled my tears with hers. How exquisitely constituted—how nobly generous is the heart of woman! No sooner did this delicate creature feel my warm tears fall on her brow, than, raising her head, and looking at me with a glance of unutterable tenderness, she exclaimed,—

"Forgive me, dearest, for inflicting pain on you. Your sympathy is a balm for every wound, and when I see you weep for *her*, whom, had you known, you would have loved, a new bond of affection seems added to that which already binds us. I have often thought, Marmaduke, that had you seen—had you known *her*—*she* must have been the object of your choice. Your dear mother had selected *her* to be your wife—not, I do believe, that she liked her better than me, for she displayed no more affection for one than the other—but because she was the elder. Yes; you must have preferred Frances; for though we were always considered to be very much alike, she was so superior to me in every way, that near her, I must have passed unnoticed."

I replied that Louisa would always have been the object of my choice; that, from the first moment I had beheld her, I loved her. She was soothed by these avowals; and with a charming *naïveté* said,

"I have sometimes trembled at the notion that had you preferred my lost Frances, how dreadful would have been my fate; for, I could not have helped loving you. But I would have locked up the secret in my own heart for ever. I never would have let any human being know it. God alone, to whom I would confess it in my prayers, should have been acquainted with the fact, and *He*, perhaps, would have given me courage to bear it."

Even now, though many a long year has passed away, though age has cast its snows on my hair, and chilled the heart once so warm, I still seem to behold the blushing cheek and tear-dewed eyes of my beautiful Louisa, as she uttered the words I have repeated.

"Be assured, my beloved," said I, "that *you*, and *you* only, would have been the object of my tenderness, and the probability is, your sister would not have regarded me with the partial eyes that you do."

"Oh! yes, she must have loved you; our tastes in all things were so exactly the same, that I feel certain on this point. And yet, to-day, on opening her desk, I found a little book in which she sometimes entered down her thoughts, and on casting my eyes over the well-known characters, I was struck with some passages, that for the first time made me doubt whether she might have felt towards you as I do. Read the lines, dearest. Tomorrow you will be her brother, and it is no sacrilege, that the eyes that have wept her loss with me should behold them."

I trembled while I took the book, yet I dared not decline reading the passage pointed out to me, lest, by so doing, I should wound or offend my sweet Louisa. The following were the lines:—

"I inadvertently overheard Mrs. Herbert this day speaking to my dear mother on the subject of her desire, that I should be the wife of her son. I have sometimes suspected from hints passing between them, that she had some idea of this, but never understood it so plainly before. How strange it is that an involuntary shudder passed over my frame as I listened, and every time I have thought of it since. I am told he is handsome, agreeable, and possesses sensibility. Why, then, should I feel this instinctive dread of him? This unaccountable presentiment that in some way or other, evil will come to me by him, or through him. It is childish—it is weak to give way to such strange fancies—nevertheless, this particular one has taken such strong hold of me, that I cannot shake it off."

My hand trembled, and I felt myself turn faint as I read these lines. How awful—how prophetic had been her fears, and how fearfully had they been fulfilled! Poor girl! Why had not some good angel kept me from crossing her path, or from yielding to the impulse to press my lips to her brow?

"Was it not strange, dearest," said Louisa, "that my dear, lost sister should have had this superstitious dread of you? But the truth is, poor Frances was, like most susceptible and delicately organized persons, disposed to be superstitious; to prove which, I will show you some other passages in this little book."

And she took it from my hand, and having turned over some of its leaves, drew my attention to the following lines:—

"For some months, I have been haunted by a presentiment that I am doomed to an early death. No feeling of indisposition—no symptom of any malady exists, to account for this dread; nevertheless, it constantly oppresses me. Even in my dreams I am conscious of it. I love to be alone; yet, in solitude, a brooding melancholy comes over me, such as a loving heart must experience on the eve of bidding an eternal farewell to all most dear to it. When I behold the opening day, I ask myself whether I may not pass away from life before its close, and when the sun is setting, it occurs to me, that I may never more see its rising. My reason tells me, that every human being is equally subject as I am to the uncertainty of life. All know it, but others cannot be so deeply, so awfully impressed by it as I am, or they could not enjoy existence as they do. And yet, who ever loved this fair world more tenderly than I—who ever was more tremblingly alive to its charms? The bright, the glorious sun; the beautiful, the pensive moon, how do I feel their influence! The azure mountains, veiling their heads in the clouds; the noble trees, waving their branches to the sighing wind; the rushing cataract, sending its snowy foam over the rocks, that would in vain impede its course; the green fields, and wild flowers that bedeck them, each, and all, fill me with delight, and bring tears of thankfulness to *Him* who made them, to my eyes; but even when their charms are most keenly felt, comes the thought that I must soon leave them for ever, and I glance around to bid them a tearful farewell.

"How often, when gazing on the beloved faces of my mother and my sister, do I shudder lest I should be suddenly snatched from them! Oh! ye so dear to me, should my sad, sad presentiment be one day fulfilled, accept these lines, traced with a trembling hand, and on which my tears fall, as an adieu. While I write, I hear the voice of my sweet sister singing one of my favourite songs to our mother; a thin partition only separates us. I will leave these sad thoughts, and go and embrace them, grateful to God that I can still do so."

Louisa's eyes perused the lines, while mine followed them. Her tears streamed down her cheeks, and mine rushed to my eyes.

"You see, my dear Marmaduke," murmured the lovely girl, "that my dear, lost sister, was very superstitious; but, alas! how have her fears been realized!—I, too, feel a vague dread of future sorrow steal over me ever since her mysterious fate. May heaven avert any greater affliction, if, indeed, a greater can occur!"

Every word uttered by my sweet Louisa inflicted a pang on my heart, and sounded like the knell of departing hope. I had entered the house, elated by the anticipation of my approaching happiness, and expecting to see the face of my beloved dressed in smiles to receive me. But how had I found her? Pale, and with eyes swollen from weeping! How unlike a bride about to be wedded to the object of her affection! How badly this argued for my ill-starred nuptials! Then the sad forebodings traced by the hand of the departed Frances;—forebodings, alas! how terribly fulfilled! Oh! if Louisa could but dream of the part I had in the fearful death of the sister she doted on, how would she shrink back affrighted from the altar, and fly from my sight! The mother, too, whose pallid lips every day pressed my brow with a maternal kiss, what would her feelings be, could she divine that mine had profanely dared to touch the forehead of her lost daughter, a brief moment ere, terrified by that profanation, she had, in her flight to avoid me, met a violent death! What a prospect for the future did the union of the coming morrow, hold out! Three persons united by holy ties—who ought to have no mystery, no concealment from each other—yet, one of these three, fully conscious that if the other two knew the terrible secret locked up in his breast, they would shun, if they did not curse him.

All these thoughts awoke in my mind, as I looked on the pale and weeping girl before me. It was yet time to fly from her presence, ere the knot was tied that must bind her destiny to that of the involuntary destroyer of her sister. Yet dolt, fool, and selfish as I was, I had not courage to abandon this lovely being, and I silenced the scruples that conscience urged, by mentally pledging myself that my whole life should be devoted to the atonement of the one fatal sin of my existence, by my unceasing efforts to render my future wife and mother-in-law happy. I knew not then, blinded as I was by an all-engrossing passion, that to render those dear to us happy, we must have the only secure basis for happiness in our own hearts—a spotless conscience, and no secrets. The heart and mind must be open as day to the wife of our bosom, so that should a cloud arise, she may be able to understand its cause, if not to dispel it. No guard must be placed on the lips,—one must be able to *think aloud* with the partner of our joys and sorrows.

Could this be my case? Alas,—no! Henceforth I must be ever on the watch, lest I should betray my terrible secret. Even in my sleep, there would be no security for me; and the undying grief of those with whom my future life was to be passed, would, I now foresaw, for ever keep alive the remembrance of the dread catastrophe I had occasioned. The veil placed by love seemed removed from my eyes. The future was shaded by the most sombre hues. I felt that oblivion of my sin was hopeless, while brought in such close contact with those who must every hour of my life recall it to my memory. But it was now too late to draw back from the engagement, of which the morrow was to witness the ratification. How could my withdrawing from it be accounted for? I had won the virgin heart of one of the fairest, and most faultless of women—a woman, whose qualities and disposition were calculated to render any attachment she formed enduring. *Her* peace must fall a sacrifice to the breaking off of our engagement, at the very day fixed for its fulfilment; and could I, as a man of honour, or a man of feeling, resolve on such a measure now? With the vanity from which none of my sex is exempt, I believed that so strong must be the attachment I had inspired, that misery, if not death, must ensue to Louisa, if I broke off our marriage. I cheated myself into the belief, that *I* could make the sacrifice of resigning *her*; so prone are we to give ourselves credit for a heroism and abnegation of self, of which we are little capable: and while thus reasoning, the indulgence of my own passion had, I fear, much more weight in my decision, than a consideration for its result on hers.

All the while that I tried to think that the non-fulfilment of our engagement must inflict misery on Louisa, the dread of losing her at the very moment she was to be given to my longing arms, was what most influenced my conduct. No! The die was cast; I would wed her on the morrow, come what might; and the possession of such a creature could not, I felt persuaded, fail in chasing gloom and unhappiness away. My love, my tenderness, and unceasing attention would, *must* render her happy, and in time banish painful recollections from her mind; and the reflection of her happiness must restore and establish mine. Inspired by these new-born hopes, I pressed my beauteous Louisa in my arms, implored her not to render me wretched by the indulgence of her grief at the approach of our wedding-day; and she, soothed by my tenderness, smiled on me through her tears, and reverted no more during the day to the subject that had re-opened her grief, although I saw, by her occasional change of colour and pensive countenance, that her thoughts were with the dead.

CHAPTER XIV.

My sleep was troubled, and my dreams haunted that night. I seemed to stand before the altar with my beloved, her hand clasped in mine; and I was on the point of placing the nuptial ring on her delicate finger, when sud-denly the shade of her sister arose up between us, and with a stern counte-nance waved me from her presence. In vain I strove to retain my place, to grasp the hand of my bride; the shadowy, but menacing figure of the dead always interposed between us to prevent the performance of the sacred ceremony; and gasping, trembling, with the cold drops of perspiration fall-ing from my brow, I started from slumber in an agony of horror. Good heavens! if such fearful visions were to haunt my couch when my bride became a sharer of it, how dreadful would be my position, and how might I betray the fatal secret! I left my bed. I walked up and down my chamber, tried to reason myself out of the terror my dreams had inspired: but my efforts to conquer it were in vain; for, when tired and exhausted, I again dropped into sleep, the same dreams returned, until, unable any longer to support them, I left my pillow at early morn, and sought in the fresh air to cool my fevered brow, and recover my self-possession.

"I hope, Sir, you are not ill," said the worthy Mrs. Burnet, when we met; "but you look so pale and haggard, that I am sure you have not slept."

I muttered some excuse for my altered looks, walked from room to room to see that all was ready for the reception of my bride and her mother, and then set out to conduct them to the church where the nup-tial ceremony was to be performed. They had laid aside their mourning dresses in honour of the day; but the laying by mourning occasions almost as much sadness as the putting it on, by reminding the wearer of the person for whose loss it had been assumed.

Louisa looked pale, and her eyes retained the traces of tears. Her mother always, since the loss of her daughter, grave and pensive, was unu-sually so on this occasion, and I felt my spirits oppressed with gloom as I witnessed the too evident symptoms of the depression of theirs. Was this like a nuptial morning? I asked myself, hurt and disappointed by this sad-ness. Was this, which I expected to be the happiest day of my life, to be ushered in with sighs and tears? Such were the reflections which my selfishness suggested; and I felt more disposed to be offended with my gentle bride for the demonstrations of sorrow which she vainly sought to conceal, than to soothe her by my tenderness. With all a woman's intuitive quickness of perception, she saw that I was mortified; and, with a feminine delicacy and tact that must have disarmed the sternest of my sex, she laid her beautiful white hand on my arm, and whispered—"Forgive me, dearest, if on the day that unites us, with so much cause for joy, I have wept; but I could not chase *her* image from my mind, recalled so freshly and vividly to it by the passages we read yesterday, and by the view of the dresses in which I have so often seen her attired: as I looked on them, I could hardly bring myself to believe she was gone for ever—that I should never see her more!"

Several of our humble neighbours, to each and all of whom Mrs. Maitland and her daughters had been endeared by acts of kindness, were in the church to witness our marriage. Louisa pronounced the sacred vows with an unfaltering voice, for which, in my heart, I thanked her; mine was, I fear, less firm: and when I attempted to place the ring on her finger, I was in such a tremor that it fell from my trembling hand. Louisa turned pale at this incident, but the ring was soon found; I put it on her finger: and when I pressed my lips to hers, I would not have changed places with the proudest monarch on earth. We received the warm congratulations of our worthy pastor and of the individuals of his flock in our immediate neighbourhood, and felt cheered by the unfeigned good-will they evinced on the occasion. The former had promised to partake our wedding dinner, and we took leave of our humble friends at the church door, to return to our home.

The walk from the church to our residence was but a short one; nevertheless, such was the languor and increased weakness of my mother-in-law, that, though aided by the support of my arm and that of her daughter, she advanced so slowly that it took us a considerable time to reach our own door. How I longed to instal my bride in the home her presence was henceforth to adorn! How impatient I felt to know whether the alterations and improvements I had made in the rooms, and the new and tasteful furniture I had placed in them, would please her! I counted every minute that fled— nay, every step of our progress, anticipating the surprise and satisfaction the arrangements I had made would afford; and my sweet Louisa, guessing and sympathising with my feelings, had banished every trace of gloom and sorrow from her beautiful face, and repaid me for my affectionate care of her parent by the sweetest smiles and fondest glances.

"Ah! there is our home!" exclaimed she; "how picturesque, how cheerful it looks! How beautifully the creepers have grown around the rustic porch; how well they look enwreathing the windows of our home! May God send down a blessing on it and us, and long preserve our dear, dear mother, to crown our happiness by her presence!"

And the gentle, affectionate creature turned and embraced her parent, into whose eyes tears started, which she turned away her head to conceal. Mrs. Burnet came forth to welcome us, and led the way into the dining-room, where a neatly-served and tempting collation awaited us, and where I embraced my bride and her mother before they seated themselves to partake of it. Everything was found to be delicious. The ladies, at my entreaties, even consented to drink a little wine, a very unusual thing with them, and I then proceeded to show them their separate apartments. My mother-in-law's was the first we entered, and so pleased was she with the neatness and comfort of its arrangements, that she affectionately pressed my hand as she declared that nothing had been forgotten.

"How thoughtful, how kind, my dear son," added she; while Louisa, touched to the heart by my forethought and consideration for her parent's comfort, threw herself into my arms and pressed me to her heart. I then led them to the rooms prepared for my bride, with which they expressed themselves to be charmed; though Louisa's blushing cheek and downcast eyes revealed that the timidity and maidenly reserve so natural to her position checked the expressions of pleased surprise to which she had given utterance on beholding the chamber of her mother. Then the drawing-room, and small, but well-stored library, were examined. These had been entirely new-furnished, and enlarged by bay-windows, which greatly improved them.

"How tasteful, how elegant, how comfortable!" burst from both mother and daughter.

"Here are your chairs, dear mother," said I, pointing out a *bergère* in each of the rooms, with abundant pillows to prop up her weak frame, and an ease-and-comfort to each, to support her legs, while a small table was placed within reach, to hold whatever she might require.

These new proofs of thoughtfulness and consideration for the comfort of her parent delighted Louisa. She thanked me with a kiss impressed on my brow; and her mother prayed God to bless me, adding that I had all my dear mother's good nature and tact in providing for the comfort of those dear to her. The pleasure afforded by an examination of their new home had exhilarated the spirits of my wife and mother. For the first time since I had known them I saw smiles brighten their countenances, and I hailed this change as a good omen of future happiness, for which I was truly grateful.

How lovely looked my bride! her delicate fairness often illumined by a rosy blush, as I whispered passionate vows of love in her ear. I felt the happiest of mortals; for I forgot in the excess of my affection, and the delight of now calling my own the beautiful creature by my side, the one dark spot that had for so many months clouded my days and embittered my nights; I forgot the gloomy cavern and new-made grave where I had so lately deposited the mortal remains of one who, had I not crossed her path, would have now been as fair and blooming as my bride, a witness and partaker of our happiness. All this was forgotten while looking in the soft and loving eyes of my own Louisa, and I blessed her for this power of banishing from my thoughts every object but herself. And yet, while blessing her for banishing from my mind the one dark cloud that obscured its sunshine, back came the sorrowful remembrance. The lonely and unsanctified grave in the cavern! with its decaying tenant uncoffined, unanealed,—wrapped not in the garments of the honoured dead, but in those worn in life, with nought to preserve that once beautiful form from contact with the reptiles that prey upon the dead, but the cloak and coarse matting in which I had enveloped it! What a sad, sad contrast did the cheerful, well-appointed, and luxurious home, to which I had brought one of the sisters, offer to the grave to which I had consigned the other! I shuddered as the thought passed through my brain, but sought to chase it by trying to fix my attention solely on the present. But remorse is not to be defrauded of its rights; and even on this, that should have been the brightest day of my life, dark clouds intervened to shadow it.

And now the hour appointed for dinner approached. Our worthy pastor arrived, and the faithful Mrs. Burnet tapped at the door to inquire whether dinner might be served, when a man on horseback rode rapidly up to the gate, of which one of the windows of the room we were sitting in, commanded a view, and rang the bell loudly. A presentiment of evil tidings made me shudder; and yet, what bad news had I to apprehend? All my happiness was comprised in the lovely creature before me; and while she was near me, well in health, loving,—and oh! how beloved!—what had I to fear? Nevertheless I *did* fear, as all must who, in the brief space allowed for perfect happiness to pause with them, tremble at every incident, however trivial, lest it should prove an interruption.

"Good God!" exclaimed Louisa, turning pale as marble, "who can this stranger be, and what brings him here to-day?"

"A stranger," repeated her mother. "Oh! heaven be praised. Perhaps he brings me tidings of my child;" and, trembling with emotion, she arose from her chair and hurried to the entrance-hall, followed by Louisa and our pastor. For me, overpowered by her words, which brought the whole scene of the late burial again before me, the thought flashed across my mind, that this stranger must be in some way or other connected with a discovery, and I reeled, and would have fallen to the ground, had I not grasped the back of a sofa, near which I had been standing. I trembled, gasped for breath, and felt so faint, that, although fully aware of how strange my absence from my wife and mother must appear at such a moment, I could hardly totter to the hall to join them. I found Mrs. Maitland in an agony of grief, supported by our pastor and my Louisa, who herself, pale as death, and tears streaming down her cheeks, was vainly endeavouring to soothe her unhappy parent. I feared to approach them, but Louisa, seeing me enter the hall uttered my name in a tone of such mingled grief and tenderness, that I rushed toward her, and she fell fainting into my arms.

"Yes, Sir," said the stranger, a rude-looking and uncouth man, who, on observing a fresh listener arrive, thought it incumbent on him to repeat his story, "the body of the young lady has been found, and no later than this very morning. Ever since the reward was offered, many have kept a sharp look out, but it was my good luck to find it, and so I galloped off as fast as I could to bring the news. I went first to the house these here ladies lately occupied, but was told as how there had been a wedding to-day, and that they were come here to live. Well, says I to myself, this is a queer world; one daughter wanting a burial, while t'other is a-marrying, and so I come off here."

This unhappy and unfeeling allusion, produced a fresh paroxysm of grief in the mother and daughter, that made me feel as though I could have annihilated the wretch who had occasioned it.

"Be silent," exclaimed I, angrily.

"Why, how can I tell those whom my business is with, all the partiklars of how the body was found with the face half eaten by the fishes, and clothes gone all to pieces, and the long hair entangled with the gravel, rushes, and stones?"

"Hold your tongue, wretch, monster," said I, half phrenzied by witnessing the terrible effect produced on my wife and mother-in-law, on hearing these fearful particulars. So tremendous was it, that I would have given boundless wealth, had I possessed it, to have been able to remove the horrible impression from their minds, by assuring them that the face of her they mourned had never been defiled or disfigured save by the natural decay that follows death, and that it had been consigned with tenderness to an earthly grave—that no profane eye had gazed on it, no rude hand touched it, and that fervent and heartfelt prayers, however unworthy the lips that breathed them, had been offered up to the throne of Grace, when the corse had been consigned to the grave! But these consolatory truths my cruel destiny had for ever precluded me from uttering, and I wrung my hands in torture, as I felt how powerless I was to afford relief to the agonized hearts of those so dear to me. Assisted by the pastor and Mrs. Burnet, I conducted them back to the drawing-room, followed, in spite of my angry reproaches, by the callous messenger, loudly urging his claims to the offered reward for finding the body, that I well knew was deposited in the earth.

"It may not, after all, my dear Madam," said the pastor, wishing to mitigate the mother's grief and horror, "be the corse of your daughter."

"But I maintain that it is," interrupted the messenger of evil tidings, "and so does every one who has seen it, for though the eyes and nose are gone and the rest of the face greatly disfigured by the hungry fishes, still, any one can see that the body is that of a very pretty young girl, and as no one else in this parish has been missing, it must be your daughter's, and I must be paid for my trouble."

"Retire to the hall," said I, frantic at hearing the feelings of my wife and mother harrowed by the fearful details of this man. "You shall receive your reward in a few minutes."

"But who is to pay the man as helped me to drag the body out of the water, and who took it to the barn where it is now lying?" demanded he.

"Go, leave the room, all shall be paid, but don't say another word."

"Ah! I see well enough how it is," replied the monster. "Ye are all vexed enough to have the pleasures of the wedding-day interrupted, and the feasting on all the good things, the smell of which is enough to make an alderman hungry, by my bringing you news you didn't want to hear, when you had all made up your minds to making merry. Sure it's enough to melt a heart of stone to think that while ye are all dressed out so fine, and living in clover here, the poor girl that ye don't as much as wear a black rag for, is lying on a barn floor, and may be at this minute receiving as bad usage from the rats, as she got from the fishes."

My mother-in-law, overpowered with horror, fell fainting on the sofa, while my poor Louisa was seized with a violent fit of hysterics. I rushed on the wretch, and would have felled him to the earth, but our pastor ran between us, and pulling him by the arm out of the room, while pointing to the two unhappy women who required my care, told me not to leave them.

And this was my wedding-day, that day so longed for, that was to have been the happiest one of my life! Never was there a house in which grief, dismay, and horror reigned more triumphantly than in mine. On whichever side I looked, faces bathed in tears met my sight, and hysterical sobs and groans, my ear. I was almost maddened, yet in the midst of my despair the consciousness that all this wretchedness had been the result of my folly, my sin, added poignancy to my tortures. Had I not concealed the corse, it would have long, long since been discovered—would have received the rites of the church—would have been interred in consecrated ground—the grave might have been wept over by those who had doted on its tenant, and time, that sole healer of grief, would have, by this hour, softened down the agony, to the effects of which I was now a witness, to a tender, pensive recollection of *one* never to be forgotten. When restored consciousness, the first words uttered by my wife and mother expressed their intention of immediately setting out for Pendine, to pay the last mournful duties to the dead.

"Take off these white dresses," said Mrs. Maitland, "and let me put on the mourning habiliments that never ought to have been laid aside until the fate of my lost child had been ascertained."

"Yes, let us go to her," sobbed my poor Louisa, so changed by grief that few would have recognized in the pale and trembling creature, deluged in tears, the lovely being, who, but two hours before, two little hours, was a blooming bride, smiling on her happy husband.

I went to my desk, took out gold enough to satisfy the rapacious wretch whose visit had turned my home from the abode of content to the house of mourning; and having dismissed him, I entreated our pastor to join his entreaties to mine, to persuade my wife and mother not to go to Pendine. I felt that the sight of the mutilated and fearful corse described by him who had found it, would be a shock fatal to both—an opinion in which he fully agreed. Long and difficult was our task ere we could induce them to abandon their project, and allow me to go in their stead, accompanied by an old and faithful attendant of Mrs. Maitland, who had been the nurse of her daughters, the pastor promising not to leave the mourners until my return. The nurse was to take with her linen and suitable habiliments for the dead, which were to be put on by her; and no strange eyes were to behold the corse, or strange hands to be employed to assist her.

I bade farewell to my bride, leaving her so overwhelmed in grief, that my departure seemed hardly noticed by her, so deep was her renewed affliction for her sister; and I, selfish as I was, felt hurt and wounded that she could see me leave her without betraying any increased emotion. *Love*, which reigned supreme in *my* heart, was, for the time being, eclipsed in hers, by awakened sisterly affection, and I, self-engrossed, could blame instead of sympathizing with her.

"Let the remains of my child be brought back and laid in a grave in the church-yard here, where mine will soon follow them," said the heart-broken mother, "or if you would have no objection, I should wish my lost child to be interred in your family vault, near my dear departed friend,—your mother."

How could I refuse so natural a request, now that we were one family? and yet, to let the body of an utter stranger, of whose life or conduct we knew nothing, be intruded into the same vault with my parents, seemed to me nothing short of sacrilege and an insult to them. Nevertheless, to this I must submit, for nothing could induce me to wound the already lacerated feeling of my unhappy mother-in-law, which I must have done, had I refused her request.

CHAPTER XV.

The shades of night had obscured the surrounding scene, when, accompanied by the faithful nurse, I left my now wretched home. The gloomy prospect accorded but too well with what was passing in my heart, and a superstitious presentiment that my future dreams and hopes of happiness would be frustrated and turned to misery, as were those of that day, filled my soul. Absorbed in moody reflections, I sank back in the carriage, reminded only by the sobs of my companion, that I was not alone. At length I conquered my reluctance to break silence by addressing a few words of kindness to the poor nurse, and this manifestation of sympathy opened her oppressed heart, and she gave vent to her feelings.

"Ah, Sir, had you known her—so beautiful, so gentle, and so good, you would not wonder at my sorrow. She was even when on earth an angel, and was too perfect to be long left us here. But to think of those delicate and fair limbs,—that lovely face, which no one ever looked on without admiring,—that long, soft, and flowing hair, I have so often combed and brushed with pride, being exposed to the impure water for long months, and to the ravenous and unclean creatures that dwell therein! Oh, it is too, too horrible, and almost deprives me of reason."

And here the poor woman gave way to an agony of grief. What, thought I, if she should discover that the body is *not* that of Miss Maitland? And then a secret dread crept over me that such a discovery might lead not only to all the prolonged sufferings of suspense, but to continued researches for the corse, destroying all hope of happiness for months, nay, for years to come. With the selfish intention of warding off this threatened misery, I, after reminding my weeping companion that all injuries inflicted on the body after life had fled were unfelt by the dead, I tried, while my tremulous voice disproved my assumption of philosophical indifference on such a point, to make her think that whether the mouldering flesh of the departed was fed on by the fishes of the water, or the reptiles of the earth, availed little. I remarked that probably no trace of resemblance might be found between the corse we were to inter and the beauteous girl she so well remembered.

"Yes, Sir," replied she, "I've been thinking of that, and have prepared myself for it. I recollect in my youth seeing the body of a woman who had been drowned, after it had been some weeks in the water, and it was so terribly altered that her friends could not recognize it, and only knew it to be hers by the dress, though that, too, was in a sad state."

A new dread crossed my mind,—might not the clothes of the corse prove that it was not that of Miss Maitland? It was true that the man who had found the body had said that they were nearly destroyed; but might not the fragments betray their texture, if not colour? This dread haunted me during the rest of the journey; and while the nurse believed I was absorbed by regret, I was wholly occupied in thinking how to remedy this new cause of alarm. Never were three hours more wretchedly passed than those of our journey. Directed by an innkeeper, on the look out for the arrival of one of the family, we proceeded to the barn in the environs of the other side of the town.

"Had the persons who found the body come to me, Sir," said the innkeeper, "I should certainly have had it moved to my house, and shown the proper respect to it; but I knew nothing of the matter for some time; when I did, I had a decent coffin, lined with flannel, made, and the body placed in it; and I took on myself—I hope I have done right—to have the torn fragments of clothes that still hung to the corse burned, for fear of their causing infection."

The weight of a mountain seemed removed from my heart at this disclosure.

"What colour was the dress, and was the linen fine?" demanded the nurse, in great trepidation.

"Both were in such a state as to render it impossible to recognize their colour or quality," was the reply. "I had the poor remains wrapped in a pair of fine sheets of mine; don't be alarmed, Ma'am," (seeing the nurse start,) "it was all done by a woman's hands,—although, to confess the truth, the operation required no little courage, such was the fearful state of decomposition in which the body was."

"Alas! alas! and shall I not be able to look on the corse?" said the nurse. "I don't think you could support it, Ma'am; but if you wish it, you can have the lid of the coffin removed, for it is not yet screwed down," replied the innkeeper.

"Then I will see it," sobbed the nurse.

And together we entered the miserable barn, where the coffin was placed on a table, with a few candles scattered around to dispel the darkness, but which only partially effected that object, leaving the greater portion of the large and rude room in deep shadow. Nothing could be more gloomy, more desolate, than the whole aspect of the barn. The servant, placed in it to watch by the dead, remained as far distant from the coffin as she could, while the finder of the body stood in the back ground, ready to prove, in case any doubt of its identity was offered, that it was, and could be no other than that of the missing young lady, and wholly and solely because no one else had been missed from the neighbourhood. The faithful nurse approached the coffin, trembling so violently that I was compelled to support her. The lid was removed, the top of the sheet that covered head of the dead was drawn aside, and a face that scarcely retained a vestige of that of a human being—so fearful had been the ravages of the fishes and of decomposition—met our view. The nurse uttered a loud shriek, and fell, fainting, in my arms; while the finder of the body, who had advanced towards the spot where it now rested, exclaimed, with a triumphant glance, "I knew she would identify it at a glance. Sure, the body of a common person never could be mistaken for that of lady. I saw in a minute that the corse was a gentlewoman."

"Yes, because a reward had been offered for finding the body of a young lady," observed the servant of the innkeeper, looking disdainfully at him; "and had you found that of a man, you would have equally tried to persuade us it was that of the missing lady."

"Why, you can't pretend to say this is not the body of the lady?" demanded the fellow, looking daggers at her. "All I can say," replied the woman, "is, that it is the body of a female, but whether of gentle or simple, I cannot even guess, so terrible is the state in which it is."

"Have the coffin nailed down instantly," said I, "for I would not have this poor woman again behold that dreadful sight."

My orders were instantly complied with, while yet the nurse was in a state of insensibility, and I had her removed to the inn.

"I thought, Sir," said the servant of the innkeeper, "that perhaps the poor mother of the dead might like to have a lock of hair, so I cut one off, and have carefully washed it. Here it is." And she took from her pocket a paper, in which a long tress of hair, as unlike both in colour and texture that of Miss Maitland as it was possible to be; but I, nevertheless, took it, and liberally rewarded her for the trouble she had taken. I then gave instructions for having the coffin provided by the innkeeper placed in one more suited to the position of the family to which the dead was erroneously supposed to belong, ordered a hearse to convey it to the village church on the following day, and proceeded to the inn, where I found the poor nurse returned to consciousness, but so weak and nervous, that I compelled her to drink a glass of wine and retire to bed; after which I wrote a letter to my bride, stating the steps I had taken, and at what hour the mournful convoy would reach the church the following day.

This was the first letter I had ever addressed to my sweet Louisa; for, being in the habit of seeing her every day during the last few months, I had no occasion to write. And now, it was decreed that the first letter she was to receive from me—and written on the day of our marriage too—was to be one in which a deep sympathy for her grief precluded those expressions of passionate tenderness which filled my heart. Strange destiny! to be called away from her the very day that made her mine, and to be unable to touch on the torture the separation caused me; nay, even to feel that our meeting on the morrow would be, under existing circumstances, as mournful as our parting had been the previous one. How clouded, how sorrowful would our honey-moon be!—that epoch, that oasis in the desert of man's life looked forward to by all men who marry for love as *"les plus beaux jours de leur vie."* But what right had I to count on a single day, nay, a single hour of happiness, after having caused the death of a fellow-creature by my folly, and entangled myself in a tissue of falsehood, from the meshes of which I felt it would be difficult, if not impossible, to escape.

There is no punishment so severe as that which results from our own misdeeds, for the self-reproach that follows them adds tenfold bitterness to their consequences. Had I not concealed the body of my victim, it must have been discovered where it fell, within a few hours after, and ere this Time would have softened the pangs of grief, and I might have hoped to enjoy a happy home; but, now reversing the case quoted by Hamlet, the preparations for the marriage-feast were to furnish forth the funeral baked meats, and Death, always so awful, had broken in on my anticipated paradise, mocking my hopes, and scaring away my dreams of love.   Such was the selfishness of my nature, that willingly would I, had it been possible, have remained absent from my bride until time had soothed the poignancy of her sorrow, and that she could receive me with smiles; so great was my dread of witnessing the grief I had brought on her, and of being robbed by it of the happiness I had looked forward to on my marriage. I was jealous, yes, absolutely, selfishly jealous, that my bride could be wholly engrossed by sorrow during the first hours of our union. Ought she not to have conquered her regret, and have thought only of me at such a time? To this unreasonable extent can selfishness urge those who yield to its blameable, its ignoble sway, rendering them insensible to the feelings of those best beloved, instead of opening their hearts to sympathy. I counted the long hours on my sleepless pillow, until, worn out, I fell into a feverish and unrefreshing slumber, from which I awoke paralyzed by terror, large drops of cold perspiration falling from my brow, and my aching temples throbbing rapidly. I dreamt that I had been absent, and returned to my bride. Her rapturous delight at our meeting could only be equalled by mine. She was in her bridal bed, looking more lovely, more exquisitely beautiful than I had ever imagined aught of mortal birth could be; and she called to me, saying, "Come, my beloved; why tarriest thou from thy bride, thine own Louisa?" I rushed to embrace her with all a lover's ardour, when, lo! her beautiful face suddenly changed to the disfigured and dreadful one of the festering corse I had seen in the coffin, the lacerated arms of which were flung around my neck to prevent escape; and so closely did they press my throat that I felt suffocation coming on, until, with a mighty effort, I burst the bonds of sleep, and, springing from the hated couch, stood transfixed with horror in the middle of the chamber. Even now that I was awake, I could not shake off this fearful vision. When I tried to remember the fair and lovely face of my bride, the mutilated and terrible one of the corse seemed to be before me, producing a loathing and horror that almost drove me mad. And now the icy coldness of my frame was turned to a feverish heat. I bathed my burning temples with water, I drank off a glass of the same liquid, and again sought my pillow. But sleep visited it no more; and, ill at ease both in mind and body, I arose at an early hour, to see that all was prepared for the funeral, at which I, knowing that the dead was a nameless stranger, an alien to the two families in whose vault her remains were to repose, was to follow as chief mourner. Oh! how I hated myself for all this deception, this sacrilege towards the buried dead, my honoured father and mother. But it must be gone on with; my folly, my madness, had rendered it necessary to deceive my wife and mother-in-law.

When I met the faithful nurse in the morning, she reproached herself for not having fulfilled the commands of her mistress.

"Oh! Sir," said she, "who could have thought that the task I had undertaken could be so dreadful, so impracticable a one. Why, the very sight of the face almost stopped the current of life in my veins; and had I, as I intended, attempted to dress the dead in the habiliments I brought, I am quite sure I should have expired long before I could complete the operation. And to think that aught so lovely, so pure, when in life, could be reduced to that fearful object which we saw—oh! Sir, it is terrible! And poor human nature, however strong the love, cannot conquer the disgust and horror such sights inspire!"

"Do not, my good nurse, I implore you," said I, "relate to your mistress or to my wife, the dreadful state in which we found the dead. It would only shock them, and aggravate their sufferings."

"You are right, Sir, I wouldn't for the world do so. The woman whom we found with the corse, told me this morning, Sir, that she had cut off and washed a lock of her hair, and given it to you for my poor mistress. This is a great relief to me, who ought to have seen that this was done, but I forgot every thing in the sickness that came over me at that terrible sight."

"I have the lock of hair safe," replied I, fully resolved to substitute the ringlet, cut by my own hand from the beautiful tresses of the departed Frances, for the coarse hair, taken from the head of the corse, which I had consigned to the fire the previous night. The kindness and attention I had shown to the nurse, had quite won her good will; but alas! this circumstance tended rather to increase my painful sensations than to diminish them, for she, poor soul, was continually dwelling on the perfections, mental and bodily, of her lost young lady, and relating anecdotes that awakened still more acutely my remorse and regret for having occasioned her death.

CHAPTER XVI.

THE funeral procession, consisting of the hearse, with its white plumes, emblematical of the maiden state of her whose remains it was supposed to convey, and the coffin, the best that the town of Pendine could furnish, covered with a pall, reserved, as the undertaker took care to tell me, solely for the gentlefolk of the neighbourhood who happened to die in the country, moved slowly along, preceded and followed by two mutes on horseback, and a mourning coach containing the nurse and myself. During the whole route back, she never ceased talking of her dear lost young lady, little dreaming that every word she uttered inflicted a wound on my heart.

"Yes, Sir," said she, "I often used to say that the two young ladies were so exactly like each other, that they could hardly be known asunder. Why, their mother, and yours too, Sir, have often mistaken one for the other; and I, Sir, I who nursed them, could scarcely distinguish between them. Miss

Maitland was of a more thoughtful nature like than Miss Louisa—Mrs. Herbert, I should say—but the troubles of yesterday had quite put your marriage out of my head.—God knows, yesterday was not much like a wedding-day, but we must bow to the will of God. Well, Sir, I used to say to my mistress, Miss Louisa is like a bright summer's morning, and Miss Maitland, like a summer's twilight, so sober, so serious; but when anything happened to make Miss Louisa grave or pensive, she looked so exactly like her sister, that it might puzzle any one to tell which was which; and ever since that sad, sad night, when Miss Maitland left the house never to return, Miss Louisa has grown more like her every day, from the thoughtful look affliction has given to her handsome face. How well I remember that sad, sad night! I sate at an open window as Miss Maitland walked through the little shrubbery, and she looked so beautiful, that I could not help saying to myself, 'Well, your face must be like an angel's.' Ah! who could have supposed that I was never more to see that beautiful face! or that the terrible one I looked at in the coffin last night could be the same! She sung a hymn, Sir, that she was very fond of singing—'Ave Maria,' I think she called it, as she walked gently along; and would you believe it, Sir, there was something so mournful, yet so heavenly in her voice, that it brought tears into my eyes? That was the last time I was ever to hear it. Well, the will of God be done!" and here the poor woman wiped away the tears that streamed down her pale cheeks. "How ever she could have fallen over the cliff, I never can imagine," resumed she after a pause. "She who knew every path, every step about the cottage, and was as sure-footed as a goat, Sir, one might say. And yet there is no other way to account for her death, woe's me, for there was not a creature, man, woman, or child, that would have hurt a hair of her head, so well beloved was she in the whole parish. She was always fond of rambling about alone in the summer's evenings, just as if she wanted to converse with the stars, or the angels above 'em. She used to say when her mother spoke of it, it composed her thoughts for bed-time, and made her sleep better. I've often thought she had, somehow or other, a notion she should not live long, blessed creature! there was something so mild and angelic about her. Well, she's in heaven, and that must be our consolation. Ah, Sir, what a different thing it is to think of the dead, sleeping quietly in their shrouds, with the same calm face we have looked on when they slept, in life, and to see them, when the poor clay is mouldering away, as we saw last night. God be thanked, my poor mistress and Miss Louisa did not see it!"

Here our arrival at the churchyard gate put a stop to the poor nurse's reminiscences. The churchyard was filled by the rustic neighbours, all the women in tears, and the men with grave countenances. Not one of them had forgotten the fair creature, who, six months before, had moved in health and beauty among their cottages, with a kind word and sweet smile for all; and consequently the sight of the hearse, with its white plumes, and the coffin supposed to hold the remains of her they had so often admired, affected them all deeply. The season too—spring—that time of promise, when nature puts forth its buds, had made its appearance; and there is something so analogous between it and youth, that, when the young descend to the dark grave just as earth is bursting to give its verdure—when the song of birds enlivens the air, and gleams of sunshine warm it,—when the very showers are like the tears of joy with which we welcome a loved and long absent friend, it increases the regret experienced.

Our worthy pastor, robed in his canonicals, and book in hand, met us at the entrance of the church. His face was pale, and his grey locks, moved by the breeze, added to the venerableness of his aspect.

The coffin was borne into the church by four of the most respected cottagers, and was followed by ten or twelve little girls, strewing the early flowers of spring on it, and singing a hymn taught them by the lovely and amiable girl, for whose death their tearful eyes and tremulous voices revealed their deep regret. These children had been the pupils of the two fair sisters, who devoted a certain portion of every day to their instruction, and were regarded by their scholars as little short of Angelic Beings.

My bride, alas! now a mourning one, was with her mother bitterly weeping in the church, having, contrary to the entreaties of the pastor, come to pay the last tribute of respect to her lamented sister. As I looked at her, my heart melted with tenderness; but that sacred fane, and the solemn duty that called us there, was no place for fond greetings. I glanced, too, into the open vault, where, from the slanting sunbeams descending from a large window near it, I could perceive the coffin of my dear mother, deposited there six months before. I shuddered at the thought that I was about to intrude into that sanctuary of my loved dead, the body of an utter stranger, whose life and conduct might have been such as to have rendered this contact utterly disrespectful to my departed relatives; but it was now too late to reflect on this painful, but inevitable result of the deception I had foolishly, madly practised, a deception that had plunged my mother-in-law and wife into a renewal of the deep grief to which I was now an agonized witness, and which had destroyed the happiness of my bridal days. How did those pale faces, and streaming eyes, reproach me for that which was known only to my own guilty heart! *Twice* I had caused her, dearest to me on earth, to feel the bitterness of losing her much loved sister, whereas, had I not concealed the remains of that admirable creature, she would only have been exposed to the *one* heavy affliction, which, by this time, would have been softened into a pious resignation, a tender memory, that would not have banished happiness from the commencement of my wedded life.

Such were the reflections that passed through my mind until the words of the Sacred Service for the dead raised my thoughts to another world.

"Lord, thou hast been our refuge from one generation to another.

"Before the mountains were brought forth, or ever the earth and the world were made: thou art God from everlasting, and world without end. Thou turnest man to destruction: again thou sayest, Come again, ye children of men. For a thousand years in thy sight are but as yesterday: seeing that is past as a watch in the night.

"As soon as thou scattered them, they are even as asleep: and fade away suddenly like the grass. In the morning it is green, and groweth up: but in the evening it is cut down, dried up, and withered."

Ah, who, while listening to these solemn truths, and beholding a fellow-creature on the point of being committed to the dark cold grave, can dare to think of earthly happiness? the whole mind becomes filled by reflections on the brevity and the awful uncertainty of life. To love with an all-engrossing passion, such as is felt while yet youth sends the blood rushing quickly through the veins, in its impetuous course banishing prudence, reason, every thing but the object beloved, seems little less than madness at such moments. All the illusions of existence appear destroyed, and the yawning grave towards which, every day, nay, every hour, brings us nearer, seems the only reality.

The sad ceremony over, I approached the two mourners, scarcely less depressed in spirits than themselves. I attempted not to offer any of the vain common-place phrases meant to console, for I knew their inutility. I merely pressed the cold and trembling hands held out to meet mine, and supporting the tottering steps of both, moved slowly from the church.

Who could have believed that it was only the morning of the previous day that I had left that sacred temple, elate with a joy so entire, so engrossing, as to banish the memory of the one terrible event that had given a colour to my life ever since its occurrence? Yet, so it was, and now I felt as if I should never more experience such emotions. Alas! we are all the creatures of circumstance, and, with our vain and boasted dependence on self, can no more resist the unseen chain that yokes us to our destiny, than can the sand on the sea shore remain stationary when the advancing and receding wave impels it along.

My poor Louisa was "so pale, so woe-begone," that one might have fancied that long sickness, as well as sorrow, and ten additional years had been added to her age, and it was plainly to be seen that this last shock had so impaired the health of her mother, as to leave little hope of her long surviving it.

What a prospect for a youthful bridegroom! knowing too, as I did, how fond, how devoted was the affection entertained by my wife for her mother, the last surviving relative she had on earth. When we reached our home, my mother-in-law, anxious to learn every particular relative to her lost child, retired to her chamber, to converse with the faithful nurse, and I was left alone with my bride. She arose, and bursting into a passionate fit of weeping, threw herself into my arms, and hid her streaming face on my breast. I kissed her beautiful tresses, and pressed her to my heart, as a fond mother might a weeping child. My very soul was filled with pity for her, and I should have despised and hated myself could I for one moment have ceased to respect her grief. The delicacy of my conduct moved her, and relieved by my tender sympathy, she poured out her sorrow as confidently as an infant whispers its first grievance to a doting nurse.

"Can you forgive me, dearest?" murmured she, "for bringing sorrow and trouble to our home, where I had hoped to have brought only love and peace. Alas! what a terrible task has been imposed on you, and on our wedding-day too! I would fain question you whether my beloved sister retained, in death, any traces of that beauty for which she was so remarkable when in life, but I want courage yet to hear the fearful details. Oh! never shall I forget the part you have taken in our affliction. You who never saw her, who knew not what a pure and admirable creature she was."

How little did my poor Louisa know how well every feature of the dead was engraved on my memory; nay, more—how vividly her own lovely face recalled that of her lost sister to my mind.

"I could have wished, dearest," said she, "that you had brought me a ringlet of that dear hair which I so often plaited; but I suppose it was changed—spoiled," and she shuddered.

"I *have* brought one," replied I, "and if you desire it, I will at once bring it to you from my chamber, where I left it on entering."

I withdrew; and having taken the ringlet, now six months in my possession, from the box in which I had placed it on returning from the funeral; first having wetted, and then placed it in a napkin to dry, I returned with it to my poor Louisa. She pressed it repeatedly to her lips, bathed it with her tears, and thanked me repeatedly for having brought her this treasure.

"How little changed!" exclaimed she, contemplating its length and silken texture. "Ah! who could imagine that it had lain so many months in the water?"

While she was yet speaking, the nurse came to request my presence in my mother-in-law's chamber.

"I have told her, Sir, of your having the lock of hair, and she desires so much to see it," said the good woman.

I took the ringlet, and placed it in the bereaved mother's hands, who implored blessings on my head for the good feeling I had shown through the whole of the painful business.

"Nurse has told me of all your kindness and thoughtfulness," said she. "Like your excellent mother, you can feel for, and lighten the affliction of others by your sympathy. May my daughter repay you tenfold for all the pain you have experienced the last two days on our account!"

It was piteous to see the doting mother contemplating this last relic of her departed child, her eyes dropping tears on it as she gazed. I did not attempt to check them, for I knew they would relieve her oppressed heart; but, by gentle means, I induced both mother and daughter to take some jelly, and a little wine and water: and when night came I led my poor Louisa to her chamber, at the door of which I pressed my lips on her brow, and praying to God that sleep might restore her weakened frame, I took possession of a bed in my dressing-room, every feeling but that of pitying tenderness subdued in my breast.

The heartless voluptuary, who thinks only of his own enjoyment, regardless of the feelings of others, can never know the self-satisfaction I experienced when, the following morning, I saw the cheek of my bride assume a less pallid tint, was assured that she had slept several hours during the night—and above all, perceived that the delicacy and tenderness I had evinced towards her sorrow were so truly appreciated, that her love for me, revealed by an artless and increased confidence, amply repaid me for the triumph achieved over every selfish feeling.

For days and weeks the gloom and sorrow impending over my home was uncheered, save by the tender, but pensive whispered words of affection exchanged between my bride and myself. Both felt that any evident demonstrations of the consolation we found in our mutual love, might appear unfeeling to the bereaved mother, on whose grief time seemed to produce little amelioration. Oh, what a deep well of tenderness lies buried in woman's heart! and how do its waters fall on the arid nature of man, refreshing and revigorating it! My whole being was changed beneath the sweet influence of my beautiful Louisa, at whose feet I was often tempted to prostrate myself, in gratitude for the possession of such a treasure. The long pent in springs of affection now gushed forth from my heart, as the water did from the rock when touched by the wand of Moses; and my lovely—my loving wife, was the enchantress that wrought this miracle. By a glance, a single word, or a pressure of my hand, she could transport me to a state of bliss almost too great for words; and often did I steal from her presence, when her mother was with her, to conceal an exuberance of happiness that might have reminded her too forcibly of her own unmitigated sorrow. But my happiness was not without alloy. When was that of mortal ever free from it? And *I*, whose folly, whose madness, had wrought such misery to those dear to me—how could I expect that so rare, so blessed a visitant, could make a long sojourn with me? And yet some foolish expectation that my marriage with her I adored would efface every care, every thought but of herself, from my mind, had beguiled me, and I was now to learn that though moments—nay, hours, of as pure happiness as ever man tasted, were accorded me, a spectre invoked by conscience, and seen only by me, would cross my path, would flit through my chamber, and sometimes haunt my couch, even when the beautiful and guileless head of my wife was resting on my heart, as she slumbered peacefully as an infant. It was true, her sweet voice, her expressions of tenderness, and her gentle smile, could exorcise for a time the spectre that haunted my memory; but alas! it would soon return, and silent, and abstracted, I would sink into a gloomy reverie, from which I would start like one awakened from a painful dream, when my Louisa laid her hand on my brow, and questioned me with fond anxiety, on the cause of my moodiness.

CHAPTER XVII.

How trifling are the incidents that can awaken a chain of thoughts which for days—ay, and for nights, too, will pursue one! Sitting one day by my Louisa in the chamber of my mother-in-law, and reading aloud to them, as was my wont, a sudden and piercing shriek from the former caused me to let fall the book, when I beheld my wife, pale as death, her eyes widely opened, and terror imprinted on every lineament, rushing wildly away. Her dead sister seemed again before me, just as she looked when starting from slumber, she cast one glance of affright at me, and fled to meet the terrible death that in the next moment destroyed her. I arose, and cried out, "Stay! oh! in pity stay!" and rushed after her. I caught her in my arms, pressed her wildly to my heart, and she faintly laughed; but casting one look at me—the paleness of my face, and the terror imprinted on my countenance, soon checked the smile, and she exclaimed, "Good heavens! my beloved, what is—what can, be the matter with you?"

I put my hand to my brow, and tried to speak, but such was my agitation, that for some time the power of articulating was denied me, and,
loosening nay grasp from Louisa, I sank trembling into a chair. My mother-in-law looked astonished, and my wife was perfectly aghast. By degrees
I recovered my self-possession; and becoming conscious of the necessity of
an explanation, I said, "Your cry, Louisa, what caused it. I fancied you had
been seized with some spasmodic attack, and——"

"You, dear, dear love, in your alarm for me," observed my wife, "showed
yourself almost as great a coward as your foolish Louisa." And she pressed
her lips on my brow, on which cold drops, wrung from it by terror, were
standing. "How foolish of me to have thus alarmed you, dearest," resumed
she, "but among other numerous follies, I have such a dread of mice, that
the sight of one terrifies me to such a degree, that I lose all self-control. I
saw a mouse run across the room; poor little animal, I dare say it was much
more frightened than I was, and I screamed and ran away."

"Endeavour to conquer this nervousness, my dear," said my mother-in-law, herself deathly pale. "Your cry and your face were so precisely like
hers," and here she burst into hysterical tears, "that I could have believed
she stood before me; and it has shaken my nerves terribly."

"Forgive me, dearest mother, and you, too, my beloved, for thus dis-
tressing you," answered Louisa, kissing her mother's cheek, and then mine;
"I am so grieved to have agitated you both."

"My lost child had the same terror of mice," observed Mrs. Maitland,
addressing me; "and her shriek, whenever she saw one of these poor little
things, seemed to ring in my ear again when Louisa cried out. It may be
only imagination; but ever since I lost my first-born, Louisa seems to grow
so like her, that although the resemblance between them was always striking, it now appears more so than ever to me."

"Would to heaven, dearest mother, that this increased resemblance
could give you any comfort," replied my sweet wife; "but, alas! I fear it only
pains you."

It was no wonder, then, that *I* was daily, hourly struck by this strong
likeness—a likeness that was ever recalling to my memory an event that I
would give worlds to forget, when the bereaved mother acknowledged its
effect on hers!

For several days that shriek rang in my ears, haunted my dreams; and I
have started from slumber in terror with the wild imagination that the dead
Frances and the living Louisa were one and the same person, and about to
be dashed down the steep precipice where the former met her death. Often
did I awaken my sleeping wife by my startings and exclamations of terror,

and she would question and endeavour to soothe me, accusing herself having occasioned this nervousness by her childish alarm about the mouse,
and thanking and blessing me for these proofs of my tenderness.

Little did she know what was passing in my breast, or how, fondly as I
loved her, I shrank from her thanks for demonstrations of terror originating in a cause that I would rather die than reveal to her. I had looked on
her sister but once, while she slumbered, calm and beautiful as a sleeping cherub, and during the brief moment that she started from the seat
on which she had reclined, and staring wildly at me, rushed away. It was,
therefore, only while my wife slept, or when anything alarmed her, that the
resemblance to the departed struck me so forcibly, and I dreaded to look
on her at these times. But now a fresh incident, by enabling me to identify
the likeness more strongly, increased my nervousness and misery, rendering me at certain moment almost a maniac. I had gone out to ride, urged
by my wife, who thought that my illness, as she persisted in calling my fits
of abstraction and startings at night, was occasioned by too much confinement within doors. I could not bear to leave her, and she, now almost
constantly occupied in nursing her mother, whose ill health caused us both
the greatest anxiety, could seldom accompany me. Having been absent
a couple of hours, I returned, and entered my mother-in-law's chamber,
when the first object that met my view was a portrait of *her* whose mortal remains were now mouldering in the grave to which I had consigned
them. Taken by surprise, I uttered a cry, and raised my hands to my eyes to
shut out the sight that had so violently agitated me, when drawn from the
adjoining room to which they had retired to conceal their tears from me, as
they had heard me enter the hall, both my wife and her mother hastened
into the apartment.

"You are ill, dearest!" exclaimed Louisa; "I see you are, for you are pale
as death. Where do you suffer?"

"Yes," observed her mother, "you are suffering severely, I see. My dear
son, where is your pain?"

"A sudden spasm at the heart," replied I, "to which I have long been
subject. I am better now."

"Give him a little camphor julep, my dear," said Mrs. Maitland; "there
is nothing so good for spasms."

I swallowed the camphor julep handed me by my alarmed wife, and to
satisfy her, promised to have a bottle of it always within reach, in case of a
return of the complaint; and having recovered my self-control, I talked of
my ride, carefully avoiding again to turn my eyes towards the side of the
room where the picture was suspended.

"We have had a great surprise during your absence," observed my mother-in-law, "and although it has agitated and made us weep, it will, nevertheless, be, when we get more used to behold it, a consolation. You have not noticed the portrait," and she pointed to it. My eyes followed the direction, and it required a strong effort on my part to look on it without betraying the emotion it produced.

"Just a week before the illness of your dear mother," resumed Mrs. Maitland, "a travelling artist, passing through our neighbourhood, attracted by its picturesque scenery, took up his abode in the little ale-house in the next hamlet. Struck by the appearance of my daughters, he offered to paint their portraits, and your dear mother, wishing to possess them, my lost Frances gave him two or three sittings, when the indisposition of my dear friend put an end to her giving any further ones, all our time and thoughts being filled up in attending by the sick-bed of our dear friend, and the artist went away, taking with him the unfinished sketch. When the terrible stroke which deprived us of my blessed child fell on us, I wished of all things to get the sketch, but we knew not the address of the painter. He, it appears by his letter, only returned from a long tour in the provinces a short time ago, and having finished the portrait, sent it down to me. It is a most striking resemblance, and when, during your ride, it arrived, I had it placed where it is now suspended, in order to have it constantly before me. Might it not, my dear son, pass for the portrait of our dear Louisa?"

I assented to the truth of the remark, as well I might, for never was there a more perfect resemblance.

And now for several hours in the day was that portrait placed before me. It seemed to possess the power attributed to the basilisk, for I could not turn my eyes from it, though the sight kept constantly alive in my breast the memory of an event that poisoned my existence, and which I would have given worlds to bury in oblivion. There were those dark and thoughtful eyes, that seemed to look into my very soul, for ever bent on me; and when I turned away to shun them, the dark and lustrous eyes of my wife met mine with an expression of such pensiveness and tenderness, that I have often been compelled to leave the chamber to conceal my emotion.

Every day increased our anxiety for the health of my mother-in-law, and confirmed my fears that she would not be long left to us. The consciousness that the loss of her daughter had dealt the death-blow to her life, was a fearful addition to the misery that poisoned mine; and as I saw the anxiety and wretchedness that took possession of my sweet and gentle Louisa, as she beheld her fondly loved mother, her last relative, fading away, I felt that I, on whom she showered the rich blessing of her affection, was the accursed cause of all her grief. I, I it was who had robbed her of a sister on whom she doted, and who was now by slow, but sure degrees, sending her mother to the grave.

The physicians called in to Mrs. Maitland held out no hope of her recovery. They pronounced her disease to be the result of anxiety and grief, and informed me that a few months must end her existence. Anxious to atone for my involuntary sin against her peace, and desirous to prove my tenderness for my wife, I devoted every hour to attendance on her dying mother. I read to her, I sate by her couch, endeavouring to beguile the long and weary hours of her confinement by every means that could suggest themselves to my anxious mind; and when she thanked and blessed me, and that my adored Louisa, with her eyes filled with tears of gratitude, would tell me that never son had more thoughtfully or tenderly fulfilled his duties to a mother, I have truly whispered, that never could I do enough to prove my devotion to both her mother and herself.

And now hope was held out to me that I should, in a few months, be a father, but the joy this intelligence afforded was damped by the delicacy of my wife's health, and the precarious state of her mother. The unceasing attention required by Mrs. Maitland's increased weakness, added to her own situation, had been too much for my poor Louisa, whose pallid face and languor greatly alarmed me. I endeavoured, and I believe with success, to minister to the comfort of both invalids; but, alas! the fiat had gone forth, and it became evident that a few days must terminate the existence of my excellent mother-in-law.

I had tried to prepare my dear Louisa for the sad event; and her dying mother, with a resignation and fortitude that proved her trust in the Almighty, exhorted her to bear, as a Christian should, this new trial. It was touching to behold and listen to these two admirable women as they spoke of that better, brighter world, to which one was hastening, and where the other hoped, when called hence, to join her: and when the hour of parting came, Mrs. Maitland sank on her pillow as a tired traveller sinks to rest, with her dying breath blessing her daughter and me, to whom, from the first hour of our meeting to the last of her life, she had evinced all the affection of a mother.

I will not dwell on the details of this sad event. In three weeks after the grave closed over Mrs. Maitland my beloved wife gave birth to a daughter; and this new claimant on her love, and the duties it imposed, I do believe saved her from the consequences of a grief that might have destroyed her delicate frame. You, my precious child, were welcomed with speechless but overflowing tenderness, and were baptized in tears, for those caused by a parent's loss often bathed your dear face, as your mother covered it with kisses. She expressed so strong a desire to nurse you, that although fearful that her strength was unequal to the task, I yielded an assent, but not until the doctor had assured me that this maternal occupation would prove the best remedy for her grief, nay, prevent her indulging it, from the knowledge that it would inevitably prove injurious to the health of her infant.

And when I beheld my sweet Louisa gradually recover her tranquillity as she watched, Madonna-like, over her child, on whose existence her own seemed to hang, I rejoiced that I had consented to her wishes, and felt my little daughter grow, if possible, dearer to me as I witnessed the consolation, the blessing, she proved to her dear mother. Far was I from imagining that the circumstance of her nursing her infant might eventually lead to exciting alarm, if not suspicion, in the mind of my wife; but, alas! so it was. Instead of allowing the little one to sleep with the attendant hired to wait on her, and who was, as the doctor recommended, to bring it to its mother once or twice during the night to receive its nurture, my wife would not consent to be separated from her nursling at night, and had a little cot placed by our bed-side, from which she could remove the baby at will. Her anxiety to supply it with its nurture kept her wakeful, previously an unusual thing with her, who was a very sound sleeper, and consequently my broken slumbers, my wild startings, and my incoherent ravings, which had become habitual to me ever since the terrible night that had deprived her of a sister, now first became known to her. Alarmed for my health, often did she awake, and, with pitying tenderness, question me. But I pleaded some disagreeable dream, or night-mare, to which I said I had been from childhood subject, and she, though evidently uneasy, urged me no more; but when the doctor paid his next visit to see her and her infant, she consulted him whether a remedy might not be found to prevent these uneasy slumbers. I happened to be in an adjoining room, whence I could hear all that passed.

"My dear husband," said she, "starts violently, utters half incoherent exclamations of falling down precipices, trembles, and, in short, when I awake him, appears in great agitation."

"I see, I see," said the doctor, a worthy man, but not a skilful physician, and whose prevailing weakness was to endeavour to conceal his professional ignorance by the use, or rather abuse, of technical terms, with the real signification of which he was not always acquainted. "I am disposed to think that Mr. Herbert's disease originates in a chronic derangement of the coronary, or gastro-epiploic artery, probably caused by a pressure of the stomachic, or hepatic plexus, acting on the cauda equina of the medulla spinalis, communicating with the pelvis viscera, and influencing the action of the pathetici nerves on the brain, the pia or dura mater of which being affected, sometimes leads to mischief."

Although annoyed that my infirmity should be exposed to Doctor Bellinden, I could not resist smiling as I listened to this incongruous medley of technical phrases, all so wholly misapplied as to prove his ignorance to any one at all acquainted with the terms.

"Good heavens! doctor, you alarm me beyond measure," observed my wife, her voice tremulous with emotion.

"You must not, my dear Madam, suffer yourself to be alarmed. With my professional experience, I flatter myself I shall soon succeed in removing the unpleasant symptoms you have named, and restore Mr. Herbert to his wonted health."

"Fool, fool," thought I. "'Thou canst not

'Minister to a mind diseased;
Pluck from the memory a rooted sorrow;
Raze out the written troubles of the brain;
And with some sweet oblivious antidote
Cleanse the stuffed bosom of that perilous stuff
Which weighs upon the heart?'"

CHAPTER XVIII.

FROM the moment I became aware that I spoke in my sleep, and that the wakefulness of my wife enabled her to observe my nocturnal uneasiness, and to overhear my words, I was seized with a terror lest my terrible secret should be revealed to her, which, acting on my already deranged nerves, increased the danger I apprehended. Never did I sink into slumber without fear and trembling, lest I should utter something to betray myself. I have lain hour after hour in enforced wakefulness, watching, to be assured that she slept, before I dared resign myself to slumber, till, worn out by fatigue, my eye-lids have closed, and even in the short and fevered slumbers which followed these long hours of watchfulness, the dread of exposing my secret haunted me. I took the prescriptions of the doctor, but alas! as I had anticipated, derived no advantage from them. Mine was a malady of the mind acting on the body, and not a disease of the body operating on the mind, and I was well aware, that to attempt to ameliorate the effect without removing the cause, was a hopeless task. But as I dared not express this conviction, I yielded to the reiterated requests of my wife, and took the potions recommended.

On the death of her mother, my wife had the portrait of her sister removed to our general sitting-room, and there it was during the day, and long evenings, confronting me with its pensive eyes, and, as if endowed with some magical power, drawing mine continually towards them. I had asked my wife not to have the portrait placed in that room; but she pleaded so strongly that it might remain, that fearful of exciting suspicions that it was disagreeable to *me*,—for latterly, every thing, however trifling, alarmed me on this point,—I let it be hung where she wished it; and thus, that image, which I would have given all I possessed to banish from my mind, was continually kept alive in it, by circumstances over which I could not exert a control, without betraying, or fancying that I betrayed, that I was actuated by some hidden motive.

I could now well comprehend how murderers, after having long escaped detection, have been so haunted by the recollection of their crimes, and having suffered such agonies by the dread of discovery, have, unable any longer to bear their misery, confessed the fact, and given themselves up to justice. Oh! could I have found some friend to whom I could confide my terrible secret perhaps I should have found relief. Perhaps a cool and impartial mind might have taught me to distinguish the difference between an accidental act of folly, followed by a dreadful catastrophe, the possibility of which could never have presented itself to my imagination, and one of premeditated guilt, for which I felt myself responsible. But with me the powers of discrimination and sober judgment were so impaired by constantly brooding over this one heart-rending event, entailing others so harrowing to my feelings, that I could no longer draw the line of distinction; and who dared I trust with the secret, that, like a canker, was preying on my life; nay, notwithstanding the blessings I still possessed, in a wife and child I adored, was rendering existence an almost insupportable burthen.

I had believed, previously to my marriage, that once wedded to my Louisa, her presence and her affection would banish the one dark shadow that obscured the sunshine of my life. But I had been disappointed. She was more faultless, more attractive than my fondest hopes had ever painted her; she loved me as only the most worthy deserve to be loved, and had given me a child on whom I doted—and yet the one fatal event was still ever present to my mind—it haunted me by day—took possession of my pillow by night—nay, even in her arms, those pure and lovely arms, that had never clasped mortal, save her mother and mine, her sister and our child, I was pursued by the recollection of the dead, hurled into eternity by my madness.

The doctor prescribed air and exercise, and my Louisa, to engage me to

adopt his advice, would walk with me, endeavouring, by a thousand nameless loving wiles, known only to the gentler sex, and practised only by the
most amiable and tenderest of it, to cheer my spirits and chase away the
moodiness, that had, by degrees, taken possession of me. A faint smile, or
a tender pressure, repaid her exertions, but notwithstanding all her efforts,
and my own, I soon relapsed again into abstraction. By a fatality, my wife
always directed her steps to the scene, which, of all others, I wished most
to avoid. She would pause to rest herself on the seat in the alcove, become
as painful as it was memorable to me; and though I endeavoured to induce
her to avoid it, I never succeeded. Indeed, the only other picturesque walk
in our neighbourhood led to the churchyard, the sight of which never failed
to renew my Louisa's sadness, and to awaken my own: so, the well-known
path that led to the home of her youth, so often traversed with the dear
and departed, became our frequent promenade in fine weather. But the
frequency of my visits to it, could not vanquish the repugnance, nay, more,
the horror I felt at approaching it. I have seen my wife, when she thought
herself unobserved, examining me with a mixture of anxiety and fear in
her countenance, whenever I betrayed any of the symptoms of repugnance
to certain places and things, which, in spite of all my efforts to conceal,
I did not always succeed in doing. This discovery alarmed and distressed
me. A thousand vague but tormenting fears began to haunt me, and my
constraints and uneasiness in her presence became consequently increased.
Sometimes I fancied that possibly I had, when talking in my sleep, divulged
enough of my terrible secret, to excite her suspicions, and that she purposely led me to the alcove, in order to try how far I could support the sight
of it.

But it were bootless to recapitulate all the wild and wayward fancies
that took possession of my excited brain; suffice it to say, that there were
moments when I suspected my own reason, so wholly had one thought
engrossed all my mind, becoming nothing short of monomania. And yet,
while doubting my own sanity, it never once occurred to me, that a similar
doubt might have arisen in the mind of my wife.

My health began to give way beneath the continual anxiety under which
my mind laboured. Sleep fled my couch, and I regretted it not, because its
absence assured me an immunity from revealing my secret to my wife,
and it was only after she arose in the morning, that, after requesting that
no one might enter my chamber, I resigned myself to slumber free from
alarm. My appetite was gone,—my body became emaciated, and my spirits
were so depressed, that I would sit for whole hours speechless, absorbed in
a deep reverie, from which I would start in alarm, if suddenly addressed.

The tenderness of Louisa often brought tears to my eyes; but alas! brought no happiness to my heart. Fondly, truly as I loved her, I began to regard her as a spy whom I dreaded; and though I felt it would be torture to tear myself away from her, I was more than half disposed to do so, for the sake of being released from the constraint her presence imposed. She would place our child in my arms, and teach the little creature to clap hands at my approach, and to present its dear red lips for a kiss from mine, and for a few brief minutes I would forget my misery, and feel happy. But then she would remark the striking resemblance the child bore to her departed sister, and ask me to look on the portrait I dreaded to behold, in order to judge of it, and, then I would return the little girl to her arms, leave the room suddenly, and rush into the open air, almost like a maniac, until recalled to a sense of the suspicions to which such conduct was likely to give rise, when compelling myself to assume a tranquil air, I would return to the house, seek my wife, and converse on some indifferent topic. I now began to dread the presence of my child, because its dear mother continually reverted to the likeness it bore to her sister.

"No consolation, no pleasure, remains free to me," would I say, "without being destroyed by some reference to the one terrible subject, that once touched upon, produces such agony in my soul." Better, thought I, stand alone in the world, deprived of wife and child, than be thus tortured. Fain would I visit some far distant region, where the sound of that name I wished for ever buried in oblivion could never be heard. Oh! how far preferable would it be than to live in perpetual terror of betraying a secret which was kept for ever alive in my memory by the frequent recurrence to the one fatal subject connected with it. But how summon resolution sufficient to fly from my Louisa—from our child? Would not she, my better half, my guardian angel, whose unchanging love was my sole blessing, pine, perhaps die, if I deserted her and our infant? Oh no! I could not leave her. Life would be insupportable without her,—and at the bare idea of inflicting sorrow on her, my own suffering seemed as nought in the balance.

I had one day been out a considerable time, when, entering suddenly, I found the doctor with my wife. I had lately noticed that his visits were much more frequent than formerly, which had somewhat alarmed me, from the suspicion that they were in some way connected with me. Was it possible that my wife had revealed to him the observations she might have made on the incoherence of my manner and conduct, when consulting him about my broken health? Both appeared confused and annoyed by my sudden entrance. Unpractised in deception, my poor Louisa could not conceal her embarrassment; and though the doctor affected to continue the conversation, it became evident to me he had chosen a fresh topic.

"By-the-by, Mr. Herbert," said he, after one of these awkward pauses in our discourse which denoted that none of the persons engaged in it were at their ease, "I don't think you are looking better. I suspect that our mountain air, though in general considered so healthy, is too keen for you, and that not only your health, but that also of Mrs. Herbert, would be greatly benefited by a change. Suppose you travel. Move about from place to place for some time. Be assured you will derive great advantage from such a step, and I shall have the pleasure of seeing you return with renovated health."

"I should like it exceedingly," observed my wife, "for I think it would do us all good. What say you, dearest?"

"If *you* wish for change," replied I, coldly, "I can have no objection; but I thought that you liked retirement, and preferred our home to all other places."

There was something reproachful in these words, as well as in the tone in which they were uttered, and Louisa's sensitive mind felt it, for she blushed deeply, and then turned very pale.

"It is very true I *do* like retirement, and prefer home to all other places," observed she, mildly; "but when health requires a change, I am ready to adopt the doctor's advice."

"I was not aware that you were in delicate health," said I. "Why did you not sooner inform me on a point in which I take deep an interest?"

"Delicate health is perhaps too strong a term," replied Louisa, blushing deeply; "but occasionally I feel a little unwell. I have had great trials you know, in the loss of those so dear to me," and tears started to her eyes.

"Always a reproach," thought I, and this unjust thought made my manner harsh, if not unfeeling.

"No one is exempt from such trials," observed I, "and those who love, or consult the happiness of the *living*, do not devote themselves wholly to a morbid grief for the dead."

No sooner had I uttered this unjust remark, than I felt sorry for it, but the presence of Dr. Bellinden prevented me from expressing my regret. Louisa turned very pale, but made no reply, and the Doctor observing the change in her countenance said, "that although Mrs. Herbert made light of her occasional illness, it was his positive opinion, that unless change of air was immediately resorted to, her health would inevitably become seriously endangered. Seek the milder climate of Devonshire," added he. "It will be advantageous to you both, as well as to the child, and let this advice be followed with as little delay as possible."

How strange, how inexplicable is the human heart! How often had I wished to leave home! How frequently had I desired an excuse for taking such a step, in the hope that in quitting it, I should leave behind the chagrin kept constantly alive by the scenes that recalled it. I had fancied, that away from them, new thoughts, new feelings, would start into life, and bring back a healthy tone to my distracted mind; but now that the proposal for going was made by another, that I was furnished with so reasonable an excuse for departing, the wish of going suddenly subsided, from the suspicion that a secret understanding on the subject of my strange melancholy existed between my wife and Dr. Bellinden, and that this was the real cause of his counsel, and not the health of my wife. This surmise offended, wounded me. Was it indeed come to this? Could the wife of my bosom, the idol of my heart, betray to any human being the suspected mental infirmity of her husband? Yet, that she had done so, seemed evident. Why were his visits so frequent? Why did they both appear so confused when I unexpectedly entered? Yes, it was clear she had revealed her suspicions of my sanity to the doctor, who, to humour my waywardness, and furnish an excuse for advising change of air and scene, had invented the fable of my wife's health requiring it. Deeply wounded, and offended by this imagined breach of faith on her part, I sat brooding over it in silence, leaving the doctor to judge me cold and unfeeling towards her, when, with all my waywardness and folly, I loved, nay, doted on her, with a passion as true and warm, as ever filled the heart of man.—I felt that I would willingly lay down my life to insure the happiness of hers—that there was no sacrifice I would not make to accomplish this, the dearest object of my existence; yet, with this conviction, I allowed her to think me careless and indifferent about her health, and let the doctor depart in the same belief—a belief that must have rendered me in his eyes the most worthless and ungrateful of men.

CHAPTER XIX.

WHEN, after dinner that day, my moodiness still continuing, notwithstanding the sweet and feminine efforts of Louisa to draw me from it, she, her fair face assuming a paler hue, and those deep and thoughtful eyes timidly turned to mine, thus addressed me—

"Dearest, as far as I can judge by your manner, it appears that you do not wish to leave our home. If this be the case, pray do not bestow a second thought on the counsel of Dr. Bellinden. My health, though perhaps a little affected by the sad events of the last year and a half, is not sufficiently deranged to render a removal from this place absolutely necessary, so do not adopt any plan not quite agreeable to you on my account."

"Are you sure, Louisa," and I looked full in her face while I spoke, "that it was *your* health that induced Dr. Bellinden to advise our removal from home?"

"I believe my health had a considerable influence in the advice," replied she, her rising colour betraying that she felt conscious of the suspicion I entertained.

"Had you no conversation with him, on *mine?*" asked I, almost sternly.

"Yes, certainly, certainly," replied she; "I spoke to him, for I was alarmed, my dear Marmaduke," and she walked gently up to me and pressed her lips on my fevered brow, "at observing your total want of appetite, your loss of sleep, your lowness of spirits, and wished Dr. Bellinden to prescribe something that might be beneficial to your health."

"Then why not tell me your intention of consulting him?" demanded I, angrily. "Am I such a child as not to be made acquainted with your thoughts, and plans, and more especially in a case so closely concerning myself?"

"My not having told you, originated in a well-meant, though perhaps a mistaken tenderness," said she, her voice tremulous with emotion. "I thought you might object to my consulting a doctor, as nervous persons frequently do, and——"

"So I am nervous, am I?" interrupted I rudely, "and am to be treated either as a hypochondriac, or a maniac."

"Oh! how you mistake and pain me," replied she, bursting into tears. "I believed that the sad, sad scenes you had witnessed since you came here, the grief you more than witnessed, for your kind heart and affection for me made you a true sharer in it, had affected your health and spirits. Could I then be indifferent to a state of health induced by your tenderness to me? Ah! no. It has sunk into my heart, and increased tenfold my affection. I have lost all but you, and our child; but *you, you* and it, are all in all to me. Can I then be otherwise than most anxious about your health; and dreading to weary you on a subject always disagreeable to those in delicate health, and more especially to persons who are nervous?"

"Nervous, nervous," reiterated I, impatiently; forgetting in the irritation produced by that word, the softness into which my feelings were relenting, as I listened to her sweet voice, and simple attempt to exculpate herself from my unjust suspicions. "Nervousness is but another name for a state of mind bordering on insanity; and you cannot suppose that it can be otherwise than most painful and humiliating to me to have a physician led to believe that such is my case?"

My wife looked at me with undissembled alarm, the excitement of my manner, the flushing of my countenance, and the anger I could not conceal, might well have confirmed a suspicion of my sanity, had such ever crossed her mind.

"I am not mad," resumed I, my anger increasing as I witnessed her alarm; "but I may be rendered so, if treated as a maniac. You, the wife of my bosom, the mother of my child, should have concealed the terrible infirmity you suspected, instead of confiding your fears to another."

"You cannot surely be serious in this charge?" said my poor Louisa, looking pale as marble, and fixing her eyes anxiously on my face. "No, no, you cannot think so ill of me?" and she burst into a passion of tears.

The truthfulness of her manner, and the guileless expression of her countenance restored my confidence; and ashamed of my conduct, I pressed her to my heart, and implored her forgiveness for my injustice and harshness. How soon was her pardon accorded me, and how gently, how soothingly did she pronounce it!

"But," observed she, "this interview proves to me that change of scene is absolutely necessary to us both. Our feelings have grown into a morbidness, that requires our thoughts to be directed from ourselves,—from our grief; and you will best prove your restored confidence in me by yielding to Dr. Bellinden's advice, and putting it into execution as soon as possible."

There was no resisting the wishes of my sweet Louisa, and in two days after we left Llandover. Every milestone that marked our increased distance from home seemed to remove a weight from my spirits; and my wife, marking the change with delight, became more cheerful than I had ever previously seen her. Every turn in the road presenting a fine prospect, called forth expressions of pleasure from her, and like a child recently from school, every novel object gratified her. It is true, in the midst of her enjoyment, a sigh would escape from her breast, and a pensive shade steal over her beautiful face, and she would lay her hand on mine, look up tenderly in my face, and say, "Oh, why is it that happiness like mine should have one alloy? Enchanted with the charming scenery we are travelling through, blessed, dearest, with you and our child, I should be the happiest of mortals if the thought of how those dearly loved ones, laid in the grave, would have enjoyed all that now delights me, had they been spared me." And her mild eyes would fill with tears, as she leant her head on my shoulder. And I, instead of wiping away those tears, and pressing her to my heart, would remain silent, and careless of her renewed regret, absorbed by my own selfish annoyance at her having unconsciously awakened a train of painful thought which I had undertaken this journey to avoid.

"What," said I to myself, "have I complied with her wishes to seek change of scene, to be thus tortured by her continually recurring to that *past*, which I would fain blot out for ever from my memory."

"Is it not strange, dearest," would she say, after a pause, "that either pleasure or grief should bring back so vividly to our minds those dear lost ones, that would have taken so lively an interest in both? Never do I behold a day of sunshine, when nature has put forth all her charms, when the balmy air fans my cheek, the odour of flowers scents the atmosphere, and the carol of birds delights my ear, without remembering that the dear companion of my youth, who once shared all these pleasures with me, who was in truth my second self, partaking all my feelings and tastes, is shut out for ever from this fair earth, and mouldering in the dark and silent grave." And then tears would again fill her eyes.

"The grave is but the portal to the temple of immortality," have I replied; "and the senseless clay mouldering there, is but the garment cast off when the soul deserted it. You should remember that those you mourn are with their God and yours, enjoying a happiness that this world never can give, and that to indulge in useless regret is weak, if not sinful."

To such reasoning, uttered, too, in a tone that resembled reproof, much more than commiseration, my poor Louisa would make no reply; but I observed that after a few such exhibitions of want of sympathy on my part, she spoke to me no more of her regrets, although her eloquent countenance, every change of which revealed all that was passing in her mind, as pure crystal does that which it contains, proved that her pensive reminiscences, though not uttered, were often awakened, and the knowledge of this kept the recollection of my dread secret continually alive in my breast. I believed that had my wife banished *her* grief, *mine* would have slumbered; and I resented as a wilful injury her awakening it, as if with her deep sensibility, and affectionate nature, she could conquer memory and regret. Sensitive natures are quick to discern even shades of feeling. It may be said of them, that they see with the heart, for frequently do they perceive what might escape the keenest eyes of ordinary persons.

Often have I noticed Louisa's lips open to address me, her countenance beaming with a tender expression, which denoted that her thoughts were of the past; when she would seem to remember something, close them suddenly, sigh deeply, and sink into a reverie. Well did I divine what was passing in her mind, and rapidly did it recall that which I would give worlds to forget. But instead of feeling grateful for her self-control in not uttering what she feared might give me pain, I felt offended at what I considered her want of confidence, and blamed that which my own conduct had occasioned.

"What," thought I, "have I gained by her forbearance in not touching on certain subjects, if her countenance reveals, as plainly as words could do, that she is continually thinking of them, and thus keeps them ever before me?" There are few things, if any, more destructive to conjugal happiness than one prohibited subject of conversation. It invariably produces a constraint that chills all the pleasure of that confidential *causerie* which forms one of the sources of domestic enjoyment. The consciousness that there is a topic that must be avoided, keeps that identical one more constantly in the mind than others, and begets reserve and timidity.

I sometimes wondered what notions Louisa had formed of the cause of my annoyance when she had referred to her lost relatives; for that she had discovered that the reference to them inflicted pain on me, I could not doubt, so carefully had she of late avoided touching on them. Had she heard me utter anything in my sleep that betrayed my feelings, or did she consider me so wholly selfish that I could not bear to be reminded of painful regrets? The first surmise alarmed, the second offended me, and then came a third that did both. Did she really think me insane, and dread exciting me by reverting to the sad events of the last year and a-half? Alas! did not these morbid suspicions, this monomania, which kept the mind continually fixed on one point, prove that, if not quite insane, I bordered closely on insanity? and as this reflection passed through my brain, I became overwhelmed with terror.

At one of the inns where we stopped for the night on our journey, Louisa happened to take up a newspaper, and began, thinking it might amuse me, to read portions of it aloud: my eyes were unconsciously fixed on her face, while hers were bent on the paper, when, after reading two or three paragraphs, I saw her shudder and lay down the journal.

"What has affected you, dearest?" inquired I; "and why do you not read on?"

"I dislike perusing painful subjects, and especially at night," replied she, "for they are apt to haunt one in sleep."

"What was the painful subject you met with?" asked I.

"Something very dreadful. A man, for many years esteemed and respected by his neighbours, and beloved by his family, has been arrested for a murder committed many years ago. The body of his victim, which he buried in a deep pit in the neighbourhood of his dwelling, has been discovered; and a sleeve-button, bearing his crest and initials, found in the pit, has led to his being accused of the crime, and arrested."

I felt the blood rush to my head; my brain seemed to burn; my eyes could scarcely discern surrounding objects; and my heart beat so tumultuously, that I fancied its throbbings must be audible to my wife, as I listened to her words. I did not attempt to speak, for I was conscious that such an effort must inevitably betray my deep emotion; but I gasped for breath, and sank back on the sofa on which I had been seated.

"Good heavens! you are ill—very ill!" exclaimed my wife, rushing to my assistance, and loosening my neck-cloth. She held to my lips a glass of water snatched from the table. I drank a few drops of it, but not without great difficulty, for the power of swallowing seemed impaired.

"Where do you suffer? what is it you feel?" demanded my wife, her face expressive of the deepest alarm and anxiety.

"Only an attack of my old complaint, spasms at the heart," replied I, in broken words, "but they have passed away now, and I am nearly well."

"Heaven be praised!" murmured she, pressing me fondly to her heart; "but indeed, my beloved, these sudden attacks are very alarming; and you must—yes, indeed you must, consult some clever physician for a remedy."

She watched every change in my face with a tender anxiety that could not be counterfeited; pressed her cool hand to my burning brow, on which it fell, refreshing it like the breath of evening coming after a sultry day; sent to the apothecary of the little town for a bottle of camphor-julep, and lavished on me all those tender attentions which only women, and intelligent, affectionate ones, can bestow on the object of their love, without being fussy or obtrusive.

Happy, thrice happy, may he consider himself, whatever be his trials, who is blessed with the affection of a pure and gentle woman; if it forms not a shield to guard him against the assaults of misfortune, it at least furnishes a salve to heal the wounds inflicted by it. This salve, this blessing, was mine; but in the ingratitude which ever forms one of the peculiar characteristics of selfishness, and in the engrossment of all my faculties in the one absorbing thought that haunted me, I prized not the blessing lent me by Providence until I had lost it, and live to mourn, with a never-dying repentance, my blindness, my ingratitude. Well and truly has it been said, that the misfortunes brought on us by our own follies are precisely those most difficult to be borne, for self-reproach adds bitterness to them.

CHAPTER XX.

WILL it be believed, that even while yet conscious of the tender care lavished on me,—while listening to the low, gentle, sweet voice, uttering only words of affectionate anxiety for my health, I could not divest myself of a suspicion that my wife either doubted my sanity, or suspected that some guilty secret was connected with what she termed my nervousness? Yes, that pure, that noble mind, incapable of suspicion, I dared to doubt. Why did she avoid reading aloud the paragraph that had so violently agitated me? She surely must have had some motives for it? And I conjured up various ones, all most alarming to me, and unjust to her, to account for so simple a circumstance as her not wishing to read a painful detail, and which she explained with a candour that would have satisfied any one with feelings less morbid, and a mind less suspicious than mine, that she was actuated by no other motive than the natural one assigned. I asked myself whether it could be possible that my sudden illness on her reading the paragraph aloud, could have escaped her notice, or could have failed to awaken suspicion of its being the cause? and conscience whispered it must be so. Truly has it been said, that "a guilty conscience needs no accuser." Mine was ever on the alert to take alarm, and reason strove in vain to subdue the fears conjured up by imagination.

I dreaded to resign myself to slumber that night, lest I should betray what was passing in my mind, and so confirm the suspicions that I believed my wife must entertain; but I could make no excuse for not seeking my pillow when the usual hour of rest arrived, though, Heaven knows, I trembled at the bare notion. Long did I resist the influence of drowsiness, but at length sleep stole on me. I dreamt that my wife held the newspaper in her hand, and was again reading aloud the paragraph that had so much excited me, occasionally withdrawing her eyes from the paper to watch the effect of the statement on me. I felt her eyes fixed on my face, not with their usual mild and tender expression, but with a cold and keen examination, that chilled my blood. From the fond wife, she seemed metamorphosed into the stern accuser, the inexorable judge. Her glance seemed to possess the fatal power of the basilisk, for, turn wherever I might, it still pursued me, till, maddened, I started from slumber, exclaiming "Hide me, hide me from those eyes, they pierce my brain, they destroy me!"

"My love, my husband, it is me, your own Louisa," said my wife, clasping me in her arms, as with distended eyelids, and gasping for breath, I sat up, trembling, and pale as death. "You are ill, very ill, dearest," resumed she, looking anxiously in my face,

"No, only a nightmare," said I, recovering from my terror. "What did I say in my slumber? Were you asleep, or did I awake you?"

"I was awake," replied my wife.

"Ay, always awake," thought I. "She never sleeps, but keeps constant vigil, to overhear my wild ravings, to verify her suspicions. Oh! this is intolerable!"

"You have not told me what I said in my sleep?" demanded I.

"Why think of it, dearest?" replied she.

"But why not tell me?" asked I, eagerly.

"You muttered something about hiding you, and of some one's eyes destroying you, and were starting from bed when I held you back, and awoke you."

I drew a deep breath, and after a brief pause, said "Yes, I now remember, my dream or nightmare was, of some creature with eyes darting fire into my brain!"

"You must not drink tea or coffee at night, my love," said my wife, "for I am sure both are injurious to your health, and impair your rest."

I slept no more that night, and when I heard the soft breathing of my Louisa, calm and peaceful as that of our slumbering child by her side, I blessed God for this proof that her mind was not disturbed by suspicions which my agitated awaking and incoherent exclamations were so calculated to excite. And as I lay awake, counting the tedious hours told by a neighbouring clock, the recollection of the paragraph in the newspaper again and again presented itself to my mind.

Here was an instance of a body, interred for many years being at last discovered, and the murderer pointed out by a shirt-pin! Perhaps the owner of the pin might have been guiltless of the crime. Nevertheless, the evidence of that pin must affix the guilt on him, and I shuddered at the possibility that when I consigned the remains of my wife's sister to her unhallowed grave, some proof of my having done so might have been interred with them. I tried to remember whether I had missed anything from my person—whether there was a chance of dropping any article, however small, that could serve to identify me; but although, after a long scrutiny, I could remember that previous to going to the cavern I had removed from my person the few ornaments I wore, I could not conquer the dread, that, unknown to me, some evidence might yet exist that I had buried the dead. Then, had not the remains found in the deep pit where they had lain so many years been *at last* discovered? Had not he who laid them there, like me, calculated that they would never be detected? Why, then, should I count so securely on the eternal concealment of the remains interred in the cavern? Might not some idle boys, less timid than the generality, find out the spot? Might not robbers, in seeking a place of concealment for their plunder, discover it; and some difference of the colour in the sand, leading to suspicion of hidden booty, tempt them to dig the spot, and find the mouldering remains.

I now recollected, with alarm, that I had never seen the cavern by daylight, so that, a difference in the colour of the earth where it had been dug, *might* betray cause for suspicion, and lead to discovery. All this, though not probable, was yet within the bounds of possibility, and I shuddered while I acknowledged it to myself. Why had I not again visited the cavern by daylight, before I left home, and ascertained what now filled me with such alarm? This would have been but a wise precaution; but no, fool, madman that I was, I blindly counted on safety, when a future day might prove how falsely I had reckoned.

Then would reason, for a brief period, assert its power, and whisper that even should the remains be found during my life, what evidence could point me out as being at all connected with their interment. Nay, could it not be made apparent by the testimony of several persons, that I had never seen the only individual missing from the time of my arrival in the country, that person being my sister-in-law, whose body was found in the river, and afterwards interred? But ingenious in self-torturing, then came the thought, that if the remains should happen to be found before the dress was wholly destroyed, would it not immediately be recognized by the nurse and other servants so well acquainted with the dead? Yes, it certainly would, and I, thoughtless, and madly confiding in the notion that the spot would never be found out, had not made away with them! Indeed, a thought of doing so never once entered my head; and if it had, I would have shrank from the task; for, to profane the person of that fair creature by disrobing her, should *then* have appeared nothing short of sacrilege in my eyes; while now, with the terror of the chance of discovery, banishing every other thought but that of self-preservation, I believed I could have had nerves to fulfil the fearful task, rather than suffer the dread that now had taken possession of me, awakened by the paragraph in the newspaper.

I writhed in inexpressible torture as these thoughts passed through my mind. And there, tranquilly sleeping, lay my wife, little dreaming that the person dearest to her in life, save our child, was enduring a mental agony that she would not have wished the most guilty to suffer—an agony that must never be revealed—and for which even her tenderness had no balm. There were moments when, my feelings excited to madness, I have gazed on her face as she slumbered, until its extraordinary resemblance to that of her departed sister almost led me to the belief that I now gazed on *her*. So did the face of the still lovely dead look, when, as the bright moon shone on it, I contemplated, in an agony of grief and remorse, its wondrous beauty. Never could I now behold my wife, without being struck by the strong resemblance which, keeping ever alive the memory of the one fatal event, embittered a life that might, without it, have been blest as was ever that of mortal. My child, too, was strikingly like her mother, and, consequently, greatly resembled her aunt; and frequently would my wife remark on this likeness, and press her little girl to her breast fondly, as if the resemblance to her lost sister rendered the child more dear to her: while, Heaven knows, it proved a fresh source of pain to me.

My moodiness and waywardness, though they failed to obliterate my wife's tenderness for me,—nay, more, I believe, even increased it, by the pity it engendered in her gentle heart,—seemed to cast a spell over us, that made itself felt by a reserve and constraint on her part, which, though originating in her affection, caused a fear of uttering anything that could excite my gloom or sadness, nevertheless, added to both, by reminding me of her consciousness that this self-control and forbearance towards me was necessary. To appear in the eyes of an idolized wife as a poor, weak, nervous valetudinarian, against whose infirmities of mind she must ever be on her guard, lest she excited them into greater activity, was most humiliating; and there were moments when, far from appreciating this angelic goodness of hers, I was ready to call in question its motives, and to resent its result. If, as was frequently the case, I caught her eyes fixed anxiously on my face, instead of meeting her glance with one of answering tenderness, I have either shrank away from it in confusion, like a criminal who cannot meet the gaze of his judge, or a hypochondriac who is offended by the examination of his physician. If she continued to look at me after I had detected her glance, I felt suspicious and hurt; if, on the contrary, she turned away her eyes, I mentally accused her of being a detected spy on my looks, instead of blessing her in the fulness of a grateful heart as she merited, for these proofs of tender interest and anxiety for my health.

And now, by slow journeys, we had reached our destination, which was Torquay, in Devonshire. We had both heard much of its salubrity, and the beauty of its scenery; nor were our expectations of the latter disappointed, for my Louisa was delighted with the beautiful villas in the vicinity, and the fine prospects they commanded; while my moodiness seemed to fade away before the influence of the mild climate, and fine natural productions it called into life.

Gratified by the improvement in my spirits, Louisa expressed a wish that we should hire one of the pretty villas, embosomed in trees, that had so strongly excited our admiration; and after a few days passed at the inn, we took possession of it.

Busied in forming our little establishment, the first week left no time for the indulgence of those gloomy reveries which had, for nearly the last two years, become habitual to me; and my wife, with all the natural buoyancy of her character, before grief and anxiety had clouded it, began to resume the smiles that added such attraction to her fair and delicate face, while I marked the change with a pleasure long a stranger to my breast. And yet, there were moments when it struck me, that these smiles were forced, the better to conceal from me the anxiety to which my strange conduct must have given birth, so ingenious is suspicion in self-tormenting, and so prone was I to see every thing through the distorted medium of my fears.

Our child, too, grew daily more rosy and playful. Often would its dear mother place her on my knee, and the child would nestle her little head in my bosom, or smile in my face, or pat my cheeks with her little dimpled fingers. At such moments, I forgot my chagrin, and felt happy; but, alas! these gleams of joy were but of brief duration. Some unfortunate allusion to the past, inadvertently made by my wife, would, in a moment, put all my happiness to flight, and leave me, if possible, more moody than before, by the sudden contrast to my late feelings.

And now I sought oblivion of my cares in reading. I perused works the most likely to excite an interest in my mind, and occasionally they succeeded in effecting this; but if certain words occurred in the page—such as rock, precipice, cavern—though merely descriptive of scenery, and bearing no reference whatever to the tragical incident that gave a colour to my life—that fatal event was instantly brought as vividly before my eyes as the night it occurred—and I fell into a train of painful thoughts, that precluded reading for the rest of the day.

My wife, always an early riser, was accustomed to walk out in the morning while I slept, accompanied by the nurse-maid and her child. She spoke of having met a very interesting lady, similarly accompanied, who had taken great notice of our little girl. This lady, after meeting my wife a few times, stopped the nurse-maid, and asked permission to kiss our child, inquired its age, which happened to be nearly the same as that of hers, who was not so large, commended the beauty of our little one, which was a direct road to the fond mother's heart; and, in short, an acquaintance had sprung up between the two youthful mothers, who met generally every morning in their walks, and finding a sympathy in their tastes, took a mutual fancy to each other. Seeing that their meetings gave pleasure to my Louisa, I had not the courage to express my dislike to her forming an intimacy with a total stranger, of whom we knew nothing, except that she lived in one of the villas in our neighbourhood, was pretty, lady-like, doted on her child, and greatly admired ours.

Her husband was absent—their first parting, as she told Louisa, and she expressed so much regret at their temporary separation, and such a desire for his return, as to convince Louisa that her new acquaintance was as fond a wife as a mother. This was an additional attraction in her eyes. A fond wife and mother must be amiable, and there *could* be no reason why she should not cultivate an intimacy, which every interview served to ripen into friendship. Had I been the cheerful companion and tender friend she had expected to find in me, she would not have experienced the desire to form a friendship with any one else; but, accustomed to the constant society of her lost sister, her second self, as she used to call her, as well as to that of her excellent and highly gifted mother, their deaths had occasioned a void in her breast, which I, in the selfish indulgence of my moodiness, had not sought to fill up; and though she still loved me fondly, tenderly, she had discovered that she, nevertheless, wanted a friend to whom she could reveal all her thoughts, without the dread of giving pain or exciting gloom, and fancied that in our handsome neighbour she had found this friend.

Speaking of her one day in terms of high commendation, she expressed a wish, if I had no objection, to invite her to spend an evening with us.

"If you have set your heart on it," replied I, "and if my society is so irksome to you as to render the presence of this new acquaintance so very desirable, I will make no objection; though I confess I have a great dislike to female friendships, and more especially to those formed by chance, and with a perfect stranger."

My wife blushed, and a shade of disappointment passed over her expressive face.

"Let us think no more of it, dearest," was her gentle reply.

"My new frie—"

And here she paused and blushed again, substituting acquaintance for friend, which she had half uttered.

"My new acquaintance is so agreeable, so artless, and so good-natured, that I thought her society might amuse and interest you, as well as me, or I should not have proposed engaging her."

"I require no society but yours," answered I, coldly; "and I had hoped mine would be sufficient for your happiness."

There was more of reproach than tenderness in the manner in which I uttered these words; and she felt it, for she turned pale, and her eyes filled with tears, which she tried to conceal.

"What, tears!" exclaimed I, sternly. "Pray wipe them away, and at once write to your new friend to come here. Put my feelings out of the question, for I should be sorry that they interfered with your happiness."

"Happiness is a strong word," said my wife, gravely. "That blessing depends wholly on you, and our child, and has nothing to do with any one else."

"Nevertheless, you shed tears when I expressed my dislike to your forming an intimacy with a woman who, ten days ago, was a perfect stranger to
you."

"Indeed, you mistake my feelings," observed my wife. "It was the coldness, may I add the sternness, of your manner, so unusual, that moved me.
You are right, I dare say. You know so much more of the world than I do,
who have passed all my life in solitude. Nay, smile not at my simplicity,
when I confess that it never occurred to me to inquire the name of my new
frie—, that is, my new acquaintance, and that if I obeyed your commands
to write an invitation to her, I should not know how to direct the note."

Far from being disarmed by this *naïve* confession, which ought to have
brought me to her feet, to solicit her pardon for having for a moment pained
her, I delivered a lecture, more resembling that of a harsh pedagogue to his
pupil than an advice from a fond husband to his wife, on the imprudence
of forming acquaintance with persons whose characters, nay, whose very
names, were unknown, and who might, under the most captivating exteriors, conceal the most reprehensible qualities.

"Be assured I shall never again fall into the error of forming any
acquaintance unknown to you," observed my wife. "But pray do not imagine, inexperienced as I acknowledge myself to be, that with regard to my
own sex, I could be deceived so far as mistake an artful or designing woman
for an innocent and amiable one; no, I feel as convinced that this lady is in
every way worthy, as if I had known her for years."

CHAPTER XXI.

ALTHOUGH the warmth with which Louisa vouched for the worthiness
of her new friend annoyed me, I could not resist admiring the purity of
mind which, judging others by a self-knowledge, endowed all with whom
she was brought in contact with some portion of the goodness with which
she herself was so richly gifted. There is no surer proof of superiority and
purity in women than their freedom from suspicion and belief in virtue; and
if this confidence in their fellow mortals should occasionally be misplaced,
its source is so admirable, that we should infinitely prefer it to that wisdom
which is the forced fruit of worldly lore, never acquired except at the cost of
that purity of mind which is one of the greatest charms of the sex. There
are many who have retained, and deservedly, unspotted reputations, and
who, wholly incapable of the slightest misconduct, yet have, unfortunately,
been placed in positions where a knowledge of the dereliction of others

from the true path has been forced on them; but this knowledge, however it may serve as a beacon, has sullied the purity of their thoughts, and deteriorated from their natural goodness, by teaching them to doubt.

The following morning my Louisa did not take her accustomed walk, and her cheeks looked the paler for the omission. I told her that this was wrong, and requested she would not forego an innocent pleasure. The truth is, that after a few hours' communing with myself, I became sensible of the unreasonableness of thwarting her desires, and anxious to atone for the formal lecture of the previous day.

While we were yet conversing on the subject, a double knock at the door was heard, and a servant announced that a lady wished to see his mistress.

The new acquaintance of my wife entered ere he had time to conduct her to our sitting-room, and as cordially shaking hands with Louisa as if they had been friends for years, explained that, fearing my wife's absence had been occasioned by illness, she had called to inquire after her health. "I should have sent," added the stranger, and she laughed joyously while she spoke, "but I did not know your name. Is it not romantic and delightful, that we should have become friends, yes, absolutely friends, without ever inquiring each other's names?" and then she laughed again, with that child-like gaiety which is so captivating in the young and handsome.

"This is my husband," said my wife, still holding the hand of the stranger, and leading her to the sofa, on which she seated herself with all the ease of manner of an *habitué*. She was singularly beautiful, possessed a most interesting countenance, with lively, but gentle manners. When looking from one to the other of these two fair and youthful matrons, both still in the flower of youth, I could not help thinking they were formed to be friends. The same artlessness and gentleness characterised both; but the cheerfulness of the stranger, probably from her never having endured any trials, was more constant and joyous than that of Louisa. Her gaiety was infectious. It was like a sunbeam, diffusing light and pleasure around her.

"Now you have made me acquainted with your husband, I hope soon to make you acquainted with mine," said the stranger: "though, by the way, you have not told me his name." And she laughed again. "But what's in a name?" resumed she "'the rose (continuing the quotation) by any other name would smell as sweet.' The ugliest name in the world could not impair the effect you produce," and she looked fondly at my wife; "and yet, somehow or other, I am sure yours must be a pretty name."

"It is,"—Herbert, my wife was on the point of uttering; but the stranger, gracefully placing her beautiful little hand on her lips, exclaimed, "No, no, you must not tell me; I would not for anything destroy the romance of our acquaintance. It will be so delightful to tell my husband (who, *entre nous*, be it said, spoils me dreadfully,) that the friend—for, mind, I insist on our being as dear friends as if we had quarrelled through our childhood, as most female friends have done—the friend, I say, whom I most love, does not know my name, and I am ignorant of hers. And then I'll bring him here, and you too will, I am convinced, become friends with him at once, for he is the dearest, *best* of human beings, and never committed a fault, unless it may be the having chosen such a little madcap as me for his wife." And her joyous laugh again echoed in the room.

It was impossible to resist the winning manners, the artless smiles, and the friendliness of this fascinating being. Even my moodiness gave way before her, and Louisa's gaiety returned.

"Now, let me see your beauteous little girl?" said she.

The child was brought in, and instantly recognised the lady, who took it on her knee, called it by a hundred endearing names, played with it until the child laughed and uttered various sounds of joy, and suffered itself to be kissed and played with, to the infinite satisfaction of the fair stranger, as well as its own.

"I must bring my little girl to visit this darling to-morrow," said she. "How I wish she was only half so pretty as yours. But I must not be dissatisfied, for my Matilda is a dear good pet, and so sweet tempered. You and I shall sit nursing together, *n'est ce pas*? like the mothers of Paul and Virginia. What a pity that one of our treasures is not a boy, for then they would be sure to fall in love with each other hereafter. See how grave your husband looks. I am sure he thinks me half mad. Don't you?" and she turned her beaming face towards me as if we had been old friends.

"No, not mad," replied I, with something like an attempt at gallantry, "but calculated to make others so."

"That is a very suspicious compliment; is it not, my dear friend?" remarked she to my wife.

"He never pays compliments," was the answer.

"So much the worse, for now it is clear he thinks that I am likely to drive my husband mad. But don't think any such thing, grave sir, for he likes my foolish ways, and says he hopes I may remain a child until I play with my grandchildren. But, bless me, only look at the time-piece. What an unconscionable visit I have paid you! You will probably never let me in again," and she put on a contrite look.

My wife and I both assured her that her visit had given us unfeigned pleasure.

"Well, then, may I renew it this evening?" asked she; "I am so solitary when my darling is put to bed, that I fall into low spirits, and grow unreasonable and impatient for my husband's return, although I know he will come to me the moment he can. My poor eyes suffer when I read long by candlelight, and as he always reads aloud to me in the evening, I am without resource in his absence. Never did he leave me before, and never will I suffer his absence again. You'll let me come, won't you?"

And she bade us an affectionate adieu, and went away, leaving us charmed with her.

"I am so glad you like her," said my wife. "There is something quite exhilarating in her gaiety, and it suits the character of her beauty, too, perfectly. She has told me so much about her husband, that I am sure he must be a very superior and amiable man."

I know not why it was, but I felt displeased at my wife's being ready to take for granted that the husband of her friend was so superior and amiable. Was it, could it, be meant as a reproach to me? I pondered over this for some time; but when the evening again brought our fair visitant in high spirits at having received a letter from her husband, announcing his return at no distant day, I yielded unconsciously to the genial influence she exercised, and we spent a few hours most agreeably. The vivacity of her mind, the sprightliness and talent that marked her conversation, exciting new trains of thought, produced a most salutary effect on me. If, for a moment, I relapsed into moodiness, she usurped the privilege of an old friend to reproach or banter me.

"You spoil this good man; indeed you do," observed she, addressing my wife. "You should not let him fancy (for be assured it is only hypochondriasis) that he is ill or low-spirited. Scold him well whenever he assumes a grave aspect, instead of looking anxious and alarmed, as I saw you do half-a-dozen times at least to-day and this evening, when he sank into a reverie. Show him no quarter, give him no time for reflection, and I will answer for it, you, as well as he, will find the advantage of my prescription."

Louisa looked timidly at me, to see how I bore this *persiflage*, and wondering that, on the very first day of my acquaintance with her vivacious friend, she should treat me so very unceremoniously; but when she observed that, *malgré* my efforts to look serious, I could not resist the playfulness of our guest, she ventured to join in the laugh in which her new friend was indulging at my expense.

The next day, and the following, a great portion of each, and the whole of the two evenings, were passed by this fascinating person at our villa, and every hour revealing some new attraction in her; and, above all, the artlessness with which she betrayed her admiration and affection for my wife, gained on my good-will so rapidly, that reserved and shy as my habits were, I lost all constraint with her, and enjoyed her society as much as Louisa did, who really, short as their acquaintance had been, already loved her as a sister.

The third evening from the first she had spent with us, the fair stranger, my wife, and I, were chatting together on as cordial terms as if we had known each other all our lives. She began forming plans for the excursions we were to make together when her husband arrived, of the visit we were to make them at their seat in Yorkshire, she clapping her pretty little hands together with child-like glee at the pleasure she anticipated, when her servant arrived with a note for her. She hurriedly opened it, blushed to her very temples as she perused it, and arose to depart.

"My husband is arrived," said she, "and instead of coming for me, as I left word he was to do, he makes some foolish excuse, and begs me to return home as soon as possible. I shall certainly give him a severe scolding for his disobedience to my commands; that is, if I can restrain my joy at seeing him sufficiently to scold. Really, men are insupportable, are they not, *chère amie?*" turning to my wife, as she tied on her bonnet, and wrapped herself in her shawl. "My tyrant," resumed she, "will soon become as unmanageable as yours, if I don't at once assert my dignity. Look there, read his absurd note," and she threw it to me, as, after having embraced Louisa, she hastily left the room, declining my offer to conduct her to her home.

"What does the husband of our charming friend say?" inquired Louisa, as, leaning on my shoulder, she glanced over the contents of the note which I had began reading. They were as follows:—

"I am this moment arrived, and, impatient as I am to see you, I cannot, for reasons which I will give you when we meet, go for you, as you wished me to do, to Mr. Herbert's.

"You see that, although you don't know it, I am already acquainted with the name of your new friends, which I learned from one of our servants, when I inquired where you were. But more of this hereafter.

"Your fond husband,
"GEORGE NEVILLE"

"George Neville," repeated I. "How very strange," the blood rushing to my very temples.

"Yes, very strange," reiterated my wife, imagining that my words referred to the purport of the note, and not to the name, which I instantly recognized as that of my old school-fellow.

"One might really be led to think that the discovery of our name presented the obstacle to which this Mr. Neville alludes," observed Louisa, the mantling blush of wounded pride and self-respect mounting to her brow. The remark offended me; and the more so, that I knew it to be founded on truth; and when I caught her eyes fixed on my face, as if waiting for an answer to her supposition, or as if watching the effect it produced on me, I turned away vexed at the scrutiny, and anxious to conceal my emotion. Instead of simply stating the fact that a Mr. Neville, probably this very person, had been a school-fellow of mine, with whom I had been on such cold terms, that a meeting could not be agreeable to either party, I gave no hint whatever of the circumstance. The motive of this disingenuousness originated in a dread of being questioned as to the cause of my coldness with Neville, to relate the particulars of which, would not only be painful and humiliating to me, but would probably impair the respect and esteem I was so desirous my wife should entertain for me.

"You don't tell me your opinion, dearest?" said Louisa, gravely.

This pertinacity, so unusual on her part, increased my ill-humour, and there was a sternness in my manner, when, affecting to forget the former remark, I reiterated the words "My opinion on what?"

"On the passage in Mr. Neville's letter that seemed to me to imply that the discovery of our name was the obstacle to his coming here."

"I had forgot all about it," replied I. "In truth, such a puerility was not worth remembering. Our name could have nothing to do in the matter; but I suppose, that knowing his wife to be very giddy and unguarded, facts which her mode of making our acquaintance proves, he meant his not coming for her a reproof, and his remark that *he* had already discovered our name, though she was still ignorant, of it as another. You must admit Louisa, that although a very charming and fascinating person, Mrs. Neville *is* very giddy and unguarded. She knew nothing whatever of us, yet forced, yes, absolutely forced her acquaintance on us. We might be the very reverse of respectable, for aught she knew to the contrary; she took not even the trouble to inquire our name, yet with an impetuosity to be met only in novels where the heroines rush into each other's arms at first sight, and vow eternal friendship, she made your acquaintance without introduction, came to our house, and established herself here with all the ease and confidence of an old friend. Is it not natural that her husband should disapprove and resent such unthinking conduct, such a perfect solecism in etiquette and worldly usage; and I shall not be surprised, if, as a punishment to her, he should let the acquaintance drop."

I said this, to prepare Louisa for the line I fully expected Neville would adopt, but it by no means answered the desired end for she observed,—

"I am so ignorant of worldly usages, that I am a bad judge on this subject, but candour obliges me to say, that when I saw a young mother, morning after morning, walking in the same path as myself, and apparently as fondly devoted to her child as I am to mine, I observed her with pleasure. Her beauty and looks of kindness attracted, her notice of my child gratified me, and when she addressed me, I was quite as willing to make her acquaintance as she was to make mine. I could have certified that *she* was good, gentle, and pure-minded, and she, it appears, at once judged as favourably of me. You men know not, cannot know, the free masonry that exists between young mothers. A glance, a smile makes them acquainted. There was the blue sky above our heads, the calm sea beneath us, the umbrageous trees, the green fields, the flowery hedgerows; the carol of birds, and the breaking of the waves on the shore, were the only sounds that broke on our ears; and with two persons so ignorant of the ceremonious etiquette of society, it is not to be wondered at that we forget the propriety, if not the necessity, of a formal introduction. I say this," continued Louisa with much more animation than I had ever previously seen her evince, "to prove that Mrs. Neville was no more culpable of giddiness or unguardedness than myself. Had I met her advances with coldness, which it never could enter my head to do, she certainly would not have come here."

"Then let this serve as a lesson," said I, gravely, "not to break from the established usages of society, for be assured certain codes of etiquette were not formed until the necessity of such were felt;" and I left the room to prevent the continuance of a discussion, in which I felt I should have the worst of the argument, so disposed was my wife to think well of her new friend, and so desirous to exculpate her from the charge of giddiness. Hitherto, Louisa had never offered any opposition to my opinions. If she adopted them not, she at least allowed them to pass unquestioned. Her warmth on this occasion, although it surprised and annoyed me, bore evidence not only to the generosity of her character, but also that she could think for herself—and this displeased me.

CHAPTER XXII.

THE next day I noticed that Louisa appeared anxious and unsettled. She frequently walked to the window, looked out, then sate down again, took up her work, or a book, and in short, exhibited indubitable evidence of what, in vulgar parlance, is termed fidgetiness, a disease, if it may be so considered, of which I had never before seen the slightest symptom in her. Well did I divine the cause. She expected an early visit from her friend, and the indulgence of this expectation displeased me, knowing as I did, that it would not be gratified.

As the day wore away without the anticipated visit, or an explanatory note why it was so long deferred, her restlessness increased, and with it my dissatisfaction. Why should she attach so much importance to seeing a person of whose existence ten days before she was ignorant? Why not be satisfied with my society alone, as I was with hers? Such reflections increased my moodiness. I took up a book, with which I pretended to be occupied, but my eye was more frequently directed to my wife's face, than to the pages.

I proposed a walk to her, but she declined, on the plea that she should be sorry to miss seeing her friend, and Mr. Neville.

"I am sure he must be a most amiable and excellent person," said Louisa, "for his wife has told me so much of his high principles, generosity, goodness of heart, and equanimity of temper, that I have formed a high notion of him, notwithstanding the mysterious passage in his letter, which I confess has excited my curiosity."

These commendations annoyed me; and the more so, as I fancied that Louisa laid a particular emphasis on the words equanimity of temper. This was a qualification which conscience whispered me I was far from possessing, for the trials I had endured had soured and irritated a temper not naturally bad; and, though well aware that I was but a cheerless companion to my gentle wife, I could not bear that she should be made more sensible of this painful fact, by the striking contrast presented by the husband of her friend, as related by his wife.

"You must not place implicit faith in the praises bestowed by Mrs. Neville on her lord and master," observed I, after one of those long pauses which so continually occurred on my part in our tête-à-têtes.

"Have you then ever met him, or heard aught to his disadvantage?" inquired Louisa, anxiously.

I hesitated at uttering the positive falsehood of denying that I had met him, and knew the nobleness of his character, so I avoided the question by saying, "I did not precisely refer to Mr. Neville, when I said the praises of husbands by their wives must not be too much depended upon. I dare say that you, dearest, boasted as much of my merits, or rather supposed merits, to your friend, as she did of her husband's?"

"No, not quite," replied Louisa, ingenuously, her cheek colouring as she spoke. "First, because she is so animated, and, so much more loquacious than I am, that she gave me little opportunity to talk; and secondly, praising one's husband seems to me very like commending oneself."

The truthfulness and simplicity of this answer did not satisfy me. I took it into my head that there was a mental reservation in it; in fact, that not liking to reveal my gloominess of temper, my habitual silence, she had avoided any mention of me.

"Yes," resumed I, "your friend is indeed very loquacious. Heaven be praised, that in this instance you do not resemble her. Such a companion would drive me mad."

"Yet you appeared amused and interested by her conversation. I never saw you smile so often before, and marking how much her gaiety restored your cheerfulness, I wished that I possessed a portion of it in order sometimes to enliven you. I, too, felt its cheering influence. It reminded me of my girlish days," and she sighed deeply, "when my liveliness used to draw smiles from——"

Her voice faltered, tears started to her eyes, and she walked to the window to conceal them.

At that moment a servant brought a note for her, which she hurriedly opened, and she blushed deeply, as her eyes ran over the lines.

"Who have you heard from?" asked I, well knowing they she had no acquaintance at Torquay, except Mrs. Neville, and consequently that the letter must be from her. She handed it to me, and then again turned to the window.

"You will be surprised, and I flatter myself as sorry as I am, when I tell you that when you receive this, I shall be some miles away on my journey to London. I had formed such pleasant projects for the next few weeks, to be passed in your society, dear Mrs. Herbert, and now my husband hurries me off to town, where business claims his presence. It is the first time I have had reluctance or regret in obeying his wishes. I should so have liked to see you again, for you have made yourself a place in my affection that absence will not destroy. Heaven bless you! Kiss your darling's lips for me, and give my compliments to Mr. Herbert. The carriage is at the door, and I have only time to add that though we may meet no more, I shall always remember you dearly.

"MARY NEVILLE."

"How very strange this sudden departure seems," observed Louisa. "Coupled with Mr. Neville's note of last night, it really appears as if he did not wish her to cultivate friendship with us, and hurried her away to avoid it."

I felt she rightly divined; yet, to avoid explanations, I was forced to deny it.

"Why," demanded I, "should Mr. Neville have any objection to his wife's friendship for you? There can be no reason that we should think so meanly of ourselves as to admit the possibility of aught so humiliating. The most fastidious can discover nothing in us to furnish a reason for avoidance, so do not, my dear Louisa, allow yourself to attach any importance to what, after all, may have proceeded from the simplest cause. Men have business connected with their properties, with which they do not always entrust their wives. They may be often called away on the shortest notice; and your acquaintance has been so brief with Mrs. Neville, that her husband would hardly have thought that any more ceremony than a farewell note could be necessary towards us."

"Yes, that I can imagine," replied Louisa. "But why say nothing of the invitation given us to visit them in the country. Why add 'though we may meet no more?'"

"You forget that Mrs. Neville is a high-flown romantic person, who, annoyed at being forced to leave a new friend, in the fervour and exaggeration of her character, writes as if she were bidding you an eternal farewell. There are many such persons in the world, who, with heads heated by novel-reading, fancy themselves wretched at parting with some imaginary friend. Mrs. Neville is one of these, and wished that her parting from you should partake the romantic character that marked the commencement of your acquaintance."

"You do her injustice; indeed you do," said Louisa. "Be assured that she is warm-hearted, kind, and truthful."

"I will give her credit for every virtue and good quality with which you, my dear, in the plenitude of your generosity, choose to endow her," replied I, "provided you let the subject drop. Think of her only as children do of the pretty butterflies that cross their path during a summer's walk, attracting them by their gay colours into a chase, which amuses for a short time, but generally ends in disappointment; for whether the insect be caught or escape, disappointment follows. If caught, its beauty is impaired, if not destroyed, by the grasp of its captor; if it escapes, it is regretted for a moment, and then forgotten. So with those summer friends formed by chance: if retained, time proves that they are much less attractive than they appeared at first; if they depart, they should be thought of no more."

My wife shook her head dissentingly, and I felt that my simile was too lame and impotent to serve my scheme of turning her thoughts from her friend.

And now we relapsed into our former dull and cheerless *tête-à-têtes*. A new prohibited subject was added to the previous ones; for Louisa, in compliance with my implied desire, never mentioned the Nevilles; although, on several occasions, the subject arose to her lips, as I could perceive by her sudden pauses in the midst of a sentence that was evidently leading to it. They often, too, recurred to my mind. Their sudden departure was a new proof of his generosity, and I understood it. He wished to avoid renewing acquaintance with me; yet how avoid it, with the intimacy that had sprung up between our wives, without betraying his disapprobation of me, and so inflicting pain on mine? To prevent this he had at once removed from Torquay; and I felt grateful for his tact and delicacy.

How strange is it that, although the memory of one fatal event haunted and filled my mind, ever interposing a dark cloud between sunshine and me, and continually reminding me of the truth of the lines of Moore— which I often caught myself repeating,—

> "One fatal remembrance—one sorrow that throws
> Its bleak shade alike o'er our joys and our woes;
> To which life nothing brighter nor darker can bring—
> For which joy has no balm, nor affliction no sting!"

I was, nevertheless, highly sensitive to the assaults of minor troubles. I keenly felt the annoyance which the untoward meeting with Mrs. Neville had brought on us; and while making light of it to Louisa, it opened old wounds, which bled not the less, notwithstanding the more recent and terrible one, that bid fair never more to heal.

There was a gravity in the air and manner of my wife ever since the abrupt departure of the Nevilles that greatly vexed me. Could it be possible that she had divined that its cause originated in some motive for avoiding any intercourse with me? Had I simply and frankly owned that we had been school-fellows, and imbibed a mutual dislike, the abrupt departure would have been at once accounted for; but no—with the unhappy desire for concealment which marked my character, I had left her to dwell on a circumstance which my own reason was compelled to admit was, to say the least of it, mysterious. Why had I not told her the truth? Conscience answered the question. The high opinion she had formed of Neville, from all that his wife had told her of him, would, I conceived, induce her to think that our mutual dislike must have proceeded from some fault on my side rather than on his. *I* should be judged the culpable person because, unhappily, I had allowed my moodiness to throw a dark shade over any good qualities which I might possess; and contrasting the equanimity, the gay and open nature of Neville, with *my* gloom and reserve, even the partiality of a wife could not prevent mine from adjudging the superiority over me to him.

It was the consciousness of this that sealed my lips about my former acquaintance with Neville; but even in the bitterness of my feelings I was forced to admit, that Neville as far surpassed me in every respect as even the bitterest of my enemies could pronounce. Oh! the pang which a conscious inferiority to a man who, if he scorns not, at least avoids one, inflicts! and yet who one has no right to demand satisfaction from.

It was not that I envied Neville. No; I truly and heartily admired the noble qualities that had won for him the popularity he enjoyed at school and at college, and which, I felt certain, would adhere to him through life; but I envied those who possessed his esteem, and bitterly repented that I had lost it. My heart yearned for a friend, but where was I to seek one? I had missed the most favourable opportunities ever afforded of laying the foundation of friendship—my school and college days. The boy who is an object of dislike in these minor theatres of life, will have little chance of becoming a popular man when he enters on the great stage of the world itself; for he not only carries with him the defects which incurred dislike, but goes forth with the reputation of unpopularity, which will be prejudicial to him through life.

I had no relations, and my marriage brought me none. Two isolated beings, Louisa and I, stood alone in the world, with no relatives or connexions to introduce us into society, or to occasionally break the monotony of our solitude. I sighed when I remembered how gratified my wife had been by the society of Mrs. Neville. How rapidly her presence and innocent gaiety had made the hours fly the few evenings she had passed with us; and I caught myself wishing that my sweet, gentle, sensitive Louisa possessed her gaiety of heart and animation, forgetful that it was my gloom and moodiness that had clouded her natural cheerfulness, and imposed a constraint which I never had encouraged her to shake off.

How did the playful gaiety of manner of Mrs. Neville draw her out, as sun-beams do the closed flower, until it expands before its genial influence, putting forth its beauty and sweetness; while I was as the cold bleak wind before which the mind of this gentle being closed itself, seldom allowing the treasures it contained to be revealed. Why could I not place her in a chosen circle, where she could soon form friends, and in which my moodiness might, if only for a few hours of every day, be dissipated, as it was in the society of Mrs. Neville?

While thus longing for an interruption to the monotony of our seclusion, I felt vexed and offended when the sadness or abstraction of my wife
betrayed that she, too, though perhaps unconsciously, desired society.
Sometimes I would make a desperate effort to shake off my gloom, and
become companionable. I would read aloud to her while she worked, or
try to keep up a conversation. But the attempt was seldom crowned with
success, because the effort was too painful to be long sustained, and I soon
relapsed into silence and abstraction again.

Our child grew into health and beauty, and was the idol of us both. In
her, we had one rallying point of affection, whence nought but pleasure
could spring; she kept alive in our hearts that hopefulness, which, without
her, would have been extinguished, for we were both fast sinking into a
state of despondency, that seemed every day to increase. Oh, offspring!
sacred blessing, accorded to mortals, who, when they no longer indulge
hope for themselves, are soothed by its smiles, delusive though they may
prove for those dearer to them than life. Surely the least selfish of all human
affections is that of parents for their children, which, leading them to look
forward to *their* prosperity when they themselves shall be no longer on
earth to witness or share it, makes them support trials and chagrin that
might else prompt them to pray for a release from an existence become
too heavy a burthen to bear. Yes, many a time did I forget my own misery,
in gazing on the fair face of my child, and in praying that her destiny might
be a less cheerless one than that of her wretched father.

CHAPTER XXIII.

Restless and unquiet, like all in my unhappy state of mind, I fancied
that I should be less miserable elsewhere than in my present abode. I proposed to Louisa to change it, and she assented with a readiness which
proved that she was no less desirous than I to leave Torquay. Indeed, ever
since the departure of Mrs. Neville, she had ceased to take pleasure in the
place, and I foolishly imagined, that in quitting it, and seeking a new scene,
she would leave behind her the remembrance of that regretted object of
her regard, of which every walk reminded her.

"Whither shall we direct our course, dearest?" asked I, willing to be
guided by her wishes.

"Where you will," was the reply, uttered in a tone of such utter despondence, as gave evidence that hope was paralyzed in her breast.

"But have you no preference?" demanded I, almost angrily, piqued by
the hopelessness of her manner.

"All places are the same to me," answered she, "and I prefer leaving the selection to you."

"Let us try Sidmouth; that, I have heard, is a healthful and quiet place, though a much less picturesque and beautiful spot than this."

"As you like," responded my wife; and it was settled, that at the end of the week we should proceed to Sidmouth.

Unfortunately, two days preceding the one named for our departure, our little girl was taken ill. The best physician in the town was called in; and after some very anxious days, during which our darling was in imminent danger, by his skill and attention she was saved, and shortly after pronounced convalescent.

Fondly as I loved our child, it was not until I saw her in a state that threatened every moment to deprive her of life, that I became aware how dear she was to my heart, and what agony her loss would occasion me. Parents who mix much in the world, and partake its amusements, can form little notion of the intensity of affection entertained by those who live in seclusion, and are in the habit of seeing their offspring many times in the day. My child was the sole sun-beam that shed a ray on my gloomy existence, and I felt, when I beheld her laid pale, emaciated, and almost senseless on her little couch, that if she were snatched from me I could no longer bear up against the weight of misery that was pressing on my heart.

I now asked myself how, with such a blessing, I had hitherto allowed despair to take possession of my soul? for the previous affliction which had clouded my life seemed light in comparison to the present threatened one. With what a different eye do we contemplate past and present trials! All the corroding grief that had followed the terrible event of the fatal night of my mother's funeral, faded away before the menaced death of my child, and I believed, as I bent in speechless agony over her couch, that if heaven spared her to my prayers, my joy would be so great, my gratitude to the Almighty so enduring, that henceforth, I would think only of atoning by every means in my power for the evil I had caused, and, triumphing over my own moodiness, bow with meekness to the chastisement inflicted by conscience, and study alone the happiness of my wife and child.

Louisa, pale as marble, watched the face of our child. No tear escaped her burning eye-lids, no word dropt from her fevered lips. Her life seemed to hang on that of her little girl, and every other thought was banished. When at length the fearful crisis was passed, and the physician pronounced that with care, we might count on the recovery of our treasure, the change from despair to joy was too great for my poor wife, and she sank fainting on the couch of her child.

It was long ere suspended animation was restored; and during her insensibility, amid the alarm and anxiety it excited, I marked with a deep pang of remorse the alteration that had taken place in my poor Louisa. No longer the blooming creature, with symmetrical and rounded form, she had become prematurely care-worn and attenuated, and a curve between her brows bore evidence that sorrow and painful thought had left their traces there. And all this sad change had previously passed unnoticed by me—by me, who, notwithstanding my waywardness and moodiness, loved her with as true an affection as ever warmed the heart of man. The truth was, there was something in the clear, calm, searching glance of Louisa, before which mine recoiled with such nervous trepidation, that I dared not often meet it; for, haunted by the dread that she might have overheard some of the words I knew I was wont to utter in my sleep, I shrank from her gaze, and consequently did not often look on that fair face, so inexpressibly dear to me.

Now, at last, the havoc wrought on it by care became revealed to me, and I trembled lest death, defeated and disappointed of his prey in my child, might aim his dart at the life of my beloved wife. There was agony in the thought, but how was that agony increased when conscience whispered that it was I who had chased the roses of health from her cheek, and planted care in her breast! Many and fervent were the vows I made, that henceforth no effort on my part should be wanting to restore peace and bring back health to *her*, although *I* might never more hope for these blessings. And during the gradual recovery of our child, I kept my pledge. I sat by my precious Louisa, day after day, as she watched over our little girl; devoted all my attention to these two dear objects of my tenderness; inventing many little amusements to beguile the tedious hours of confinement to the sick chamber of my little daughter, who became so fond of me, that she could hardly be persuaded to allow me to leave her room. I procured the most dainty food, to tempt the feeble appetite of Louisa, and evinced such tenderness towards her, that by degrees she began to look more like her former self, and to treat me with the same confidence that marked her manner during the first months of our union. And although this restored confidence often led to her unconsciously inflicting many a wound that lacerated my heart, by references to the past, and by pointing out the increased resemblance of our child to her departed aunt, I suffered no symptom to escape that could reveal my pangs, while she, in the full belief that my nervous system was restored to a healthy state—a belief that filled her with delight—no longer felt under the same constraint as of late.

The daily visits of the worthy physician, Doctor Western, had led to an intimacy with us which, heightened by gratitude for his having, under heaven, saved the life of our child, ripened into friendship. He had brought his wife and daughter, amiable and well-educated women, to visit my wife, who, finding them intelligent and agreeable, derived so much pleasure from their society, that she encouraged their attention; and one or other of them looked in most days, and often passed the evening with us.

My child's health being perfectly re-established, and my wife's much improved, we saw no reason to decline a pressing invitation from Dr. and Mrs. Western to drink tea with them, to meet a few friends. Accordingly, having seen our darling asleep, and left her nursemaid employed with her needle in the room, we proceeded to the Doctor's abode. Some fourteen or fifteen persons formed the circle assembled there, and in two of the number I recognised, with no pleasurable feelings, my old fellow-collegian, Mordaunt, with whom I had fought a duel, and in his wife, the ci-devant Miss Melville. Dr. Western, according to the old fashion peculiar to provincial towns, introduced his guests to each other, and as my name was pronounced, I noticed Mordaunt and his wife exchange glances, in which surprise was much more visible than satisfaction. They bowed coldly when the introduction to us took place. The husband looked embarrassed, and the wife—who, from a pretty, shy, and timid girl, was grown into a flaunting, over-dressed, coquettish-looking woman—bridled, tossed her head, affected to cast down her eyes when she met mine, and, in short, behaved as absurdly as a weak and silly country boarding-school girl could possibly do. It happened, by chance, that Louisa was seated between the mistress of the house and Mrs. Mordaunt, who stared at her, if not rudely, at least with a degree of curiosity that seemed greatly to surprise the object of it. After gazing at Louisa intently, she often turned her glance to a large mirror on the opposite side of the room, as if to compare her own face and form with those of my wife, and then she would bridle, simper, and toss her head again. As I looked on her, I felt ashamed that I ever could have admired, or fancied that I loved such a being, for the contact with Louisa was so much to her disadvantage, as to draw attention still more to her showy, and, I may add, vulgar style of beauty, and ill-chosen finery. Never had my wife appeared to greater advantage than contrasted as she now was by Mrs. Mordaunt. Her calm and beautiful face, her distinguished air, the classic shape of her small and finely turned head, with its luxuriant raven tresses bound round it, and the simple elegance of her dress, combined to render her one of the most charming creatures ever beheld.

"Have you been long at Torquay?" inquired Mrs. Mordaunt.

The question being answered, and after a short pause, Mrs. Mordaunt observed, "How very ill Mr. Herbert is looking. I hardly recognised him, he is so very much changed. I knew him when he was at Oxford," continued the lady; and she simpered and cast her eyes down. "I dare say you have often heard him speak of me?"

"Not that I remember," replied Louisa coldly.

"Perhaps not as Mrs. Mordaunt," resumed the lady, "but as Miss Melville, I'm sure he has spoken of me."

"No, I never heard him speak of any one of that name."

"Then, I am sure it was because he was afraid of making you jealous, that he did not tell you how desperately in love he was with me, and how he wanted to marry me, and how he fought a duel about me with Mr. Mordaunt, and how I preferred Mr. Mordaunt."

Not a single syllable of this speech escaped my ear; and as I listened to it, I felt that I could, with pleasure, see her who uttered it consigned to the darkest cell of the county jail, as a punishment for her vulgar loquacity on the present occasion.

Louisa looked at her with undissembled astonishment, and there was a degree of natural *hauteur* in the stateliness of her air, as she replied,

"I confess, Madam, that my husband has never confided to me his boyish attachments."

"How very odd!" said the incorrigible Mrs. Mordaunt. "Now, my husband has told me of every flame he ever had; and very jealous he makes me sometimes, when he talks of them, and praises them up to the skies. I was quite a simpleton like when I married him, but lately come from school, where Mrs. Dobson, the mistress, had taught us that we must seldom speak, and then hardly above our breath; cast down our eyes whenever any gentleman looked at, or spoke to us. I came to Oxford to live with my aunt Mrs. Scuddamore; and Mr. Herbert, your husband, was the first young man I knew. He thought when he saw me casting down my eyes every time they met his, just as Mrs. Dobson had taught her young ladies, that I was in love with him, and so perhaps, I might have been, if I had not just then seen Mr. Mordaunt, who was so free and easy in his manner, and so flashy in his dress, that he took my fancy at once, and I thought no more of Herbert, who was so shy and melancholy like. Quite sentimental, as one might say. Well, I married Mr. Mordaunt, and ever since we have led such gay lives, going about from one watering-place to another, and leaving each the moment the novelty is worn off. We are never dull, for Mr. Mordaunt goes to the billiard-room or coffee-room of every place, where he soon makes friends. He is so free and easy, and he brings them home and intro-

duces them to me, and we make pick-nick parties, and hire horses and ride
about the country, and go to the plays, where there are any, and play cards
at night; and as I am generally the only lady of the company, all the gentlemen are so polite and attentive to me, you can't think."

Louisa became more reserved and stately in her manner, as Mrs.
Mordaunt with *naïveté* revealed the mode of life she and her husband had
adopted; but Mrs. Mordaunt's loquacity was not to be checked, and after a
short pause, she resumed.

"O! 'tis such good fun having three or four gay young men constantly
about one. They bring me novels from the circulating libraries, and such
funny novels! How I laugh when I think how shocked Mrs. Dobson, who
is the greatest prude in the world, would be, if she saw them; and would
you believe it, they have taught me to smoke cigars, which I have got at last
to like, though I hated them at first, and used to quarrel with Mordaunt
about, for he is an inveterate smoker. Do you smoke?"

"Certainly not," was the brief reply.

"Well, I can tell you, that the most fashionable ladies at Paris smoke,
and they are called lionesses. Why, I never could make out, not because
they smoke I suppose! What makes Mr. Herbert look so ill?" resumed the
silly woman. "Perhaps it was from being crossed in love. I have heard people say, that first love is, after all, the only true love, and he certainly was
quite desperate about me."

Seeing that Louisa made no reply to this speech, Mrs. Mordaunt looked
spitefully at her, and added, "I am sorry I told you this for I see it has made
you jealous. Don't deny it," (my wife had attempted to speak) "for it's only
natural after all. Why, I was made very jealous myself the other day when
we met at Exeter Mr. and Mrs. Neville. He had been a fellow-collegian of
Mordaunt, and she had been an old flame of his, and had refused him. I had
heard Mordaunt talk so much about her beauty and sprightliness; though,
for the matter of that, I don't think anything of her beauty, a pale-faced
thing; and as to sprightliness, she isn't, I am sure, half so sprightly as I am,
when I'm in the humour. I am a perfect mad-cap. I blacken the men's faces
with cork when they fall asleep. I pin paper to the skirts of their coats, with
'send the fool farther' written on it, and I win wagers by *jumping* over the
chairs."

My wife instinctively drew her chair nearer to that of Mrs. Western,
who, engaged in deep conversation with an old lady on the other side, was
unconscious of the annoyance she was suffering under.

"As I was telling you," resumed Mrs. Mordaunt, "I was quite jealous
of Mrs. Neville. I was angry and offended that she had refused my hus-

band, and yet, as Mordaunt said in his funny way, I would have been more angry if she had accepted him, for then *I* could not be his wife. And I told Mordaunt, that if he wished to flirt with his old flame, he was welcome, for I would flirt with Mr. Neville, who is such a handsome man. But neither husband nor wife were at all disposed to flirt. Mrs. Neville kept Mordaunt at as great a distance as if he had never proposed for her, and as to Mr. Neville he hardly seemed to notice me. He told Mordaunt that he had been driven away from Torquay, owing to finding that an old college acquaintance of his, with whom he did not wish to hold any intercourse, was staying there, and with whose wife Mrs. Neville had struck up a great friendship."

What were my feelings as I listened to the unexpected turn the conversation had taken, and marked its effect on my wife. Her cheeks became for a moment covered with deep blushes, and then turned deadly pale, but she struggled to conceal her emotion. "Are you ill?" enquired her tormentor; "You look as pale as a ghost."

"No, not at all," replied my wife, making a desperate effort to appear calm and unconcerned.

"We only arrived to-day," observed Mrs. Mordaunt, "and we brought a letter of introduction to Mrs. Western, from a cousin of hers, which we sent as soon as we came, and so we were invited here. Now, that I think of it, I am sure the person Mr. Neville wished to avoid was Mr. Herbert, for I remember all his fellow-collegians avoided him; nobody could tell why, but some thought it was because he was so very strange and mopish-like that they fancied he was a little crazy."

Louisa's paleness was now really alarming, and fearing that she might fall from her seat, I approached her.

"I fear, dearest, that the heat of the room is too much for you," said I. "Shall we return home?"

"No thank you, my dear," was the reply; "I only felt a slight return of the pain I suffered under last week, and it is now quite gone, so pray do not be uneasy."

I could have knelt and worshipped her for the composure and dignity of her demeanour, and the affectionate tone in which she spoke to me. What a proof of her self-control! It even imposed on her silly and heartless neighbour, who looked embarrassed, if not alarmed, but soon recovering her habitual flippancy, she addressed me.

"I hardly recollected you, Mr. Herbert," observed she, "you are so dreadfully changed. I hope you have not been ill. Oh you need not look so shy, for I have told Mrs. Herbert all about your having been in love with me at Oxford."

"I really had quite forgotten that circumstance, madam," replied I, gravely, "and had you not told me of it, I should still have believed there was some mistake."

"Mistake indeed!" reiterated the lady, "I wonder you can deny it when——"

But here Dr. Western, observing the paleness of my wife, came up, and drawing her arm gently within his, insisted on leading her to the next room, and making her drink some wine and water, and I accompanied them, leaving Mrs. Mordaunt in the middle of her sentence, and looking highly indignant at my denial of her statement.

"I fear, my dear Madam," observed the doctor, "that you have been talked to death by Mrs. Mordaunt. Her husband it was, who told me that he feared you were suffering under the infliction of what he termed her mad spirits and unguarded gossipping, so I went to the rescue. Mr. Mordaunt was very frank, and to a comparative stranger too," added the doctor, "for he told me that his wife was a regular mad-cap, and was always getting herself or him into scrapes by her tongue."

My wife faintly smiled, and introduced some other subject, avoiding to let Doctor Western know that her paleness had been at all produced by the loquacity of her neighbour. We waited by Louisa's desire, until the party had broken up, and she exerted herself so successfully to appear as usual, that no one save me could have discovered that while thus calm, nay even cheerful, in appearance, her heart was a prey to anxiety and chagrin.

CHAPTER XXIV.

My poor wife little dreamt that I had heard the whole of Mrs. Mordaunt's conversation, and that I had writhed under the communications she had made. For a proud, a sensitive man, to hear revealed to the object of his affections, the person on earth whose esteem he most wished to preserve, such disparaging statements, was humiliation, was torture. To have my pure-minded, my high-souled Louisa, led to believe that I could ever have bestowed a thought on the vulgar, giddy, garrulous woman, whose appearance was now divested of every personal attraction, and whose manner and bearing reminded one of what might be expected from a female rope-dancer or rider at Astley's, was too mortifying to be borne. But to have her led to believe that I could have wished to marry such a person, was so derogatory to me, that I felt ashamed to meet her glance. But painful, humiliating, as all this was, there existed still stronger

motives of chagrin for me in the disclosures made by Mrs. Mordaunt. Had
she not revealed the suppositions entertained by herself and others with
regard to my sanity,—suppositions so calculated to confirm the suspicions
of my wife on this point, (if indeed, as I feared, she had formed any such,)
or to give birth to them if they had not previously existed,—and had she
not denounced my duplicity, nay more, my want of veracity, with regard to
my former acquaintance with Neville, and the termination of it, a fact that
explained at once the motive of the sudden departure of him and his wife
from Torquay,—my silence and concealment on this topic must inevitably
lead Louisa to form the most disadvantageous opinion of me. If I had not
been conscious of the wrong being on my side, why should I have withheld the truth from her? My heart was lacerated as reason whispered these
truths to me, and I cursed the hour, when, under the influence of a puerile
amour propre that made me shrink from confessing to the partner of my
life my former acquaintance and subsequent coldness with Neville, I had
concealed the truth.

Not a word of reproach escaped the lips of Louisa, not even the most
distant allusion to the conversation of Mrs. Mordaunt, or to that odious
person herself. It may be easily imagined that I did not refer to a subject
fraught with pain and shame to me, although it occupied my thoughts
nearly to the exclusion of all others, for many days, ay, and nights too,
after. Those alone who are of a nervous temperament, and who have experienced painful trials, can know with what terrible power all subjects of
chagrin return to the pillow in the silence of night to torture and chase
sleep away from him who most needs its refreshing balm! The cares which,
during the day, are felt difficult to be borne, acquire tenfold power in the
night, when only those with ruined health, or wrecked peace, count the
tedious hours, and long for the light of day to scare away the shadows that
encircle them.

I watched Louisa with anxious eyes, to discover the effect produced
on her by the disclosures of Mrs. Mordaunt, but the only change I could
observe was an increased paleness and sadness. Her manner to me was as
kind as ever; nay, there seemed to me to be a sort of pitying tenderness in
it, such as fond mothers evince towards their sick and suffering offspring.
Yet far from being soothed by this gentle forbearance and pity, it offended,
it irritated me, from a belief that it originated in her conviction of my
intellects being in a most unsettled state, and I became again captious and
gloomy, in spite of all my lately formed good resolutions.

Instead of reproaching myself for this relapse, I, with all the sophistry
of selfishness, asked whether it was my fault that some evil destiny—some

malignant demon—was continually pursuing, irritating, and compelling me to break through my wise resolves. Was it my fault that the wife of Neville had crossed our path, and forced us, as it were, into acquaintanceship? Was it my fault that Mordaunt and his odious wife had come in contact with us, and that she, in defiance of every rule of good breeding, or decency, should have in one brief interview disclosed to my wife, an utter stranger, circumstances from which, had she been the oldest, dearest friend, a woman with common sense or delicacy would have shrunk from even hinting at. No, it was clear to me at least, that I was the victim to a train of events over which I had no control, and from which it was useless to endeavour to escape. I was born under an unlucky star, from the malign influence of which it was in vain I tried to struggle: so I abandoned myself to the moodiness that cast its dark shadow over my home, and was daily destroying the peace of my admirable wife. Oh! the vanity, the folly, which leads erring mortals to believe themselves the victims of destiny—a belief so subversive of the courage and principle which enable us to resist adversity. No, conduct is Fate, and had I paused to reflect on the trials of my life, I should have found that all of them had originated in some fault of my own.

My wife and I called two days after the party at Dr. Western's, to take leave of the family, we having decided on quitting Torquay. The doctor was from home, but we found Mrs. and Miss Western in the drawing-room, into which we were ushered. I detected a look of surprise and displeasure in the countenance of Mrs. Western, as the servant announced us, which indicated that our presence was neither expected nor desired. Coldness and constraint had taken the place of the former cordial greeting we had been accustomed to receive, and the change in the manner of our hostess and her daughter was so visible, that we abridged our visit and took leave, heartily regretting that we had paid it.

When we left the house of Dr. Western an observation on the marked coldness of our reception arose to my lips, and I was on the point of giving it utterance, when the reflection, that it must have originated in some communication to my disadvantage, made by Mr. or Mrs. Mordaunt, occurred to me, and checked my comment. I could not bring myself to touch on a subject that must inevitably lead to the disclosures made to my wife by Mrs. Mordaunt, although conscious that she could not help feeling that the treatment we had just experienced must be attributed to the cause I had rightly divined. Louisa was silent and thoughtful during our walk; but as I glanced at her face I noticed that a deep blush was spread over it, even to her very temples, and I groaned in spirit, that *I*, who would have laid down my life to have saved her from one pang of regret, should be the means of drawing on her a coldness and contumely, when she merited only esteem and respect. But was I to submit to such treatment like a coward, conscious of having forfeited all claim to consideration? No, it was not to be borne! I would at once write to Dr. Western, and demand an explanation of the change in the manner of his wife and daughter when we visited them that day. I wrote a letter, and waited with no little impatience for an answer.

The doctor came, instead of writing, and I, seeing him from my window, went out to meet him, in order that Louisa should not know of our having an interview in my house, at which she was not to be present. He was considerably agitated when we met, and I, scarcely less so, but more versed in concealing my emotion, I appeared calm, and, to avoid interruption, proposed our walking towards the country.

"I am much pained, I assure you, Mr. Herbert," said he, "that Mrs. Herbert, for whom I entertain so high a respect, should have experienced any annoyance from any one under my roof. My wife and daughter are so little skilled in the usages of society, that they have been, I fear, less urbane than could be wished, and——"

"Pray, Doctor," interrupted I, "say no more on this point, but simply inform me of the cause of the change in their manner. I surely have a right to demand this."

"I really am most pained. I hardly know what to do or say," said the doctor, and the embarrassment and agitation of his countenance and manner fully proved the truth of his assertion. "But I acknowledge, Sir, that you have a right to question me, and therefore I waive my own feelings in consideration for yours. The truth is, Mr. Herbert, Mrs. Mordaunt, whose garrulous propensities know no bounds, paid my wife an early visit, when I was absent from home, and related a whole pack of nonsense, probably wholly unfounded, but certainly to your disadvantage. Had I been present, I should decidedly have informed her that I never listened to ill-natured gossip; and if I could not succeed in checking her, would at least have prevented my wife and daughter from being influenced by her statements; but unfortunately——"

"Excuse me, Doctor; but pray inform me of the substance of her communications; for little importance as I attach to the opinion of such a silly and absurd person, it becomes necessary for me to know what statements she could have made that produced such an effect on your family."

"Why the only point in a confused mass of gossip that I could make any sense of was,—pray excuse me for repeating anything disagreeable,—that at college you were disliked; nay more, avoided by your fellow-collegians, who held no intercourse with you; and that when you challenged Mr.

Mordaunt to fight a duel, you could not find any gentleman who would go out with you as a friend, until her aunt, Mrs. Scuddamore, prevailed on an old officer, a friend of hers, to accompany you. The lady added, that a Mr. Neville, whose wife had been staying here lately, and who intended prolonging her sojourn had, when her husband arrived, been hurried away the following morning, to prevent her associating with Mrs. Herbert and you. This statement, which I dare say is by no means correct, conveyed an impression to my wife and daughter, that there must exist some very strong grounds for this avoidance of you and Mrs. Herbert; and, unfortunately, before I could have removed this impression, you arrived a short time after Mrs. Mordaunt had left my house."

I thanked the doctor for his frankness, accepted with a cold stateliness his apologies and regret for the annoyance inflicted by his wife and daughter, but declined receiving a visit from them, which he pressed on me, and we parted.

Traces of tears were discernible in the eyes of Louisa when I returned home, but she, nevertheless, assumed a faint smile when I entered, and commenced talking of indifferent subjects, as if to turn my thoughts from painful ones. This tact and delicacy of conduct on her part, which ought to have produced only gratitude and tenderness on mine, led to irritating suspicions that wounded me. Why did she so carefully avoid recurring to the communication made to her by Mrs. Mordaunt, or to the marked change in the manner of Mrs. Western and her daughter? What could be more natural than that she should remark on it to me? Yet not a single word on the subject passed her lips though, from the increased pensiveness of her countenance, and the traces of tears in her eyes, it was but too evident the subject painfully occupied her thoughts. Could it be that she believed the statements, and dreaded to provoke the fearful infirmity attributed to me? To defeat these terrors, I felt that I must henceforth be ever on my guard; that I must impose an incessant control over my words and actions; and the conviction of this necessity produced such an additional constraint, that my moodiness returned in spite of every effort to banish it.

I walked to the reading-room at Torquay, and from thence wrote a letter to Mordaunt, demanding satisfaction from him for the statement made by his wife to the family of Dr. Western. I added, that I would remain at the library until his answer was sent there, which I requested might be as soon as possible He did not let me wait long, for before I could have expected to hear from him, the following letter reached me:—

"MY DEAR HERBERT—If you will allow me to address you on the terms

of good-fellowship peculiar to old college chums, I hope you will not expect
me to be answerable for the sayings and doings of my wife, who is the
most incorrigible gossip that ever a man was tied to. Ah! Herbert, you had a
lucky escape from her. She is everlastingly getting me into scrapes with her
tongue, and neither advice nor menaces can check it. As to giving satisfaction—which, I suppose, means nothing more nor less than going out to
fight—I must decline it; for, having established my character for courage
by our former duel, from the consequences of which my health has never
wholly recovered, I have determined on never again fighting. But I am ready
to call on Doctor Western, and contradict every word my wife may have
said; and also to give from under my hand the most complete denial of the
truth of any of her assertions to your disadvantage, as well as the strongest
apology I can write for my wife's unfounded gossiping. In fact, I am ready to
do anything you wish, except to fight, and am already sufficiently punished
by being cursed with a wife who would embroil me with half the world if
she could. Little did I think, when I married a girl who was always blushing
and casting down her eyes, that she should turn out the greatest hoyden and
gossip in the world. I longed to go up and shake hands with you the other
night at Dr. Western's, but I did not know how you might take it; but be
assured, my dear Herbert, that I am very truly yours,

"W. MORDAUNT.

"P. S.—On reflection, I think it best to send you at once an apology; and
when I have dispatched this, I will call on Dr. Western and contradict all my
wife's statements."

The apology was as follows:—

"MY DEAR HERBERT—Accept my heart-felt regrets and humble apology
for the mis-statements made by my wife, which I trust you will look over,
and attribute to her incorrigible habit of gossiping. I acknowledge that
every syllable she uttered to your disadvantage was wholly untrue; and I
cannot express half the regret I feel that you, for whom I entertain the highest esteem and respect, should be for a moment annoyed by her. Believe
me, my dear Herbert, sincerely yours,

"W. MORDAUNT."

Disgusted with the cowardice which dictated these epistles, I blushed
for the man who could have written them; and although I longed to show
them to Louisa, a sense of shame for the baseness of the writer checked
the impulse.

I had been some time absent from home, and when I returned I found my wife looking even more pale and languid than when I had left her. Her spirits, too, in spite of her endeavours to appear cheerful, were more depressed. I questioned her about her health, declared my conviction that she must be unwell, and proposed sending for Dr. Western; but at the mention of his name a blush overspread her face, and she promptly and firmly declined seeing him, adding that she felt sure she should be better when we left Torquay, for that the climate was too soft for her, after having been so long accustomed to the keen air of the Welsh mountains. In the course of the evening Dr. Western came to show me the letter of Mordaunt. Louisa was present when he was announced, and motioned to leave the room, but I requested her to stay; and then, after many humble apologies for his wife and daughter's reception of her at their last interview, he handed me Mordaunt's letter to him, and I gave him the apology addressed to me. Both were shown to my wife, and her eloquent countenance flashed with indignation and contempt as she perused them.

"I wonder you could have condescended to notice the gossip of such a woman, or demand satisfaction from such a man," said she, proudly, to me. "You should have treated both with the contempt they merit."

And she threw the letters carelessly on the table.

"Yes, Mr. Herbert," observed Doctor Western, "such persons are indeed unworthy of notice, and I shall never cease to regret that my wife and daughter should have placed the least faith in the assertions of Mrs. Mordaunt, who shall never again be permitted to enter my doors."

I had suspected that Louisa's was a proud nature, but her whole manner during this interview convinced me that my suspicions had underrated the extent of this peculiarity in her. The conviction offered no balm to my wounded mind; for, aware by sad experience of the pain inflicted on the sensitive by the contumely of even those they value not, I felt the deepest sympathy for her.

CHAPTER XXV.

THOSE who have passed their youth in the seclusion of a country residence, surrounded by humble, but faithful followers, who, knowing and liking them from infancy, are prone to magnify their good qualities, and to pass over their defects—are precisely those who are the most keenly alive to aught that betrays a want of esteem and respect towards them. A contact with others of the same grade in life, commencing in childhood, by

imperceptible degrees, habituates persons to the trivial slights and annoyances that, in their little world, as in the great one, for which it serves as a
preparation, never fail to occur. Louisa's childhood and girlhood, passed in
Wales, with no society, save that of her sister and mother; and mine, who
loved her nearly as fondly as did her own, and looked up to with little short
of adoration, as she and her family were by their humble neighbours,—had
never been prepared for those annoyances to which a contact with general
society invariably exposes the proud and sensitive.

The first wound, and it was a profound one, inflicted on her pride, was
the unlooked for departure of Mrs. Neville, and the letter holding out no
prospect of future intercourse, after all the plans of long visits to be mutu-
ally paid. Conscious that her own life, and that of her parents, could offer
no cause for avoidance, she, naturally enough, concluded, that something
in my past conduct must have furnished the motive; and this conclusion
filled her with sorrow and shame. To bear a dishonoured name, was terrible to a creature with her proud and lofty spirit; but to love one who
was shunned and avoided,—that one, too, the husband of her choice—the
father of her child—was torture. Then came the reflection, that never had
she heard me refer to former friends or companions,—never knew me to
receive letters from, or write to any such,—though all who had been at a
public school, and at college, must have formed acquaintances. This reflection, which might never have presented itself to her mind, had not the
conduct of the Nevilles given rise to it, now flashed on her, inflicting all the
pangs peculiar to wounded pride and womanly delicacy. Then came the
recollection of my frequent fits of deep abstraction, my constant moodiness, and my strange ravings during my troubled slumbers.

Some cause must exist for all this; and coupling with it, the avoidance
of Neville to come in contact with me; how, with all her affection for me,
could the wife of my bosom fail to think—though the thought was agony—
that I had committed some crime in the eyes of society, that banished me
from its pale? Nevertheless, she ceased not to love me. A heart like hers was
too noble to turn from him, to whom it had vowed allegiance, because all
others avoided him: and, with a heroism to be found only in woman, she
determined that whatever might be the sin that had sent me forth from
society, *she* never would shrink from the object of her first, her only love,—
the father of her child. Oh! if her tears—her prayers—the sacrifice of her
unspotted life, could wipe away my guilt, how willingly would this angel,
accorded to me by a pitying Providence to walk by my side through the
gloomy vale of life, have offered them? And I, contemning the pangs she
was enduring, incapable from my grosser nature, and less elevated mind,

from appreciating a character like hers, remained in ignorance of the inestimable blessing lent me; and, instead of kneeling to her as to a guardian angel, and pouring forth to her all the errors of my youth, and the consequences they had entailed, (leaving only my one dread secret unavowed), maintained a reserve calculated to confirm her worst fears, and saw not the fatal effect her anxiety and wretchedness were producing on her delicate frame.

But let me not anticipate. Believing that the Devonshire air did not agree with my wife, I determined to direct our course to London. In that vast metropolis, I hoped that both our minds might be directed from the *triste* thoughts that had taken possession of them, by the busy crowds that would beset our path, and by the various scenes of amusement it presents. When I consulted Louisa on the subject, she merely answered, "where you will; all places are alike to me." The tone of deep despondence in which this was uttered, pained me deeply, and I endeavoured to discover whether she might not prefer some other place. But with her, as she said, "all places were alike;" an assertion that proves such internal happiness, as to be independent of places; or such misery, that no hope is entertained that any change can bring relief. Alas! the latter was the case with my poor wife; and I—I who had entailed unhappiness on her, was angry that she should so keenly feel it. Often have I noticed tears fill her eyes, as they bent on our child, whose rosy cheeks offered a sad contrast to the pallid ones of her mother, and whose dimpled smiles seemed to mock the sorrowful countenances of the author of her being.

Arrived in London, we took up our abode at an hotel in Albemarle-street, until I could procure a small ready furnished house.

The noise and the bustle of the moving mass in the street, drew the attention of Louisa, and seemed, for a short time, to divert her from the sadness that was become habitual to her; but after some time, a sense of our loneliness in that vast world, where each individual composing the great crowd, hurried on, intent upon his own business or pleasure, struck her; and sinking back in the carriage, tired and exhausted, I saw tears drop from her closed eye-lids, while our little girl clapped her dimpled hands, and laughed aloud in delight, at the various novel objects presented to her view in the vast Babylon, now seen for the first time.

The next day I sallied forth, alone, in search of a house, Louisa feeling too much fatigued to accompany me. I first proceeded to my old acquaintance, Mr. Vise, with whom I had lately kept up no intercourse, and found that he had been some time absent from England. I was annoyed at this circumstance, for he was the sole acquaintance I possessed in London, and had always evinced a desire to oblige me. After looking at several small houses, none of which pleased me, I at last found one likely to suit in Wilton-street, and the terms being agreed on, I was leaving it, when the mistress of it told me, she expected a reference, as it was always her custom to demand one: she hoped I would excuse her being so particular, but in London it was absolutely necessary.

The disadvantages of my isolated position never struck me more forcibly, nor more painfully, than at this moment. How could I avow to a stranger that I did not know a single person to whom I could refer? After an awkward pause, I took courage to say, that not liking to trouble any of my friends, I would, if equally agreeable to her, pay a month's rent in advance, and continue to do so while I remained in her house.

"Well, Sir, your appearance is so respectable, that I will, for once, break through my general regulations," replied the landlady; "and I dare say I shall have no reason to regret it."

It was agreed that we should take possession the following day, and I returned to the hotel. On ascending the stairs I met a lady, who no sooner saw me than she exclaimed—

"Bless me, if it is not Mr. Herbert! I am so glad to see you," and she seized my hand, and shook it cordially. "But you must come into my room, I have a thousand things to say to you," and she still held me by the hand, when, at this moment, Louisa, who was crossing the corridor from her sitting-room to her bed-chamber, stood before us. Seeing our recognition, Mrs. Scuddamore, for it was no other than her, immediately said—

"Your wife, I suppose. Pray, introduce me. Mr. Herbert and I are old acquaintances, ma'am, and I am very glad to meet him again. Will you walk into my room, or shall I have the pleasure of going to yours? It's quite the same to me. I'm a soldier's widow, almost an old soldier myself, and never stand on ceremony."

Louisa looked at her with surprise and timidity, while I, who would willingly have avoided meeting her, saw no means of getting rid of her proposed visit, and so led the way to our sitting-room.

"Upon my word, Mr. Herbert, I congratulate you on your choice in a wife," said Mrs. Scuddamore. "A very charming young lady, but looking a little delicate, I am sorry to see. You are aware, I suppose, that my poor brother is dead. Yes, poor man, he is no more. He was an excellent person, but as ignorant of the world as a child: knew nothing of life, at least of military life, and never could comprehend its codes and regulations. Poor Captain Brady, I grieve to say, is also dead. His death was a severe blow to me, it broke the last link of my military associations. Ah! Mr. Herbert, it is sad to think how all one's old friends pass away. I was reading an Army List this morning—I always do read the Army List as regularly as when my dear departed Colonel was alive—and I could hardly find an old brother officer still remaining. Poor Captain Brady has left me all he possessed. It was not much, but it proved his attachment to the widow of his commanding officer. You remember how well he behaved when I had him to go out as your second? You have heard, I suppose, that my niece married one of your adversaries? I never approved the match, because I knew Mordaunt to be so deficient in courage, that, had he been in the regiment of my lamented husband, he would have insisted on his leaving it. How my niece, who knew my sense of honour, could have married him, I cannot make out! She is greatly changed, and I cannot say for the better, for she has turned out a hoyden and a gossip; and, had she been the wife of any officer in Colonel Scuddamore's regiment, I would have either conquered her levity and habit of *bavardage*, or have had her sent to Coventry. Ah! Mr. Herbert, you had a happy escape from marrying her. And pray what was your wife's maiden name?"

"Maitland," was the reply.

"Any relation to Major Maitland, who exchanged from the 62d Foot to the 87th; a brave man, and a very good soldier."

"No relation, ma'am."

"Perhaps she descends from General Maitland, who, for a long time, commanded the Fusileers, and was remarkable for keeping his regiment in the highest order? A little of a martinet, to be sure."

"No, ma'am, I never heard of any such relations."

The nurse here brought in our child, and Mrs. Scuddamore, having looked at her, said—

"A boy, I hope; if so, I will use my influence at the Horse Guards to procure him a commission when he is old enough."

The sex of the child being explained, an expression of deep disappointment stole over the face of Mrs. Scuddamore.

"I am sorry," said she, "for I think it is a pity that there should be so many girls in the world. What can one do with them? whereas boys can always be put into the army or navy, and serve their king and country. Are you going to dine at home, good folk? If so, I will order my rations to be served in your room, and join your mess. It will be more sociable, and I hate dining alone."

What could we do but submit as well as we could to this infliction—and a very great one my wife and I felt it to be? How did we rejoice that we had secured a house, into which we were to move the following day; for to be longer exposed to the free and easy manner of Mrs. Scuddamore, we both felt would be unbearable.

In due time, the dinner was served. Mrs. Scuddamore's rations, as she termed a mackerel, *bœuf steak aux pommes de terres*, and her half pint of sherry, being placed on our table; and during the repast, she ceased not to pass in review the different regiments with which that of her husband had been quartered, and the improvements which she had effected, interspersed with various military anecdotes, which she related with great spirit, to the no slight astonishment of my wife, who was almost disposed to think her an old soldier in female guise.

"I am looking out for a house," said the lady; "I can't afford an expensive one, being, as soldiers say, on half-pay; but I must pitch my tent near some of the military establishments, where I can, daily, see and converse with the old soldiers: for I am like a fish out of water when I don't see red-coats."

I had hoped that for once Louisa might have been amused by the originality of Mrs. Scuddamore—so unlike anything she could ever have met with before—but I was disappointed. Her coarseness and freedom of manner excited only disgust in the mind of my wife, who shrank from her with instinctive dread. Some allusion having been made to Wales, Mrs. Scuddamore said, *à propos* of Wales,—

"Did you know that beautiful young girl whose sudden disappearance was noticed in the provincial papers, and whose body was found, six months after, in the river? I remember an artist, who is a distant relation of mine, showed me a charming portrait he made of her, but a few weeks before her tragical death."

I felt Louisa's eyes were fixed on me, and I would have given worlds to appear unmoved; but the effort at self-possession was beyond my strength. A cold shudder passed over my frame, and I was conscious of turning very pale.

"Are you ill, Mr. Herbert?" inquired Mrs. Scuddamore. "Do let me ring for a glass of *liqueur des braves* for you; or, perhaps, a little brandy and water would be better. You really look quite livid."

Before I could frame a reply, if, indeed, I could have found utterance for one, my wife said, with a sorrowful but calm countenance,—

"Alas! madam, the tragical circumstance to which you referred occurred in our family; the person whose loss we must ever deplore, was my sister."

"Indeed, I am quite shocked. Your sister! I had not, I assure you, the slightest notion. If I had, I would not of course have alluded to it. Your sister was it, or Mr. Herbert's? for *he* seems to feel so *very* much, that I——"

"My sister, Madam," replied Louisa, "but Mr. Herbert, although he never saw her, took so deep an interest in our affliction, and had such a painful and melancholy duty to perform towards the dead, that all reference to the sorrowful subject affects him powerfully."

And she wiped away the tears that chased each other down her pale face, and gave me a look of mingled affection and gratitude, the latter sentiment re-awakened by the recollection of my conduct on the sad, sad occasion so painfully brought to her mind. I could have fallen at her feet and embraced them, for this proof of her utter freedom from suspicion, and the sacrifice of her own feelings to mitigate the effect on mine! And I had doubted the candour of this admirable creature, and suspected, ay, no later than a few minutes before, that the glance she gave me when the obtuse Mrs. Scuddamore introduced this fatal subject, originated in a curiosity to know how it would affect me, and in a desire to discover my terrible secret!

"And was it never ascertained how she met her death?" resumed our callous tormentor.

"Never," replied my wife. "But, spare us, Madam, the subject is too painful, the wound too recent to be *touched;*" and she covered her face with her handkerchief, and wept in silence.

"I am sorry to have grieved you," observed Mrs. Scuddamore, "but to those who, like me, have seen a field of battle with hundreds lying dead and dying, covered with ghastly wounds and gore, the death of one single individual, and by so easy a death as drowning, appears so light and different to what it must to persons like yourselves, who have never witnessed such scenes, that I did not think I should have pained you by recurring to the loss in your family."

Mrs. Scuddamore left us, to our great relief, a short time after, and when the door had closed on her, my wife exclaimed,

"O! never, dearest, let me see that odious and unfeeling woman again; she has made me feel quite ill and nervous."

CHAPTER XXVI.

We removed into our new abode in Wilton-street the following day, taking especial care to conceal our address from Mrs. Scuddamore. Louisa was pleased with the house, and the landlady, who was waiting to receive her, took such a fancy to her and our little girl, that she unlocked some of her store of ornaments and comforts, which she never, as she carefully explained to us, had given the use of to any of the tenants of her dwelling, "unless," said she, "as in the present instance, when the lady was more than ordinarily nice."

And now, having established ourselves, I determined to amuse my wife by showing her the sights of London. It gave me pleasure to see the interest she felt in the fine arts, and how intuitively her pure though uncultivated taste led her to admire the best productions, while she turned from all meretricious ones. I, too, felt amused during the hours in which we visited the public and private galleries, for which we obtained admission, as well as the studios of the most remarkable artists; and not only did the mornings pass pleasantly in this manner, but the sights seen furnished topics for the evenings. We visited the theatres, too, and Louisa, passionately fond of music, was delighted with the opera. The ballet startled her unsophisticated notions of propriety so much, that after the first she witnessed, she expressed a desire never to see another; and I did not attempt to change her opinions on this subject, having formerly felt some surprise how modest women could tolerate the indelicate exposure of so many of their sex.

There are few things more agreeable than accompanying the woman one loves, to the places worthy of attention, in a large capital. The originality of Louisa's mind, and the natural good taste she possessed, lent a fresh attraction to whatever we saw; and as I noticed the pleasure *she* experienced, and felt the advantage I derived in having my attention drawn from my own sad thoughts, I was disposed to regret that I had not sooner brought her to London. Even the isolation in which two persons, without acquaintances, but who love each other, find themselves, draws them more closely together, and in the vast crowd of strange faces, and in the loud hum of unknown voices, they turn with increased tenderness and dependance to each other. After some weeks passed in sight seeing, I began to fear that Louisa was over fatigued by the exertion; for her appetite failed, she grew thin, and pale, and got a slight cough. She made light of all this, and when I wanted to call in a physician, dissuaded me from it, saying, that now she had seen all the London sights, she should have time to recover from her fatigue, and get well again. Thinking a little country air might be of service to her, I took her, and our nurse and child, every fine day on some little excursion in the environs of London, and the beautiful scenery so charmed and delighted her, that the exhilaration of spirits it produced lured me into the hope that she was really deriving benefit from them. But, alas! the relief was only temporary. Fatigue and exhaustion followed every exertion, and, no longer to be blinded by her assertions that her indisposition was not of a grave character, I called in a physician of the highest repute, to attend her, and awaited his sentence with as much terror, as a culprit ever did that of his judge. Yet, though filled with a terror that almost paralysed my mind, I could not bring myself to think that *I could* lose her! How could I bear to live without her who was the very soul of my existence, the strong tie that bound me to life? No, the blow was too terrible to contemplate, and like many a wretch under similar misfortune, the consciousness of my utter inability to support it, led me to believe it impossible.

The physician came, and although his guarded manner might have imposed on any one less deeply interested in ascertaining the truth than I was, it did not deceive me. The questions he put, at once revealed to me that he suspected consumption to be the malady he was called in to minister to, and the answers were, alas! but too well calculated to confirm his worst fears. And she, looking beautiful as ever, her eyes even more lustrous than when in perfect health, and a light pink spot on each cheek, appeared as calm and fearless while replying to his inquiries, as if only the most trivial malady was in question.

"Any pain in the chest and side?" demanded the physician.

"Yes; but not a great deal."

"Cough troublesome; and more especially at night?"

"Yes, rather troublesome."

"General feverishness, followed by languor?"

"Yes, but after all I really do not feel nearly as unwell as Mr. Herbert seems to think," and a smile, half playful, half reproachful to me for needlessly alarming myself passed over her lips.—The Doctor wrote a prescription, recommended the least stimulating regimen that could be adopted, milk to form a principal part of her food, and then withdrew.

I attended him to another room with a beating heart, longing, yet trembling to inquire his opinion of his patient. The gravity of his countenance prepared me to expect nothing favourable, yet when he confessed his fears that the case was a pulmonary one, the shock nearly overcame me. He recommended change of climate, said her youth was much in her favour, advised her going to Nice, with as little delay as possible, and laid great stress on the necessity of her mind being kept quiet, and her spirits cheerful.

"If you betray your alarm, Sir, it will naturally have a bad effect on her," added the physician. "Come, you must really bear up. I will look in again to-morrow, but I advise no time being lost in your trying the efficacy of a milder climate."

I swallowed a glass of water, and hastened to join my dear Louisa, forcing a cheerfulness of aspect and manner, while my heart was a prey to wretchedness. All my efforts could not conceal from her that I was agitated; perhaps it was my assumed cheerfulness, so unreal, that revealed the truth, but no sooner had I entered the room, than looking affectionately at me, she exclaimed, "You must not, dearest, be alarmed about me; I assure you there is nothing of any serious consequence the matter. If there was I would tell you at once."

Alas! this very security on her part, was one of the general symptoms of the fearful malady I suspected the existence of, even before the physician had verified the fact.

I feared that the huskiness and tremulousness of my voice might betray my emotion, and hesitated for some time before I dared speak.

"I see that the doctor has frightened you, dearest," said she, placing her hand in mine. The hand was burning, and bore fearful evidence of the truth of his opinion.

"No, my love," replied I, "he has not frightened me; but he told me it is absolutely necessary for the health of us both, that we should go to a milder climate."

I feared she might be averse to going abroad solely on account of her own health, but knew that if she was led to believe it necessary for mine, she would at once consent; so therefore I used this artifice.

"I knew you were not well," said she; "I was quite certain of it for a long, long time, though you would not acknowledge it, and if the doctor thinks going abroad will do *you* good, I have not the least objection, though I don't think it at all necessary for *me*."

I pressed her to my heart, and thanked her for this ready accordance to my wishes, adding that I hoped she would be ready to leave England in two or three days.

The preparations for our journey were soon made, and within four days from the first visit of Doctor Harford, we were *en route* for Nice.

And now a new epoch seemed marked in the page of my troubled life! The one terrible event that had coloured it, and which had fixed itself in my memory with a tenacity that defied every effort to weaken its impression, now faded away before the new and all-engrossing feeling of dread, occasioned by the danger of my wife. This dread haunted me by day, and left me not even in my dreams. I would gaze on that beautiful face, instinct with the soul's meaning, and ask myself, could it be possible that death had already marked her for his prey,—that in a few months, it might be hidden in the dark and silent grave! I would listen to the tones of that low, sweet voice, and shudder at the thought that it might soon be hushed for ever, leaving no echo save in my tortured heart, until the menaced calamity seemed too mighty, too overwhelming for possibility, and I have said, "No, no, it would be too, too dreadful; all else but this I could bear."

The belief that I was ill awakened all the tenderness of my adored wife,—a tenderness so soothing, so touching, as to increase mine to torture. No, not even in the intoxication of passion, when, in all her bridal charms, she first blessed my fond arms, did I love her as now,—*now*, when I dreaded that every day might bring our separation nearer.

Yet still she declared she felt no worse, though every exertion proved that there was less strength to bear it than before, and the increasing alteration of her form betrayed the ravages of disease. Her cough, too, became more troublesome, her nights more restless; but she bore all without a murmur; and so placid was the state of her mind, so cheerful her manner, that few could have believed that her life was in danger.

We only stopped on the road a sufficient time to rest her, and reached Nice by easy journeys, in little more than a fortnight after we left England. But even in that brief time, a fearful change had made itself visible in my wife's state of health. Her features had assumed a sharpness, her eyes seemed to have entered more profoundly the large dark orbits in which they were set; her chest, formerly so symmetrically round and prominent, appeared flattened and narrowed, and her finely formed throat, as if too weak to support her head, rested languidly on one side, always requiring a pillow to rest on.

And yet she talked of her recovery as if it were a thing to be by no means despaired of; formed plans for the future, that future which my foreboding heart told me was not reserved for her, and chided me when she detected in my countenance or manner, any indication of the alarm which filled my breast. I procured the most comfortable lodging that was disengaged at Nice, but even that was very inferior to what she had been accustomed to in England, and greatly did it pain me to see that no effort or expense could secure her the many little articles of luxury, so essential to an invalid, confined wholly to the house.

I went to an English physician established at Nice, the morning after our arrival, and he accompanied me to the hotel, to see Louisa. His first injunction was for her not to leave the house while the *bise*, as he termed it, was set in, as at present, for it was most trying to invalids. It was, therefore, a week or ten days after the lodging procured had been ready for her reception, before she could be removed to it, and when she was, a fresh cold, although every possible means had been adopted to guard against it, had been taken, which produced increased irritation in the chest. Still, not a complaint escaped her lips. It seemed as if increased suffering only called forth more prominently new proofs of that angelic sweetness of temper and patience for which she had ever been remarkable.

Oh! the torture, the agony of beholding a creature dearer, ten thousand times dearer to one than life, supporting the most acute disease, and yielding without a murmur to the decree of the Almighty! At length, the total prostration of her strength gave her, as I believed, the first notice of her real state. She had been every day lifted in my arms from her bed to her sofa, and hitherto had been able to assist herself a little in the operation, and to clasp my neck while I conveyed her. But on this occasion, I found she was utterly helpless from weakness, and her fragile hands dropped listless from my neck, unable to continue their grasp. A passion of tears followed. She wept long, and looked at me through her tears, with a glance full of such unutterable tenderness and regret, that, unable to conceal my emotion, I sobbed aloud.

"I see, I feel, dearest, that I must soon go hence," said she. "It was so sweet to be cared for, to be nursed with such tenderness as I have been by you, that I forgot, in the happiness it afforded me, that danger might lurk in the illness that called forth such precious proofs of love. To leave you now, when I know how dear I am to you, and to leave our child, too,—oh! it is a terrible trial for your poor Louisa;" and she wept afresh, while I pressed her to my heart, and she reclined her head on my shoulder. "And yet, it seems impossible, too," resumed she, "with all this hoard of love here," and she pressed her hand to her heart, "with all the bright hopes of a life to be passed with you and our child. Yes, it does seem as if it cannot be true that I am to be torn from you."

"Let us hope, dearest, that you may yet be spared," whispered I, though my heart belied the hope I would fain give.

"No, no, do not cheat me with false hopes, but try to give me courage to bear the doom that awaits me. Teach me to support our coming separation as I ought, as a Christian woman, who trusts in the mercy of her Redeemer, should, and who looks forward to being re-united to those loved on earth, in that better world, where no partings are."

But, although resigned to the will of her Creator, and daily preparing her mind and mine, for the earthly separation she knew to be inevitable, any amelioration in her state, a better night, a day more free from pain or cough, gave her hope that her life, if not saved, might be prolonged; and it was only by the increased sadness that stole over her when she found the hope illusive, that I knew it had been indulged.

I could not bear to leave her presence, and she, dear and gentle creature, seemed to forget her pain when I was near her, and never slumbered so calmly as when she knew I was seated by her side.

CHAPTER XXVII.

EVERY day that brought my beloved Louisa nearer to the last, betrayed some new trait of that noble heart, and that gentle spirit, which rendered the thought of leaving her still more insupportable. My habitual moodiness had produced a constraint on her part, that prevented her from revealing to me those vast treasures of the heart and mind, in which hers were so rich. Although, from the commencement of my attachment to her, I had believed her to be one of the most faultless of her sex, I little imagined the strength of her intellect, the overflowing tenderness of her heart, and the utter guilelessness of her nature. The terror occasioned by her illness, driving every other care from my mind, and bringing forth the deep, the engrossing affection she had inspired, had convinced her, that whatever might be the waywardness of my manner, or the uncertainty of my temper, I fondly, truly, loved her. This conviction had destroyed all constraint or reserve on her part, and, for the first time, I became sensible of the treasure I possessed.

She would sometimes, with the artlessness of a child, confess the awe, the dread, with which I had inspired her, often making her doubt whether I indeed loved her; or whether I had not found her too simple and inexperienced, to make a friend and companion of. How my heart reproached me while I listened to these artless revelations of her pure mind!—a mind so free from taint, that when my moodiness or inequality of humour pained her, she sought to discover some error in herself to account for it, instead of censuring me. And this was the creature I had considered a spy on my thoughts,—who I believed more than half suspected me of madness! O! ye to whose care some young and guileless creature is confided—who has never previously left a mother's wing—who has never known aught of the world, save that which a fond mother, or a faithful preceptress has revealed—who looks up to you for all the hopes of happiness in this life, and whose heart, overflowing with tenderness, waits but to know you will value it, to pour forth its rich stream of affection on you! deal gently,—deal mercifully towards her. Do not mistake her timidity for dulness;—her sensibility for ill humour. Give her confidence in herself—in you; and when she first learns to reveal those thoughts, only previously confided to a mother or sister's ear, do not mock the first fruits of an inexperience which is one of the peculiar charms of youth. You expect only perfume from the rose, and should be satisfied if you find only innocence in youth.

Of how much happiness had I robbed myself by not duly appreciating my sweet Louisa,—by not sufficiently mastering my moodiness, to draw forth the charms of her mind! But no; it was not to be! Destiny, in blessing me with such a creature, only required that I should know how to prize the rare gift; and I, blind and selfish, could remain insensible to such merit, and believe myself wretched, while I possessed one blessing so inestimable, as to supply the place of all others, had I been wise. Now,—now that heaven was about to withdraw the gift, of which I had proved so unworthy, what would I not have given to retain it, if but even for a few fleeting months?

Never had I loved Louisa with half the fervency, the passion, the tenderness, as since I knew I must lose her; and far from the continual contemplation of this event rendering me more reconciled to it, every day, every hour brought increased agony. *She* found strength in religion. It had been early and carefully implanted in her mind—had grown with her growth, and strengthened with her strength—and now, in her hour of need, it failed her not. It taught her to look with confidence to a meeting with those she loved, and left behind on earth, in another, purer, world; and dried her tears at the thought of a separation, which, without the hope of a re-union hereafter, would have terribly added to the bitterness of death. Alas! *my* religious education had been far less carefully attended to. My poor father, brought up a Protestant, had abandoned the faith of his fathers, to please the wife he loved almost to adoration; and she, satisfied with this proof of his attachment, was content when she saw him follow the rites of her Church, without inquiring whether a conviction of its truth had taken root in his heart.

For my mother, her religion partook of all the enthusiasm of her character and temperament. While my father, the object of her passionate love, was left her, her God was adored with all the blind idolatry of a fanatic; but when death snatched him from her, in spite of all the prayers, tears, and vows she offered up for his recovery, despair took possession of her heart. Her God became a God of terror, to be propitiated only by unceasing grief; and surrounded by all the insignia of sorrow, she passed the remainder of her life in the practice of all the austerities of the Roman Catholic creed.

Before I left her, I used to shrink with instinctive dread from her gloomy oratory, and her ceaseless tears; and, unhappily for me, in after years, I found no one to implant in my mind those sacred truths, which form the only sure basis of that religion, which is at once the guide through this life, and the hope for another. I ventured not to doubt, but my belief possessed not the hearty conviction, the pious fervour, that appertains to the faith of a true Christian. Thus it was, that I lacked the strength accorded to my admirable wife, and allowed despair to fill my heart, while hers was supported by hope in the mercies of her Redeemer. Blind must I have been, when her angelic patience, and resignation, failed to bring conviction, that only from *above* could it have been accorded her. I saw the effect, but I traced not the *cause*, and yet, never was cause more apparent.

Whether those about "to shuffle off this mortal coil" are endowed with quicker or finer perceptions than those in health, or whether affection, strong even unto death, enables them to penetrate the hearts of those dear to them, I know not; but my suffering wife became conscious that my faith wanted the earnestness of conviction that now formed her consolation. She questioned, she exhorted me to open my soul to the truth, and I listened to her, as I would to an angel, had the Almighty allowed one to descend from heaven, to remove the film of worldliness from my eyes. I embraced her faith, because it held out to me the sole refuge from despair—the prospect of meeting her in heaven.

The *vent de bise*, so often and severely felt at Nice, had disappeared, and the advent of milder weather, and occasional gleams of sunshine, had induced the physician to yield to Louisa's often repeated request, to be taken out for a little air in a wheeled-chair. This indulgence, promised for the first favourable day, had long been looked forward to with pleasure by the dear invalid, and from an early hour in the morning, when she saw the sunshine illumine the windows of her chamber, she had been impatient to go forth. I took her in my arms down stairs, placed her in the chair, supported by pillows, and walking by the side of it, bent down to catch her feeble accents.

We had only proceeded a short distance from our lodging. when we met one of the many groups of valetudinarians so often encountered at Nice. In this case, the invalid was a man, and evidently in the last stage of consumption, and a woman, so wholly occupied by him as not to appear conscious of surrounding objects, walked by the side of his chair. The two chairs met on the pavement; the occupants glanced at each other with that mingled sentiment of pity and interest awakened by the similarity of their fate, peculiar to invalids, and at the same moment, I recognised in the poor faded shadow, propped up by pillows in the chair, my old school-fellow Neville. His wife,—for it was Mrs. Neville who walked by his side,—turned her head at this moment, and her eyes and those of my dear Louisa met. In a moment Mrs. Neville was by my wife's side, pressing her hand in hers, and speechless with emotion, trying in vain to address her, while poor Neville, reaching forth his hand, exclaimed:—

"My dear Herbert, this is no time for remembering old differences. Let us forgive, as we hope to be forgiven, and forget, if, indeed, we have either of us had any real cause for coolness, which I doubt."

I clasped his offered hand, while his warm-hearted wife said, "This, dearest, is my amiable friend, Mrs. Herbert, of whom I have so often spoken to you." And Louisa smiled, and nodded kindly to him.

"This," said Neville, "is a sad meeting, but I am glad it has taken place. I have often since my illness thought of you, Herbert, and wished that we might meet. My dear wife formed such a regard for yours, that I regretted and reproached myself for having taken her away from Torquay. It was wrong—it was unkind, but you will pardon it, will you not?"

I met Neville's kindness in the self-same spirit that prompted it. My heart had been softened and ameliorated by the state of my adored Louisa, and when I beheld him, whom I had last seen in the pride of health and manhood, reduced to his present pitiable state, my heart had no place for aught save regret and regard.

My countenance, I suppose, as well as my manner, revealed my feelings, for Neville again took my hand, and while he warmly pressed it, said, "You will come and see me, Herbert, will you not? and my wife will go and see yours."

"And your darling little girl, where is she?" inquired Mrs. Neville of Louisa.

"Here, dearest friend," replied Louisa; "and she is, thank God, in perfect health. And yours, is she here?"

"No, I left her in England with my mother, that I might devote all my time to him," and she gave a look full of tenderness to her husband.

Both invalids were drawn to the same spot, the most sheltered one in the whole vicinity of Nice, and Mrs. Neville and I walked by the chairs, conversing with their occupants. I learned from Neville, that a neglected cold, caught by sleeping in a damp bed, the very time he was coming to join his wife at Torquay, had fallen on his lungs, and defied the treatment of all the physicians he had consulted: that after unavailingly testing their skill, he had been ordered to Nice, "where they have sent me to die, Herbert," added he, dropping his voice, that his wife or mine might not hear him.

"Yes, I feel it is so, but I must submit to the will of God. But I was so happy," and his lip trembled, "that it is hard to die, to leave her, on whom my soul dotes. But you also, Herbert, you have your cares. Your poor wife, I fear, is very ill."

I shook my head, and tears rushed into my eyes, for I could not form words to tell him that I had lost all hope of saving my Louisa.

"I am so glad," said my wife, when we returned from her little drive, "that we met the Nevilles, and that you and he are reconciled. I cannot express the pleasure it has given me, dearest, for now you will not be left quite alone when I am taken from you, and our child will have one kind friend."

"Poor Neville will not be long spared to his wife," said I, anxious to turn her thoughts from herself, and unable to bear the frequent recurrence she was in the habit of making to her own death.

"Yes," observed she, "I fear her heavy trial will soon come. He seems as near the last parting on earth as I am. But I think our being brought together seems like something providential to both parties, and this interposition of the Almighty's goodness, if I may be permitted so to consider it, ought to be received with gratitude, and not slighted."

She made me visit Neville that evening, and he insisted on his wife going to sit with mine, while I remained with him. Our lodgings were luckily very near each other, and by this arrangement, the invalids were never left without society.

Neville, always frank, noble-minded, and kind-hearted, had lost none of the qualities that had rendered him the most popular boy when at school, and the most esteemed man at college. But, in addition to these qualities, he had acquired others in the school of affliction, to which he had lately been subjected, that were calculated to endear him more than ever to those who had opportunities of knowing him. He had more charity, more forbearance towards others than formerly, and severely censured himself for not having sought to correct the errors in me, which had induced him to think ill of me, instead of casting me from him, and resisting those advances on my part, towards a renewal of intimacy, which proved that I was disposed to like him.

"The truth is, my dear Herbert," would he say, "I was vain of my foolish popularity, and although I felt drawn towards you, your reserve, your pride, and shall I confess it, your assumption of worldly wisdom at an age when according to my notion it was a very poor substitute for generosity and good fellowship, had turned all our companions against you, and I swam with the stream, instead of honestly telling you why you made enemies, and giving you a chance of righting yourself. Then it was both wrong and unfeeling of me to break off the friendship that had sprung up between our wives, by carrying off mine so abruptly. It inflicted pain on her, and must have hurt the feelings of Mrs. Herbert. I had no right to do this on no other grounds than that you had been less popular at school and at college than myself, and I assure you, Herbert, I have often of late regretted it."

At such moments I have exposed my whole heart to this generous friend, keeping the one fatal secret alone concealed. Even that sometimes trembled on my lips, but I had not courage to reveal it. The shock might be too much for his weak state, and what right had I to agitate, to distress him? My conscience told me that if I was a victim to one single impulse, indulged with no guilty intent, but which had led to the death of the object, I had no right to enchain to my destiny the sister of that object, between whom and myself her death ought to have interposed an insurmountable barrier. No, I dared not hazard the loss of his friendship so lately proved, so dearly valued, so soon to be closed by death, by the avowal of my terrible secret! But I told him all the circumstances of my childhood, the perversion of my better nature by the cynical counsel and example of Mr. Trevyllan, the pride that checked the avowal of my errors, and prevented my vindicating myself, or at least openly resenting the avoidance of my companions. He comprehended, he pitied me, severely blamed himself for not having sooner understood me, and shielded me under the ægis of his popularity and power over his companions.

Poor Neville! Never did a kinder, warmer heart beat in a human breast than his! It was no wonder that his wife adored him, for he possessed every quality to conciliate affection and command respect! She was no longer the gay, sprightly creature I had seen her at Torquay. Subdued to pensiveness, her high spirits fled with her husband's health, and pale and care-worn, she looked as if fifteen years had been added to her age. Her frequent visits were a great comfort to my dear Louisa, and in the confidential intercourse established between them, a promise was asked, and given, that through life Mrs. Neville would prove a friend to my daughter, nay more, a protectress, should death deprive her of a father.

When I looked on my wife and on Neville, two beings so rich in every estimable quality, fast sinking into their premature graves, I have thought that if the Almighty would yield a prolongation of their lives to our prayers, existence would be henceforth to us who loved, who almost idolized them, a boon, a blessing, to command our eternal gratitude. But, alas, this blessing was not for us! The fiat had gone forth, and prayers and tears were unavailing to stay the terrible stroke impending over our heads.

CHAPTER XXVIII.

THERE is something peculiarly touching in witnessing the triumph of virtue, combined, as great virtue invariably is, with superior intellect, in the last stages of life. The patience, the resignation, the thought for others, outliving every selfish feeling.

Thus was it with my beloved wife, and with my dear friend. My soul, long darkened by error, and overshadowed by one memory so harassing as to render life a scene of gloom and trial, instead of a blessing, seemed to be illumined by the glorious light that now broke in on it from those two admirable creatures, who, like setting suns, give forth the brightest light when about to vanish from our view. How pure, how ennobling, were the thoughts uttered by their lips, lips that were alas! soon to be sealed by death; and how eagerly, even in the midst of my grief, did my ears drink in the wisdom which emanated from minds already freed from the soil and influence of earthly passions. I seemed, all unworthy as I was, to hold communion with angels, and my grosser nature became purified by the contact with them.

"You must unlearn the worldly wisdom acquired under the tuition of Mr. Trevyllan," would Neville say to me, "before you can be able to make friends, or to appreciate them. Suspicion, though it may sometimes preserve a man from being duped, erects a barrier between him and his fellow men that for ever excludes sympathy and friendship; and far better is it to suffer some inconvenience from misplaced confidence, than to shut up one's heart from the genial influence of good will. Think well of mankind *en masse*, even though *en détail* you may find some unworthy specimens of the genus, for good thoughts beget a healthy mind, whereas evil ones—and suspicion is ever evil—corrodes the mind that once receives it as a guest. A suspicious man is never a truly wise one, just as a superstitious man is never a truly religious one. To have lived some years with so admirable a woman as your wife, Herbert, ought to have vanquished the error grafted on your character by your unfortunate intimacy with your guardian."

I dared not tell Neville that my suspicions had sometimes lighted on the all-faultless creature with whom he believed a contact would suffice to banish them for ever. No! I restrained my tongue, though Heaven knows how contrite a spirit reigned in my heart, as I remembered the humiliating fact.

And now the attending physician prepared us for the fast approaching death of Neville; and the agony of his poor wife was as intense as if she had not been several months inured to the terrible certainty that she must lose him. She left his side no more; and twice every day did my dear Louisa insist on my going to them. Oh! God of mercy! pardon me, if, when writhing in agony with my own grief, and when I beheld that young pair, also tortured by their coming separation, I dared to question thy goodness, for not vouchsafing to spare *his* life in pity to the poor creature who doted on him, and for not granting me that of my adored Louisa.

"Let my remains be interred in the English cemetery here," said poor Neville to his wife, in my presence, a few hours before he breathed his last.

"My friend Herbert will see the last duties paid, and relieve you, dearest, from the painful details consequent on such situations. Return to England, my beloved, as soon as your presence can no longer be a solace to the wife of my poor friend, and ever continue to be to him as a sister."

Even up to the last hour, his thoughts were turned to the good of others, his noble nature maintaining its influence over a frame reduced to a shadow by pain and disease.

He retained his senses to within a few minutes of his death; pressed my hand and bade me farewell; blessed his absent child; and holding the hand of his wife within his, while he murmured prayers and blessings on her head, resigned his soul to the Almighty, and expired without a groan.

Never did I witness grief like that of the bereaved widow; for now that the restraint which the dread of afflicting him had imposed, was removed, her sorrow mastered her reason for many hours. She could not for some time believe that he was indeed dead, and addressed to the ears, now sealed for ever. the passionate words of endearment that had been wont to fill them with delight. But when she found that all was over, that the husband who had never ceased to be the lover, whose lips had never uttered a harsh word to her, and the tones of whose voice were still ringing in her ear, was gone for ever, her despair was so wild, that I trembled lest she should destroy herself.

I left her to the care of the physician, and with a heart almost broken, returned from the dead—to the dying.

"Your poor friend is released, is he not?" said my wife, as I entered her chamber. "I saw it by your countenance the instant you came in. Ah! my poor Mary, how my heart bleeds for her! Come near me, dearest. You are ill, worn down. But God will repay you for your kindness to your departed friend."

She pressed her transparent fingers to my brow, and kissed my cheek, but the burning heat of her hands and lips betrayed the fever that was consuming her, and made me tremble.

"I have been thinking, dearest," said she, "that if your poor friend's remains are to be resigned to earth here, I should like to have mine interred near them. In a strange land it seems less desolate to be buried near some one dear to those most dear to me. Promise me this shall be as I wish."

Her lips quivered, and her voice became tremulous with emotion; and I, losing all self-command, my feelings having been so excited by the death-bed I had left, and the dying one by which I stood, groaned aloud, and fell insensible on her bed. Her silver hand-bell soon brought her maid into the room, but it was not for many minutes that their united efforts could restore suspended animation to my frame.

"Oh, my God! do not forsake him," exclaimed she fervently; "but grant him resignation to bow to THY will, and to live for the child it pleased thee to grant us. Oh! this grief of his disturbs my soul, and draws it back with a mighty effort from the contemplation of that world, where I hope to be reunited to him, to this vale of tears, where the thought of his sorrow, when I shall have left him, fills me with anguish."

And now that I felt aware that the hours of my adored wife's life were drawing to a close, I could not bear to absent myself even for a moment from her presence. Yet she, ever unselfish, would insist on my going to her bereaved friend, Mrs. Neville, whose sorrow awakened all her sympathy. On me devolved the painful duty of giving instructions for the funeral; but further than sparing her this chagrin, I could be of little use, for she refused to be comforted, and it was only by talking to her of her child, that I could for a moment draw her attention from the dead. There she sat, all day, silent and motionless as a statue, looking at the remains of her husband, until a burst of violent grief would break the stillness of the chamber of death, after which she would again resume her fixed gaze on that pale face, as if she expected to see some change in its marble aspect. By her desire I had a sculptor to take a cast of the face. But even while this operation was performing, she could not be persuaded to leave the room, but watched its progress with as much anxiety, as if the dead could suffer pain from it. With her own hands she smoothed the pillow in the coffin, on which his head was to be placed, and when the corse was laid in its last narrow bed, she left it not for a moment, until it was found absolutely necessary that the coffin should be nailed down. That scene was terrible! and the witnessing it shook my nerves so much, that I lost all power of being of use. Happily for her, a deep swoon, the effect of mental and bodily exhaustion, ensued, and for some time she lost in insensibility the consciousness of her misery.

I attended the remains of my poor friend to the grave, a solemn and melancholy ceremony which his poor wife could not be dissuaded from being present at, although her trembling limbs were scarcely able to support her languid frame.

When the coffin was lowered into the grave, she would have fallen to the earth, had I not sustained her fainting form. Poor bereaved woman! she felt that she was now alone, and desolate; her child, whose presence would have reminded her that she had still a tie on earth, and duties to perform, was far away; so it could not be wondered at, if, stunned and overwhelmed by the blow that had crushed her heart, she prayed for death to reunite her to *him* she had lost. I had much difficulty in getting her to leave the cemetery, when the last sod of earth was laid on the grave. She clung to the spot with passionate tenderness, for it had now become dear and sacred in her eyes, and she preferred it to all others on earth.

To return to that home where *he* was *not*, but where every object reminded her of him, would, I felt assured, be more than she could bear, and at the suggestion of my dear wife, a vacant apartment in the house in which we lodged had been prepared for the reception of her poor friend. I ordered the carriage to drive to it, and asked her whether she would not spend an hour with my Louisa. I really felt afraid to leave her alone, and yet I could not remain longer absent from the couch of my dying wife.

"She cannot go to you," said I, "and will be comforted by seeing you."

She hesitated long, but at length consented, and we entered my wife's room. The sight of her poor friend, reduced to the last extremity of weakness, a breathing shadow she might be called, had, as I anticipated it would, a powerful effect on Mrs. Neville. She became more calm, and tears, hitherto almost denied her, flowed in abundance down her pale cheeks; as reclining in a chair by the bed-side, my dear wife holding her hand in hers, she listened to the feeble accents of her friend.

"My stay on earth must now be short," said my adored Louisa, "and it would be most kind in you to remain with me in this house to the last. With my dear friend and my husband by my dying-bed, I shall pass away to another world more calmly; do not, therefore, refuse this my last request."

"But I shall put you to such inconvenience; I am sure I shall."

"No, all has been arranged in the hope you would not refuse my wishes; a room is ready for you, and your maid is already here."

My wife, with all a woman's tact, made a point of occupying her poor friend continually, so as to leave her as little time as possible to devote to grief. She asked her to read the Bible to her twice a-day, to join her in prayer, and to give the anodynes prescribed by the physician. She would place our child in the arms of our friend, and exhort her to remember her own absent one, who would prove a blessing and a comfort to her; and thus, by employing her, interrupted the constant contemplation on her heavy affliction, that would otherwise have wholly destroyed her health, already greatly impaired by anxiety, confinement, and grief.

"Ah! my beloved friend!" would Mrs. Neville say, when my dear Louisa spoke of her fast approaching end, "how I envy you who are going where my adored husband is gone, while I may live for months, ay, years separated from him."

"You forget that you are a mother, that *his* child is a sacred legacy bequeathed to you by him," would my Louisa reply; "and that when you are summoned hence, *he* will expect to know how you have fulfilled the task he assigned to you. You must live, if it be the will of *the Most High*, to perform your duties, and you must not shrink from them."

For me,—the scenes I had lately witnessed, and the sight of my adored wife on her death-bed, had taken such an effect on me, that I felt as if I could not long survive her. Nor did I desire it; for with the selfishness inherent in man, and aware that with her would depart my every hope of happiness on earth, I wished for nothing so much as death to unite me to her. I forgot that I was a father, that it was my duty to struggle to live for the sake of my daughter; or if I did remember her I silenced all paternal solicitude with the conviction that Mrs. Neville would be a mother to her as she promised; and worn out by grief and anxiety, I longed to lay down the load of life, and to be laid in the grave with my beloved Louisa.

I sometimes betrayed to her this desire, but never without her severely reprehending it.

"What!" would she exclaim, "are mortals, like cowards in the field of battle, to wish to fly from their duty the moment that hope no longer cheers them? Oh, no, my dearest husband! you must not wish to leave your post while a task remains to be fulfilled, nor desire to join me, until the Almighty sees fit to summon you."

Often have I been jealous and offended by her wishing me to live after her. I thought it betokened a want of affection; for I could not, with my selfish nature, judge her high and noble one. I felt that were *I* on the bed of death, I should rejoice to know she should soon be called to follow me; hence, I could not comprehend the difference of our sentiments on this point. Alas! it was not given to me to know her worth, until I had lost her.

CHAPTER XXIX.

THREE weeks after I followed my friend to the grave, my beloved wife resigned her gentle spirit into the hands of her Creator. Although long prepared for this heart-rending event, I found myself as unable to support it, when it arrived, as if my foreboding heart, and tortured mind, had not foreseen that it was inevitable. Her dying farewell to our child, and to me, achieved the measure of my despair; and within an hour after she had breathed her last, I was wildly raving, under the influence of a sudden attack of brain fever, from which, for several weeks, the physicians believed I could never recover. During its violence, I imagined myself dead, and believed that I beheld my lost wife, crowned with more than mortal beauty, in the regions of the blessed, holding out her arms to welcome me. Methought I approached to embrace her, when her dead sister interposed between us, and exclaimed, "Away, sinful man, thou who in life presumed to attach thy evil destiny to her sinless one; think not that here, where only the good are permitted to join those loved on earth, thou canst be reunited to her."

"Hinder him not, dearest sister," said my wife. "He loved me on earth, and I loved him,—oh! so fondly, that even in the grave he was not forgotten. He was my husband, and the commands of the Most High are, that those whom God has joined, no one may put asunder."

"Thou knewest not, my sister, that this sinful man sent me, whom thou didst love, whom thou didst mourn with such bitter tears, to an early, an unhallowed grave?"

"Oh! say not so, say not so, it cannot be."

"Yes, it was even as I say. When, fatigued by a long walk, I sank to slumber, as was sometimes my wont, on that seat where thou and I had often reposed, this man approached, and heedless that sleeping innocence is under the protection of Heaven, he dared, even on the evening of the day that saw his dead mother consigned to the grave, to steal on my slumber, and to profane my virgin brow with his lips. Terrified, I burst the bonds of sleep, and fled from him. He pursued me; I felt him gaining on my steps, his scorching breath moved my hair, and I rushed more wildly on, until my foot struck against a stone. I stumbled, tried to recover myself, and in the effort fell headlong over the steep precipice that bounds the narrow path."

"Oh God! oh God!" exclaimed my wife; "can this be possible? And this man, the destroyer of my sister, dared to wed me, knowing in his heart that I would have preferred the most lingering, the most cruel death, to allying myself with him! And he is the father of my child, the niece of her he sent to an early grave!"

I tried to speak, to call Heaven to witness that when I obeyed the impulse of a wild desire to press the brow of the sleeper, no thought of guilt entered my mind. That, when I pursued her, it was with no evil intent, but to entreat her pardon, and to reveal my name. But my tongue clove to the roof of my mouth, and not all my efforts could produce utterance.

"Oh, Almighty!" exclaimed my wife; "can this man, whose head has so often rested on my bosom, whom I loved better than I ought to have loved aught but Thee, have intentionally destroyed the life of my sister? Oh! grant him the power to vindicate himself from intentional guilt, or, if speech be denied him, oh! grant me the power to read the truth in his heart."

It seemed to me at this moment as if the veil of flesh that envelopes the soul was rent asunder by Divine will, and that the heart thus exposed, its secrets could be deciphered as easily as written characters when brought to the light.

"Look there, behold!" said the spirit of my departed wife, addressing that of her sister, which still interposed between us, "no crime was meditated. The unhappy man meant no evil, and severely has he suffered for the fatal indulgence of an impulse which, hadst thou not awoke, would never have wrought the fatal consequences that ensued. Have I not, in my mortal state, witnessed his wakeful hours, his troubled sleep, his days of gloomy preoccupation, and his despair, without knowing the cause? O! join me, my sister, in entreating at the throne of the Most High, pardon for him who was my husband."

"And can mortal love still exist when life is over?" said the sister. "Thou pleadest for this sinful man, as though thou still lovedst him. But thou knowest not what a tissue of deception and falsehood he wove to conceal the result of his sin, and which has so greatly aggravated it. Did he not, when he found my poor mangled body, palpitating with the last pangs of life, only wait until my heart had ceased to beat, before he drew it into a cavern at the base of the precipice where I fell? There he left my remains until it pleased him to come under covert of the night, to dig in the same cavern, a grave into which he consigned them with no minister of God to pronounce a prayer, no fond eye to drop a tear over them. Why left he not my corse where it fell, and where it might be discovered, and restored to my distracted friends? But no; he added the pangs of suspense to their terror and grief at my mysterious disappearance, and deprived my poor remains of the rites of Christian burial, in a consecrated grave, where the tears of a fond mother and sister might sometimes fall. Nay, more, did he not, some months after, consign the corse of a stranger to the vault where the remains of his parents then reposed, and where those of our mother now rest, passing them for mine? And can this sacrilege be forgotten? Canst thou urge aught in his favour?"

The brow of my wife, over which a halo of light played, that gave a divine expression to her countenance, now seemed clouded by care. She bowed her head for a few minutes, as if overcome by grief, and then lifting her tearful eyes to heaven, said, "Yes, I can still urge thee to join me in imploring his pardon from the Almighty. If God could pardon those who caused *his* death, and implore forgiveness for them, from *his* Father on High, saying, 'Lord, they know not what they do;' mayest thou not follow the bright example, and entreat pardon for him who surely as we read his heart, knew not what he did, when he pressed his lips to thy brow?"

"When he has expiated his sins by long suffering and repentance, perhaps I may listen to thy pleadings, my sister, and join thee in praying for his pardon; but he must undergo many trials and persecutions before this can be; and never shall he approach thy presence in heaven until, purified by long sufferings, he has effaced the stain of his sins by his tears."

And now the power of utterance seemed restored to me; for throwing myself on my knees, I cried in bitter agony—

"Have pity, oh! have pity on me!"

At this moment I felt myself seized by powerful arms, and in defiance of all my struggles and resistance, I was lifted from the floor, and laid on my couch. I saw figures moving around my bed, heard whispering voices muttering—

"His delirium still continues. He might have been seriously hurt in thus throwing himself out of bed, and you must not take your eyes off him, even while he appears to sleep, lest he should injure himself."

"Why, he raved so strangely, Sir," said another voice, "that he really quite frightened me."

"Stuff—nonsense!" replied the first speaker; "who would mind the wild ravings of a man in a brain fever? If I had not thought you had better nerves, I would not have recommended you as a proper person to take charge of the poor gentleman by night, now that his own servant and Mrs. Neville's are so worn out with fatigue from sitting up with him."

"I'll take better care for the future, Sir," was the answer; "but he threw himself out of bed so suddenly, and began crying out, 'Pity, pity,—have pity on me,' so loudly, that I was quite confounded like. The poor gentleman seems to have a wonderful deal of trouble on his mind."

"Never busy yourself about his mind, that is not your business," observed the other speaker, whose voice I now recognised to be that of the doctor who had attended my poor friend Neville and my lost wife; "only attend to his person, and take care that during his delirium he does not injure himself."

My senses were now perfectly restored, but such was the extent of my weakness, that I could hardly move. Perhaps it was this total prostration of strength that for the time being vanquished the fever of the brain, and subdued, to a certain degree, the violence of my grief for the loss of my

wife; for although I remembered her death,—nay more, every word of that
last farewell, which had so agonized me as to bring on the attack that had
nearly killed me, I no longer felt the overwhelming grief I had previously
experienced. Perhaps a strong frame is required for violent grief. Mine was
reduced to such weakness that as well might I have sought to use bodily
force as to endure strong mental agony. My dream was vividly remembered, so vividly that I could almost believe, that instead of a dream it had
been a reality. And then came the recollection of what the man left to take
care of me had said to the doctor of my strange ravings, and the great
trouble that he believed pressed on my mind. What, if I had uttered all
the conversations that my delirium had framed in that terrible dream, and
thus had betrayed my dreadful secret to a stranger? There was torture in
the thought; and I now found, that although too exhausted for the indulgence of violent grief, I was still accessible to terror. Oh, man! selfish to the
last! thou canst outlive grief for those dearer to thee than life; thy feelings,
benumbed by bodily weakness, may remain torpid to the appeals of love
and memory; but let thy personal safety, or rather, let me think, thy honour
and reputation, be menaced, and thou canst feel as acutely the danger as
if in health.

I had not only a dread, but a secret conviction that in my ravings I had
betrayed my secret, and to a stranger, too, who might be disposed to make
the worst use of it for his own advantage. Drops of cold perspiration fell
from my brow, wrung by terror, as I reflected on all this. What must I do to
remove the impression made on this strange man by what I had uttered in
my ravings? Here was selfishness and cunning still exerting their combined
influence over me, although life scarcely fluttered at my heart, or kept my
pulse still beating.

I stole a look at the man through an opening in the curtains, and never
did I behold a worse countenance. Large shaggy eyebrows, projecting over
small, deep-seated eyes, remarkable for a mingled expression of malignity
and cunning; a low and narrow forehead, retreating towards the roots of
the hair; a large and ill-shaped nose; a wide and very coarse mouth, and a
peculiarly short chin. He was a tall man, of a powerful and muscular form,
with herculean limbs, and a very short neck, and his ears were the largest
and flattest I had ever seen. No peculiarity in his appearance escaped my
attention. I felt instinctively that this man, so unfavoured by Nature, might
henceforth have a baleful influence over my destiny. I mentally measured
his powerful frame with my own now weakened one, and acknowledged
that, even in my days of health, I could not struggle with him without the
certainty of defeat.

There is always a disagreeable sensation experienced in the conscious-ness of inferiority in physical force to other men, but when this conscious-ness of inferiority is felt towards one whom we may have cause to dread, in whose keeping a secret of vital importance to us may be, how much more annoying does it become! The man, while I was examining him, seemed wrapt in deep reflection. His brows were curved, his coarse lips strongly compressed, and from time to time he darted furtive glanced towards my bed.

After a pause, he shook his head, and muttered, "Yes, yes, something profitable maybe made of this. I'll bet anything that, light-headed as he may be, there's some crime or another at bottom, in which he has been concerned, and that he lets out in his sleep, mixed up with his insane rav-ings. Why, he has not passed a single night since I have been called in with-out talking of having destroyed some woman, and of having hidden her body in a cavern. All this can't be the pure raving madness of a brain fever. No, no, there's something in it, I'm sure; and as he can afford to pay for my keeping his secrets, why, I'll be hanged if I don't make him come down handsomely,—that's all."

Though this soliloquy was uttered almost in a whisper, not a syllable of it escaped my ear, and terror took such possession of me, that it required a strong effort of my volition to prevent the violent trembling with which I was seized from becoming visible by the movement of the bed.

A thought occurred to me to try if I could not impose on him by affect-ing to talk in my sleep. I breathed hard, uttered a few words, and he instantly stole to my bed-side, and bent down to listen.

"Will no one come to release me?" demanded I, keeping my eyes closely shut, and breathing hard, as if I slept. "They hurled me over a steep rock, and when I fell mortally wounded, they dug a hole and threw my body into it; and no one will release it, though I call night and day for deliverance."

"That's a new go, however," murmured the man; "I never heard him talk of being killed himself before. It has always been some woman who fell over the rock, and whom *he* buried in a cavern. I hope he hasn't been talking nonsense after all, and that there's something of truth at the bot-tom of all his raving."

"If they would take my body out of the pit," resumed I, "I should then be taken directly to heaven."

"The devil you would," said he; "I am not quite so sure of that, though. I must find out all I can concerning him," continued he. "The nurse knows more about him than the rest. I'll pump her, and discover where he comes from."

CHAPTER XXX.

To listen to this designing ruffian, arranging his plan for discovering my home and past life, filled me with alarm. Yet how could I counteract his schemes?—how prevent the nurse from answering his questions? To put her on her guard would excite suspicion in her mind, that there existed some cause for concealment, and this would be dangerous.

Oh! the torture of feeling my bodily weakness to be such, that I could not turn in my bed without assistance, and to know that a villain was bent on discovering a clue to a secret, partly revealed in my ravings, but which I could die rather than have exposed. There were moments,—to such fearful crimes may terror of the discovery of guilt lead one,—Heaven pardon me for the sinful thought! when, had I but the strength to carry my desire into execution, I could have strangled this wretch, while he dozed, as he sometimes did, in a chair by my bed-side, and so have secured his silence, and prevented his further researches into my past history. I thought not of the consequences that must inevitably ensue from his being found dead in my room—so wholly does the mind become blinded to the sense of one danger, in the burning, the mad desire to escape from another—or, if I did, I fancied it would be easy to account for it, by saying he had been seized by apoplexy.

"Yes! Yes!" thought I, and I clenched my teeth, and the spirit of a fiend seemed for a few minutes to have entered my heart, urging murder. "Had I but the strength, *he* should soon be silenced for ever."

I had conceived a hatred the most intense against this man, who, without any provocation on my part, had turned eavesdropper; noting down the ravings of delirium of a fellow-creature, worn down by grief, and reduced to death's door by fever, in order to discover some secret, for the keeping of which he could enforce payment. That night's experience taught me how fortunate it sometimes is, that man has not the power to work the evil he wills; for alas! there are those so weak in principle, and so prone to act on the impulse of the moment, that crime is often only escaped, by the want of power to perpetrate it.

I was surprised to find how much the sense of my grief was dulled. I felt like one who had received some severe bodily injury, to lull the pain of which, some strong anodyne had been administered; and who was fearful of even thinking of the wound, lest he should awaken the dormant agony. It is asserted by physicians, that two maladies cannot act on the human frame at the same time; and I believe a similar rule holds good with regard to the mind; for, judging by my own experience, I should say, that two strong passions cannot sway a man at once.

The terror excited in my mind by the wretch in my room had so filled and engrossed it, as to deaden, if not banish, for the time being, my sorrow for the death of my beloved wife; and yet, when my alarmed imagination pictured the danger that might result to me from the villain so bent on discovering my secret, I blessed God that *her* peace could not be disturbed by the success of the utmost extent of his malice. No, she, heaven be praised, was safe. The discovery of my guilt could bring no blush to her cheek, no pang to her heart, and gentler tears than any I had lately shed filled my eyes, as I thought of her in her peaceful grave, where I longed to repose beside her. Then came the thought of my motherless child, and my tears flowed faster. Poor innocent! my heart yearned to embrace her; but yet I must not ask to have her brought to me; I must still for a few days assume the mask of delirium, in order to deceive the spy who was watching me, and cheat him into a belief that the words uttered by me when I slept were but the ravings of insanity. I lay tranquil and overpowered by lassitude and exhaustion, during the long and tedious days that followed my return to consciousness. My own servant generally remained in the room, but I affected not to recognize him, and pretended to doze when he looked at me.

At night the strange man took his place, and then my terror commenced, lest I should sleep, and in my slumber betray my secret. Often was I obliged to pinch my limbs, and pull my hair, to keep myself awake, while pretending to sleep, and in my simulated slumbers, uttering incoherent words to deceive the designing wretch who was carefully noticing every syllable that escaped my lips.

In proportion to my desire *not* to sleep was the drowsiness that stole over me every night, filling me with terror for its possible consequences, while during the day, when the man I feared was absent, I had little inclination to sleep.

One night, while I pretended to slumber, I saw this man take the candle in his hand, approach it close to my eyes to ascertain if I indeed slept, and then, having repeatedly passed the light before my closed lids, he searched in the drawers of the looking-glass and commode for something, leaving not a single one unopened. At length he found a bunch of keys; I heard them jingle in his hand, and with them he tried to open my writing-box. The patent lock foiled his attempts, and then, with a half-suppressed oath, he searched the drawer of the dressing-box, in which he found my watch, to the chain of which the key he sought was attached. He seized it, opened the writing-box, and began examining its contents; but, finding nothing to gratify his curiosity, or to confirm his suspicions, he muttered curses, and taking up the portrait of my beloved wife, opened and examined it. I could have killed him for the profanation. That picture I had induced her to sit for in London, when I first began to be alarmed about her health. It was an admirable resemblance, and I would not, so highly did I value it, have confided it to the hands of any creature on earth, save to those of her friend Mrs. Neville, or her old nurse at home.

"Hoh! hoh!" muttered the wretch, "this, I suppose, was his wife, and a devilish pretty creature she must have been, if she had not such a sickly look. I don't like your whey-faced women, not I, give me a buxom wench, with roguish eyes, and rosy cheeks, that's the girl for my money."

I cannot describe the mingled feelings of anger and disgust which I experienced, as I listened to this ruffian commenting on the portrait, and comparing it with the object of his own vulgar taste. There are some persons who inspire us with such repugnance, that we would not, could we avoid it, permit their glances to fall on any woman dear to us—but when the beloved object is no more, her memory becomes so sacred in our hearts, that we shrink from the notion of her portrait being profaned by the gaze of vulgar eyes. And there I lay inert, and powerless to avenge the insult, though almost suffocated with rage against the offender.

The wretch still held the portrait, and looked at it. "Yes," resumed he, "she must have been a pretty creature before she grew sickly. I dare say 'twas his sulky temper that spoilt her health. The nurse-maid confessed to me, when I questioned her, that although he was an affectionate husband, he never was a cheerful companion to her poor mistress; but, from the beginning, was a gloomy, melancholy man. That's what convinces me he must have committed some crime or other, that he's always afraid will be found out. What else would make him so gloomy and unlike other men?" And now he laid down the portrait, and renewed his search in the writing-box. He found a purse with some eight or ten guineas, counted them over, and then paused, as if hesitating whether or not he should appropriate them. Some slight noise disturbed him; he let fall the purse into the writing-box, hastily closed the lid; and approaching my bed he stealthily examined me; but I kept my eyes closed, murmured a few words as if in sleep, and so deceived him.

"I really was startled," muttered he; "to be caught with his purse in my hand, and his writing-box open, would be an awkward job. By Jove, it was lucky for him that he did not awake and see what I was about, for if he had, there was nothing left for me to do but to place the pillow on his face with one hand, while I clutched his throat with t'other, and so made an end of him; and, when all was over, I'd have called up the house, and sworn that he had been seized with a fit."

My blood seemed to congeal in my veins as I listened to these words, which, though pronounced in a whisper, I heard distinctly, owing to the silence that reigned in the room, and my sense of hearing, always acute, having now become more so from the abstemious regimen I had lately undergone. I shuddered at the thought of being in the power of a ruffian who, I felt convinced, would not hesitate to commit murder, if he deemed it necessary for his own ends.

"I've half a mind to take these ten shiners for my own use," muttered he. "The chances are, the owner will never recover to claim them; and, if he should, he will forget all about 'em, so much has he suffered since he put 'em here, and so crazy has he been. But no, let's have a care. Suspicion would fall on me; and it's likely enough that chap, his servant, has looked at this here writing-box as well as I have; *he* knows the money was here, and would soon guess who took it. No, I'll not take a guinea of it; I'll resist temptation for once, and try to make my money by getting that there fellow who is sleeping so soundly in my power, instead of putting myself into his, for sake of a few paltry guineas."

So saying, he replaced the purse and its contents into the writing-box, arranged the papers in the state in which he had found them, locked the box, put back the watch in the drawer, and, having again examined to see that I slept, resumed his place by my bed-side, and I, breathing loudly, muttered incoherent ravings now and then, to which he listened attentively, occasionally exclaiming—

"Psha! stuff! he doesn't let out anything worth hearing of late, but talks a pack of nonsense."

I could no longer sustain my present painful position, so wholly worn out was I in body and mind by sleepless nights and feverish anxiety; so, the following day, after the surreptitious opening of my writing-box, I affected to awake as if from a troubled dream, and demanded to see the physician. My servant was rejoiced to find that my reason was restored; and, when the doctor came, I inquired for my child and Mrs. Neville so collectedly, as to convince him that the fever had wholly subsided, and that nothing remained to be done, but to endeavour to restore my strength by a more nutritious regimen. He promised, that when I was a little stronger, I should see my child, of whose health he gave me a most satisfactory account.

"I should be glad," said I, "to have no one to sit up at night in my room, it disturbs and prevents me from sleeping."

"You are still too weak, my dear Sir, to be left alone at night," replied the physician.

"But could not a bed be arranged for my own servant on the sofa?" demanded I.

"Certainly, if you prefer it, and I will immediately give instructions that your wish shall be carried into effect."

What a weight seemed to be removed from my mind by this arrangement. Yet, fearful that the wretch I so dreaded might again enter my chamber, I said, that I wished the man who had sat up with me might be sent away, and remunerated for his trouble.

"Has he not satisfied you by his attention?" inquired the doctor.

"He has, I believe, behaved well enough," replied I; "but invalids are, I suppose, prone to be fanciful; and I confess I should be glad to have him sent away."

"Then he shall be dismissed at once," observed the doctor, good naturedly; "I will give him his *congé.*"

A great weight was removed from my mind in the certainty that I should see this man no more; yet my conscience reproached me for not informing the doctor, who had recommended him, of his having opened my writing-box and examined its contents. A secret dread of exciting his vengeance deterred me from taking this step; and as he had actually *not* robbed me, however well disposed to do so, I excused myself for my want of moral courage in not denouncing him, by the reflection, that as he had not rendered himself amenable to the law, I might be justified in concealing his intended turpitude. I confess that it was no sentiment of humanity that checked me from informing the physician of what he had done, but simply the selfish dread of exciting his hostility to aid the cupidity that was urging him on to discover my secret, and to make it a profitable speculation.

A bed was made up for my servant in my room, and when I became assured that he was fast asleep, an assurance given in the most convincing, but least agreeable mode imaginable, namely, by his loud snoring, I experienced a sense of relief, and freedom from constraint, that was a positive comfort. *Now* I could resign myself to slumber, of which I stood so much in need, without the dread that a sordid spy was watching my pillow, and listening with interested and evil intentions to every word that might escape my lips while I slept. It was a positive luxury to feel myself secure to enjoy refreshing sleep and the disagreeable nasal sounds that unceasingly reminded me of this fact, however unbearable I should have considered them under different circumstances, were now considered only as proofs of my safety from *espionage.* How deep, how unbroken were my slumbers that night!

Such was my total prostration of strength, that even imagination and memory remained quiescent, the body being too weak to nourish them, and not a dream troubled my repose. I awoke refreshed, and was glad to hear my servant still snoring as loudly as when I dropt asleep; and when I called him to procure me the sustenance which my weakened frame required, I listened with satisfaction to his humbly expressed hopes, "that his being such a heavy sleeper, and sometimes rather given to snoring, did not disturb me." He would have been doubtless surprised, had he been told that to these peculiarities so calculated to annoy an invalid, I owed the calm and refreshing sleep I had derived such benefit from.

"Well, Sir," said he, "how some persons do lie! why, would you believe it, Sir, Figgins, the man who sat up with you at night, said, as how you kept talking in your sleep all night long, so that he could not close them for a minute, and I can declare I never heard you say a single word all the time."

I readily believed the assertion, for I must indeed have had the lungs of a Stentor, to have talked sufficiently loud to have broken the slumber of poor Thomas, who seemed to feel an increased sentiment of attachment towards me in consideration of my not having reproached him for his infirmity of snoring.

"Yes, Sir," observed he, as he opened the shutters and drew back the curtains, "Figgins must be a great story-teller, for when I wanted not to leave you, Sir, at night, when you were so poorly, he said I snored so desperately, that were I to remain in your room, you could not get a wink of sleep; and as he told this tale to the doctor, he insisted that I should not stop in your room at night."

Well did I divine the motive of Figgins wishing to watch me at night, though experience taught me that his statement with regard to the snoring was not untrue.

"I'm glad he's gone, Sir," resumed Thomas, "for of all the prying, inquisitive chaps I ever met, he's the worst. Why, he used to cross-examine me as closely as barristers do a witness in a court of justice, about where you came from, Sir, and every particular about you, and your family affairs; and when he found he could get nothing out of me, he began to question Mary, and I was obligated to tell her not to gratify his impudent curiosity about what did not concern him."

CHAPTER XXXI.

I FELT a secret dread as I listened to the revelations of the good and simple Thomas, for they but too well proved the determination of the artful
and designing Figgins to follow up, if possible, the clue he believed he had
discovered to some secret connected with my past life. How unfortunate
that chance should have thrown so dangerous a man in my path, and especially, at a period above all others, when I was incapable of exercising over
myself the constraint practised when free from fever. Alas! we are ever the
slaves of chance when our own errors have plunged us into difficulties! Had
I not a terrible secret pent up in my breast, I should have had nothing to
dread from the prying disposition of Figgins, or the cupidity that led him
to wish to turn it to profitable account. No, every day's experience taught
me that to myself, and myself alone, I might date my misery. Every event
that had entailed disquiet, had originated in my own error. Nothing aggravates the sense of misfortune more than the consciousness that it has been
brought on by our own faults—If we can blame another it seems some
mitigation to our chagrin; but when we know that we only have been in the
wrong, our self-reproach increases our suffering.

In three days after my release from Figgins, my health had so much
improved, owing to the refreshing and uninterrupted sleep I had enjoyed,
that the doctor consented that I might see my child. The dear little creature
was brought to me; and the sight of her black dress, and smiling face, as she
recognised me, produced an effect on my feelings not to be described.

"Papa, papa," exclaimed she, holding out her little arms to come to
me, and "Mamma, mamma," followed, although the nurse made signs to
her, that the words must not be repeated. The passionate grief, quelled
by extreme bodily exhaustion, and by the terror awakened by the odious
Figgins, now revived afresh, called into action by the sight of my daughter. A child, and more especially a young one in deep mourning, is at all
times a mournful object. That a creature should be deprived of a parent,
when it most requires its tender care, strikes the beholder with sadness, and
the unconsciousness of the bereaved little one of its loss, and its innocent
smiles, offering such a melancholy contrast to its sable habiliments, add to
the sadness awakened by the contemplation. But when the child calls one
father, when one knows that its mother, the most lovely and faultless of
created beings, is no more, when one traces in the dear child's sweet face
the likeness of her laid in a premature grave, whom one would have died

to save, how keen is the agony, how bitter the grief that fills the heart! It is then that the truth of the well known lines, "I weep the more, because I weep in vain," is felt, and one turns with distaste from the world that no longer contains the object in whom our all of love and hope was centered to that lonely grave, in which rests all that was mortal of her. I almost smothered my child with my kisses, while my tears fell fast on her delicate face.

"Don't ki, papa," said she, looking fondly in my face. "Mary says, dear mamma, who is gone to heaven, will be angry if I ki, and so she will if you ki," and she wiped my eyes with a handkerchief she found on my bed, and told me to be good, and then kissed me again and again.

How much of her adored mother's gentleness and affection did I discover in her child, and with what tenderness did it fill me! Great as was my sorrow, I felt that I was no longer alone in the world. I had still something to live for, some one to cherish. A sacred bequest had been confided to me by the angel I deplored, and I vowed that henceforth I would devote my life to discharging the duties it imposed. The artless prattle of my daughter continually turning to her lost mother, melted me to a womanly softness. The tears, hitherto denied, now flowed abundantly, and relieved me, and I blessed the innocent creature to whom I owed this relief.

The following day I was able to be moved to the sofa in the sitting-room, and it was arranged that I was to receive a visit from Mrs. Neville. The thought of this meeting shook my nerve greatly. How many recollections of other and happier days must it awaken in my mind! Our loss had been the same; but she, happily for her, had not a single sin of omission or commission towards her husband with which to reproach herself, while I was towed down by the consciousness of having by my abstraction and moodiness caused my inestimable wife many hours of anxiety and wretchedness. How many bitter memories of instances of this now arose to wound me! How often had I noticed her heavy eyes and tear-stained cheeks when I had more than ordinarily indulged in these fits of gloom, which she felt she had not the power of charming away! And I, cold, unfeeling, and selfish, had forborne either to conquer the gloom which afflicted her, or attempt to persuade her, that it was constitutional, depending on the state of the nerves. How the consciousness of having pained the dear departed aggravates grief, those only can comprehend who have endured this misery! The grave! the atoning grave! while it banishes every recollection of error in those over whom it has closed, if error they had, brings before us, oh! how vividly, even the trivial annoyances we have inflicted on them, now when it is too late to offer atonement. What would we not give to possess the conviction that we had never grieved, never vexed them? This conviction I fully believed would be Mrs. Neville's panacea for sorrow when time should have softened the first sharp pangs of regret, and I envied her this consolation, which conscience told me never could be mine.

When the next day, at the appointed hour, she entered my room, I positively started with astonishment when I beheld her altered appearance. Pale as marble, and reduced almost to a shadow, she was hardly to be recognized by those who had, like me, seen her in the bloom of health and beauty. She approached the sofa on which I reclined, extended her hand, which was so icy cold as to chill mine, and tried to speak, but a tremulous movement of the lips, and a faint and indistinct sound alone followed the effort. She sank into a chair, and after a silence of many minutes, which I had not the courage to break, she at length found words.

"I have only waited for your convalescence, Mr. Herbert;" said she, "to quit Nice. I could not bear to leave the husband of my dear friend, the friend of my—beloved—husband," her agitation increasing as she referred to those so dear to her, "while his life was in danger! Now that Dr. Farrington assures me you are safe, I mean to depart and join my child. If you wish to consign yours to my care, be assured I will as faithfully fulfil the duties of a mother to her as to my own."

"Thanks, thanks," replied I; "but I have not the courage to part from her. She is now all that remains to me," and here a passionate burst of grief interrupted my words.

"I thought you would be unwilling to part from her," observed Mrs. Neville; "but remember, should circumstances arise that may occasion a change in your sentiments on this point, I will be ever ready to receive her with affection, and to afford her a home with me. Here is my address in England. Let me often hear of your dear child's welfare and of your own. I offer no attempt at consolation, Mr. Herbert, to a grief like yours, for I too well know how utterly vain and useless it would be; but recollect, and the recollection will be necessary when the bitterness of regret makes you feel that life has lost its charm, that those whose loss we must ever deplore, have confided a sacred, a solemn trust to us to fulfil—a trust for sake of which we must vanquish all selfish feelings, and consent to live. And now, farewell. May the Almighty grant you resignation to *his* will, and may you find in your dear child a consolation and a blessing!"

She once more extended her hand to me, and quitted the room, leaving me overpowered by contending emotions, but grateful that I might count on a true friend to my child, while life was spared to this amiable and exemplary woman.

The next day she left Nice, after having gravely exhorted the nurse on the subject of my daughter, promising to be ever a friend to her if she carefully discharged her duty to her charge. And now once more, all ties between the world and me seemed broken. In losing sight of Mrs. Neville I stood alone with my motherless child, the world before me where to choose my path, no one offering a less gloomy prospect than another. I no longer lived in the actual—the present. My thoughts were all with the past, in that past which at the time appeared, Heaven knows! anything but happy, but which now regarded through the mist of bitter tears, and the sadness of memory seemed bright as a rainbow in a troubled sky. But the rainbow itself, if analyzed, is it not found to be composed of the tears of the sky? Such is past happiness, only bright when reflected on from a distance. How I could be otherwise than blest while my adored Louisa was lent to me on earth, I could not in my present misery imagine. Her presence, her affection, ought to have been a solace under every affliction; and I must have been the most ungrateful of mortals; nay, more, positively mad, not to have felt it to be so. Yet I was conscious that even while I possessed this inestimable treasure, there were hours, days, and months in which I was most wretched; while now, could she but be restored to me, every other ill in life would appear light, and I would abandon my whole heart to the happiness of calling her mine. Oh, God! why is it that we know not the value of the blessings thou hast vouchsafed to lend us, until we have lost them for ever, and the consciousness of our ingratitude for them is added to our sorrow? I now wondered how I had outlived the blow that had destroyed my peace. I must surely have a harder heart than most men to bear up against it; and I almost despised myself for this insensibility. I resigned myself without a struggle to the grief that every day increased, rather than diminished. It seemed an infidelity and ingratitude to the memory of my beloved wife to forget her even for an hour; and I sought to feed this morbid sorrow by continually gazing on her portrait, and recalling proofs of her tenderness and devotion the most calculated to keep alive regret. Well has the great Italian poet Dante written—

> "Nessun maggior dolore
> Che recondarsi del tempo felice."

Alas! I now experienced the truth of these lines as I pondered with an agonized heart on past happiness.

When my child was brought to me every day, I used to gaze on her sweet face, tracing the resemblance to her sainted mother, and listening to her innocent questions. She would chide me when my tears could not be controlled—tell me it was naughty to cry—and then kiss me, and say I must be good.

I found, that the affection a father feels for his child while its mother lived, is very different to that which he experiences when she is no more, for the love and sorrow for the dead mingles with the tenderness for the living, and gives it a stronger character. Pity also adds its weight, reminding us of the deprivation that has fallen on the dear little creature, in the loss of a mother, a loss that never can be replaced—for we know, that no step-mother, should we ever be disposed to give our daughter one, could supply that inexhaustible well of affection to be found in the maternal breast. A sense of duty, and a kindness of heart, may, and sometimes does prompt a conscientious discharge of the duties of a step-mother, but how different, how cold is this duty, in comparison with the undying anxiety and love of a real mother. And as I made these reflections, I vowed, that even if time should calm my regret, although I believed this to be impossible, that never should the place of my lost Louisa be filled either in my house, or heart, that never should her child have a stepmother.

A melancholy task was now before me, but I feared it not, for it was congenial to my feelings. It was, to open different boxes that had belonged to my wife, and to transfer their contents to others, in order to diminish the vast quantity of luggage that had been deemed necessary for her comfort, and that had accumulated during our travels, and to send all that was not required for our use to England.

To perform this task, I had to enter the chamber in which my adored wife had breathed her last, and which had been left precisely in the same state as when she inhabited it. There was the bed on which she had last reposed—the pillow on which her head had last rested. It still bore the impression, and many and bitter were the tears that fell on it as I pressed my lips to the place.

The odour of violets still pervaded the chamber, and all things in it. It was the favourite perfume of my Louisa, the only one she used, and her dresses and handkerchiefs were impregnated with it. This delicate odour, so strongly associated in my mind with her, so fondly loved, so deeply mourned, stole over my senses, awakening agony, and long and bitterly did I weep, before I recovered sufficient calmness to resume the task that had brought me to the room.

There was the chamber, just as she had left it, every thing speaking to me of her, but where, oh! where was she? Alas! that fair form, that lovely face, on which my eyes had so often gazed with delight, were withering in the cold grave, and her, for whom I had thought this chamber not half good enough, was now shut in a narrow coffin! "Fool, fool," thought I, "it is but the mortal coil, the earthly envelope of the bright soul that is confided to the grave. That clay, over which thou wouldst still drop thy burning tears, would be as insensible to them, as is the dust with which it will soon mingle. The spirit, the immortal soul that animated it, is with its Creator in heaven; and let that be thy consolation. Wouldst thou, ever selfish, ever pining for thine own comfort, presume to wish her, who is now with her Almighty Father, freed from all care, and enjoying the reward of a life of virtue, back on earth, to suffer again the ills to which all of human kind are heirs?"

I tried to think I could not be so selfish, but, alas! the leaven of that human taint still fermented in my heart; and could wishes and prayers have recalled her to life, with all its trials, she would have once more become a denizen of earth, and her happiness above would be immolated to mine below. Who that has idolized a creature as I did my Louisa, can, during the first pangs of grief, learn to think of her as an unembodied spirit in the unknown realms of bliss! Those realms which imagination can never realize, and in the attempt to contemplate which the mind becomes dazzled—bewildered! when one dear to us departs on a journey to some far distant clime, where we have never been, how is our regret increased by the vastness of the distance, and our ignorance of the region! We seek every source whence we can derive information of it, and as we become acquainted with its nature, customs, and habits, we feel more reconciled, because we can, in some sort, realize the image of our beloved one in the scenes we have been studying. But when the King of Terrors snatches her from us, to that world, at the portal of which (the grave) we must leave her, that shadowy region, of which we know nothing but that which religion teaches, of which we can learn nothing, though we search every volume ever written by man, of which no traveller who has journeyed there has ever been permitted to return to tell us of it.—Oh! then do we feel the bitterness of grief: nor can the hope, the faith, that the spirit whose departure has steeped our life in gloom, is in heaven, conquer the selfishness, the anguish of regret!

If departed souls were permitted to revisit this earth, to hover near us, to give some sign that we were remembered, even in the regions of the blessed, what a consolation would it be! But this is denied. The Almighty, for *His* own all-wise purposes, has not thought fit to grant this boon for which every bereaved and sorrowing heart has longed, and prayed in vain during the first months of the sharp agony of grief.

CHAPTER XXXII.

I OPENED the wardrobe containing the clothes of my wife. The *robes de chambre* that had last enveloped her fragile form, were the first articles that met my view. "Oh, God!" cried I, "that these delicate fabrics can still retain their freshness, when she for whom they were made, who so lately wore them, is mouldering in the grave! Are we not like shadows that flit through life a brief span, to go hence and be no more seen? Life is all unstable! We know not when we shall be called away; we cannot count on a single day of existence."

This conviction, however alarming it ought to be to the erring, is, nevertheless, the greatest consolation to the mourner, and fondly does he cling to it. Death is the only certainty on earth. Every thing else is fleeting away, but *that* is sure; and as we contemplate the habiliments of the departed, the objects that appertained to them, the letters they wrote, the books they read, we feel as in an unreal and shadowy world, on a river ever flowing to the sea of eternity, where our frail bark can cast no anchor, and whence the next wave may bear it off for ever. I almost doubted my own existence, so absorbed was I in the contemplation of death, or, if reminded of it, it was only by the pangs of grief.

How many times were the dresses of my departed wife pressed to my lips, and bathed in the tears that fell on them! How many tender recollections did they evoke! What appeals to the heart did they make! "No never," exclaimed I, "shall these robes be worn by another, save by her child. They shall be kept until she becomes old enough to use them, and I will often look at them, to keep alive in my breast the image of her who wore them, fresh as it now is."

And could my treacherous memory, or faithless heart, require such mementos to keep alive that image? I was angered with myself as this thought occurred; but such is man. Even in the midst of sorrow he has a presentiment, that unless death should soon summon him away, a day may come, when the anguish he is enduring will soften into a gentler feeling, become a pensive sentiment, and that the sight of such mementos may be necessary to revive fond memories of the past. He has seen others live on when robbed of all that made life dear. He has seen the deepest mourners come back to the busy world, after a year or two has elapsed, since they fled from it in agony. He has seen smiles return to the lips whence he believed they were for ever banished, and pleasure sparkle in the eyes where it had been drowned by tears. He learns to know the frailty of man, and the brevity of grief, by having witnessed the conduct of others, and in anticipating the possibility of similar results in himself, he loathes his own nature.

Having filled the trunks with the contents of the wardrobe, performing the operation with as light a hand as if the dresses could feel a rough touch, I proceeded to open the writing-box of my lost Louisa. A little *sachet*, filled with her favourite odour of violets, was at the top, and beneath it was her blotting-book. My hand trembled when I drew it forth and opened its pages; amid which I found the well-remembered diary of her poor sister, and one also kept by herself, which I had never previously seen, or suspected the existence of. The first leaf contained the following notes.—

How my heart throbbed and ached as I perused them! And yet I hesitated whether I should read on. I doubted whether I had a right to make myself acquainted with her secret thoughts. I feared I might find passages that would aggravate my chagrin, and I was already so wretched, so hopeless, that coward-like, I shrank from any increase of woe. But then came the reflection, that nothing could increase my sorrow, so deep, so overwhelming did I feel it to be at that moment, and although I suspected that jealousy and selfishness sharpened the edge of my curiosity, I nevertheless read on.—

"I have seen *him*, and though his long and severe illness has left him pale, emaciated, and helpless as an infant, I was greatly struck with his appearance. Perhaps the impression was heightened by these very circumstances, for nothing appeals more to the heart than these silent indications of suffering, and in a man, too, who is less liable to them than woman.—His face is very expressive, and to my taste, very handsome; yet there sometimes steals over it a cloud of sorrow and anxiety, which proves his thoughts are not with the present. This is but natural in his position; the loss of such a mother as his must be deeply felt, and I who knew and loved her so truly, can well sympathise in his regret. He must possess great sensibility, for my mother has told me that the interest he took in our terrible afflictions, was as warm and profound as if he had known that angelic being, whose loss we must ever deplore. He constantly raved of her during his delirium, and even wept her loss. This alone, were he even plain instead of being attractive, would make me"—(here a line was drawn through the word love) "esteem him" was substituted.

"I have seen him again—he improves greatly on acquaintance. His languor, his low spirits, and his frequent abstraction, increase my interest for him. One who thus deeply mourns a mother, must have a tender heart, for I have heard that in that busy world whence he has come, such deprivations are soon forgotten. Yet how can such afflictions be effaced from the heart, before time, the consoler, has healed the wound. Alas! do I not experience the truth of this?—Do I not every hour, nay, every minute, feel that mine is a grief that will ever endure, although it may be softened.

"There is nothing that awakens attachment, I do believe, so strongly as sympathy in sorrow. Well has Schiller said:—

'The tie that binds the happy may be dear,
But that which links the unfortunate is tenderness unutterable.'

I don't think, handsome and clever as I consider Mr. Herbert to be, that he would have made such a deep impression on me had we not been stricken by grief. Perhaps my dear mother's constant commendations of him,—her having repeated to me his raving of my dear sister, joined to my affection and gratitude to his excellent parent, have aided to increase the sentiment. I must not, however, allow myself to like him too well. But have I now the power to check this too strong preference? I fear not; and *I* blush as I record the unmaidenly fact of liking one who has not owned a passion,—nay more, who may never feel one for me. But pity for his languid state opened my heart to a stronger feeling. And yet there is an inexpressible softness in his eyes when they meet mine, and an earnestness in his manner when he addresses me, that lead me to think I am not indifferent to him. But, perhaps, all men—that is to say, young men—assume these indescribable looks and manner when they address young women. I know so little of the world, how should it be otherwise? having always lived in such total seclusion, that what I take as indications of a preference for me, may be only the general mode adopted by men towards the youthful of my sex. I have never known—never even seen—another young man, except the artist who made a sketch of my adored sister, and his manner was deferential, and nothing more. How I wish I knew whether Mr. Herbert's attention to me is more than mere politeness would dictate, or simply gratitude for my mother's and my attention.

"There is a melancholy expression in his eyes when he gazes on me that goes to my heart. How I should like to dispel *his* grief,—though Heaven knows my own still lives with all its pangs and regrets. Perhaps it is the intensity of it that has so softened my heart, as to have rendered it more susceptible of affection. How often do I question myself how I can live on,—how I can permit another object to replace in my breast that dear, dear sister, who, till lately, wholly filled it? It may be that Heaven, in mercy, has decreed that this new, this engrossing affection, should occur to save me from despair! Who shall circumscribe the pity, the goodness of God!

And if without *His* will, even a sparrow cannot fall,—may not I, a human
being, however frail and erring, hope that His commiseration and mercy
descends to me. If *He* has willed that my adored sister, the half, the *better*
half, of myself, should be snatched from me, her fate shrouded in a mystery, that adds all the pangs of suspense to horror and grief,—may *He* not
have vouchsafed to grant this new sentiment to preserve me from—madness? There have been moments when my brain throbbed with such agony,
and such a sense of despair came over me that I trembled for my reason.
And could it be otherwise? Who could bear to think that a creature dearer
than life itself should suddenly disappear, leaving no trace behind—no clue
to lead to a discovery of her fate? Oh God! oh God! is not here cause for
despair—for madness? Had she died in my arms; had I closed those dear
eyes, every glance of which is so fondly remembered; had I seen her laid in
her silent grave, every duty to the loved dead faithfully, tenderly fulfilled;
and could I daily visit it, and drop my tears over the spot, it would be a
comparative happiness. I should then know that her dear remains were
safe from insult, that her spirit was with God. But this terrible mystery, this
fearful suspense,—oh, it is heart-breaking! If thou art still an inhabitant
of earth, oh, most beloved sister, how bitter must be the grief which thou
art condemned to endure, for thy compelled separation from us, and the
agony thou knowest it must inflict on us!—I can write no more, my tears
fall so fast that they blind me."

"We found him better to-day. The pallor of sickness is giving place to a
faint tinge of red in his cheeks. His voice, too, is less weak and tremulous.
Yet he is unwilling to admit this improvement. Is it that he fears his admission to convalescence would no longer offer a motive for our visits? Yes, it
must be so; and may I not receive this little *ruse* on his part as a proof that
our presence is a source of pleasure to him. How ingenious I am in finding
food for hope! Heaven grant I may not deceive myself—and yet may not he
derive comfort from having his solitude broken by the friends of his dear
mother, unable as he still is to leave home? Who possesses such power to
soothe and console in sickness and sorrow, as my mother?—and may not
this power in her make him most desirous for a continuance of her visits,
without any reference to mine? It is most probably so; and I, vain and simple, have fancied what I hoped. I feel more sad and dispirited than of late;
such is ever the result of indulging false hopes."

"Yes, he is certainly making daily advances to convalescence. He looked
much better to-day. I used to think that much of the beauty of his face

might be attributed to its paleness and pensive expression; yet now that these gradually disappear, I begin to think he appears to even greater advantage.—How strange it is that I should know, or rather feel, that he is looking at me, when I dare not lift my eyes to his face.—This frequently occurs. Can I be wrong in thinking that these fond glances,—the softened tone of his voice when he speaks to me, must mean something more than mere ordinary attention. Oh no, he does, he must love me!"

"Heaven be praised, my fears, my doubts are over. He loves me, and we are affianced! How much can a few short hours accomplish! How much of joy, and alas, of sorrow too, can be crowded into them! I accompanied my dear mother yesterday as usual, to visit him, determined to examine more closely than ever whether or not I was deceiving myself into a belief of his affection. He looked so much better in health that my mother, thinking our daily visits no longer necessary, confessed to him that her increasing weakness warned her that the exertion was too much. And I, ungrateful and selfish, had not remarked the change in her aspect, had not noticed the fatigue which these daily walks had occasioned.

"As the avowal fell from her tremulous lips, I gazed on her face, and noted with a sharp pang of the heart, how pale, how care-worn it had grown. I arose, and bursting into a passionate fit of tears, pressed her in my arms, forgetful of all but that I might lose her. Then it was that he avowed his love for me, and entreated that she would accept him for a son. Oh, the mingled feelings of joy and sorrow of that moment! He spoke better than man ever spoke before. He was all tenderness to me, and dutiful devotion to my mother. She consented to our union, and blessed us; and it was agreed that he should henceforth come daily to our house. He insisted on walking back with us, and proved he was quite equal to the exertion; nay more, acknowledged that he had tried to conceal his recovery, lest we should discontinue our visits, or think his too frequent ones importunate. Why should joy and grief follow so closely on the steps of each other? Tears streamed down my cheeks, and my frame trembled like the leaves of the aspen, as I listened to the fondest vows that ever escaped the lips of man. Such a deep sense of content thrilled my soul, and agitated my frame, that I thought I should have fainted. Oh! my sister, why art thou not here, that I might weep tears of joy and thankfulness on thy bosom, that I might whisper in thine ear, how for long and weary days, and sleepless nights, my hopes have been dashed to the earth by torturing doubts. But now there is an end of doubt, he has asked for my hand, I feel my happiness poisoned by thy absence, and by the uncertainty of thy fate."

"I have learned to distinguish his step from that of all others, and to know his knock at the door. Nay more, to *feel* when he is approaching, before I can see him. Strange prescience of love, how mysterious art thou!

"Now that my attention has been drawn to my dear mother's declining health, I find myself frequently examining her face with an extreme anxiety.—Yes, she has grown very thin, and very pale, and her eyes have lost their bright expression of intelligence—Oh, God of mercy, deprive me not of her too; in pity leave me my mother!"

CHAPTER XXXIII.

"My whole being seems changed within the last two days—I am no longer the same person since I have known that he loves me, that our destinies are to be henceforth inseparable until death! That surely is one of the most trying hours in woman's life, when the man she has long loved in secret, authorizes her affection, by the avowal of his own! He told me he had loved me from the first, and had only been withheld from declaring his passion, by the sorrow in which both of us were plunged. How I approve this delicacy on his part. My dear mother is pleased, though not surprised, at the proposal for my hand. She feels all a mother's tenderness for him, for her attachment to his parent disposed her to like him, and the deep sympathy he evinced in our affliction, rivetted the chain of affection. He too, entertains a sincere regard and respect for her, which is testified by his dutiful attention."

"His visits are now those of an affianced husband. He comes early and stays late, and yet time flies so rapidly when he is here, that the hours seem to have wings. His fits of gloom and abstraction are much less frequent, and he is occasionally even gay; but gaiety is not natural to him. No, his is a thoughtful mind, a melancholy temperament, and this it was that attracted me towards him. I am sure I never could have loved a lively man, one who could make me laugh. Such a one may be a very amusing companion; but could not, according to my notions, excite a deep attachment. Women are born to love but once, and although they may sometimes be mistaken, and fancy that a real passion, which is but a preference, that subsides when the object is better known. I feel by my own experience, that the deep emotion, the all-engrossing sentiment of love can never be twice felt, and that the peculiarities of the beloved, though not attractive to others, become so to her who loves. I would not have my betrothed changed in aught, except that I should like to see his occasional moodiness dispelled, by happiness to be derived from my affection and devotion. Grant me, O God! but the power to render his life a scene of peace and content, and I shall be the happiest of women.

"What a solemn trust is the happiness of a man we love, when he confides it to our care! With what a firm resolution to guard it religiously, should we accept the responsibility! and with what a deep sense of gratitude to the Almighty, should we kneel and thank Him that we, by no merit of our own, but by His mercy, are endowed with the power of preserving it.

"They are unjust who say that love is a selfish passion—I am sure it is not so with women, at least, not with the good of our sex. We live in another, *his* well-being is far dearer to us than our own, and I believe that there are few of us who would not sooner resign the beloved to another, whom we thought could confer happiness on him, than retain him after the discovery that *we* could not bestow it. Who could bear to behold the beloved unhappy, with the heart-breaking, withering consciousness, that she possessed not the power to soothe, to cheer him? Heaven preserve me from ever feeling this—it would be the only misery I could not endure."

"Still no tidings of my adored sister; although rewards have been offered for intelligence—Oh! this terrible suspense. Never do I press my pillow without a shudder at the thought of where her dear head may now rest. We avoid speaking of her, for it excites such agony in us all, but she is constantly in our thoughts—my dear mother and I, are not more overpowered by any reference to her, than is my betrothed husband, and this sympathy in our grief, for one he never saw, increases my tenderness tenfold. I often wish he had seen, had known her; yet, had this been the case, could he have loved me, who am so inferior to her?"

How often during the perusal of this artless journal, did my tears fall on it, and how bitterly did my conscience reproach me for my own unworthiness of the treasure I once possessed. To be so loved, and by one so pure, so admirable, was indeed a blessing I did not merit, a blessing I was not capable of duly appreciating, until I trembled in anticipation of its loss, and was smitten by the realization of my worst fears—I groaned in agony—I called on her to take pity on me, as if my prayers could be granted, until overcome by my grief and remorse, I sank powerless on the couch on which I had thrown myself. How vividly arose her lovely image before me, such as she was when she had written the early portion of that journal! How

well did I remember the suffusion of her fair and delicate cheeks, when
I entered her mother's dwelling of a morning; the mild radiance of her
eyes as they met my impassioned glance! And had I not found her all that
my warmest, fondest imagination had ever pictured? Had not the excel-
lence of her nature, the noble simplicity and guilelessness of her mind,
fully equalled the matchless charms of her person? And this creature with
more of heaven,—oh! how infinitely more!—than of earth in her composi-
tion, had been mine, had loved me as only the unerring, and the excellent
deserve to be loved, and yet while thus blessed, I could, forgetful of the
treasure I possessed, give way to gloom, to moodiness, and embitter her
life; nay more, abridge it, by my conduct.

An irresistible impulse led me to take up the journal again, although
every line of it planted a dagger in my heart. Well was she avenged by the
tortures I now endured for every pain I had ever inflicted on her; and I experienced a melancholy satisfaction in my own sufferings in the vain belief
that they might be accepted as an expiation for my wrongs to her.

How long, how intimately may we live with a being most dear to us,
without being acquainted with the thoughts that are every day, every hour,
passing through her mind. A look, a word, may chill the confidence that
was springing to her lips, inspiring a dread of not being understood, or of
not meeting sympathy. And then she poured out in secret the overflowing
measure of her heart on paper, carefully concealing what ought, ay, and
what would have been poured into the enraptured ears of a husband, who
had not ceased to be a lover, had he not permitted the foul fiend, moodiness, to scare away the confidence of love. I must have been mad to have so
acted, but now, too late, reason had resumed her empire over my brain, and
tortured memory, lashing me like the fabled furies, allowed me no rest.

Again I resumed the perusal of the journal, though certain it could only
bring me increase of woe.

"All is settled, and in a few days I am to be his. Oh! the happiness of
belonging wholly, of being entirely dependent on the husband of one's
choice. 'To love, honour, and obey!' How easy seems the fulfilment of
this solemn engagement! I would not for all the wealth of Eastern climes
wed a man whom I could not conscientiously swear before the altar of
God to love, honour, and obey—Even should his commands be sometimes
opposed to my own wishes, would it not be still sweet to sacrifice them to
his? Would it not be a new proof of love, and duty, although he may never
discover that inclination was opposed to it; and who, that has a heart filled
with tenderness, but must rejoice in every opportunity of expending a por-

tion of its wealth on the beloved? I feel that the utmost indulgence of my own wishes could never afford me half the gratification that must ensue from yielding them to his. It is with this conviction that I will pledge my faith to him at the altar, that I will through life make the study of his happiness the object of my life."

"My future husband has arranged that my mother is to leave her home and partake ours; and this has been done with a delicacy, a kindness, that enhances the favour he has conferred on me. This arrangement was proposed the day he owned his love, but had it been less frequently, less warmly, less affectionately urged, it might not have been accepted by my dear mother. It has given the finishing touch to my happiness, and has, if possible, increased my love to my betrothed. May heaven enable me to repay him for all this goodness, this attention and forethought to my comfort. Often did the notion of my poor mother in her solitary home, when I should have left her, present itself to my mind, before she consented to live with us; and it formed the sole sombre shade in my anticipated happiness: but a timidity I could not vanquish, checked my naming my wishes; now my betrothed has removed this shade, and left me nothing to desire. How is every blessing, every good, enhanced by its being derived from the person dearest to us in life! Great blessings seem greater, and even trivial ones assume an importance from the medium through which they are vouchsafed. I feel such gratitude towards my future husband, that ingratitude, a crime that always appeared peculiarly odious in my eyes, now seems doubly so, and is the sin I should feel least disposed to pardon."

"How wonderful is the influence of love on the heart that truly feels the passion! Mine is so filled with a desire that all of human kind should experience a similar blessing, and with pity for those deprived of it, that though never uncharitable, I am more than ever disposed to sympathize with my fellow creatures. Surely a spark from the divinity is granted to us when love enters our hearts, when it can thus fill them with charity and commiseration. This belief soothes and comforts me, for I could not bear to think that love was a selfish passion.

"Why is it that there must ever be some drawback in happiness? Is it that poor mortals are not formed for so great a blessing, without alloy; that they are unworthy of it?—Yes, it must be so; and we should accept with humble gratitude that portion which it has pleased the Almighty to accord us, instead of ungratefully murmuring that our share has not been so great as our vanity and presumption may have led us to expect. The alloy to my happiness springs from the occasional gloom I notice in my betrothed. And yet, may not this gloom be accounted for by the loss of his mother, scarcely six months dead, and who died ere he could receive her parting blessing? My grief for that sad event, and, alas! for even a still more terrible one, has been soothed, that I, perhaps unreasonably, expect that as *his* love has been my consolation under such heavy affliction, *mine* ought to have become his."

"He is making great alterations and improvements in his house for our reception. He need not have gone to such expense as I fear he has incurred, for I should have been well satisfied with an humble home with him. He has asked me many questions not only about my peculiar tastes, but also about those of my dear mother, that they may be taken into consideration in the furnishing arrangements. His attention to my mother is quite touching, and is one of the most gratifying proofs of his affection for me."

"This has been a melancholy day, and my spirits droop sadly. To leave the home my dear lost sister shared with us, in every part of which we can identify her with past days of happiness, is a new trial, though I leave this home for that of my beloved. In that dwelling I, fortunately, can also call up her dear image to occupy the places she was wont to fill in it, when she lived——

"When she lived—Oh! God, and does she no longer live? must I abandon all hope of ever again beholding her on earth? Ah! yes, it must be so; I can no longer cheat myself with a hope, that every day proves fallacious. Were she snatched away by aught save death, some tidings must have reached us of her. She could not so long have been kept concealed! Never do I look on the river without a shudder, for some secret presentiment tells me, that in its bed she may have found a grave! I remember how in the twilight hour she was wont to wander along the path near the edge of the rock. If in that uncertain light, and absorbed as I have often seen her, she approached too near the precipice, and fell over it into the water, she may have been swept away by the current far from the reach of those employed to search for her! Oh Heaven! to think of that lovely face, those flowing tresses, that delicate form exposed to such a fate: my brain grows dizzy, my temples throb, and my heart aches with agony, as I dwell on it. Oh! for a Lethean draught to drown these terrible thoughts; yet no, ever beloved sister, I would not, if I could, forget thee.

"To-morrow, I am to be his, and am to leave this house. I have been to her chamber, have packed up her clothes, books, and papers. Oh the pain of the task! But I dared not let my dear mother perform it. How vividly did the sight of all these things bring her image before me! Of how many incidents did they remind me. To think that these habiliments should still retain their pristine freshness, while she who wore them is—but no, I dare not trust myself to finish the sentence.

"In her desk I found a book, in which she had occasionally noted down her thoughts. It is now all that remains of her. Strange! I find on perusing this little journal that she had a sort of mysterious instinct that her fate was to be in some way or other connected with my future husband.—I felt myself grow cold, and a shudder pass over me, as I read the passage.—But now that I have reflected on it, may it not have been that she had a presci- ence that he might love either herself or me, and in either case would he not have been connected with her destiny? Yes, this must be the significa- tion of the passage.

"I have wept many tears over her little journal. She felt a foreboding of an early death. Her abstraction, her occasional sadness, and her lively tenderness for my dear mother and me was kept alive by this presentiment. Dear, blessed sister! I thought I had loved thee, fondly, dearly, before thou wert snatched from us, but I knew not until now how unutterably dear thou wert to my heart.

"He has gone home, and for the last time alone. To-morrow we are to be united, never more to be separated until death.—He came all joy, in the anticipation of to-morrow, and found me with eyes swollen from weeping, and spirits subdued beyond my power of concealing my chagrin. He seemed pained, and hurt, as well as surprised at my sad face and deep emotion; and to account for it I permitted him to read the cause. It greatly moved him. He changed colour several times as he perused the pages, and his hand really trembled when he read aloud her presentiment that he was to be connected with her fate. How I love him for this deep, this womanly sensibility. He fell into frequent musings during the day, and though no less tender, was thoughtful and pensive up to the moment of our parting."

CHAPTER XXXIV.

"'LET no man say hereafter, this shall be a day of happiness,' says the proverb, and never did I feel the wisdom of the warning so deeply as now. This, that was to have been a day of happiness, how is it changed! Oh! may the wretchedness of my nuptial day, not prove an omen of that which is to follow it. But I must not give way to superstitious forebodings. Heaven knows, that 'sufficient unto the day, is the evil thereof.' This morning I pledged my faith to him at the altar, and was welcomed—Oh how fondly welcomed!—to be the mistress of his home. From the moment that I entered it, fresh and most pleasurable surprises met me at every step, all due to his forethought and ever-watchful affection. The house is a little paradise, so embellished, so filled with all that can gratify the eye, and contribute to comfort, that the first glance given to it would prove that a fond, a tasteful, a generous lover, had presided over its arrangements, to receive the mistress of his heart. Unused to aught save simple comfort, the elegance of every thing around surprised me. In every room fresh surprise and pleasure awaited me, but most of all in those appropriated to my dear mother's use. Nothing that could contribute to her ease and comfort, has been omitted, and tears of gratitude started to my eyes, when I beheld how gratified she was by these proofs of my husband's filial thoughtfulness and affection. I heard her, when she thought she was unobserved, murmur a prayer for his happiness, and I felt I never loved her so fondly as at that moment. We went from room to room, wondering, and admiring, and I thought that were my lost, my beloved sister, but with us, never was human felicity greater than mine would be. Yes, I thought of her, as I ever do when aught occurs to give me pleasure,—it is so natural to wish her to share it. But six months of sorrow—oh! that grief should so soon become consoled—had accustomed, though not reconciled me to her loss, and latterly I have learned, such is poor human nature, to look forward to happiness without *her*, who once formed its chief ingredient. But terribly have I been punished for my obliviousness! A couple or so of happy hours had only glided by, they seemed but minutes, when a man rode hurriedly to the gate. I saw him first, and my heart instantly foreboded some coming shock, although it divined not what. My happiness seemed too great for any addition, and the happy must ever tremble for the stability of their bliss. This man brought the intelligence that *her* remains, the remains of my adored sister, had been found in the river! And this on my wedding-day! The messenger, a vulgar and brutal man, entered into details relative to the state of the dear remains, that caused my flesh to creep, and filled me with a sickening horror, never to be described. Oh God! Oh God! to think of that lovely being defiled by—I cannot finish the sentence, it is too, too terrible. This unfeeling man made coarse allusions about my marriage, that cut me to the very soul. Oh! why did I consent to marry until the remains of my dear Frances had been found, and consigned to a consecrated grave? It was wrong, it was indelicate! But yet, my dear mother advised, nay, pressed my marriage. She said it would make her mind more easy to know I had secured a protector, that it would make her less fearful to die. But this man's coarse allusions have shocked, have alarmed my conscience, and I now wish I had postponed these ill-omened nuptials, until at least a year had elapsed since we lost my beloved sister. It was too soon to think of happiness! They who only count months since the date of an affliction, and behold the mourners with their tears wiped away, and smiles once more returning to the lips, know not, cannot know, the hours of sorrow from the first wild and frantic outbreak of it, to the different stages when tears relieve the heart. And then comes memory, calling up vividly images, that again make them gush forth in agony, and imagination lends her aid to prolong anguish, by painting happiness that might have been ours, had death not dashed it to the ground. All these stages the mourner must pass through. But who sees them? True sorrow is ever shy of exposing its depths to casual observers, and only in privacy gives way to its anguish. How often, after a short respite from grief, passed in the society of those dear to us do its pangs return in the solitude of night, to reproach us for having, even for a brief hour, forgotten our dead!

"Perhaps we ought to have evinced more satisfaction at the finding of the dear remains of my sister, than we did; and so we should have done, had the messenger who came to announce it arrived on any other day. But we had wound up our feelings to a high pitch, and the unexpected change from happiness to renewed grief, was too sudden, too terrible, to meet us prepared to bear it as we ought. When the first overwhelming shock was somewhat softened down, it was decided that my husband was to accompany our old nurse to Pendine, where the loved remains are resting. She will, it is hoped, be able to identify them, which my dear husband could not. He set out with her almost immediately, to see that all due respect be shown, and to accompany the funeral here.

"Oh! what an evening have I passed! Compelled to stifle my own grief, in order to endeavour to soothe that of my mother. All around seems changed. These rooms, that charmed me in the morning, look gloomy and funereal now; *he* is gone, and the severe wound inflicted by my dear sister's death, has opened afresh, and bleeds more than ever. What a terrible trial for him, too!

"The night wind seems to have a portentous and an unearthly sound. The birds of night mingle their wild cries with it, as they hover near my window; and as I gaze around, my eyes dread to encounter some shadowy object, so fearfully excited are my overstrained nerves. Ah! can it be, that I should dread to behold thy blest shade, my sister! *I*, who have so often, within the last six months, prayed in the silence of night, that it might be accorded me to behold thee, even if but for a minute! But oh! the fearful difference between what my imagination pictured, and the terrible reality! Hadst thou gone down to the grave in all thy virginal and unprofaned beauty, the shade would have been associated in my mind with that living loveliness, I so well, so fondly remember.

"But now—after six months exposure to the deforming, the defacing influence of the turbid waters, in which thou hast lain, and contact with the inhabitants therein that dwell,—imagination, terrified by the fearful images that present themselves, invoked by the terrible details of the messenger, turns in horror away, to shut out the appalling sight; and affrighted reason trembles lest it should be overthrown. Thou, who wast so fair—so pure—my sister; why wast thou not doomed to a milder fate? Why?—But let me not impiously question the decrees of Providence!

"How like a troubled dream does the latter part of the past day appear! A day that opened so brightly! And *he*, my beloved,—my husband,—what a task he has to fulfil! How shall I ever reward him sufficiently for what he is undergoing for my sake! May heaven grant him health and courage to fulfil it! I will pray to the Almighty—to that throne of mercy, whence only consolation can be derived in such trials.——"

"I am more calm. Oh! the soothing influence of prayer! I have prayed for my husband for the first time; and, as I pronounced the word husband, a blessed ray of consolation seemed to enter my soul. No! I cannot be quite wretched while *he* is spared to me.

"A letter has just reached me, from him. How thoughtful of him to write! Strange! that this, the first letter he ever wrote me, should be on so sad, so grievous a subject,—a subject that precluded all expression of love, or reference to the position in which we stand to each other. I love him the more for this delicacy to my grief. Few men would, I believe, be capable of such forbearance.—To-morrow I shall see him again, to part no more. The funeral will take place, and he will accompany it. We shall meet in the church,—in the church, where her dear remains will be laid!"

"In the church to-day I met the living and the dead—both so inexpressibly dear to my heart. The house of God was filled with our neighbours— come to offer the last mark of respect to the honoured dead. There was not a dry eye in the church. Yesterday, the same humble friends witnessed a different scene. They attended my marriage: some strewed flowers on our path,—all blessed us!—What may not a day bring forth! The coffin, borne by neighbours, was followed by my husband. Oh! how death-like was the paleness of his face. I thought—but it might only be fancy—that he rather avoided than sought my mother's glance and mine. And I, although a shudder passed over my frame at finding myself so near that dear corse I had so often prayed to see, but never more may behold, and that my heart seemed to die within me,—yet could not resist turning to him in this solemn hour of trial, for consolation to bear it. What a touching ceremony is the burial one! How faints the heart when the earth rattles on the coffin of one dearer than life! Oh! my sister, when last we parted, who could have believed we were to meet no more on earth? That the coffin that contains thy dear remains, was all of thee I should ever again behold! Oh! that dark and dreary vault, where thou art laid! But there, also, sleeps her who so fondly loved thee,—thy early, thy constant friend,—the mother of my husband; and there, too, will those who will never forget thee be likewise laid! Now, alas! all suspense is over. We know where thy remains rest; we can weep over the spot!

"The sad, sad ceremony over, my husband joined us. How cold and trembling was his hand, when it pressed mine. We none of us could speak, and were almost blinded by our tears.—He and I supported my dear mother to our home; but he made no vain attempt to offer consolation.— He evinced the deepest sympathy in our sorrow; and, had he known her whom we mourn, he could not betray more regret. The wound that had become nearly healed, now bleeds afresh; and I feel as if I had only now lost my sister.

"Our good nurse says he is an angel, and that his grief for the dead, and his kindness to her, cannot be described. My dear mother was melted greatly by this account, and again blessed him solemnly. He has brought us a long lock of her hair—that beautiful hair of which I was so proud. Strange to say, it exhibits no mark of deterioration from its long exposure to the water, but is fine and silken as ever. Even this is a consolation, and takes off from the horror I experienced, when imagination pictured her, after the details of the man who found her. The treasures of the East would not tempt me to part from this ringlet. My dear mother, too, values it beyond all price, and has bathed it with her tears.

"My husband conducted me to my chamber to-night, imprinted a kiss on my brow, and betook himself to the dressing-room that adjoins it, in which there is a small bed. How this delicacy and consideration for my feelings touches me, and endears him still more to my heart!—I can hear him every time he moves in the next room, and I feel a confidence, a relief, in knowing he is so near me.—He speaks.—He seems to suffer.—Shall I awake him?—No, I have not courage to enter his room. His dreams are probably haunted by the painful events of the last two days. Heaven bless and comfort him! He little knows, that, unable to sleep, I am noting down my thoughts as an occupation, a melancholy one though it be, through the dreary hours of this long night.—He breathes more calmly now, and has ceased to rave. Dear, precious love, may nought henceforth disturb his slumbers, and may the consciousness of a painful duty, so tenderly, so admirably fulfilled towards the living and the dead, procure him calm and refreshing sleep.—I, too, will seek my pillow.—"

"I arose early this morning, and was dressed before my husband was awake. *My husband!* there is something sweet and comforting in the very sound of these two words. They assure me that I have a tender friend, a sure protector for life!

"What a holy institution is marriage! By it, two destinies are mingled in one; two human beings, frail and weak as mortals ever are, acquire support and strength in mutual reliance. The woman, the weaker, feels confident in the protection of her husband, whose arm will shield her through existence, from those dangers which beset the path of her who stands alone, and the man knows, that he has secured a fond companion, a sympathizing friend, a tender nurse, should sickness overtake him—one, in short, who will share his cares as well as his pleasures. Yes, marriage is a blessed institution! Grant me, O God! the grace never to violate a single one of the sacred duties it imposes."

"He came to me the moment he was dressed, and pressed me fondly in his arms. I wept on his breast, for my feelings were touched by his tenderness, and I thought of *her* who was yesterday laid in the grave; whose fate, alas! was so different from mine. Oh! why was a similar happiness to mine not reserved for her, for *her* who so well merited every blessing! He seemed to comprehend the cause of my tears, wiped them gently away, and whispered—

"'May I never bring a tear to these dear eyes; and may I have the power to console you, my sweet Louisa, for all the chagrin endured during the last months.'

"We descended to the breakfast-room; he placed me at the head of the table; my dear mother, having had a sleepless night, was now slumbering; and thus our first morning repast was taken *tête-à-tête*. Every little incident gave him pleasure. The pouring out his tea, the seasoning it to his taste, called forth expressions of affection and gratitude; and we both felt that a *tête-à-tête* breakfast is a most delightful thing, even though sorrow has banished joy. Then came good Mrs. Burnet to receive orders for dinner, and she looked so pleased to see me at the head of the table, that my dear husband told her *she* must still be housekeeper, as he intended to occupy my time so much as to leave me none for managing household concerns. Then followed his consultation about what I best liked for dinner. He remembered what he had seen me prefer at my old home, and also our dear mother's favourite dishes. How thoughtful, how kind!—Then I would insist on having *his*, and a little contest ensued, which ended by his saying that I should have it all my own way, and good Mrs. Burnet went away smiling, as if she thought us both children. How puerile seem all these little details, and yet what happiness did they not confer on me while passing? But do not puerile details occupy a great portion of existence? and may not the spirit which presides over them greatly tend to infuse happiness,—or,—the reverse? What is, what can be trifling that elicits or proves affection? My dear mother will breakfast in her room, and I must go to see that her morning meal does not go away untasted. He has made me promise to ask admission for him to go and wish her good-morrow."

CHAPTER XXXV.

"Of all the modes taken by a man of sensibility to prove his affection for the woman he loves, there is none that so perfectly convinces her of it, as his attention and kindness to those dear to her. I feel the truth of this when I see the thousand different little marks of assiduity to add to her comforts, and gratify her tastes, which my husband shows to our dear mother. There is a respectful tenderness in his attention to her, that fills me with satisfaction, and greatly touches her feelings. I should be miserable if my husband betrayed indifference to my mother, or only treated her with mere politeness. Why is it, that in the midst of so many causes for happiness, I am often low-spirited, or rather, I should say, why do I frequently detect symptoms of gloom in him on whom my happiness depends? I tremble for his health, for I observe in him a certain susceptibility of nerves, so unusual even in women, as to justify my fears that he is far from well.—He admitted the other day that he had been attacked by spasms of the heart, and the dread of a return of them, has haunted me ever since. I was greatly vexed with myself lately, when overcome by my foolish, but uncontrollable terror of mice, I saw one run along the room, and, like a silly child, I screamed aloud and rushed away. He echoed my cry, and turning pale as marble, seemed ready to faint, and it was some time before he recovered the shock. What watchful tenderness, what doting love! But I must be on my guard not to startle or alarm him henceforth."

"Must we ever tremble for the health of those dear to us? My dear mother's state gives me great uneasiness, and when I betray it, she tells me that she feels she must soon leave me. Even my dear husband, ever so desirous to give me comfort, holds out no hope of her restoration to health. Dear, dear mother, and must I lose thee? Can no healing art bring back health, no filial tenderness, and untiring devotion prolong thy precious life? I cannot fix my eyes on that dear pallid face, without tears starting into them, at the notion that it may soon be hidden from my gaze for ever.

"The physician whom my husband summoned from Pendine, said that the case was hopeless. A total breaking up of the system, as he termed it, occasioned, I am sure, by the loss of my beloved sister. The lowness of my spirits on account of my dear mother's declining state, has such an effect on those of my husband, that I feel the absolute necessity of assuming a cheerfulness, which, alas! is foreign to my heart. He too is deeply affected about her, and watches over her with as much care tenderness as I do. Oh! what a blessing was accorded me, when heaven, in mercy, vouchsafed to unite my destiny with his!"

"I have been ill for some weeks, which is peculiarly unfortunate, for I have no time to devote to my own ailments, all being engrossed by those dearer to me, oh! how infinitely dearer than self.—I have endeavoured to conceal my illness, but it has not escaped the observation of my dear mother, and husband, in whom it has excited great uneasiness.—I know not what can be the matter with me, the sensation, and sufferings I experience are so totally different from any I have hitherto known.—Perhaps they are produced by my anxiety about my dear mother, which increases every day. I must lie down, I feel so faint."

"The cause of my long indisposition has been explained to me by my dear mother, and has filled me with joy. I too am to be a mother,—am to have a creature to love, and who will love me, as I have been loved by my parent, and as I love her! What a gushing tenderness pervades my heart at the thought, and oh! how vast a capacity for affection is the heart endowed with, when, after bestowing so large a portion on the two dear beings who already occupy it, there still remains enough to dispense to the dear creature with whom God is to bless me.

"My mother is greatly pleased, and took occasion to explain to me that this new tie enjoined a self-control over my anxiety for her, and a resignation to her approaching departure, positively essential to the health, nay, probably to the very existence of my child. Heaven grant me courage to bear all trials; but oh! how hard is the task, to *conceal* anxiety like mine—how impossible to vanquish it.

"Every day betrays an increased debility in my dear mother, and I can no longer cheat myself into the hope that her life can be prolonged beyond a few brief weeks, perhaps—days. Her mind retains all its firmness, and she is perfectly resigned to die.—Would to God that I could contemplate the impending blow with the same courage!"

"It is now some months since I have opened my little diary. How much has since occurred, fraught with the deepest interest to me.—I have become, alas! an orphan, and a mother. One of the dearest bonds that bind us to life, that between a mother and her child, has been rent asunder, and a new one no less endearing has been granted me, the last event following the first three weeks after.—I may not, must not touch on the sad details of her last hours, and the heavy affliction that followed, lest such reflections should prove injurious to my infant, whom I nurse. This dear creature has awakened unutterable emotions in my heart, and taught me that a sweet fountain of love lay hidden there, to gush forth when I heard its first cry. How mysterious, how wonderful is nature, and what blessings has it in store for those who open their hearts to receive them!

"To feel one's infant pressed to one's breast, its dear soft lips imbibing sustenance from the maternal fount, its sweet eyes occasionally turned on its mother's face, and its delicate little dimpled hand resting on her bosom, gives a happiness so intense that tears of joy and gratitude fill her eyes, and a deep sentiment of religion pervades her heart. What delight to watch over the dear creature while it slumbers, and to mark the heavenly smile that so often plays over its half-open lips.

"At such moments, I feel assured that the legend, which tells that in their sleep infants hold converse with angels, is true. What mother gazing on her slumbering child could doubt it? Would that the sleep of my dear husband was as calm and refreshing as that of our child. But alas! this is far from being the case; his startings, and wild ravings often terrify me. His dreams are haunted either by a terror of falling down precipices, or else the sad catastrophe which caused my dear sister's death seems acted over again, and before his eyes, for he calls aloud to her to stop, and turn from the dangerous path.—He betrays evident marks of annoyance, when he thinks I have heard the incoherent ravings. He knows they alarm me for his health, and consequently he would wish to conceal them from me. Dear, good, unselfish being, ever thinking of others, and neglecting self."

"My husband must be very ill, although he strenuously denies it to me.—He passes whole hours without sleep, and when over-tired nature finds relief in slumber, he starts from our couch, shudders, and raves of falling down precipices, or of witnessing some one else do so.—Then his days are passed in silence, and sadness. A faint and sickly smile, now become so rare as to be remarked, repays my solicitude and unceasing efforts to cheer him.—Yes, he must be seriously ill; how else can his moodiness be accounted for?—Can it be that he has ceased to love me? No, my own heart tells me that this is impossible, for love like mine must keep alive his affection. Or, is it possible that I have lost the power I formerly possessed of making him happy? Nothing cheers, nothing amuses him; and I begin to fear that his melancholy is infectious; I feel such a disquietude and gloom creep over me, after I have been for hours unsuccessfully endeavouring to win him from the long and moody fits of abstraction into which he is so prone to fall.—If I know my own heart, I think I can be sure that no puerile sentiment of wounded vanity on discovering that, with all my devoted affection, I do not, cannot, render him happy, actuates me, or produces the deep chagrin I experience.—No, so wholly free from the taint of vanity, or selfishness, is my love, that I would submit to any suffering could I but see him happy.

"There are moments when I catch his eye fixed on me with an expression of suspicion and distrust that wounds my very soul! What can be the meaning of all these symptoms of estrangement and misery? Oh, that I should live to see them! I have several times prayed him to let me consult a physician; but he refuses, and dislikes my touching on the subject. Teach me, O God! to discover in what I have failed in my ardent efforts to render him happy, and endow me with the power to win him back to peace and happiness.

"I have been reflecting on the possible cause of the gloom into which my beloved husband has fallen, and carefully examining my own conduct in order to discover by what sin of omission or commission I have erred. The result is, that I think the afflictions that have fallen so heavily on us have impaired his health, and that the monotony of our existence here, by offering no interruption to divert him from his melancholy, has allowed it to take such hold of him, that he succumbs to its influence.

"For me, who have ever been used to a life of unbroken seclusion, this monotonous mode of existence has many charms; but for him who has been accustomed to other scenes, to the excitement of a brilliant capital, with its various pleasures, this lonely place must be dull and joyless. I, too, am deficient in that animation and those colloquial powers, acquired by intercourse with the busy world, and a knowledge of society, which so greatly assist to beguile the weary hours, and to dispel *ennui*. I must force my spirits to amuse him, and conquer the timidity that often checks my efforts from the fear of their not being crowned with success, when I would give worlds to ensure it. Buoyed up by his affection into a false estimate of myself, I dreamt not that a day would come when it would no longer be in my power to amuse, to interest him;—that my want of talent would become so evident to him, that he would feel how much he had at first over-rated me. That woman who 'makes to-morrow cheerful as to-day,' in a seclusion like ours must possess many qualifications in which I, alas! am wholly deficient; and this consciousness of my own demerit serves to increase my timidity, and impose a constraint on my endeavours to please."

"He has consented to see a physician, and has taken the medicines pre-scribed for him, yet no relief has been derived from them. Could he be persuaded to leave this, and for a time to enter into the busy scenes of life, perhaps this despondency, this *tedium vitæ*, might be conquered. I will use my utmost endeavours to accomplish this point, on which my hopes now solely rest.—How many pangs have I endured before the conviction of my own utter want of power to enliven, or contribute to his restora-tion to health, became impressed on my mind! Oh! could I but behold him restored to his wonted state ere the demon of *ennui*, introduced by ill health, had taken possession of him, I might again know peace. Happiness I never more can know, now that I am aware that his depends not on me.

"I had the portrait of my dear departed sister removed from my dear mother's room to our general sitting one, and, strange to say, this annoyed him. He was not angry, he never is; for, notwithstanding his moodiness, he never gives way to ill-humour; but I could see that although he yielded to my request to allow it to remain where I had placed it, he would have pre-ferred not having it there; and I would now have it removed were it not that I fear offending him, after having so strongly pleaded for its remaining. I often catch him with his eyes fixed on the portrait—his face so pale, and its expression so sad, as to bring tears to mine. Is it that the sight of the picture brings before him the fearful contrast the face of the dead offered when he beheld it? That sight was too dreadful! it shook his nerves so terribly that he has never been well or happy since. I thought, when I became his, it was impossible that my love for him could increase; but I knew not, until I had seen him ill and desponding, how sickness and sorrow draw the heart of a wife more closely, more fondly to her husband.

"It is unfortunate, that having but two walks in our neighbourhood, he dislikes both. The one leads to the alcove, so constantly resorted to by my dear sister and myself, the other, to the churchyard, where the remains of those so dear to us rest. This last walk makes us both melancholy; but he dislikes the other even more, and is ever more nervous when we are there. I suppose he thinks it was near the alcove that the fatal misfortune occurred, for the pathway is there very narrow, and the precipice most steep. He turns pale as marble when he looks at the precipice, and there is a wildness in his glance that alarms me. How great must his sensibility be! when I who *knew*, who doted on my sister, feel her loss less acutely than he does, who never beheld her until in her coffin.

"There are some natures so susceptible, so highly sensitive, that a deep and painful shock cannot for years be banished from the mind. *His* is one of these, and although his own happiness, and, consequently mine, is impaired by it, I cannot help loving and valuing him the more for this peculiarity, which my dear mother often told me was rarely to be found in men. I find myself often watching over him as a doting mother does over her child when it first attempts to walk alone, such is the extent of my tenderness for him."

CHAPTER XXXVI.

"My blessed child improves in beauty and intelligence every day. Her resemblance to my dear sister is remarkable, and endears her still more to my heart. Strange to say, my husband appears vexed whenever I refer to this resemblance, but so he does when I speak of my lost Frances, who is continually in my thoughts. I dare say that he thinks my regret would wear away, if I less frequently made her the topic of our conversation. Some kind motive, I feel sure, always actuates him, even when he seems displeased.

"I have of late often seen Doctor Bellinden, and consulted him about my husband's health, which gives me increasing uneasiness. The doctor thinks change of air absolutely necessary; but knowing his dislike to such a measure, I suggested that were it recommended on account of my health instead of his, my husband would, I felt sure, be more disposed to adopt it.

"'I shall utter no falsehood, my dear Mrs. Herbert,' observed the worthy doctor, 'when I say that your health requires a change of abode, for you have looked very delicate of late; nursing has weakened you, and a milder climate would be advantageous.'

"My husband entered unexpectedly at that moment, and I felt, and I fear looked like, a criminal detected in some crime. He betrayed evident symptoms of displeasure when the doctor stated that he had been recommending change of air for me. Remarked that he had not been made aware that I was unwell, and, in short, behaved so differently to his usual kind manner towards me, that I fear the doctor went away thinking him harsh and stern, if not indifferent about my health.—I would not for worlds that he should be misjudged, and I was greatly pained that he should appear, what I know he is not—unkind. How continually do I find it necessary to remember past and present kindness, to prevent my giving way to the regret occasioned by the change in my husband's manner, from passionate love to a kindness meant to atone for its cessation."

"I have had a most painful scene with my husband. Alas! alas! that I should have to record such an event! I endeavoured to explain away his annoyance about my detected consultation, with Dr. Bellinden. Why was I so unthinking as to use the word nervous, when referring to his case? It offended him, and increased his displeasure. I must never again employ that unlucky word. Would that I could divine what is agreeable, and the reverse, to him, in order to avoid ever giving him pain. I never before saw him really angry; and to know that my inadvertence aroused his displeasure, has pained me to the heart. Persons of such deep sensibility as he possesses, should be treated with the utmost forbearance and delicacy; and I, who would rather die than displease him, have proved myself greatly deficient in the last. I made a desperate effort to recover my self-control and courage, and happily succeeded in persuading him to follow Dr. Bellinden's advice. We are to leave Llandover in two days, for Devonshire. Heaven grant the change of air and scene may be productive of good to him! I believe there was some truth in the good doctor's opinion,—that my health also required change of place. I feel a sense of fatigue and oppression very often; but my thoughts have been so wholly occupied by those dear to me, that I have not had time to think of self.

"Since I have discovered that his happiness does not depend on me, I feel less anxious to live. To sleep beside my mother and sister in their quiet grave, until awoke by the last trumpet, no longer alarms me, as it would have done, when I believed he would be wretched without me. Alas! have I not learned the bitter truth, that he is wretched with me, notwithstanding my fond, devoted affection; and after this, what charm can life offer? But no,—I must not thus abandon myself to despair. My child; my dear, blessed child, requires my care; and I must not forget the duties a mother has to fulfil. How disposed is the human heart to selfishness!—when disappointed in its cherished hopes, it leads one to wish for death. I must check this proneness to discontent—I must fix my thoughts on the solemn obligations into which I have entered—and, instead of thinking of my happiness, endeavour, with all my mind, and all my strength, to secure that of my husband and child. If I cannot be the object of his passionate love, as I once was, let me at least be his tender nurse,—his kind companion, whose society he would miss, if deprived of it—and I will not murmur—will not long for that calm slumber in the tomb, with those who so fondly loved me."

"To-morrow we depart. I stole out alone to visit the spot where my mother and sister are laid, and to drop my tears on the stone beneath which they repose. I could not leave them without many a heart-felt pang; and were I disposed to be superstitious, I should own that a secret presentiment seemed to forbode to me, that I beheld that spot for the last time. But am I not in the hands of my 'Father, who art in heaven;' and in this trust, why should I fear? He knows what is best for me; and to His will do I bow."

"It is now many weeks since I opened my little journal. I sometimes ask myself why I commenced? and why should I continue it? The want of some one to whom I could *say* what I write, first led me to note down thoughts and events; for I soon discovered, that even to the beloved of one's heart, one cannot always open its secret recesses. I think, too, that the habit of noting down one's thoughts may be useful in enabling us to correct our failings. How often have I detected my own selfishness, when I read some of the passages to which it had given rise, and endeavoured, not always I trust unsuccessfully, to correct it! Selfishness is the bane of happiness, for it leads us to think only of our own disappointed hopes, when we should be exerting ourselves to console those of others. On the ruins of selfishness should the foundation of pity be erected.

"Our journey here was through a country presenting the most beautiful scenery at every turn. My husband enjoyed it, and every mile that marked our distance from Llandover seemed to remove a weight of sadness from his breast.—How glad I am that I won his consent to our leaving home! Already his health seems improved. He eats with a better appetite, and I, seeing this happy change, feel as if the principle of life were renewed in my frame. His tenderness, too, has returned, and happiness once more smiles on us. Grant, oh Almighty! a continuance of these blessings.

"Won into confidence by a belief in the restored tenderness of my husband, and my feelings softened by this belief, I took courage to pour out the long-suppressed emotions that filled my heart. I ventured to tell him all that was passing in my heart; how, even in the midst of happiness the memory of those dear departed ones, would glide in to make me sigh that they were not partakers of my felicity.—Alas! I met no sympathy! Why do I pine for it? and by revealing my thoughts, draw down on myself some remark, so like a stern reproof, that my frightened heart shrinks in alarm before him who uttered it.—Perhaps I am unreasonable in expecting sympathy. Men do not feel as women do, I am convinced; and probably my husband is not different from the rest of his sex in this particular, and consequently is not to be blamed. But his nerves are so excitable, that I fancied he could understand mine.

"While on our journey, a proof of this excitability was given me; for, on my reading in the newspaper, the details of a detected murder, committed by a man, previously believed to be a worthy individual, and greatly beloved by his family, my husband was seized with a violent spasmodic attack, that terribly alarmed me. It is most painful to behold him at such moments; and for hours after I cannot recover the shock, though I affect to make light of it to him. That night, he uttered the most incoherent ravings, trembled,—and at length, gave such evidence of mental, as well as bodily suffering, that in pity I awoke him from his perturbed sleep. For some minutes, his agitation was so great, that he did not recognise me. He questioned me in visible inquietude, whether I had heard his ravings;—said he had had a frightful nightmare, during which, a person with eyes of fire seemed bent on destroying him.

"The least shock of the nerves brings on these fearful attacks the following night—attacks, which prove a highly sensitive nature—such a one, as I might look to for sympathy. Would to Heaven that I could vanquish this growing discontent! It is wrong,—it is sinful; and often, perhaps, originates in my inexperience and want of knowledge of mankind. How many women, far superior to me, may have more cause for complaint— Complaint! No; I will efface the word, for it is one that should never be used towards a person we love.

"This is a charming place: the verdure so luxuriant,—the foliage so umbrageous,—and the productions of nature so rich and various. The sea, too, oh! how sublime and ever beautiful it is! What thoughts of immensity—of eternity—does it awaken! I feel as if I should never be tired of gazing on it, and of listening to the murmur of its waves. I am glad we came here. He, too, seems to like it. Oh, may every breeze bring healing on its wings to him!

"We have got a pleasant house, and I have been making it look more like a home, with flowers and books scattered around. He smiles at my attempts at housewifery, and expresses himself pleased with my arrangements; but the smiles are but faint and sickly ones, and he frequently falls into his old fits of silence and abstraction, quite forgetful that I am near him. Sometimes it occurs to me that he must have some secret cause of chagrin, which preys on his heart, and destroys his health, and then I become so wretched, that I long to throw myself on his neck, and entreat him to let me share his pain, whatever it may be.

"Is it not one of the privileges of a wife to partake the troubles of a husband, as well as the joys? and why should I forego it? I torture my brain with vague and painful imaginings of the probable or possible cause of his chagrin, until I become so alarmed at the wild images my anxiety have conjured up, that I rub my eyes like one awakened from some frightful dream. My very soul melts with tenderness for him when I behold the gloomy reveries into which he falls.—I could weep over him as a fond mother weeps over her only child when danger menaces it; and with this love and pity in my heart, I must hide its overflowings, lest I annoy, instead of soothing, or comforting him.

"When, as often happens, he catches my eyes anxiously bent on his face, he looks angry, and even reproachful. I frame some phrase to address him, to explain my anxiety, my deep sympathy; but the sternness of his glance causes the words to expire on my tongue, and it is with difficulty I can check the tears that rush to my eyes. What misery can surpass that of seeing the object of our most tender affection, him whom we would die to save from chagrin, betraying a wretchedness, the cause of which we cannot divine, and the effect of which we are not permitted to soothe?

"A mystery seems to impend over him. He writes to no one; receives no letters: or if he does, they are never referred to. He never mentions the name of any friend, or even acquaintance, or makes allusion to his school or college life. He is yet so young, that of the busy world he can have seen but little. How then account for his deep melancholy, his abstraction and reserve? But hold! Have I a right to question, to pry into his past days? Am I not rather enacting the part of a mere suspicious acquaintance than of the tenderest, truest friend? If he withholds confidence, is it right, is it delicate in me to form a single conjecture as to the cause of his troubles? And yet, Heaven knows, no idle curiosity urges me on to desire to become acquainted with aught he may wish to conceal. It is his evident unhappiness that creates the wish to know the cause, and the longing desire to mitigate the effect.

"I have become a very early riser, and walk out, accompanied by my child and her nurse, along the shore. The dear little creature opens her bright blue eyes to gaze on the seas when the sun makes it look like a vast sea of molten gold. How interesting it is to mark every token of awakening intelligence in one's child! Mine—but perhaps the partiality of a mother influences my judgment—appears to me to be peculiarly intelligent for her age.

"For some days, in my early walks, I have noticed a very beautiful woman, accompanied, like me, by her child and its nurse.—We looked at each other every time we met, as if attracted by a mutual sympathy. This morning the fair stranger stopped when we encountered each other, and asked permission to kiss my little one. She lavished commendations on its beauty; and by that sure and short road to a mother's heart, made a very favourable impression on mine. I could do no less than embrace her child, a dear, nice little girl, but certainly much less pretty than mine; and in ten minutes we were the best friends in the world, walking side by side, and chatting as familiarly as if we had been acquainted for years.—We parted, promising to meet next day. My new friend would have our little girls to kiss each other; and a pretty sight it was when their nurses approached their dear little faces, both the fat, dimpled little creatures, smiling and cooing as they were brought lip to lip. The two mothers shook hands cordially, and then we separated; neither knowing or having inquired the name of the other, or, I venture, to say, having even dreamt of it."

CHAPTER XXXVII

"My new friend improves greatly on acquaintance, although at our first interview I thought her so agreeable as not to need any additional charm. She is beautiful, without the slightest semblance of vanity or affectation, and full of vivacity, so tempered by womanly gentleness, that it exhilarates the spirits without ever incurring the risk of bordering on levity. Her husband is away, and this is their first separation. She speaks of him with an emotion that proves how fondly he is beloved, and refers to him continually. He will soon join her here. I know so little of my own sex, having associated only with my husband's mother, my own dear parent, and my ever lamented sister, that I cannot judge comparatively of women; but if all are like those I have named and this new friend, then must they be indeed entitled to be termed the good, as well as the fair sex. How all these dear ones to whom I have referred would have liked my new friend!—Again I have forgotten to inquire *her* name, and she has not asked mine.

"There is an indescribable charm in a friend of one's own sex and age, and especially in one who loves her husband and child as I do mine. Such a ready sympathy springs up spontaneously between women similarly situated. They can say all that they think to each other, without fearing a cold remark, or being misunderstood. They can prattle of their husbands, their children, their gardens, and a thousand things, which men care not to hear. Already I have told my friend of the grief I have experienced in the loss of my dear sister and mother; and her eyes filled with tears, as she held out her hand, and said, 'Let me be a sister to you; I never had a sister, and have always longed for one. Now you are the very person I should like to be my sister, for already I feel drawn towards you, more than to any woman I ever knew. A sort of magnetic influence attracts me to you. Do not reject my affection, for I never offered the gift before.'

"This frankness and *naïveté* won me. I reached out my hand to meet hers, and then she playfully insisted that our little girls should enter into the same pact of friendship, both of us smiling as we placed their plump, dimpled hands together."

"My husband seems to look somewhat coldly on my new friendship. I proposed to him to invite the object of it to come and spend the evening with us; but he received the proposition so formally, not to say discouragingly, that I abandoned the project. He said he disliked female friendships, and above all, with persons who were strangers; but added, that if his society were so irksome to me, that I required that of another, he would yield his own objections, and I might write the proposed invitation. I, of course, would not accept this sacrifice; and he rather sternly cautioned me against forming acquaintances with persons whose characters, nay, whose very names I was ignorant of, and whose exteriors, however captivating, might conceal the worst qualities. All this may be true, and I admitted his superior wisdom; but as far as regards my new friend, I feel as convinced that she is all goodness, as I do that I live and breathe. Is there not something in the heart that prompts us to put faith in some, strangers though they may be, while a secret instinct warns us against others?"

"I did not take my usual walk this morning, although the sacrifice of giving up meeting my new friend really gave me pain. My husband betrayed a dissatisfaction at our meeting, that decided me on staying at home, for I would infinitely rather forego any pleasure, than act contrary to his wishes.

"What will she think of my absence after the friendship to which we pledged ourselves only yesterday? I like her so much, that it grieves me to think we may meet no more, or that she should imagine that I am insensible to the affection she has professed for me. But any thing is better than offending my husband, or adding to his low spirits by an opposition to his wishes."

"He has evinced great kindness. Has told me he wishes me to resume my matinal walks; and so, to-morrow, I hope to meet my interesting and charming friend. His wish for me to resume my morning walks, I consider as a tacit sanction to meet my friend."

"I am so glad! While conversing with my husband yesterday, our servant entered, and announced that a lady wished to see me; and ere he had finished the sentence, my friend was in the room, looking so bright and joyous, that the effect produced on me was as if a sunbeam had shone in to cheer and warm me.

"'I called to inquire if you are well,' said she, 'for I was really rendered uneasy by your absence from our favourite promenade. I would have sent, but I did not know your name:' and she laughed like a pleased child, 'How delightful, how romantic,' resumed she, 'to have formed a friendship, that I feel will endure without knowing each other's names!'

"I presented my husband to her, and even his dear, serious face relaxed, from its usual grave character, as he looked at her smiling and beautiful countenance, and listened to the clear and sprightly tones of her sweet voice. I marked with pleasure that he quite partook of my admiration for my friend; and her lively sallies, and total freedom from affectation, had a most beneficial effect on his spirits. She is one of the most fascinating creatures imaginable, and no one can resist her winning manners, and artless graces. Now my dear husband can comprehend how I was attracted towards her at once, and will no more accuse me of imprudence in having formed a friendship for a stranger.—She has offered to come and pass the evening with us, to which we have joyfully assented, and we then parted the best friends in the world."

"She spent last evening here, and her society lent wings to time. Never had I seen my husband so cheerful before. She drew him out into conversation with perfect ease, excited him into vivacity, nay, even occasionally bantered him, but in such a feminine, playful, yet gentle manner, as to induce him to throw off his reserve. Would to God I possessed her gaiety and talent for conversation, for then I might beguile the long evenings, which hang so heavily on my husband. I never so thoroughly felt my own inferiority to him until I saw how she could amuse and interest him, drawing out the stores of information which he possesses, and which have been hitherto as a sealed book, which I, alas! have no key to open. And yet this sense of my own inferiority begets no envy, no jealousy in my breast. It only makes me wish that I was more capable of interesting and amusing him, and could chase away the moodiness that I now begin to think must originate in *ennui*.—I do hope that the society of this charming woman will bring comfort to me, and cheerfulness to my husband, and that her husband will prove as great an acquisition to mine as she is to me. A man requires the society of his own set to keep up the tone of his mind, and I am sure the husband of my friend must be precisely the sort of man I should like to have as a friend for mine. All that I have seen of her leads to this conclusion. She could not love him so fondly as she does, were he not of a very superior character to the generality of men, so quick-sighted, well-informed, and highly gifted as she is."

"Another day has gone by, the greater part of which my dear friend has been here, both during the day and evening. Her society acts as an exhilarating cordial on the spirits of my husband, and like genial sunshine on mine. I am amused, as well as surprised to see how frankly and gaily she chides my husband whenever he for a moment relaxes into moodiness, while I, who have now been so long his wife, would tremble even to chide or banter him on the subject. But then I am so different, so timid, and so fearful of inflicting pain on him. I begin to think that the more we love, the less can we exhilarate the spirits of those dear to us.

"With my charming friend, I find all the vivacity of my girlish days returning. I can enter into her lively sallies, nay, hazard some in turn when we are alone; but I know not how it is, I have grown so timid, from the fear of displeasing my husband, that in his presence I have not courage to venture to be amusing. Perhaps, were he to throw off his gloom, I might acquire courage; but a curve of his brow, or a pshaw, would freeze me into silence in a moment. I count on the happy influence of my friend's vivacity over him, and that which a contact with her husband may produce. She tells me that he always acquires a great influence over the men he likes. How I hope he will like Marmaduke!"

"I have been, and am, greatly moved by something strange and unaccountable that has occurred. My friend was passing last evening with us, when a note was brought her. She had been talking with delight of the expected return of her husband in a day or two, and forming various plans for excursions to be undertaken *en partie carrée*, to every place worthy of attention in this neighbourhood, and of a long visit which she insisted we must pay her at their seat in the country.—She tore the note open hastily, her eyes sparkling with pleasure; but no sooner had she perused a few lines, than, blushing deeply, she arose to depart, saying, that her husband had returned, and required her presence at home.—She declared she would scold him severely for not *coming* for her, instead of sending, if in the joy of seeing him she could find nerve to scold.

"'I really must check this commencement of insubordination,' said she, or something to that effect, 'lest my husband should become a tyrant, like yours; read this note,' continued she, throwing it on the table; and, embracing me, she hurried away.

"I took up the note, which Marmaduke wished to see. It stated, that though impatient to behold her, he could not, for reasons he would explain when they met, go for her to *Mr. Herbert's*, as she wished him to do. 'You see,' continued the note, 'that although you don't know it, I am already acquainted with the name of your new friends, which I learned from one of our servants, when I inquired where you were.'

"No sooner had my husband seen the signature, 'George Neville,' than he repeated it aloud, adding, 'How strange!' and betraying symptoms of great agitation. I ventured to observe, that it appeared as if the discovery of our name had been the cause of Mr. Neville's not coming; but this remark offended Mr. Herbert, who turned from me in anger. Why is it that I so frequently give offence, or pain, when nothing is so far from my thoughts as to do so? It had occurred to me that he might have formerly known this Mr. George Neville; that they might have quarrelled, and did not wish to meet; but it appears my supposition was erroneous.

"When I asked my husband's opinion on the matter, he looked angry, and said the subject was not worth thinking about; but he greatly pained me when he added some severe reflections on the giddiness and unguardedness of Mrs. Neville, in making acquaintance with strangers, which he said might have offended her husband, and to reprove her, he had declined coming to our house for her.

"I confess, these reasons were unsatisfactory to me, and the strictures on my charming friend, while yet her kind words were ringing in my ear, and her parting embrace fresh in my memory. I could not resist vindicating Mrs. Neville, or at least sharing the blame, if blame was to be found, for our having so unceremoniously formed our friendship; but my attempt to exonerate her from censure was not only wholly unsuccessful, but greatly displeased Mr. Herbert.

"I have been nervous and anxious all the morning expecting to see or hear from my friend. No tidings have reached me of her, though the hour when she used to come has long gone by.—But this delay may have originated in her being so much occupied by her husband after his long absence. I can easily fancy that were mine just returned, after a separation of some weeks, I should be disposed to postpone my visit to the dearest of friends. Mr. Neville, too, may be a ceremonious man, and desirous not to come here until later in the day. In short, many circumstances may have kept them away. My husband proposed my walking out with him; but I declined, because I was afraid of missing my friend when she comes.

"I know not how to account for the dislike my husband has conceived against Mr. Neville; but that he has conceived it, is quite clear to me, for when I repeated some of the commendations bestowed on him by his wife, they were received with a sneer, and a certain air of incredulity that pained me. He also commented with severity on the loquacity of my friend, and, in short, plainly betrayed that he had imbibed a strong prejudice against both husband and wife."

"The day has passed away, but brought neither visit, nor letter from Mrs. Neville! How strange! I could settle to nothing, so anxious was I to see or hear from her, in consequence of the mysterious note of her husband last night, and I found myself involuntarily going to the window every ten minutes, to watch for her coming, until, having discovered that my anxiety had been noticed, and was offensive to Marmaduke, I constrained myself to my chair, and took up some needlework as an occupation. What can have prevented her coming, or writing to me?"

"I have at last heard from Mrs. Neville, but her letter affords no clue to the mystery of her husband's strange note of last night, although it confirms my fears that he wished to avoid meeting us. What can be the motive of this avoidance? I am lost in conjecture. And every imaginable motive for conduct so unaccountable pains and distresses me.

"Mr. and Mrs. Neville departed for London early this morning! Her letter was a farewell, written in a constrained, but nevertheless, an affectionate tone. It contained no reference to any future meeting! And this then is the end of a friendship, from which I promised myself so much happiness, and hoped the low spirits of my husband would derive relief! Mrs. Neville had repeatedly told me that her husband would remain some weeks here— that his letters stated this intention, and yet he remains but one night. She made me promise, too, that we should go on a visit to them, and now does not even revert to the subject! Can it be possible, that Mr. Neville has some cause for avoiding an interview with Marmaduke? Yes, it must be so. My husband knows something to his disadvantage, and Mr. Neville shrinks from confronting him. This explains the depreciating tone adopted by Marmaduke, when I repeated Mrs. Neville's commendations of her husband, although he would not reveal the cause. That any cause could exist for Marmaduke wishing to avoid *him* is out of the question. Poor dear Mrs. Neville, how it grieves me that the husband she so fondly loves could ever have done aught to make him avoid mine! It must be a terrible humiliation to a woman, to know that him she *loves* has reason to shrink from confronting any human being; and she is one to feel this so keenly, that I pray she may never suspect it. How generous, how noble it was of Marmaduke to find plausible excuses for the sudden departure of the Nevilles, rather than betray, even to me, what he knows! And I could accuse him of severity, and incredulity with regard to Mr. Neville's high qualities, while he was generously concealing his evil ones.—Good, dear Marmaduke!"

"It is strange how often I find my thoughts reverting to my sweet friend Mrs. Neville, though, seeing that the subject is a disagreeable one to my husband, I avoid it. There is something peculiarly annoying in having any prohibited topic with a person dear to one, for it invariably presents itself more frequently to the lips than any other; and one is compelled to be continually on one's guard, lest it should escape them. I feel sure that I never should have continued this Diary, could I have conversed unreservedly with Marmaduke. This little book is the safety valve for thoughts that must not be uttered to him!"

CHAPTER XXXVIII.

"A LONG time has elapsed since I last opened this little book. Much anxiety and grief have fallen to my share, but much good also has been accorded me by the Almighty. Perhaps the trials I have endured were mercifully sent to arouse me from the stupor of discontent, into which I was falling; for, since the mysteriously sudden departure of my friend Mrs. Neville, my spirits have given way, and, forgetful of the blessing I still enjoyed, I ungratefully pined for the loss of one I had anticipated. We had decided on leaving this, when two days previously to the one named for our departure, my darling child was taken dangerously ill, and for many days I trembled for her life. Oh! the agony of those days, when, watching every change in that dear face, I felt that, were my child snatched from me, I could not support existence. How puerile then appeared all the annoyances I had lately undergone! What was then to me the loss of Mrs. Neville's friendship? or the motive which led to it? Had I not my child—my husband? Oh, yes, I merited chastisement for such weakness, such wilfulness! I merited the terror that for days and nights tortured my soul; but I merited not the mercy shown me in the escape of my child from death, and in the restoration of my husband's tenderness.

"How unceasing was his care, how terrible his anxiety during this trial. Should aught ever again occur to vex me, let me remember all his goodness and tenderness during my darling's illness, and every other annoyance will be forgotten.

"I, too, have been very ill, so ill, that I feel it will be long ere I regain my strength.—I had felt indisposed for some time prior to my child's dangerous malady, and the anxiety I underwent proved too much for me. I can hardly regret what I suffered when I daily beheld the tender assiduity of my beloved Marmaduke to both his invalids.—Oh! the blessing of marking how inexpressibly dear and precious we are to his heart!—of seeing how wholly self is forgotten in his care of us! Our child has grown so fond of him, that she would fain never have him out of her sight; and he, dear, good soul, submits to her *exigeance*, not merely with patience, but with pleasure. I have forced him out to have a little air, and note down these few lines while he is absent and my darling sleeps.

"The alarm excited by our illness has awakened the slumbering tenderness of my husband. It beams in his eyes, which are continually turned to us; it betrays itself in every word he utters, and in every intonation of his voice. The state of languor and debility to which I am reduced is not without its charm to me. To lie on the sofa, almost helplessly, wholly dependent on him, and nursed with a tenderness, not to be described, is indeed most soothing. If I fall into a doze, his dear face watching over me is the last object I behold; and when I awake, there is the same glance of affection to greet me! It is sweet to live thus cared for, and even death would be robbed of his terrors when love stands by to soothe the dying to the last."

"A long chasm in my Journal, but only mercies and good to be noted down. The roses of health have returned to the cheeks of our child, and my strength seems restored. Happiness is the best of all medicine, as I have experienced; for I believe, under Heaven, it has cured me. But I must not undervalue medicine, either, for to Doctor Western's skill in the treatment of my child, what do we not owe!—He has pronounced that we may both now travel, and thinks that change of air will be beneficial to us; so, it is arranged that we are to depart in two or three days.

"I shall never forget the attention of Doctor Western and his wife and daughter. They have been daily visitors during my illness, and have dropped in many evenings to cheer us their society. They are amiable and worthy persons, and I greatly esteem them.

"We have received such a pressing invitation to pass this evening with the kind Westerns, that we have consented to go. They are to have a few friends; and although I feel little inclination to meet strangers, they made such a point of our spending the evening, that, without appearing ungrateful, I could not decline going. I must conquer this growing dislike to society, for I think going into it may prevent my dear husband relaxing into low spirits again; and what would I not do to guard against the possibility of this."

"Would I had not gone to Doctor Western's party last night: nothing but mortification awaited me there! I am pained, hurt, and humiliated.—A presentiment of evil warned me not to go. Had I obeyed it, how much annoyance should I have been spared! So happy, too, as I have lately been in my husband's restored tenderness, and my re-established confidence in it. Now my mind is all confused; my confidence shaken; my self-respect humiliated. That he ever could have loved, or even fancied he loved, the coarse, the vulgar woman we met there, seems so impossible, that if I had not heard her assert it in his presence, I should have wholly disbelieved the statement. Oh! how mortifying it is to discover that the only man ever loved—the husband of one's choice—could have ever dreamt of selecting for a wife, a woman from whom any man possessing delicacy, or a sense of propriety, must shrink in disgust.—I feel the blush of shame mount to my very brow, when I think of this Mrs. Mordaunt—so unfeminine, so full of levity, and so bold! And I, so proud of his preference, so certain that I had been the first, the sole object of his affection! Nothing lowers a man as much in the estimation of a right-minded woman, as to know that he has soiled his heart, and given such proof of want of refinement of mind, as to have loved such a woman as I saw last night. I dared not meet his eye, lest he should read the disgust with which her presence inspired me, and consequently discover how changed must be my opinion of him. And now is revealed the cause of Mr. Neville's sudden departure, and the breaking off of his wife's friendship for me. Oh, what would I not give, that I had never heard the things told me by that coarse woman, Mrs. Mordaunt! or, having heard, that I could forget them.—To have the man whose name I bear,—to whom I looked up with such respect—disliked, avoided,—despised. My whole being seems changed: I am by turns angry, indignant, and scorched by a sense of burning shame! That cruel woman insinuated, too, that he was suspected of being crazy, as she termed it. Oh, my God! what am I to think?

"This last terrible stroke almost deprives me of reason, while giving rise to the most fearful suspicions. I bless God for being, through *His* mercy, enabled to conceal the awful shock I had received. Stunned—tortured—as I was, I would not, for worlds, have let my unhappy husband know by word or look, what was passing in my mind. I feared several times that I should have fainted, so overpowered was I; but, even in that trying hour, I prayed for help, where alone help can be found,—and it was accorded to me. Pity— the most profound and tender pity—filled my breast for my poor husband. I could have wept over him, as a fond and forgiving mother weeps over a child, who had been her pride, but who is no longer so; yet, who though shunned by all else, will never be deserted or reproached by her.

"Oh! my unhappy Marmaduke!—Now is revealed the fatal cause of all thy nervousness!—thy sleepless nights,—thy incoherent ravings,—thy deep despondency and moodiness! But I have sworn to hold to thee in sickness, as in health; in sorrow as in joy; and faithfully will I fulfil my vow. Never shall a word or look lead thee to suspect, that I know that which would bring the blush of shame to thy brow,—a sense of humiliation to thy heart. Henceforth, I will be thy solace in all thy trials, if thou wilt let me, though all others keep far aloof.

"Oh! wondrous power of love, that acquires strength even from misery!—that can cling to its object through every trial—even that most bitter one—shame for his errors. And has he not need of all my pity, all my love, now that I can no longer bestow on him my esteem, and that he has lost that of the world? Why did he not trust me with the truth? Why permit me to hear evil of him from another? Heaven knows, he might have confided in me! Whatever may have been his sins, when I united my destiny with his, I did it in no light spirit; but firmly and solemnly determined to share all of evil, as well as of good, that awaited him. Should the whole world forsake him, am I not the more called on to supply, as far as I can, the loss of that society and countenance, which a sensitive mind like his must feel so severely. Yes! marriage is a holy—a blessed institution—and, even in this heavy hour of trial I feel it to be so, when it gives me the privilege of sharing his trials—his sorrows, even though I may not have the power of mitigating them. He little knows the deep sympathy they have excited in my breast, while he imagines that I am ignorant of them.

"Perhaps his reserve—his concealment—has originated, *not* in a want of confidence in me, but in dread of giving me pain. I catch at excuses for his conduct, as a drowning wretch catches at straws. Alas! such is the poignant anguish which even the bare notion of his unworthiness inflicts, that I would resign life itself to be able to absolve him from gui—no, I will not, cannot write the word guilt, as applied to him; I will, in spite of all that I have heard, all that I may hear, maintain that he can have only committed some error, and that he knows not guilt. Could I love him as I do, were he guilty of crime? I, who even shudder at the sound of the word!—But I must not probe my heart too much on this point, lest I find my sense of morality give way, and acknowledge, in the words of Moore's song that once made a strong impression on me:—

'I know not, I ask not, if guilt's in that heart
I but know that I love thee whatever thou art.'"

"I have been treated with an indignity that, in spite of my firm resolution not to allow myself to give way to the sense of mortification such treatment must inflict on any person with sensitive feelings, has deeply wounded me. How long will it be ere I get accustomed to meet with insult,—ere my feelings become hardened to bear it?

"Who could have expected that worthy individuals like Mrs. and Miss Western could have so acted as to wound my feelings so deeply? Instead of the cordial greeting we had been accustomed to receive from them, the most marked coldness and constraint, without any attempt to conceal that our visit was unacceptable to them, were so visible to us that we remained but a few minutes at their house, where we had gone to bid them farewell. I felt my husband's arm tremble as mine leant on it when leaving the house. I dare not trust myself to look in his face from the dread of increasing the painful emotion under which I felt assured he was suffering, and I uttered not a word on the subject, which I was sure occupied his thoughts as well as my own.

"My poor Marmaduke! And is it come to this? Did I induce you to leave our secluded home, where at least insult could not meet us, to expose you to it here? Though scorched by the blush of shame, Heaven is my witness, that I forgot my own wounded feelings to think only of his. Why will he not confide to me the cause of the treatment we have experienced, and thus give me the opportunity of pouring the balm of affection and sympathy on his wounds? Never will I refer either to past affronts, or notice future ones, by word, look, or deed: his home shall never be disturbed by his being

reminded of the annoyances met with abroad, but I will endeavour to keep
him away from meeting those who might renew painful recollections."

"I have discovered that my husband demanded an explanation of
Doctor Western of the cause of the treatment to which we were subjected
at his house, and the doctor having told him that was owing to some slanderous statements made by Mrs. Mordaunt to his wife and daughter during his absence from home, Marmaduke wrote to demand satisfaction of
Mr. Mordaunt. O my God! what fatal consequences might there not have
occurred, had Mr. Mordaunt accepted the challenge? How fearful to think
of this senseless, this unchristian mode of proceeding, tolerated by society! An unworthy man, (Mr. Mordaunt, I am persuaded, is one,) injures,
or his wife injures, a worthy one. The injured demands satisfaction, and
runs the risk of killing, or being killed by, the man who has wronged him.
And this is deemed satisfaction for an injury! It is not enough then that a
man's feelings may be wounded, but he must expose his life to the chance
of a pistol-shot, or his conscience to the terrible chance of shedding human
blood—of sending a fellow-creature out of the world!—Why should not
a code of true honour be instituted, by which a man whose conduct was
ungentlemanly, should incur the punishment of being excluded from society, without being allowed the right to challenge any of those on whom
he wished to avenge his angry feelings? Why not have courts of honour,
as well as of law to try culprits accused of having violated the established
regulations of its codes?

"How much self-reproach have I merited for accusing my husband of
not seeking an explanation of the insults offered to us (not a hostile one)
while he was busy in demanding satisfaction. When I reflect that he might
now be a murderer; or, oh! terrible alternative—be no longer among the
living—my blood runs cold, and I feel I can never be sufficiently grateful to Providence for his safety. I discovered the whole affair not from my
dear husband, but from Doctor Western, who came here to make the most
humble apologies for his wife and daughter, and who showed us the letter of apology from Mr. Mordaunt. I also got from the Doctor the letter
of Mr. Mordaunt to my husband, which, I believe, Marmaduke did not
wish me to see. Oh the baseness of this pair! The husband meanly giving
up his wife to obloquy, as a slanderous gossip, everlastingly bringing him
into scrapes, and he trying by submission to escape the consequences her
folly and wickedness entailed on him.—I felt such contempt for both, that
I regretted Marmaduke had condescended to notice their slander; nevertheless, his manliness in calling the husband to account, proves he did not
dread meeting any charge against him."

CHAPTER XXXIX.

"My husband has left the choice of where we are to go to me. But to me all places are alike—I dread solitude for him, his spirits being depressed by it, and perhaps in a crowded city we may best escape coming in immediate contact with those *he* may wish to avoid, or who may wish to avoid him. I tremble at the bare notion of his encountering any one, formerly known to him, whose coldness might provoke him into a duel, now that I am aware he has not the same objection and horror of the system of duelling that I entertain. My poor Marmaduke! how I pity him, and how I love him!

"We arrived in London yesterday. What a vast world of a place it is! The crowds, the noise, stunned and alarmed me, and a sense of isolation stole over me, that made me draw closer to my husband's side. Not so our child: she laughed, and clapped her little hands as she gazed on the passing throng, while we drove through the streets to the hotel, where we are to remain until we have procured a house. I know not whether it is the fatigue of the journey, or the confined and less pure air of the town that has disagreed with me, but I feel so weak, and have such a pain in my side and chest, that I cannot make the slightest exertion without a sudden faintness coming over me. I must conceal this from Marmaduke, for he is so easily alarmed about my health."

"I have seen such a woman; but no, let me not call her woman, for she much more resembles a man. She is the aunt of that disagreeable Mrs. Mordaunt, who occasioned me so much pain at Torquay. My husband knew her at Oxford, and by chance we encountered her in this hotel, where she has been staying, and she would, *bongré malgré*, force herself on us.— Through this masculine creature I discovered that Marmaduke really had intended marrying Mrs. Mordaunt, for the aunt said he had a happy escape from her. I wish that I had never known that he could have thought of so coarse and vulgar a person as a wife! Mrs. Scuddamore,—so is the aunt named,—inspires me with as much dread as an old rough soldier could do: so *brusque*, so unfeeling, and continually talking of military affairs. Perhaps, had I been in good health and spirits, I might have smiled at this strange creature's sayings and doings, but, ill and nervous as I feel, she alarmed and disgusted me. I hope I may never again meet her, and so I am sure does Marmaduke. How she had harassed my feelings, and his, by dwelling on the sad, sad death of my dear sister, even after she was told how nearly we were related. I forget every pang Marmaduke has ever inflicted on me when I see how acutely he still feels that terrible event. It is such a proof of his tenderness of heart and affection. Ah! never can I forget how he behaved when, on our wedding-day, he went off to perform the painful duty to the dead. How unselfish, how kind was his conduct all through! Oh! let me always have the consolation of reflecting, that whatever may have been the errors of his youth before I became known to him, from that hour his conduct has been irreproachable! Is not this something? Ah! How much to be thankful for!"

"We moved into our new abode yesterday, and I hope its quiet, after the bustle and noise of a crowded hotel, will do me good. My husband is all kindness and attention, his spirits, though not high, they never were, are more even, and free from moodiness, and our dear child is a constant source of interest and pleasure to him, as she is to me. The owner of this house, too, appears to be an excellent woman, and has busied herself to make our rooms as comfortable as possible.

"I wonder whether I shall ever get accustomed to the crowded streets and constant din of London!

"The pain in my chest and side increases rather than diminishes, and I can scarcely force myself to eat, my appetite has become so bad. I have often heard that London produces bad effects on those accustomed to the pure air of the wild mountains of Wales, but I had no idea the influence could be so powerful."

"I have accompanied Marmaduke to the public galleries, and to the studios of the most esteemed artists, and have been delighted with some of the pictures and statues I have seen. A new source of pleasure has been opened to me, and I feel a love of art developing itself rapidly in my mind as I behold its chef-d'œuvres. I am surprised when I discover that an instinctive feeling leads me to prefer only the best works. So uncultivated as my taste has been by never having contemplated the works of good masters, or indeed any masters at all until now, it seems strange that this instinctive taste should at once declare itself. I feel it with satisfaction, for the pleasure it conveys takes my thought from painful reflections, and furnishes agreeable topics of conversation for the evenings. Marmaduke delights in fine pictures and statues; I should be greatly disappointed if he did not share this taste with me. Every innocent pleasure that diverts attention from painful thoughts, is a boon from the Giver of all good, as the wild and beautiful flowers that spring from the hedge-rows that border a road on which we are travelling, beguile us from a sense of its weariness. Methinks that were I a constant dweller in London, I should be a frequent visitor to the public galleries, as a relaxation to my mind, and an anodyne to soothe or make me forget pain."

"I get no better,—nay more, I fear that the pain in my side and chest increases. The sense of fatigue certainly does, for I am conscious of it, even in the midst of the enjoyments so lately opened to me. Perhaps the excitement they occasion may be the cause, for I, ignorant as I am, experience an enthusiasm as I contemplate these productions of master minds, of which I did not believe myself capable. I could not define the beauties in them that fascinate me, nor reason on them, but I feel, acutely feel, the admiration they create."

"Yes, a crowded capital, with the ever-moving sense of busy life it presents, is the best place for those who have thoughts from which they would fain escape, or who are isolated in the world. The constant demands on attention, the novelty of the objects that attract it, and the various reflections they excite, occupy the mind, and fill up the hours. My dear Marmaduke, I can perceive, derives the same advantages from our sojourn here that I do, which makes me rejoice that we came hither.

"Nothing has occurred since our arrival to give us pain, except the encounter with Mrs. Scuddamore; and even that had its good side, for the heartiness and cordiality of her manner towards Marmaduke proved that she could know nothing to his disadvantage at Oxford; for a woman with her stern notions of honour would not have evinced such warmth and good will, had there been the slightest accusation, or even suspicion, of aught injurious to his reputation. How often has this consolatory reflection come back to me since I saw her, inducing me to overlook all that displeased me in her.

"Still tormented by the pain in my chest, and increasing debility, which renders every exertion fatiguing, I carefully conceal both from my dear husband, for he is so much more cheerful than he used to be, that I cannot bear to disturb his serenity by any alarm about me, and I well know the least hint of my being ill would make him anxious and unhappy."

"I have been to the Opera, and one or two of the other theatres. The music of the first surprised and delighted me;—it was a new, an engrossing pleasure. It soothed, it entranced me, and drew from my eyes the sweetest, softest tears that ever visited them. What a potent spell does fine music exercise over a sensitive person! Every note seemed to find a vibration in my heart, until, hurried away from the actual present, into another, a brighter world, I forgot every care, every sorrow I had ever experienced, and was alive only to a sweet, a delicious melancholy, such as is sometimes awakened by an air heard in happier times, and in other scenes. And yet the music was all new to me! I suppose it was the weak state of my nerves that led to this powerful effect on them. Into what unknown realms of thought does music lead us; and how weak seems language compared with it! To me there is something mysterious and religious in it, something that lifts the soul to its Creator. Such at least was its effect on me, for although in no sacred fane, but in a theatre dedicated to pleasure, and crowded by gay faces, a solemn, a holy feeling stole over me as I listened to the music of "Moïse," and turned away from the stage which disturbed my associations, to resign myself wholly to the magic of Harmony. No; music, I feel, could never be a light pleasure to me! I only stayed a short time during the ballet. It displeased, it annoyed me, to see women exhibiting their persons with such a reckless oblivion of the modesty inherent in our sex. Through what a long process of mental demoralization must these poor creatures have passed, before they arrived at this state of indelicacy! And yet loud were the plaudits, reiterated the clapping of hands, that marked the admiration these feats of dexterity excited;—and this before so many women presumed to be irreproachable. It appeared to me that this frantic applause of indecency was an affront to all my sex. It seemed to convey the insulting thoughts of the applauders, that women, designed for such holy purposes,—to be the sweeteners of home, the tender wives, the devoted mothers, the dutiful daughters,—should thus profane their sacred calling, for the amusement of the idle hours of Sybarites. And yet, women looked on, unabashed, unwounded;—nay, shared of the admiration of the male sex as was demonstrated by their smiling faces, their tapping the fronts of their boxes with their splendid fans, some of them even applying their white gloved hands to the palms, in imitation of the men! I turned from the sight, grieved to have witnessed it, and will never again see a ballet. When will women comprehend and fulfil their mission?

"While I believed my illness was concealed from my dear husband, he was anxiously noticing every symptom that indicated it, and this morning used all his persuasions to induce me to see a physician. I have promised, that if I do not derive benefit from the daily excursions into the environs which he proposes, I will yield to his wishes, but I trust that fresh air will restore my strength. His tenderness, his attention melts my heart. He accuses me of not thinking enough of my health. Well may I forget illness when his dear and watchful love guards me! Oh, the happiness of knowing, and feeling, that one is so unutterably dear to another!

"We have been making the most delightful excursions into the country. How beautiful are the environs of London! Reclining on cushions in a boat, with my husband and child close to me, and gliding over the smooth and transparent bosom of the Thames, a blue sky over our heads, and just enough of sunshine to warm us, I feel that I could for ever pass my days in a sort of dreamy existence, without the fatigue of motion. We have been repeatedly to Richmond,—beautiful Richmond, and to Marlow, passing by the stately woods of Cliefden.—How varied, how enchanting the scenery, and how delightful to contemplate it with those we love! Health ought to come with the soft and balmy breezes that fan my brow, and play with my hair, yet it has not made me feel sensible of its approach. Perhaps it is only a blessing deferred! But am I not in the hands of *Him*, Who best knows what good is for his children?

"Never since my marriage have I felt so happy, so blest as of late. The tenderness of my dear Marmaduke, the growing beauty and health of our dear child, and an indescribable, but sweet calmness of spirit that has come over me, makes me often wonder how I could have been so wretched at Torquay—how I could ever have for a single moment believed, nay even suspected that my husband could have erred—could have merited reproach or avoidance. I blush to have judged by appearances. Heaven be thanked, I never revealed to him that I did so, or I could never meet his glance.

"I suppose I caught cold on the water, for lately I have been annoyed by a cough, which is very troublesome, and at night especially. This new ailment has awakened afresh the alarm of my dear husband, and he insisted on calling in Doctor Harford."

"The Doctor has been here, and has divined every one of my symptoms. The pain in my chest and side, and the frequent attacks of fever. Dear Marmaduke looked as pale, and anxious, while the Doctor was questioning me, as if my malady was of the most serious character, nor could my assertions of the reverse quiet his anxiety.

"Dr. Harford has recommended me to be taken to a warmer climate, with as little delay as possible, and said it was also necessary for my dear husband. He named Nice, to which place we are to proceed in three or four days. This advice makes me fear that my disease is of a more serious nature than I imagined, and yet I do not feel ill, that is, not so ill as to make me apprehend danger. Dear Marmaduke is evidently alarmed, although he endeavours to conceal it from me. He little knows that I am so well acquainted with every change in his expressive countenance, that I can read it as easily as an open book.

"I strongly suspect that his saying that the Doctor thinks a change of climate necessary for him, as well as for me, is a mere pretence, urged lest I should object to going on the continent on my own account solely, while he knows I would go any where that could do *him* good."

"I have had another bad night. My cough was much more troublesome than hitherto, and to-day I feel feverish and uncomfortable. My God, can it be, that I am to be taken from my husband—my child? Now, too, when I am so happy, so desirous to live! A pang of agony shoots through my heart, as I contemplate the possibility of parting from those to whom it clings with a love stronger than life. My husband—my child! Oh! spare me, Almighty, to those whose happiness is bound up in me. I am yet young; let me still stay with them, if but for few years longer. But if this must not be; if thy fiat has gone forth, grant me, oh! in mercy, resignation to submit to *Thy* will, and vouchsafe unto my husband courage to support the impending blow. My tears fall so fast, they blot the words I write, and blind me. I must hasten to remove the traces from my eyes lest he should return, and suspect the cause.

"Death is now ever before me; it haunts my pillow; it fills me with terror and anguish every hour! And can it be that I must soon go hence, and be no more seen? Be hidden from the light of day, behold no more the bright sun, the fair earth, and all it yields of sweet and beautiful? I who love nature as a child loves its mother, whose heart thrills with pleasure when I behold her charms! But all these blessings I could resign without a murmur, could I but remain with those I dote on, in the most dreary clime that ever chilled the human heart. In the wilds of Siberia would I make my home, could I but be left with my husband and child. And will this heart that now throbs with affection, this brain filled with agonizing thoughts at the bare notion of being torn from those so dear, soon be but as the clod of the valley, insensible to all, even to the wild grief of him who will so deeply mourn my loss? Is there no medicine, no skill, that can prolong my life? I will close this journal, nor lose a single one of the few hours that may remain to me, in noting down the agony of this too fond heart. Pardon me, O my God, for this impious impatience, and want of submission to *Thy* will. Grant me fortitude to bear what *Thou* thinkest best for thy suffering servant, and grant resignation to my dear husband, to whom this weak heart clings with too great a love, to bear parting, when I am summoned hence.

"To-morrow we depart for Nice. My poor dear husband still indulges hope of my recovery, but my increasing want of strength warns me that it is delusive. I must, by degrees, prepare him for our separation, that he may be better enabled to meet the blow."

CHAPTER XL.

THE effect produced on my feelings by the perusal of this artless disclosure of the sentiments of my lost wife, may be more easily imagined than described. It seemed, if that could be possible, to increase the love I had borne to her, and to aggravate ten-fold the sorrow her death had occasioned me. Every pang I had ever caused her rose up to reproach me; and as I felt the soul-harrowing conviction that I had embittered her life, nay, more terrible still, abridged it by the anxiety to which I had given rise, I wept in agony, and loathed myself.

I could not lay down the journal until I had perused every line. I refused sustenance, and remained locked up in the chamber until I had concluded the diary—at one moment melted to tenderness by the avowals of her affection, and the next almost maddened by the overwhelming sense of my own unworthiness. And while she had been writing many of these pages, I, selfish and incapable of duly appreciating the treasure I had lost, was accusing her of being a spy on me, attributing the watchfulness of anxious love to curiosity, or a more unworthy motive. And *she*, who so loved me with all my faults, whom my moodiness and wayward temper grieved, but never disgusted, she was in her early grave, sent there through the cares and uneasiness I had entailed on her gentle heart! What tears, although every one sprang from a source opened by torture, and flowed like molten lava, scorching the eyes whence they fell, could atone for my sins to her, who had been the angel-guide vouchsafed to me by the Almighty?

No longer was my grief torpid, as immediately after my return to consciousness from the brain fever it had been. Despair had now taken possession of my soul. Fate, I deemed, had done its worst, and hopeless for the present, I was reckless for the future.

I had destroyed the most peerless creature that man had ever been blessed with; and now, *now* when it was too late to make atonement,—to throw myself at her feet, to bathe them with my tears, to confess my unworthiness, and avow my adoration, I discovered my injustice, and the pain it had inflicted.—My child, too, how had I wronged her, by depriving her of such a mother—one who would have trained her so admirably in the path of rectitude; one who would have presented her so bright an example of every virtue! Again and again I perused the journal. I slept with it under my pillow when in bed, and referred to its artless pages often during the night and morning. Never did the most passionate lover read the first letter accorded him by the object of his idolatry, with the same engrossing interest that I perused this diary; and although it inflicted torture, I would not have resigned it for all the world could grant.

I had not yet ventured out of doors, although my physician was anxious I should try the efficacy of air and exercise to restore my shattered health. His reiterated request on this subject at length induced me to go out to drive, and having ordered the coachman to proceed in the direction recommended by the doctor, I no sooner got out of the sight of the latter, than I desired the man to conduct me to the English Cemetery. To that spot my heart yearned to go ever since I was capable of bearing the exertion. I left the carriage at some distance from the gate, and, with trembling steps, entered the sacred resting-place of the dead. I soon discovered the spot; white marble monuments had been erected over the graves of my adored wife and my lamented friend, by Mrs. Neville, and as I perused the name and age of my lost Louisa I felt like a culprit, as conscience whispered that I it was who had consigned her, while yet so young, to a premature grave.

How strange, how terrible, are the feelings experienced on beholding for the first time, the spot that holds the mortal remains of one who was our all of life, our sunshine, our blessing! The conviction of our desolation seems never to have struck us so wholly, so overwhelmingly, as now. I sank on the cold earth beside the marble, and bathed it with burning tears; I called on the dead, as if she who had ever answered me with words of love could now hear me; and, forgetful of how unfit I was to die, I prayed for death, to be reunited to her. The sun shone out, and its beams played on the white marble, but I turned from its cheering influence, heart-stricken by the thought, that although it might warm the marble, it could not warm the precious deposit it contained. The birds chirruped gaily as they flew from tomb to tomb; but, for the first time in my life, their notes wounded my ear. Why should there be sunshine, and notes of joy, when all my sunshine, all my joy, was interred beneath the marble beside me? It seemed unnatural—cruel—and aggravated my sense of misery. I would fain have had the bright luminary of day veil its face in clouds, nature itself put on its gloomiest aspect, the birds forget to sing, and all around become shrouded in darkness, like that which filled my soul.

And must I go hence, and leave her in a foreign grave, her whom in life I could not bear to quit for even a day? And now days, weeks, months, and years may roll on, ere I am summoned to take my everlasting rest beside her! I determined that the first step I would take should be to add a codicil to my will, desiring that wherever I might chance to die, my mortal remains should be conveyed to this spot, to be interred by those of my adored wife. How eagerly does the despairing wretch catch at anything, however puerile, that holds out the slightest prospect of even a momentary relief of his woe! The thought of assuring the certainty of being buried in the spot on which I then reclined, seemed to bring the hope of death nearer, and in some sort to console me, though, notwithstanding this hope, I found it difficult to tear myself from the grave of my wife, even when the deepening shades of evening warned me to begone; and I should hardly have found resolution to go, had I not heard the coachman, alarmed at my long absence, entering the cemetery to come in search of me! I could not bear that he should profane the spot by his presence, nor witness my grief; so I turned away with a breaking heart, and, entering the carriage, was driven to my desolate home.

A cheerful fire blazed on the hearth, commanded by my thoughtful physician, lest I should be chilled on going out for the first time after so many weeks' confinement to the house. It gave an air of comfort to the room; and the light from it fell brightly on the ornaments and furniture around. I thought of the deepening gloom of the cemetery, of the cold grave in which my loved one was sleeping; and, giving way to a passionate burst of tears, I rushed into the dark chamber inside, and, flinging myself on my bed, remained there for the night.

And now my doctor became urgent with me to leave Nice. He declared that change of air and scene was absolutely necessary; and that if I did not, without delay, remove, a low nervous fever, which was hanging about me, would certainly grow into a chronic ailment, most direful in its effects. I questioned him, whether such a malady was likely to occasion death. But he shook his head, as if divining the motive of the question, and answered, "No, not death, but a state of suffering to which death would be infinitely preferable—a state bordering on insanity."

My own sensations warned me that this might be, for there were moments, nay hours, in which my grief was so overwhelming, that I felt that reason tottered on her throne, and led to a growing desire to abridge, by my own hand, a life that was become insupportable to me. I therefore determined to leave Nice, and my arrangements were just completed, my farewell visit, an agonizing one, paid to the cemetery; when the evening previous to my departure, I received the following letter, in an unknown hand. The signature, however, revealed the writer, and as I glanced at it, an instinctive presentiment of evil and danger flashed through my brain.

"Sir," wrote this vile wretch,—"when I sat up with you during your illness, you let out in your sleep a secret, that you would rather die, I am persuaded, than have known to the world. That secret is in my keeping, and it depends on you, whether or not it will remain so. You will easily guess to what I allude, but in case your memory should fail, I will at once go to the point. You, for reasons best known to yourself, but which may easily be surmised, threw your sister-in-law down a precipice, by which she was killed, and you buried her in a cavern. So convinced was I that what you were raving about every night must have some foundation in truth, that when I was dismissed by your doctor, I availed myself of the information I picked up from one of your servants, about where your home was, and set off, regardless of expense and trouble, to Wales, being well convinced my long journey would prove a profitable one. Arrived at Llandover, I went to your house, made acquaintance with your housekeeper, by representing myself as having lived in your service; informed her of the death of your wife; and, after a few days' close inquiry as to whether any young lady had ever fallen down a precipice, I discovered that your sister-in-law had *accidentally*, as was believed, met her death in this way, and that it occurred a short time before you were married. It instantly occurred to me, that had her death been purely accidental, why should you, and so long after the matter, too, be continually raving of it, and accusing yourself of having thrown her over the cliff? I will not tell you *all* the discoveries I made. Let it be sufficient to state that I have found the body, that I have concealed it where you can never discover it, and that if you do not buy my secresy, I will disclose the whole fact, and have the body brought forward, in proof of my assertion. Five hundred pounds will buy my silence, and you shall hear of me no more; but refuse these moderate terms, and I will at once have you arrested as a murderer, and brought to condign punishment. I know you intend leaving Nice to-morrow morning; but go where you will, I will pursue you, and carry my threat into execution.

"I remain yours to command,

"JAMES FIGGINS.

"P. S. I will call for an answer."

Amazed, confounded, terrified, my senses were overwhelmed, by this unexpected blow! I reeled under it, my brain grew dizzy, and reason denied its aid to guide me through the fearful danger that threatened to destroy me. Whichever way I looked, danger beset my path. Exposure, ignominy, and a scaffold, arose in terrific array before me, and no mode of escape, save suicide, presented itself to my agonized brain. I rushed to my chamber, locked the door, tore off my neckcloth, bared my throat, and seized a razor, when, at the moment I opened it, with desperate intent to inflict a deadly wound, the voice of my child crying out, "Papa, papa! mamma is come back!" arrested my hand. I cast the instrument of destruction from me, hastily resumed my neckcloth, opened the door, and found my child in her night-clothes, trembling with cold, outside it. Half frantic, I caught her up in my arms, and wildly pressed her to my heart. "Papa!" said she, "mamma came from heaven to my bedside, and kissed me, when I was asleep, and I awoke, and got out of bed, and ran to tell you, for I knew you would be so glad."

I dropped into a chair, still clasping my child, that little creature, who had been, through the interposition of the Almighty, my preserver from the terrible sin of suicide—from a felon's grave.

The alarmed nurse now entered. She had left my child sleeping, while she descended for a night light. The dear creature had dreamt that her blessed mother was returned, and, mistaking the dream for reality, had ran to tell me the happy tidings, and thus, by little short of a miracle, had my life been spared. The dear child could not be persuaded that she had not seen her mother. She persisted in asserting it, and maintained that she was sure that dear mamma was still behind the curtain of her little bed.

This intervention of Providence made a deep and lasting impression on my mind. When my child was removed from my chamber, I sank on my knees, and humbly implored pardon for the terrible sin I had dared to meditate, and offered up prayers that never more might I be tempted to such evil thoughts. My mind was all in a tumult! The reflection that my poor child might now have been an orphan, had not her dream led her to my door, made me tremble, while I owned the goodness of God in having vouchsafed this mercy.

But what was to be done with the wretch who was waiting for my answer to his diabolical letter—to the serpent who had entangled me in his folds? Stunned by the terrible emotions of the last hour, acting on a frame exhausted by mental and bodily suffering, and with a brain maddened by conflicting feelings, a release from the terror inspired by the vile man who menaced me seemed the object in life the most desirable at that tremendous crisis—I had lost the power of reasoning. I could not see the possibility of proving my innocence of actual guilt against his nefarious charge; and in a moment of madness, I sent him a cheque for the sum demanded—and thus sealed my doom, by admitting the truth of his assertion.—I placed myself in the power of a fiend, whence never more could I

extricate myself, and the sum paid to secure his secresy, would furnish the
terrible proof of supposed guilt.—Yet that night I slept more calmly than
for many a previous one. Thus have human beings been known to dance
over a volcano ready to explode and destroy them.

CHAPTER XLI.

I AWOKE the next morning in a very different frame of mind. The folly,
the madness of having yielded to the threats of the villain Figgins now
struck me so forcibly, that I could hardly comprehend how I could have
perpetrated it.

A night's calm and refreshing slumber, the first enjoyed for a long time,
had produced such a salutary effect on my nerves that the menaces which
had the previous night almost irritated me to insanity, by filling me with
terror, were now looked on in quite another point of view.—Such is the
weakness of man, and so do his actions depend on the state of his nervous
system!

Now, when it was too late, I could see, and intensely feel, the terrible
false step I had taken, and writhe in agony when reflecting on the consequences it would inevitably entail. I loathed my own moral pusillanimity,
which, instead of leading me to resist the demand made on me by a scoundrel, whose menaces I should have, in common policy, defied, induced me
to comply with it, and by so doing, placed me for ever in his power.—Yes,
now, indeed, had I signed my own condemnation—henceforth must I feel
myself the slave of a villain. Why had it not occurred to me, when I got
the demand, to send off at once for the doctor, and tell him of it? He was
a sensible, as well as a kind man, much esteemed by the civil authorities at
Nice; and had I appealed to him, there was little doubt that he would have
extricated me from the clutches of the wretch who meant to make me the
prey to his mercenary scheme of extortion.

The artful plot would have been nipped in the bud. The representations
of the villain Figgins would have been received as a vile calumny, hatched
to work on the fears of a nervous invalid; and my courage in exposing it
would not only have had the best effect as a proof of innocence of the
charge, but would also have defeated any future scheme of him who sought
to extort money from me.

How well, how clearly could I *now* see all this, although the previous
night I could perceive nothing but ruin, urging me on to suicide, in order
to escape exposure! O God! how could it have been that my reason was so

wholly prostrated, that fear, base, ignoble fear, should thus have conquered me! It *now* was evident to me that the threats of Figgins were founded on no more stable basis than that created by his own suspicions. My ravings had excited these; he journeyed to Wales to discover some cause for them—had found that my sister-in-law had been supposed to fall down a precipice, and having thus ascertained that a *part* of my expressions uttered in sleep bore reference to that sad event, he concluded that those relative to interring the dead in a cavern, must also bear reference to a fact, and thus built up his accusation on surmise. It was clear that had he pushed his inquiries further, he would have learned that the young lady was buried, (as was generally believed,) in the vault of my family; and, consequently, would not have searched for the body in the cavern. But working on my fears, he had made the experiment of asserting that he had found the body, an assertion which I now felt firmly persuaded was utterly false, but which my insanity in crediting would confirm him in his suspicions. Oh, the agony of reflecting on all this, and despising myself while did so!

Now was I well aware that had I defied Figgins and sought protection of the law from the knavery he was practising against me, I must have perfectly succeeded in crushing his attempt at extortion; and as I examined, and closely sifted every circumstance connected with that fatal event, which had so darkly coloured my fate, I felt assured that nothing to criminate me could have been brought forward. It could have been proved that I had never beheld the young lady, of whose death I was accused of having been guilty. My worthy housekeeper and other servants could have borne evidence that I had not left my chamber that night until summoned from my bed, where indisposition retained me, by the servant of Mrs. Maitland; I had joined him in search of the missing young lady, at the risk of my life. Even had the body buried in the cavern been exhumed, and identified as that of Miss Maitland, how could it be proved that I had interred it there? Nothing but my incoherent *ravings* uttered when under the influence of delirium, occasioned by a brain fever, could be produced to connect me with the circumstance, and even this could only be adduced against me by Figgins, whose unsupported testimony would have no weight.

How strange and incomprehensible did it now appear, that never previously did this same mode of examination occur, or if it did, never did it produce the same satisfactory effect on my reason. A film that had hitherto obscured my sight, and prevented my beholding all the circumstances of the case in their true colours, seemed to drop from my eyes. Good God! had I for years been blind! Had I borne hours, days, weeks, months, of torture, and only now learned to reason calmly, sensibly, on facts? Could it have been proved, even had the body in the cavern been brought to light, that when I had seen, and caused the other corse to be interred in my family vault, I could have known that it was *not* that of the person missing, whom I had never seen; and even if I had, would not the state of decomposition in which it was, have prevented the possibility of recognition? Had not the clothes of the dead been buried before my arrival, and had I not brought the nurse with me to identify the body? Yes, I was secure, perfectly secure, from the danger menaced by the vile Figgins, had I not, from moral cowardice, placed myself in the snare he had planned to entrap me.

I groaned in agony, as the truth now appeared before me, divested of all the terrors with which formerly my alarmed fancy and shattered nerves had clothed it, but which at present reason proved to me I, and *I* alone, had rendered dangerous by yielding to the menaces of Figgins. And I had embittered the life of my adored Louisa, ay, had shortened it, by the moodiness, the misery, I could not hide from her, when by the exercise of my reason I might have seen that I had nothing to dread from discovery, and when I knew myself to be perfectly innocent of any intention to her, whose death I had unfortunately caused.

But the same lucidness of intellect which enabled me now to see that all the terrors which had assailed me during so long a period, rendering existence almost a burthen, had been groundless, displayed, oh, how vividly! the danger I had brought on myself by buying the silence of Figgins—I felt that henceforth I must unresistingly submit to his extortions.

To brave him hereafter, armed as he was, with this proof of my conscious guilt, would be impossible; and, as I gloomily looked forward to a prolonged existence, over which this villain could hold a power, which, like the sword suspended by a hair over the head of Damocles, might at any moment fall on me, I longed for death! What was I to do?—where was I to escape from my tormentor? Had I even paid the five hundred pounds he had extorted from me in money, direct from my hand to his, no proof could be brought forward of the fact, except his assertion; which I could deny; but no!—as if to affix the seal to my own ruin, I had given the wretch a cheque on my banker at Nice, whose books could always serve as evidence on this point. And how explain the having given a man, who had been for only a short time employed as a servant in my family, so large a sum of money? What credible motive could I assign? Never did a barrister, engaged to defend a client, whose case was desperate, examine with a cooler, a more searching eye the evidence to be produced against him, than I now did my own case; becoming every moment more firmly convinced, that *I* had furnished the only evidence that could injure, and that must one day, sooner or later, destroy me.

Could it be borne that I was to hold immunity from the consequences of implied guilt, only by continuing to pay the heavy price exacted for it, by the wretch who held me in thrall? Would not the facility with which I had yielded to his extortion, induce him to levy it again, and again, until he had wrung from me the fortune of my child, and left me a beggar?—The thought of destroying this man here crossed my mind; and I, who had in all my misery, found consolation in reflecting, that whatever I might suffer, I was innocent of intentional guilt, now contemplated murder; nay, was ready to commit it, could I but find a safe opportunity. But how was this to be found?

Ay, there was the point; and I conned over every possible chance in which my personal security might not be endangered by the crime I meditated. Could I not seek a secret interview in some retired spot with my enemy, and, armed with a pistol, shoot him through the head? Then came the recollection that I had no pistol, nor indeed any weapon of destruction; and to go out and buy one might excite suspicion, for probably every place where guns or pistols could be bought would be examined, after a man had been shot, in order to discover to whom any had been sold. This project must, therefore, be abandoned for the present at least; and who knows, whispered Hope, but that death, a natural death, involving me in no guilt, may release me from him. He, no more than others, bears no charmed life. One of the same casualties may end his days that so frequently abridge those of other men. Let me, therefore, not despair, at least not until he renews his demands; and let me seek some distant spot, where he may lose the clue to discover my abode.

What a fearful abyss is the heart of man! even that of one not naturally prone to evil! No sooner is his personal safety involved in danger, than he who would under other circumstances shrink with instinctive horror from committing crime, begins to contemplate it without disgust or dismay.— And I, who would not injure aught that had life, who would recoil with pity from witnessing human suffering, could now meditate depriving a fellow-creature of life, and ardently desire an opportunity of accomplishing this sinful project!

Let no man hereafter say, "this or that crime would *I not* perpetrate." Or, if such confidence in one's own integrity may ever be indulged, it can only appertain to him who has been brought up in the love and fear of God; who is prepared to bear every trial with which it may please Providence to afflict him, rather than forfeit the blessing, the inestimable blessing, of a quiet conscience, and the trust that he is walking in the path in which he should tread. Many are those who have passed through life unconscious of their own weakness, and who, because they have not been tempted, believe they would not have fallen. Let such, with humility, return thanks to the Almighty, that they have not been tried, and learn to pity their less fortunate brethren.

The more I reflected on my culpable weakness, the more did I begin to doubt my own sanity. This doubt was my sole refuge from a growing self-contempt that was corroding my mind; for it was less mortifying to believe that my intellects must have been impaired, than to think myself the moral coward which my conduct towards Figgins would imply.

CHAPTER XLII.

I LEFT Nice next morning, after taking leave of my good doctor, in answer to whose inquiries of where I intended to direct my course, I stated that it was my intention to proceed to the north of Italy, where I should probably remain a considerable time. To countenance this misrepresentation, made solely with a view to mislead Figgins, I proceeded to Turin, whence I meant to journey to Naples, hoping that I might sojourn there some time, free from the dread of being followed by my evil genius, for such did I now consider this wretch to be. How did I miss my adored Louisa, when I again took possession of the carriage she had been wont to occupy with me!

Every contrivance that had been arranged in it for her comfort brought a pang to my heart; and as I gazed on the front glasses that used to reflect her beautiful face, I almost expected again to behold it.—My own pale and care-worn countenance alone met my view, and my sable habiliments increased its death-like pallor. My child and her nurse occupied one of the front seats; my lost wife's maid had returned to England with Mrs. Neville. Often would my little girl draw me from a gloomy reverie by calling "papa, and mamma," and the nurse would shake her head, and hold up her hand in reproof; but I ordered that she should not be checked in speaking of her mother, and the dear child, pleased with this freedom from the constraint imposed on her, kept continually uttering the word "mamma," generally adding to it, "Mamma is gone to Heaven."

My grief had been rudely broken in upon by the terror occasioned by the wretch Figgins. That so solemn, so sacred a sentiment should be crossed by the ignoble one of fear, and of fear too of such a low villain, maddened me. I hated him with an intensity which no words could express; but alas! I equally feared him, for I was but too well aware that by my own wild terror I had placed my fate in his vile hands. To find myself in some retired spot, where I could, free from interruption, abandon myself to the regret that was now consuming me, appeared to be the natural aim of my tortured heart! While I could conjure up by memory the image of my departed wife, could recall her sweet voice, her beautiful smile, and her fond words, I seemed still to retain something of her, something that pacified, that consoled. I tasted "the luxury of woe," the sole enjoyment left to the heart-stricken mourner. But when this indulgence was denied; when a terror, for feeling which I despised, I loathed myself, took possession of me, profaning the shrine where only the sainted image of my Louisa should be, I became hopeless, miserable—lost in gloomy abstraction, from which not even the voice of my child could sometimes draw me; I was insensible to all around; I noticed not the scenery through which I passed, I cared not whither I went. Morose and silent, sunshine or gloom alike failed to attract my notice.

A return of indisposition detained me several days at Turin, and my servant, alarmed, sent off for a physician. This gentleman, luckily for me, was an intelligent, as well as a humane man. He soon perceived that my disease was more of the mind than of the body; and having learnt from my servant the heavy affliction I had lately sustained, applied himself to soothe and calm my irritated nerves, endeavouring, by every means in his power, to divert my thoughts from self, and the chagrin that was preying on me.

Dr. Martelli possessed extensive information, with a facility of imparting it seldom granted. He was at once a Christian and a philosopher, and the charity prompted by the influence of the tenets of the first, was ably supported by the philanthropy and wisdom which he had acquired in the school of the second.—He excited my interest; directed it to scientific subjects requiring a more than ordinary attention; led me on to examine theories and systems to which I had never previously turned my thoughts; made me consult the best books on the subjects, sent me from his own well-stored library; and so judiciously treated me, that ere I had been more than a fortnight under his care I felt better. He used to come and spend the evenings with me, revealing the treasures of his noble mind, and keeping my poor one so occupied, as to leave me unconscious of the flight of time.

I could not, before I had experienced the advantage, have believed that it was possible such a salutary effect could be produced on me by any human being; but now I was ready to admit, that if God, for His own wise purposes, permits such wretches as Figgins to cross our path in life, *He* who gave the bane, bestows the antidote in such men as Dr. Martelli! What an expansive mind was his! How full of pity for mankind, and how desirous to ameliorate its condition! With great sensibility, reason so well regulated its impulses, that he was never its dupe.—He analyzed his own feelings as closely and correctly as he would the causes and effects of the maladies he was called in to relieve; and this habit and power of self-analyzation enabled him to administer consolation to the minds of those entrusted to his care while applying remedies to the body.

Had I not feared to remain so near Nice, I would have continued my abode at Turin; but the communication between the two places was too direct, and too frequent, to permit me to feel comfortable while within the reach of Figgins; so I proceeded on my route to Naples, leaving my new friend, for such he had in truth become, with unfeigned regret.

My mind had in some degree recovered its tone, although a deep melancholy still pervaded it. Mine was not a grief to be soon vanquished, but it had become more calm, more reflective. It formed a part of myself; I wished not to lose it, for I should have considered it nothing less than a sin of ingratitude to cease to mourn for my lost Louisa. My child, too, now began to be an object of interest and pleasure to me, and the more so, that her resemblance to her departed mother seemed to increase every day. I loved to trace the likeness, and the dear little creature, encouraged by my fondness, became even more familiar with me than with her nurse. She had all her mother's sweetness of temper, and gentle nature, which was revealed whenever anything occurred that might have irritated a child with a less placid disposition; yet she possessed a degree of sensibility seldom met with in one so docile and equal tempered. Before we reached Naples, she had so endeared herself to me, that I could hardly bear her out of my sight; and she, dear child, was never so happy as when with me.

Dr. Martelli had given me a letter of introduction to an old friend of his at Naples, a man of great erudition, and owner of one of the best libraries there. He had described this friend as a *savant*, devoted to literary and scientific pursuits, who mingled rarely, if ever, in the busy world, but who would be sure to receive with kindness any person recommended to his notice by him. I was almost tempted not to call and leave the letter. I dreaded making a new acquaintance that might draw me into others; but recollecting the advantage I had derived from Dr. Martelli's society, I conquered my repugnance, and left his letter and my card at the door of Il Signor Bertucci.

I had taken up my abode at the Victoria Hotel, and had been so fortunate as to secure a sitting-room commanding a view of the Bay, and of the Villa Reale. The weather was beautiful, a cloudless sky, as blue as it was ever represented in those *aquarelle* drawings, so highly tinted as to make one doubt of their accuracy, was reflected on the unruffled bosom of the sea, which resembled a vast lake; and so joyous, so beautiful was the scene that I beheld from my window, so genial the air, that even I for a few minutes was sensible of its influence, and acknowledged that the description of the charms of Naples which I had hitherto believed to have been exaggerated, did not exceed the reality. To the right of the hotel rose an amphitheatre of steep tuffa rocks, seen above the stately dwellings of the Chiaja, crowned with picturesque buildings, intermixed with gardens and groves.

The Chateau St. Elmo, with its turrets and spires, was conspicuous; and extending from it were the green heights of the beautiful villas of the Floridiana and Belvedere, with their stately terraces glittering in the sun; and beyond them the convent-crowned steep of the Camaldoli. The Villa Reale, separating the Chiaja from the sea, which laves its wall, with all its flowering plants and rare trees, lay in front; while in the distance were seen the Isles of Ischia and Procida, set as sparkling jewels in the azure sea.—In the middle of the bay, Capri rose as a giant, to protect its entrance; and to the left, lay the coast of Castelamare, and the heights of the vine-covered Sorento. I gazed on this scene of enchantment until, half intoxicated by its bewildering beauty, I closed my eyes. And then came the reflection of, where was she who would have shared my rapture at this view, and tears started to them.

Oh! if she who was sleeping in her far-off grave, could be restored to me, what more on earth could I desire? but wanting her to share my pleasure, an aching void was felt in my heart, and I arose and left the window.— My child was at that moment led into the room by her nurse, and after embracing me, she would have me take her to the window I had so lately quitted. She looked around for some time in speechless pleasure, and then clapping her little hands joyously, exclaimed "Oh, how pitty! how pitty!" Even while partaking the repast prepared for her, she kept continually turning her eyes to the window, uttering, "Papa, how pitty," to the evident surprise and satisfaction of the waiter, who had rarely, perhaps never, seen a child so young, sensible of the beauty of the view from the Victoria. This enthusiasm was not shared by the nurse, who seemed no more moved by the dazzling scene, than if she were contemplating a turnpike road, of the most ordinary description, while she observed to me, "Miss Herbert, I am afraid, Sir, is not quite well, she has been very restless and fidgetty ever since she has been in the hotel, and I suspect she is a little feverish, for she wants to be at the window, which shows she requires air."

If the pure atmosphere and exquisite beauty of the scene before me surprised and delighted me by day, it was no less lovely by night; for no sooner had the short twilight, which falls so suddenly, and fades into night so rapidly, disappeared, than the moon, bright a "one entire and perfect chrysolite," arose in unclouded radiance, its beams quivering on the rippling bosom of the blue sea, and silvering the objects around.

The lights from the windows of the lofty buildings that front the bay and crown the range of the amphitheatre, that forms the back ground, fell like columns of bright gold across the silver-tinged undulations of the calm sea, giving it a most brilliant and wonderful effect. Boats filled by gay parties, whence the sweet sounds of music were wafted to the shore, dotted the bay, casting their dark shadows like little islets on its bright surface, while the phosphorescent lights produced by every stroke of the oars gave the whole scene an almost magical effect. I gazed, marvelling at its beauty, but my mind was not attuned to the scene; and those before whom, when bowed down by sorrow, some brilliant exhibition is suddenly presented, can alone sympathize in my feelings as I did so. It was like a jar of discord in the midst of harmony, and I turned from it in increased gloom.

And there were hundreds contemplating, with pleasure, that bright and ever-moving picture which awakened only sad thoughts in me! Alas! to enjoy such sights the mind must be tranquil, the heart content. The mourners bearing their loved dead to the grave, turn not with a keener pang from the encounter of a joyous throng of vociferous merry-makers, than I did from the exhilarating prospect commanded from the window of the Victoria, and the sounds of light laughter from the gay crowds passing beneath it.

The next morning, before I had finished my breakfast, Il Signor Bertucci was announced. He had, as he told me, come to offer his services as a cicerone, adding, with urbanity, that he entertained so high an esteem, and so warm a friendship for Doctor Martelli, that he would feel pleasure in being useful to any one recommended to his acquaintance by him.

Signor Bertucci was tall and slight, appeared to be about fifty years old, had a high and intellectual brow, around which, a few locks, tinged with silver, clustered, and had that paleness of complexion peculiar to studious men. I never saw a more benevolent expression of countenance, nor met with a more pleasing manner. The ease of a well-bred man of the world, was mingled with a certain gravity that proved he was a thoughtful character. I felt a strong prepossession in his favour before we had spent half an hour together, and accepted his offer to conduct me to the Musée Borbonico. The nurse, as was her habit, brought my little girl into the room, to see me before I went out, and had I not previously been disposed to like my new acquaintance, the interest which he immediately conceived for her, would have achieved the conquest of my good-will.

"It is only when I behold children like this," said he, "that I regret not having married. My youth was so devoted to study, that I feared a book-worm like myself would have made but a sorry husband to a fair wife. Women, and more especially the youthful and handsome, expect to engross a greater portion of their husband's time than a studious man would be disposed to give. Hence disappointment would ensue, and consequences result which I never had courage to contemplate, so I am now a solitary old man, instead of being like you, Sir, a happy father. To educate a creature like this," and he patted my little Frances's head, "to train her mind, and to see it expand, must be a source of the most enviable happiness."

The child, as if she could comprehend his kind feelings, smiled in his face, and extended her hands towards him, and when he took her up in his arms held her rosy lips to his to be kissed.

"The Romans," said he, "ages ago, pronounced the English to be angels, when they first saw them at Rome; and looking on this beautiful child, I feel disposed to agree with the Romans in opinion, for I never saw so lovely a creature. How cold, how cheerless seems the life of a solitary recluse, shut up with his musty tomes, when compared with the ever increasing interest of such a companion as this. You smile, Sir, but an intelligent child is the most interesting companion in the world."

CHAPTER XLIII.

FORTUNATE was it for me, that I made the acquaintance of Il Signor Bertucci, for my mind, not strong enough to lean on itself, required com-panionship with one of a more vigorous calibre to sustain it, and prevent its subsiding into the moodiness to which it was prone. Constitution and temperament have much influence in forming the character of man. My health, never robust, had become uncertain, and every disease made a more serious impression on it than on that of others, while such was the nervousness of my temperament that I shrank from general society, with an innate dread, lest in it some annoyance might await me.

Nothing is more calculated to convey an unfavourable impression of a man than his avoidance of society. There ever enters some portion of wounded *amour propre*, in the opinions men pronounce on those who are unwilling to form acquaintance with them, and consequently their stric-tures are never charitable.

At Signor Bertucci's, I met several of my countrymen, who eagerly sought his acquaintance, so general was the appreciation of his erudition, and urbanity, and who perceiving his good will towards me, were willing to accept mine, on trust of his well known high reputation. An unconquerable timidity on my part, led to my holding back from their advances, and every acquaintance thus avoided, became from that hour, a secret, if not an avowed enemy.

"I must," some of them said, "know that there was something against me or I would not betray such extraordinary coldness to my own countrymen." They could discover no reason why *their* acquaintance should not be readily accepted, but they were ready to divine why *mine*, notwithstanding their having sought it, might be objectionable. Others accused me of an insolent *hauteur* which merited correction; but none suspected that delicate health, joined to constitutional shyness and reserve, were the sole causes of my avoidance of them. There happened to be some three or four English noblemen at that time at Naples, and they were appealed to by these gentlemen, to declare whether they had ever known me in England, or heard anything to my disadvantage there. Their avowal that they did not know me was received by their compatriots as nothing short of a proof of my unworthiness.

Not to have the honour of the acquaintance of such distinguished noblemen argued that I must be some very obscure individual, who, conscious of his own demerits, naturally shrank from forming acquaintanceship with those who might be so condescending as to make advances to him. All this, and much more, was insinuated to the Signor Bertucci in a mode very likely to have prejudiced him against me; but he, like his countrymen in general, was little disposed to listen to slander, whether openly expressed or cautiously insinuated. He shrugged his shoulders, told my enemies that his friend Dr. Martelli would never have introduced an unworthy acquaintance to him, and continued to treat me with a kindness of which I was deeply sensible.

"Your countrymen, Mr. Herbert," said he to me one day, after we had grown into habits of closer intimacy, "are strange people. I suppose that their tempers are soured by the frequent changes in your climate so injurious to the nerves, for I have known many, and never met above two or three who were not disposed to decry each other. If acquainted, they have told me such spiteful things; and if not, have formed such severe, and often unjust, conclusions of those they meet. They expose all the faults they detect, assailing their possessors with poignant ridicule, while to the unknown they attribute all imaginable evil. What can be the cause of this, if your northern climate be not to blame? I have been acquainted with several Englishmen, and found them sensible, well-informed, and agree-

able, when I met *only one* at a time; but the moment a second appeared
in the field, the good qualities of both became immediately deteriorated.
Hauteur, reserve, and dislike, marked their manner; and I have discovered
afterwards, that no other cause existed for the exercise of these disagreeable indications of *mauvais goût*, than that they were not of the same politics,
had not been brought up in the same university, did not live in the same
clique, or did not hunt with the same hounds. Strange causes, *n'est-ce pas*,
for dislike? and strangers, observing their manner of treating each other,
would very naturally be led to conclude that one, if not both the individuals, had committed some action that ought to exclude him from society.

 "Your countrymen are considered proud; but the peculiarity of decry-
ing each other, to which I have referred, induces me to think that, *au con-
traire*, they are deficient in pride; that is, at least, national pride, which is,
perhaps, the only pardonable one. What can be a surer indication of this,
than the way in which they expose the defects, known or suspected, of
each other? Now, we Italians endeavour to conceal the errors of our fellow-
countrymen. If we know no good of them, we abstain from attributing
evil; and when we meet those with whom we are unacquainted, we treat
them with the same civility we should exercise towards any other gentleman in the society; and are really pained to hear anything said to their
disadvantage before strangers, thinking it may give a bad impression of our
country. How often has it occurred to me to hear one Englishman say, 'O!
so you know Mr. A. or B.?' and I have answered, 'Yes, I have that pleasure.'

 "'You call it a pleasure, do you?'

 "And a sarcastic smile passes over the lips of the speaker.

 "'Yes, I really think it a pleasure, for he is well-informed and
agreeable.'

 "'Indeed! I was not aware of this.'

 "And the gentleman draws up his head, and looks supercilious.

 "'Perhaps you are not well acquainted with him?'

 "'No, I have not that honour; and, to say the truth, I do not desire it.'

 "And he looks more contemptuous than before.

 "'If not an indiscretion, may I venture to inquire if you know anything
to his disadvantage?'

 "'Why, perhaps not positively so, but he is a person not belonging to my
circle.'

 "'He might possibly, if questioned, say that you did belong to his,' said I.

 "'But as mine is far superior to his—in fact, mine is the *exclusive* circle, he could not say, that is, he could not think himself as well placed in
society.'

"'But, pardon my ignorance, do tell me what constitutes the difference of the two circles?'

"'The difference is perfectly defined by us, but to a foreigner I really can hardly make it understood. The exclusive to which I appertain are a set of men of high birth, good fortune, and certain pretensions to *savoir vivre*, which are acknowledged by the *haut ton*. We draw around us a *cordon sanitaire*, which we permit not to be passed. We live together, frequent the same clubs, dine at the same houses, pay our court to the same women, reside in the same quarter of the town, and vote all whom we do not admit into our *coterie*, to be quite of another grade in society.'

"'But is it not the extreme of injustice, first to exclude men, and then blame them for the exclusion?'

"'How, without exclusion, could we keep our circle sufficiently select?'

"'Does talent, fortune, or station, ever induce you to give an *entrée* to this circle of yours?'

"'Not often; and never until the individual possessing any of these advantages has been recognised by the world in general, and by the world of fashion in particular, as being worthy of this distinction.'

"'And when you meet in foreign lands a fellow-countryman, who belongs not to your circle at home, you avoid him, even though you may know him to be a perfect gentleman?'

"'Most decidedly, for were we to form any acquaintance with him abroad, we should be compelled to leave him off in London.'

"'What, if you found him clever, agreeable, and amiable?'

"'Yes, for otherwise we should have all our clique enquiring, "Where on earth did you pick up that strange man? Has your new friend a house?" "I dare say he lives at the other side of Oxford-street, and thinks the denizens of Portman-square and Portland-place vastly genteel!" This is what our set would say, and end by entreating one not to introduce the strange man to them.'

"'And pray what is the harm of living at the other side of Oxford-street, in Portman-square, or Portland-place? May a man not live where he pleases in London?'

"'Not if he wishes to belong to the best society, that is to the exclusive—*par exemple*, to mine. We live in certain parts of London, and vote all who inhabit the places which we reject, bores—vulgar—*mauvais ton enfin.*'

"'But can the street or square in which a man resides, change his character or claims on society?'

"'Not his character, but certainly his position.'

"Such, Signor Herbert, have been the reasons often given to me by some of your countrymen for avoiding the acquaintance of others of their own nation, men, I assure you, whom I have found clever, well-informed, and perfectly gentleman-like."

I confessed to Signor Bertucci that I had mixed little in society in England, and had very few acquaintances. Indeed none among the aristocracy, because it had so fallen out that I had never met any of that class, and even if I had, my station in life, that of a private country gentleman of small fortune, living in a very secluded part of Wales, must have prevented my making any advances towards persons so much my superiors in rank and fortune.

"You were right, Sir," observed he. "Unequal positions in life, present a great obstacle to agreeable association. The great expect a certain homage from those beneath them in station, a homage which a man of independent mind, and conscious of his own worth and respectability, would seldom be disposed to offer to mere rank or fortune. Every man is best in the circle in which his birth and merit has placed him, where *he* is not compelled to look up, nor his associates obliged to look down."

Often did my new friend come and spend his evenings with me at the Victoria hotel, and still more frequently did I pass mine in his home. Together we constantly visited the Musée Borbonico, and inspected the treasures it contained. He was deeply skilled in antiquarian lore, and loved to make his knowledge of it available to others. He was a patient investigator of all connected with his favourite study, but maintained none of the fanciful hypotheses, in which so many antiquaries indulge,—hypotheses that, instead of elucidating the subjects much more frequently, tend to involve them in doubt. He could, from the extent of his researches, as readily class the age to which any object or work of art belonged, as an able geologist could ascertain by the different strata of lava found at Pompeii, which of the various eruptions that have visited that ancient town, had deposited it. Nor was his knowledge confined to the lore of the ancients. Perfectly conversant with the history of the middle ages, he was no less skilled in the interesting memorials they have left behind.

A mind so filled with knowledge, and so ready to bring forth its stores for the advantage of others, afforded me a source of instruction and pleasure, which kept my thoughts from dwelling on the grief that still preyed on my heart. There it lay, slumbering occasionally it is true, but often awaking; and, like a child on first being aroused from sleep, demanding the object that had been dearest.

Signor Bertucci accompanied me to the interesting environs of Naples, was my cicerone at Herculaneum and Pompeii, and made me acquainted with all concerning them. It was when contemplating these celebrated places, so long hidden from the world, that my grief was least bitterly felt. I was reminded of the brevity of life and human suffering, as I gazed on the wrecks of ages before me,—wrecks that have so long survived the beings who had raised, who had inhabited them. As well, thought I, might we be inconsolable for some beloved friend who sets out on a journey some time before we can follow to join him, as sorrow as I have done for that most beloved one, whom I may soon be summoned to join. What are we but fleeting shadows, that glide away, and are in as short a time forgotten, as the flowers that droop and fade, ere autumn has passed! But the sunshine—the gaiety of Naples, and its joyous denizens, produced only dissonance in my feelings; so, having seen all most worthy of attention in it, I proceeded to Palermo, deeply regretting Signor Bertucci, from whose society I had derived so much consolation and instruction.

My child was now my constant companion. The genial clime of Italy had operated on her frame and mind, as on the plants confided to its soil. She had grown rapidly; her health was more vigorous, and her young intellect expanded, as a flower opens its petals to the smile of the sun. She noticed every thing novel around her; would listen with delight to the songs of the sailors, as our vessel floated over the blue Mediterranean, and would clap her hands with transport, when she beheld the sun-beams playing on its bosom. "That child has already the temperament of a poet," had Signor Bertucci often observed, when he noticed the pleasure she took in objects seldom remarked by children. "I can behold it," has he said, "revealing itself as light does through a vase of alabaster. May it tend to her happiness, and the restoration of yours! We live again in those dear to us, after our own hopes have been dashed to the earth; and you, my friend, will once more be able to endure sunshine, when you witness the delight it gives your daughter."

Often have I prayed, that the cares and sorrows that had fallen on my head might avert misfortune from my child. Nay, it soothed me to think that as a certain portion of misery must be dealt out to mortals, that in the large one that had fallen to my share had been included that meant for my offspring. I would watch over her whilst she slumbered, keep off the flies and musquitoes from her pillow, observe every change in her lovely face, listen to her soft breathing, and murmur blessings when she smiled. She seemed every day to grow more like her lost mother, and this increasing resemblance made me dote on her still more. She, too, loved me fondly,— was never so happy as when seated on my knee, her head nestling in my breast, or her dear dimpled arms twined around my neck. Even the sailors as well as the passengers took a fancy to the dear little creature, she was so sweet tempered, and so lively. Every one had a smile and a kind word for her, which she failed not to recognise by kissing her hand, and nodding to them when they passed. A doting mother never felt more pride at seeing her child admired, than I did at witnessing the homage offered to mine. She was now the sole object of interest to me in life,—the only possession of which I could be proud. No wonder then that I loved her with all the intensity of passion peculiar to a nature like mine,—that she became my idol!

Arrived at Palermo, its picturesque beauty, even though seen after that of Naples, struck me with surprise and admiration. Being so much less frequented by strangers, too, than the city I had left, I felt that I should be more at my ease here, and I rejoiced that I had come, though I still regretted leaving the Signor Bertucci, and could not hope to meet at Palermo so accomplished an acquaintance, or so kind a friend. Determined to make some stay in this beautiful place, I engaged a small but charming villa, in the vicinity of the very fine one of the Prince Buttera, and, in a few days, was comfortably established in it, assisted by the banker to whom my letter of credit was addressed, and who procured me the villa on much more moderate terms than I could.

CHAPTER XLIV.

THE interest awakened in my mind by the society of Signor Bertucci led me to a course of reading that filled up many hours of the day; and when I laid down my book, I would devote some time to my little daughter, whose intelligence afforded me a never-failing source of pride and gratification. The novelty of the scenes around me, awakening new trains of thought, and the habit of reading I had lately acquired, proved so salutary a medicine for my diseased and morbid mind, that I began to taste the blessings still left me, and to look back on the past as a troublous dream. Had this love of reading possessed me during the first year of my marriage, what a difference might it not have produced in my fate, by withdrawing my attention from the one sad subject of my incessant contemplation. Unfortunate must that man be who has no fixed occupation, and who seeks not to give himself that most delightful of all—study. The mind must be employed or it reacts, and becomes a prey to every chagrin that assails it. Ask the mourner when bowed down by grief, whence he has derived relief, and he must confess that study alone afforded it. The pleasures of society, the gaieties of life, but aggravate the pangs of regret; but the solitude of a quiet room, and a book that engrosses the thoughts, offer a balm that with time brings consolation, without banishing that pensive memory of those we have lost, which we should hate ourselves were we not to cherish it. And yet when reading the works that most interested me, often have I laid them down with a sense of painful regret, that she to whom my memory so constantly reverted had never shared with me the new gratification I had discovered. How would it have sweetened many of those long and wretched hours when, wholly absorbed by gloomy reflections on the past, I was laying up a store of future misery! for the habit of indulging such, grows on the unhappy individual who gives way to it, until, his feelings rendered morbid, he becomes wretched himself, and is the cause of wretchedness to others. My beloved Louisa too, had a natural taste for reading, and had I encouraged it, would have been solaced by having her thoughts drawn away from painful subjects. How many hours might I not thus have snatched from care, and what a new bond of sympathy might I not have established between us, by the perusal of the same works, the cultivation of the same tastes.

The banker to whom my letter of credit was addressed, invited me to his house, and introduced me to two or three English merchants established at Palermo, who were desirous of showing attention to me as their countryman. They were sensible, well-disposed men, wholly occupied in making money, and consoled for present devotion to business, and the sacrifices it entailed, by the prospect of returning to their native land some years hence, when a sufficient fortune had been amassed to satisfy their notions of comfort. They had already passed many years at Palermo, and the snowy locks that shaded their furrowed brows denoted that they had turned the sunny side of life, and made a considerable progress in the descent of that hill, at whose base lies the open grave that awaits them. Nevertheless they were talking with vivacity of future plans, when they should be enabled to leave off the toil for gold, and return to enjoy the remnant of their days in England. They had lived in the admirable climate and beneath the cloudless skies of Sicily, until habit had palled the sense of the blessings bestowed by both, and looked forward with pleasure to the cold and cheerless clime of their native land, the disagreeableness of which they had forgotten in their long absence from it. They thought not that habit had rendered the mild and genial atmosphere they had now so long and thanklessly enjoyed, necessary for their health, and that, arrived at the winter of life, that country to which they longed to return was little suited to warm the blood chilled by age, or to enliven the spirits depressed from the same cause.

"Strange!" said Mr. Mitford, one of these English merchants, to me, "when we first came here, my wife and I were enchanted with Palermo; the constant sunshine, the clear and light atmosphere, and the gaiety of the people delighted us. But now we are tired of all this, and long to exchange it for England. That is the country in which to sit down and expend the fortunes acquired elsewhere. There a man is valued for his wealth; here, no one cares what his fortune may be. He is not a bit the more valued for it, for the necessaries, nay, even the luxuries of life are so cheap, that those who do not possess one quarter of his wealth can enjoy as many comforts as he does, and he has not even the pleasure of knowing that he is envied for his riches. Now, in England every one knows when a man is wealthy, and more still, people are always prone to magnify his fortune, and to treat him with the consideration it inspires. The necessaries of life are dear, and the luxuries unattainable except by the rich, so that a wealthy man knows that he is in the possession of many advantages denied to the less fortunate than himself. The rarity of sunshine, and the frigidity of the climate, induces him to adopt all appliances to atone for the absence of the one, and the chilliness of the other. When a man is sunning himself in a beautiful conservatory into which the windows of his sitting-rooms open, and is warmed by a *calorifère* diffusing warmth and equal temperature around his dwelling, he need not regret the sunshine and mild climate of Palermo, which he only shared in common with the poorest Lazzarone in the place."

Such was the reasoning of the Englishmen at Palermo, and such I believe is the reasoning of most of my countrymen when far from home, and making money to enjoy themselves when they return to it.

With such men I had nothing in common. I was content to share the sunshine of Sicily with the very insects that basked in it, and liked it all the better, that the poor enjoyed it too. This want of sympathy in our tastes and feelings soon made itself felt. They discovered that I was deficient in patriotism, in finding so much good elsewhere than in my native land, and I found them illiberal and purse-proud, so our intercourse, after some time, was reduced to occasional formal visits, and never grew into friendship.

When I had been about a month in Palermo, walking out one evening, to my surprise and dismay I encountered the man on earth I most wished to avoid, and who I had hoped never again to behold. Figgins, the odious Figgins stood before me. He gazed insolently in my face, never even touching his hat as he approached me, and said, "I see you are more surprised than pleased at this meeting. It however was inevitable, and as I want to speak to you without interruption, we had better walk outside the town."

"You can have nothing to say to me," replied I, "that I can wish to hear;"

my thoughts running on what course I had best pursue in the present emergency, as on my conduct *now* I felt that my future position with this ruffian must depend. Should I appeal to my banker, and the English merchants I knew, for their aid against a fellow who had formed a plot to extort money from me? These thoughts glanced much more rapidly through my mind than I can indite them, but not so rapidly as not to betray irresolution by my countenance, to him who was eagerly examining it. Even in the brief interval I remembered that my intercourse with my banker was but slight, and that my countrymen, mortified that I had not evinced a greater desire to cultivate their acquaintance, had latterly treated me with only a distant civility. I should therefore, in all probability, find them little disposed to judge favourably of me in a case which required a more than ordinary good-will to insure me their assistance to defeat the mercenary scheme of Figgins, and this conviction operated to quell the lagging courage I was endeavouring to summon up to resist him.

"Since you left Nice," said this scoundrel, "I have been unfortunate at play. I had been so lucky with you, that I determined to try still further my luck; but fortune, the blind jade! has jilted me, and again I am obliged to have recourse to you. I want money, and therefore I have followed you here."

"You have no claim on me," answered I, anger and hatred operating so powerfully on me, that had a pistol been within my reach, I should not have hesitated to have shot this wretch.

"No claim on you?" repeated Figgins; "well, that's cool, however. I'll make you know, ay, and feel too, that I have a claim, and the best of all claims, that of the strong over the weak, the innocent over the guilty. The same reason that made you buy my silence at Nice still exists, and is strengthened by your having once paid for it. I will instantly go and denounce you to a magistrate, unless you comply with my demand. Ay, you may look as furious as you like. Had you bodily strength enough to do it, you would kill me on the spot, and so get rid of me, as you did of the poor girl you murdered; but I could master ten like you, and so you feel at this moment, so it's no use your trying your tricks with me."

O! the rage, the intense hate, that filled my breast as I listened to this wretch! A demon seemed to have entered my heart, banishing from it every feeling of man, and planting in their stead a thirst of vengeance that maddened me.

"It's no use putting yourself in such a passion," said Figgins, with a malicious sneer; "what's the good of it? You'd be but as a child in my hands, if we came to try our strength, and all the anger in the world won't change me. Money I want, and money I will have; and I swear, that if you don't come down with the sum I require, I will instantly go and denounce you. I asked you too little before: I was a fool for not knowing better the value of your secret: I *now* am wiser, and therefore, insist on five hundred pounds more. That sum paid, you shall not be troubled by me again."

Why, oh! why did my good angel then sleep? Why did not the insolence of this hardened villain rouse me into resistance? O! shame to manhood, to stand paltering thus with a wretch, instead of defying him! Yet, such was the dread his threat of exposure had inspired in my soul, that, fascinated like the hapless bird which drops down to the serpent who menaces it, I yielded to the instinct of terror, and basely condescended to make terms with this ruffian.

"When I gave you so large a sum before," said I, "it was with the perfect understanding that never more were you to make any demand on me."

"Nor should I," interrupted he, "had I not been so unlucky at play. But what was I to do when the money you gave me was all gone at the gaming-house? It was like a dream, and when I looked at my empty purse, I felt as if you had never filled it. There was nothing left for me to do, but to make you fill it again, so I determined to follow you, and here I am. You thought to deceive me by changing your route, but it was useless. I have my spies every where, and you can no more hide yourself from me, than I can live without money, and that's one of the most difficult things I know."

"But were I to give you money, the sum you have named is absurd, and out of the question; what security should I have that you were never more to make any demand on me?" observed I, covered with shame and confusion at parleying with such a villain.

"What security?" repeated he, with a derisive smile; "why, my word of honour, to be sure. What other security can I give?"

"*Your* word of honour!" said I; and a portion of the contempt and abhorrence he inspired was expressed in my countenance.

"Don't provoke me, don't provoke me," replied he; "for if you do, I may demand double the sum I have named; and I am as obstinate as an Irish pig when I am made angry."

"Will you swear, on your oath, that if I give you two hundred pounds more, you will never again appear before me, nor address me by letter?"

"Just as if my word of honour wasn't quite as binding as my oath!" And Figgins leered in my face, while I groaned in spirit, being fully convinced that no more reliance could be placed on one than on the other.

"I can only give you two hundred," resumed I. "Mine is not a fortune to admit of throwing away such sums."

"Do you call throwing it away, when your character, your very life, depends on my silence?" demanded he. "You cannot impose on me. I know as well as you do, that to save my life you would not give me a guinea, were you not in my power; and I am not at all disposed to throw away my advantage over you."

Stung to desperation by his insolence, I declared that I would give no more than two hundred, let the consequences be what they might; and after some attempts on his part to extort more, which I resisted, he at length consented to accept that sum; and I desired him to meet me on the same spot in an hour from that time, when I would bring him the money.

"Why not give me a cheque on your banker here?" said he.

"Because I don't choose it," replied I, angrily.

"Only take care of what you are about," observed Figgins; "for if you play any tricks, I'll go at once to the magistrate, and have you arrested."

I glanced scornfully at him, and walked towards home to get my letter of credit, and proceed with it to the banker's for the money. I noticed that he followed me, at a little distance, keeping me in view all the time until I entered my house; and when I again left it to go to the bank, he never lost sight of me. There must have been some indication of the tumult of my mind in my aspect or manner, for the banker asked me if I were unwell. This simple question embarrassed me, and I stammered out that I had only a slight head-ache.

"You must take care of yourself, Mr. Herbert," observed he. "This climate, genial and fine as it is, is apt to disagree with strangers at first; and you really look feverish, and ill."

I proceeded to the spot where I had appointed to meet my persecutor, bearing the gold in a small sack, which I had great trouble in preventing my banker from insisting on sending to my house by one of his clerks.

Figgins had dogged me the whole time, and now, having walked on before me to the place of meeting, stopped, and waited for my approach.

"Lay down the money," cried he. "I don't want to come too near you. You may have a pistol as well as a sack of gold in your pocket; and I don't want to tempt you to commit another murder."

"Wretch!" exclaimed I, "he who should rid the earth of you, would render a service to the world."

"Come, come, no hard words if you please. Remember, I have never killed any one yet, and that's more than you can say," replied he.

I threw the sack to him, and turned away, maddened by the sense of my dependence on such a villain.

CHAPTER XLV.

FROM this hour, I felt that there was no security for me from the base wretch who was the master of my destiny. I had the conviction that he would pursue me wherever I might go, and that I should never escape from his power. Who could describe the deep sense of shame, the bitter humiliation and misery this thraldom must inflict on a man possessed of one gentlemanly feeling, one noble sentiment. I writhed under it, and loathed myself for having meanly, basely, yielded to the first attempt at extortion of Figgins.

What was I to do, where was I to fly, in order to elude his vigilance? Again my tortured mind became a prey to despair, and lost the energy to resist the morbid gloom into which I was sinking. When I embraced my child, that creature dearer to me a thousand times than life, her sweet and innocent smiles seemed to reproach me for having entailed dishonour and disgrace on her name.

Although her blessed mother had escaped the bitter pangs that my exposure must have inflicted, had she lived, was not my child's destiny endangered? Could I count for a day, an hour, on the silence of Figgins, who, when I least expected it, might suddenly stand before me as of late, and dictate terms again?

How could my fortune, far from large, resist the heavy inroads made in it by the extortion of this man? Yes, this fortune which should have been the provision of my daughter, would inevitably dwindle away under his demands, until beggary became my portion; and Oh, how infinitely worse! that of the daughter on whom I doted. Would it not be better for me to lay down the load of life, now too heavy to be borne, and thus escape the fangs of the monster whom I dreaded? But to leave my child to rush, unbidden, into the dread presence of my offended God! Oh! no; I dared not commit the foul crime of self-murder; and yet existence was hateful, was insupportable to me. My brain throbbed in agony, my reason was bewildered, as I reflected on my terrible condition. Human aid it was vain to expect. I had permitted myself to be so closely entwined in the fold of the serpent that held me, that I saw no possibility of rescue. But this utter despair of human aid reminded me of Heavenly succour. I knelt and prayed for support to my Heavenly Father, and felt calmed and strengthened when I arose from my supplications.

For some days after my interview with the vile Figgins, I never went out without expecting to meet him. Every man of his stature that I beheld at a distance I imagined to be him, and I was disposed to turn back, so much did I dislike encountering him; but I worked my courage up to confront him, and was repaid for the effort by discovering the person, whose height was similar, not to be him. Haunted by the dread of another demand from him, my very dreams presenting his odious countenance and abominable leer, I felt that change of scene was absolutely necessary to divert my thoughts from this one painful subject which now engrossed them, banishing gentler and holier ones, as well as the *one* terrible event that had entailed all the misery of my life.

That event, which for years had filled my mind, had faded away before the actual danger that this wretch Figgins menaced me with. The dread of him became a positive monomania. He assumed gigantic proportions, and demoniacal propensities and power in my troubled slumbers. He grasped me in his iron arms, he held me, balancing me as if a helpless infant over steep precipices, projecting far into the sea, into which I expected every moment to be hurled. At other times my dreams presented him dragging me into a court of justice, at which presided gibbering fiends, who laughed aloud when he denounced my crime, and held out their arms to seize me, when, screaming in terror, the large drops wrung by agony falling from my brow, I awoke, to thank Heaven it was but a dream.

I began to tremble for my reason. The agitated nights, the impending dread that haunted me through the day, could not, I felt, much longer continue without driving me mad. Sometimes it occurred to me to travel in the East. In that remote quarter of the globe I might elude my tormentor, and drag on the remainder of my days free from dread. But then came the thought of my child. I could not bear to part from her; and to expose her to the risks and dangers of Eastern climes was not to be thought of. In all my misery, her smiles, her artless affection, were the only drops of balm to sweeten my bitter cup of life; and, as I gazed on her beautiful face, so like her blessed mother's, I felt that, rather than it should ever wear the blush of shame occasioned by the exposure of her wretched father, I would submit to every privation, every humiliation, that man could undergo.

Now that my abode at Palermo was known to Figgins, I became so unsettled and nervous lest he should return to extort money from me, that I determined to leave it and return to Naples, where, after a short stay, I would travel homeward. Two or three days after I had formed this resolution, my banker called on me, and after some apologies for the liberty he was about to take, but which, as he asserted, a sentiment of good-will towards me prompted, he told me, with much circumlocution, that reports very prejudicial to my character had been circulated by an Englishman of low manners and habits who had lately left Palermo.

"The fact is," said he, "this person, in a state of intoxication, obtruded himself into the news-room, which is an establishment supported by subscription, for the sole use of Sicilian gentlemen, and to which, by courtesy, the English merchants resident here are admitted, but have not the privilege of introducing others. Seeing some of his countrymen enter, the individual in question forced his way into the room in spite of the representation and remonstrances of the porter; and when one or two of the English gentlemen explained to him that strangers were excluded, he pulled out a considerable sum in gold to prove his respectability, declared he could bring you to certify that he was a gentleman, and had only come to Palermo to visit you; and these asseverations not being deemed satisfactory reasons for violating the regulations of the establishment, he grew irate, insulted all the members who were present, and anger, combined with intoxication, having wholly mastered him, he swore that, little as the members seemed to think of him, he could make you, whom probably they respected, tremble at his nod. These strange expressions excited the curiosity of some of those present, who, piqued by your evident avoidance of cultivating an acquaintance with them, are not favourably disposed towards you. By affecting to doubt the insinuations of this low man, they stung him into asserting that no later than the preceding day he had compelled you to give him no less a sum than two hundred pounds, which he made you go to your banker to procure, which sum he declared he could show them; nay, more, that he could compel you to give him as much more whenever he pleased, as he held your fate in his hands. I was not present when this scene occurred, but soon after, two of your countrymen called on me, and inquired whether you had not the previous day drawn from my bank two hundred pounds in gold. I acknowledged that such had been the case, little thinking that, by so doing, I was confirming the evil suspicions these persons had formed of you. I knew not the motive of their inquiry, and only discovered it to-day, when I found that the vile insinuations of a low drunkard had been received as evidence against you, and that your countrymen have been searching every where for this man, in order to have him examined, and an investigation made into your connexion with him. I have come to inform you of this disagreeable affair. The man who has caused it, left by the packet early the next morning for Naples; but the persons who have made themselves so officious here have written to their correspondent at Naples to gain intelligence of this man, giving a minute description of his person and dress, by which they hope to discover him, they not having been able to ascertain his name."

My feelings during this statement can be easily imagined. Shame, rage, and terror, in turn assailed me. I made a violent effort to conceal my emotion, but it must have been an unsuccessful one, for the banker, with much good nature said, "I see you are shocked, disgusted, and no wonder; that your countrymen should lend credence to the assertions of a man evidently of a low station in life, and by their own account intoxicated while he made them, does seem as strange as it is uncalled for. I have expressed my sentiments on the subject to them, but finding that they were determined to busy themselves in the matter, I have thought it a duty I owed to you, to make you acquainted with the business."

I thanked Signor Magatti with as much calmness as I could assume. I feared to deny having seen the wretch Figgins at Palermo, lest by so doing I should compromise myself still more. In fact, my having drawn the two hundred pounds on the day he had named, which could be only known at the bank, and to myself, unless *he* had been informed of it by some one in the bank, or by me, was a positive proof of at least a portion of his assertion. Then the gold he had displayed furnished another evidence against me, and I felt so inextricably involved that I knew not what to offer in my own defence. At length I ventured to say that though I did not acknowledge the right of the two gentlemen named to interfere in my concerns, it had become positively necessary for me to set out with as little delay as possible for Naples, in order to discover and punish the impostor who had dared to make use of my name. There was no need for me to affect indignation, for my bosom swelled with it, and my anger had such an influence with Signor Magatti, that he entered warmly into my feelings, and appeared convinced that I had been slandered. "Had you not better see, or write to your two countrymen here?" said he, "you may quote me as your informant of the active part they have taken in this affair. Or I will go with you to them, for I really think the sooner their tongues are stopped on this subject, the better."

I felt that were I to decline his offer, it would make him think ill of me, and this I was unwilling should be the case, for I knew that he was on terms of intimacy with Signor Bertucci, and would in all probability inform him of my refusal to confront those who had so unjustifiably taken a part against me. And yet, with all my pride and reserve, how painful was it for me to seek these men, and to enter with them on a subject so humiliating. But it must be done. I must drain the cup of mortification to its very dregs, or leave Signor Magatti to believe me culpable; so I assented to his proposal, and set out with him to seek my countrymen. I found them at home, and not being together, they were less untractable than might otherwise possibly have been the case. I stated the cause of my visit, which each in turn seemed to anticipate the moment I entered his abode; for never did I behold two men more confounded than when I demanded by what right they had, on the faith only of some low and drunken ruffian, presumed to attribute crime or guilt to me, or to take on themselves to institute inquiries on the subject.

My indignation and anger, which were unfeigned, seemed to convey to them a conviction that I had nothing to fear; and in proportion to my spirit, became their want of it. They evidently had not expected that I would have thus boldly confronted them; and when I threatened legal proceedings, they expressed the utmost regret at having been misled by the assertions of the drunken man they had seen, and offered any, or every apology I might choose to dictate.

Il Signor Magatti was delighted at my triumph, repeatedly reminded my two spiteful and malicious countrymen that *he* had never for a moment given the slightest confidence to the vile insinuations of the unknown person, and had urged them to observe the same course. The crestfallen gentlemen looked very contrite, and declared they would immediately write to their correspondents, to take no further steps in the affair, as the whole had originated in error.

Encouraged by their shame and confusion, I felt my spirit increase; and, with a haughty air, I assured them that I would immediately proceed to Naples, and use my utmost endeavours to have the man in question arrested, and compel him to explain the hints he had dared to give; and I added, that I trusted, if he was arrested, that they would be ready to come forward, and prove the words he had used. This they promised to do; and I left them, coldly accepting their reiterated excuses and regrets.

"Give me your hand, Signor Herbert," said Signor Magatti. "You have behaved like a man, and a brave man too, jealous of his honour and reputation. It did my heart good to hear you rate those gentlemen, and to observe your *fierté* while you did so. They were made heartily ashamed of themselves, and they deserved it; for between you and I, they are extremely malicious. Never does a noble traveller from your country visit Sicily, that these two do not instantly make us acquainted with some history or anecdote to his disadvantage. One is ruined by his extravagance, and is obliged to get out of the way of his creditors. Another has lost his fortune by gambling, and another is so immoral that he is glad to leave his own country, where he is too well known. In short, there is no end to the propensity to scandal of the individuals we have left; and if they are to be credited, there is not to be found in all your country an honourable man, nor a spotless woman.

Such persons greatly injure their own land by propagating such reports, and I rejoice that they have been reproved by you. And yet how prone are we all to error! How given to think ill of our fellow men! I assure you that I, even I, who am not disposed to misjudge, fancied that you were not over-willing to confront these gentlemen.—Yes, I misjudged you, my dear Signor Herbert, until I saw the anger that flashed in your eye, the honest indignation, and noble *fierté* you evinced when reprimanding these men."

I was glad that I had been able to screw my courage up to the scene I had gone through, when I saw the good effect it had produced; and I took leave of Signor Magatti, leaving him impressed with a most favour-able opinion of me, although the striking fact of my having drawn the two hundred pounds in gold from his house, the day in which the wretch Figgins had boasted of my having given him that sum, offered such an incontrovertible evidence against me that one would have thought it could not have been passed over. But such is the influence of money. To give so large a sum away, argued that I must be richer than was imagined, and to be rich is always in favour of a man, more especially when he who attacks his reputation is known to be poor.

CHAPTER XLVI.

Now fully impressed with the conviction that not even his own interest could bind the odious Figgins to secresy, and that with his habit of inebri-ety, he would during those hours when he was no longer master of his reason, disclose as at Palermo, his power over me, I became more than ever wretched, when I reflected on my own position. How was I to escape from the reach of this harpy,—where hide myself? In what a labyrinth of misery had I involved myself, and where was I to find a clue to lead me out of it? Then came a hope that Figgins's habits of intoxication might abridge the term of his life, and he dead, I might pass the remainder of my life free from alarm! But then came the recollection of how many aged men I had seen who had all their days indulged in a similar habit to Figgins. He was probably inured to intoxication, and might live to torture me during all my days.

Oh! the misery, the despair of knowing my peace, my honour, to be in the hands of one of the most despicable miscreants on earth, without the power of securing his silence, or of ridding myself of his exactions!

Existence, held on such terms, instead of being a blessing, was a bur-then, an intolerable burthen, and had not the Almighty forbidden self-murder, I would have laid down the load. Of one change in myself, I had cause to be thankful, and I was so, deeply, humbly, thankful; for I now felt that, to free myself for ever from the power of the vile Figgins, I would not, could the mere movement of a finger effect it, occasion his death. No, as yet I was unsullied by guilt, and though, by my own folly and madness I had increased the penalty, I would not for worlds add to my present wretchedness, the consciousness of crime, the weight of remorse. I remembered when at Nice, the desperate thought of destroying Figgins had crossed my mind, and I thanked God, that now, whatever my sufferings might be, such a thought returned to me no more.

I sailed from Palermo the next evening, my plans for the future totally unsettled, and haunted by the dread, that as my persecutor had traced me thence, notwithstanding the *ruse* I had put in practice to deceive him when I quitted Nice, so would he be able to discover my retreat, wherever I might direct my steps. Oh! could I but lay open my position to the Signor Bertucci—he, such a sensible, as well as such a kind man, and who had evinced such a warm interest for me and my child. But how convince him that I was *really* guiltless, when I had nothing but my own assertions to offer in proof. The whole affair must appear so strange, so improbable, as to be almost incomprehensible. No; I could not bring myself to relate what must excite his incredulity; I could not encounter his altered countenance, when I had revealed my secret. I must submit to the fate that awaited me, a fate brought on by my own folly, but not the less bitter for that.

Arrived at Naples, I called on my only friend there, the Signor Bertucci. He was surprised, but pleased to see me again; had many new subjects of interest to talk to me about in the recently discovered buildings and antique bronzes of Pompeii. The glass found there also, refuting some learned hypothesis, relative to the ancients not having applied glass in their windows, lately published by an erudite *abbate*, afforded him an opportunity of revealing some of the vast antiquarian lore, in which he was so well versed; and, as I listened to his reflections, I almost envied the calmness of mind, that permitted such researches, and enabled him to be so eloquent on them. I told him of my desire to visit Pæstum, and to explore the beautiful country between Naples and Salerno. He expressed his regret that he could not accompany me, and advised my leaving my child and her nurse under his protection, during my absence, alleging that the accommodation to be found on the road, was not suited to a little creature, brought up so luxuriously. I did not wish to impose so much trouble on him, and knowing that the kind hostess of the Victoria would herself attend to the comfort of my daughter, I determined to leave her at the hotel, for the few days I should be absent, the Signor Bertucci promising to call and see her every day.

I longed to be alone: to ramble at will through a picturesque and beautiful country I had never previously explored. I fancied it might prove a diversion from the painful thoughts that haunted me, forgetting that sorrow and memory accompany the wretched wherever they go. I took leave of my daughter,—merely telling her nurse and my male attendant that I should be absent a week, but not stating whither I was going,—and two days after my return to Naples, proceeded to Castelamare, *en route* for Salerno.

Never had a fairer day been granted in Italian climes. The sky, blue and bright, was reflected on the sea, with a tint as rich as ever the purest sapphire gave forth; and, as the sun-beams fell on the sparkling water, millions of brilliants seemed to glitter on its translucent breast. The dark azure of the mountains, brought near by the light and transparent atmosphere, bounded the horizon on my left, while the rippling waves broke in circling eddies on the shore at my right, with a soft and monotonous sound, most soothing to the senses. Myriads of pearls, formed by the foam of the broken wavelets, floated and glittered on the sand, like broken hopes, dispersing almost as soon as formed, and wafted away with the revolving tide.

Could I behold, unmoved, the enchanting views that presented themselves before me? There lay Capri, like a precious gem set in the sea; the sunshine playing on it, and bringing out its varied hues; and to my left, stood Vesuvius, in grim repose, yet with something menacing, too, in its aspect,—something, reminding one, that it might again overwhelm the smiling scene around, and spread desolation, where industry had almost effaced the traces of its former ravages.

Vesuvius was to the glowing picture, what the sight of a cemetery is in a beautiful landscape. It reminded one of the instability of what we are enjoying, and I turned from it as chastened, as a man in high spirits rushing from a scene of brilliant pleasure feels, on encountering a funeral procession of some young and fair victim to ruthless Death. Having left Castelamare with its dark green foliage, its olive woods, and vineyards, crowned by cliffs and isolated towers, I proceeded to La Cava, through a country full of the most picturesque and romantic scenery. Here a rustic bridge spanned a broad and sparkling stream, that jumped and gambolled over broken rocks and shining gravel, while perched on high, stood wild rocks intermingled with grotesque-shaped trees, presenting just such scenes as the pencil of Salvator Rosa loved to paint. We recognize his pictures at every turn of the road, and are reminded of his having often wandered through the spots we are now exploring.

The white towers erected for pigeons along the left of the road, with the blue sky for background, and the flocks of these birds winging their course from tower to tower, gave great animation to the scene, and the picturesque costumes of the peasants encountered, added to the beauty. All that I had heard of the country between Castelamare and Salerno fell short of the truth. It was beautiful beyond the powers of description; and as I paused to admire it, the thought of her who was sleeping in her distant grave,—of her, whose heart would have been filled with delight when gazing on such scenery, brought tears to my eyes. Every thing that touched my heart, whether in Nature, or Art, awakened my regret for my lost Louisa. It was as if every noble and tender sentiment were so closely associated with her memory in my heart, that never more could they be separated. Even when I prayed to the Deity, her pure spirit floated in my thoughts as an angel interceding for me at the Throne of Mercy, as a pitying soul redeemed from sin, looking down from its own beatitude on the unhappy being she had loved so well. She was with me in thought, through the whole of this journey. Alone, with no curious or indifferent eye to mark my emotion, I abandoned my whole soul to the tender melancholy that stole over me, as I thought of her. Again her low sweet voice seemed to sound in my ear; her pensive, dark, and loving eyes met my glance, though I was passing through scenes where she had never been, and where consequently it might be supposed they could awaken no memories of her. But all that was beautiful, all that appealed to my heart, evoked the recollection of her whose image was buried in it, and though I travelled in search of recreation from care, my love and sorrow accompanied me.

I stopped a day at Salerno, so rich in associations of the middle ages, but I took little interest in its sights, and the mouldering folios shown me. The blue sky, and bluer sea, the distant sunlit mountains fading into the most delicate hues, and the luxuriant vine branches trailed from tree to tree, had more attraction for me than the objects to which strangers are led by the self-elected ciceroni of the town. I, however, suffered myself to be conducted to the church of Santa Maria Maggiore, once the temple of Vesta, and saw the antique Sarcophagi now converted into a Mausoleum for the modern dead, but I little heeded the erudite histories of the place and its treasures, recounted to me in a doubly nasal tone by the ciceroni, and gladly returned to the sea-shore, where, having engaged a boat, I was rowed some distance on the bay, whence Salerno with its tower-crowned cliffs had a striking effect. I returned to the Alberga for a late dinner, and again wandered forth to the shore. It was the Ave Maria time, and as the sound of the hymn was borne to me by the evening breeze, a deep religious feeling filled my soul. I felt, that in a strange land, far from all I knew, amidst a people who were not even acquainted with my name or country, the same Almighty God worshipped in my own land was here adored, and no place could be strange to me, where at the same hour, earnest hearts offered up the incense of prayer to Him. Oh! blessed tie of brotherhood, why should a difference in the forms of worship ever separate human hearts? The hymn borne to me on the breeze, was addressed to the mother of God, but that did not prevent *my* soul from ascending in prayer to *Him*, nor did I condemn those who offer their vows to that most pure and blessed of women, who was chosen to be his mother, though theirs was not my faith. To me, worship to the divinity, when sincere, in every form is sacred, and I pity the hard of heart, who can condemn the followers of any religion, which they believe to be true, and hug themselves in the selfish belief that those only of one creed can be saved. Who dares put a limit to the pity and mercy of God, towards his erring and ignorant creatures!

I left Salerno for Pæstum early next morning, refusing to take an escort, as was advised by the innkeeper. I was told of persons robbed, and in one instance murdered, through want of this precaution. But what had I to dread? The loss of the small sum I carried with me, could only occasion a temporary inconvenience, and my carriage and dress indicated so little of patrician wealth that much could not be expected in the way of ransom for me. I would offer no resistance, if assailed, and consequently dreaded no ill usage. The landlord shook his head, and said the English were always self-willed, and hoped I might not suffer for it as a poor young couple from my country had done, who, while yet in all the elysium of the honey-moon, had met their deaths returning from Pæstum, by the hands of some brigands who attacked them. The driver, he added, could tell me all about it, for he drove the hapless pair that very day, and had been severely beaten. I questioned the man as we journeyed along, and he related the story to me.

"A fairer couple, Signor, I never saw. They were young, rich, I believe,— generous I found them, the husband handsome and manly, the wife, so youthful, as to be almost still a child. She was fair as the finest pictures of the Madonna. Her cheeks like two roses, her eyes blue as the sky, her hair rich as our vine branches, and borne by every breeze like their tendrils. They were like two happy children escaped from school, joyous in their liberty. They used to turn from looking at the heavens, and the blue sea, and gaze into each other's eyes, as if every thing they saw together made them dearer to each other. And she would lean her small hand on his shoulder, and he would encircle her delicate waist with his arm. And sometimes they used to sing too, Signor, such beautiful duets. One might easily know how well they loved, by the way their voices kept time together. It seemed as if the notes of both came from the same breast; I warrant me, this road never before nor since heard such voices. They reminded me of birds, now rising high into the air, and then sinking down, as if they brought back a little patch of the blue heavens with them, so clear, so beautiful did they die away. Every one noticed their love. The men and women at the Albergo, who waited on them at their repasts, spoke of it. They said they were always gazing at each other, and when they passed before the mirror, they never looked in it, but turned to look at each other.—'Now said Annunciata'— and Annunciata, Signor, is a clever girl, 'when a woman prefers looking at her lover's face, to seeing her own in a mirror, it is a sign of the greatest affection. They are too happy,' said Annunciata, 'such happiness never lasts long.' Poor young creatures, how will they bear to live, if either should cease to love! Providence looks jealously on such bliss on earth, for when it is so great, what greater can be reserved up there, Signor?" and he pointed to the sky.

"Well, Signor, I took them to Pæstum, and they were pleased. Every thing, in truth, pleased them—they were so happy. And they made sketches of the temples, and each said the drawing of the other was most like, and they showed them to me; and though I could not really see which was the most perfect, both were so very true, the Signora pressed me so much to decide that, seeing what would most please her, I said the Signor's drawing was the most like. And she clapped her small hands for joy, and gave me a piastre, while he said I was quite wrong, for hers was a much finer drawing. They say, Signor, that we don't like to see happiness in other persons' eyes; that we like to see it only in our own. But I assure you, I had grown so fond of this young pair, that it gave me pleasure to see their great happiness. And yet, I never saw them kiss. Annunciata wouldn't believe me when I told her. And once, when the Marito was raising her hand to his lips, before me, her cheeks grew redder than any rose, and she drew away her hand, and he seemed to understand that it was not pleasing to her, in my presence; and then she thanked him with such a look as I never saw before—never shall see again. No, Signor, with all their love, they were as modest and innocent, as two *bambini* at play. One felt that they were pure in heart.

"What a bright day it still was when we turned our backs on Pæstum! Often did they stand up, to look back on it, until we had got too far away to see it. I was advancing at a quick pace, when all of a sudden I heard a shrill whistle, and saw heads pop up from behind a hedge, and guns aimed at the carriage, while loud voices called on me to stop. I determined to put the horses into a gallop, and began whipping them, but the Signora cried out to me to stop, and in accents that went to my very soul, implored her husband to make no resistance. He had arms in the carriage, and was well disposed to use them, but there was such agony in her entreaties that he yielded to them. The brigands came up and demanded money.

"'Give them, oh! give them,' said the Signora.

"The gentleman looked angry, and I am sure was thinking how easily—for he was a strong as well as a brave man—he could drive them away, when, they more angrily demanding the money, he stooped down to take the sack that contained it from the bottom of the carriage, when one of the brigands, thinking he was looking for his pistols to shoot them, aimed his gun at him. The Signora saw him take aim, and quick as lightning threw herself between her husband and the brigand to save the former, when—oh! unhappy day—the gun was fired, and the same shot pierced both bodies! Never, never, shall I forget that moment. Both fell back mortally wounded, and I, Signor, maddened at the sight, reproached the murderer with such bitter violence, that he was only prevented murdering me also by the other brigands, who disarmed him, but not until he had terribly beaten me with the butt end of his gun. The brigands, having rifled the carriage, fled, and I, mounted on one of the horses, galloped off for aid to the next house. To this the poor Signor was borne, while the Signora was taken back to the wretched hostelrie at Pæstum, there being no more room at the house to which the husband had been taken. They were insensible when they were separated, but I, Signor, my heart bled at the notion that even in death they should be parted. He died in a few minutes; *she* lived two days, believing all the time that *he* was recovering, and would soon be brought to her, and that she herself was in no danger. She spoke of her husband continually, raved of him in all her delirium, and died, Signor, talking of the unutterable happiness she experienced at being again reunited to him.

"Yes, Signor, Annunciata was right. They were too happy to live, but it was a pity that they who could not bear to be asunder a moment, should not have died together, though perhaps it was all through the mercy of God; for as the Signora lived two days after her husband, it would have been too cruel for her to know he was gone from earth before her."

This simple narrative powerfully affected me, and the changes of countenance, and voice, as well as the tears of the narrator, proved his sorrow. "Yes, better," thought I, "was it that they died while yet their happiness had known no cloud, their garland of life had not faded, nor lost a single flower. Theirs, if short, was a blissful existence, loving and beloved. What could life yield that they had not already enjoyed? Their cup of happiness was full to the very brim, and none of the dregs had yet touched their lips." But then came the thought, that had they lived to bless, and be blessed by a child, to feel that most pure and unselfish of all love, that of a parent to his offspring, which looks beyond the grave to the happiness of its object, might not their felicity in life have known increase? My heart swelled with tenderness, for my own child seemed to rise up before me; and as I thought how bitter the pang of leaving her alone on earth, while yet in the helplessness of child-hood, I admitted that it was a mercy accorded to the youthful pair, whose fate had excited such sympathy in my breast, that they were spared this pang. I dwelt on the youthful wife in all her charms, which must have been great to have made so profound an impression on the simple man, who so fondly remembered the happy pair. I felt sure she must have resembled my lost Louisa. But, far happier in a husband, she had experienced no trials like those to which one terrible event in my life had subjected my dear lost one. She had not met with moodiness and abstraction, where *she* had garnered up *her* heart; *her* days had been all sunlit, and when the night, the night of existence came, she slept in the same grave with her husband.

CHAPTER XLVII.

THERE was something in the desolation of Pæstum, analogous to the state of my feelings. There stood the work of man in ruins, while the mountains, the sea, and the hills, the work of God, remained unchanged. A cloudless sky, and a dazzling sunshine, seemed to mock the time-touched temples, once the boast of other centuries, and still magnificent in their decay. There was not a fissure in them that was not distinctly revealed by the bright light shed on each and all.

The stateliness, the fine proportions of these works of antiquity, stand-ing boldly out against a sky as darkly blue as the purest ultramarine, had a most imposing effort. They sobered, they awed my feelings. How puerile seemed the wreck of man's fleeting, transitory happiness, while contem-plating these grand wrecks of ages!—these monuments of a bygone race, whose works have so long outlived even the names of the architects and founders, as to give rise to various apocryphal hypotheses concerning their history! A miserable building used as a wine-shop for the postillions who drive travellers to Pæstum, and as a stable for their horses, stands at a little distance from the temple, and two or three reed huts erected as a shelter for shepherds, form a striking contrast to the temple of Neptune.

A swarthy shepherd clothed in sheep-skin, his bronzed bare legs, and sandalled feet reminding one of a statue, or a squalid looking mendicant, attracted from his wretched hovel by the sight of a carriage, might be seen hovering around to entreat charity. I walked from the temple of Neptune to that of Ceres, through long grass, interspersed with wild plants and bushes, growing in rank luxuriance; but not one of the roses, for which Pæstum was once so famed, met my view.

I sat down on a broken column to contemplate the scene. Its desolation, instead of irritating my morbid feelings, soothed them.—Life seemed a dream, a feverish dream, soon passed, and its griefs, fleeting like our days, scarcely worth a thought, when the brevity of our existence is brought before us by the sight of objects like the temples I was gazing on, and which countless generations have, like me, looked on, and passed away like shadows, leaving no trace behind.

I arose, and proceeded to the fragments of the walls and gates of the once proud city. No solemn procession, no joyous crowd, no busy population now passed through them. No hum of voices, no sound of chariot-wheels were heard; the wind slept, for not a breath of air moved the branches of the cactuses or aloes growing amid the fragments of sculpture strewed around. I felt that could I have obtained cleanly accommodation, however plain and simple, I should have liked to prolong my stay at Pæstum, but the hostelry was too filthy to be thought of, and after having waited until the setting sun cast a roseate hue on the temples, and made the hills to wear a rich lilac tint, I was warned by my postillion that it was time to depart.

"The Signor," said he, "is not like some Inglesi who came here early this morning, and who, having walked through the temples, betook themselves to the *cabaret*, where they have ever since been carousing over the provisions and wine they brought with them from Salerno, and smoking and singing. They say the temples are not worth looking at. Yes, Signor, I heard them myself, for I understand English, having served an English merchant some time at Naples—Giovani, who keeps the inn, says they have done nothing but abuse the place, and drink until they scarcely retain the power of moving."

I heard the voices of this "rabble rout" as I entered the carriage, singing obscene songs, interrupted by hiccups and oaths, and rejoiced not to have met the individuals themselves, whose presence would have greatly impaired the pleasure, melancholy though it was, which the contemplation of Pæstum had afforded me. Leonardi, for so my postillion was called, beguiled the tediousness of the journey from Pæstum to Salerno by singing. He sang of the shepherd who leaves his humble home, and fond wife and children, to guide his flock to some distant pasture, where for months he is to be separated from those dear to him, and dwell in his comfortless and solitary exile, with no companions but his sheep and dog. His sole consolation is that the sun which shines over *his* head, brightens also the home of his beloved ones; and the stars, the bright eyes of night, which look down on him while he prays ere he sinks in slumber, meet the glance also of his poor wife; thus by the blessed sun by day, and blessed stars by night, he feels not wholly separated from his dear ones, and it will be sweet when he rejoins them, to tell his wife, as they together gaze on the golden sun, and silvery stars, how often they spoke to him of her.

Then he sang of the lover stealing at night to the lattice of his beloved, and awaking her from her slumbers by his song. He tells her that while she sleeps he is near, and hopes that in her dreams she may show less severity to him than when she is awake. He blames the harshness of her parents, who will not let their daughter wed one who is poor in all but love, and paints that love is better than gold to make a wife happy.

The voice of Leonardi was not unmusical, and he sang with considerable feeling, while I leaned back in the carriage in a dreamy reverie, glad to be withdrawn from my own sad thoughts by those vague and more pleasing ones suggested by his simple songs. Pleased at the commendations I occasionally bestowed on his voice, he ceased not to sing until we arrived at Salerno; and I believe the silver I gave him was less gratifying to the kindhearted fellow than my approbation of his songs.

The fumes of sundry savoury preparations issued from the kitchen of the Albergo as I entered.

"It is the supper of some Milordi Inglese, who are expected," said the host in an apologetic tone, on seeing that I turned from the strong odour of oil, onions, and cheese, with distaste. "They are brave milordis, pay like princes, and drink *Corpo di Bacco!*—like Bacchus himself. They took all the provisions in my house with them this morning to Pæstum, and as much wine as would have served eight Italians, though they were but three Inglesi; and they ordered the best supper and wine Salerno can produce, to be ready for their return."

Fatigued by my journey, and desirous to seek my pillow, I despatched my repast, the frugality of which, and the diluted wine with which I washed it down, must have given my host but a mean opinion of me. I certainly could not pass for a Milordi Inglese with him, as profusion and gross habits are what Italian innkeepers, in remote districts, consider the peculiar characteristics of the class they so designate. I sought my bedroom, and found, to my annoyance, that it communicated by a door with a rude sort of *salle* à *manger*, in which a table was ready laid for supper for three persons. I instantly conjectured that it was intended for the riotous trio whom I left deep in their Bacchanalian orgies at Pæstum; and anxious to avoid such a vicinity, I descended to the landlord, and endeavoured to make him give me the chamber I had occupied the previous night, or any other more remote from that to be occupied by the expected guests. But I urged in vain. Every other room was filled, my late chamber was now in the possession of two ladies, and he had no other.

I had not long enjoyed the slumber induced by fatigue, when I was awoke by loud voices, and reiterated demands for supper.

"More wine, bring more wine," cried a voice that seemed familiar to my ear.

"Are you afraid of not being paid?" vociferated the same person; and I heard the chink of a well-filled purse, shook, I concluded, to display the owner's wealth.

"Ay, ay," said another speaker, "he need not be afraid of your not paying. You're the prince of paymasters, as well as of good fellows, and the very one to give these d–m–d Hitalians a right notion of the English."

"Why yes, I flatter myself I'm rather a good specimen of my country. I like an idle life, and love to live on the fat of the land wherever I may be."

"Ay, my hearty, and you are right too. A short life and a merry one, say I. But after all, this here country is but a poor affair for a man with plenty of the ready rhino, to throw away his time in. The Hitalians are a set of spooneys. Know nothink of sport, and what's a country without sport, I should like to know?"

"You are right, Motcombe. No man of spirit can henjoy life where there is no sport, and for my part, if I could find myself back in hold Hengland again, I'd never wish to stir hout of it."

"I say, Bradstock, why did you leave that there Lord Ardingfield? They say he's as rich as a Jew."

"Ay, and as fond of his money, too. Why, to tell you the truth, it wasn't much of a place after all. He *would* pay his own bills; and when a man does that, what can his valet make by him? Then he made a fuss when any of his things disappeared, and things *will* disappear when noblemen are travelling, going from hinn to hinn; you take, don't you?"

"Yes; and so did you, too, I suspect, Master Bradstock; hah, hah, hah." And this attempt at repartee occasioned a general hilarity.

"Not much, I can assure you; for I saw very soon *he* was not precisely a sort of chap as would stand my *taking* ways."

"But it wasn't wise to throw up the place, and so far from home, too;

you have heard the wise old saw, 'never throw out dirty water till you have got clean,' and a devilish good advice too."

"But if a place throws *you* up, or that you see its coming close to that point, who wouldn't take the *h*initiative, and *give* warning instead of waiting to *get* it?"

"Then there is the advantage of being able to say when one hoffers for another place, 'I left hat my own haccord; I was not *sent* away.' Eh, Bradstock?"

"Certainly, Motcombe. It makes hall the difference."

"What infernal hinns these here Hitalian ones are! Here have I been ringing this here bell for the last twenty minutes, for supper, without being hable to get hany one to hanswer. Yes, Hengland is the only place to live in. But here comes supper at last. I hordered that no maccaroni should be sent hup. I can't abide the sight of it. Maccaroni looks to me for all the world like boiled tobacco pipes. Would you believe it, when I told 'em to give us a good hot devil, they stood as if I really wanted the hold gentleman himself, and the cook began crossing himself. Come, gentlemen, let us set to. I see we have devilled cutlets, devilled chickens, and devilled beef-steaks; after which the Marsala may pass hoff as sherry."

The repast was done ample justice to, as far as I could judge by the clatter of the knives and forks, and the comparative silence, interrupted only by half distinct exclamations, from mouths too much filled to articulate plainly, and invitations to drink wine.

"What a regular humbug that there Pæstum is," said Mr. Figgins, for by this time I ascertained that the voice familiar to my ear was no other than his, and though I trembled at his proximity, I listened attentively to the ribald jests going on between him and his companions, in the hope of hearing his plans for the future, when wine had rendered him unguarded and communicative.

"Yes," resumed he, "it may well be called Pæstum, for it's a regular pest, and nuisance too."

"Bravo, bravo," reiterated his guests. "A capital hit."

"To come hall the way from Naples to see two hold tumble-down temples, that's not worth turning one's head to look at."

"You're quite right, Figgins; but—"

"Now, didn't I tell you, Bradstock, never to call me Figgins again? It's a d–mn–d low name, and I can't habide it."

"Pardonnez-moy, as the French say," replied Mr. Bradstock, "but it was an hoblee."

"A what?"

"An hoblee, as the French call it. I was going to say that it's the nobility and gentry that's to blame, for sending so many people to see sich places as Pæstum. They purtends, for it can be nothink in the world but purtence, that they find 'em charming, or as they say, very hinteresting. I'm sure I've heard that there silly chap, Lord Hardingfield, rave habout 'em to his friends, has if they were the finest buildings in the world. And what are they to the Temple in London, I should like to know, where you may see the steamers running hup and down the Thames, hevery ten minutes, while you are walking in a garden filled with flowers? And to think of the lies of people! Hang me, if I haven't heard that chap, Hardingfield, talk scores of times of the roses of Pæstum, and I'll be sworn there isn't a rose in the whole place, for I looked all around to find one."

"Talk of *our* lying," observed Mr. Motcombe; "why, hang me, if the hupper class, as they call themselves, don't lie ten times more. Lord, love ye! I've heard some on 'em tell such thumpers, when I've been a-waiting at table, as made me wonder how they had the face to do it. Why, would you believe it, I've heard one of 'em say that the hearth, yes, the hearth we live on, moved around the sun."

"No, d—n me, that's too much, Motcombe, you made that yourself. There's no man in the world would have the himpudence to tell even a hidiot that the firm earth, with all the thousands and thousands of mountains, rocks, castles, palaces, and cities on it, could move up into the clouds to march round the sun! What would become of the buildings, ay, and of the people too? Why, they'd be capsized, and dashed to pieces, and who would there be left to tell the story?"

"Don't himagine I was such a flat as to believe such a himprobable lie," answered Mr. Motcombe; "I honly mentioned it to show how lords and gentlemen can lie when they set about it."

"Lord, that's nothing," said Mr. Bradstock. "I've heard many things quite as himprobable. What do you think of my hearing one on them there chaps of lords talk of there being mountains in the moon, and the marks of a volcanor, I think he called it, visible through a tell-his-cope."

"And I," observed Figgins, "once heard one on 'em say that the moon shines with a borrowed light."

"Come, come, that's a good un," remarked Mr. Motcombe. "I'd like to know who's the lender?"

"The chap said it was the sun, and they were all such d—mn–d flats, that not one of 'em seemed to doubt it. In fact, they all of 'em took these lies, as if they were hestablished truths that no one questioned."

"And to think such spooneys, such snobs, should be masters of thousands, owners of fine castles and palaces, while we, who have ten times more sense, should be hobliged to wait on 'em. 'Tis too bad, ain't it?"

"But all the world knows their folly; for don't every one of whom they buy take 'em in, in a manner that none but fools would submit to? and when we hadd per cent. to what we buy for them, have they the sense to discover it, tho' the greatest fool among our class would see it in a jiffey?"

Here, overcome by weariness, I dropped asleep, and so lost much of their discourse.

CHAPTER XLVIII.

I SUPPOSE I could not have slept long, when I was awoke by a loud chorus, singing, or rather screaming, a bacchanalian song. For a few minutes I could not remember where I was, or what all this clamour could mean; but when recollection came, I shrunk with disgust at the odious vicinity of the noisy revellers, and from the fumes of tobacco which impregnated my room. The song over, I heard one of these ruffians ask Figgins what he intended to do with his money.

"Why not set up a cock-pit at Naples, and bring over fighting-cocks from England?" said the speaker.

"A devilish good speculation," observed Motcombe. "It would be sure to be well supported by the Henglish who come to Naples, and there's always a plenty on 'em, and it would give these spooney Hitalians a notion of sport."

"And suppose you brought out some good bull-dogs, and made 'em fight once or twice a week? You could get good subscriptions for entrance to see the sport, and turn a handsome sum by betting."

"It's a low trade, and I hates what's low. I'd much rather live like a gentleman. Do nothing, but go about from place to place amusing myself," replied Figgins.

"That's very well, but have you money enough to keep up always an idle life? for be assured, my good fellow, after one has been living like a gentleman for some time, it seems harder than ever to be obliged to go to work again. I know it by hexperience."

"But I have got a bank that will never fail," answered Figgins. "When my money is gone I know where to get more."

"You're a lucky fellow, my boy, that's all; and I wish you'd put me in the way of making gold also."

"And me," observed Motcombe. "God knows, I want money badly enough. Just give us a hint how you have managed to have your purse always well filled, though you open its strings so freely, live like a fighting-cock, and treat your friends like a prince."

"Why, because I've my wits about me. If I wasn't born with a silver spoon in my mouth, and I know full well I wasn't, I've made myself one. Poverty, it is said, sharpens the wits, and I believe it. Mine ought to be sharp enough, for no one knows better what it is to want a dinner. I was always thinking how I could gain enough to become independent of service, and at last I hit on the means."

"There's a good fellow, let us into the secret."

"No, no! Every man for himself. My wits have worked me a mine. Set yours to work also, my fine fellows, and see what you'll make of 'em. I asked no one's advice how to make *my* fortune, and I'll tell no one where mine lies."

I trembled like a guilty wretch while his companions were questioning Figgins. I dreaded every moment that he would, now that he was under the influence of the wine he had drank, disclose my secret, or at least furnish a clue to it; and the weight of a mountain seemed removed from my breast when I found he was not disposed to satisfy their curiosity.

"Come, let us have some brandy," said Bradstock.

"This here wine is poor washy stuff," observed Motcombe, "for all the Hitalians praise it. It is made in Sicily, is it not?"

"Talking of Sicily," interrupted Bradstock, "you were there lately for a short time, Figgins, were you not?"

"And what if I were," replied Figgins angrily. "What is that to you? Ain't I at liberty to go where I like? And once for all, I tell you Bradstock, I don't like being called Figgins, and I *won't* be called so. I told you that I will answer to no name but Howard. That's an haristocratic one, and sounds well. It belongs to one of the noblest families in Hengland, and has such a genteel air with it!"

"Well, my good fellow, I meant no hoffence, but when a man has known another so many years by one name, he is apt to call him by it."

"As for hoffence," observed Figgins, "I hallow no man to hoffend me, for hif he does I turn my back on him, and stand no more treats."

"Well, my dear Howard, 'pon my honour it was only a slip of the tongue. Why, do you think I'd say anything to vex you, after being friends for the last ten years? I remember well we struck up our friendship when you were in that scrape about the jewels that were stolen, and which I helped you to dispose of."

"And about which the poor waiting-maid was transported," observed Motcombe.

"If you think I'm to be frightened by your ripping up old bygones, you're mistaken, gentlemen, I can tell you," said Figgins, his voice indicating suppressed rage. "Many a guinea I've given you both, when I could ill afford it, to induce you to hold your tongues about that awkward business. But that was when I was a servant and depended on my character for bread. Now, the case is different. I know where to get money whenever I want it, and all you could both say and swear, can't stop the bank I draw on."

"Don't be too sure of that, Mr. Howard."

"No, don't reckon too much on that," said Bradstock.

"What, do ye mean to threaten me, after all I have done for ye?" demanded Figgins, in a rage.

"Done for us," repeated Bradstock; "what have you done that you should reproach us in this vulgar way? Lent us a few pounds occasionally, and invited us to dinner, or to make an hexcursion, because you wanted our society, being tired of your own."

"I advise you, now that you intend to set up for a gentleman, to learn to behave as sich," observed Motcombe. "Whoever heard a gentleman reproach another with having lent him a few pounds, or with having given him a few dinners?"

"Hold your tongues, and don't tell me how gentlemen behave; I know all that much better than you do. But when two fellows, filled with good food and wine, which hasn't cost 'em a stiver, begin to open old sores that ought never to be touched again, they must expect that a man will speak his mind. I don't want to quarrel with you, if you don't provoke me into it. So, let us have some brandy, shake hands, and forgive and forget."

"Yes, yes, forgive and forget," echoed both the men. "It's foolish for old friends to quarrel."

"I'll go down stairs, and see if I can't make the master of this house fork out some Rosolio," said Figgins. "It's rare stuff, made in Sicily, where I drank plenty of it." And I heard him staggering out of the room.

"He's a regular cocktail," observed Bradstock, "and deserves a sound thrashing."

"And should get it too," said Motcombe; "only that were we to give it him, it would stop the supplies in future; and one never knows when one may want them. My motto is, that 'It's better to *use* than *abuse* a friend.'"

"D–mn such false friends, say I," replied Bradstock, "But we must find out how he comes by all this money of late. We may be able to turn it to account."

"I suspect he went to Palermo for money," observed Motcombe; "for I know he lost a round sum playing at blind hookey with some chaps at

Naples, and was short of cash the day before he went away. He stopped only a very short time, and returned with his pockets full of money."

"There's some mystery in all this, and I hoped we'd have got it out of him when he was tipsy; but he's such a fox, even when in liquor, that he's too deep for us."

"I say, do you know how much he has about him?"

"Not exactly, but I should think a handsome sum."

"Suppose we were to rob him when he's asleep. In an inn like this the robbery could be put on some one else; and he's too much in our power to prosecute us, even if he knew us to be the thieves."

"A good thought; and we'll share the money."

"Certainly. You sleep in the same room with him. When you hear him snoring, take his purse, and hand it to me. I'll be waiting outside the door for it. You had better hand me his watch, and yours too, for it must appear as if *you* also were robbed."

"But we may be searched, and where will you hide the money and watches?"

"I'll take care of that, so don't be uneasy. I hear him coming up;—is it agreed on?"

"Yes; here's my hand on it, and mind you are outside the door to receive the stolen goods."

"I'll be there—mum!—not a word more—for there he is."

"I told you I'd get you some Rosolio," hiccuped Figgins, "and here it is. I've tasted it, and I can tell you, it's the genuine article, neat as imported, as they say in our country. This here spooney made great difficulties in letting me have it. Fancy what a flat he must be to refuse giving liquor to a man who can pay for it! You'd not catch an Englishman doing that, would you? The fool said he was afraid we'd kill ourselves with so much drink, and that he'd be blamed for supplying it."

I heard the host now speak. He requested them to go to bed, and drink no more: warned them that they would severely suffer in their healths from such terrible excess, and that the character of his house would be endangered by it. They understood enough of Italian, to make out that the host wanted to prevent them from drinking any more, and began calling him abusive names.

"They had not," they said, "egg-shell heads, like Italians, who could only drink sour lemonade, or as sour wine of their own making. No; *they* were men with sound pates."

The host retired, shaking his head, turning up his eyes, and invoking half the saints in the calendar to bear witness, that *he* had warned these drunkards, and that it was not *his* fault if evil came of their excesses. The Rosolio was highly praised; and, if I might judge by the noise of the glasses, done ample justice to. The voice and accents of Figgins became so thick, as to be almost unintelligible; and he complained that he did not know what had come to him, but he believed he saw double.

"For—only—just—now," said he, bringing out his words with an effort, and with a pause between each, "I'll be hanged if I didn't think I saw you two fellows filling my glass twice oftener than your own—a thing that I know to be impossible—for you are both too fond of good liquor to let me have a double share."

I heard the host called; heard the three men stagger out of the room to their sleeping apartments; and, disgusted and horrified beyond measure by the scene to which I had been a listener, I was so troubled, that I hardly knew what step I had best take. After a few minutes' reflection, it occurred to me, that it would be highly culpable to let the innocent host, or the character of his house suffer, by allowing the intended robbery to take place. And yet, how prevent it without involving myself with the miscreants who had planned it, and making my vicinity known to the ruffian I so much wished to avoid? At length, I resolved to steal down stairs, and tell the landlord that to prevent danger to his house, in case of Figgins having a fit, he being the most drunk it would be wise for him, and one of his men, to have a pallet placed in the passage, outside the door of Figgins's chamber, so that if he were seized with illness, assistance could be promptly afforded him.

"Ah! Signor, I feared something serious would come of all this drinking. These three men, brutes they should rather be called, drank at supper and after, no less than eight bottles of Marsala, the strongest wine we have, Signor; and he, who ordered every thing, came down himself, and insisted, in spite of my remonstrances, on having three bottles of Rosolio taken up to his friends."

"Go up at once, and take your place at the door of the drunken man's room. It is the only way to prevent danger to you," said I. And the host, impressed by my manner with the urgency of the case, immediately followed my advice, and thus prevented the intended robbery.

I left Salerno early next morning, long before these base men had awoke from their slumbers. The landlord descended to receive the amount of my bill; but he had taken the wise precaution of leaving his man at the same spot where both had passed the night.

"I never closed my eyes for a moment, Signor," said he; "and in the night one of these persons came from his bedroom towards that where his two companions slept, but, seeing us, went away; and the other got up two or three times, and opened the bedroom door, softly—looked out—and told us we need not remain, for that his companion was quietly sleeping off the effects of the wine he had drank. Indeed, we could hear him snoring loudly, but I would not leave my post."

I felt relieved when I had quitted the Albergo, and breathed the fresh air; the atmosphere of the inn, charged with the mingled odours of the libations and tobacco consumed by the knaves, caused me to experience head-ache and sickness, and created a disgust, which their moral turpitude served well to increase in my mind.

"What wretches to be let loose on society," thought I; "of what are they not capable! With such associates how soon might I not expect another demand from the vile Figgins! And was this system of exaction and plunder to go on for ever? Was I to be always the prey of a ruffian, dead to every feeling, who lavished on his infamous companions the money wrung from me? Was the patrimony of my child to be thus squandered until exhausted; and when no more remained to buy the silence of Figgins, might not the exposure and disgrace, to avoid which I had sacrificed it, fall on me, and stain the name of my daughter?"

Such were the bitter reflections that filled my mind as I retraced my steps to Naples, to rejoin my child.

I determined to remove her to Sorento, for at least a few weeks, and then decide where I had best go in order to avoid the pursuit of Figgins. With what different feelings did I repass the same route, which only three days previously had afforded me so much pleasure as almost to banish, for the time being, the recollection of the wretch who rendered my life so miserable. Now the beautiful scenery was scarcely noticed, or, if looked at, the hated image of my tormentor presented itself, and destroyed every picture. There were moments—and I shudder as I recall them—that the hope occurred that this vile man might, sooner or later, meet his death at the hands of his infamous companions, or from the effects of the orgies in which they encouraged him; and that thus I should be released from his power. But better thoughts arose, and I felt it would be a heinous sin to desire the death of one so steeped in guilt as to be indeed unfit to die.

CHAPTER XLIX.

I FOUND my daughter well, and, in my partial eyes, increased in beauty and intelligence. I lost not a moment, after our things could be packed, in setting out for Capua; whence I led the postillion who drove me to believe I

was immediately to proceed to Rome, as soon as I had looked at the antiquities in the vicinity of the town, to be conducted to which, I demanded a
cicerone at the inn.—I listened patiently to his prolix account of the ruins
we were examining, in order to give time to the Neapolitan postillion to
leave Capua; and seldom, I dare say, had he found any stranger devote so
long a time to the task.

When I returned to the inn, I ascertained that the postillion had left for
Naples; and, having ordered dinner to be got ready, that no chance should
occur of my overtaking him on the road, I strolled out until it was ready.
The repast proved that Capua no longer maintained its ancient renown
for enervating, by its luxuries, those who stopped in it, for never was a
less tempting dinner beheld; and when a very small portion of it was
despatched, I, to the evident surprise of the nurse and my man-servant,
ordered post-horses, and arranged that they should take us to Castelamare,
where I intended to pass the night, and proceed next morning to Sorento.

A douceur to the postillion won his assent to this measure; and, as I
had calculated it would be dusk before we should pass through Naples, our
doing so would not be known, and I should consequently elude the vigilance of Figgins to discover my abode. I had heard him the previous night
announce to his companions his intention of not returning to Naples for
two days, and then coming by sea, so I felt sure I had no chance of encountering him on the road.

My plan succeeded perfectly. I arrived late at night at Castelamare, and
left it early next morning for Sorento; the exquisite beauty of the scenery
of which made me rejoice that I had chosen it for a temporary séjour. I
engaged a house by the week, in the environs, and, in a few hours, was
comfortably established in it.

Those who have not seen Sorento, and its neighbourhood, can form no
notion of the beauty of the place. Orange groves in abundance surround
the town, the golden fruit amidst its green boughs, shining beneath the
azure sky, while the snowy flowers sent forth their fragrant odour to every
breath of air. The sea bathed the town with its blue and pellucid waters,
which broke on the shore with a soft and gentle murmur. White villas
peeping from orange groves, intersected the surrounding country, while
majestic pines and cedars lifted their dark green branches on high.—Never
had I beheld aught so lovely as Sorento, which far, infinitely far, surpassed
my expectations, as well as every description I had heard or read of it. No
gloom, no sorrow, could resist the benign influence of the beautiful scenery and balmy air of this earthly paradise. Here I felt that if free from the
pursuit of the wretch Figgins, I could for ever dwell, and wear away life,

unsated with the charms of such an abode. Day after day I rambled in the environs; one day ascending the steep hills that encircle the town, and the next exploring the sea-girt grottoes along the picturesque shore.—Or I would enter a boat, and sail on the smooth and sparkling sea for hours, pause before the house where the unfortunate Tasso, when fortune frowned on him, came in his misery, to seek an asylum with his sister. In this humble abode he found the repose denied him in a palace, and his tortured heart was soothed by sisterly affection. The recollection of his fate drew me from the contemplation of my own troubles, and I was ready to admit, that if the great and gifted poet could not escape a life of misfortune, men of the common herd, like myself, should not hope to be exempted from its heavy trials, but learn to submit to them with patience. How long was this noble poet the solitary occupant of a dreary cell! Shut out from the light of Heaven, and not permitted to breathe the fresh air—tortured almost into the insanity which his cruel persecutor wished to have it believed he was fallen—how must he, with the sensitiveness which forms one of the peculiar characteristics of poets, have felt the terrible privations and hardships to which he was condemned! And I, who could wander at will among the beautiful scenes that courted my eye, who could bask in the sunshine, or recline in the shade, as inclination prompted, had counted myself among the wretched of earth's sons, and had longed to lay down the load of life!

Before the heavy afflictions of the great and gifted, we become ashamed of having been wholly engrossed by our own; and this I experienced now.— I had so often with terror, mingled with deep humility, doubted my own sanity, that I felt a peculiar interest and sympathy in the fate of Tasso; and now, while wandering where his steps had often turned, I fancied I could identify his thoughts and feelings with my own. This going out of oneself, as it were, is a relief, for while we experience sympathy for the griefs of others, we forget our own, or at least remember them less bitterly.

I formed an acquaintance with the good pastor of Sorento. Struck by my melancholy countenance, and deep mourning, he came to offer me all the consolation in his power, the use of his library, and occasional companionship, if acceptable to me. I was glad to avail myself of both; for his frank and gentle manners, as well as his benevolent aspect, conciliated my good will. I resumed my habit of reading, and with a book in my hand would wander out to some secluded spot, where, stretched on the ground, I would for hours peruse some favourite author, occasionally laying down the volume to gaze around on the bright and beautiful views that on every side met my eyes.

My grief for the loss of my beloved Louisa became softened down into a tender melancholy that I would not, if I could, forget. She was often present in my thoughts. Her affection was remembered with fervent gratitude, and the idea of ever replacing her was as foreign to my mind, as if triple the years I now numbered had been added to my age. Her image was enshrined in my heart, and there worshipped as is that of a saint by a devotee, who would think it little less than sacrilege to expose the object of his adoration to other eyes.

My child grew daily more like her dear mother. Not only did her features and the expression of her countenance strikingly resemble those of her parent, but the tones of her voice often made my heart thrill, so similar were they to my wife's.

My acquaintance with the good pastor had now grown into an intimacy that was not without charms for me. He was a simple and pious man, who knew little of the world except through books, and who devoted all his time to his religious duties, and to works of charity. To him, the poor of his parish never appealed in vain, either for pecuniary aid, or Christian counsel. He looked on his poor neighbours as his peculiar charge, and often were their wants relieved at the expense of his own comforts. For them he had studied medicine, and kept a dispensary, attending not only to the care of souls, but also to the cure of bodies; and constantly occupied for others, he had hardly time to think of self. His was indeed a useful life, and it brought "its own exceeding great reward" in a tranquil mind, and a heart filled with charity for human kind. The erring found him ever ready to commiserate the consequences of their sins, while pointing out and reproving their faults, and the good were encouraged to persevere in goodness by his approbation.

With Il Padre Maroni I visited the poor, learned to become acquainted with their wants, and through his hands to relieve them; and found so much simplicity and frankness, joined to kind-heartedness among them, as to wholly conquer the prejudices strangers are so prone to imbibe against the natives of all countries but their own, and which, through either indolence, or want of opportunity, they seldom take the pains to correct.

Il Padre Maroni was greatly beloved in his neighbourhood. Never did he pass the door of a peasant, that a blessing did not follow his steps. The very children lisped his name with pleasure, and ran to meet him, and kiss his hand when he appeared. These grateful creatures began to like me too. The favour and confidence shown me by their worthy pastor was a passport to theirs; and I felt pleased with their frank cordiality, and encouraged it by every kindness in my power. There is a charm, when far from one's native land, in meeting good-will from strangers. How little, too, does it cost to conciliate it with a people so simple and naturally grateful as the Italians are! When I witnessed the increase to their comforts, which very trifling sums could effect, I experienced a self-reproach at thinking how little I had done at home for the poor in my neighbourhood; and I wrote to the good clergyman of my parish, and sent him money to distribute to them.

This step quieted my conscience a little; but I was reminded how much good the large sums I had lavished to buy the silence of the vile Figgins would have effected, and I writhed as it occurred to me that I was still, in spite of my precautions to elude him, liable to another invasion, whenever his purse should become empty. Had he not discovered me in Sicily, when I believed myself secure in his ignorance of my whereabouts, and had he not told me that it was in vain for me to endeavour to conceal myself from him? I trembled lest he should trace me to Sorento, where I had, for the first time for years, found a little repose; and a consciousness of my insecurity again poisoned the peace I had lately been enjoying. I had come to Sorento, to have breathing time in its seclusion to determine on my future plans to avoid Figgins.

Yet although no day passed by without my having thought of this man, I had postponed forming any resolution, and, like a school-boy during vacation, enjoyed the present reprieve from care, leaving painful reflections to the future. Why, thought I, should I anticipate trouble before it comes? If Figgins discovers I have been at Naples, he will learn that I left it for Rome, and will believe I have returned to England. At Capua I was unknown, and as no person in Naples is aware of my being here, I may surely count on being safe.

Thus I reasoned with myself. But although it is said that we are prone to believe what we wish, it was not so in my case. A latent presentiment that this wretch would discover my abode, took possession of my mind, and I felt that I should, sooner or later, be driven from Sorento. And as this dread haunted me, I became more than ever attached to the place. No one over whom the doom of exile from the home he loved was impending, ever clung more to the yearning desire to continue in it, than I now did to remain in this enchanting spot.—Every time I gazed on its beauties, I sighed at the thought that I could not count on making it my home; for to return to Wales, to the scene of that event which had changed the current of my life, and poisoned my happiness, I felt to be impossible.

We are all more or less influenced by those near us. The chameleon, which is said to take its colour from the object in closest proximity, could not be more affected than I was by the person with whom I had the most frequent intercourse. Il Padre Maroni's simplicity of heart and goodness had drawn me into a sincere regard for him; I liked his society, and a portion of the calmness and tranquillity of his life seemed to be infused into mine while we daily met. He was with all his simplicity and ignorance of the world, and its usages, so right-minded, so charitable, and so pious, that an atmosphere of purity and goodness seemed to surround him, from which I dreaded to remove myself, as much as ever the inmate of a convent dreaded to quit the peaceful solitude, where he had found repose, to enter the busy world, of which he felt an instinctive terror.

I had experienced from strangers, wholly unprejudiced, either for or against me, by any previous reports, a good-will that on increased intimacy, had grown into friendship. The friends I had made were among the most excellent of men, Doctor Martelli at Turin, the Signor Bertucci at Naples, and Il Padre Maroni at Sorento. The regard these worthy individuals had conceived for me, had in a great measure vanquished the timidity and mistrust implanted in my breast, by the avoidance and dislike evinced towards me by the companions of my youth.

I had, in truth, previously to my sojourn in Italy, believed that I was fated to pass through life without a friend, and my heart pined for this blessing, which the last days of my dear Neville had taught me to appreciate. Now that I had secured a friend, on the stability of whose attachment I felt that I could count, I could not bear to leave him, and Sorento consequently became dearer to me than ever.

CHAPTER L.

MORE bitterly than ever did I now reproach myself for not having boldly met the first demand of Figgins with defiance. My utter folly and madness, in having acceded to it, had sealed my doom. That act of insanity had alone placed me in the power of a wretch, whose reckless extravagance would entail a frequent recurrence of his exactions, and I should not only drag on existence in perpetual terror of exposure, lest in his fits of inebriety he should betray my secret, but with the conviction that my whole fortune could not suffice to satisfy the ever-recurring demands I anticipated that he would make. Rendered gloomy by these reflections, I sought to dissipate them, and wandered forth into the balmy air. I directed my course to my favourite walk, the brow of a hill on the opposite side of Sorento, commanding a view of the sea and surrounding country, so vast and beautiful, that often had the contemplation of it chased painful thoughts away, and soothed my distracted mind.

I took a volume from my pocket, and stretched beneath a group of chestnut trees, whose foliage afforded a shade from the too fervid rays of the sun, I was deep in its contents, when the sound of approaching footsteps met my ear. A presentiment of evil flashed through my mind, and yet it was no unusual thing for persons to visit this spot, which was pointed out to strangers as commanding the most extensive view in the environs, and often previously had persons visited it while I was there. But the truth is, the state of my nerves had rendered me superstitious, and I had remarked, that when thinking more than ordinarily of certain persons, it had frequently occurred, that I had either seen, or heard of them very soon after. I had thought the previous day and night a good deal of Figgins, and no sooner did I hear the approaching footsteps, than it instantly flashed on me that they were his. I kept my eyes still fixed on the page, but the letters seemed to dance before them, and I was wholly unconscious of their sense. The footsteps came nearer, and at last paused close by me. Still I turned not, though a tremor thrilled my frame. A forced cough, as if to arrest my attention, failed to draw me from my book, and then a hand was laid on my shoulder, from the contact with which I started as if a serpent had stung me, and beheld the hated Figgins standing by my side.

"I am sorry to have started you so," said he; "I coughed on purpose to rouse you, but you were so taken up by your book you never heeded it. It's an advantage you gentlemen possess over us, that you can find pleasure in reading. It's only one of many advantages you have, and we poor devils would be badly off, if we did not sometimes by a lucky chance get some hold on the rich in order to draw away a little of the gold which they don't know what to do with. Now if I could find pleasure in reading, I need not be driven to gaming and drinking, to pass away my time, and then I would not be obliged to come back to you for money."

"When I last foolishly consented to give you so considerable a sum at Palermo," said I, assuming as severe and stern an air as I could summon up, "it was on the express condition that you should make no more demands on me."

"That's a condition easier made than kept," replied he. "If I had been lucky at play, you would not have seen me; but as I have not, here I am. I want three hundred pounds. It's no great sum after all, so you need not make a bother about it. Every thing has got so dear, that money vanishes before one thinks it's half gone. Time hangs so devilish heavy on my hands, that I can't get rid of the old codger without pitting him against the blind jade Fortune, or drowning him in wine. Now if, as I said before, I could pass away whole hours, as you do, in reading, I should require less money; but then, on t'other side, I do more good to trade than you do."

The cool effrontery of this speech so excited my anger and indignation, that I felt disposed to hurl the wretch who uttered it from the top
of the declivity where we stood. Conscious, however, of my own inferior
strength, prudence prevented my making the attempt, although I could not
master my muscles sufficiently to prevent my countenance revealing my
feelings. Figgins noticed this, for he assumed a quieter demeanour.

"I do not wish to enter on the subject of your tastes or propensities,"
observed I, with *hauteur.* "The point in question now is, whether or not I
will consent to furnish means for their indulgence; and I tell you, that seeing how you have lavished the two large sums I have been already so foolish
as to give you, on the pledge that you would never trouble me again, I must
positively decline any further advance."

The fellow looked at me inquiringly, as if to see whether he had really
understood me rightly, and seeing the determined expression of my countenance, his became flushed with rage into a dull crimson hue that increased
its ferocity.

"So, then," said he, "I am to understand that you will not come down
with the sum I demand? Think well what you are about before you provoke
me. Once I have let out the secret on which your character, ay, and your
life too, depends, it will be too late to repent that, for the sake of a few
paltry hundreds, which you can well spare, you allowed me to bring you to
justice. Ay, you may look big, and pretend to doubt my power to ruin you,
but you are no such fool as *really* to have the slightest doubt on the subject,
for you're not the man to have given me five hundred pounds for nothing,
and two more to the back of 'em, if you were not perfectly certain that you
were wholly in my power. It's all folly holding back, or argufying the topic.
By this time you ought to be well convinced that I am a determined man,
and will go through with whatever I take in hand. You saw how I defeated
your cunning scheme to deceive me when you went from Nice to Turin,
and how I found you out at Palermo. And, last of all, when you wanted me
to lose all trace of you, by pretending to go to Rome, and then only went to
Capua, where you stopped, and came right off here, fancying yourself safe
from me—here I am, come to prove to you that you can no more get rid
of me, go where you will, than you can be quit of your shadow. Every step
you take I am made acquainted with, and will continue to know while we
both live. You are like a poor fly caught in a spider's web; every move you
make to escape only serves to entangle you more and more in the meshes
of *my* net, as happens to the silly fly in that of the spider. Once for all, you
can't help yourself, so don't let us waste time in words, but give me the
money."

"When I committed the folly of giving you money before," answered I, "it was wholly through a dread, that if you repeated the words I uttered in my delirious ravings, I should be thought actually insane; and as I have a child, to whose future prospects such a belief would be most injurious, all the world dreading to form an alliance with the offspring of a madman, I gave you the money to prevent your letting that supposition get abroad."

Figgins screwed up his mouth and whistled, looked at me with a vulgar leer, and then said, "Oh, that's the dodge, is it? But you forget that I went to Wales, *not* to inquire whether you were mad, or not, but to find out whether any lady had fallen over a rock, (I knew she had been *thrown*,) and to search for the body, which I found, and have ready to bring forward as evidence against you."

My nervous system terribly shaken by this recurrence to the one fatal event of my life, I no longer felt the courage or firmness that but a few minutes previously had animated my breast. The loudness of Figgins's voice alarmed me, lest some English traveller might by chance be within hearing; and I suppose my altered countenance revealed to him that this was the moment to take advantage of my returning weakness.

He elevated his tone still higher, and almost screamed his threats. "Yes," cried the wretch, "I will at once go before a magistrate and give you up to justice. I have been too quiet, too patient with you, that's what I have been; but I'll be so no longer, I'll send you to the hangman, and then I wonder whether it will be worse for your daughter, on whom you pretend to dote, to be known as the child of a man that was hanged for murder, ay, and for the murder of her own aunt too, or as the child of a madman, which you so much dreaded that you have given me some hundreds not to run the risk of it. A likely story indeed! You may tell that to the marines, but I'm too old a sailor to believe it. But I'm wasting time in talking to you, and so I'll be off," and away he walked.

Oh! the misery, the madness of that moment! my brain seemed to be on fire. I trembled in every limb—the agony of years was compressed into one terrible shock. I seemed to behold a gazing crowd pressing around me, a scaffold with all its fearful apparatus reared high in the distance, and the burning brand of shame impressed its indelible stamp on my brow, searing and entering it like a hot iron.

Overcome by mental torture I fell to the earth, and lost in a long and deep swoon the consciousness of my misery. When I recovered, I saw the wretch Figgins on his knees, bending over me. I shuddered, and closed my eyes to shut him from my sight. I found the burning taste of brandy in my mouth and throat, and really thought he had forced me to swallow some deleterious mixture while I had been insensible. I felt a bottle applied to my lips by this man, and it was only by using my utmost exertions that I could prevent him from pouring its contents again into my stomach.

"Come, come, don't be so obstinate and foolish!" said he. "It was a devilish lucky thing for you that I happened to look back and saw you fall, for with your tight cravat, and nobody near to help you, you would certainly have been strangled had I not come to your aid. And it was quite as lucky, that I happened to have my dram bottle not empty, for it was the brandy I forced down your throat that brought you back to life; and a pretty sight of trouble I had to open your teeth, which were clenched as tight together as if you were dead. If you have any gratitude in you, you must feel obliged to me for saving your life. What would have become of your poor child, in a foreign land, if you had died here?"

I was so weakened and exhausted by the shock on my nervous system, that when Figgins mentioned my daughter, with reference to her isolated state had I not recovered, that a violent fit of hysterical tears and sobs ensued; nor could I subdue them, although well aware that this unmanly exhibition of effeminate weakness would encourage him to make future demands.

"Come, come," resumed Figgins, "don't give way to your feelings. Nothing grows on a man so much as nervousness, if indulged. How much better would it have been for you to have given me the money I asked, than to have aroused my anger, and forced me to be harsh with you."

The wheedling tone he assumed was precisely that which an artful nurse might adopt towards a foolish, spoilt child; and while it made me hate him still more than before, were that possible, made me despise myself for the weakness which led him to presume to use it.

"Leave me," said I. "I wish to be alone."

"I will do no such thing," replied Figgins. "You are not in a fit state to be left to yourself. Why, at this very moment, you tremble like an aspen leaf, and require some one to lean on to reach home. It's all nonsense our quarrelling. We can't do without each other. My silence is absolutely necessary for your character—for your life—and your money is indispensably necessary to me."

I was so paralyzed, so overpowered, that I was no longer capable of resisting the artful pleadings of this villain. Not that they made any impression on my reason, for even while he spoke, I knew that I was lost if I yielded. But my tortured brain and exhausted frame, now undergoing the terrible re-action of excitement, impressed me with a conviction that both must give way unless I could free myself, though even but for a temporary

release from this harpy; and to gain this reprieve, mean and cowardly das-
tard as I was, I once more consented to make terms with him.—I remained
silent for some time and Figgins again renewed his demand.

"I will pledge myself, and this time I swear I will keep my pledge, not
to demand a single shilling from you for three years to come if you will
give me the three hundred pounds I want. In three years much may happen—death may release you from me; or you may die, and so be freed from
any future demand from me."

Three years' freedom from seeing or hearing from this miscreant
appeared to my bewildered mind, at that moment, cheaply purchased at
the expense of the sum required; but a latent notion that he would break
through this engagement, as well as he had done through the two former
ones, suggested itself. But even this suspicion did not hinder me from yielding to his demand, so desirous was I to be rid of him, if only for a short
time. "For this once," said I, "I will give you the money but, remember, if
you break faith, expect nothing more from me. Call at my house, and tell
my servant to come to me here. I will go to Naples to-morrow, get the sum
wanted from my banker, and if you will meet me on the Mola, I will give it
to you."

"Ah! I see you are too proud, or too revengeful—perhaps both—to take
my arm to reach your house. Surely I'm as good as your servant for this
service?" And Figgins looked angry.

"I will be candid with you," said I. "I do prefer my servant's arm to
yours."

"More fool, you," observed he,—"Your servant respects you, because he
knows nothing of your guilt, and you are not in his power. You have brought
yourself to my level through my knowledge of your crime, and need not be
so very proud and squeamish as to refuse my arm when I offer it."

"I know more of you than you imagine," replied I, angered by his insolence. "I am well acquainted with your past life, and the robbery of the
jewels, for which the unfortunate lady's-maid paid the penalty."

He gazed at me for a moment, in speechless astonishment, his face
becoming deadly pale, and then, in evident embarrassment, said, "I don't
know where you have picked up that old story, not a word of which is true;
but no matter, true or false, what is it to you? Were you to charge me with
it, you have no proof to bring forward, whereas, I can bring home to you
the crime which has placed you for ever in my power; so the less you refer
to bygones the better, I can tell you. And why can you not give me a cheque
on your banker, which I can present and get cash for at Naples, without
your having the trouble of going there?" demanded he.

"Because I do not wish it," replied I.

"Ah, well, it doesn't make much difference as long as I get the money," said he; "and to-morrow I will be on the look-out for you on the Mola. At what hour will you be there?"

"At three o'clock."

"Goodbye, till then; I'll send your servant to you."

And away walked Figgins, whistling as he went, leaving me a prey to bitter reflections, among which, a deep sense of shame at my own pusillanimity was not the least. My servant came to me, stating that a stranger had called at my house to tell him to do so, and I was glad to find that Figgins had not gone in person. Returning to my house, I encountered this vile fellow in company with two villanous looking men, who it instantly occurred to me, must be his companions at Salerno. He looked at me, but gave no mark of recognition; and although my servant remarked the circumstance of that impudent fellow Figgins not having taken off his hat as I passed, I was glad, that, by not doing so, he had avoided drawing the attention of his companions to me.

CHAPTER LI.

THE interview with Figgins had so shattered my nerves, that the evening that followed it was spent in a state of such despondency and mental prostration, that although I had recourse to an opiate, I could not obtain a single hour's repose during the ensuing night, and I arose the next morning so ill and nervous, that I was little equal to the visit to Naples. However, it must be undertaken, but I felt so weak and languid, that dreading a return of my fainting fit of the previous day, I determined to take my servant with me. I was haunted by the reflection that the vile companions of Figgins, who had drawn a conclusion that he had, on a former occasion obtained money by his visit to Palermo, would now date the reinforcement of his finances to his excursion to Sorento; and furnished with this clue, and perhaps aided by his indiscretion, trace me to be the donor of his riches, and naturally enough concluding that such large sums would not be given without some very urgent reason, discover that Figgins held me in his power. They, I had found out at Salerno, entertained the worst opinion of him, and would not be slow to set all their cunning to work to ascertain the secret by which he obtained such liberal supplies, for the purpose of turning it to their own profit.

"What, then," thought I, "if instead of one harpy, I should have three

pouncing on me?" and I trembled at the bare notion. "Had I not heard
the indiscreet boastings Figgins had made to his associates? And were not
they precisely the persons most likely to leave no means untried to discover
his secret, and convert it to their own advantage? Of their cupidity had I
not had oral demonstration? That their curiosity and suspicions had been
excited, their accompanying Figgins to Sorento proved, and justified my
belief that they were bent on not losing sight of him. Might they not have
followed him to the spot where our interview had taken place, and have
thus traced the money he was about to receive to have come from me?"

As these thoughts passed through my mind, inflicting indescribable
torture, I felt that I must leave Sorento, and again endeavour to elude the
wretch who embittered my existence.—But where was I to go? Had he not
traced me when I believed myself out of his reach? Had he not baffled all
my schemes to evade his search? At length it occurred to me that in the
Diario di Napoli of the previous morning, I had read that a packet was to
sail, on the evening of Thursday, (this was Wednesday,) for Malta. I would
engage accommodation in it for myself and family; send back my servant
to discharge my bills, and remove my child and her nurse to Naples the
following morning, arranging that they were to drive direct to the Mola,
where they were to embark without having gone to any inn, and where I
would be in attendance to see them on board. I would, after I had given the
money to Figgins, pretend to return to Sorento; instead of doing which, I
would go to an hotel where I was not known, remain *incognito* there until it
was time to meet my child and her attendants on the Mola.

By this, as I thought, well-concocted plan, I would defeat the cunning
Figgins to discover my retreat; and yet a dread crept over me that as he had
hitherto, by what means I could not divine, discovered my movements, so
might he ascertain that I had gone to Malta. It was, however, worth trying,
and having arrived at Naples, and after writing to Il Padre Maroni, to say I
was suddenly summoned to England, which letter my servant was to take
back to Sorento, I proceeded to my banker's; and in addition to the three
hundred for the odious Figgins and sufficient to discharge my rent and bills
at Sorento, I drew a considerable sum to take with me to Malta, in order
that even my banker should not know that I had proceeded there. I then
went to keep my appointment with Figgins, whom I found with blood-shot
eyes, and swollen countenance, giving every indication that he was either
still under the influence of intoxication, or that he had not yet slept off
its effects. I advanced to the least frequented part of the Mergellina, and
motioned to him to approach me. When he drew near, there was such an
expression of stolid brutality in his face, that I saw at a glance something
had gone wrong with him.

"Here is the money," said I, handing him the gold.

"It's all right, I dare say," observed he; "but since we parted, I have got into a terrible scrape. I haven't been to bed all night, and have a head-ache enough to split my skull. I have two friends, and pretty friends they are too, who made me play with them last night when I was so tipsy, as not to know one card from another, and they have won a hundred pounds from me, and insist on being paid. This will only leave me two hundred; not enough to keep me going for three years, as I promised. Give me therefore another hundred, and I'll break off with these sharks, who stick to me like leeches, feast like fighting-cocks, at my expense, and when they've made me drink more than my head can stand, get me to play with them, and win my money. They are two regular blood-suckers; and if I wasn't in their power—"

Here he stopped and looked embarrassed.

"Go away, go, as fast you can," said he; "I see them coming, and they must not see us together."

He walked off in an opposite direction, and I turned away into a house, the door of which happened to be open, to inquire whether or not lodgings were to be let there; taking care to prolong my conversation with the servant of the house, until they had time to be out of sight. I then went to an hotel, where I had never stopped before, and having despatched my servant to Sorento, remained within doors the rest of the day, nor left the inn the following one, until the dusk of the evening, when I drove to the Mola to meet my child and her attendants; and they having arrived soon after, I took berths for them and myself, and had my carriage put on board. There were so few passengers, that I was enabled to have the best cabin for my daughter and myself, and having taken possession of it, I did not leave it during the voyage, lest any one on board should recognize me, and so betray the place of my destination.

My last interview with Figgins had convinced me that I could hope for no rest while I remained within his reach. It was clear that his vile companions were not only determined to plunder him, but to discover the source whence he drew the money that supplied their reckless course of extravagance. He, it appeared, had just sense enough left to guess their aim; but in the state of constant inebriety which they encouraged him in, how long was it probable that he could retain sufficient reason and prudence to defeat their machinations, and guard the secret they were so anxious to discover!

How fortunate I considered myself to have got away from Naples, and to have left no trace behind me of whither I had gone. I reflected on the retribution which had fallen on the wretch Figgins, who while plundering me in the belief that I was wholly in his power, was himself the prey of the two villains who had no more mercy on him than he had evinced to me. How bitterly had he reviled them, apparently wholly unconscious that he himself was pursuing precisely the same system of conduct to me that he so censured in them. But thus it ever is with selfish and unprincipled men, who are ready to let fall the whole weight of their condemnation on whoever tries to wrong or injure *them*, but who wrong or injure others without one sentiment of remorse.

We arrived at Malta after a safe but tedious passage, and the sound of my native language, and the uniform of British soldiers, gave me a feeling of security not experienced since I had left England. The cleanliness of the place too, pleased me, and before many hours had elapsed, I found myself established in a comfortable abode, where I hoped to enjoy some tranquil days, free from the presence of the odious Figgins.

My daughter grew more companionable every day, and my happiest hours were those passed with her. Never did the most enthusiastic Dutch florist watch over the opening petals of his choicest flower, with such interest and delight, as I did over the opening intellect of my child. Her facility in acquiring every thing I taught her, seemed to me little less than miraculous, and her memory in retaining what she learned, was equally surprising. Often while pressing my lips to her open brow, did I vow, that never should it wear the blush of shame for me, if the sacrifice of my own feelings, nay, of my existence itself, could prevent it. To be loved by this pure and innocent creature as I was, was the one drop of comfort vouchsafed to sweeten my bitter cup of life, and to remain blameless in her eyes when arrived at womanhood, and worthy of her affection, seemed to me to be the sole end and aim of my existence.

I had been about three weeks at Malta, when walking one day at Valletta, I encountered Figgins accompanied by his villanous associates. My feelings at this encounter it would be vain to attempt to describe. The conviction that henceforth it would be useless to endeavour to escape him, took possession of me, filling me with a terror that almost shook my reason. The companions of Figgins stared at me with inquisitive glances, but *he* took no notice of me, and passed as if I were a perfect stranger. Encouraged by this prudence on his part, I mustered up courage enough to take another turn, and confront the trio, and this *manœuvre* seemed to put an end to the suspicions of Figgins's companions, for they no longer examined me with searching glances, but I observed they looked anxiously at every respectably dressed man they met, and then glanced at Figgins, who seemed aware that he was watched.

I returned to my home, my mind filled with presentiments of evil. I had not only Figgins now to dread, but his designing and unprincipled companions, whose cupidity, excited by the knowledge that he had some means of obtaining large sums of money, would leave no scheme untried to discover the source whence it flowed, and by acquiring *his* secret, convert it to their own account. The conversation I had heard between these two miscreants at Salerno, when he was absent from the room, had made me aware that they were capable of any turpitude, and I trembled at the dread, that, instead of having one ruffian to contend with, I should find myself in the toils of three.

That evening a letter was brought me, the contents of which were as follows:—

"Did I not tell you that it was in vain you tried to hide yourself from me, and that, go where you might, I should soon find you out? I am no blunderer. I have my spies every where; and were you to go to the most remote spot on the globe, there would I discover you. But while you cannot escape from me, I, in turn, am entangled in the snare of two of the greatest brutes on earth. They have found out that I am supplied with money by some one, and, full of suspicion, have guessed the truth, or something very near it. They are too knowing to believe that I could get money for nothing, and suspect it is for holding my tongue about some secret dangerous to him from whom I obtain it. These rogues have fastened themselves on me. They live wholly at my expense; they cheat me at cards; and leave nothing undone to inveigle me out of *my* secret and yours. I'll own the truth to you. My firm belief is, that if they could worm out the secret, my life would not be safe in their hands. They would get rid of me somehow or other, in order that *they only* should draw away your money for keeping the secret; and though you may think me extravagant and unreasonable in my demands on you, I'll be sworn you'd soon find the difference if you had to deal with them, for they would strip you of every shilling you possess; and when they had made you a beggar, would, in all probability, show you up to justice. I tried to escape from 'em at Naples, and embarked, as I thought, cunningly enough, without their knowing a word of my intention of coming here. But no sooner had we got out to sea, when the two rogues, to my utter surprise and dread, appeared on deck, and reproached me bitterly for having, as they said, attempted to play them such a trick. They watch me night and day; and I confess I am afraid they will do me a mischief. They got all the money you gave me at Naples out of me, as they did what you gave me at Palermo. My life is made miserable by 'em, and I never go to sleep without dread that, as they watch me, *I* may let out the secret in *my*

slumber, as you did to me. It's no pleasure or comfort to me now to get
money from you, when I know these cormorants, these wicked robbers,
will drain me of every shilling of it. I hate 'em worse than poison; but what
can I do? They are two against one. I am afraid to drink with 'em, and afraid
to refuse when they force the liquor on me. I'm tired of high feeding and
wine, which, like a fool, I at first thought I should never get too much of.
The very sight of these two villains makes me tired of life and every thing
in it. I see but one way left to save myself, and to keep our secret close from
them, for I can't answer for it when they make me tipsy, or when I talk in
my sleep. The way I see, you will, I know, object to, nor can I wonder at
it; but I'm sure it's the only safe plan; and that is, for you to let me live in
your house, find me in every thing I want, and leave me something to live
on in your will, in case I should last the longest. This is the only way for me
to get out of their hands; and don't refuse my offer, or it will be worse for
us both. I'll say it's my intention to return to service, as all my money is
spent. Let you inquire at the inns for an English servant, and I'll go round
to each of 'em to offer myself, if a situation should be open. So you see the
whole thing will appear quite natural. Once in your house, I'll make 'em
understand that you don't allow followers, nor let your servants go out.
They, finding that they can make no more out of me, will either go away
or let me alone. Whatever crimes you may have committed, you are still a
gentleman, and I'm sure I'll be safe under your roof.—Do follow this advice
for both our sakes. If you refuse, it may be the cause of our ruin. I will pass
under your window to-morrow morning early; and if you drop a bit of
paper, with 'Yes, or No,' on it, that will do.

"J. FIGGINS."

CHAPTER LII.

My agitation while perusing this production was so great, that my
hand shook so violently it could hardly retain the paper.—Indignation at
the terms of equality which it contained, mingled with terror, for my reason, even in the midst of my dread, admitted the prudence and wisdom of
Figgins's suggestion. He felt his own weakness in the hands of his ruffian
companions, and the consequences likely to result from it, and he besought
me for my sake, as well as his, to rescue him from his perilous condition.
And yet with the perfect conviction of the reasonableness of his advice, as
well as of the danger of his being left with his present associates, my pride
could not brook being treated by him in a tone of fellowship, and I angrily
threw his letter from me, and trampled it under my feet.

Then came other and more bitter thoughts. "Was I, who revolted from the occasional sight of this man, to consent to have him a fixed resident beneath my roof, and be compelled to see him perpetually?" To bring a person of such licentious habits into the same house with my daughter, and her female attendant, seemed to me nothing short of profanation, and I shuddered at the notion. Reflections of minor importance, but, nevertheless, very embarrassing, followed. I had at present the precise complement of male servants that I required, consisting of my own personal domestic, and a man engaged at whatever place I resided, and discharged when I left it. This number had been found sufficient for the service of my small establishment, and on what plea could I add a supernumerary to it, without exciting surprise on the part of the servants already in my employment? Although I had never encouraged any remarks from my valet on Figgins, I could see that he had left an unfavourable impression on him; and then flashed across my mind the recollection, that at Sorento my servant had seen Figgins pass close by me, with his worthless companions, without paying me the mark of respect of taking off his hat, so universally offered by every servant when he encounters a former master! What would *he* think of my again taking into my service a man who had betrayed this want of respect? Would it not give rise to suspicion, as well as to surprise? Yes, I felt it would, it must; and yet these minor evils must give way, before the great one of leaving Figgins any longer exposed to the machinations of his designing associates.—But what if he, once an inmate beneath my roof, should forget his position, and presume to be familiar, or insolent? Might I not be compelled to exclude him, and by so doing, draw down on me his anger and vengeance? My mind became unhinged and confused, as all the advantages and disadvantages which might be produced, by whichever line of conduct I adopted, presented themselves to it.

I paced up and down the room almost like a maniac, endeavouring to acquire sufficient coolness to form a resolution, but so many contending feelings tortured my excited brain, that I feared to trust to its decision. I undressed, and threw myself on my bed, in the hope that a few hours' sleep might tranquillize me; but an opiate, to which I had recourse, failed to calm my senses or induce sleep, and after an hour or two's fruitless efforts to repose, I left my couch, and opened the window to cool my fevered brow by the night breeze.

This refreshed and relieved me; and now I was better able to sift and compare the *pour et contre*, of consenting to the proposal of Figgins; and when morning dawned, I had formed my determination to have an interview with him, to state explicitly the conditions on which I would accede to his request and the line of conduct I expected him to pursue.

When I looked out on the starry heavens, so bright, so calm, not a breeze agitating the leaves of the orange trees in my balcony, and not a sound to be heard but the gentle murmur of the waves as they broke on the sea-girt isle, a deep sadness filled my soul. All nature seemed to slumber; mankind had found temporary solace from the cares of life, but this solace was denied me. I, I alone, waked, while others in a sweet oblivion lost the sense of chagrin. Was it not enough that I was haunted by regret for the one terrible event that had clouded the sunshine of my existence, that I mourned with undying grief the loss of that angelic being whom ruthless death had snatched from me, but I must now be tortured by finding myself in the power of one whom I despised, whom I loathed; and to escape the greater evil of my secret being discovered by two wretches even more base, if possible, than himself, I must receive him beneath my roof, and bear his odious presence, until death to him or me should relieve me from this galling penance?

How strong was the contrast afforded by the tranquil and beautiful scene commanded from my window, and the troubled thoughts that filled my breast! "O Nature, lovely beneficent Nature!" thought I, "am I never more to be permitted to enjoy the blessings thou canst bestow? Have I learnt to worship thee,—to feel my heart melt into tenderness and gratitude to the Creator, as I contemplate thy charms,—only to know that gnawing cares so torture me, that, even the innocent pleasures thou canst confer I am too wretched to taste, and that only in the grave can I hope for rest?"

At length, the grey dawn was followed by the rosy-streaked clouds that herald morning. Another day was opening, bringing to some a continuation of happiness,—to others, as to me, a prolongation of woe,—to all, a short-lived leaf in either the garland of bright flowers that illumine, or the cypress-wreath that shadows life with gloom. The coming day, like the preceding one, must fleet away, and bring us so many hours nearer to the goal to which we are all hastening—the grave. It is only the wretched that find consolation in this reflection; and often in my misery had I invoked it as now. But as the day became brighter, I was reminded that I must write to Figgins, and I seized a pen, and disguising my writing as much as I could, I wrote, "Be at my door, this night, at half-past twelve."

I had only time to twist the piece of paper, and put one or two brass coins in to prevent its being blown away, when I saw him for whom it was intended appear. I watched narrowly to be certain he was not followed, and when he approached near the house I threw down the little parcel, saw him take it up, disappear quickly, and I closed my window, and once more threw myself on my bed.

When my servant came to me at my usual hour of rising, I said to him, that should he happen to hear of an English servant wanting a place, I should be glad to engage one.

"I beg your pardon, Sir, but I really think that with the Maltese man we now have, who is a sober, steady, active, and willing man, there is quite enough to get through the work, and more too."

I had anticipated this observation; and though annoyed, was not taken by surprise by it.

"Very likely," said I; "but I do not so much want a servant to do the work now, but a person who, in case I should be summoned suddenly to England on business, which is more than likely, could accompany *me*, while I should leave you with my daughter."

This implied confidence mollified him, though I could see he was by no means pleased at the notion of my engaging a new servant.

"But, pray, Sir, I beg pardon for asking, in what capacity is the person you require to be until you may be called to England?"

Here I felt puzzled what answer to make, and he increased my embarrassment by looking me steadily in the face, with an expression of anxiety and curiosity.

"The servant I intend to engage," said I, "must make himself generally useful."

"Am I to understand, Sir, that he is to be put over me? For if this is to be the case, I would rather at once resign my place."

Why did not my reason suggest to me at this moment the advisability of taking advantage of the suggestion, and letting my servant go away? But thus it ever was with me; my weakness and tergiversation always prevented my profiting by the opportunities thrown in my way to render my position less embarrassing, while there was yet time to take advantage of them; and it was only when too late, that I became sensible that I had thrown them away!

Before giving myself time for a moment's reflection, I replied that the new servant was by no means to be placed above my present one; and, although still looking dissatisfied, he expressed his willingness to remain in my service.

I wrote a few lines, to be left at the inns and library at Malta, stating that an Englishman might hear of a situation with a gentleman who required a servant; and having sent them to be posted in the halls of those places, I walked forth, some hours after, ill at ease.

Almost the first persons I encountered were Figgins and his companions. None of the trio appeared to notice my presence, which afforded me an opportunity of observing them. Figgins looked depressed and fatigued, his associates flushed and angry. The two latter seemed to be quarrelling with him, while he appeared to maintain a dogged silence. I turned soon after, and walked near enough to them to overhear some of their words.

"Humbug, regular humbug," observed one. "We're too old birds to be caught with chaff. Where you found money before, you can find it again; for you'll never get us to believe you came to Malta for any other purpose than to follow some one on whom you have some claim."

"Yes, yes," said the other man, "it's no use whatsomever to try and himpose on us. We're not to be done, I can hassure you; so out with the truth, or let us have some money. There's nothing to be made here. The natives are too sharp, and as for taking in the English officers here, it's not to be done."

I was afraid of being noticed by these men, if I continued any longer near them, so I turned away, convinced by what I had overheard that at least a portion of Figgins's statement to me was correct.

Slowly and heavily dragged on the hours during the remainder of that day. I wished for, yet dreaded the interview I had arranged with Figgins. I entertained such a strong personal antipathy to him, that his presence was absolutely hateful to me; and yet believing as I did that the project he had suggested was the sole one that could separate him from his designing associates, who, sooner or later, might discover his secret and mine, I was desirous that he should be removed from contact with them.

Restless and agitated, often did I pull out my watch to see the time for our meeting was drawing near.—An unhappy wretch, condemned to undergo some terrible operation under the knife of a surgeon, which he knows must be submitted to, or that his life will pay the forfeit, never experienced a greater desire to have it over, or a greater dread of the pain to be endured.

At length the whole family had retired to rest. All was silent in the house; and giving a sufficient time to allow my servants to be wrapt in sleep, I stealthily opened the hall door, and in a moment Figgins stood within it, in evident trepidation. I closed the door noiselessly, made him take off his shoes, lest a creaking sound on the stairs should disturb any of the inmates, and guiding him by the arm, though I shrunk with disgust from his touch, I led him to my room, taking care that the doors of both the adjoining ones should be secured.

He dropped into a chair the moment he entered; and this act of impertinent familiarity produced an instantaneous and disagreeable effect on my temper. He noticed it, I believe, for he said,

"I really can hardly stand, I'm so weak from agitation. I feared up to the very last moment that they would pounce out on me, and follow me here. Such a life as they have led me ever since we came to this place! They will insist on pouring wine and spirits down my throat, do all I can to prevent it; and it is only by pretending to be tipsy, and falling into a sort of lethargic sleep, that I can save myself from being destroyed by them, they are so anxious to make a beast of me. To-night I took to my bed, pretending to be ill, and they, thinking me safe for the night, went out to drink, so I got away. They have picked my pockets while I made believe to sleep, and have ransacked my box. But they found nothing that could help them to make out where the money has come from. They're so mad that they can't get the secret out of me, that I sometimes think they are half disposed to murder me:" and he turned pale and cast a glance of fear around him.

"I believe," observed I, "that you are in actual danger with these ruffians with whom you have connected yourself."

"Ah, Sir!" replied Figgins, "being in people's power," and he looked at me, "makes one keep bad company."

The application of this remark came so home to my feelings, that as I glanced at this wretch seated in my presence I keenly felt its force.

"But though convinced of your danger," resumed I, "and willing to extricate you from it, it is only on certain conditions that I can consent to receive you beneath my roof."

"Bear in mind, Sir," observed he, "that the danger is not solely confined to me. You are also exposed to it, therefore in saving me, remember, you save yourself too."

This reflection vexed me, although I could not deny its truth. It was plain I had to deal with a man who would not let me think that he was imposed on as to the motive of any service I might render him.

"The conditions on which I can receive you," resumed I, "are as follows:—You must always remember that you are my servant, and must treat me with the respect due from a servant to his master."

He screwed up his mouth on one side in a comical way, and answered, "I suppose I must, before others."

I did not condescend to notice this impertinence, but resumed, "Your habits must be orderly, your conduct steady and sober."

"Oh! as for being sober," observed he, "I've got such a sickener of drinking ever since I have been bullied into it by the two villains that have fixed themselves on me, that I don't think I'll ever take to it again as long as I live, and as to being orderly, it's easy to be that when one's sober."

"But I wish to have an explicit understanding with you, a positive engagement, that you will be sober, orderly, and respectful while you continue in my house, before I consent to your entering it," said I, assuming as grave and dignified a manner as I could put on, for the purpose of awing Figgins.

"It is my intention to behave as well as I can, but no man can pledge himself, weak as all men are, never to break through good resolutions. If you don't like me, and I don't like you, which may very probably be the case, why, we can part whenever I am wholly out of the clutches of the two rogues from whom I want to get away; and if ever I come within their reach again, I'll give you leave to call me the greatest fool alive."

I was compelled to be satisfied with this vague, undefined promise, if promise it could be called, and having told him who made it to go round to the places where I had posted up the notice that I wanted a servant, and then to present himself formally at my house, I dismissed him from it as stealthily as I had admitted him, first taking especial care to ascertain from the window that no one was lurking near to see him depart, a precaution, I must do him the justice to say, he evinced as great an anxiety about as I did. I retired to my pillow, sick at heart—and Heaven knows, little disposed to sleep.

CHAPTER LIII.

I DID not leave my bed until late the following morning, and was only just done breakfast, when the Maltese servant (my English one having gone out to execute a commission for me) announced that a person wanted to see me. This person was Figgins; and I was glad he had come during the absence of Thomas, who knowing him since Nice, would very probably have expressed the bad opinion I guessed he entertained of him, and having done so previously to my engaging him, would, doubtless, think it strange that I should then have done so.

I settled all preliminaries with Figgins as quickly as I could. It was agreed that he was to enter my house the next day; and he then told me, that he had, ever since his sojourn at Naples, prepared his troublesome companions for leaving them, as he had oftentimes stated his intention of going to service again, could he but find a suitable place; a declaration, he said, which they wholly disbelieved, from having previously known that he had possessed large unaccountable, or at least, unaccounted for, sums of money.

The truth was, the vain boastings of Figgins, when in his cups, had convinced his unworthy companions, that a fellow of intemperate habits, and with the power, however attained, of gratifying them, never would—never could—return to service again. Now, however, that he was putting his intention into effect, it remained to be seen what plan they would pursue; and on this point, I felt quite as nervous as Figgins.

When Thomas returned from executing the commission I had given, he told me, that while absent he had heard of more than one servant wishing to enter my establishment.

"I engaged one while you were out," said I, affecting as much indifference of manner as I could; "and it happens to be the man who was in my family, when I was ill at Nice."

"You don't mean Figgins, Sir?" asked Thomas with a look of such utter astonishment, as brought the blood to my face, to conceal which, I turned and affected to be busily occupied turning over the pages of an account-book on the table.

"Yes!" replied I; "it is Figgins."

"Well, Sir, I am sorry you have engaged that man; for, if the truth must be spoken, I have not a good opinion of him."

I felt my face glow, and my ears tingle, but I took care that he could not see my countenance.

"Had you any positive cause for your bad opinion?" inquired I.

"First, Sir, he was not a sober man then, and was so prying and inquisitive, that he never ceased asking questions about the family, and where they came from. In short, Sir, all manner of impertinent questions. I told you of this, Sir, after you got better; and I thought you, too, Sir, did not like him to sit up or be near you."

"Did you tell me?—I had forgotten all about it; but now I do remember something faintly about it. I wish I had recollected before I engaged him. Now—it is too late,—I have hired him."

"I'm afraid he has not mended with regard to his drinking," observed Thomas; "for I saw him once at Palermo, perfectly tipsy, and here, also, walking about with two very ill-looking fellows, no more sober than himself. Don't you remember, Sir, the day you were taken ill out walking at Sorento, when a strange man came to tell me to go to you; how, when you were returning home, leaning on my arm, we met this very Figgins, with the two men who are now at Malta? and he must surely have been very tipsy then, for though he passed close to you, Sir, he never so much as took off his hat, or even touched it when he saw you."

"How very odd that I did not see him," observed I; "but probably, he no more saw me than I did him."

"Don't you think, Sir," resumed Thomas, "that you could get off taking him, by making him a small present for the disappointment?"

"No, no! having hired him, I will give him a trial," replied I. "Curiosity is a very common defect; and I am sorry to say there are few sober servants, like you, to be met with, Thomas. Send your young lady to me, without delay" (I saw he was about to make another attempt to induce me to get rid of Figgins). "Go quickly, for I want particularly to see her."

Thomas withdrew, evidently surprised and annoyed, leaving me pained and embarrassed, though not at all surprised, at the result of our interview; and it required all the winning wiles, and fond caresses of my child, to restore me to aught resembling composure.

When Figgins presented himself, towards the evening, he looked so pale and haggard, that I guessed he had had some very disagreeable scene with his worthless companions; and this presentiment increased my own nervousness. He was, however, perfectly sober; and this was some comfort, for I feared he might have indulged in a parting potation with his companions, and have borne unmistakeable proofs of the fact. I walked out, as was my usual custom, and saw, at a distance, the odious associates of Figgins, apparently in deep consultation together. An instinctive dread of encountering them, led me to turn my steps in another direction, although I had no definite notion what I had to fear, or what excuse they could make for addressing me.

I returned home and Figgins opened the door to give me ingress. He whispered in my ears as I entered—

"I want to speak to you when all are asleep, and will go to your room."

I nodded assent and passed on. What could he have to say to me? A thousand painful conjectures presented themselves to my mind, each and all fraught with annoyance.

When Thomas served tea, I noticed a great change in his aspect—he looked offended and gloomy, seemed desirous to speak to me, but I gave him no opportunity, as I affected to be deeply occupied with a book.—At length he broke silence, and after apologizing for interrupting me, begged leave to have my permission to take the key of the hall door to his room every night.

There was a certain manner in making this unusual, though simple request, that was meant to elicit my attention and inquiry to the cause, but I asked no question, and merely said I saw no objection to it.

"If I might, without offence, Sir," said Thomas, "say a few words to you, I should be glad."

I answered, "Yes, certainly;" although there was nothing I more wished to avoid at that moment than any representation relative to Figgins, which I fully anticipated would be the subject on which Thomas proposed speaking.

"Not wishing, Sir, to draw blame on, or to injure a fellow-servant, I have never told you that a continued correspondence has been kept up between Miss Herbert's nurse and Figgins, ever since you left Nice. Indeed, before you left it, so great an intimacy subsisted between them, that when he went to Wales, he wrote to her from thence. She wrote to him from Palermo, from Sorento, and from Malta, Sir, the very day after you arrived here.—I always noticed that he came to wherever you were, as soon as he could hear from her; and there was such a mystery made about the letters, and such a desire to conceal from me that any were passing between them, that had not accident made me acquainted with the fact, I should not have known it. Nurse used to give her letters to him to the Faquino to put in the post, charging him especially not to let me see them, and the man thinking it was only a bit of fun, or some courting going on, used to let me see the address. Thinking Figgins a bad fellow, who would deceive and make a fool of her, for she is quite a simpleton, I spoke to her, and advised her not to keep up any more correspondence with him; but she said he would soon become a rich man, and had promised to marry her, and make a lady of her soon, provided she always wrote to him from whatever place she went to. I thought it my duty, Sir, to tell you this, for it would be a pity to have the poor simpleton of a woman led astray by this fellow, and this is *one*, (and he laid a peculiar stress on the word *one*,) of the reasons why I am so sorry he has been hired."

So now the mystery of how Figgins was kept aware of my movements, whatever pains I took to conceal them, was disclosed. And how cunningly the rascal had suborned this weak and silly girl to give him the information he required!

I listened with perfect astonishment to the statement of Thomas, wondering how I had been so stupid as not to have hitherto suspected the channel through which Figgins became aware of my movements: but it was too simple, too natural to be divined. His boast of having everywhere emissaries who would reveal my residence to him, wherever I might direct my course, was too imposing not to have been credited by me, who in my terror of this miscreant, had invested him with a sort of melodramatic power and effect, that greatly served his purpose of working on my fears. I was shocked as well as surprised at the revelation of Thomas, but assuming as calm an aspect and manner as I could, I merely said, "I wish, Thomas, you had told me all this before; I should then have been on my guard, and would certainly not have hired this man; as it is, I cannot discharge him *merely* because he has been corresponding with the nurse, although it will be well to prevent their associating while they continue in the same house."

"That will, I fear, be difficult, Sir, for the foolish woman is much attached to Figgins, or Howard, as he used to call himself while he was away, for he changed his name for a fortune, as nurse said; but this change of name, coupled with the rest of his conduct and habits, looks very suspicious in my mind."

When Thomas withdrew, I sank into a chair confounded at the discovery of the manner in which I had been duped by Figgins, and his tool, the nurse. How little had I dreamt, while I was puzzling my brains to plan my escape from him, that I carried with me an agent of his, who would defeat all my schemes! How stupid, how foolish did I now appear in my own eyes! I felt humiliated, and more angry than ever with myself, but what availed my anger? I could not change a single one of the annoyances of my position, and nothing was left but to bear it as best I could. Nothing adds more to self-reproach (always a painful thing to bear) than the perfect consciousness that the evils we are undergoing have been entailed by our own folly. This aggravation to mine had long existed, but this last discovery greatly increased it. I now perfectly remembered Thomas having told me at Nice that Figgins had been questioning the nurse very frequently and closely relative to me, my abode, and other particulars; and yet this information which ought to have placed me on my guard, and taught me the probability that he might turn this weak woman to account, in discovering my whereabouts, had never once entered my thoughts. What so natural as that, finding this tool ready to his hand he should employ her, so that while I, believing I was taking effectual means to defeat any search he might make for me, fancied myself securely hidden in the labyrinth I had formed, his agent, mocking all my schemes, could send him a clue to defeat them!

When the house was at rest, the stealthy tread of Figgins announced his approach to my room.—Every creak of the stairs as he ascended alarmed me, lest Thomas too should overhear it; and when he entered the chamber, I arose and locked the poor to preclude interruption.

"I wished to tell you what passed between Motcombe, Bradstock, and myself," said Figgins, "but as it's rather a long story, I suppose you'll not object to my sitting down;" and he dropped into an easy chair, vis-à-vis to mine. How I longed to punish him for this liberty, but I dared not provoke him. "I took care," said he, "to let those two infamous rogues be present, when I noticed the paper posted up, requiring an English servant—'Hallo!' observed I, 'this seems to be something to suit me: hang me, if I don't go and offer myself.'

"'And who'll give you a character I should like to know?' said Motcombe.

"'Yes, yes, my boy,' puts in Bradstock, 'who'll say any good of you?'

"'That's my affair,' says I.

"'Now, come Figgins, make an end of all this mystery and fool's play. What's the good of it? We are too deep to be done by you—your scheme of entering service again can't take us in;—you think that when you are in place we'll go away, and you'll be rid us, but it's no such thing. We'll stick to you like leeches, get your neck into a scrape as sure as you're alive; whereas, if you go share and share alike with us in the booty you have made, or may make, we'll lead a jovial life, and keep each other's secrets.'

"I tried all I could to persuade them that there was no secret in the case; that the money I had spent so freely with them, came from a relation who died; that it was now all gone; and that I had no resource to make a living but by going to service. They wouldn't believe me, do all I could, and swore they'd never stop until they found out the truth. I pretended there was nothing to find out, and I came off here to offer for the situation. When I went back I met them, and when I told them I was engaged they would hardly believe it. That's one of the disagreeable things among fellows like them, they never believe a word they say to each other. When at last they found I was coming here, Bradstock had the impudence to propose to me to let 'em in at night, to rob this house. Yes," seeing me look surprised, "hang me if he hadn't?

"'The packet will sail in two days,' said Motcombe, 'and the night before, you can open the door to us, or hand out whatever valuables there are in the house, and we'll be off early in the morning, and no one will find us out; nor will you get into a scrape, for we can cut through the lock of the door from the outside, without much noise, which will bear you harmless, for no more suspicion can fall on you than on any other servant in the house.'

"I told them I never would turn a robber; and then they twitted me because of a great past scrape I had the misfortune to fall into; and said, 'In for a penny, in for a pound.' I was already enough in their power to ruin me, and it was no use holding back now.'

"The truth is, I am in their power, that's the long and short of it, and heavily have they made me pay for it; but I'm so tired of being bullied and plundered, that, I'd almost rather give myself up to justice, than drag on life in their clutches. I know they're no better than myself, and I believe, on the contrary, they are much worse; but, if I was to try to show them up to the law, they'd swear away my life. They're two to one, and hold by each other against me."

I experienced a loathing sense of degradation as I listened to Figgins's acknowledgment of his own turpitude. I felt that an inferior, a menial, must have indeed formed the very lowest estimate of the character of his employer, before he could thus venture to lay bare his guilt to him. To do so, was a tacit avowal of equality between them, a sort of mode of showing that it was taken for granted, that both were embarked in the same boat. Pride is one of the last qualities that forsakes him who has long indulged it; and serves as the medium by which his punishment for sin is most frequently inflicted. I had passed through humiliations enough, Heaven knows, to have crushed mine, yet it still survived in my breast, as the pangs I endured whenever it was assailed but too well proved.

"I have now told you the whole truth," said Figgins, "and have prepared you for whatever these villains may write against me. They'll do all they can to hurt me, I know, but, I'll keep out of their way, and remain within doors till I can find out if they're gone from Malta. In the mean while, keep the windows well bolted, and the door secure, at night, for fear of accidents, and fire-arms loaded will do no harm."

I dismissed him for the night, ashamed of the interview.

CHAPTER LIV.

THE following day Thomas informed me, that he had been grossly insulted by Figgins because he had told that individual that he must not go into the nursery, and had informed the nurse that she must not sit in the room assigned to the men-servants.

"You'll find, Sir," said Thomas, "that it won't do to keep this man. He has a violent and ungovernable temper, and is by no means disposed to submit to the regulations of a steady family. I was sure it would be so, and am sorry to find I was right. The two fellows he used to walk about with, are continually hovering about this house since he came into it, and they are such suspicious-looking persons, that I cannot help thinking they mean no good. I must, however, say, Figgins shows no desire to see them, for he hasn't been once out since he entered your service, and he requested me in case they should call to inquire for him, to say he was out, or was not to be seen. Judging from his manner, Sir, I should say he was afraid of them."

"That argues in his favour," observed I, "he has probably discovered that they are worthless, and wishes to keep up no further intercourse with them."

"I'm afraid, Sir, there's not much to choose between them. But, at all events, I hope you will give your own instructions to nurse and to Figgins, relative to their keeping apart."

"Should they infringe your orders, Thomas, I certainly will."

The remainder of the day passed over quietly. I heard no more complaints. I sat up later than usual that night reading, and was about to retire to my bed-room, when I heard a noise at one of the windows on the ground-floor. I listened attentively, and became certain that some person or persons were endeavouring to force open the window; but they were so cautious in their efforts, that every five or six minutes they discontinued them, lest the noise should be remarked. The warning given me by Figgins of the intention of Motcombe and Bradstock to rob my house, now flashed across my mind. This warning proved his good faith to me, at least. I hesitated for a few minutes what I had best do, and then seizing a poker in my hand, the only weapon within my reach, having no arms, I descended to Thomas's sleeping room, and awoke him, though not without some difficulty. Indeed his snoring, which was so loud as to be audible at a considerable distance, had been, I conclude, heard through the window, and had encouraged these miscreants to attempt to force it, believing that the noise they made would be lost in his.

While I was yet shaking Thomas's shoulder to arouse him, I heard Figgins leave his room, and in another moment he stood before me. He looked significantly at me, and exclaimed, "There are robbers trying to force the window; I have got pistols," and he pointed to a case in his hand— "I hope you have arms, Sir?"

"No, none," replied I.

"Hush, make no noise," resumed Figgins, "my advice is, that we keep perfectly quiet; let them force the window, and I will shoot them, one after another as they enter."

Never shall I forget the demoniacal expression of Figgins's countenance as he spoke. The triumph of a ferocious hatred and vengeance flashed in his malignant eyes, such as may be seen in the face of some fierce animal about to pounce on its prey.

"No, no," replied I, "I want no blood shed. I wish to guard my property, but not to wound or kill the robbers."

"What! would you spare 'em—spare such villains as these, who wouldn't mind a pin killing us all?" said Figgins, forgetting in the excitement of his hatred and thirst for blood, that he was betraying, before Thomas, his knowledge of the robbers.

This oversight on his part did not pass unnoticed, for Thomas looked sharply at him, and remarked "Oh! *you* know the robbers, do you?"

Before he could reply, I cried out, "Who's there? We're armed; and your blood be on your own heads if you compel us to fire."

We instantly heard footsteps rapidly retreating from the window. Figgins, frantic with rage and disappointment, rushed to the hall-door to open it, but the key not being there, his anger knew no bounds. He uttered oaths and execrations at not being able to get out and pursue the robbers, cursing his luck at missing such a chance of destroying them.

"That fellow is a wild beast rather than a man," said Thomas, *sotto voce*, shuddering as he looked at me; "I am sure he would rather kill a man than not."

"Who took the key away?" demanded Figgins. "Had it been in the lock, I would have pursued the villains, and brought them down."

"I took the key," replied Thomas.

"What, did you take me to be a thief?" said he, angrily.

"I make it a point always to take the key at night," observed Thomas, calmly.

"Let the police be informed in the morning, Thomas, of this attempt," said I; "and inquiries be made to detect those who made it."

"And if they should be discovered, Sir, I hope you will prosecute them to the utmost extremity of the law," observed Figgins. "But it was a sin, ay, and a shame too, to have let them off, when I could have shot them as easily as rats are shot when running into a trap."

We all retired to our beds again; the dislike of Thomas to Figgins increased tenfold by the discovery of his warm desire to shoot the robbers; while I could perceive that Figgins, on his side, had conceived a strong aversion to Thomas, from the circumstance of his having taken out the key of the hall-door.

For me, a vague dread of danger to come was more predominant in my mind than gratitude for that recently escaped. Men so desperate as the late companions of Figgins were not likely to remain inactive; and that they would draw trouble on me, I felt a strong presentiment, although the precise manner by which they might accomplish it I could not divine.

The next morning Thomas went to lay information before the police; who, after taking down his report, sent persons to examine the window, and note down the state in which it had been left. It was found by the marks that the tools used in the attempt must have been those generally employed by burglars. This circumstance the police thought might lead to the discovery of the perpetrators of the offence; and a diligent search was set on foot for their detection.

While Thomas was absent on this errand, Figgins stole to my chamber.

"I told you, Sir," said he, "that these villains proposed to me to rob the

house. I know what they are capable of. Oh! why did you prevent me from
shooting them? I could so easily have done it, and had the law on my side
too. 'Twas folly, 'twas downright madness to have stopped me. Once rid of
those two villains, *I* should have been at rest, and in peace for the rest of
my life; and *you*, too, would have found the benefit, for then I should not
be compelled to come and fix myself on *you*, which I am sure must be disagreeable to *you*, and is anything but pleasant to me. I hope, however, they
are both off by the packet that was to sail this morning; but what security
have we that they mayn't come back, when the attempt to break into this
house blows over?"

"If they have gone," said I, "your best plan would be to take the opportunity of their absence, to leave Malta, and go to some place where they
cannot find you out. I will furnish you with means to depart, and regularly
send you a yearly stipend of fifty pounds a-year, wherever you go to."

"Ah, you don't know them!" replied he, "if you did, you wouldn't reckon
so confidently on my escaping from their clutches. No, my only chance was
their death, and *you* have made me lose that," and he shook his head, and
looked bitterly at me. "They are, as I said before, two against one, when I'm
alone. While I stick to you, we are two and two, and it will go hard against
us if we don't prove a match for 'em."

Angered by his familiarity, with some portion of my old *fierté*, I drew
up, and desired that he would not presume to include me in any league,
offensive or defensive, against the two bad men in question.

"Don't drive me raving mad!" exclaimed he. "What's the use of this
false pride with me when we're here alone together. Are we not in the same
boat, and exposed to the same danger? and should we not combine our
efforts to balk whatever schemes these villains may form against us?"

"I have nothing to do with these men, and they can have nothing against
me; why, therefore, should I fear them?"

"You may yet find to your cost that you are mistaken," observed Figgins.
"Your safety depends on me—that *you* must now as well as I do. Now,
unfortunately, I am in *their* power, as *you* are in *mine*, and if they were to
take any steps against me, and I was brought into a scrape, I cannot answer
for your secret not being exposed. Let us understand each other, once for
all; while I am safe you shall be so. The whole thing hinges on this."

A knock at the door announced the return of Thomas, and putting his
hand to his lip, in token of silence, Figgins hurried from the room to admit
him.

"The first person I met in the street, Sir," said Thomas, "was one of
the suspicious looking fellows I used to see walking about with Figgins.

He appeared quite unconcerned, and swaggered by me as if nothing had happened, and yet I can't help thinking he and his friend were the very men who forced the window; for if you noticed, Sir, Figgins let out that he suspected *who* the robbers were; and what makes me think all the worse of him, he seemed most anxious to shoot 'em in cold blood, which, considering they were so lately his constant friends and companions, looks very strange. The police have all set to work to discover the burglars, and I hope will find 'em out."

It was clear that Thomas entertained the worst opinion of Figgins, and what was infinitely more embarrassing to me, took no pains whatever to conceal his opinion from me. Indeed, he seemed actuated by a desire to disclose his sentiments on this subject, in order to prepare me for some anticipated mischief. How strange, then, must it appear in his eyes, that I should still continue to retain a man of whom he had formed such suspicions! I felt ashamed to meet his eye, and yet could not bring myself to rebuke him for his evil thoughts of Figgins, although every indication and expression of them was a reproach to me. How had I lost the respect of my servant; and, alas, forfeited my own!

I walked out after breakfast, and encountered only one of Figgins's late companions. He eyed me narrowly, and walked on in the direction of my house, while I proceeded in a different one. Where could his associate be? Had he left Malta, and wherefore? I found myself thinking a good deal of these bad men, and wondering what they were going to do; and when, conscious of my vague anxiety about them, I endeavoured to reason myself into the belief that they, or their actions, could be nothing to me, a presentiment of evil to come through them could not be conquered, and an undefinable alarm connected with them haunted me. Here was I, meeting at every step Englishmen, from whom, although personally unknown to me, I might have claimed assistance to defeat any conspiracy formed, or forming against me, were I not in the power of Figgins. But I trembled at the bare notion of his being confronted with any one, however determined he might be to guard my secret. There was something in his appearance and manner well calculated to impress persons with an unfavourable opinion of him, and create surprise, if not suspicion, that I should retain such a servant. I felt, that by one act of folly, of madness, in yielding to his threats, I had placed myself out of the pale of sympathy with the worthy portion of my fellow-men, and that I must continue to drag on life, a prey to perpetual anxiety and terror.

When I returned home, Thomas, on admitting me, related that one of Figgins's late associates had, soon after my departure, knocked at the door, and inquired to see the servant who had entered the establishment a few days before. "As Figgins had requested me to say he was out when any one wanted to see him," said Thomas, "I told his friend he was not within."

"'I know *he is* within,' replied he, 'and I am determined to see him.'

"'I have told you he is not,' repeated I, 'so it's no use your keeping me from my work.'

"'Tell him that he'll find himself mistaken, if he thinks that he can shake off, or conceal himself from *old friends*,' answered he, 'and be sure to add, that the most dangerous *enemies* are made out of old friends, when people try to get away from 'em.'

"There was something so malicious and spiteful in this man's look and manner, that I just thought I'd bring down his impudence a little," observed Thomas, "so I said,—'the new servant is out with the police, looking for the robbers who tried to get into this house last night,' and I fixed my eyes on his face while I spoke. I assure you, Sir, he turned as red as fire, when I said the words; but he tried hard to look unconcerned.

"'Oh! he is, is he?' said he, 'Give him my compliments then, and tell him I'm glad he remembers the old proverb, "Set a thief to catch a thief."' He was then walking off, but he returned and said, 'Pray what's the new servant's name?'

"'Why, as you're his friend, you surely must know,' answered I. He looked vexed, but gave a sneer, and said:—

"'When a man goes by more names than one, his friends don't always know by which to inquire for him; but tell the new servant, whether he is now Mr. Figgins, or Mr. Howard, that Mr. Motcombe is on the look out for him,' and away he went.

"Figgins had been listening to all that passed, hid behind the door of the waiting-room, off the hall; and when the door was closed, he came forth, Sir, as pale as a ghost, and absolutely trembling. 'What are you so afraid of?' asked I.

"'Afraid,' repeated he, his lips shaking, 'I—am not afraid, I'm only surprised at the rascal's impudence.'

"And ever since, Sir, he seems all over in a twitter, quite cast down like, though he tries all he can to hide it. He asked me to let him have a glass of brandy, and when I refused, he gave money to the kitchen woman to go off to the next shop to bring him some. Now, Sir, I've told you all that passed, that I should not be blamed if any thing happens; but it seems to me to be very dangerous to have a man in the house who has such persons coming after him, and threatening him. They must know something very bad against him."

CHAPTER LV.

TOWARDS the evening of the day of Motcombe's visit to Figgins, I was disturbed by clamour and the sound of quarrelling in the servants' offices, a very unusual circumstance in my house, for Thomas, aware of my nervous temperament, and abhorrence of noise, always took especial care to maintain quietness among the servants. It instantly occurred to me that Figgins must be the cause of this tumult, and consequently I did not ring the bell to inquire; but the clamour increased, and at length Thomas rushed up stairs, and, in great agitation, entered my room.

"I have been struck by that drunken sot Figgins, Sir," said he, "who has been drinking spirits ever since the visit of Motcombe this morning, and is now so intoxicated, that when I tried to prevent his going to the nursery, he struck me, and tore my clothes, as you see. I intend going for the police, to take him away, for it is impossible to submit to such usage."

I felt the blood rush to my face, but conscious of all the mischief that might occur if Thomas put his threat into execution, I observed that it would be better to let him sleep off his inebriety, and that I was sure he would be sorry for his bad behaviour when he came to his senses. While I was yet speaking, I heard him staggering up the stairs, and in another moment he came into the room, his face bloated and crimson, and his eyes flashing with anger. Never had I beheld a more revolting object.

"I say," exclaimed he addressing me, "will you allow this blockhead to insult me, and dictate where I am, or am *not*, to go?"

"Leave the room at present," said I, "and go to bed; to-morrow I will hear what you have to say."

"To-morrow!" reiterated he. "That's a good un, howsomdever. You will hear what I have got to say now; and, what's more, *you shall* too. Come, come, don't think to frighten me with your grave looks. You know well enough that if I chose to speak, you'd soon be glad to cry peccavi; and, what's more, if you don't at once turn this here impudent rascal out of doors, I *will* speak out. I'm not going to be bullied and brow-beat by a fellow like this. I'm not to go and see the nurse when I like!—I'm not to smoke, forsooth, because you dislike the smell of tobacco! I'm not to get drunk when I like!—in short, I'm to be a slave, and under the orders of this here numskull, when I ought to be treated as well as yourself, seeing as how I have you wholly in my power, as you well know."

"Had I not better go at once for the police, Sir?" said Thomas, looking perfectly thunderstruck.

"No," replied I; and approaching Figgins, I made a strong effort to *appear* calm,—to be *really* so was beyond my utmost effort. I spoke to him: "Let me advise you to go to bed; to-morrow you will regret having behaved ill. Do, Figgins, retire to your room."

"Not until you have turned this rascal out of the house, and made me upper servant to rule over all the others. It isn't much to ask, when I might command you; yes, *you*," and he stared provokingly in my face. "When I might show you that, for all you pretend to be *my* master, I am *yours*."

The astonishment of Thomas, at hearing all this, could only be equalled by the mingled emotions of rage, shame, and indignation which filled my breast. I absolutely trembled from the violence of my feelings, although I did all in my power to prevent this symptom of agitation from being seen.

"You had better sit down," said Figgins, "for you're in such a taking you can hardly stand, and I'll set you the example." And he sank into the most comfortable chair in the room.

"I can't remain and see you insulted in this manner, Sir," observed Thomas; "and if you will not allow me to go for the police to take this man away, or to turn him out myself, I really must leave the house."

"Leave the house! Why, that's just what I want, what I've been driving at," exclaimed Figgins. "So, go along; and never let me see your face here again as long as you live."

"Do not leave the house Thomas," said I. "You see this man is so much intoxicated that he knows not what he says or does."

"What, do you ask the rascal to stay before my face, after I have told him to go?" demanded Figgins, furious with passion; and rising from his seat, he approached me in a menacing attitude.

"If you dare to lift your hand against my master," exclaimed Thomas, placing himself between the ruffian and me, "I will throw you out of the window."

Figgins aimed a blow at him, but in the exertion lost his balance and fell on the floor, striking his head so violently against the table that the blood rushed from the wound, flowing over the carpet. He turned so very pale, that for a few minutes I really believed he was either dead or dying. He was totally insensible too; and Thomas also imagined that all was over with him.

Shall I confess the truth; shall I expose the turpitude of my own hardened heart, and acknowledge that a gleam of joy passed through it, when I believed I was for ever released from the power of the wretch who had so lately insulted—tortured me; and who held my honour—my very life, in thrall? To be rid of him without sin or crime, without having even willed his death, was as if the weight of a mountain had been removed from my breast! But better feelings came. That he should rush before his offended God in a state of brutal inebriation, with all his sins on his head, was so shocking, that I busied myself in using every effort to restore him to life as strenuously as if his existence were desirable to me.

"Oh, Sir!" said Thomas, "he is not worthy of this care. You could do no more by a good man than by this wretch."

"Humanity, Thomas, has its laws, and they must not be violated. The more unworthy is this unfortunate man, the less fit is he to die; and the more is it my duty to save him if possible."

"I hope, Sir, you may never have cause to repent this humanity," observed Thomas; "but I fear this wretch will be a torment to you as long as he lives. Forgive me, Sir, for presuming to forget the difference between us, and for speaking to you so freely. I know not how, nor why, this man dares to threaten you, and behave as if you were in his power; but that he does so is quite clear; and that you, Sir, permit it, I grieve to say, is equally so. I cannot stay in the same house with him, to be a witness to all this. I could not,—indeed, Sir, I could not,"—and tears started into his eyes,— "stand it. Oh! Sir, how sorry I am to see you so ill-treated!" and he put his handkerchief to his eyes, and positively wept.

While he was speaking, I was occupied in binding the head of Figgins with my handkerchief, and in forcing a little cold water into his mouth.

"Do go for a surgeon, Thomas," said I, "and let us try to save this unhappy man."

"But, if when he comes to himself again, Sir, he should insult you before the surgeon, which he is quite capable of doing, if only speech is granted him?"

"No; the loss of blood will have brought him to his senses, and he will say nothing offensive."

"Well, Sir, your orders shall be obeyed; but for God's sake, Sir, and for your own, and your child's sake, get rid of this man; for be assured, he will bring disgrace on you and your house, and set all your servants talking disrespectfully of you; and no honest man will remain in your service, while he is in it."

So saying, Thomas left the room, and hurried off in search of a surgeon, while I bathed the forehead of Figgins with cold water, and endeavoured to restore him to consciousness. At length, he heaved a deep sigh, opened his eyes, and looked at me.

"Where am I!" exclaimed he; and then seeing the blood, which had stained his clothes, he shuddered, and inquired what had occurred to him.

"I have been struck, and half murdered," said he; "I see it all now. You wanted to get rid of me, that your secret might be safe."

"Unhappy man," replied I, "your own intemperance has been the sole cause of the state in which you find yourself. After insulting me grossly, you wanted to strike Thomas for no just cause, and in aiming a blow at him you lost your equilibrium, and in falling hit your head against the leg of the table."

"I don't believe a word of it," observed the obtuse wretch. "I'm quite sure you did it, or got that rascal Thomas to strike me, when I could not defend myself, but I'll have my revenge."

At this moment the surgeon arrived with Thomas; and Figgins, with dogged sulkiness, allowed his head to be examined. The wound was found to be deep, and the loss of blood occasioned great weakness. Figgins was removed to his room, where being placed in bed, the surgeon dressed the wound, and offered to send a nurse to attend on his patient.

"He has very narrowly escaped being killed; a half an inch more to the right would have been fatal, and as it is, I am not prepared to pronounce that he will recover," said he; "he is evidently a man of intemperate habits, and a wound like this is much more dangerous with such, than with a sober person. I rather suspect a concussion of the brain, from the lethargic appearance of the patient, and the dilation of the pupils of the eyes."

I requested the surgeon to visit Figgins as frequently as he considered it necessary, and he promised to return again in a few hours.

When he had left the house, Thomas said to me, "Pray, Sir, allow me to say a few words to you. This bad man is now reduced to a state that will, in all human probability, detain him in his bed for many weeks. Why should you not take this opportunity of leaving Malta, he being unable to obstruct your departure, or to follow you, for some time at least?"

I felt my face flush at this open avowal, that Thomas was aware that I was in Figgins's power, and that it was desirable I should escape from him. To what a position was I reduced! And how was my pride, that besetting sin of my nature, humbled! I wished to make some attempt to disprove the justice of Thomas's opinion, but I had not nerve enough to do so. I felt that I could not deceive him, that he had drawn unerring conclusions from all that he had seen and heard, and that I could not blind him. Yet the suggestion he had given me of leaving Malta, made such an impression on my mind, that I wondered it had not occurred to me. Yes, this was the time to leave Malta. I remembered with satisfaction that Figgins hardly dared go to England, since there it was that he had committed the crime known to his two companions, Motcombe and Bradstock, and for which an innocent person had been punished.

How strange that it had not previously occurred to me that my best chance of escape from him would be to go to England! But the truth was, I had for some time almost lost the power of coolly calculating the most advisable step to adopt; and, constantly kept in terror by Figgins, I deferred from day to day coming to a decision, which the conduct of this wayward and impracticable man might render abortive.—Yes, Thomas was right, this was the moment to go to England, and I would the next day, by which a packet was expected to arrive, give out that it brought me letters requiring my immediate presence at home.

The packet arrived that very evening. I went to the post-office myself, returned to my house, and announced that by a packet which would sail the next day, I would leave Malta. I ordered every necessary preparation to be made, and desired the nurse to hold herself in readiness to embark.

To my utter astonishment, however, she declared her intention of not leaving Malta until Figgins was recovered. She stated that she had been affianced to him ever since we were at Nice, and that to leave him under present circumstances was out of the question.

And this woman had been the nurse of my child from her birth, and had been treated with the utmost indulgence and kindness ever since she entered my service. She had always professed to love my daughter fondly, and the little girl was warmly attached to her.—Yet she could abandon her charge at such a moment, and for the sake of one of the most worthless and unprincipled men on earth. I sent for her, reasoned, advised, and argued with her, but in vain. Figgins had so completely succeeded in wholly blinding her, alike to her duty and interest, that all argument was useless. The foolish and selfish woman believed that her services could not be dispensed with, and that it being impossible for my daughter to undertake a voyage without a female attendant, I should be compelled to postpone my departure.

Thomas, however, came to my relief in this dilemma. He had some time before heard of an Englishwoman who had lost her mistress, the wife of the Colonel of a regiment stationed there, and who desired to find some person returning to England, and requiring her services for the voyage. The widower would give her an excellent character, and she would be ready to embark on short notice. This seemed the very thing, and I was delighted to be able to dispense with the ungrateful nurse.

Thomas went off to engage this woman, and I wrote to the Colonel to obtain her character, which proved perfectly satisfactory. I placed a sum of money at my banker's, to satisfy all demands likely to accrue from the illness of Figgins, and for his maintenance, arranging that the surgeon should continue his attendance while necessary; and I embarked the following morning for England, much pleased at observing that my daughter was quite reconciled to her new servant, and bore her separation from her old one much better than I had anticipated.

CHAPTER LVI.

OUR voyage was a prosperous one. My daughter bore it well, and before its termination I had ascertained that her new attendant merited the high character I had received of her, so assiduous and unceasing were her attentions to her youthful charge, who, in return, evinced great fondness for her. My resolution to come to England had been so suddenly adopted, that I had no time to form any plans relative to where I should settle when I arrived there. My first wish was to see Mrs. Neville, in order that my child should have the advantage of her protection—for I already felt that a father, however fondly attached to a daughter, cannot supply the place of a judicious and affectionate female friend. How had I been deceived in the nurse, who I believed to be so entirely devoted to the child, that nothing could induce her to leave her; yet, who deserted her charge for the sake of the worthless Figgins! I pondered over the future during the voyage, but it was for my daughter, not for myself, that I formed projects.

Once more I touched the shore of England, but the joy felt by others on returning to their native land was not experienced by me. I returned to it even more gloomy, more hopeless, than when I left it; for then my beloved, my ever lamented Louisa was in life, and although in very delicate health I hoped that a milder clime might restore her, and prolong her existence for many years to come, to bless and comfort me—I came back without her, leaving her dear remains in a foreign grave. I again gazed on the shore we had both watched from the deck, as it receded from our sight, but I now looked on it *alone*, no fond arm pressed mine as then, no sweet voice whispered that "with me all countries would be welcome to her." How well I remembered even the slightest incidents of that brief voyage, and what a flood of tenderness rushed through my heart as they were recalled!

I had no friend to greet my return to my native land. Any kindness I might experience from Mrs. Neville, I felt assured I should be indebted for solely to her memory of the affection entertained for me by the dear departed, and commiseration for my lonely state; and how poor a consolation was this mere tolerance for that exquisite tenderness I had been wont, in other and happier times, to meet with from my matchless, my blessed

Louisa! The heart, ever disposed to seek affection, never feels the want of it so deeply as when, after a long absence, one returns to the land of one's birth.—There it is so natural to look for it, that its deprivation is felt with increased bitterness; and as I reflected that no heart would beat quicker at my approach, no hand be stretched out gladly to meet mine, I drew my daughter closer to my side, and felt that she was now the sole tie that bound me to life, the sole object from which I could hope for affection. But the love of children who could count on? Had not my daughter appeared to love her nurse fondly, yet how soon was she forgotten? How then could I hope that, if separated from her, I should be remembered as tenderly as my heart yearned I should be? And as these reflections passed through my jealous mind, I animadverted with dissatisfaction on a circumstance that had previously greatly gratified me—namely, the readiness with which my daughter had parted from her nurse, and the rapidity with which she had forgotten her. By what a different standard do we judge the conduct of those dear to us to others, to that by which we regard it when the possibility of its ever coming home to ourselves presents itself.

I took my daughter by the hand, and was leaving the Point at Portsmouth to proceed to the inn, when my name was called aloud. A few minutes previously I had been moodily reflecting on my isolated state. It then appeared a cause for additional gloom that no friendly voice would hail me, no amicable hand be stretched forth to clasp mine as I once more touched my native land. Yet now that I heard my name pronounced, the sound of recognition, far from giving me pleasure, grated harshly on my ear, and could I have avoided meeting the individual who uttered it, though ignorant who it might be, I would have done so.

"Mr. Herbert, my dear Mr. Herbert, how glad I am to see you!" said the voice, and in a moment after I felt my hand grasped by that of Mrs. Scuddamore, who, more robust and rubicund than ever, uttered a torrent of congratulation on my return to England, of expressions of pleasure at being on the spot to welcome me, and of condolements at the severe loss I had experienced.

"I read the melancholy event in the newspapers," continued she. "I was quite prepared for it, for poor Mrs. Herbert looked the picture of ill health; and when a woman has a bad constitution, what can be expected? The longer she lived, the more you would have suffered, for let me tell you that few things in life are more trying than to watch a candle a long time going out, for such is the illness of a consumptive woman."

Oh! how I loathed this unfeeling creature!

"But let me not detain you. Let us walk to the inn. We positively must dine together, and talk over old times. I am at the George."

"I am going to the Crown," said I, anxious to avoid her.

"Not a single room to be had in it," observed she. "I tried to get lodged there, but the house is full, so you can't help yourself. I arrived at Portsmouth last night to meet an old brother officer whom I expected from Malta—Major McCulloch, an excellent soldier—a *leetle* bit of a martinet. *entre nous*, but that's a fault on the right side. He's coming over on leave to take possession of a little fortune left him in Scotland by a distant relative. He also expects a step in his promotion. I can't understand what has prevented his coming in the same packet with you. He wrote to me that he would, if possible, sail by the next that would leave Malta. I was so sure that he would come, that I engaged a room for him at the George, which you can have, and ordered dinner for two, which you can share, and save me expense, without costing you any more than you would otherwise pay."

How I groaned in spirit as I heard her coolly arrange my movements without ever consulting my wishes on the subject.

"I think I will at once proceed to London," said I, anxious to get rid of her.

"What, and expose your little girl, who looks so delicate, to such fatigue on coming off a long voyage?" said she. "It would be perfect madness, my dear Mr. Herbert; nay, more, perfect cruelty. No, no, you must give her and yourself too, some repose—you positively must."

And now for the first time she looked at my daughter, and with much the same glance with which a drill-serjeant examines a raw recruit, who has just joined his regiment, or a horse-dealer inspects a new purchase.

"A pretty child, upon my word, a very pretty child!" observed she; "but looks very delicate, like her poor mother. Requires care—great care. Asses' milk, the constant use of dumb-bells to expand her chest, and some months' drilling, under a good soldier, would do her a world of good. I have just a man in my eye for this, an old soldier of my regiment, now a pensioner in Chelsea Hospital. He has got the rheumatism so badly, that he is often months without being able to move; but when he *can* walk, I know no man so good for drilling young people, and setting them up."

All the time she was carrying on this monologue, I was considering how I could escape from her. I knew it would be no easy task, but her society was so insupportable to me, that I was most desirous to get rid of it. She, however, had taken possession of my arm, and relinquished it not until we reached the inn.

I had some difficulty in procuring a chamber for my daughter and her attendant, for the inn was, as Mrs. Scuddamore had represented, nearly full. That lady, always fertile in resources for emergencies, proposed a *shake-down*, as she termed it, for Miss Herbert, in her room, and a stretcher for her maid.

"I have been too long accustomed to rough it in campaigns abroad and at home, to be disposed to make difficulties, and could sleep as well on three chairs joined together, ay, or even on the ground, as in a regular bed," said the Amazon, much to the surprise, if not the admiration, of the hostess of the inn, who gazed at her with undisguised wonder.

I remained in my own room with my little girl, until summoned to dinner by the waiter. I found Mrs. Scuddamore already seated; and, like an old soldier, as she professed and prided herself to be, examining the wine, and smelling the soup.

"I have my doubts," observed she, "about that soup being made of fresh meat; or, if made of fresh meat, it has certainly been re-heated, a thing I can't bear."

The waiter, more than half-offended, declared that such things never occurred in the establishment to which he belonged, and eyed Mrs. Scuddamore with peculiar suspicion during the rest of the repast.

"This is a quality of beef that my dear departed Colonel Scuddamore never would have tolerated. No, he carefully examined the meat furnished for the soldier's rations, allowed no peculation, no private understanding between the quartermaster and the contractor. 'My soldiers,' he used to say, 'must have the best, and *only* the best meat;' and he made it a point to taste their soup, and other food. Ah! *he* was a model of commanding officers: and if I am better acquainted than other women are with many useful things—I owe it wholly to him."

Dinner over, and the waiter withdrawn, Mrs. Scuddamore, with that absence of feeling and tact which was peculiar to her, inquired into the particulars of my poor wife's illness and death; but I declined entering into them, on the plea that the wounds were too recent to be touched, without a degree of pain that I was unable to encounter.

"Strange!" observed she. "Now, when I lost Colonel Scuddamore, it afforded me the greatest comfort to speak about him. But this, I suppose, originated in my having been so accustomed to see the killed and wounded *en masse*, when I accompanied my husband on foreign service, that I was used to death. Nothing gives courage so much as witnessing such scenes. And now tell me, did you know Major McCulloch, at Malta?"

I replied in the negative.

"Then you had a great loss," observed she. "He is a capital soldier, and no wonder, for he served many years under the command of Colonel Scuddamore. I will be confidential with you, Mr. Herbert, the Major will become my husband as soon as he gets his Lieut.-Colonelcy. He proposed for my hand the year after I lost the Colonel; but I told him, that to marry any officer of an inferior grade in the army to that which my former husband bore, was out of the question. He then extorted a promise, that when he received his promotion, I would become his. I wanted to wait till he became a full Colonel, but he said, that as neither of us were young, and both had seen a great deal of hard foreign service, it would be folly to wait for so long a period; so I yielded, though I do think it rather *infra dig.* for me to lose rank by becoming the wife of a Lieut.-Colonel, after having so long been the wife of a full one. The Major says, 'Where should we find persons to suit either of us so well as each other. We have seen the same countries, been engaged in the same scenes; we both revere the memory of the gallant Colonel Scuddamore. You know *me* to be a brave soldier, and I know you to be the very best soldier's wife I ever met. Our winter evenings will pass rapidly, talking over old times, by our fire-side, and our incomes joined will secure us the comforts of life.' What could be urged against such a rational project? Now, Mr. Herbert, that I have told you my plans, do, pray, let me know yours. You are come home, I conclude, to marry Mrs. Neville, the widow of poor Neville. I heard you had both arranged this affair at Nice, when you lost your wife, and she her husband."

"Then you were greatly misinformed," observed I, red with anger. "Mrs. Neville was in too great affliction for the loss of a husband she fondly loved, to admit of so preposterous, so indelicate and so indecorous a proceeding; and as for me, I should hate and despise myself, were I capable of such conduct."

"So, then, you are *not* engaged."

"Certainly not; and if I know myself, I never will give a successor to her whose loss I must ever deplore."

"But, my dear Mr. Herbert, you are still a young man. It would be madness at your age to remain single! I have not yet told you, that your old flame, my niece, Mrs. Mordaunt, is become a widow. Yes, positively she is free, and has inherited a very pretty property from her late husband. Poor fellow, you would never, I am sure, guess how he met his death? He was killed in a duel—shot through the breast. I knew him to be so deficient in courage, that when I was told a ball was lodged in his body, I said, he must have swallowed it then, for he never would have stood to be fired at. But he did though, for all that, for his wife, who has a little of my notions of honour, insisted on his going out with a gentleman, whose wife had, she said, insulted her; but who I really believe, *she* had insulted, for the husband of the other lady challenged Mordaunt, and he wanted to make an apology, as he was always ready to do, and she would not let him. Yes, Mrs. Mordaunt would make you an excellent wife, for her income is good, she is full of gaiety, and never out of spirits. You were once desperately in love with her, and you know the old song,

> 'On en revient toujours
> A ses premiers amours.'"

Though little inclined to mirth, heaven knows, I could not forbear smiling at the earnestness with which Mrs. Scuddamore recommended me to marry her niece, and the *naïveté* with which she revealed that to her the unfortunate Mordaunt owed his death.

There was something so ludicrous in such a recommendation, that I could not forbear laughing, but Mrs. Scuddamore saw nothing risible in the affair, and thought her niece had acted perfectly right in compelling her husband to fight, even though his death was the result.

Having exhausted her military intelligence, the fruit of a constant and sedulous perusal of the Army List, Gazette of promotions, exchanges, and obituaries of the last few months, I wished her good night, having given a very vague answer to her proposal of breakfasting together next morning. I arranged to depart for London at a very early hour, and having paid the bill of our dinner and tea, and left a few lines of farewell for her, giving no clue to my address in town, I sought my pillow, leaving instructions to be called at daybreak.

I got away from Portsmouth long before Mrs. Scuddamore was awake, rejoiced to have escaped from so troublesome an acquaintance, and determined to avoid her and her odious niece by every means in my power.

I entered London once more, but under what altered circumstances! I took apartments at Moffat's Hotel, in Brook-street, desiring to be as near Mrs. Neville's house as possible; and having seen my daughter and her attendant installed in their rooms, I hurried off to inquire if Mrs. Neville was in town.

CHAPTER LVII.

I FOUND Mrs. Neville at home, and although the first sight of me brought tears to her eyes, by recalling the sad events at Nice to her mind, her reception of me was kind, nay more, cordial. Her daughter was with her, and a more interesting and intelligent looking child I had never seen. Strikingly like my poor friend Neville, I could not look at her without being reminded of him. Though still pale and delicate, Mrs. Neville had recovered a portion of the beauty and attraction which had won my dear lost Louisa's admiration when first they met. Sorrow had given a more serious character to her countenance than it wore when I first beheld her, but all the feminine softness and touching grace peculiar to it, still existed; and whatever she might have lost in brilliancy and vivacity, she had gained in mildness and increased gentleness. One could not gaze on that pale but still lovely face, or that fragile figure, without feeling that long sorrow had wrought the change visible in her, and an increased sympathy, and deeper interest, were excited for her. When she learned that my daughter was at an hotel, she pressed me so cordially to permit her and her attendant to take up their abode with her, that although I hesitated to part from my child, even for a short time, I could not decline.

"You can come and see your little girl as often as you like," said Mrs. Neville, "and as I have generally a few intimate friends and relations who drop in to spend the evenings with me, it will give me pleasure if you join my quiet circle when you have nothing better to do."

Grateful for this kindness, invaluable to one like me, who had no friends or acquaintances to welcome me, gladly did I promise to avail myself of it. Hitherto my eyes had been wholly occupied in looking at Mrs. Neville and her interesting daughter.

As I glanced at the pensive but beautiful face of the beloved friend of my adored wife how many sorrowful thoughts were recalled to my mind. My poor Louisa seemed again to rise up before me; my dear, my only friend, Neville, seemed to live again, so closely associated were these dear lost ones with her who was now present.

Something of this feeling was also experienced by Mrs. Neville, for I saw tears start to her eyes frequently while we conversed, and the tremulous movement of her lips betrayed her emotion. I noticed too that she more than once turned her eyes to the side of the room where I was seated, and when I arose to depart I glanced at the wall. Upon it were suspended two portraits, so strikingly resembling my beloved Louisa and poor Neville, that I could not for several minutes withdraw my gaze from them, though tears almost blinded me.

"I ought to have prepared you for this surprise," said Mrs Neville, "but I was afraid to trust myself to speak. The faces of both were so deeply engraved on my heart and memory, that I was enabled to make these portraits, which are constantly before my eyes. They were painted *con amore*, and constitute one of my greatest consolations."

It was some time before I could recover my self-possession, so deeply affected was I by these pictures, and my emotion was the truest homage I could offer to her who had produced them.

Mrs. Neville sent her carriage to the hotel for my daughter and her attendant, and I took my leave of her, promising to join her in the evening, and hastened to give instructions to have the wardrobe of my little girl removed to Brook-street, filled with gratitude that she had so kind, so judicious a friend, under whose protection she could be placed.

My next visit was to my old friend Vise, but a brass plate, with another name than his, informed me that he no longer inhabited his old place of abode. I knocked, and was admitted, and in answer to my inquiries, was informed that Vise had been dead some time. Poor fellow! how my neglect and long silence towards him now smote my conscience. He, who had from the first moment of our acquaintance been so invariably kind and friendly, and had taken such a warm interest in my affairs. I knew not until this moment how much I liked poor Vise, and now, it was too late to prove to him that I was not ungrateful. He must have died thinking me so, and this reflection pained me.

"Should you wish to see his executors, the address can be given you," said the person who had answered my inquiries. "It has been left here in case it should be asked for."

I took the address, and hurried from the house, where no longer, as heretofore, I had a friend.

I had arrived at no very advanced period of life, yet how had I seen the few dear to me, or to whom I was dear, snatched away from existence! On whom could I now count in my native land for friendship, or good will? On no one save Mrs. Neville, and she, I felt fully conscious, was only interested for me out of regard to the memory of those dear to her who had loved me. This feeling of isolation, always peculiar to a solitary man, came stronger on me than ever, and I almost repented having resigned my daughter, though even but for a temporary period, to any care but my own. Under my own roof I could seek her presence when I pleased, could lose the depressing sense of my loneliness in her fond caresses and artless prattle. Now I should have to look for her in the house of another, should be compelled to consult the convenience of those with whom she was domiciled for the time of our interview, and its duration—perhaps have witnesses to it, before whom I could not give way to that expansion of heart, that doting tenderness, of which she was the sole object. I could not, as I had been wont to do, bend over her little couch to bless her slumbers, or receive her kiss when she awoke. Now that I had, by my own consent, parted from my darling, I seemed to require her presence more than ever, and shame alone prevented my going to Mrs. Neville's and revealing my weakness, and reclaiming back my little Frances.

To chase away these thoughts, I walked to Mr. Goldey's, one of the executors of poor Vise. I found him at home, and on sending in my card, I was admitted to his office.

"I have heard my poor deceased friend often speak of you, Sir," said he, looking at me through his spectacles. "He was snatched away very suddenly, and in the prime of life I may say. Not above four or five years older than I am." The speaker looked to be at least twelve years the senior of my poor friend.

"Of all tenures, Sir, and as a lawyer I am conversant on such matters, none are so precarious as that of life. There are so many flaws in the title, Sir, so many clauses of forfeiture, that no man can count on a peaceable or long possession."

The air of self-complacency with which Mr. Goldey uttered these truisms, might have amused me under other circumstances, but now that I was saddened by the loss of poor Vise, I was more disposed to be impatient than diverted by his pompously uttered common-places.

"Death, Sir," resumed he, "is of all creditors the most stern and unbending. He claims, ay, and compels, too, payment of the debts due to him, even from those who never discharged any other. Not that our late respected friend Vise, was one of those who neglect their worldly affairs, for there was no man more just in his dealings, or more punctual in the payment of his debts. Never was sued in his life, until the King of Terror, as poets term him, brought his action, without serving him with due notice, got a verdict against him and carried him off.—Poor Vise did not, however, forget his old friends. He has remembered you, Sir, handsomely in his will, which has been properly administered to; and when your identity is satisfactorily proved, you can receive your legacy, amounting to no less a sum than five thousand pounds, as well as different articles belonging to you confided to his trust, each, and all of which he took especial care should be labelled, and a regular list of them made out, in order to prevent the possibility of mistake or litigation."

I inquired the particulars of my poor friend's illness, and the precise time of his death?

"The doctors differed, as they generally do, as to his disease. One asserted it was of the liver; another, said it was dyspepsia; a third, declared it was ossification of the heart; and the fourth, insisted that it was an affection of the lungs. The only point on which all agreed, was,—that each had applied precisely the wrong treatment,—so poor Vise's friends had the annoyance, in addition to their regret, of thinking that he might have been saved, had he been differently treated. If a poor, unfortunate patient is in danger with *one* doctor, I leave you to imagine, Sir, how little must his chance be with four. From the beginning, I saw it was all up with him, and the result but too well justified my fears. Death, at all times a disagreeable thing, becomes much more so when it carries off our contemporaries; and though poor Vise was five years, at least, older than me, nevertheless I might, in some sort, consider him a contemporary; and his death alarmed me considerably. Such events come as warnings to us, Sir; and never do I lose a friend, or does a misfortune occur to one, without my thinking that it *might* have happened to myself: and the satisfaction experienced that it has *not*, greatly mitigates the regret felt for others. Indeed, a sensible man may reconcile his feelings to every affliction that befals *others*, by reflecting that such might be his own lot; and *his* escape soothes all sorrow."

I left this selfish being, thoroughly disgusted with him, while he, I verily believe, imagined that he had exhibited a degree of good sense and philosophy, that must have made a most favourable impression on my mind.

How strange and incomprehensible is the mind of man! I had been months—nay, more—years, without ever bestowing a single thought on him whose death had been that day announced to me; and, had I remained abroad, I should probably have continued equally oblivious of him; and now—I could think of nothing else! I recalled his various acts of kindness and good nature to me—the expression of his countenance on these occasions—the tones of his voice and puerile details of his person and dress, as vividly as if I had seen him only the previous day. The proof that, however I had forgotten him, *he* had not ceased to remember me with affection, awakened a sentiment of strong self-reproach in my heart; and the regret I now experienced, caused me to reflect, that there was something in my nature, if not in that of all mankind, that disposed me much more to painful, than pleasurable emotions, since he whom living, I seldom, if ever, bestowed a thought on, now when dead, gave me regret.

When walking back to my hotel, the crowds in the streets, the hurrying to and fro, the noise, the bustle, the air of deep occupation of all those I encountered, struck me with as much surprise as if I had never previously beheld this scene.—How different from the comparatively deserted streets of the continental towns, in which life and its business seemed to stagnate!

"Here," thought I, "a man might long escape being found," and the thought of Figgins pursuing me flashed through my mind. "Here an obscure individual, of more than suspected character, would long pause before he dared to prefer an unsupported charge of criminality against a person known to be of respectable station in society." And a feeling of security nerved my frame, long unknown to it. I fancied that in busy, crowded London, with its active police ever within call, my tormentor would be afraid to assail me. That a charge of conspiracy might enable me to get rid of him, should he presume to follow and attack me, and, let me also add, a consciousness that my pecuniary independence would greatly befriend me against any charge brought by an impoverished man of his class, added to my newly acquired courage—Figgins in London and on the continent were two different persons. In a foreign land he stood a better chance of frightening me to his wishes, because there I had less protection against his nefarious schemes than at home. And as these thoughts passed through my mind, it occurred to me that I ought to go to my property in Wales, and take steps to guard against any future attempt on his part to bring testimony of the crime of which he supposed me to be guilty.

Yes, painful as the effort would be, I would go to Wales, to that spot where, notwithstanding the one terrible event that had obscured the sunshine of my life, I had enjoyed some hours of as exquisite happiness as was ever vouchsafed to mortal! But now, *she* who had bestowed this bliss was sleeping in her distant grave; and I must enter the abode once graced by her presence, every room in which must remind me of her—must make me feel more poignantly the loss of that happiness I must never more hope to find. How impressionable is the human mind! How many thoughts had passed through mine during the few hours that had elapsed since my arrival in London! They had been so various and exciting, that days, nay, weeks, seemed to have glided away, instead of hours, since I left my hotel; and, morally and physically fatigued, I threw myself into a chair, and closed my eyes, as if to shut out thought.

I was aroused from my reverie by the announcement that my solitary dinner was served; and having slightly partaken of it, I dressed for my evening visit to Mrs. Neville, and proceeded to her house.

She had considerately given instructions that I should be shown to the sitting-room assigned to her daughter's use, where I found my sweet Frances waiting, with her attendant, to receive me. The dear child rushed into my arms, and fondly embracing me, exclaimed, "Oh! dear, good papa, how kind of you to let me come here, where I am so happy with dear Matilda Neville to play with; and her mamma, who is so fond of me. Won't you leave me with them, dear papa, and come and see me every day?"

I felt a chill strike at my heart at this artless address of my daughter's. Was this, then, the reward of that doting affection I had lavished on her, for the pang it had cost me to part from her, for even a short time? Already was her new playmate preferred to me; and her first words to me on meeting, were to prefer a request to be left with her new friends! Stunned and pained, I disengaged myself gently from her embrace. I felt disappointed, grieved—here, where I had garnered up all my affection, all my hopes, I was doomed to find only disappointment, and I mentally accused my child of ingratitude and selfishness, when the unsophisticated little creature was only following the dictates of nature in revealing the pleasure she experienced at finding herself, for the first time, with a playmate of her own age, to enjoy her sports. It was I who was selfish and unreasonable; but so I ever was, allowing my morbid feelings to govern me.

After passing an hour with my daughter—an hour that, instead of being one of pure pleasure, was poisoned by the thought of her preferring her new friends to me, I joined Mrs. Neville's circle in the drawing-room. It was composed, for the greater part, of near relatives, and a few intimate friends, to whom I was presented. The conversation proved that the visitors were intellectual and accomplished; yet, it was wholly free from the pretension and desire to shine, which but too frequently impair, if not destroy, the agreeability of such society. Mrs. Neville formed the focus around which this circle moved, and though no longer playful, animated and brilliant, as when I first knew her, the seriousness, if not pensiveness of her manner, free from all moroseness, or misanthropy, invested her with a new charm.

I took an opportunity of informing her of my intention of departing for Wales next day, and she so earnestly requested me to leave my daughter with her, that I consented.

CHAPTER LVIII.

I LEFT London at an early hour in the morning, taking no servant with me; and in the post-chaise which conveyed me on my route, had ample time for reflection. I remembered, now for the first time, that the bequest of my late friend Vise, would not only prevent the fortune of my daughter being impaired by the sums I had given, or might yet be called on to give to Figgins, but add considerably to her portion; and although, heaven knows, never fond of money, this thought pleased me, for aught that could tend to make *her* lot in life a more fortunate one, was regarded by me with an interest, that nothing appertaining exclusively to my self could awaken.—I lived but for my child. The present—the future—were contemplated solely with a reference to her welfare; and if I trembled in an agony of terror, at the possibility of my name being disgraced by a charge preferred against me by Figgins, it was because *she* bore that name, and that a charge of guilt against me would entail discredit on her. Knowing my perfect freedom from guilt, my conscience no longer inflicted pain on me. Time and reflection had soothed the torture endured during the first year after the fatal event that had blighted my existence; and when death had snatched my beloved Louisa from me, whose peace would have been inevitably destroyed for ever by the disclosure that I had been, even unintentionally, accessory to her sister's death, I no longer dreaded with such intense horror, the chance of discovery, as when the blow might have crushed her. But then came the thought that my daughter's prospects might be ruined; and again I was a trembling coward, ready to make any sacrifice to preserve the name *she* bore from dishonour.

Every mile that took me further from my child seemed to increase the overflowing tenderness I felt for her; and as I gazed on the lofty mountains that rose up between us, I wondered how I had found courage to leave her, and was ready to exclaim with Goldsmith, the poet,—

> "Where'er I roam, whatever realms to see,
> My heart untravell'd fondly turns to thee;
> Still to my *daughter* turns, with endless pain,
> And drags at each remove a lengthening chain."

He who has never experienced misfortune, and, above all other misfortunes, that of having lost the object of his most tender love, can form no idea of the disgust of life with which he turns from the syren, Hope, who would again cheat him with smiling prospects for the future. For *himself* he expects not—he seeks not happiness again. He knows it is buried with her who once constituted it; and he desires not, even were it possible, to find it through any other medium. But when he is a father—when a child of her he loved is bequeathed to him—the happiness to which he no longer aspires for himself, he would fain transfer to his, to *her* offspring, and losing his selfishness, his very identity, as it were, in the all-engrossing interest awakened for her child, he would gladly purchase its exemption from the ills of life at the price of his own misery.

How often did my memory recur to the last time I traversed the route I was now pursuing! I was then hastening to my mother, in the hope to receive that blessing, which, alas! I was doomed never more to hear her dear lips pronounce.—I was then wretched, as the bare possibility of arriving too late presented itself, and I looked on that as the utmost misfortune that could befal me.

I little dreamed, that, heavy as that must be, a still heavier one menaced me, and I hurried on to my fate, thoughtless as victims approach the altar of sacrifice.

Now I was journeying to the same goal—alone, as then—but with a heart still bleeding for one I had never seen when I had previously traced this route. How widely different is the solitude of one bereaved of the object which made the charm—the *all*—of life, and that of him who has yet to learn the blessing of having found this object! Now an aching void was left in my heart, never more to be filled; and the grief I felt was in proportion to the difference which the actual present bore to the happy past.—It seemed wondrous to me how I had supported existence before I knew my Louisa, so wholly had she changed its entire current; and yet it was surely more wonderful how, after having been blest with her, I could drag on life when she was no more!

I reached my now desolate home, at a late hour of the third evening from my departure from London. The post which brought the letter, announcing my return, had arrived some hours before, and my humble, but faithful friend, Mrs. Burnet, had made some preparations for my reception.—A bright fire, a clean hearth, and lighted candles, took off from the gloom that always pervades a long-deserted abode; but alas! the light only showed me the serious, but lovely face, of my departed wife's sister, which might be mistaken for the portrait of my lost Louisa, so striking was its resemblance to her. It made me shudder; and yet I could not withdraw my eyes from it.

I attempted to taste the light supper prepared by Mrs. Burnet, who pressed me so anxiously to eat a few morsels; but I could not swallow, and it was only after having drunk a glass of wine that I could answer her affectionate inquiries for my daughter, so wholly was I overpowered by the agonizing feelings awakened by the sight of the objects around me.—There was my lost Louisa's chair, and the footstool on which I had so often seen her delicate feet resting. Her work-table and tambour-frame were still in the places where she had been wont to use them; one of her favourite volumes, with a rose between the leaves, still lay on a small table near her chair, and a pair of her gloves was beside it. How did I press these mementos of happier times to my lips, and bathe them in my tears, as the thought that she whose presence had been the only sunshine that had ever cheered my gloomy existence, was now slumbering in her distant grave, between which and me a wide sea rolled. It seemed but a short time since I had left the spot I now found myself in, bearing with me my beautiful, my adored companion, blooming in youth and health, or, if the rose had paled on her fair cheek, it was from her tender solicitude for me. Yet, oh!

how much sorrow and agony had I endured since that period.—How many days of wretchedness and sleepless nights! Every thing around me seemed so exactly like what had been before I left my home, that I could hardly reason myself into the conviction that *she* was gone for ever. There were moments in which I indulged the illusion that she might have gone to her chamber, and that when the door which led to it opened, she would enter! Then came back the terrible truth, and that I could even for a moment have doubted it, filled me with dread that I must be losing my reason, to have had such hallucinations.

Mrs. Burnet spoke not of my lost wife, although I saw by her mournful countenance that her thoughts were with the dead. I was grateful for this forbearance, for I could not have borne to have talked on the subject that occupied all my thoughts. To turn me from bitter memories, Mrs. Burnet reverted to other topics.

"There was a strange man came here, Sir," said she, "who said he had lived in your service at Nice."

I became all ear, though trembling with emotion, as I listened to this preface.

"I really think he was not right in his head," resumed the good woman, "for he did nothing but ask the strangest questions, and all about one subject, which was whether any lady had ever been thrown down from a precipice in our neighbourhood; who had been suspected of the crime, and whether the body was ever found, and where buried? I lost all patience at his minute inquiries, and then he went round to all the neighbours, questioning them. And when he heard how poor Miss Maitland had been so long missing, he seemed quite pleased, which showed he must be crazy to be glad of such a misfortune; and after, when he learned that the corse had been found in the river, and had been buried in the vault in the church, he seemed quite sorry, and wanted to know whether it had been identified by those who knew the deceased, and whether any marks of violence had been discovered on it.

"I don't know whether I ought to repeat this low man's words to you, Sir," continued Mrs. Burnet; "but would you believe it, Sir, he had the impudence and wickedness to ask, if you, yes, Sir, positively you, had never been suspected of throwing the young lady down the precipice? This made the persons to whom he spoke, so angry, that they would hold no further talk with him; and, afterwards, he brought a spade and mattock and went digging up the ground about the precipice, for several days,—some say, in hopes of finding buried treasure. He, at last, went away, and we have heard no more of him, ever since but I am sure he was mad."

My feelings while Mrs. Burnet related all this tale to me cannot be described. Terror, and horror, predominated! To hear a subject discussed, which I never could even think of without shuddering, tortured me almost beyond the power of endurance; and yet I felt the necessity of concealing, though I could not vanquish, my deep emotion. The effort nearly convulsed me; but Mrs. Burnet was no prying spy to watch whatever demonstrations of grief, or agitation, I might betray; and any symptoms of such that she might notice, she would naturally attribute to anger and indignation caused by what she had narrated.

"To think, Sir," resumed she, "of a crazy fellow coming here to ask, whether you had not loved, and murdered a young lady, whom I and many others could prove, on oath, you never saw, till you beheld her in her coffin; for you may remember, Sir, she disappeared the very evening of my dear lady's funeral, when you were very ill in your bed; and many persons, as well as me, could prove you had never, since you returned to find your blessed mother no more, left this house, by day or night, except to attend her interment, until you were called from your sick-bed, to join in the search of poor Miss Maitland, the night she was first missed."

It was highly consolatory to me to find that Mrs. Burnet's memory was so accurate in every particular connected with the fatal night that had destroyed my peace. Her evidence, if ever required, would fully acquit me of any charge brought by the vile schemer Figgins; and corroborated as it could be by the neighbours who were cognizant of the facts she detailed, I felt that I had little to dread, even if denounced by the wretch who had taken such advantage of my terror.

I determined that I would once more visit the cavern, and ascertain whether the mortal remains of my poor sister-in-law still rested where I had interred them, or whether the statement of Figgins, that *he* had removed them, was founded in truth. I assumed as calm an aspect as I could, affected to believe with Mrs. Burnet, that the strange man of whom she spoke must be mad, and then pleading fatigue, retired to my bedroom—that which had been my nuptial chamber!

There stood the toilet-table of my lost Louisa, her dressing-stool, and her easy-chair, with their delicate flounced coverings. The mirror with its lace draperies, the snowy pillows with their embroidered trimmings. In short, all that distinguishes the *chambre à coucher* of a woman from that of a man. The very atmosphere of the room was redolent of the mingled perfume of violets and vervaine, her favourite odours, which, contained in *sachets* of her own making, had been carefully preserved in the wardrobes and commodes by Mrs. Burnet, and still sent forth their scents. An

Æolian harp, placed in a window of the adjoining dressing-room, occasionally breathed its unearthly sounds, as the night-breeze swept over its chords. How frequently had I listened to its fitful music, when she who placed it there was by my side! Now it seemed to breathe a requiem to her shade, every note thrilling my heart with sadness, until, unmanned, I flung myself into a chair, and lightened my tortured breast by an uncontrollable fit of tears.—I wept long, for the fountain of grief, once opened, could not be soon closed. I experienced a sense of relief from tears, and throwing myself on my couch, slept for some hours. When I awoke, I found that it was only a little after twelve o'clock. I had retired so early to my chamber that I could hardly believe that only so small a portion of the night had passed; and now finding that some hours of darkness might still be counted on, and that all was silent in the house, I arose, and determined on proceeding to the cavern, provided I could find a lantern and a spade.

With stealthy step I entered a small room not far distant from my bed-chamber, appropriated for the keeping of all objects not in daily requisition, and there I found the lantern formerly used, and having placed in it one of the candles of my chamber, and locked my room door inside, I opened a window, and stept noiselessly into the garden; in the tool-house of which I found a spade, as I had expected. I had put some phosphoric matches in my pocket, to strike a light when required; and wrapping myself in my cloak, I took the well-remembered path, and with a quick beating heart, hurried on to the cavern.—Not a human being did I meet,—not a sound, save that of the night birds, met my ear.

I entered the cavern, and lit the lantern with a trembling hand. I stooped down close to the earth, to examine whether any portion of its surface had been disturbed since I last saw it, and almost fell to the ground, when I beheld evident traces that it had.

Yes, some one *had* been digging here, and had taken so little pains to restore the former evenness of the surface, that the inequality was very perceptible—"Good God!" thought I, "the story told by Figgins was not untrue!" And yet the spot that had been dug up, was not precisely that in which I had placed the corse. There was still a chance that he had not discovered the body, and this chance nerved my arm to apply the spade more vigorously to the closely bound soil, rendered harder by the amalgamation of earth and sand. Large drops of perspiration fell from my brow on the ground, as I worked through it for nearly two hours, when my spade met a different substance. Oh! how I trembled! and how rapidly did my heart beat!—I loosened the earth, and drew forth a portion of the matting which enveloped the corse. Beneath it a fragment of the cloak I had wrapped around the dead was revealed, and having thrown out several spades-full of the soil, the form, shrouded in its covering of matting and cloak, met my eyes. I fell on my knees and breathed a prayer of thankfulness to the Almighty, for this little less than miraculous escape of the dead from the prying search of Figgins. He had opened the earth in more than two or three places, within a few feet of that spot which contained what he sought; but the precise one was so knit together as to offer strong evidence of never having been disturbed since I had closed it, that I felt assured, he had not dug it, while other spots disclosed that they had been disturbed. What was I next to do? I was so fearful of *not* finding the corse, that I had not thought of what would be advisable to do with it until now. Although shuddering at the contact, I raised the corse in my arms, and to my utter amazement found it so incredibly light, that at first it occurred to me that I held only its envelopes, and that the remains had been abstracted. That was a terrible moment! I laid down the light burthen on the earth, and trembling with the mingled emotions of anxiety and terror, I rapidly tore off a portion of the matting and cloak, when the interior drapery met my touch, and beneath it a skeleton-like form, to which no substance like flesh seemed to adhere. I dared not look on what had been the face—that face, whose rare and exquisite beauty had been kept fresh in my memory by the wonderful resemblance which that of my departed wife bore to it, and which still lived in my daughter! And yet it was necessary to ascertain that the remains were those which I had placed there! I held the open lantern close to the shrouded form, and with averted eyes, groped with one hand to remove sufficient of the cloak to reveal some part of the corse, which I could turn to glance for a moment at, when uncovered, when the candle fell from the lantern, and before I was aware that it had done so, matting and cloak were in a blaze! Terrified, bewildered, I lost all self-control, all reason! I rushed wildly to the opening of the cavern to seek assistance, forgetting that none could be met with there; or, if a human being could be encountered, the discovery of my terrible secret must be the inevitable result.

CHAPTER LIX.

Even on the outside of the cavern I could hear the crackling of the flames, and see the bright reflection illuminating the sides of the rock at the entrance, and casting forth a stream of light to the spot where I stood. I wrung my hands in helpless, hopeless, despair. Could the dead feel the fire that encircled it in its embraces, raging more fiercely every moment,

I could not have experienced a greater degree of terror and dismay than filled my breast then! The lurid flames streamed forth from the mouth of the cavern, falling on the sand and on the water like columns of molten gold. Oh! what would I not have given for some vessel to fill with water to throw on the fire,—but I was powerless, and could only writhe in agony as the blaze mounted still higher.

Hardly conscious of what I did, I again entered the cavern, and gazed on the flames, when, Oh! horror! through them, as through a transparent vial, I could behold the face of the dead brightly tinted by their reflection; and, uttering a loud cry, I fell to the earth! How long I remained insensible I know not; but when consciousness was restored the fire was over, and the smouldering ashes still smoking, alone revealed what had occurred.

The first light of day-break now pierced the cavern. Oh! how dreary, how desolate, was its aspect, as only partially illuminated, the distant portions still remaining in deep shadow, while the pale light of day fell on the funeral pyre. Aroused to a sense of danger, I felt that these traces of some mysterious crime must instantly be removed. I collected the ashes of the matting and drapery, which, alas! were mingled with those of the dead, and filling my cloak with them, although my hands recoiled with instinctive horror from the contact, I emptied the contents into the water, and saw them quickly hurried away, and dispersed by the rapidity of the current.

Having then shaken the cloak as carefully as I could, to remove every particle of the ashes from it, I placed in it the scorched skull, shorn of the beautiful tresses that had formerly graced that once lovely head, and the half-carbonized limbs, that could have betrayed them to have appertained to a human being. I then filled up the now empty grave, and by repeatedly stamping on it, and strewing dust over the surface, restored it to its former appearance.

Having enveloped the head,—the word makes me shudder even now,— and the bones into as small a parcel as I could, I hastily pursued my way to my house, like a criminal, glancing from side to side, lest some shepherd should be leading his flock from the fold, or some early milkmaid should be abroad to milk her cows. Every sound alarmed me, every shadow terrified. The carol of the birds to welcome morning, was, for the first time, distasteful to my ear, by reminding me of the advance of day, and that consequently others, like myself, might be abroad. My fears, however, were groundless: I met not a human being; and, having entered the window by which I had left my house, I placed my sacred burthen on a table, and gasping for breath, sank into a chair to recover my self-possession.

Grown more calm, I replaced the lantern where I had found it, took out a portion of the clothes contained in a large trunk I had brought with me, and removing from my cloak the deposit it had enveloped, I wrapped its contents in a large dressing-gown, which I placed in the trunk, taking care to secure the key in a secret drawer in my writing-case. I then removed every trace of soil from my cloak, brushed it, scraped my boots, and carefully washed my hands, emptying the contents of the basin into the garden, and then, unlocking my chamber-door, went to bed. But sleep refused to visit my couch, notwithstanding the intense sense of fatigue I experienced. The thought of the scene I had witnessed, and the recollection of the contents of the trunk in my room, prevented me from having even a few minutes' sleep, greatly as I required it; and when, at eight o'clock, I rang my bell for Mrs. Burnet, my pale face and haggard countenance alarmed the worthy creature so much, that I had some difficulty in preventing her from sending for Dr. Bellinden. Some strong coffee proved a stimulant that so greatly revived me, that Mrs. Burnet's alarm subsided.

"I was thinking, Sir," said she, "that it was very stupid of me not to have thought of opening your trunk, and arranging its contents in the drawers."

I trembled at the bare notion, but making an effort to conceal my agitation, I answered, "that as my stay would be only for a day, I would not have my trunk unpacked."

Seeing that she glanced at the trunk, whose size must have given her the idea, that for so short a visit it was unnecessary to bring so large a one, I said something about having intended to have stayed some time, but that I found the place reminded me so much of the past, and affected my feelings so powerfully, that I could not support a longer continuance there.

"I don't wonder at it, Sir," replied the worthy woman; "I thought you looking extremely ill last evening when you arrived, but you appeared so much worse this morning, when I first entered, that I really believe your health would suffer by a longer residence here." And she sighed deeply, and tears filled her eyes while she spoke.

I walked out after breakfast, and called on the good pastor of our hamlet. His reception of me was most kind and affectionate—my altered appearance had evidently touched him., for I saw his eyes become moist more than once while he spoke to me.—He expressed a hope that I was come to make some stay, but, when I stated that I found I had not yet acquired sufficient strength of mind to support the sight of a place where I had once been so happy, he shook his head, and answered, "that he feared it." I placed a sum of money in his hands, for the poor of his flock, and then proceeded to call on Dr. Bellinden. This son of Esculapius no sooner saw me than he held out his hand, not to shake mine as might be anticipated, but to feel my pulse.

"Good God! Sir, how ill you are looking," exclaimed he.

"Yes, I have not been well of late," and I endeavoured to withdraw my wrist from his grasp.

"Do you know that you ought to be in your bed, Sir, instead of walking about. You are ill, seriously ill, Mr. Herbert. Your pulse is up to one hundred and twenty, and hard and wiry. Not the least moisture on the skin. You should return home, and go to bed directly."

I answered that it was only the fatigue occasioned by a rapid journey and want of sleep that had occasioned the symptoms he had remarked, and that, as I was called back to London immediately by business, I should not have time to lay up, and profit by his care and skill.

"Are you quite sure that you feel no uneasiness in the crico-arytenoideus lateralis?" demanded the doctor, still examining my countenance.

"Not the least," replied I, wholly ignorant of the signification of the technical words he had uttered.

"Well, that is strange," resumed he, "for you certainly appear to me to have some affection connected with the muscles of the glottis. Yet now, that I look more narrowly, I begin to think that you have a derangement of the levator labii superioris ulæque nasi. Yes, certainly, you have, and a very disagreeable and troublesome complaint it is, if not attended to at once."

"I confess," answered I, "that I do not know the sense of the words you have just pronounced, consequently cannot say whether I feel any symptoms of the malady or not."

"Ah!" and the doctor sighed deeply, "when will science, and above all, the science of anatomy and physic, be so generally diffused, that every educated person will be able to give an accurate description of his symptoms, and in the proper terms. Then there will be no mistakes in my profession—none of those fatal errors which originate, *not*, as is too frequently but falsely attributed in the want of skill in physicians, but in the want of accuracy in describing their complaints, so prevalent in patients. The levator labii superioris ulæque nasi, to simplify to the unlearned, I designate the sneering muscle, Mr. Herbert; and yours, I am persuaded, has an unnatural tension, for I have been looking at it the last ten minutes."

For once, the Doctor had guessed nearer the truth than usual; for, little disposed to smile, heaven knows, something like a sneer had involuntarily passed over the muscles of my lips, at his pedantry, and desire to take possession of me as a patient.

"Be assured, Mr. Herbert," resumed the Doctor, "that Pope never wrote a truer or a more philosophical line than that which says—

'The proper study of mankind is man.'

It is by studying man that I have arrived at a knowledge of physiology, that, had I but a more extended field for the exercise of my talent, would render me celebrated."

I bade the self-complacent Doctor farewell, leaving him far from being satisfied at what he considered my wilfulness and obstinacy, in not yielding to his advice. Little did Pope think that the line quoted so gravely would be taken as bearing reference to the physical instead of the moral state of man!

And I could reflect on such things, ay, and even for a moment smile at the weakness of the poor Doctor, while my own mind was even at the moment conscious of still greater weakness, and that my heart was oppressed at the thought of the contents of the trunk in my chamber. Frequently during the day did I feel in my waistcoat pocket to be sure that the key of my writing-case was safely lodged in it; because in that writing-box was the key of the trunk! When I entered my house, I walked straight to the bedroom to see that the trunk had not been touched; and often did my eyes turn to it with a mingled sentiment of horror and dread.

I had ordered post-horses for an early hour on the following morning. Oh! how I wished the long evening, and longer night, was over; for I shuddered at the thought of being alone to gaze on objects that wrung my heart with sorrow, by reminding me of my lost, my adored wife, and of passing the night in the chamber with the trunk. What fearful dreams might it not occasion, the bare sight of it agitating me so violently!

My scarcely-tasted dinner removed, I summoned Mrs. Burnet to come and sit with me, so much did I dread being alone. It was no supernatural fear that haunted me, no, it was the fear of my own sad thoughts—my own troubled dreams, which tortured and unmanned me.

I encouraged the inquiries of my worthy house-keeper relative to my daughter. She had endless questions to ask, all betraying the deep interest she felt for this last scion of a house she had so faithfully served.

"And Jenny, the nurse, Sir," said she, "I suppose she is in London, with dear Miss Herbert?"

"No," replied I, "she preferred remaining in Malta, and I left her."

"What! let her young lady come back over the sea alone?" observed the good woman. "Oh, what an unnatural, ungrateful creature she must be! It is fortunate that her poor widowed mother is in her grave, for it would have broken her heart, to know that her daughter had behaved so ill. But to speak the truth, when I heard that wicked, crazy fellow, who came here, speak of her as *his* intimate friend, I began to fear *she* could not be good for much. Ah, Sir, when a foolish girl has no steady, elderly woman, or strict mistress to look after her, she is sure to fall into a scrape."

When the word mistress had escaped Mrs. Burnet's lips, her changed aspect, and timid glance at me, disclosed how much she regretted her inadvertence in having used a word so carefully guarded against since my arrival. Poor, faithful creature! with intuitive tact and tenderness, she knew that the wound in my heart was still too recent to bear the touch, and could not forgive herself for reverting to it.

When at length it was time to retire to bed, she offered me some syrup of hops, from her little store of medicines, kept for the use of her poor neighbours.

"A few drops, Sir, will calm your nerves, and procure you a tranquil night. Often have I known my dear lady, your honoured mother, obtain a few hours' rest, when her deep grief kept her waking."

How these few words brought back to my mind that deep grief I had so often witnessed, and, alas! after the first few weeks, so little sympathized in. The darkened chamber, and the pale mourner, with tear-stained cheeks, again seemed to stand before me. How little did that fond mother anticipate that her son, who had been so insensible to *her* sorrow, would so soon become a prey to his own. A merciful Providence has, in pity, veiled the future from us—for those who might have courage to support their own heavy trials, would surely sink could they but know the troubles ordained to fall on those dear to them. As this reflection arose in my mind, I prayed that my child might be spared the misfortunes I had undergone, and my heart was melted with tenderness as I thought of her.

The syrup of hops produced a most salutary effect. I enjoyed some hours of refreshing slumber, and awoke more calm than I had been of late. Thankful for this relief, I possessed myself of the bottle, and after having partaken of an early breakfast, and seen *the trunk* safely consigned to the interior of my chaise, *malgré* the reiterated representations of my good housekeeper that it would incommode me, and that it might be securely attached by cords behind the carriage, I placed funds in her hands to enable her to extend her charities to the poor; and wringing the hand that warmly clasped mine—its owner with streaming eyes and faltering lips praying for blessings on me and mine—I entered the chaise, and was driven rapidly away from the spot endeared to me by a thousand fond but mournful recollections, which rendered a sojourn in it too painful to be borne, until time had softened the bitterness of regret, and could enable me to look on the objects and scenes that now tortured me with less anguish.

CHAPTER LX.

INSTEAD of proceeding directly to London, I determined to go to Portskewell, a little village not far from Chepstow, remain there a day or two, then cross over to Clifton, and thence go to London. Never for a single hour—nay, more, for even half that period, did I forget the contents of the trunk, to which my eyes were continually reverting. The horror I experienced at contemplating this unseemly receptacle of all that remained of the once lovely being to whom they appertained, far from diminishing, increased; and as I reflected that I could not give these sacred relics the rites of Christian sepulture, I groaned aloud, and beat my breast in despair.—When I stopped for the night, I had the trunk conveyed to my chamber, though well aware that its proximity to my couch would debar me from slumber; but I feared to allow it to be out of my sight, lest by some unlucky chance it might be opened, and its contents being revealed, lead to suspicion and investigation.

Arrived at Portskewell, after the most painful journey I ever made, I took up my abode at a small inn, near the water's edge; and early the next morning, opening the trunk, and enveloping a portion of its contents in a Scots shepherd's plaid, I concealed the skull in a large silk handkerchief, which I slung to my waist beneath the large cloak I wore, and walking to the shore, hired a boat "for an hour's pleasure," as I told the owner, though my lips almost refused to utter the words.

"You had better let me, or one of my lads accompany you, Sir," said the boatman, "for sudden squalls often come on here, which are dangerous for those not well accustomed to the management of a boat."

I declined the offer, however, and so peremptorily, that the man said, "just as you like, Sir, it's all one to me," and I entered the boat, still grasping the shepherd's plaid; which I never let out of my hand, until I had placed it on the seat by me. The owner of the boat pushed it from the shore, and I took the oars and rowed towards the opposite coast; the boatman remaining at the water's edge, as if watching how I managed his little vessel, until it was nearly out of sight.

I then removed the limbs from the plaid, and let one drop into the water; proceeded in another direction, and let another fall, and so one by one, always changing my course between each fragment I consigned to the deep, till all had disappeared. I then, removing the handkerchief, immersed the skull, and, with a beating heart and distended eyes, beheld the circling

eddies close over it, as it sank many fathoms deep into its watery grave! I
then refolded the plaid as it had formerly been, and, with trembling hands,
rowed back towards the shore, within a short distance of which I continued, until my violent emotion had subsided, when I landed, and, ordering
the boatman to have his boat ready for another excursion in a couple of
hours, as also for the same hour the following morning, I retraced my steps
to the inn.

This measure was adopted to avoid exciting suspicion by my solitary
excursion that morning; and it was, perhaps, well that I had recourse to it,
for my host, while serving breakfast, observed that the boatman had been
there to inquire whether I had left any effects at the inn, in case I might not
return with his boat.

"Did he suspect my honesty, then?" demanded I, "or was it that he
feared my want of skill to manage his little vessel?"

"Perhaps a little of both, Sir," replied the landlord, laughing; "for old
Will Stevens thinks as much of his boat as of his sons, and couldn't make
out why you, whom he instantly took to be a landsman, should prefer row-
ing yourself, when you might have one of his lads to row you. Will is a
sharp old chap, and rather given to be suspicious. He fancied that you were
come to this out-of-the-way place to hide from your creditors; and that all
your worldly goods were concealed in your large plaid, you seemed so careful of it, he said; or under your cloak, and so was uneasy: but when I told
him you had left plenty of luggage here, he was quite satisfied."

I said that, my health being poorly of late, my physician had ordered
me to move about as much along the sea-coast as possible, and to be on
the water, and row myself, which he thought would be good for my chest.
This explanation seemed perfectly satisfactory to my host, who, I dare say,
as long as his best rooms were occupied, his larder put in requisition, and
his wine ordered, cared very little for the motive which led his customers
to Portskewell.

A weight of anxiety seemed removed from my heart, since the remains
of the dead had been consigned to the deep. No longer did I put my hand to
my waistcoat pocket, to assure myself that the key of my writing-box was
safe; no longer did I dread the possibility of the trunk being opened in my
absence. Nevertheless, I could not divest myself of a feeling of horror, when
I reflected that my hand, which should have shielded the sacred remains of
my wife's sister—the lovely, the pure creature, whom my folly had doomed
to a premature death—had consigned them to a watery grave. I wondered
how I had found nerve to get through this painful ordeal; but the dread of
discovery, of exposure, of having the name of my daughter sullied by my

supposed guilt, had steeled my nerves, and enabled me to pass through this last painful trial, as it had through the heavy previous ones.

Though most desirous to leave Portskewell, I remained there two whole days, passing the greater portion of them on the water, and always alone. On one occasion I affected to let drop my plaid, before I stepped into the boat, taking care, as I did so, that the folds should open; and when Will Stevens took it up from the strand, I called out to him to take great care of it, as I would not lose it on any account, and requested he would fold it up, as before. On another, I purposely let my cloak fall from my shoulders, and noticed that the sharp old man narrowly watched my person, as if he expected to see something concealed on it.

I left this retired spot, where, having no occasion to make my name known, or no gossipping servant to reveal it, I was recognised only as the "gentleman;" which designation stood at the top of my bill. I proceeded to London, as rapidly as I could, for I impatiently longed to behold my daughter, and to press her once more to my breast. I felt as if I had been months absent from her; and my fond heart prompted the question whether *she* had felt this separation as deeply as I had? Yet my reason whispered that, at her age, with kind friends, a charming playfellow, and so many novel objects and scenes to attract her attention, it would be unreasonable to expect that I should be remembered with such engrossing tenderness by her, as she was by me. I found myself already forming excuses for any little disappointment she might inflict on me, by a less demonstrative mode of betraying her affection than I could have desired; and determined to be pleased—to be happy was, alas! out of the question.

I hurriedly exchanged my travelling dress for a more suitable one for such a visit, and hastened to Mrs. Neville's.—How quickly beat my heart, and how my hand trembled, as I knocked at the door! I was ushered into the library; and, in a few minutes after my daughter was in my arms! After pressing her again and again to my heart, I put her from me, that I might gaze on her.

Never had I seen so great an improvement as that effected during the short time she had passed with Mrs. Neville. The good taste of her kind protectress had effected this improvement in her dress, in the arrangement of her beautiful hair, and in her carriage; and the example of her charming playmate, had taught her a more feminine manner. I had thought her so perfect before, that I had been blind to the defects in her dress and deportment, until now, that I witnessed the vast revolution operated in both. She looked more like than ever to her angelic mother, and I was proud and grateful for the change.

The dear girl's caresses were so warm—so affectionate—that I, fastidious and jealous as I was disposed to be, at the least semblance of a diminution in her tenderness for me, felt perfectly satisfied, and expressed to her the dictates of my doting fondness.

Encouraged into confidence by my caresses, the artless child, clasping my neck with her arms, exclaimed,—

"Oh! dear papa, I am so happy with dear, good Mrs. Neville, and dear Matilda! Won't you let me stay with them always?"

What a sharp pang was that which shot through my heart, as my daughter uttered these words!

"Then you could do without *me*, Frances," said I, reproachfully.

"No, papa! I could not do without you for a long, long time; but while you went into Wales, or were travelling about to other places, and I had dear Mrs. Neville to love me dearly, as she does, and dear Matilda to play with me, and walk with me, when our lessons are over—I could do without you for a short time. It is so pleasant to have some one who is like a mamma, to buy one nice dresses, and to see that they are nicely made, and properly put on; and that one's hair is nicely arranged; and to have some one who is like a sister, to play with, and not to be always with a nurse, who isn't at all like a lady, and who can't answer any of the questions I ask her,—who is always saying, 'I'm sure, Miss, I don't know',—and, 'I wish you would not ask so many questions. Young ladies ought not to be asking questions.' Now, there has been so many things, papa, that I wanted to know, and that nurse could not tell me."

"Why did you not ask me, Frances?"

"Because sometimes when I asked, you did not seem to hear me, dear papa; and you looked so sad, that I thought my questions tired you, as they did nurse. But I ask dear Matilda every question that comes into my head, and a great, great many do come, and when I ask any that she does not know, she goes to her mamma, who tells me so plainly,—so nicely,—that I understand it, and never forget it after. And dear, good Mrs. Neville likes me to ask her questions. It never tires her a bit, papa. Oh! I am so happy here! I am always glad when I awake in the morning, for I say to myself, I shall have such a pleasant day with Matilda; and at night, when I am going to sleep, I think how nice it will be to have the next day, like the day before."

Although pleased at the knowledge of my dear child's perfect happiness, and most truly grateful to those kind friends who constituted it, so strong was the leaven of selfishness which pervaded my nature, that I could not vanquish the regret I experienced at discovering that she could be perfectly happy away from me. I, however, smoothed my brow, when a message came from Mrs. Neville, that she should be glad to see me in the drawing-room, was delivered to me; and tenderly embracing my daughter, I permitted her to rejoin her young companion, while I proceeded to the tea-table. Mrs. Neville's reception of me was kind, and cordial. Her own feelings had taught her to sympathize with mine, at reviewing the scene of my former happiness. My pale face was a proof to her of the chagrin I had endured since we parted, and she endeavoured to soften it by the commendations she bestowed on my child. When I attempted to express my sense of obligation for the wonderful improvement I discovered in her, she declared that Frances was so sweet-tempered and intelligent a child, that it was a positive pleasure to instruct her, and greatly tended to the advantage of her own daughter by the emulation it excited in their studies.

When I returned to my hotel, I found my servant in a state of considerable alarm.

"Would you believe it, Sir," said he, "soon after you left to go to Mrs. Neville's this evening, the two ruffians Bradstock and Motcombe came here, and asked to see you. They were so pressing, that the porter called me to satisfy them that you were not in the house, and they assumed such an insolent and bullying tone, that I am sure, by the looks and manner of the waiters who happened to be in the hall, as also by the porters' manner, that they took these vile fellows to be creditors, or in short, Sir, some persons who had a claim on you. They had evidently been drinking, and smelt of tobacco so strongly, that the porter and waiters were anxious to get them out of the hall.

"'Tell your master that it's no manner of use to deny himself to us,' said one of them.

"'Ay, and let him know, that our business is of such importance to him, that he'd better not trifle with us,' observed the other in a menacing tone.

"I assure you, Sir, I was quite ashamed and confounded by their impudence, and I know it has occasioned much talk among the waiters."

"Let me know when they call again," said I, assuming as unconcerned a tone as I could; "and mind, if I ring the bell while they are with me, you send for the police, to whom, if they attempt to be insolent, I will give them in charge."

This last part of my instructions seemed to give peculiar satisfaction to my servant. His countenance brightened up at once, and he said, "Ah, Sir, you will be doing a real service to society in exposing such scoundrels, and in delivering them up to the law!"

Although fully convinced that these men could really do nothing more than endeavour to extort money from me by menaces, which they were unable to enforce, I nevertheless could not close my eyes during that night.

All exposure of suspicious circumstances—and that there were such connected with my case I was fully aware—occasioned me such uneasiness,
that I writhed at the bare notion of publicity being given to them.

To yield to the threats of these wretches, in the hope of buying their
silence by gold, would, I knew by past experience, be unavailing; yet such
was my reluctance to have my name brought before the public, and subjected to the comments of the world, that though aware no proof of guilt
could be brought against me, and consequently that I must be acquitted of
any charge preferred, I would have made a very large pecuniary sacrifice
to prevent the affair in question being agitated. I knew, however, that if I
once yielded to menaces, I should ever more be subjected to a repetition
of them, and that the having yielded would establish a proof that I feared
those who had extorted money from me. My mind fully made up on this
point, I had again recourse to the syrup of hops given to me by my worthy
housekeeper, and by its aid procured, towards morning, two or three hours
of sleep; and having dressed, and drank a cup of strong coffee, I awaited in
no slight anxiety the threatened visit of Messrs. Bradstock and Motcombe.
They did not make their appearance until two o'clock, and both bore evidence of their having had recourse to brandy to strengthen their courage.

CHAPTER LXI.

PRIDE is sometimes of use! Mine had been so outraged by the attempt
made to intimidate me by the vile men who now stood in my presence,
that indignation lent me courage to assert my own honour, and repel their
insolence. I stood up as they entered the room, and looking sternly at them,
inquired their business with me.

"I think you must have some inkling of it," said Bradstock.

"Not the slightest," observed I.

"Come, come, Mr. Herbert, it's no use shamming ignorance," interposed Motcombe; "we are the friends of poor Figgins, whom you attempted
to murder at Malta, because you were afraid he'd let out your secret to us.
He has told us all, and you must now pay for our silence, as well as his, or
we will declare what we know before a magistrate, have you arrested, and
delivered up to justice."

It was evident that my calmness and sternness had somewhat daunted my
villanous assailants, for though they endeavoured to appear confident, and
free from fear, there was a trepidation in the manner of both that betrayed
their surprise, if not their alarm, at finding me so cool and collected.

"If you expect to intimidate and extort money from me, by some conspiracy hatched up between you," answered I, "you will find yourselves greatly mistaken. I shall not only firmly resist any such attempts, but punish, as far as the law will admit, those who undertake them."

"Well, we'll see who'll have the best of it," said Bradstock, "we know where the body of the lady you killed is now lying. Figgins went to Wales on purpose to have the proof, and removed the body, for fear that you would have it made away with. It's safe enough, I can tell you, and will prove against you yet."

"It's no wonder, after having killed a poor young creature, and your own sister-in-law into the bargain," remarked Motcombe, "that you should attempt to murder poor Figgins, in order that your secret should die with him. But he's alive; and although the split you made in his skull has touched his brain a little, he has his senses sometimes, and doesn't forget a single point in all he found out of your wickedness."

"No, not a point," rejoined Bradstock; "we've got him safe enough to be ready to bring him as a witness against you, in case you are so blind to your own interest as to compel us to proceed against you."

"What's a few hundred pounds, ay, or a few thousands even, in comparison with exposure, and the probability of being hanged?" demanded Motcombe. "We don't wish to be too hard on you, Mr. Herbert; indeed we don't. We would not like to make your daughter—a fine little girl she is, too—an orphan; but we must think of our own interests; and if chance has put a secret on which your character, and more, your life depends, in our keeping, we must be paid for it; we must not cheat the offended laws of our country, as the judge says when he is pronouncing sentence of death on some poor devil for a crime not one half as deep as yours, unless we can reconcile it to our consciences by receiving wherewithal to make us comfortable for the remainder of our lives."

It then occurred to me, that unless I could have some proof of the attempt of these men to extort money from me, I should not be able to prefer the charge against them; and, although very unwilling to temporize with such men, I was compelled to do so on the present occasion.

"Supposing I were disposed to avoid the publicity of a trial, which I am, however, perfectly convinced must terminate in my favour," said I, ashamed of my own enforced duplicity, in leading these vile fellows to imagine for a moment that I would yield to their attempts at imposition, "what may be the extent of your pretensions?"

They looked triumphantly at each other, concluding that they had succeeded in alarming me; and, after a short pause, Motcombe said that "fifteen hundred pounds, paid down, which could be five hundred for each of the three acquainted with my secret, could not be considered unreasonable."

"But what security should I have," demanded I, "that no further sum would ever be asked?"

They looked embarrassed; and then Bradstock offered to sign a paper, by which they should pledge themselves never more to claim anything at my hands.

"As I do not wish this interview to be prolonged," observed I; "suppose you consult together, elsewhere, the lowest terms you will accept for your silence, and send or bring me the written conditions. But I advise you to be moderate in your pretensions or I decidedly will not give anything like the sum you have named."

"Very well, Sir, we will furnish you with our terms in writing," replied Bradstock; "but I really don't think we can take much less than the fifteen hundred. Your character is worth more than that, set aside your life, Sir, which would be in great danger."

"Yes, certainly," added Motcombe; "Mr. Herbert's character and life are worth twenty times that paltry sum, more especially with such a nice young lady for a daughter. Oh, what a terrible thing it would be for her to have her father bring disgrace on her name, or perhaps to have him hanged!"

How my blood boiled, and how I longed to punish the scoundrels! But I checked my anger, and told them that the next day I would expect to receive their terms; and they removed towards the door to withdraw.

Before they left the room, however, they turned to me, and Motcombe said, "I mean no offence, Sir, but I think it as well to tell you that it will be quite useless for you to attempt to give us the slip, as you did Figgins, more than once."

"Yes," added Bradstock, "we'll be constantly on the watch, and are too sharp to be caught napping."

I disdained to reply to these insolent hints, and they withdrew, leaving me fully determined, when furnished with a written proof of their conspiracy to extort money from me, to deliver them over to justice.

My servant made some excuse for entering my room, soon after the departure of Motcombe and Bradstock. His countenance betrayed deep dissatisfaction and disappointment; and he ventured to say, "I expected every moment, Sir, that you would ring the bell, that I might call the police to take charge of the two rascals who have just gone. I saw them leave the house in high spirits, as if they were content with the result of their visit here; and it went to my heart to see the waiters and porters looking at them with surprise and suspicion as they marched off. They were remark-

ing, too, how long those shabby fellows had stayed with you, and what
business you could have with such men."

"My intention of employing the police with regard to them, is only
postponed, not abandoned," observed I. "It was absolutely necessary for
me to have positive proof of their conspiracy to extort money from me,
in order to proceed against them. That proof they will furnish to-morrow;
and when they come, I will, as soon as it is in my hands, ring the bell for you
to have the police summoned."

"And right glad I shall be to see the rascals taken up, and punished for
their scheming. Figgins let out to me, when he was tipsy, that they were the
greatest rogues he had ever met, and that his life would not be safe in their
hands, if they got him in their power. They wanted, he said, to get secrets
from him that he never would entrust them with. I assure you, Sir," added
Thomas, "that he was mortally afraid of them."

"Only imagine these men accusing me of attempting to murder Figgins,
and inflicting that wound on his head which you saw him receive when he
fell, and hit it against the table."

"Is it possible the villains dare make such a false charge against you,
Sir?" and he opened wide his eyes in astonishment and indignation.—"After
such a proof of their infamy as this, it can't be doubted, Sir, but that they
are capable of anything," replied Thomas.

It now occurred to me that it would be necessary for me to consult a
lawyer for the prosecution of Motcombe and Bradstock, and remembering
that Mr. Goldey, the executor of my poor friend Vise, was one, I determined to go and state the case to him. I found him at home, and when I
informed him that I wished his aid in a legal matter, he could not conceal
his satisfaction.

There are two classes of persons towards whom the wise declare a man
should never have any reserve when he consults them, namely, a physician
and a lawyer; and that however humiliating to one's *amour propre* may be
the revelations, not a single circumstance of the case, physical or moral,
should be omitted. I was compelled to remember this counsel several
times, while relating the facts connected with my case to Mr. Goldey, for I
felt aware that however favourably he might be disposed to judge from the
good opinion entertained by our mutual friend Vise of me, proved by his
liberal bequest, there were circumstances but too well calculated to convey suspicion against me in the disclosures I was making, and my natural
pride and reserve revolted from uttering them. I was, however, compelled
to begin at the beginning, in order to make him comprehend the whole
case. I narrated the idiosyncrasy which, from childhood to manhood, had

marked my character—the pride, the shyness which made me shrink from aught that could cast even a shade on my name.

"Yes, yes, I understand," observed he. "Our late friend, in speaking of you, often remarked that you were the proudest and shyest young man he ever knew."

I related the state of grief and excitement occasioned by arriving too late to receive the blessing of my mother, after travelling night and day without refreshment or sleep, in the hope of finding her still alive. I mentioned particularly the not having left the house from the moment of my arrival until that on which I attended the funeral of my mother, immediately after which I returned home so much exhausted by fatigue and sorrow, that I went to bed with symptoms of brain fever, and sank into a troubled slumber from which I was awoke several hours after by a loud knocking at the door, occasioned by the servant of a lady in the immediate neighbourhood, a friend of my deceased parent, but whom I had never seen, coming to inquire whether a daughter of the lady's had been to my house, for that she was missing, and could no where be found. I stated the effect produced on my already excited mind by this news, for that, although I had never seen the lady nor her daughters, I had discovered, through my mother's letters, that both were beautiful and amiable, and that she hoped one of them might become my wife, so I felt no common interest towards them. I narrated every circumstance connected with my accompanying their servant, ill as I was, in his search;—of the deep regret occasioned by its being unavailing;—of the notion entertained, and repeatedly expressed to me by the servant, that the young lady must have fallen over a steep precipice near her favourite walk, where the path was very narrow; and of the violent attack of brain fever which followed, keeping me many weeks confined to my bed, during the nights of which I continually dreamt that I saw the young girl fall over the precipice, nay, sometimes that I threw her over, and uttered the most incoherent ravings. I stated, that so great was the shock on my nerves, that for many months after, whenever assailed by illness, these dreams and ravings returned;—that up even to the present time, if attacked by fever, to which I was peculiar liable, I was harassed by the same dreams.

I related my marriage, the discovery of the corse of my wife's sister on the day of my wedding; its interment in my family vault; my subsequent bad state of health, and removal into Devonshire; my wife's delicate constitution; her being ordered to Nice; her death; my grief, and its consequences; return of brain fever; Figgins being engaged to sit up with me at night; my incoherent ravings leading him to imagine me guilty of a crime, and his taking advantage of his supposed discovery to extort money from me, when, with broken health and shattered nerves, I was rendered incapable of resisting his menaces.

"But surely," said the lawyer, who had been making notes of my communication, "you were not so—(he paused to find a less harsh word than that which arose to his lips)—so incautious as to betray your fear of his threats, by yielding to his extortion? Or if you did, I trust there was no witness to your giving him money, no proof that you had done so?"

I was so ashamed of my folly, my madness, that I was greatly tempted to conceal the fact of my having given him a cheque, and for a large amount too; but convinced that this proof might be produced against me hereafter, I acknowledged the truth.

"This, Mr. Herbert," said he, "is the only bad feature in the whole of your case; the only evidence that can be brought against you. How very unfortunate it is that you gave him a cheque! Gentlemen should know enough of law to keep out of such scrapes as furnishing evidence against themselves;" and he shook his head, and looked very grave. "A large sum, too, you say?"

I named the precise one. He shook his head again, and looked still more grave.

"This will have a very bad effect, a very bad effect indeed, before a jury, should the case come to that. In all countries, and more especially in England, where money is so highly appreciated, it is always taken for granted that a man does not part with any considerable portion of it without some cogent reason, Mr. Herbert. What pretext can we allege for your giving so large a sum to the man in question? He was not an old servant of yours; was not empowered by you to disburse money, pay bills, or keep cash in hand for you. There will, consequently, arise a foregone conclusion, that you must have been in some way or another in this man's power, and that the money was given to secure his silence. What has become of him? And how have the men who now conspire to extort money from you, become cognizant of the supposed secret, with the disclosure of which he first, and they now, menace you?"

I stated my belief, that they had taken advantage of his habits of intoxication to get him to reveal it, when he was no longer master of his reason.

"I perceive," said Mr. Goldey, "that yours is, indeed, a very nervous temperament, and this peculiarity has unhappily involved you in difficulties, from which it will be no easy task to deliver you; for you have, unfortunately, furnished the only dangerous evidence against yourself. But we must try our best to extricate you; and remember, above all things, that you do not allow your nervousness to influence you again in yielding a single point to those villains who have conspired against you. Have these fellows prosecuted as soon as you have the proof of their conspiracy to produce. *Your* taking the first step in this affair will be in your favour, but you must make up your mind, Mr. Herbert, whenever publicity is given to this business, to find that many persons will be disposed to judge you severely, solely from the fact of your having given Figgins so large a sum. The value of money is, as I before observed, so duly appreciated in England, that few will be inclined to believe you would part with it, unless from a positive necessity."

I requested Mr. Goldey to draw up a brief, and to lay it before the most eminent counsel, and then I returned to my hotel in a state of mind that might have excited the pity of my bitterest enemy.

CHAPTER LXII.

Soon after I entered my temporary home, a letter signed by Motcombe and Bradstock was brought me, with an intimation that they waited for an answer.—I rang for my servant, and gave him instructions to have these men traced to their lodgings; and having desired the waiter to inform them that they might call the next day for a reply to their letter, I enclosed the proof of their conspiracy, which fortunately was so explicit as to furnish the clearest evidence against them, to my lawyer; and requesting him to accompany me to a magistrate, from whom a warrant for their arrest could be obtained, I walked to Mrs. Neville's to see my daughter.

Again the artless child referred to her desire to remain always in her present home; but seeing by my countenance that the wish pained me, she added, "and I want you too, dear papa, to come and live here with dear Mrs. Neville."

Such was the moodiness of my feelings that I received this innocent proof of the undiminished tenderness of my poor little Frances as an indication of cunning which displeased me, and only replied to it by inquiring whether, as it was impossible for me to live in Mrs. Neville's house, *she* would prefer leaving it to go with me, or stay altogether with that lady? With the instinctive tact of her sex, the dear girl, instead of answering my question, put one to me, "But why," said she, "can't you come and live here, dear papa? There is such a nice room, where no one sleeps, that I am sure good Mrs. Neville would give you; and as she gives me leave to call her mamma, you would give Matilda permission to call you papa, would you not? and then we might all live together, and be so happy! Do let me ask Mrs. Neville to let you come and live with her, and be Matilda's papa, as she is now my mamma."

"No, Frances, you must never say a word more on this subject; but tell me at once whether, as I cannot live here with you, you prefer staying with Mrs. Neville and Matilda, or coming away with me?"

The dear child looked pained and embarrassed, but after a pause, replied, "If you, dear papa, will ask Mrs. Neville to let Matilda come and live with you and me, then I will prefer living with you."

I saw that the happiness of my child depended on her remaining where she was, and although the effort cost me a severe pang, I determined to sacrifice my own happiness to hers; and if Mrs. Neville were willing to take charge of her altogether, to resign her to her care, provided that I was permitted to defray all the expenses which such an arrangement must incur. I sought an interview with her, and before I could introduce the subject which led me to desire it, she opened it herself, by hoping that I had no intention of taking away Frances from her. She added, that she had conceived so warm an interest for the child, and her daughter was so much attached to her, that she desired nothing so much as to retain her. I had much difficulty in inducing her to consent to my defraying all the expenses which this increase to her family, as well as for masters in all the different branches of education and accomplishments, would occasion; and it was only when I declared that this was the sole condition on which I would leave my daughter with her, that she consented to have three hundred pounds annually placed at her banker's for my daughter's expenses. I wished to speak to her on the subject of the law-suit likely to take place, in order to prepare her to judge favourably of me before the trial. I thought that having taken charge of my daughter, it was only proper that she should be made acquainted with aught that might militate against my character, ere yet it was too late to free herself from the charge, in case she should wish to resign it. But my tongue refused to frame the words, my lips to pronounce them; so I determined to write her that a conspiracy had been formed against me, which compelled me to seek protection from the laws of my country: and assuring her of my perfect innocence of the crime of which I was accused, I added, that I could not allow her, who offered a home to my child, to remain in ignorance of any charge that might, though but for a short time, impeach my character.

On returning to my hotel I wrote this letter, and my lawyer having arrived, I entered a carriage with him, and was driven to a magistrate, to whom he was well known, and where, having sworn information against Motcombe and Bradstock for a conspiracy, a warrant was issued against them.

I had now passed the Rubicon—there was no longer any power of retreating.

"Oh, had I but taken this step," thought I, "when first the vile Figgins began his system of extortion, how many hours of torture might I have been spared, and how free should I now stand from the suspicions to which my weak, my mad compliance with his threats, must inevitably subject me!"

I received that evening an admirable letter from Mrs. Neville, stating her implicit belief in my freedom from guilt, whatever might be the accusation brought against me; but adding, that were it possible she could suspect the friend of her lost husband, or that even the appearance of criminality might involve him in ruin, she could never forget that she had pledged herself at the death-bed of the mother of my child, to prove a parent and a protectress to her, should it ever be required, and that never should she prove faithless to that solemn promise.

This generous, this noble-minded woman's letter brought tears to my eyes, while it removed a weight of care and anxiety from my breast. Let the ordeal, through which I was to pass, terminate how it might, my child would escape the evil consequences it would entail on her unfortunate father. Safe beneath the roof of one of the most faultless and respectable of women, where nought but good example and virtuous precepts could reach her, she would grow up to be an ornament to her sex, and conciliate the regard of the estimable circle of friends who surrounded her admirable protectress; while should I selfishly retain her with me, she would be exposed to the solitude and friendless position into which my destiny had plunged me, and might suffer from the suspicions to which my folly, my madness, must subject my character.

The following day, Motcombe and Bradstock were brought up before the magistrate and committed for trial. Irritated to the utmost degree against me, they loudly proclaimed my guilt of the charge, to conceal which, they had in pity, as they alleged, consented to receive certain remunerations. They maintained that they could furnish indubitable proofs of my having committed murder, and displayed such undaunted assurance, that Mr. Goldey was greatly alarmed at the turn things were likely to take, as also at seeing that the charge had already produced a strong impression against me in the minds of all those who had been present at the examination.

"This will be a very serious inconvenience, if no worse," whispered he; "the charge they have made is not bailable, and it will be very annoying to you to submit to confinement, until the trial comes on."

"How! confinement did you say?" exclaimed I. "Surely the unsupported evidence of two such scoundrels cannot subject me to such treatment?"

"I fear it will, though," observed he, "for the law is very strict relative to such charges."

To be sent to a prison!! There was degradation, wretchedness, and madness, in the thought! And yet this had I brought down on my own head; the consciousness of which fact only served to increase my misery. My total ignorance of the law had led me into the fearful position in which I now found myself placed; and bitterly did I execrate the folly that had wrought the evil. Why had I not previously to indicting Motcombe and Bradstock, inquired the possibility of a result like the present to myself from such a measure?

These reflections were now, alas! too late, and nought was left me but to conceal as well as I could the agony of my mind, and await the evil I had brought on myself.

The magistrate now received the charge of my accusers. They were sworn, and I was committed to prison,—there to remain until my innocence should be proved; while they were condemned to the same doom.

Mr. Goldey's countenance had assumed a very grave and anxious expression; and although he attempted to offer some common-place consolations to me, it was evident that he was far from thinking as lightly of what had occurred as he wished me to believe. The magistrate and he spoke some time together in a low voice; and I heard the words, "The bill may be ignored, and then your client will recover his liberty," uttered by the former. "At all events, the trial will very soon come on," returned the magistrate.

"A gentleman of family and fortune," said Mr. Goldey; "highly esteemed and respected, and only accused by two fellows of infamous character."

"So much the better for your client," replied the magistrate. "I am very sorry that he will be put to a temporary inconvenience; but it can't be helped, Mr. Goldey; and of course you can arrange that he should suffer as little discomfort as possible. There are good rooms in the prison, and these Mr. Herbert's position and means will enable him to have."

Mr. Goldey accompanied me in the carriage called to convey me to my new hateful abode, as well as two of the police; and, drawing my hat over my eyes, I sank back to avoid being seen by the passers.

To describe my feelings would be impossible. Weak and helpless as a child, my terror almost deprived me of reason; and when I entered the massive walls of the prison, and heard the heavy gates closed after me, I was ready to abandon myself to despair. Mr. Goldey arranged with the jailer, for all the amelioration which money could produce in such a dwelling, and remained with me until the hour when visitors are dismissed. What would I not have given to have had him remain with me! But it was impossible; so I saw him depart with a moodiness that alarmed me for my own sanity, now when I most required all my reason.

Soon after he had departed, the turnkey inquired whether I would not have some supper. "You can have what you like, Sir," said he, "and wine fit for any gentleman. We know how to treat gentlemen here."

"Yes, let me have some wine and water," replied I.

"Take my advice, Sir; drink the wine plain—'twill do you more good; for when a gentleman hasn't been used to such places as this, his spirits are apt to sink just at first; and wine does him good."

I drank a few glasses of the wine, which cheered me a little, and soon after fell into a deep but troubled sleep, from which I was awakened at an early hour by the noise occasioned by the opening of the doors, and the clanking of the chains, keys, and bars. For a few minutes I could not recall my senses sufficiently to remember where I was; but when I looked around and beheld the iron barred windows and style of the chamber, too soon did I become conscious of the place, and of all the painful events of the previous day.

I had never formed an idea of the interior of a prison; and even the modified form in which I now beheld it, struck me with dread and disgust. The mixture of unclean finery and sordid squalidness in the furniture, was offensive to the eye; and the odour of the ill-ventilated chamber, into which the fresh air was seldom allowed to penetrate, was no less so to my nasal organs.

I groaned in spirit when I reflected that in this odious room I might be compelled to remain some time; nor did my spirits improve when the turnkey brought me the morning newspapers, giving, in the police reports, the particulars of the examination and committals of the previous day, headed by a charge of murder against Marmaduke Herbert, Esq., a gentleman of considerable fortune, by two men named Motcombe and Bradstock, against whom Mr. Herbert had sworn information for a conspiracy to extort money from him.

This publicity, although anticipated, tortured me. I fancied that henceforth, wherever I might go, every eye would be turned on me, that already I was prejudged and found guilty in public opinion. I dreaded even to meet the glance of the turnkey, and would have desired not to see even my own servant, whose services, however, I could not dispense with. Had I been actually the guilty wretch which Motcombe and Bradstock accused me of being, I could not have shrunk more from observation than I now did, although morally certain that the result of a trial must exculpate me from guilt, even if it could not exonerate me from the suspicious appearances to which my own madness could alone have given rise. How I loathed my past cowardice, and yet my present pusillanimity was scarcely less reprehensible!—The changed aspect of my servant when he presented himself in my prison, although it proved the deep interest he felt in my situation, testified also the alarm it excited in his mind. I could perceive that my present abode seemed to furnish him with a solution to the mysterious circumstances connected with Figgins's visits to Naples, Sorento, Palermo, and Malta, and finally to my admitting such a man beneath my roof. In short, I saw, or imagined I saw, that my own servant had prejudged me; and although his assiduity to serve me had increased rather than diminished, I was more disposed to feel humiliated by, than grateful for it, so prone is a proud mind to reject even kindness, if accompanied by aught that can irritate. I felt inclined to remain in bed, rather than go through the fatigue of dressing, which would bring me into more immediate personal contact with my servant, for while appearing to be occupied with the newspapers, though, heaven knows, I hardly knew what they contained save what related to me, I had no necessity to address him; but I mastered this inclination, and, making an effort, rose to be ready to receive Mr. Goldey's promised visit.

CHAPTER LXIII.

I counted the hours, but still Mr. Goldey came not. What could occasion his protracted absence? A thousand vague fears connected with it tortured my mind, the most prominent of which was, that he believed me guilty, and would see me no more! My reason in vain combatted this dread, a dread that gained ground every minute that marked the progress of time by my watch, which I kept continually looking at. I tried to find consolation in the consciousness of my innocence of the crime with which I was charged, and in the reflection, that of dishonour and guilt alone should a man be ashamed; but alas! I had not now to learn, that reason is often unable to vanquish the terror of imagination; and that, to a proud and sensitive mind, the dread of the exposure of its weakness is almost as appalling as if crime, and not folly, were to be revealed.

At length Mr. Goldey arrived; for hours had I expected him. Oh, how long and tedious had they appeared, before he made his appearance! Little had I ever imagined that his presence could give me such satisfaction as I now experienced at beholding him.

He looked fatigued and anxious, and I suppose my countenance had revealed to him how much inquietude the delay in his coming had occasioned me, for he said, "I couldn't come sooner, I assure you I couldn't, although I tried all in my power. But I had so many places to go to, so many persons to see, that every moment since I arose this morning at an early hour has been filled up. I trust, however, that my time has not been thrown away. Fortunately for you, the bill of indictment preferred by those scoundrels against you will be brought before the proper authorities to-morrow, and I indulge sanguine hopes that it will be ignored, in which case you will immediately be restored to your liberty, which will be a great point gained, for I was fearful there might be a delay of several days here."

I could have embraced him as he uttered these words, and yet I believed them to be too good to be true.

Mr. Goldey lost not an opportunity like the present to launch out into all the technicalities of his profession, the greater number of which were, in truth, utterly incomprehensible to me. But no longer did I feel disposed to find fault with them, nor with the more than ordinary degree of self-complacency with which he pronounced them. I felt that he was now invested with very different character in my eyes, to that which I had regarded him in our first interview. *Then*, he only appeared ridiculous; *now*, he was the sole person on whom I could count to extricate me out of the difficulties in which I had so unhappily placed myself. I listened with breathless interest to his legal phraseology and was sorry to see him take his departure, although, as he assured me, it was for the purpose of attending to my case.

When left alone, my gloomy thoughts, banished during his presence, returned with increased force; and, when I sought my couch, I only slumbered a short time, when I started from it in terror, believing myself to be in a Court of Justice, invested with much more awful solemnity than any such court ever was. I seemed to behold the malicious faces of the opposing counsel; the alarmed ones of my own. The cool assurance of the witnesses against me,—the embarrassed manner of those on my side,—the contemptuous looks of the crowded audience—and the stern glance of the judge. My brain seemed seared by fire and cold drops, wrung by agony, fell fast from my brow. Mrs. Neville and my daughter seemed to be present, and gazed on me with sorrow, mingled with horror—until my child, the burning blush of shame glowing on her lovely face, and indignation flashing from her eyes, tried to hide her countenance with her handkerchief, and uttering a piercing shriek, fell, lifeless, to the earth.

Such were my dreams,—and sleep became no longer "tired nature's sweet restorer," but a fearful dream which tortured and thrilled me with terror. When awaking from such troublous dreams, and looking at my prison, I wondered how I ever had the courage to draw such misery on myself, by instituting legal proceedings against Motcombe and Bradstock, when, by the sacrifice of fifteen hundred pounds, I might have purchased their silence, if not for ever, at least for some time; and in that time death might snatch me from their power, or rid the earth of them. Was not the unusual courage on my part, which urged me to resistance, an outbreak of folly—of madness? And I dwelt on the question until, as on many previous occasions, I strongly doubted my own sanity.

Mr. Goldey sent me the brief he had drawn up to be given to counsel; and as I perused it, I was compelled to acknowledge that, notwithstanding the innumerable instances of tautology and technicalities, which rendered it tedious, and obscured its sense, he had omitted nothing of all that I had stated to him. The following day Mr. Goldey came to me early.

"I still hope," said he, "that the bill of indictment against you will be ignored this day, and that you will be restored to liberty. I cannot think, that on hearsay evidence, which, after all, is the only evidence those rascals can bring forward, a true bill will be found. We can, if it be thrown out, as I expect, proceed against the parties for false imprisonment and perjury; nevertheless, it will be necessary to summon friends to give their testimony to your character on the trial; and the more highly respectable and well-known they may be, the better. Think over those with whom you have most lived in England, and make a list, as well as of the individuals on the Continent with whom you have been on habits of intimacy."

He looked surprised and pained, too, when I related to him, how extremely circumscribed was the circle of my acquaintance in my native land, and explained the cause of its being so limited. To do this, I was compelled to enter into a brief story of my school and college life,—my unpopularity and wounded feelings, during both,—reminiscences fraught with pain and humiliation to me; and these feelings were increased, as I marked how little he seemed to comprehend or enter into them.

"It would require a philosophical casuist, well versed in the study of men's minds, to fully understand the peculiarity of yours, Mr. Herbert," said he; "while I am only a lawyer—a mere practical man of business, knowing more of law than of human nature, and only able to judge of the minds and feeling of others, by comparing them with my own. I know that at school, the first boy with whose conduct towards me I was offended, I would have had a pugilistic combat with; and at college, I should have resented any symptom of coldness, or avoidance towards me, by instantly and indignantly demanding satisfaction."

I could perceive that Mr. Goldey more than suspected me of want of proper spirit; and this suspicion having wounded me, endeavoured to explain to him, that an excess of pride may sometimes lead to a conduct which may bear the appearance to a want of it.

"Possibly!" replied he; "but as I am no casuist, I do not comprehend these distinctions. According to my notions, the greater the degree of pride, the more unbearable would be the least approach to insult, and the more prompt the attempt to repel and chastise it."

I felt I must remain a coward in Mr. Goldey's eyes, as it would be utterly useless to endeavour to make him comprehend my character; yet I made one more effort to justify my courage, by telling him of the duel I fought at college.

But even this fact did not seem to elevate me much in his estimation, for he merely observed—"that he believed all men might be brought to fight if their anger were once excited to a certain point."

The renewal of my friendship with Neville, whose character he happened to know stood very high in the opinion of those with whom he was acquainted, he considered a strong point in my favour. The esteem also of the two individuals to whom I was best known, testified by their bequests to me, might be of use, and the respect of the only persons in my thinly inhabited neighbourhood, the clergyman and doctor, who could be called to speak of my character, would have weight, as also of the only foreigners with whom I had lived in intimacy in Italy;—all these, men of high reputation, and whom it would be needful to summon to England.

"Men, or rather boys, know not," said Mr. Goldey, "how great is the importance of their making friends at school, and at college. It gives the colour to their future lives, for he who has no friends at these places, will seldom make any elsewhere, and no one can say how requisite they may be at some period or other of his existence."

The truth of this assertion could not be doubted, and my life offered an illustration of its wisdom; but who in early youth is governed by prudence, or forethought, or can conquer his natural character, if reserve and pride happen to constitute its most prominent features?

The ensuing day the bill of indictment against me was ignored, and I was liberated after three days passed in prison, my sole redress being to bring an action for false imprisonment and perjury against men, already sunk too low to suffer from any additional charge.

I returned to the hotel, where I had taken up my abode previously to my arrest, but was met by such cold looks, and scrutinizing glances, as intimated that my return there was as little desired as anticipated.

"Your apartments, Sir," said the waiter, "are now occupied by another gentleman, who has engaged them for some months. We really did not expect that you could resume them, after having seen in the papers—"

I cut short his speech, by asking whether there were no other rooms empty which I could take by the week or month?

"I will go and inquire of Mr. Moffat," replied he, and he left me in the hall to be stared at by several other waiters and servants, who came there as soon as they heard of my arrival. The man speedily returned, and said that there was not a single room empty in the house, although I had during his brief absence overheard another waiter inform a gentleman who came to engage apartments, that they had several.

Mortified and humiliated beyond measure, I was about to leave the house, when I was informed that Mr. Goldey, although he had paid my account which had been furnished to him, had omitted to settle for the room in which my luggage had been put; and, "How much is the sum?" demanded I, greatly annoyed at being detained in the hall to be gazed on by the vulgar herd assembled there.

"Only a guinea a day, Sir," was the cool reply, and I paid it, as I would readily have done thrice the amount, to get out of the house.

My servant went up to the room, to have my luggage removed, while I proceeded to Mr. Goldey's, leaving instructions with him to follow me there. My brain seemed to burn, and a sense of shame and degradation, bowed me down. I fancied that every eye was upon me, that every one recognised the lately liberated prisoner charged with murder. When I related the conduct of the hotel-keeper, Mr. Goldey said,

"I, by all means, advise you to let me proceed against this fellow. He has no right to refuse accommodation to any gentleman who conducts himself properly in his house."

And then followed a string of legal technicalities, to which, Heaven knows, I was ill disposed to listen at that moment.

"The question now is to procure me a lodging in some other hotel," observed I, impatiently.

"True, true," answered Mr. Goldey; "I know one, where you will find yourself very comfortable; although it is not what is termed a fashionable hotel."

He instantly sent one of his clerks to engage rooms for me, who soon returned to announce that all would be ready for my reception in a few minutes. Meanwhile, a hackney-coach, laden with my luggage, was driven up to Mr. Goldey's door, and my servant stepped from it, with a face crimsoned with anger.

"Would you believe it, Sir," said he, "those rascally fellows had put all your things into a damp loft, although they had the impudence to charge you a guinea a day for a room, in which they pretended they kept them. But I have given one of them a lesson he will remember for some time; for when he told me they never took in criminals, nor jail-birds, into their hotel, but only the first quality in the land, I just gave him a box in the face that loosened some of his teeth, I'll be sworn."

"There you were wrong, very wrong," observed Mr. Goldey; "never take the law into your own hands. We might have brought an action for defamation against this fellow, and got damages."

"What, Sir, would you have me stand by, and hear my master insulted?"

"Certainly, for the law would have given your master redress."

My servant did not seem to relish this opinion, for he shook his head, as much as to say, that he preferred a summary act of justice, to waiting for a protracted legal one.

I drove to the hotel, where, having taken some refreshment of which I stood greatly in need, I proceeded to Mrs. Neville's, to see my daughter, and return thanks to that excellent woman for her kindness. I discovered from my child, that my absence had been accounted for by her protectress informing her that I had been suddenly summoned from town on business of importance, and that the precise time of my return was uncertain.

My unexpected visit filled my daughter with joy. She embraced and clung to me for several minutes, and I, melted by her fondness, could scarcely retain my tears. I had a short interview with Mrs. Neville, who had seen in the newspapers the statement of my arrest, and, to prevent its being talked of in her establishment, had destroyed the papers, so I was not pained by inquisitive looks from her servants, which I felt to be a relief.

Nothing could be kinder than the manner of Mrs. Neville. She hinted, but with the utmost delicacy, that it would be now incumbent on me to vanquish the natural reserve and shyness which had hitherto prevented my forming acquaintances, or friendships. That for my daughter's sake, I ought not to live isolated, and added, that surrounded as she herself was by the friends of her dear husband, an opportunity would be afforded me of cultivating intimacies with persons who, knowing me to have been his friend, would feel disposed to give me a kind reception. I felt the wisdom and friendship of this advice; but the publicity of the charge brought against me had so much increased my nervousness and timidity, that however convinced of the necessity of the exertion to conquer these peculiarities, I did not feel equal to it.

Mr. Goldey deemed it necessary that intelligence should be obtained of Figgins, so I wrote to the medical man, at Malta, to whose care I had confided him, to inform me of his actual state, and whether he was still there.

In due time, I received an answer, stating, that Figgins was in prison at Malta, where he had been lodged, as an accomplice in a robbery committed by two Englishmen, who had absconded, and for whose apprehension a reward had been offered. The abuse of strong liquors, acting on the fevered blood of this man, had rendered the wound in his head of a more serious character than had first been anticipated. His intellects were occasionally impaired, and his wretched female companion had met with great ill-usage at his hands. A subscription had been raised for her at Malta, and she had embarked for England a short time previous to the date of the letter I now received.

Mr. Goldey thought it advisable to have Figgins transferred from the prison at Malta, to one in London, in case his presence or evidence might be required; and the necessary steps being taken to effect this transfer, the order was sent out. I ventured not to give any opinion in my own case, for I saw that Mr. Goldey was disposed to suspicion whenever I interfered; so, though I did not in the slightest degree oppose Figgins's being sent to England, I entertained a secret dread that his presence would greatly tend to create prejudice against me. If, when beneath my roof, his appearance was disreputable and disgusting, how much more so must it have become, by his increased habits of inebriety, and the reckless squalor that generally is induced by a long sojourn in prison! But the die was cast; I had placed myself in the hands of my legal adviser, and must abide the consequences.

CHAPTER LXIV.

In a few days after the receipt of the letter from Malta, the unfortunate woman who had been the nurse-maid of my daughter, came to implore my pardon, and to entreat my charity. She had discovered my abode through having met my servant by chance in the street, and traced him to it. The misery and destitution to which the unfortunate woman had been reduced by Figgins, who had not only plundered her of her wages, but robbed her of all her clothes, disarmed my anger. She told me that while Figgins was still under the doctor's care, his two infamous companions, one of whom had been absent from Malta for some time, and had only a day or two returned, came to the lodging, to which the doctor had had him removed, commanding the strictest abstinence to be observed,—these men constantly plied him with brandy, in defiance of the doctor's injunctions and her representations, until he became delirious. She was sure they wanted to cause his death. They questioned her closely about me, and when Figgins was out of his mind, they cross-examined him about some secret concerning me, which they said he possessed, and for concealing which, I had given him large sums of money. Figgins raved about my having murdered my wife's sister by throwing her over a precipice, and of his having gone to Wales and discovered the body.

They noted down every word he uttered, and when they got out all he knew, or imagined, for he was seldom an hour in his sober senses, they used to pour spirits down his throat, in spite of all she could say to prevent it. "It was from his ravings that I, for the first time, discovered that he had made a fool and a dupe of me, Sir," said the wretched woman, "and that instead of being in love with me, as he swore over and over again, he only pretended it, in order to know all about you, Sir, and about your movements. At Nice, he was always asking me questions about your place in Wales. Whether there were high rocks near it, and whether any lady had ever been killed there? I thought it was no harm to tell him that the only lady ever supposed to fall over the cliff was Miss Maitland, the sister of my poor mistress. He then said he'd go to Wales to satisfy himself that I bore a good character in my native place, before he'd make up his mind to marry me; and as I knew he could not hear anything against me, I was quite pleased that he should go, for I thought when he came back we should be married.

"When he returned to Nice, he said he must put off our wedding until he got some money, which he expected very soon, and which would enable us to set up in business; and he made me promise that wherever you went, Sir, I should immediately write and tell him, in order that he might know where to come to marry me, the minute he got the money he expected. So I wrote to him from every place you went to, Sir, and he behaved very well to me until he took up with his wicked companions, Motcombe and Bradstock; and then he took to drinking, and became quite another man. Still, as he always swore he'd marry me, I like a fool wouldn't leave Malta when I thought him so ill. His companions took every shilling he had, and then he asked me for my wages, telling me he'd soon have plenty of money. And when my wages were gone, he made me sell my clothes, and Motcombe and Bradstock got the price of them from him, for he was afraid of them, and dared not refuse them anything. I was then left penny-less, and with only the clothes I wore; and he used to curse and strike me, Sir, because I had no more money to give him; and his bad companions wanted to insult me, and abused and even beat me, because I wouldn't listen to their infamous proposals. They used to go out at night and rob, and bring the stolen property to Figgins's lodgings.

"I had remained in the house you had, Sir, the owner having allowed me to stay there, and keep it clean until it was let. These bad men often wanted to come into it, but I would not let them, and never saw them except twice a day, when I used to go and see how Figgins was going on. One night an attempt was made to break into the house, but I heard the noise, and gave such an alarm, by screaming out of an upper window that the robbers had to run away; and I could take my oath that they were Motcombe and Bradstock, for it was a moonlight night, and I saw them almost as plain as if it were day.

"They broke into another house that night, and brought the plunder to Figgins's lodgings; and, would you believe it, Sir! they wrote a letter to the police, saying where a part of the property could be found, for the hand-writing was discovered to be Bradstock's; and they escaped from Malta, leaving Figgins to suffer for their crime. He was taken up and thrown into prison, and the Doctor, out of pity, made a subscription to take me back to England. I never thought, Sir, there could be such wickedness in the world. I have lost my character by my folly, and have become a miserable, broken-hearted creature, with no one to blame but myself."

I wrote a note to my lawyer by this unfortunate woman, authorizing him to give her pecuniary assistance, and place her in a lodging, to be ready in case her evidence should be required. I was afraid to give her money myself, lest it should be deemed that I was tampering with a witness; but though inclined to save this unhappy woman from further degradation and misery, I laid a stern prohibition on her ever going to see my daughter, in case she might discover her abode.

"I forgot to tell you, Sir," said the nurse, "that the last robbery commit-ted by Motcombe and Bradstock was on an officer at Malta, who, being on the point of coming to England with all his effects packed up, had removed from the barracks to the inn nearest the point where persons embark, and was having a take-leave dinner with his brother officers, when these thieves entered his room by the window, and having stolen all he possessed, sailed for England by the very packet that he was to have come in. One of the robbers dropped a silk pocket-handkerchief in the room, by which, it being marked with his name, he was known to be the thief. The officer came over in the same packet with me, Sir, and I heard he was determined to offer reward for their apprehension, and to prosecute the thieves."

"What is the officer's name?" inquired I.

"Major M'Culloch," replied the nurse.

It flashed across my mind that I had heard the name before, and, after a few minutes' reflection, I recollected that it was of this very individual my old acquaintance, Mrs. Scuddamore, had spoken when I met her at Portsmouth, on my arrival in England, to which place she had gone to meet her expected friend. Nothing, I felt, could be more favourable to my case than to have the real characters of Motcombe and Bradstock proved. The establishment of the fact of their robberies would inevitably cast a strong doubt on their evidence, and render their charges more than suspicious.

I saw Mr. Goldey the following day, and he, too, thought the arrival of Major M'Culloch a very fortunate circumstance. It occurred to me that it might be possible for me to leave the Major to prosecute these men for robbery, and proceed no further myself.

"The more I reflect on this business," observed he, "the more do I feel convinced that, for your own sake, you should institute the strictest inquiry, to bring every circumstance to light concerned in this disagreeable and painful affair: otherwise, the charge made at the police-office by these scoundrels, and your being committed to prison on it, will give rise to a thousand rumours and suspicions, which can only be put an end to by a public investigation."

Again did my moral pusillanimity prompt me to avoid the measure advised by Mr. Goldey; but he got so angry when I uttered a few words indicative of this desire, that I no longer betrayed my feelings, but merely observed that I had imagined the indisputable proofs of the guilt of those who impeached my character, as also the ignoring of the bill against me, would prevent the necessity of a trial.

"So it might," replied my lawyer, "if the world were prone to judge all who are accused, fairly, instead of harshly. But as, unhappily, in society men are more ready to listen to attacks against their fellow-men, however unworthy of credence those may be who make them, than to doubt the alleged guilt, because the accusers are vile, it becomes the positive duty of those assailed to justify themselves from the least stain attempted to be cast on their characters."

There was a sternness in the nature of Mr. Goldey that precluded the entire and perfect confidence which a client should repose in his lawyer. I had originally fully determined to conceal nothing from him, except my knowledge of the death of my wife's sister, and the mad conduct on my part that followed it, and led to all my subsequent troubles. That part of my history I felt sure he would doubt, for he was such a matter-of-fact man, and possessed so much plain common sense and self-control, that he could not be made to comprehend that any person not positively mad could draw on himself the suspicion of a fearful crime, by concealing the body. I felt that his eyes would be ever on me, if I revealed all these circumstances,—that he would believe me to be a murderer—or a—maniac.

The astonishment he had betrayed, and the reproaches he had uttered, when I confessed my having given Figgins a cheque on my banker for the large sum he had extorted from me at Nice, had prevented my revealing other facts to him, with which I was aware he ought to be made acquainted:—as, for instance, the embarrassment into which his boastings at Palermo had got me there, and my having allowed a man of whose infamy I could not entertain the slightest doubt, to become an inmate of my house at Malta. I felt my heart beat quicker with wounded pride and shame at the thought that these facts, so calculated to injure me in public opinion, would, nay must, come before the world in any investigation that might take place. I anticipated the anger and disgust Mr. Goldey must experience when he, too late, should discover my disingenuousness and folly in withholding from him what it was of such importance that he should know. Yet with this conviction, I could not bring myself to tell him the whole truth, and like an idiot—a madman—I preferred leaving him to learn the facts that would redound so much to my disadvantage, from evidence in a court of justice which he had no means to refute, or even to palliate the evil effect of. To a man of a less rugged and stern nature, more skilled to comprehend the weakness of his fellow beings, and to sympathize with them, I could have revealed the whole truth, and prepared him to make light before a court of justice of circumstances really important in the case. But to let him remain in total ignorance of them I knew was madness, and yet I allowed this to be, rather than meet his suspicious or contemptuous glance, such was the weakness, the pusillanimity of my nature! Often did I put the question to myself, whether I, who was, Heaven knows, little disposed to incredulity, would believe the history of my own troubled life, if related to me by another? and I groaned in spirit as my reason told me that I could not; and that the utmost extent of my charity could not go the length of absolving the individual who revealed it, from strong suspicion of crime, if not from absolute condemnation.

As the healthy and vigorous can seldom sympathize in the sufferings of the sick, nay, are disposed to disbelieve in their amount, so are those blessed with firm nerves and cold temperaments, prone to judge harshly the moral maladies which they never experienced, and to attribute the results to guilt never for a single moment contemplated, however the appearance of it may exist. A lawyer should be like a judicious and skilful physician. He should encourage the confidence of his client, as the doctor does that of his patient, until every symptom of the case is revealed, that a palliative, if not a remedy, may be applied.

CHAPTER LXV.

THE following day Mr. Goldey learned, at the office where Motcombe and Bradstock had been examined and committed to prison, that a Major M'Culloch had been there to lodge information against them, for a robbery committed on him at Malta, and as my servant had them traced to their lodgings two days before their arrest, he was enabled to furnish the address, and a warrant of search was issued to a constable.

At the lodgings, nearly the whole of the Major's property was found, a small portion of it only having been disposed of. Other property had also been discovered, which proved that these men had been active in their depredations, and amongst the rest of the spoil, was a gold watch, chain, and seals, a showy shirt-pin, snuff-box, and some clothes, which my servant recognized having belonged to Figgins.

While all this additional evidence of the culpability of Motcombe and Bradstock was furnished, these knaves had not been idle in prison. An attorney of a low grade was induced, by the hope of reward which they held out, to enlist in their cause against me; and he drew up under their instructions a brief, every charge in which they swore that they could substantiate. I was accused of having murdered the sister of my wife, whose body I had concealed in a cavern, near to which the crime had been committed. I was further charged with having given large sums of money to a person of the name of Figgins, who had discovered my crime, and whom had I afterwards attempted to murder, lest he should betray my secret. The said Figgins, they asserted, had been greatly distressed for money a short time, yet was, soon after, living extravagantly, and in the possession of a gold watch, a snuff-box, and other expensive trinkets, as well as of clothes fit for a gentleman. That they knew that I had tried to conceal my abode from the said Figgins, and had gone secretly from place to place for that purpose; but that he had, through the means of a female servant in my establishment, been always kept aware of where to find me. That they knew the said Figgins to have expended hundreds in a short time. That when he was without money at Naples, he had followed me to Palermo, and had, in a few days after, returned, well stocked with cash. That, having a strong suspicion that he was paid for keeping some important secret, probably a crime, of which he often gave hints when intoxicated, they had formed a plan to detect it, and for this purpose, one of them had gone to Palermo, where he learnt that a person answering in every respect to the description of Figgins had been there, and had been seen to meet Mr. Herbert in private. That Mr. Herbert had gone in person to his banker's, and had drawn for two hundred pounds, which, when the banker offered to send to his house by a clerk, Mr. Herbert declined, and took charge of himself, the whole amount being, by his desire, paid in gold. That the following evening Figgins, being intoxicated, had attempted to intrude himself into a reading-room, open only to subscribers, and on being excluded, boasted as a proof of his respectability, that he was the possessor of, and could produce two hundred pounds, being precisely the amount which Mr. Herbert had drawn from his banker. That Figgins said he could have as much more whenever he liked, and that Mr. Herbert, a gentleman of great fortune and family, was his friend, would answer for him, and that he could make Mr. Herbert do whatever he pleased. That the boasting and insinuations of Figgins, coupled with his intoxication and low manners, had excited strong suspicions in the minds of the banker, and other gentlemen at Palermo, who were cognizant of these circumstances, that Figgins had some extraordinary power over Mr. Herbert. That he had avowed that he could make that gentleman tremble at his nod, as he held his fate in his hands. That some of the English merchants resident at Palermo, desirous to institute an inquiry into this mysterious transaction, had search made for Figgins, who they had found had sailed for Naples the following day, whither these gentlemen had immediately written to have inquiry made about him, in order that the connexion between him and Mr. Herbert should be sifted, and if his influence over the latter originated in crime, it should be, for the sake of justice, laid open.

The bankers at Nice and at Palermo were summoned to come to England to give evidence of the payment of the money made by them, or to furnish, through the English Consul at both places, attested proofs of these facts.

The merchants at Palermo, who had taken the strongest part against me, were written to, to send statements of the cause of their suspicions. My servant was served with notice to attend the trial, and the nurse, whose arrival in England was discovered, received a similar one.

Disappointed in their scheme of extorting money from me, and maddened by my having handed them over to the law, Motcombe and Bradstock, urged on by a spirit of vengeance, had stopped at no falsehood, no perjury, to injure me.

My lawyer was in high spirits at the proofs furnished by Major

M'Culloch, of the robbery committed by these vile men at Malta. Keen in the pursuit of criminals as a sportsman after game, he exulted in the anticipated certainty of their punishment.

"The counsel I have employed," said he, "are of opinion that the known infamy of your accusers, as well as their accusation having only been made after you had commenced a prosecution against them for a conspiracy to extort money from you, and, above all, the bill of indictment against you being ignored, renders your going into a formal defence almost a work of supererogation."

"And I also am of that opinion," observed I.

"What! you would allow your name to be bandied about as one who had never cleared up his reputation against charges of crime of the most serious nature, or who had compromised with his accusers?" replied Mr. Goldey; "the charges and your committal to prison have been published in the newspapers, bruited about in society, and cannot now be silenced except by the decision of a court of justice. You know little of the world, Mr. Herbert, if you are not aware that a charge against any man, however respectable, although preferred by persons of known disreputability, will always find credence among a certain class of individuals, so much more prone are they to believe in guilt than in innocence. The class I refer to is, unhappily, a more numerous one than that disposed to be indulgent, and should a trial not clearly disprove the charges made by these scoundrels, your name would be henceforth a mark for vituperation, and must eventually lead to many actions on your part, for defamation. One of the peculiarities of our time, Mr. Herbert, is a dread of being duped, not only as regards our pecuniary affairs, but our opinions. Hence many men, not naturally malicious, are ready to pronounce every individual not belonging to the immediate circle of their friends guilty of any crime brought against them, lest they themselves should be laughed at for an excess of good nature, which they imagine to mean nothing less than weakness, and of which they would feel ashamed. It is with these persons, as with those who set up to be connoisseurs of old pictures. They are ever prone to pronounce the specimens exhibited to them not to be originals, because they know that there are more copies than originals in the market, and in fear that the accuracy of their judgment should be called in question. Every man now-a-days would prefer being considered a sharp fellow, who cannot be imposed on, rather than pass for a generous-minded one who could."

Though aware of the truth of Mr. Goldey's opinion, I nevertheless now heartily regretted having employed him. I wished I had fallen in with a legal adviser less addicted to carrying measures to extremities, and could not help suspecting that a love of litigation, and the profits to be derived from it, had a much greater influence over him than a regard for my reputation. I felt an increasing repugnance towards him growing on me every day. At our interviews, and they were now frequent, I fancied that his searching and stern eye was often on me, and that its expression was full of suspicion. Had he divined that, after all, there was something held back from him, and that I had some strong, some hidden motive, for wishing to avoid a trial? In proportion as this fear grew on me, did my dislike to him increase; and yet, when I examined the purport of his actual words, I could find nothing to justify my suspicion; and with the pertinacity peculiar to nervous persons, who are ever prone to be self-tormentors, I referred to his looks for a motive for my inherent dread of him, when in his words I could not discover one. Alas! it was in the consciousness of my own disingenuousness towards him that this fear of him originated, although I was unwilling to admit it, even to myself.

I went every day to see my daughter, and marked with heart-felt satisfaction her progress in her studies and accomplishments. Yet even this solitary source of comfort was not without its alloy, for as I saw her expand into health and beauty, becoming every day more attractive, and noticed her easy and graceful demeanour, her gentle and polished manners, the facility with which she acquired all that was taught her, and her retentiveness of the knowledge and accomplishments once acquired, I experienced a deep pang, at reflecting that one so calculated to excite attention and fascinate regard, should bear a name at which the finger of scorn might one day point, marring the brilliant prospects and position in society to which she might otherwise so naturally aspire. I would have her name as bright, as spotless as herself; I would not that even those unconnected with her who bore it, should ever draw a stain on it; how then did I shrink at the notion that I, her father, her only living relative, should, by my own madness, have drawn suspicion of crime on myself, and if guilt could not be proved, at least expose my name to the suspicions of the world, by certain inexplicable circumstances connected with my past life.

Partial insanity, the most charitable cause that could be alleged for my strange conduct, must prove highly injurious to her; for to wed a girl, however charming, who was suspected of having a taint of insanity in her blood, would be as insurmountable an objection to most men as to form an alliance with one whose father had incurred dishonour. In either way my daughter, the sole object of all my affection, of all my interest in life, must suffer by me, and I loathed myself as this mortifying reflection passed through my mind. Why had I not been a man bold in the consciousness of having really committed no crime, instead of a pusillanimous idiot? Had I been the first, I would have repelled with indignation and scorn the first menaces of Figgins, and by defying him have saved myself from the suspicious circumstances which my yielding to them had entailed on me.

Although it was now too late to dwell on these painful reminiscences, I could not banish them from my thoughts; and, heartily despising myself, I felt that my daughter must one day or other have cause to blush for, if not to hate me.

Mad as had been my moral cowardice in submitting to the threats of Figgins, I now considered the late effort to resist the attempt at extortion made by his vile companions as no less a proof of insanity, knowing, as I ought to have done, that in prosecuting them, circumstances must be revealed which would inevitably implicate me in suspicions, from which I could not extricate myself! How far wiser and better would it have been to have silenced them by the sacrifice of a few hundreds—ay, or even a few thousands—than to have stirred up this fire, which, though it must burn them, would sear me so deeply as to leave indelible marks through life!

There are persons—and I unhappily was one of those—who are born to be miserable! Let it not, however, be imagined from this assertion that I was a fatalist; no, my belief was founded on the influence exercised over individuals by their peculiar temperaments, depending much on the health of their parents, and the character of those with whom their childhood was passed.

The elasticity of my mind was greatly impaired by the being, for so long a time, a constant witness to the passionate grief of my poor mother, to control which no effort was ever made on her part; and subsequently by my being subjected to the baleful influence of my guardian, Mr. Trevyllan, whose gross selfishness and evil opinion of mankind had passed like a simoom over my youthful mind, destroying every bud of promise, every plant of goodness that might have grown to maturity in it. With this moral blight came also a physical one: morbidness of feeling was accompanied by weakness of nerves; and an unhealthy pride, that made me shrink from degradation, was, alas! unsupported by the self-respect that should have shielded it from subjecting itself to aught like insult.

All these peculiarities, so fertile in producing future misery, had never been corrected. They grew with my growth, and strengthened with my strength; and even now, when I could reflect and philosophize on them, I had not the power to vanquish or mitigate them.

Aware that my name had been mixed up in the police report with those of the vile wretches whom I had prosecuted for conspiracy, and whose charges against me had led to my imprisonment, I could not bring myself to resume my evening visits to Mrs. Neville, notwithstanding her repeated entreaties, lest I should encounter at her house some person not disposed to meet me under present circumstances. She, with the kindness which ever characterized her, endeavoured to induce me to come, until, finding me so averse to comply with her reiterated solicitations, she ceased to urge me; and then, with my wonted habit of turning every thing into some cause for self-torment, I was pained that she no longer pressed me to join her evening circle, and attributed her not doing so to a consciousness that my presence would not be acceptable to the individuals composing it.

This suspicion goaded—tortured me; and I conclude, produced, though I did not intend it, some striking change in my manner to this admirable woman. She, however, maintained the same kind and cordial behaviour to me, and evinced every day an increased interest in, and a more tender affection to, my daughter, who in return, doted on her and her playmate.

Often, ungrateful and selfish as I was, did I listen, with a moodiness of mind and a jealous heart, to the constant praises bestowed by my innocent child on her benefactress and companion.

"Yes," thought I, "*they* are all and everything to her, while I am as nothing. Her happiness no longer depends on *me*; my presence has ceased to be necessary to her. Why did I permit this, the only tie that binds me to life, to be loosened? Why allow others to usurp that place in the heart of my child that should be occupied wholly by me?"

At such moments I was frequently tempted to reclaim the possession of my daughter, and to take her to some far distant region, leaving the suit to which Mr. Goldey attached such vital importance, to drop to the ground, and the world to form its own uncharitable conclusions on my flight. But could I now tear my child from those to whom she was so fondly attached, without inflicting such chagrin on her affectionate heart as might injure her health, and impair the elasticity of her spirits? Would it not be cruel, nay barbarous, to deprive her of the only protectress on whom I could rely in case of my death—the only friend who constituted her happiness? Could I bear to behold her pining away in some distant land for those so dear to her and for those comforts and elegances which habit had now rendered necessary to her? No; of this selfishness I was not yet hardened enough to be guilty, and I offered up this sacrifice of my own happiness to that of my beloved child.

Anxiously did I watch her manner to me, during every visit I paid her. Did I perceive the slightest shade of indifference on her part, the least demonstration of a desire to abridge the length of my stay, I grew jealous, and moody; and the indications of dissatisfaction, the motive for which the dear innocent girl could not divine, inspired her with a timidity, and fear of giving offence, that led every day to a decrease of confidence and cordiality between us. I mentally accused her of a want of gratitude for the sacrifice I made in permitting her to remain with her new friends,—a sacrifice which I thought should have called forth in her a livelier affection to me,—while she was wholly unconscious how much it cost me to make it, or, in fact, that it was a sacrifice at all. How frequently do we accuse those dear to us of not duly appreciating acts of kindness, of the extent of which they are ignorant, or of the self-denial required to carry them into effect of which they never even dream!

Sometimes Frances would look towards the time-piece on the chimney, with an anxious eye, after I had been for some minutes silently brooding over some fancied evidence on her part of impatience to leave me; and I would quit my chair, deeply hurt, and coldly bid her farewell, when she, flinging her arms round my neck, would exclaim, "How sorry I am, dear papa, that Matilda and our governess are waiting for me to go to Madame Tussaud's wax-works, and it is now the time, for I should have liked to stay longer with you!"

CHAPTER LXVI.

THESE *naïve* explanations of the causes of her looking towards the time-piece sometimes disarmed my displeasure; but not always was I so reasonable, for there were days when my nerves, affected by a sleepless night or troubled dreams, and painful reflections, I was rendered irascible, and although my tongue did not utter reproaches, my heart formed them. "What," thought I, "can this creature, on whom I so fondly dote, and whom I see but for a short period once a day, grudge the brief time devoted to me, and long to get released from my presence, in order to seek some puerile gratification!"

I judged my dear and innocent child as if she were a woman to whom every feeling of my breast was laid open, who, aware of the sacrifices I was making for her, and of the jealous pang of a too fond heart, trifled with and neglected me—I forgot that over this burning lava of love was a deep and hardened incrustation of reserve that concealed the fire. That the coldness of my manner, superinduced by the habit of moodiness, must naturally operate to render a girl of Frances's age shy and embarrassed with me, and that not possessing the power of amusing or interesting her, I ought not to wonder that she preferred the society of those who did. "If she knew how I love her," would I sometimes say, "she would not prefer any one to me?" forgetting that it is the natural impulse of every human being to prefer those who most contribute to his or her happiness; and a cool and dispassionate examination of my own peculiar case, had I been capable of making it, would have convinced me that with all my boasted love, I did not personally contribute to that of my daughter. "Would she be less happy were I a thousand miles off?" was a question I often asked myself; and the answer was, "No," for there she would not have to support a daily visit, rendered uncongenial by the gloomy countenance, grave manner, and fits of abstraction and silence, of her unhappy father. There were times when these reflections tortured me; yet, strange to say, at other moments they occasioned a vague sense of relief, by the conviction that if any revelation or suspicion in the forthcoming trial should cast dishonour on my name, and consequently render a residence in my native land insupportable to me, it would be some consolation to know, that my absence, however prolonged, would not interfere with the happiness of my daughter, although my separation from her must bring protracted sorrow to me. "When I have offered up this last and greatest sacrifice," thought I, "I shall have at least the consciousness of feeling that I allowed no selfish motive to interfere with what I believed to be best calculated to ensure her welfare, and a day may come when she will understand how well I loved her."

On my way to Mrs. Neville's one day, I encountered Mrs. Scuddamore, escorted by an elderly man with a certain military air, which instantly led me to guess that the individual must be the Major M'Culloch of whom she had spoken. I would willingly have avoided this meeting, for I had an instinctive dread of the well-known frankness and *brusquerie* of the lady, which, always disagreeable to me, would be, under present circumstances, still more so. But I had approached too near her, before discovering our proximity, to permit my crossing the street, or turning back, without subjecting myself to the charge of rudeness. On drawing close, I recognised in her companion a face familiar to me at Malta, which convinced me that he was indeed no other than Major M'Culloch.

"Well met, my dear Mr. Herbert," said Mrs. Scuddamore. "I have been several days endeavouring to find out your address. Give me leave to introduce Major M'Culloch, Mr. Herbert. The Major has also been in search of you; but, as I told him, one of the innumerable disadvantages of not belonging to the military or naval profession, is the difficulty which occurs in finding out gentlemen in London who are not regular residents there, and whose names consequently are not inserted in the 'Court Guide,' whereas at the United Service Clubs soldiers and sailors are soon found. I pity all those who do not belong to the army or navy, but more especially the first service, to which, from being so long attached to one of the finest regiments in the army, I naturally give the preference."

While Mrs. Scuddamore was uttering this speech Major M'Culloch drew himself up as if on parade, protruding his chest and holding up his head, while he looked somewhat sternly at me, only making a very formal bow when we were introduced.

"The Major wished particularly to have some conversation with you," returned Mrs. Scuddamore. "My lodgings are near at hand. I reside in Gilbert Street. We may adjourn there, if you have no objection; or, if you prefer it, we can call on you if you give me your address?"

Unwilling to be exposed to the visits of this very unceremonious lady, I told her that I had a call to make in Brook Street, after which I would proceed to her abode; and I hurried off to Mrs. Neville's, where, after staying a much shorter time than usual with my daughter, I walked to Gilbert Street, where I found Mrs. Scuddamore, and her friend the Major, waiting my arrival.

"The subject on which I wished to speak to you, Sir," said the latter, "is connected with two men, against whom, if I may credit certain statements in the newspapers, you have commenced proceedings for a conspiracy to extort money from you. It so happens that these men have robbed me at Malta, and I also have commenced a prosecution against them. A considerable portion of my property has been discovered at their late lodgings, but although I can certify it to be mine, it will not be delivered up to me until after the trial for robbery is over. It occurred to me, Sir, that you could identify these scoundrels as being the same individuals who attempted to break into your house a few nights before they plundered me. A man of the name of Figgins, a person against whom considerable suspicion has been excited, declared, when arrested for having some stolen property found in his lodgings, that these men had been the thieves, and to injure him, against whom they bore great malice, they had brought the plunder there in order to implicate him. Figgins told me that, when beneath your roof, these same persons had proposed to him to join them in robbing your house. Now, this proposal proves that they must have known him to be dishonest, or they would not have made it; and Figgins positively asserted that you, Sir, as well as he, saw them; and that you prevented him from shooting them."

While the old soldier spoke, he eyed me sternly; and I, considerably embarrassed by this new proof of the indiscretion of Figgins, felt the blood mount to my face.

"Figgins misinformed you, Sir," replied I. "I perfectly well remember that an attempt was made to break in through a window in my house at Malta, and that the robbers, alarmed by hearing that we were on the alert, hastily retreated, but I did *not* see them, and consequently could not identify them to be the persons now in prison."

"Did Figgins express his conviction that these men were the individuals who attempted the burglary?" enquired Major M'Culloch.

"If he did," answered I, "the assertion has escaped my recollection."

I saw the Major glance suspiciously at Mrs. Scuddamore, and this increased my embarrassment.

"Come, come, my dear M'Culloch," said she, "let us be open and candid. There is nothing like being so, you may be sure; my good friend Mr. Herbert knows me long and well enough not to take offence at plain speaking; therefore I will not mince matters. The Major, Mr. Herbert, thought it strange that a gentleman of good birth and fortune should have been some time at Malta without ever having been seen at the Governor's table, or elsewhere. This he considered rather suspicious." (I felt my blood boil at the word.)

"I explained to him your extraordinary shyness and reserve when at college, and your not being on habits of acquaintance with a single fellow-collegian, so that it could not be wondered at if the same shyness and reserve prevented your making yourself known to the Governor, and becoming acquainted with the officers of the Garrison, as all gentlemen stopping at Malta for some time do. Then the assertion of the man Figgins, who is suspected to be no better than he should be, that you saw the thieves breaking into your house, and prevented him from shooting them, struck him as being so extraordinary, that he formed a very erroneous opinion of you, which I have left nothing undone to remove."

"The opinion of Major M'Culloch, who is an utter stranger, cannot be of the slightest importance to me, Madam," said I, haughtily. "Nor do I acknowledge his right to question or comment on my actions."

"Now then, my dear Mr. Herbert, don't allow yourself to be hurried into anger, and to mistake that for offence, which is only the result of my friendly feelings towards you," observed Mrs. Scuddamore.

"Pardon me, Madam," answered I, "but I really cannot comprehend how your friendly feelings towards me can justify this gentleman's suspicions and comments;" and I looked sternly at the Major, who in return drew up his head with an air of offended dignity, and opened his mouth to speak, when the lady laying her hand on his arm, requested him to permit her to speak first.

"When my friend here arrived from Malta," resumed she, "I spoke to him of you, Mr. Herbert, and with those expressions of esteem and regard, which ever since our first acquaintance I have entertained. The high terms I lavished on you drew his attention."

"It is strange," observed the Major, "that a gentleman of the name of Herbert has lately been at Malta, and that a servant who had been in his service, a man said to bear a very bad character, had accused him of having attempted his life; a statement that would have led to a judicial inquiry, had not the surgeon who had been called in by Mr. Herbert declared that the wound on the servant's head had to his certain knowledge been inflicted by Figgins's falling, when in a state of extreme intoxication, and knocked his head against the sharp edge of a table. This surgeon declared that *he* was immediately summoned to Figgins, whom he saw a few minutes after the accident, and that Mr. Herbert had evinced great humanity on the occasion; and previously to his departure from Malta, which took place the following day, had left ample means in his hands to provide for the comfort of, and medical attendance on, Figgins. That he had endeavoured to remove the false impression which had taken hold of Figgins, relative to his master's having struck him, but that such was the state of that man's mind, induced by constant habits of intoxication, that he could not be reasoned with. Then followed Figgins's declaration that his master had recognized the robbers who attempted to break into his house at Malta, and had prevented him from firing on them; as also, that although he had recognized them, he had not informed the police of this point."

"All these extraordinary statements produced an unpleasant impression at Malta, and gave rise to various reports to your disadvantage, which I, having learned from my friend here, endeavoured to refute; and being perfectly convinced that could we but find you, you would at once explain any circumstance that now appears strange and mysterious, I have been looking out for you everywhere. So long the wife of a brave and distinguished officer, and, as you have not now I believe to learn, having derived from him those nice and decided sentiments on the point of honour which should be the guide of all, I could not allow your name to be mixed up with aught derogatory to it, without frankly acquainting you of the circumstance, and enabling you to put a stop at once, and for ever, to such base falsehoods.

"The opinion of my friend here may not, as you have said, be of any importance to you, Mr. Herbert, but it has great weight with me, for as he will soon become my husband (indeed we only wait until he is gazetted, as I could not think of wedding any officer of a lower rank in the army than the late ever lamented Colonel Scuddamore), I wish that a gentleman for whom I really feel a sincere regard, should stand as high in the esteem of my future husband, as he does in mine."

"And I, Sir," added the Major, "am well disposed to judge favourably of any gentleman whom Mrs. Scuddamore honours with her friendship; for I know her chivalrous sentiments on the point of honour, and that no partiality could induce her to overlook the slightest deviation from it."

"The simple circumstance of my having commenced proceedings against the men who robbed you, Sir," observed I, "a step which must elicit every circumstance connected with them and Figgins, ought, I should have supposed, to have convinced you, as well as this lady, that I could have nothing to dread from any of the individuals, and should have saved me from being catechised—a process always painful and insulting to the feelings of a gentleman: ladies are, of course, privileged; and Mrs. Scuddamore is peculiarly so in my eyes, from a lively recollection of former kindness, when, a raw and inexperienced youth, I stood in need of her good advice and assistance. But permit me to add, that if your confidence in her high sense of honour and judgment is not sufficient to induce you to abstain from forming injurious suspicions of a man she has favoured with her esteem, I must prefer not at present entering into disagreeable details, and wait for my justification in your good opinion until the trial of those whom I have indicted for a conspiracy against me shall have effected this point."

And, bowing respectfully to Mrs. Scuddamore, and coldly to Major M'Culloch, I left the room, notwithstanding that the lady made a move to prevent my withdrawing. I believe this step on my part was injudicious, but my pride was wounded, and I obeyed its dictates without reflecting on future consequences.

In due time, letters were received from Malta, Naples, and Nice, sending the affidavits of the surgeon, and the testimonials of the few friends I had known in those places, in favour of my character and conduct while in habits of intimacy with them.

Figgins was transferred from the prison at Malta to one in London; and a few days after his arrival, he wrote me a letter, which he induced the turnkey of his prison, by the promise of a large reward from me, to have put in the post-office. The turnkey delivered the letter to the gaoler, and he, deeming it expedient, as a chance of leading to the truth, opened it, in the presence of witnesses, and then, carefully taking a copy, resealed and forwarded the epistle to me. Its contents were as follows:—

"SIR,—As I now believe you had no intention of making away with me at Malta, and find that those rascals, Motcombe and Bradstock, have played me false all along, I wish to make amends for whatever harm I may have done you, and also to get these scoundrels punished for perjury and conspiracy. If you will pledge yourself to give me five hundred pounds more, I will swear, before any court of law they bring me to, that the whole story they have said I let out, is a lie. I will swear you were never in my power in any way; that I never suspected you of murdering your sister-in-law; that I never discovered her body where you concealed it; in short, that the whole story is a hum got up by these rascals, to get money from you. You may depend on me *this* time; for I really wish to serve you, and to punish those who tried to ruin me, by bringing their stolen goods to my lodging when I was too ill to see what they were about, and then writing to the police to tell 'em where to find the plunder. One line from your hand to say 'Yes,' is all I require.

"J. FIGGINS."

I trembled with the mingled emotions of indignation, shame, and fear, as I perused this letter; but the first feeling prevailing over the others, and thoughtless of results, I seized my pen and wrote to Figgins that I was surprised at his daring to address me; and to state that if he wrote any more letters, I would not receive them. This answer, as was afterwards proved, had been opened by the gaoler, and tended greatly to remove the suspicions entertained against me, occasioned by the numerous falsehoods circulated by those ever on the alert to prejudge and condemn all who are accused.

CHAPTER LXVII.

IT had been deemed expedient by my legal adviser that proceedings should also be commenced against Figgins for a conspiracy, the first menaces to extort money from me having originated in him. This step was, I felt, fraught with danger to me. What might not be drawn out to my disadvantage from an examination of this man? For although he could bring no evidence that could really criminate me before a jury, enough might transpire to throw a deep and indelible shade of suspicion on my character. I dared not oppose the advice of my counsel and lawyer, for I felt that such a measure would greatly prejudice me in their opinion, so I remained a silent observer of a line of conduct on their part, the result of which I could not help foreseeing must, with my sensitive feelings, prove fatal to my happiness.

Figgins, angered to the utmost degree by my stern refusal to accede to his scheme, had now become as vindictive, if not more so, than Motcombe and Bradstock. He vowed that he would be revenged, and bring to light the crime which, as he alleged, his conscience had often reproached him for having so long concealed.

An early day was named for the trial, and never did a criminal, conscious of guilt, experience a greater degree of trepidation and terror than did I, who had no actual crime of which to accuse myself. Distracted and restless, I was more than half tempted to fly from England for ever, and forfeit at once my reputation and honour; but then would come the reflection, that such a step would put the seal on any suspicion that might be awakened on the trial, and therefore I chose the lesser evil, and remained.

I had frequently recourse to opiates to deaden the agony of my mind during this time, but alas! they failed to relieve me; for, during the stupor they induced, I was haunted by incoherent, but fearful, dreams, as torturing as my waking thoughts; and I really believe that, had this state of mind continued some time longer, insanity or death must have soon ensued. I had not the consolation experienced by those who start from a fearful dream, to bless God that it was *only* a dream, and then again sink into slumber.

Oh! no. When I awoke, and recalled my scattered senses to consciousness, I shuddered at the thought, that the reality of my position was as agonizing as the troublous visions whence I had started! Then I would remember every incident of my life, and as I traced effect to cause, I would imagine that I saw the hand of Omnipotence in all, even to my having brought down on myself the terrible ordeal which I alone could have invoked.

Never shall I forget my feelings when Mr. Goldey told me it was positively necessary that I should attend the trial, and appear in the witness-box the following day. My utter ignorance of all judicial proceedings had left me unprepared for this necessity, and not the utmost exertion of my self-control could prevent my exposing the dismay and horror with which the contemplation of such a measure inspired me. I staggered to a chair, and gasping for breath, inquired if there were no means of escaping this great annoyance?

"None whatever," replied Mr. Goldey. "But you are pale as death, Mr. Herbert," observed he. "One might suppose that it was *you* who were to be tried, and not those scoundrels whom you are prosecuting! Your nerves are, indeed, in a very fearful state, and when this trial is over, I should strongly advise you to consult a skilful physician, in order that some treatment should be had recourse to, to remove their irritability. I have, it is true, in the course of my practice seen instances of prosecutors and witnesses more nervous than the guilty. We all know how the poet Cowper suffered when called as a witness; but you, my dear Sir, are really so excited, that I can no longer wonder that these rascals, having, by some means, discovered your extraordinary nervous susceptibility, have availed themselves of the knowledge to endeavour to extort money from you."

At another time, and under different circumstances I should have felt wounded and offended at the freedom of my lawyer's remarks; but now, having the sense to perceive that the unusual extent of this nervousness furnished the sole explanation or excuse that could be offered for my having yielded to the menaces of Figgins, far from resenting the comments of Mr. Goldey on the subject, I confessed that my nerves were so shattered ever since the deaths of those dear to me, that I had no control over them, and was alarmed even about the most puerile things.

"All this comes from an idle life, Mr. Herbert," said my lawyer. "A man without a profession or occupation, which keeps his mind from self, is ever prone to become nervous, or, in other words, a hypochondriac, indulging the strangest fancies, and unfit for the world and the complicated trials it imposes. Business takes a man from morbid thoughts; it makes him think less of self, and more of others, and this of itself is a great blessing; for, depend on it, Mr. Herbert, that if we expend on self only, the interest and thoughts that should extend to our fellow-beings, we destroy our own happiness, for *self* is the worst object on which a man can allow his mind to be wholly engrossed."

The eventful morning of the trial arrived. Oh! how I trembled at its advent. Mr. Goldey came for me, and noticing my pallor and trepidation, advised me to take a glass of wine and a biscuit. I had not thought of this expedient to support my drooping spirits; but I acquiesced to his proposal, and having swallowed the wine, I entered a carriage with him, and was driven to the court, where the counsel retained for me were already in attendance. I seemed in a dream, a vague sense of terror filled my breast; and yet, the wine I had drank, by stimulating my nerves, and quickening the circulation of my blood, lent me a sort of desperate courage, that enabled me to conceal my alarm. "Those scoundrels," I overheard Mr. Sergeant Vernon say to Mr. Goldey, *sotto voce*, "have got Messrs. Burton and Vyner on their side. I wish they had any other counsel, for as our client is so nervous a man, and these gentlemen are apt to use, if not abuse, the latitude allowed to our profession, they may inflict pain on him. The lawyer is a sad scamp, so great a disgrace to his profession, that I heartily wish he was struck off the roll. He may truly be called the rogue's friend, for all his clients are among that class, which can find no other."

"Very true," replied Mr. Goldey; "but that fact is so well known to the Bar, that his clients suffer by it."

How quickly beat my heart as I heard this conversation, and how did I summon up my courage to appear calm and collected! And now the case was called, Herbert, *versus* Motcombe and Bradstock, by the crier, and I was placed in the witness-box. The court was densely crowded, and every eye was fixed on me. It seemed to my excited mind, as if from every one of those multitudinous eyes, there issued a beam, aimed expressly at me, which entered my brow, and seared my brain; yet, I allowed not my eyelids to droop, to shield me from these burning beams shot at me; but, wound up to a desperate pitch of courage, preserved a calm demeanour. Motcombe, Bradstock, and Figgins, were in the dock, and my heart quailed within me, as I met their demoniacal glances, so expressive of intense hatred and vengeance. The case was opened by my counsel, and while he stated every particular of it, my eye wandered through the court. Seated by the judge on the bench, I recognized, with a painful emotion, the noble lord whom I had formerly met at Naples, and who, because he had not previously known me, had so charitably concluded I was not worthy of so great an honour. His glance was at once stern and triumphant. It seemed to say, that the man who was not of *his* acquaintance, might be capable of any evil. Major M'Culloch was not far distant, and alternately looked from me to the dock, with a severe countenance. As Mr. Sergeant Vernon proceeded in a luminous and eloquent speech to state the case, a solemn silence was maintained in the court. A considerable impression seemed to have been produced by his discourse. Many a face was turned to mine, with a mingled expression of curiosity and interest; and as my eyes glanced over them, my courage seemed to revive at these symptoms of sympathy.

"My client," said Mr. Vernon, "must not be judged severely, if, when reduced to a state of illness and nervousness, occasioned by severe domestic afflictions, and far from his native land, with no friend near to counsel or support him, he was wanting in the energy, which, under other circumstances, would have enabled him to repel the attempts to extort money from him, with the same firmness with which he has withstood it in England. Those acquainted with mankind, and who know how powerfully affliction operates on the nervous system, will comprehend the temporary weakness that led him to fall a prey to the machinations of a designing villain, and will not allow themselves to imagine the least possibility of crime to have ever existed, where only the results of depression of spirits, and broken health, can be found."

The letter from Motcombe and Bradstock, naming the sum, and the conditions for which they would bind themselves to molest me no more, was here produced. I was sworn, and proved I had received it, and believed it to come from them, as also the particulars of the interview with them, and their menaces. I was then subjected to the cross-examination of the counsel for the defendants, and he put many subtle questions to me, all calculated to excite the prejudices and suspicions of the jury against me.

"Why," inquired Mr. Burton, "did you not at once, and indignantly, refuse compliance with the demands of another person, who had previously compelled you to pay him large sums? Remember, Sir, you are on your oath."

"My client," observed Mr. Vernon, "is not bound to answer that question at present. My brother Burton forgets that that the evidence against his clients, having proved the conspiracy, he has nothing to do with any other case."

"My clients have already declared," resumed Mr. Burton, "and are now willing to be sworn, that Figgins had informed them that Mr. Herbert had, at different times, given him large sums of money, to induce the said Figgins to conceal his knowledge of a murder committed by Mr. Herbert, of which payments, evidence can be furnished."

A murmur ran through the court, and again every eye was turned on me, while I, ready to drop to the ground, and wishing, in the sharp agony that wrung my heart, that it might open to hide me, was obliged to support my trembling frame against the bars of the box.

And now Mr. Burton stated the case for the defendants; and most artfully was it constructed, omitting nothing that could serve his clients or inculpate me. The statement was listened to with breathless attention; and, as it proceeded, I could perceive that it produced a strong impression against me. When concluded, Figgins was the only evidence called to substantiate the charge. His appearance was even worse than I had anticipated—his face bearing all the disgusting marks of intemperance; his countenance expressive of hardened impudence; and his dress, the remains of his former vulgar finery, completed as revolting a picture of a man of habitual low habits and vices, as could be seen.

Being sworn, Mr. Burton demanded—"Did you inform Messrs. Motcombe and Bradstock that Mr. Herbert had given you large sums of money to conceal his having committed murder?"

"Never!" was the concise reply.

"Remember, you are on your oath!"

"So I do."

"By the virtue of your oath, you never made any such disclosure to them?"

"Not I.—I wouldn't be such a fool as to tell a secret for nothing to them, when I could get as much money as I pleased from Mr. Herbert for keeping it."

A suppressed murmur in the court was again audible.

"Recollect yourself!" said Mr. Burton. "How should my clients know your secret, if you had not revealed it to them? I don't think it likely that Mr. Herbert" (and here the speaker looked cunningly at me) "would have told it to them."

"No, I don't think he would," replied Figgins, his swollen lips distended into a grin, "for Mr. Herbert wasn't given to talking about it!" and he looked impudently at me while he spoke.

"Then you persist in swearing that you never told your friends how you obtained so much money?"

"Never!"

"Your memory, I am afraid, is not very good. Recollect, you often drank with my clients: and the old saying has it, 'that when the wine is in the wit is out.'—You may, when you had drunk more than usual, have placed this confidence in your companions."

"Not I—I knew them too well for that;—I wasn't going to give a cow, which gave me such good milk, to them who would soon leave not a drop for me."

CHAPTER LXVIII.

No cross-examination could extort from Figgins an admission that he had ever told Motcombe or Bradstock what they had sworn he had revealed to them, although every reply he made to the queries of their counsel implicated me as deeply as he could.

The evidence called for the defendants being now closed, and their statements wholly disproved, the judge summed up; and the jury brought in a verdict against them for conspiracy to extort money, and for gross perjury: and the judge, having pronounced sentence of three years' imprisonment and hard labour, they were removed from the dock; while I received the congratulations of my counsel and of Mr. Goldey.

And now the case against Figgins was called; and my counsel stated it at length, calling evidence to prove Figgins having pursued me from place to place, to extort money. The counsel for the defendant then cross-examined the witnesses; and the result was, that my servant, who was one of them, admitted facts but too well calculated to excite the strongest suspicions and prejudices against me.

"In what capacity did Figgins first enter the service of Mr. Herbert?" demanded Mr. Burton.

"He was engaged to sit up at night with my master, when he was ill with a brain fever," was the reply.

"How long did he remain?"

"I believe about ten days, or thereabouts."

"When he was discharged, did he remain at Nice?"

"No; he left Nice, and was absent some weeks."

"Did you know where he went?"

"I heard from the nurse-maid that he went to Wales."

"When did he return?"

"The evening before my master left Nice."

"What was the impression made on your mind relative to Figgins, while he attended on your master?"

"I formed a bad opinion of him, from observing that he was addicted to drinking, and was of a prying, inquisitive turn."

"Why did you think him prying, and inquisitive?"

"Because I often overheard him asking the nurse-maid questions about my master and his family."

"What were those questions?"

"He inquired whether any young lady had been missed, or had ever fallen down, or been thrown down a precipice in my master's neighbourhood? and whether any one had been accused or suspected of the murder?"

"What did you think, when you overheard these questions?

"I thought he was half crazy, or tipsy."

"When did you see him again?"

"The evening before we left Nice."

"Where did you see him?"

"He brought a letter to my master's lodgings."

"Who for?"

"For my master."

"Was an answer sent to that letter?"

"I heard there was; but I did not deliver it."

"Where did your master next proceed?"

"To Turin."

"Did he lead the persons at Nice to believe that he was going remain at Turin?"

"I understood he was going back to England."

"Where did he go to from Turin?"

"To Naples."

"Did he make some stay there?"

"Yes; some weeks."

"Where did he then proceed?"

"To Palermo."

"Did Figgins come to Palermo?"

"He came to Palermo some short time after. I saw him one evening in the street, and he appeared to be the worse for liquor."

"Did you speak to him?"

"No; I avoided him, for I had a bad opinion of him."

"Did it not strike you as strange that Figgins came to Palermo?"

"I did think it odd; but as he had no settled place of abode, I thought he might be going from one place to another, to look for a situation."

"How long did your master remain at Palermo, after you saw Figgins there?"

"Not long."

"Where did your master proceed to, when he left Palermo?"

"To Naples."

"Where did he then go?"

"He took an excursion of some days into the country, to see some antiquities."

"You did not hear where?"

"No."

"When your master returned from this solitary excursion, where did he go next?"

"We all went to Capua, as we believed, on our road to Rome."

"Did your master say he was going to Rome?"

"I don't recollect whether he told me so; but I know I understood it to be so."

"How long did you remain at Capua?"

"Only a few hours."

"And where did you then go?"

"We returned to Naples."

"What—on the same day?"

"Yes; the evening of the same day."

"Did you go back to the same hotel?"

"No."

"Where did you go?"

"To another hotel at Naples, whence we proceeded to Sorento."

"Did your master take all his luggage with him to Capua,—and did the owners and persons at the hotel think he was going on to Rome?"

"Yes; they all thought so."

"Did you not think it very odd that your master should try to mislead people into a belief that he was going to Rome, and then only go as far as Capua?"

"I did think it strange."

"How long were you at Sorento before Figgins came there?"

"Not long."

"Did you see him?"

"Yes; I saw him there."

"Did anything particular strike you, connected with his presence at Sorento?"

"Yes, I remember that during the time he was there, a person came one day to the house, to say that my master was taken very unwell at a certain spot near the town, where he was often in the habit of going, and wanted me. I went, and found my master looking very ill, and seemingly agitated. He leant on my arm, and walked slowly home, being very weak, and as we passed through Sorento to the house, I saw Figgins walking with Motcombe and Bradstock, and I was surprised that he did not take off his hat, or even touch it, to my master."

A murmur through the Court was now heard, and I *felt* that all eyes were on me.

"What happened next?"

"The following day my master went to Naples, and from thence I got orders to bring Miss Herbert, her nurse, and all the effects of my master to Naples, where we were to arrive late on the following evening, and to drive *direct* to the Mola, where my master was to meet us. We were not to go near the hotel."

"What next occurred?"

"We did as we were ordered, met my master on the Mola, and by his directions, we embarked in the packet, which in half-an-hour after set sail for Malta."

"Did you suspect that there was any mystery, or attempt at concealing his changes of residence on the part of your master?"

"I did think there was a desire that our embarking for Malta should not be known."

"Were you long at Malta before Figgins made his appearance there?"

"No; only a short time."

"Did you not think it very strange that Figgins should follow your master to every place?"

"I did think it odd."

"Did Figgins come to Malta alone?"

"I don't know, but I saw him walking with Motcombe and Bradstock at Malta."

"Did he come to your master's house?"

"Yes, and my master engaged him as a servant."

"In what capacity?"

"My master never told me. He only said that Figgins should not have any power over me."

"Did your master want an additional servant when he engaged Figgins?"

"I did not think he did."

"Figgins then was an extra servant?"

"Yes."

"Did your master know that Figgins was a man of intemperate habits?"

"I believe he did."

"Had you ever suspected that your master disliked Figgins?"

"Yes; I had seen when he was dismissed at Nice, that my master disliked him."

"Yet after this, and knowing him to be a drunkard, he took him into the house, although he did not require an additional servant?"

"Yes."

"Did you not think this a very strange proceeding?"

"I did consider it rather extraordinary."

"Having, as you have acknowledged, a strong personal dislike to Figgins, did you make any observation to your master when he re-engaged him, or did you wish to leave his service?"

"I certainly did make some representations on the subject, and I did wish to leave."

"What was the conduct of Figgins while in your master's service at Malta?"

"It was very irregular."

"Did he indulge in habits of intoxication?"

"Yes; he was generally in liquor, and smoked—a thing never before permitted in the house."

"When remonstrated with on this latter point, *did* he leave it off?"

"No, he became very abusive."

"What were his occupations?"

"He really did nothing."

"Did he appear to entertain the respect and submission generally shown by servants to their employers?"

"No; he did not."

"Did you not suspect that there must be something very wrong, when an extra servant is hired, and not only does no work, but drinks, and smokes, against the regulations of the house?"

"I confess I thought there was something very incomprehensible in it; but my master had been always so worthy a gentleman, such an excellent husband and father, and so kind to his servants, that I could not bring myself to think that he could be to blame, and therefore I imagined that his sorrow for the loss of my poor mistress had so disturbed his mind, that he was no longer the same as formerly, and did not keep the same regularity and strictness as before."

"Do you remember an alarm having been given that some robbers were endeavouring to break into the house at Malta, one night?"

"I do."

"Who first gave the alarm on that occasion?"

"My master."

"Did Figgins wish to have the robbers fired on?"

"Yes."

"Who prevented this being done?"

"My master."

"Did Figgins seem to know who the robbers were?"

"He did, and from what he let out at the time, I guessed he meant Motcombe and Bradstock."

"Did your master take any step to discover the robbers?"

"Yes, he did; for he sent me to the police-office to report it."

"What occurred after?"

"Figgins got very much intoxicated the following days, and smoked; the smell of the tobacco infected the house, and when I remonstrated with him, he became violent and insolent, and even intruded himself into my master's presence in a very disrespectful manner; and in attempting to strike me, he lost his balance, fell down, and hit his head violently against the leg of the table."

"What did your master do on that occasion?"

"He showed the utmost humanity. Staunched the wound which bled profusely, and sent off immediately for a surgeon."

"Did not Figgins accuse your master of inflicting the wound, and with the intention of killing him?"

"Yes; he did."

"Can you swear that your master did not strike him, or push him down?"

"Yes; I can positively swear he did neither."

"What do you suppose was the motive that led your master leave Malta so soon after the accident that occurred to Figgins?"

"I really don't know, but I concluded he wished to return to England."

"Did it not occur to you, that he wished to leave Malta while Figgins was unable to follow him?"

"I believe some such thought did come into my head."

"Did you think that your master was afraid of Figgins?"

"I thought he was very shy of him."

Here closed the cross-examination of my servant, and the case of Figgins was stated by his counsel. It openly accused me of murder. Stated that his suspicions being excited by hearing me continually raving in my sleep of having thrown a lady over a precipice, and having buried the body in a cavern, he had determined on finding the body, and bringing me to justice. That he had gone to Llandover, in Wales, had made inquiries, had found that a young lady, my sister-in-law, had been supposed to have fallen over a cliff, and he had dug in several parts of a cavern in the neighbour-hood, had discovered the body of a female, which he had removed to another place, in order that should I wish to have this proof of my crime put aside, I should not know where to find it.

A murmur prevailed in the court, and all eyes were turned again on me. The statement detailed the sums of money Figgins had received from me by menacing to reveal my guilt. The evidence that could be furnished by the banker at Nice, who had paid the amount of my cheque for 500*l.* to Figgins, as also the evidence of the 200*l.* in money paid by me into his hands at Palermo, corresponding precisely with that sum drawn by me from my banker at Palermo. The statement of these facts produced a great sensation in Court, and I felt like a convict awaiting sentence of death. Oh, the agony of that hour! Never, never can it be effaced from my memory!

The statement went on to tell how Figgins having renewed acquaint-ance with Motcombe and Bradstock, and having lavished large sums in feasting them, they formed suspicions that he had some means of obtain-ing money, which they were bent on discovering. How they made him tipsy repeatedly, to discover his secret. How he, fearful of betraying it, fled from them; how they pursued him from place to place, until he, alarmed for his personal safety, and also, lest when intoxicated he might betray the truth, had sought a private interview with me at Malta, and had insisted on my taking him beneath my roof for protection against the machinations of these men, in whose power he was to a certain degree, by their knowl-edge of some former offence which he had committed. How these men followed him to my house. How he had refused to see them, and how they had uttered menaces against him. How they had proposed to him to let them enter my house at night to rob me. In short, not a single detail connected with the whole affair was omitted; and although my counsel tried by a rigorous cross-examination to impair the testimony of Figgins, they could not succeed.

During the statement of the circumstances which I had so foolishly, so madly, concealed from my legal advisers, I felt the blood recede from my heart to my brain so violently, that I expected nothing less than that a stroke of apoplexy would fell me to the ground, and put an end to my shame and torture. I saw, although I dared hardly meet their eyes, the looks of astonishment and anger that were exchanged between my counsel and Mr. Goldey. I saw that their confidence in my innocence was destroyed, that I was in their opinion, a lost—a degraded wretch.—The judge summed up the evidence, and the jury having withdrawn for a considerable time, returned and pronounced a verdict against Figgins for a conspiracy to extort money from me; but expressed their unanimous opinion, that so serious a charge as murder having been sworn against me, and the evidence of Figgins not having been refuted, they thought that I should be committed to prison, until, on a formal trial, I could be able to disprove the charge made against me. This opinion seemed to be that of the whole Court also, for a murmur of approbation was audible, until the Court was called to order by the judge. Sentence of imprisonment for two years was pronounced on Figgins, who was removed from the dock, while I was given in charge to be conveyed to a prison once more, there to await the result of a trial, the crime of which I was accused not being a bailable one. Mr. Goldey approached me, his eyes flashing with anger.

"Why, in the name of common sense," exclaimed he, "did you conceal the facts that came out on the trial of Figgins from me and from your counsel? You have destroyed your character for ever, for even an acquittal after the trial, now become inevitable, could not remove the obloquy which the uncontroverted evidence of to-day has cast on your reputation."

"I wish to speak to my counsel to-morrow," replied I; "and although I cannot, Mr. Goldey, exculpate myself from the madness of not revealing all you this day heard, be assured that I am not only innocent, but that no proof of crime can be brought forward against me."

He shook his head incredulously, seemed doubtful whether he would continue to act for me; but yielded, when I requested him not now to desert me, and to let me see my counsel early the following day.

My feelings on again entering the prison may be more easily imagined

than described. I was a crushed—a ruined man! The burning brand of
shame seemed to sear my brow, and my heart was pierced with anguish.
For how many days, weeks, nay months, might I not pine in this hateful
prison, before a trial liberated me from it? And during this period to bear
the stigma of guilt, to be prejudged by hundreds—thousands; oh it was
agony! And my child, my pure, my beautiful child! how bitter was the
pang with which every recollection of her was fraught! How long might
it not be before I should again behold her? and when that blessing might
be accorded me, how could I bear to meet the glance of her, on whose
name I had drawn down disgrace and dishonour. How could I meet Mrs.
Neville, knowing that although a trial might acquit me of murder, it could
not destroy the damnatory evidence of Figgins, which proved me to have
bought his silence with hundreds of pounds, and to have received a ruffian
of the lowest, basest habits, beneath the same roof with my daughter.—
Nothing but conscious guilt, or insanity, could be received as an explanation of these proofs of criminality, and I writhed in an agony of mind,
compared with which, all physical torture is light, as my reason pointed out
the extent of my disgrace and its consequences.

CHAPTER LXIX.

THAT was indeed a fearful, a terrible night! I trembled for my reason,
and prayed that, if I must lose it, it might not be destroyed until I had
seen my counsel, and enabled him to comprehend the peculiarity of my
unhappy character, which had led step by step to my present misery and
disgrace.

Mr. Sergeant Vernon came to me early the following day, accompanied
by Mr. Goldey. I had been so struck by the intellectual physiognomy of this
gentleman, as well as by the benevolent expression of his countenance, that
I felt I could reveal to him that which I could not bring myself previously
to disclose to Mr. Goldey. Not wishing, however, to offend the latter, I did
not object to his being present while I unbosomed myself to Mr. Sergeant
Vernon; nay, I proclaimed my own blameable disingenuousness with Mr.
Goldey, entreated his pardon for it, and then confessed that, finding he did
not or could not comprehend my wayward temper, habitual reserve, and
nervousness, which had occasioned all the wretchedness in which I now
found myself plunged, I had not moral courage enough to confide to him
the circumstances brought forward the previous day by Figgins on the trial,
lest he should believe me culpable.

"Why, this is downright madness," exclaimed Mr. Goldey.

"There is more madness in all men," observed Mr. Vernon, mildly, "than people imagine. Who can say that, on some subjects, *all* men may not be more or less mad. Do not let us interrupt Mr. Herbert, whose peculiar nature and character I must examine, as an anatomist does the subject which he dissects, in order to discover the malady that destroyed life. Keep nothing from me, Mr. Herbert. Remember that you are confiding your errors to a man who has so long and so profoundly studied mankind, that he has learned to pity and sympathize with their misfortunes, while tracing effect back to cause."

Encouraged by his mildness, I opened my whole soul to Mr. Vernon, and left not a single secret in it unrevealed save the one which every trial, every misery, had been based—namely, my having involuntarily occasioned the death of my wife's sister, and having concealed the body.

He listened with breathless interest to the narration; comprehended how the weakness and nervousness, induced by intense grief and long illness, had led to my falling an easy prey to the machinations of Figgins; how, having once yielded to his menaces, a dread of exposure of that fact precluded my seeking redress for a conspiracy, although perfectly conscious of my own freedom from guilt.

How great was the contrast offered between Mr. Vernon and Mr. Goldey on this occasion! The first understood every minutiæ, every shade of my sensitive and nervous nature; the second could only view me as a maniac. I told Mr. Vernon of my anxiety to have the trial brought forward as soon as possible; furnished instructions to have the good clergyman and doctor of Llandover brought as witnesses; as also my housekeeper, and the nurse of my wife's sister.

Fortunately for me, the Courts of Law were still sitting, and in a fortnight the trial came on. Often during that period did Mr. Vernon visit me, and, by his sympathy and kindness, alleviate the gloom of my prison. He possessed great influence over Mr. Goldey, and used it to remove from his mind the evil impression produced by the evidence of Figgins.

"I see nothing to be made of his confession," said Mr. Goldey, "except to account for his yielding to the scoundrel Figgins's extortion through insanity."

"Leave all the defence to me," would Mr. Sergeant Vernon reply; "and you will find what can be made by the exposure of a morbid pride and an over-excited sensibility, when worked upon by a not unskilful hand."

Figgins was sent down to Llandover, in the custody of four policemen, who were to be present while the cavern and adjoining ground were to be opened in search of the body he had asserted that he had removed.

After a laborious and strict search, not a trace of any such evidence could be found; and when upbraided by his guard for the useless expense and trouble he had caused, he acknowledged that he *never had* found a body, and only pretended to have made such a discovery in order to alarm me, and that he might obtain the money he intended to extort from me.

This confession, made before the four policemen, had a great effect on public opinion. The day of trial came, and I appeared as a prisoner in the dock.

The counsel for the prosecution stated the case, but could bring no evidence to support the charge, except Figgins, who acknowledged before the Court, that he never had found the body, and only suspected the murder from hearing my ravings when in a brain-fever.

How differently sounded in my ears the murmur that was heard through the Court on this admission, to those which had so terribly wounded them on the former trial! Now, pity and sympathy were expressed in that murmur, and every eye turned towards me, beaming with compassion. The witnesses from Llandover proved the mysterious death of my wife's sister, as also that I had never seen her. The death of my mother, my grief, and the severe illness, which was the result, were stated. My housekeeper proved, that from the hour I arrived at Llandover I had not left the house, except to attend the funeral, and that when that sad ceremony was over, I returned home direct, and shut myself up in my room, absorbed in grief. She swore (good, worthy creature! how little did she think she was swearing that which was untrue), that I could not leave my chamber without her being aware of it. That I was ill in bed when Mrs. Maitland's servant knocked at the door to state that one of his young mistresses was missing. That she entered my room to inform me of the circumstance, and that I, although very ill, had left my bed, to join the servant in search of the young lady, and had passed the night in exploring every spot which it was deemed likely she might have visited. She bore evidence to the dangerous brain-fever that resulted from the fatigue, cold, and anxiety of that night. She related how, in the fever, I kept raving that the young lady had fallen, or had been thrown down from a precipice, the general belief in the neighbourhood being that she had slipped from a narrow pathway, her favourite walk, over the cliff. She stated how Mrs. Maitland, the mother of the lost young lady, had nursed me through this brain-fever, and had become fondly attached to me from the interest I had taken in her misfortune. The whole circumstances of my recovery, my attachment to Mrs. Maitland's second daughter, my marriage, the discovery of the body of the long-missing young lady on the very day of my nuptials, were narrated. My going off with the nurse, who was to identify the body, my humanity and tenderness on the occasion;—the interment of the body in my own family vault, my care and affection to my mother-in-law, and passionate love to my wife;—the deep gratitude of my mother-in-law to me up to the last moment of her life, were recapitulated, and excited a great interest in the Court.

The old nurse was then called. She proved the identifying of the body (forgetting, poor old creature, in the weakness of memory, brought on by age, that she had fainted when brought to the coffin, to look on the dead), and even spoke of the beauty still to be traced in the face,—that terrible face, which I could not think of without shuddering!

The clergyman spoke of my high reputation in my neighbourhood,— of my charity, and unimpeachable moral character: as also of his having attended the funeral of Miss Maitland.

The doctor gave his testimony in my favour, and so satisfactory was all the evidence, that nothing now remained, but to destroy the effect produced by the only facts proved by Figgins, namely, my having given him large sums to conceal the charge he made against me—of having murdered my wife's sister.—Why, if innocent, as was now proved, by so many witnesses of good character, had I yielded to his menaces? This query was addressed to the Court, by the counsel of Figgins. Mr. Sergeant Vernon replied to it in a speech, in which he so luminously and eloquently detailed the effect of violent grief and sickness on the nervous system; giving many illustrations to exemplify his statements, that not a single person in the Court refused credence to his admirable hypothesis. He called medical men, of high professional reputation, to prove, how often men of nervous temperaments, but of strict honour and probity, who were utterly incapable of a crime, had yielded, under the excitement of a dread of censure, to the menaces of a villain, and given vast sums to prevent an unfounded accusation being made against them.

He traced my history from boyhood. My extreme sensitiveness, amounting, in many instances, to a positive morbidness. The horror of exposing my name, and of drawing a painful notoriety on that of an only and adored child, blinding me, at the moment, to the danger and evil consequences likely to result from my reprehensible weakness, in buying the silence of a man from whose worst malice, I ought to have well known, I had, in reality, nothing to dread. Never was the idiosyncrasy of a nervous hypochondriac so well laid open and defined as by Mr. Sergeant Vernon; and the countenances of his hearers revealed the compassion he had created in their breasts for me.

How powerfully did he describe the various emotions and conflicts of my agonized mind, during so long a period! and with what tact did he bring forward the testimonies in my favour, not only from my neighbours in Wales, but from the two intellectual and well-known *savans*, with whom I had been on the most friendly terms in Italy, all vouching for the irreproachability of my moral conduct while known to them, and to their perfect confidence in my worth.

My heart was melted to a woman's softness, as I listened to these details; but, though filled with gratitude to heaven, and to the good man who defended me, my pride—my indomitable pride and sensitiveness—made me writhe in torture at being thus held up to the public, as a poor, weak, and idiotic hypochondriac. I could not bear the pity I marked in the eyes of the crowded audience, whose murmurs of compassion reached my ear. Their pity brought no balm to the long-festering wounds inflicted on my feelings; and, in the morbidness of my excited nerves, I questioned myself whether an acquittal, achieved by revealing my moral infirmities, was not as difficult to be borne, if not as degrading, as a condemnation.

The jury brought in a verdict of not guilty; and the judge, in a discourse remarkable for good feeling and knowledge of the human heart, pronounced my acquittal, regretting the annoyance to which I had been exposed, through the machinations and perjury of a vile fellow, who, basing his scheme of extortion on the incoherent ravings of delirium, which he had listened to when I was in a brain-fever, and judging of mankind by his knowledge of one bad specimen of it—self, had, for so long a period, rendered me his prey, until, finding that I would no longer continue to be so, he had tried to avenge his disappointed cupidity, by boldly charging me with a terrible crime, of which he had wholly failed in establishing a single proof.

Many individuals of the highest respectability had come forward after the trial to congratulate me, and express their satisfaction at its result; but such was the shock inflicted on my nervous system, that even their sympathy gave me pain. I felt persuaded that I must henceforth be regarded as little less than insane, and that to be pointed at by the finger of pity was almost as humiliating as if that of scorn were directed to me. I determined to leave my native land for some distant one, where, unknown, I could wear away the remainder of my life, leaving my child with the admirable protectress I had found for her.

I regulated all my affairs, amply rewarded Mr. Vernon, whose luminous exposition of my unhappy state of nerves had exonerated me from the fearful dilemma in which my folly—my madness—had placed me, and then prepared to depart.

"Never again," said Mr. Goldey, "will I believe a man culpable, however appearances may be against him, until a trial has decided his case. I acknowledge, Mr. Herbert, that had you revealed the whole case to me, I could not have believed that a man, conscious of his own innocence, could become the prey of a scoundrel like Figgins. Mr. Sergeant Vernon has proved to me how much the actions of a man may be influenced by the state of his nerves, a fact I never before even imagined, and henceforth I will not forget the lesson."

I dared not trust myself to take leave of my daughter, lest I should find myself unable to part from her; and my reason told me that I best consulted her happiness in letting her remain with Mrs. Neville. Our farewell would, I felt, be a trial I had not courage to support, and the sight of my agony might leave an impression on her ductile mind injurious to her future peace.

I wrote a long letter to Mrs. Neville explanatory of my feelings; entreated that a portrait of my daughter should be sent me every year, that I might mark the changes from childhood to womanhood, which I was not to have the bliss of witnessing; and having sent that excellent woman and her daughter costly gifts, as poor proofs of my gratitude, I left England, and, directing my course to Sorento, engaged the house in which I had resided when previously there. I preferred it, because in it I could picture my child in the rooms she had inhabited, and I could gaze on the little bed she had slept in. I found the good Padre Maroni at Sorento, as usual, constantly employed in works of piety and charity, in which I have endeavoured to aid him; and am often gratified by the visits of my worthy friend the Chevalier Bertucci; and, passing most of my evenings in the society of the good Padre, years have rolled on, Time bringing healing on his wings, as he draws me further from the days of my heavy trials, and nearer to that which will reunite me to my beloved and never-forgotten Louisa.

At the close of each day I murmur to myself, "A day nearer;" and this thought is as sweet to me, as the sight of the bed where he is to repose is to the weary traveller at the end of a long and most fatiguing journey. The narrating the events of my troubled life has filled up many an hour of my self-imposed solitude; and I have been soothed by the thought, that when I am no longer a denizen of earth, my daughter will know why I left my native land, and made the sacrifice of consigning the charge of her youth to one with whom I believed her happiness would be more secure than with her father.